CORAL BEACH CASEFILES

• PETERSON SYNDROME •

Published in Canada by Engen Books, St. John's, NL.

ISBN: 978-1-77478-160-9

Reprinting material originally presented in: *Roulette, Ghosts of the Past, Ignorance is Bliss,* and *Becoming.*

Distributed by:
Engen Books
www.engenbooks.com
submissions@engenbooks.com

First hardcover printing: April 2024

Cover Image: Liz LeDrew
Cover Design: Matthew LeDrew

"The Black Womb lives, thanks to Smoke and Mirrors, Matthew LeDrew's third novel in his saga. Released by Engen Books in 2009, it is a mature and complex tale with many twists and turns that is sure to please fans of action, drama, horror and mystery. If not for a dip in the middle portion, this would easily be the best book – thus far – in the series. As it stands, it may be the most entertaining." - Jay Paulin, author of *Emma Awesome*

CONTENTS

Introduction
by Matthew LeDrew

So, this set of four novels is interesting to me as I look back with hindsight and personal growth. Their approach to storytelling, and how that approach has changed for me over time, means that these novels likely wouldn't be written the way they are if I was writing them today. Perhaps they wouldn't be written at all. This often leads to them being overlooked, as some novels are sure to be when your bibliography stretches inevitably towards fifty plus titles, but as I look back through them to write this introduction, there is merit here. I had things to say, and I had things to say that weren't always received.

But, let's rip off the band-aid: why wouldn't these novels be written today? Well at the time I was very enamored with, and was indeed employing a strategy of, *skip no time*. What this comes down to is, when telling sequential stories, how much time are you allowed to skip between "episodes?" Nowadays I'd skip a lot, years even. But there was a period of time in my twenties when I was infatuated with the idea of showing *every second* of a character's development, laying small hints of what formed their worldview that would not be paid off for long stretches of time. But because this is a crime drama, that means that there are great sections of this work not focused on the crime: they're focused on the people solving it.

That makes this book a fun mix of things. Is it a horror-thriller? Often, yes. A teen-sleuth detective novel where the young protagonists are often put in very adult danger? Yes, of course. Something akin to a superhero origin? Sometimes. But also, let's call a horse a horse: it is also a *soap opera*. In the same way that people are shocked to learn that 90% of the time the X-Men are not fighting Magneto, they're in arguments over who is sleeping with who, that is this book. It is teen angst paired with life-and-death stakes and sometimes grisly crime.

Modern stories by me aren't like this as much. If anything, they're about obsessed characters that fail to connect with other people, so the kind of attachments that happen in this book are much more of a struggle.

I was focused on showing *every episode* for a very brief window of time. Famously, when I first wrote the books staring Xander Drew, I wrote them out of order. In order I wrote: *Black Womb* (now the first book in the series), *Smoke and*

Mirrors (now the third book), *Faith* (now in a sequel series and the fourteenth book starring the character), *Family Values* (15th), *Fate's Shadow* (16th), *Moments* (18th) and the 19th book that was formally titled *Lover's Spat* but now likely will not be. I skipped wide passages of time between each book, but even then, *I knew what happened* in the space skipped.

I had this logbook where I kept track of every main event in my character's lives. I had it in my head that if the books ever made it big, there might be spin-off material (comics, television, whatever) and that those mediums might want those stories. I'm also a firm believer in habitus as a writing form, the idea that the writer should know everything that happened to a character and *everything* that informs a character, even if they're not going to show it.

But as I reached the end of *Lover's Spat*, I wrote myself into a corner and I struggled to work my way out of it, and I started to look back on those plans, those in-between episodes. I remember sitting in the spare room in my aunt's house, staring at the screen, that damnable blinking curser, and deciding I would write *something* just to get words out, and wrote a random scene from the planner set in the time I'd skipped. And woo, it got the juices flowing. I loved it. It was a high so high I didn't look back for years: I knew what was coming, I could foreshadow, play with time, allude to things down the road. This was going to be *fun*.

And so when I started writing, I only wrote the big, impactful stories. And then once I hit my mid-thirties I again decided I only wanted to write big, impactful, life-changing events in the lives of my characters. But there was a long stretch of time in my twenties when I was living in the day-to-day life of Xander Drew, Cathy Kennessy, and Mike Harris, and these four books are the absolute meat of those stories.

So these were the stories written in the middle chapter of my life and the middle chapter of a series. Middle chapters tend to get overlooked. Everyone remembers *Fellowship of the Ring* and *Return of the King*, but nobody talks about *The Two Towers*. Such is life. But as a result, there's meaning in here that's gone unexamined. I liked these stories more than I thought I would, going back. This is not a misshapen collection: it had something to say, some of which still hasn't been puzzled out by readers. So if you're reading this, give the material in these stories a second glance, see if you can pick up what I was putting down when I was definitely less polished.

And while you're at it, spare a thought for Mandy Peterson. I would never write a character like her today; I wouldn't be able to.

Matthew LeDrew
April 04, 2024

BOOK FOUR

ROULETTE

PROLOGUE

"This is ridiculous," he sighed into the phone clamped between his ear and shoulder, sifting rapaciously through the mound of paperwork covering his desk. Unable to find what he was looking for, he rubbed his hands through his thick black hair and sighed, listening to the voice on the other end of the line. "I'm sorry, I was mistaken. That was ridiculous."

He was drenched in sweat even though fall was in full swing, and there were three fans going in the room almost at all times. The guidance office was like a furnace and showed no signs of improving. Even opening the window didn't seem to do much good, and only served to frustrate him more. The heat had always agitated Dr. Warren O'Toole, and lately he felt as though it was bothering him more and more.

"Listen, just listen for a sec--" he snapped, then immediately dialed back his tone. He took a deep breath and fixed a smudge on his coke-bottle glasses. "I'm sorry. But I've got a pile of paperwork on my desk that I'm told is only going to get bigger. There are people actually suing the school for what--"

He stopped again, leaning back on his chair as the person on the other end of the phone responded to him. He let his eyes creep over the desk until they landed on a tan folder, the name scrawled on it completely illegible to anyone but him. He flicked it open, revealing the student-ID photo of Derek Smith clipped to the top left hand corner of the document. He flicked through the pages, raising an eyebrow at how short it was, then tossed it into the nearby trash bin with many others.

"No, I wouldn't consider the memorial service a success." he laughed, suddenly sitting back up. "And I don't think anyone else here would either. I think it would be considered to be the exact *opposite* of a success. Yes, actually. A mass murderer almost taking out a gymnasium full of students and faculty, myself included, is considered a failure in my eyes. Come to think of it, I don't blame the parents for suing at all, I..."

The voice on the other end of the line was audible even without his ear to the phone now, the reception full of static but its message all too clear.

"Fine. But administration is blaming me for this one, and that's not fair. The idea was mine, but there is no way I could have known. And the kids... jeez, these poor kids. There's denial and regression and... well, fear. They're just watching each other constantly now, wondering who else might be capable of something like that."

He paused, listening intently for a moment.

"That'd be great. Listen, the second I come up with something to make this right, you know I will... yes... yes, of course. Beyond that, these kids need my help. Well, if someone were writing me a blank check then I'd have plenty of ideas, but since..." There was another tense pause. "...Yes, I understand completely. We do all want the same thing. Nobody wants another Derek Smith or Adam Genblade, that's for damn sure." A sly smile spread over his lips. He pumped the air triumphantly, took a blue pen out of his breast pocket and clicked the quill out before starting to scribble something down. "Thank you, sir. Yes, yes, I'm sure that'll help. I've got an idea right now that I think will do everyone some good. Yes. Yes, thank you."

He hung up the phone, clutching the yellow post-it note between his thumb and forefinger. He looked at it intensely for a moment, as though it were some great adversary he'd just overcome. He wiped the sweat from his brow, turned his head toward the nearest fan and let it blow air onto him for a long moment before reaching out and picking up the phone. "Jenny? Tell Shnieder I'm coming to see him." He smiled, getting to his feet and straightening his tie.

CHAPTER ONE: EVALUATION

-Click-

Cathy Kennessy's eye twitched slightly, turning on her heels at the sound as it came from behind her. She was wearing a pink dress covered by a jean jacket and looked like a character from some mid-nineties teen soap. Her long, dark hair spread out from her head to its fullest length as she spun, a look of alarm filling her nearly black eyes.

A series of small cuts and scrapes danced along her right cheek and chin, like those she received when she was a child while running through the forests and parks around town, as tree branches slapped her in the face only to be brushed off as if they were nothing.

-Click-

These marks, however, were hardly as innocent. A little more than a week ago, someone she had thought was her friend had dragged her through the trees behind her school. He had been a friend to so many, yet he had taken the lives of nearly ten percent of the school's population over the course of the previous month. As he was in the act of trying to take yet another loved one from her, she shot him in the back. Through the shoulder, actually, and the irony of the situation had not been lost on her. After all, Derek had stabbed her in the back, and as Sara had always said when she was alive, turnabout was fair play.

-Click-

Flame seemed to erupt from Xander Drew's hand as he flicked the flint on a concealed lighter again, this time with better results. Orange fire shimmered to life next to his thumb, casting weird and eerie shadows onto his face. He low-

2

ered himself to the heat, letting it light the cigarette that was lodged between his lips. There was a sound of burning paper as the cherry caught and he finally let the lighter die, placing it safely back into his back pocket. He took a long drag then leaned back onto the brick wall of Coral Beach High School.

He was wearing his black leather jacket again, but it had been the first time in months he'd been seen wearing a white shirt. Cathy took this as a good sign. Ashes tumbled down and left charcoal tracks on his loose shirt as he tapped the cigarette, seeming not to notice the mess he was making on himself. After a moment, he exhaled, sending a long spiral of smoke spinning toward her.

She wrinkled her nose at the smell, then stepped back a pace away from him. "Since when do you smoke?"

"Since when do you care?" he retorted, avoiding her eyes as he took another puff. His face was splashed with heat as the grey clouds emanating from his mouth danced along his un-combed, auburn hair.

Frowning, she waved her hand in front of her face. "You smell like feet," she observed, trying to stay upwind from the stench. It wasn't easy in such a confined area. They were standing in the only area of the school's park that the teachers had a hard time seeing from most angles, and was therefore designated the smoking ground by its students. Butts littered the dirt everywhere, so much so that you couldn't take a step without treading on at least five. She snatched the pack out of his hands and pointed to the grossly vulgar image of a human lung that was portrayed there. She tapped the message next to it twice to draw his attention to it. "Can't you read, dumbass? Each one of these things takes five minutes off of your life. It adds up to years over time."

Xander nodded, exhaling right into her face. "True. But those are the last years, and they suck anyway. No sex, so what's the point?"

"Plus, they make you impotent," she chimed, raising a finger triumphantly as she reread the back of the packaging.

Xander did not respond to that, merely taking another puff.

"They'll kill you, y'know," she added, handing him the pack and giving up, trying not to breathe in deeply as she leaned against the wall close to him.

"Didn't you used to say that to Sara?" he asked, and this time he looked at her. His eyes were baggy and the skin around them was beginning to look grey. He hadn't slept in days, and it was obvious. The signs of fatigue were beginning to overcome him, the stress of the past few months weighing him down. "And Jamie too, right?" he chuckled, looking away as he finished his smoke and tossed it to the ground, not bothering to extinguish it. "Yeah, you were always the little anti-smoking activist, weren't you? Well, guess what? Smoking didn't kill Sara and it didn't kill Jamie," he said, almost smiling as he spoke. "Derek did."

Cathy shuddered, trying very hard to brush off what her friend had just said. Suddenly, she could feel the cold gun in her hands again, her fingers tight around the trigger as she prepared to pull it. Most people knew enough not mention Derek's name around her. That either made Xander the bravest person she knew, or the stupidest. "You're a jerk," she spat at him angrily, curling her lip slightly.

3

"That I am," he nodded, his breath thick with nicotine. "But, you're the one who saved me, so we've got you to blame for that, don't we?" He smiled. Suddenly, the tension was gone again. He was her Xander again, the boy she used to play Nintendo with until their thumbs went numb.

She smiled at him, despite all her efforts not to. She glanced around the corner, making absolutely sure that nobody was there before getting a little closer to him, her voice hushed. "How are you doing, anyway?" Her normally soothing touch grazed his shoulder and he winced, telling her what she wanted to know.

"I'm doing better," he lied, smiling though the pain. "It hurts less now. I think the reason it hurt so much before was because it was healing nerves."

"You can do that?" she asked, more than a little skeptical.

"I guess. I don't see why not. After all the beatings I've been getting lately, you'd think I'd have some nerve damage. What other explanation is there?"

She nodded once in consent, filing that information away. Right now, they needed to arm themselves with as much knowledge as possible if they were ever going to beat this thing, and they'd have to do it together. So far, she'd managed to gather that whatever it was inside him could heal just about anything, but that the time it took to recover was equivalent to the severity of the injury. When Xander had gotten stabbed a while back, it had taken a little over a minute to heal. But when he'd gotten caught in an atomic explosion it had taken him weeks to heal. During this healing period, all of his other powers tended to 'burn out' from overuse. He still wasn't completely over that ordeal yet, and that's why he was still aching now. Cathy suspected that when he lost the enhanced healing ability, his body's natural healing factor went with it. But there wasn't much to base that on yet.

She'd also taken careful note of what transformed him. High emotional stress, the spilling of blood, and unconsciousness were on the list, and it seemed that more and more reasons for it to flare up were appearing every day. The most disturbing of all the things she'd observed had to have been the transformation itself, though. To see blackness and hatred envelope her friend's body like a suit, an adhesive liquid made up of all the rage and hatred a man could ever feel... It was like Xander just disappeared, and there was something else coming toward her, with his voice and mannerisms.

"You still there?" he asked, waving a hand in Cathy's field of vision.

She snapped her head toward him, blinking twice. "Sorry. What were you saying?"

"Not much," he sighed, staring out at the town through the chain link fence that surrounded the playground. He was silent for a long time, twirling a stone back and forth between his fingers.

She traced his field of vision, her eyes scanning the horizon. Not finding anything specific of interest to look at, she decided not to ask.

"She loved this view, didn't she?" he asked finally, sitting down on the grass somberly.

Cathy nodded, taking the hint to sit down right next to him, shuffling up

4

against him. "She did," Cathy said, resting her head on Xander's shoulder as they both stared out at the calm streets. A yellow Beetle was parked in front of a bungalow, but otherwise the roads were bare.

"She'd sit right here and look out there all recess and dinner hour, just watching things happen even though nothing ever did. She used to say that this was what she thought of when someone said *home*. The nicest spot in town; calm and quiet," he continued, smirking a little. "'This is when people are at their best, Xander. Everyone just walking to and from, wherever they need to go, their minds wandering. When people walk a familiar street, their minds go to their default setting. You can really tell who a person is by the way they walk,'" he chuckled a little, recalling the girl's insistent rambling.

"Yes, she did," Cathy smirked, remembering those exact words.

Xander sniffed once, pretending to wipe his nose. "She'd ask me so many times to just come out here and sit with her while she had a smoke; to do nothing and talk about stupid crap and watch the people walk back and forth all day long. And I don't think I ever did it once, Cathy." His voice was quavered now, despite his best efforts to hide it. His lips crunched in disgust. "Not once."

Slowly, Cathy stretched her arm around him, pulling him a little closer. "We thought we'd have forever with her, you know. Everyone did. But she was taken from us before she was supposed to be."

"By Derek," Xander spat, his top lip curling savagely.

Cathy shivered slightly, and he felt the motion of it through his jacket.

"It's weird, but... it was almost easier when I thought I had done it," he almost laughed. "It wrapped everything up nice and tight. Now that we know he killed most of those people... it's like that wound has been opened again. In a lot of ways, it's easier to heal nerves than that. I just don't know where to go from here... what to do with this."

"Xander?" she asked quietly, straining her eyes upwards to get a slight glimpse of his face.

"Yeah?"

"Will you come out here and go people watching with me tomorrow?"

There was a long silence, then. After a moment, he reached up and began to stroke her black hair slowly and softly. "Sure," he said, almost too low for her to hear.

⋀⋅⋏

Across the playground, Julie Peterson was sitting on a wooden picnic table beneath a tree that was losing its leaves. She twirled a red sucker against her tongue playfully, staring over at Cathy and Xander.

Next to her, two boys melted at the sight of her nonverbal innuendo, laughing at one another as they fawned over her. Tommy Irons was a junior, but at well over six feet tall most people mistook him for a senior until he opened his mouth. He wore the same faded denim jacket in summer, winter and fall, typically over a tee-shirt displaying whichever band happened to be his favorite that week. Today, it was Dave Cadlecott Band, a local metal group that specialized in

5

massive pyrotechnic displays and fundamentally bad music.

The boy next to him was called Sud by the majority of the student population, as well as most of the faculty. He was much shorter, coming in at almost exactly five feet tall, with a shaved bald head and massive arms that seemed to travel down forever past his kneecaps.

It wasn't as though Julie needed to put on an act to gain the attention of the opposite sex; she did that just fine all on her own. A brunette with natural blonde highlights, her green eyes sparkled as if she were some kind of untapped fountain of energy and zest. That was how her friends described her, anyway. Most people just called them bedroom eyes. She had freckles across the bridge of her nose that were especially noticeable just then, as the sun beat down upon her cheeks. She was getting a tan already, her forehead and chin beginning to burn and peel in some places. Still, it did little to deter her beauty. She smiled from around the lollipop, her ivory teeth seeming even brighter when compared to the deep red of the candy in her mouth. A movie-star smile, they said. She was wearing a red tube top and a tight, black mini-skirt, covered with a sleek leather jacket. Principal Shnieder had already tried talking to her twice about the appropriateness of such attire, but had since given up all together.

Tommy hung his head mere inches from her smooth, silky legs, and was mumbling about a dance coming up this Friday, or something of that nature. He was *always* mumbling something of that nature. *As if I'd be caught dead going to a dance with a troglodyte like him, anyway,* she thought, rolling her eyes. She could barely hear them anyway. Her thoughts were across the playground, where Cathy and Xander still sat, chatting about the view from the brick wall. She crinkled her nose a little as she watched them; Xander stroking the other girl's hair slowly, rhythmically, tickling her ears a little with each and every pass.

Julie let out a long breath from her nose.

"...and I figured, with the way you are, we could..." Tommy continued rambling on, oblivious to the fact that Julie had stopped paying attention to him minutes ago. He wore a sly smile and elbowed Sud at key points in every sentence, punctuating his innuendos as if they weren't already painfully obvious.

"Excuse me?" Julie interrupted, turning her head sharply from the happy scene over to Tommy's chubby features. She'd only caught a few words, but they had been enough to make her cheeks grow livid with anger. Her hair danced around her as she swirled, her gaze accusing the young man before he even had a chance to defend himself. "What do you mean, 'the way I am'?"

Tommy looked at Sud and shrugged. "Well, you know," Tommy pressed, moving toward Julie and laying his hand on top of hers. "You slept with the old guidance counsellor, right? I figured if you'd have that greasy old troll, then you shouldn't have any problem with - "

Julie shoved Tommy's hand away, getting up from the picnic table quickly. Wooden splinters stuck to her skirt and tried to keep her there, but she got up anyway, barely affording either of the boys a second glance. "You thought wrong," she said simply, brushing her hair back and trying to hide the expression of pure disgust that she knew just *had* to be bubbling over her features. She stopped suddenly, though not of her own will. She turned back around to see that Tommy had grabbed her by the wrist, his long, filthy fingernails digging into her skin.

"Where you think you're going?" he asked harshly, pulling her back a little.

Sud smiled devilishly.

"Let go of me," Julie demanded, struggling against the older boy's grip.

"We were talking. It's impolite to walk out on somebody right in the middle of a conversation, y'know," he continued, smirking.

"Impolite," Sud echoed, uttering the first words he had spoken, possibly in weeks.

There was a loud shuffling sound as the school loud-speakers cut in before Julie could utter several *very* impolite phrases. "Julie Peterson, please report to the Guidance Office, please. Julie Peterson, to the Guidance Office."

She felt a cold shiver run down her spine as her entire body went numb. The words had sliced through her like a knife, penetrating her tender flesh as if it had no more consistency than silk.

Tommy let go of her arm, raising both hands above his head in mock surrender, a broad smile spreading across his angular chin.

Julie watched him for a moment, then forced herself to turn away and finally got her legs to work again, slowly making her way across the playground toward the school.

"Hey," he laughed, slapping Sud playfully against the chest. "Looks like she's finally ready to break in the new guy."

Sud laughed, the sounds coming out in massive, hard bursts like shit from someone suffering from the world's worst case of constipation. She pretended she didn't hear it as she pulled the back door to the school open and walked in.

"Why do they call them a pair of pants, anyway?" Xander wondered aloud, rubbing the fabric of his denim jeans between his thumb and forefinger. He gazed at a few specks of dirt against the black fabric, flicking them off without even realizing he had moved. When he spoke it was a mumble, one that made his entire body quake. He felt light and weightless, as though the slightest breeze might carry him away. He told himself that it was the cigarettes. That he wasn't used to smoking and just felt a little light-headed. If anyone had asked what was wrong, he could have convincingly said so. But he couldn't lie to himself with anywhere near the same effectiveness.

"Um... what?" Cathy muttered in a voice deeper than she usually used, her voice mushed because of the odd positioning of her head, propped up against Xander's arm.

"Why do they call them a 'pair of pants'? I never did get that," he replied absent mindedly, almost detached from the conversation he himself had started. Her hair tickled his nose, and filled his enhanced sense of smell with her presence. She smelled amazing to him, even if it was only shampoo. Herbal Essences went a long way, nowadays.

Cathy thought for a moment, raising an eyebrow. "I'm not quite sure I follow you," she admitted finally.

"Okay," Xander began, shuffling slightly to get comfortable enough to explain his point. "There's a pair of shoes, because there's two shoes, right?" he asked, marking off the point on one finger.

"Right," Cathy acknowledged, nodding once.

"There's a pair of socks, because there's two socks, right?" he continued, again annunciating his words by tapping another finger.

"Right," she repeated, her voice rising in pitch a little as she became intrigued as to where he was going with this.

"So why do they call them a pair of pants? There's only one. It doesn't make any sense," he concluded, flapping his hands against his knees hopelessly. All around them, the playground continued to bustle loudly with life and the vibrancy of youth.

"You require mental help," she offered, stroking his hand with mock sensitivity. "It's all right. We'll get you a nice padded room. It'll be white... you like the color white, don't you?"

"Shut up," he groaned.

She smiled as her voice became even more patronizing, as if she were talking to a small child. "We'll even let you keep the part of your brain that they take out."

He narrowed his eyes at her, squinting his frustration. "I'm being serious here. Shouldn't there be a reasonable explanation for this? Why aren't they called pant, or something?"

Cathy furrowed her brow, moving her head to give him a look this time. She grunted heavily, her body voicing its distaste at being removed from the comfortable position she'd found herself in. "What the hell is the matter with you?" she started, trying not to laugh. "That sounded so stupid. Can you imagine if we actually called them that? 'Hey Mom, I need twenty bucks to buy a new pant', or 'hey, Mike, check out my cool new faded jean.'" She tisked, shaking her head in dismay. "I think we've just stumbled on why you were never a trend-setter, Drew."

"Mark my words," he warned humourously, shaking a finger at her. "One of these days, kids'll be saying that just like you did then."

"Frig off."

"No, really! And you'll look at your grandkids..." he made his voice become straggly and old, his finger quivering to emulate an old man's, "and say: 'In my day, we used to call them pants,' and they'll roll their eyes at you and go, 'No, grandma. They're called pant. Christ, grandma doesn't know anything. Why can't you be more like Jeremy Drew's grandpa?'"

"You're an idiot," she tried to say, but she couldn't seem to stop herself from laughing long enough to get the words out.

A high-pitched whine squealed its way over the intercom system, the sound arching back on itself and making Xander scream, his body lurching forward as he grabbed his ears so tightly that he drew blood from around the lobes. When the squeals finally subsided, they were followed by a loud shuffling sound as the school loudspeakers came to life. Principal Shnieder's voice blared: "Julie Peterson, please report to the Guidance Office, please. Julie Peterson, to the Guidance Office."

Xander huffed, turning to look quizzically at the intercom. He got up and stepped away from the smoking section and out into the main body of the playground, his eyes scanning the assembled student body. Cathy got up and walked to his side, eyes wide as they both watched Julie stomp her way across the playground and over to the school's twin blue metallic doors, then disappear from sight. He opened his mouth and tried to find words, then closed it again as he failed to.

Cathy wrapped her fingers around his shoulder. His bad shoulder. But he was too numb to notice. "What just happened, Xander?" she asked in a small voice, turning to look at him.

He did not return her gaze as his eyes returned to their natural state of blue. "I don't know," he admitted regretfully, taking a step out onto the grounds just so that he could catch a glimmer of the Guidance Office out of the corner of his eye. "Nothing good, that's for sure."

⋏⋏

Mr. Larkin swept his way slowly past room 135, the steady sound of his broom making Mike Harris' eye twitch every time the stiff, worn bristles scraped against the tile floor. It sliced through the thick, unbearably humid air of the computer room like a serrated knife, cutting little slits in his sanity with every pass. The freckles that dotted his features seemed to dance across his flesh as his muscle contorted out of control. His sleepless eyes lazily, yet desperately, tried to keep their focus on the screen, but kept darting back and forth to the hallway. The slow, steady hum of over-clocked computers surrounded him, their monitors emitting an unnatural heat that attached itself to the skin over the boy's brow. He attempted to wipe it off, but that thin sheet of sweat kept returning, time and again.

A small vein in the side of his head, just barely covered by his short blonde hair, was pounding fiercely to the beat of a wild jungle drum. The glow of the computer screen only seemed to be making the burgeoning headache worse.

That wasn't the worst of it, though. His body was assaulting itself in more ways than that. Pangs of guilt shot up from his gut as his mind broke the barriers of time and space, traveling back weeks until he was in front of Julie Peterson's front door again, standing side by side with Derek Smith, about to save the day.

What was that old saying? Burn the village to save it? he thought, as the pangs got so sharp that he thought he might throw up. He choked it back as soon as he tasted something almost like orange juice in the back of his throat, his face turning white as his cheeks began to take on a greenish hue. Sweat still leaked from pores all over his body. His armpits, his chest... even his knees were drenched in perspiration. He could hear his breath before it even left the chamber of his

9

mouth, further adding to the noise that was surrounding him, coming at him from every direction. His side ached, the wound he'd received over a month ago still flaring angrily in reaction to the signals his body was sending. He was beginning to see a correlation between the flaring of the stab wound and when it was going to rain, but that theory hadn't really been perfected yet. It was possible, though. His mother could tell the weather when her right middle toe started acting up, so he couldn't see any reason the six-inch gouge in his side couldn't spring to life in response to barometric pressure as well.

When it rains, it pours.

His eyes became bloodshot as he tried to focus on what Mr. Bartlett was babbling on and on about. He was a portly man with unkempt hair and fingers like soot-covered sausages, his voice small and meek as he tried to instill the wisdom of the WYSIWYG computer system. Usually, Mike couldn't seem to get his head past the unmistakable funky scent of dampness that wafted in a three-foot radius of wherever the man stepped, his shoulder-length brown hair bobbing vibrantly as he walked with a little bounce in every step.

After a second of forcing himself to concentrate, Mike gave up. He reasoned that even if he did manage to learn whatever technology Bartlett was trying to teach them this week, by next week it would be rendered obsolete and thrown into the dumpster out back along with the moldy crap left over from lunch.

Like teenagers.

Mike looked around the classroom at all the kids there, each of them talking loudly and caught in their own little worlds, trying to drown out the monotone teacher who spoke with all the flare of Ben Stein. So easily they'd forgotten what had happened over the past few months: the deaths, the murders, the betrayal. They'd all moved on so quickly that you'd think it had never happened at all. Like maybe it was nothing more than a violent daydream. And if nobody remembered? Would all the death and suffering have been for nothing, then? Had he sacrificed everything just so that things could stay the same as they always had?

No.

As the beat in his head increased, he fiddled with his coat pockets to see if he'd remembered to bring any Advil today. He sighed, finding nothing but an old penny and an ungodly amount of lint. The constant thump of the beat seemed to quicken in pace, as if to mock his inability to find relief from the pain. His hands gripped the desk in front of him, his nails making long gouges in the wood. He wouldn't look to his left, just as no other child in that classroom would. To his immediate left was an empty desk that had been filled only weeks ago by Derek Smith.

Everything had seemed so clear when they were on Julie's front porch. She'd been too scared to testify against the men who'd hurt her, so they'd have to make her even *more* scared not to testify. He let out a disgusted grunt, giving himself a headache as his mind kept trying to justify its own thoughts, only to be shot down by another thought process, looping back around on itself until his mind was one big knot. He'd once heard that hindsight was 20/20. He assumed whoever said that had never been faced with a real, honest-to-goodness moral choice.

We caught Phillips, didn't we? The side of his brain concerned with self-preservation argued, his interior monologue almost pleading with him. *Didn't we save lives? Cathy's life, even? Everyone in school said that Derek and I were saints. That we'd done what everyone else was afraid to. Even Julie said so, though her tone had been less than convincing.*

All around him, everything was loud. Even the walls seemed to buzz with noise as he tried to drown all of it out. Click. Scrape. Buzz. Scrape. Thump. Beat. Mumble. Scrape.

Then, directly behind him, a new sound emerged. Tommy sat there, tapping Sud on the shoulder to gain the absent-minded boy's attention. "Hey," Tommy smiled, and it was suddenly all that Mike could hear. The bully's voice was thick with malice and sinister desire. "You think I got a chance with the Peterson slut, or what?"

Mike slammed both of his fists down upon his desk as hard as he could, cracking the wood and sending splinters jutting into the meat of his hands. He turned sharply to face Tommy and Sud, his face a mix of infuriated reds and sickly greens. "Shut the hell up!" he boomed, pointing a finger at them, making the two boys jump back in their seats. "What the fuck is wrong with the both of you? Don't you have any common sense at all?"

Suddenly, everything was quiet except for the sound of Mike's own heavy, labored breathing as his lungs trembled, trying to regain all of the oxygen lost during his outburst. Mr. Bartlett and all of the other students in the class stared at Mike in unison. The teacher even dropped his chalk, which plummeted to the floor and landed with a small tap. Mr. Larkin poked his head around the corner, a look mixed with fear and amusement painted on his withered old features.

After what seemed like a forever-long silence, Tommy and Sud began to snicker simultaneously, unable to hold it in any longer. They roared then, pointing at the still red-hot Mike, as if he had told some hilarious joke or dropped his pants.

Suddenly, the intercom again buzzed to life, defusing the hazardous scene for another moment. Silently, Mike prayed that it would be for him. Or at the very least, that the Principal would say something interesting enough to distract the class' gaze from him for at least twenty seconds.

"Alexander Drew, report to the Guidance Office please. Alexander Drew to the Guidance Office."

Again, the entire class fell into a collective muteness, Mike included.

Well, he commented mentally, cocking his head to one side. *That should do it.*

Xander stared at the wall where a crucifix hung, a carved likeness of Christ himself hung there in eternal suffering. It made him uncomfortable, the Lord's eyes gazing down at him as if to ask for help. One more person he couldn't save. The Womb flinched and he thought he heard it moan, a sound not unlike one's stomach rumbling after a lengthy period of fasting. He was scratching at his wrists nervously until he realized that those were the exact spots where he himself had been crucified just over a month ago. Xander forced himself to cease.

"Hungry?" the pencil-necked man that sat across from him asked, the words distorted by the man's hands, firmly planted in front of his face. His black hair had been combed low over his brow, and in his current position it was almost impossible to see his eyes beneath the glare of his glasses. It was haunting, like looking at a robot.

The sudden question startled Xander, snapping his head back to attention. He'd almost forgotten that the sunlight-deprived guidance counselor had been there, having already gone a full five minutes in complete silence. Xander's eyes shifted from one direction to the next, as he tried to grasp the question he'd just been asked. Finally, when the older man didn't get the hint, he had to say it. "What?"

O'Toole raised his eyebrows, which allowed Xander a split-second glimpse at his pupils, Warren O'Toole explained himself. "Sorry. I heard your stomach growling. Are you hungry?" he motioned toward a small cooler in the corner, offering Xander some of the contents.

"No, thanks," he smiled in return, letting his face sink back into a frown. He hadn't eaten in days.

"Do you eat as much as you should, Alex?" O'Toole asked, whipping out his little notebook and scribbling something down, presumably the question he'd just asked.

"I eat when I'm hungry," Xander responded cryptically, raising an eyebrow at the oddity of the question. He sat up straighter in his chair, trying to see exactly what the good doctor was writing. "And people usually call me Xander."

O'Toole smiled. "Yes, of course. It's signed to most of your tests after grade four. That's an odd nickname. How'd you get it?"

"Why do you want to know that?" he responded, growing increasingly defensive as the man prodded into areas of his life he preferred not to venture into on a regular basis.

"Why do you answer a question with a question?" O'Toole said, looking up from his notebook for a moment.

"Same to you."

O'Toole laughed. "Yes, I guess that is true," he chuckled a little while longer, and then flipped to a new page in his book. "You're right, though. That's not really any of my business. I was just making small talk."

"Hmm," Xander grunted. "What's this for again?"

O'Toole looked up, ultimately making direct eye contact with his 'patient.' "Oh? This is for me. Just getting assimilated into my new job. You understand that, don't you, Xander? What it's like to find yourself thrust into a new situation with no idea how to get out of it?"

Yes. He cursed inwardly, looking away. But when he spoke, he said, "No. Why would I?"

"Well, I understand there have been some tragedies around here lately, Xander. How do you feel about that?"

"Quite honestly, I don't feel much of anything about it," he snapped, lying blatantly.

"Yes, well," O'Toole stammered, again jotting notes, "that's perfectly normal after the loss of loved ones for a little while, especially in kids your age. But sometimes that fear and angst can fester and express itself in other ways. Like eating disorders or issues dealing with rage... even sleep disorders like sleepwalking."

Xander stirred noticeably.

"Do you have any of those problems, Xander?" O'Toole pressed.

Again, Xander shifted. "Nope. Not-a-one," he avoided eye contact as he spoke, and the counselor seemed to find that interesting. He marked something quickly along the sidebar of his notepad.

"Still, emotional distress such as this could mount itself into your subconscious, affect things there... hypno-therapy has come quite far, you know. It has let many patients release things in a hypnotic state so that they don't bottle them up and explode in real life, see? And it's simple -" he reached into his drawer and pulled out a small pocket watch, just like the kind they used in the movies.

The True Womb surged uncontrollably, and Xander leapt from his seat. "Um, what did you say this was for again?"

O'Toole looked up, placing the watch harmlessly upon his desk and checking the time, "It's so that I can better understand the students in this school. This is just something to let you know that you have somebody to talk to if you need it. It's really for you."

"This is for me?" Xander repeated.

"Yes?"

"You have no interest in this at all?"

"Professionally? No, not really," he smiled warmly, convincingly even.

"Then why are you taking notes?"

There was a silence, and the smile quickly wore off of Warren O'Toole's face. He let out another chuckle, but this one was lower and much less good-humored than the last. He folded the book shut, held it up to Xander, and said "This? This is just for me. It's nothing."

"Hmm."

"Well, Xander, I - "

"Do I have to be here?" Xander cut him off, taking one step back toward the door and starting the zipper on his leather jacket.

"Excuse me?" O'Toole begged, his voice getting a little whiney and irritated. He removed his glasses and rubbed the bridge of his nose, then put them back on and resumed his gaze at Xander where it had left off.

"You said this was for me, right?" Xander repeated, motioning his hands to try and get the shrink to finish the thought for him.

"Yes."

"So, if I don't want to do this now, I don't have to?"

"Of course not," O'Toole smiled, spreading his arms broadly and happily. A little too happily, but now that was just being paranoid. "You're free to go whenever you want! Julie stayed for a good twenty minutes, though."

That stopped Xander in his tracks, but he decided not to take the bait by pressing the matter further. "Well, if I don't have to be here, then I have to go meet -"

"Mike and Cathy?" O'Toole interjected abruptly, checking a small card calendar on his desk.

"Yes, what about them?" he asked, feeling heat rise to his cheeks as he turned back.

"Nothing. I was going to call them in right after you left, is all."

Xander nodded, "Well, that's... not who I was going to see," he said, barely even able to sound persuasive to himself. "So, I still have to go now," he opened the door and was half way out when O'Toole called after him.

"Ever been to Los Angeles?" he almost yelled, struggling to gain the boy's attention.

Xander turned slightly, barely intrigued. "No, why?"

O'Toole smiled, flipping his hand as if to disregard the comment completely. "No reason. I'm going to be heading there soon... just wondering if you'd ever been."

Xander stared at him for a moment, trying to figure the perplexing little man out. When he got no answer, he turned and exited the room without another word, slamming the door behind him.

Julie Peterson stared at the combination lock in front of her, her fingers grasping gently at the dial as she struggled to recall the code to get it open. She bit her lip and cursed, unable to make the numerical sequence come into her mind. All that she could think about was O'Toole and his questions, and all the answers that she hadn't had.

"How are you feeling?"

No response.

"Are you nervous about being here?"

Yes.

"How have you been sleeping?"

No response.

"How is your family?"

My cousin Amanda's fine. Mom's freaked.

"How are you?"

No response.

"Anything new you want to discuss?"

No response.

She had wanted to answer that last question, badly. So much of what was happening now was new that it hadn't been a matter of what to say, it had been a matter of where to begin. There were the problems with Phillips -- like court dates and the statements she still had yet to make. She still didn't trust most of the people around her, and it seemed the feeling was mutual. Tommy and Sud hadn't been the first to throw a sexist comment her way in the last month, and something told her that they wouldn't be the last either. She'd trusted Derek, but he'd betrayed her trust to Mike and forced her to tell everything that had happened to her... and now Derek was in jail and she wasn't sure how she felt about Mike anymore.

Then there was Xander.

He'd seemed so brave fighting Derek. She wasn't quite sure what it was, but something had changed him in the last few months. Then again, *everyone* had changed so much in the last few months; she wasn't surprised that nobody else had noticed. A month ago, Xander wouldn't have been caught dead near any type of social event. Then, there he was, barging into one to save the day. It was a side of him she'd never seen, never considered, but one that she liked.

She huffed, putting down the lock and walking away from it, deciding that she could go to Lit without her books again and that the teacher probably wouldn't notice.

The last question O'Toole had asked still bothered her as she walked down the hall toward class, though:

"Have you ever been to California?"

No response.

CHAPTER TWO: FIELD TRIP

"Please, tell me you're joking," Principal Shnieder sighed, rubbing both his hands against the bridge of his nose. The small man looked almost dwarf-like behind the large mahogany desk that took up the majority of his office, cluttered with papers and knick-knacks that students had given him over the years. There was a mug that read 'world's best teacher' perched on the side furthest from him, and a Newton's Cradle sat to his immediate left. The man himself looked like something out of the *Wizard of Oz*. His nose was large and bulbous and his eyes small and red around the edges. His ears seemed to be half the size of his head and stuck off like their attachment to him was tenuous at best. There were frown lines dragging down the sides of his face that made him look like he was in a bad mood even when he was smiling, which, at the moment, he was not.

"I'm completely serious," O'Toole said without a second's pause, tossing a pile of files and a map onto Shnieder's desk. Someone had scribbled on the map in a red felt tip marker, marking a path from Maine to California, with a circle around Los Angeles. "These kids need a vacation, sir, and they're eight months away from having a real one. If they don't get a break, one or more of them is going to snap again. This... this 'field trip' could be exactly what the doctor ordered... if you'll pardon the pun."

Shnieder cocked an eyebrow at him, either not understanding the joke made or not finding it amusing. He took a brief glance over the files that had been spread out before him, and then at the map. "But why this?" he asked, tracing his fingers along the line O'Toole had marked.

"Because travel is good for us from bottom to top. It cleanses the mind, touches the soul, lightens the heart and usually relieves stress. It could mean letting these children bond in a new experience that has nothing to do with the horror that went on in this town, and maybe make some new friends as well. It's like a... baptism of sorts, I suppose."

Shnieder chuckled, thinking O'Toole had made another joke... then stopped abruptly when he realized he hadn't. "And just how do you expect us to send these students, Warren? Plan on breaking open the piggy bank for no reason other than your whim and the fact that your last attempt to give these students 'guidance' was a complete failure?" He looked like he had more to say, but there was a knock at the door and a young brunette girl popped her head in. "Not now, Jennifer." he almost snapped, and the girl closed the door again promptly. He sighed, turning his attention again to O'Toole. "It's a wonderful idea, Warren... but we can't financially justify sending these students to another *state*."

O'Toole grinned as he began rummaging through his briefcase. "Well, our Science Club has been grossly under-funded for quite some time now, and this could be a fine way to make it up to them."

Shnieder rolled his eyes, running a hand over his bald scalp. "We don't *have* a Science Club, Warren."

O'Toole removed another file from his briefcase and tossed it softly onto the paperwork and maps he had handed Shnieder a second ago, grinning from ear to ear. "We do now, sir."

⋏⟨⋏

Tommy Irons ran his hand along his throat, tracing what was left of the slice that Derek had made. The flesh there was still bumpy and scabbed in places, and he resisted the constant urge to pick at it. It was still tender to the touch, and more often than not it hurt to speak. Not that that prevented him from doing it, it just meant that when he became agitated half way through a conversation, he felt he had a valid excuse to stop.

He was wearing a turtleneck sweater to hide the mark, even though everyone had seen it being made. It was like anything else that happened in this school... everyone would pretend it didn't happen as long as you did.

Alone in the cafeteria, he stared down at the camera in his hands. It was an old automatic manual-load. Even though his parents had gotten him a digital one last Easter, he still preferred this one. There was more to it. With the digital one, all he had to do was snap the picture and it was done. With this one he could snap it, develop it, crop and compose it manually, and frame it. There was more time and enjoyment put into each and every print, and part of him loved it. He looked at the dial on top, set to nineteen out of twenty-four. He wasn't sure what was on most of the filmstrip, but he was sure that at least some of the pictures were things that he didn't want to deal with.

Glaring down at it, he opened the hatch and exposed the film to light.

He breathed a sigh of relief, then took out the ruined film and let it fall to the floor, again bringing his hand up to his throat.

Somehow, it hadn't made the pain go away as he'd thought it would.

O'Toole stared at Xander Drew from across the hall as he walked over to him, burning a hole into the boy's scalp. He had a devilish smile on his face as he approached where Xander sat with Mike and Cathy, like a child who had done something wrong and gotten away with it.

"Pack your bags," he said bluntly as he reached them, pulling out three slips of paper and handing them toward the three.

Mike narrowed his eyes and was about to make a retort when Xander did it for him: "Say what?"

"Pack. Your. Bags," O'Toole smiled, speaking softly as though Xander were challenged in some way. "You're all going to Los Angeles with the Science Club. The school is arranging an all expense paid field trip to the West coast, and it could be a lot of fun. I'll be going, too. I think it'll be an opportunity to show the students that I'm not a bad guy... just a bad shrink." He said that last bit with a humor and swagger that suggested he thought he already knew what their answers would be.

"We're not in a Science Club," Cathy pointed out, raising a finger.

"You are now," O'Toole replied sharply, making Cathy retract her finger as if it had been nipped.

Xander grabbed one of the sheets and glanced over it. It was a permission slip to be signed by his parents. He quickly handed it back to O'Toole. "Sorry. I hate to drive. I get car-sick."

"We'll be flying," O'Toole corrected between gritted teeth.

"My ears pop, too. Just can't take the pressure."

"Well, too bad," O'Toole sighed, tossing all three slips into Mike's lap. "This excursion has been made mandatory for all those victimized by Derek Smith... who all happen to be members of the Science Club. Shnieder's orders. It's either go, or you can relinquish yourself to me for three hours after school, *every* day, for the next three months."

Mike scoffed, finally speaking up. "That's blackmail. You're saying if we don't go, you're going to force us into therapy?"

"Well, you do have issues," O'Toole grinned. "But no. If *either* of you doesn't go... *Xander* will be forced into my sessions."

Xander huffed then looked from O'Toole to Mike and Cathy and back again. "When do we leave?"

O'Toole smiled in return. "I thought you'd come around. You have two weeks. Don't be late."

"This blows."

Xander glanced over at Cathy from across the pool table, a smirk finding its way onto his face for half a second. He turned back toward his balls, surveying the situation glumly. The Factory was nearly deserted and a thin layer of dust and dirt had settled on the floor, reminding him of the after-hours bars that seemed to feature in every Western movie ever made. Three of the lights overhead had burnt out a few days ago, yet nobody had bothered to replace them. The cooler wasn't stocked with anything that was inside its best before date, several of the less popular video games had been unplugged to save power and the glowing green puck was stuck inside the air hockey table. No matter how flawed it became, it was still home.

"That's an understatement," Mike agreed from between gritted teeth, lowering himself to be at eye-level with his stick as he aimed for the bright yellow one-ball, careful to line it up with the corner pocket. "The trip blows. The fact that Tommy and Sud and Julie and all the other people that pretty well want us dead are going blows. It all, to generalize a statement, blows."

"So, what you're trying to say is...?" Xander teased, motioning with his hand for Mike to complete the thought.

Mike leaned his mouth over to Xander's hand, as if talking into a microphone. "It *blows*," then, thinking for a second, he added, "But that's off the record," he returned to his game, sinking the one ball effortlessly, smirking as he lined up for the two.

"It's not that record that bothers me," Xander grumbled, drawing a look from Cathy. "It's what's on my record."

"What's that supposed to mean?" Cathy inquired, picking up on her friend's distress and walking over as Mike shot at the two, missing completely and allowing the cue ball to bounce harmlessly off the side.

Xander sighed. "I don't know. Nothing, I guess. Maybe I'm just being paranoid."

"Paranoia is just a word for people who realize more than the average person," Mike murmured.

"Plus, we've been given plenty of reasons to be paranoid lately," Cathy reminded him, reaching over and fixing the collar of her friend's black leather jacket, then touching Mike's hand softly.

Xander leaned down, preparing to bank the cue and slam the dark blue two-ball into the side pocket, having no other shot thanks to Mike. "It's just like this game." Xander said, almost to himself, as he tapped the pool table. "This is a hard shot. I always end up having to do things the hard way. But when I look back, I discover that there was no easy way. Somewhere along the way, life stopped giving me the luxury of making choices, and now I'm stuck shooting blind," he closed his eyes and let the shot rip, sinking the ball perfectly. "Course, sometimes everyone gets lucky," he smirked, turning to Mike. "Did you find out what O'Toole said to Julie?"

Mike rolled his eyes. "Basic garbage he said to everyone else. Why do schools even have guidance counselors? If they're not being useless, then they almost always turn out to be evil," he felt Cathy cringe then squeezed her hand in apology.

Xander shook his head. "He was looking for something. Don't try to tell me he wasn't."

"Now you're being paranoid," Mike said with exasperation, patting Xander on the back. "The job's getting to you, man."

"No," Cathy chimed in, thinking about her own interview with O'Toole. "I saw it too. The questions he was asking... they could have been about anything. Rape, what's been going on at the school lately... things that me and Julie could relate to. But..."

"But?" Mike strained, trying to see what he was missing.

Xander finished the sentence solemnly, "*But*, if they were taken in the right light, they could have been about the Black Womb," he said the last piece with a hushed voice, spying some kids at a table not far from them. Feeling them, really. He squared up his shot on the three, trying to make his conversation appear casual.

Mike rolled his eyes, throwing his hands up into the air and away from Cathy. "You've been watching way too many of those creepy pasta videos, man. You're whacked. Completely, totally whacked. You realize that you're whacked, right?"

"I'm not saying he's another Alpha or something, just-"

"What?" Mike interrupted, practically screaming his objection. "Just what?"

"I got a bad feeling."

"Me too," Cathy added.

"But I've got my feeling *here*," Xander announced, using the end of his stick to tap his right side.

They were both silent for a moment.

Mike clucked his tongue, and nodded with an excess amount of sarcasm in the motion. "That's great. We're going to be stuck in a small hotel room together, and you're getting in touch with your inner serial killer. Very comforting."

Xander grimaced at his best friend's words, gaining a pity-filled look from Cathy. "After what happened with Phillips," Xander nearly spat, focusing his frustration into his shot as the True Womb again began to show itself, reeling within his system, "I just don't want to take any chances. If we slip up again..." he hit the cue ball weirdly and it slunk to the side, tapping the eight ball. The pitch-black orb rolled softly, quietly into the corner pocket, slowly rolling down through the tunnels of the game table.

CHAPTER THREE: SCREAM

Los Angeles, California.

It is the largest city in the state of California by population and the second most populous city in the United States. Often abbreviated as L.A. it is a 'global city' whose affairs have direct and tangible ramifications on a world scale through more than just socio-economic means, having an estimated population of 3,950,400 people and spanning 470 square miles. The Greater Los Angeles Area, encompassing a larger area of five counties, has an estimated population of over 17.7 million people. At night, the city shines. It shimmers to life as fluorescent lights buzz on, giving the streets their character, each one with its own personality. The smog that blankets the city doesn't seem as concerning as it is lit aglow from street level. In the day, the sun is the brightest object in view... at night, it is Los Angeles.

In recent years, the city has seen a record low in violent crimes... only 29,737 violent acts a year, of which 481 were homicides, nearly triple the amount of some neighboring countries for that year. Criminality peaked ten years ago with 1,096 homicides and 245,129 property crimes. The year before, Los Angeles recorded 1,025 murders. According to research conducted by the LAPD quarterly, L.A. is home to 152,000 gang members organized into 1,350 separate gangs and has led to the city being dubbed the 'Gang Capital of America.'

West 33rd Street is considered to be one of the more affluent areas of the city. At its core, it is a business sector, with skyscrapers rising up so high that on most days people on the ground might never see its top through the thick soup of fog. City planners had made efforts recently to make the area more inviting for real estate and housing developers, developing man-made parks of grass that were a sickly green, rather than lush and inviting. The end result had been a checkerboard of nature and steel that made neither camp truly happy. The business community had not been able to expand into the area taken up by the parks, and the park was in the constant shadow of the buildings and never allowed to grow.

Wendell Voters took one last puff of his cigarette before flicking it into the street, watching the cherry spark and bounce in all directions when it hit the pavement. He held onto the last breath of smoke, holding the glass door to the building open with his other hand, before letting it escape from his lungs with some reluctance. It wasn't that he wanted to keep the smoke in so much as he didn't want his break to be over. In a twelve-hour shift, he only got two. He glanced over at the trees in the park, taunting him with their freedom as he watched the smoke join the glowing fog. He headed back in, pulling on the door twice to make sure that it was locked securely, then glared apprehensively down the corridor at the uncomfortable plastic chair behind the security desk as if it were an electric chair as he started walking toward it.

His blue eyes were sunken into his chubby face, and he had the beginnings of a beer gut. The blue and white uniform that hung loosely over him bore the name 'Shane' in several places, and his blonde hair had been cut short in the style most beat cops around the city used.

Wendell had been working this job temporarily for the last five years. He still felt the need to use the word 'temporarily' in his job description because he was still only doing it until he got into police academy. After six years of effort, the test results on his last try-out had been the worst of his life, and now he found it hard to get up in the morning and come to work for nearly minimum wage.

He'd come to hate the people that he worked with more than anything else. Every few months there would be a new one, fresh out of college without a friend in the world and still hungry for his mother's cooking. They'd be Wendell's best friend for the first few months, bringing him coffee in the mornings and saying pleasant words every time they passed by his desk, but after a pay raise they were always too good for him.

Last year his wife had given birth to their third, and he'd asked his boss – the very *head* of this branch of Shane enterprises—for a raise. He got a look like he had asked the man for a kidney, and instead received several coupons for ten dollars off a meal at a restaurant a few blocks over: a restaurant whose cheapest meal was fifty-nine dollars plus tax. He had used them as a birthday present for his brother.

As he pulled out his chair and sat down, he took a quick pan of his surroundings. The main hallway went up for nearly twenty feet before peaking at a blue-tinted window. The walls that came down from it were the natural grey of steel and concrete, stylized in a way that he had heard a number of the interns refer to as 'art deco'. The floor was tiled in a colour somewhere between clear skies and faded green limes, with little silver and gold flecks in it every now and again.

He sighed.

The view from this desk had been very impressive to him for the first month, but ever since then it was what he imagined hell would be like.

A red light started to blink on a large panel of switches and monitors in front of him, and he leaned forward. It was the light representing the top-left monitor for the sixteenth floor, but there was nothing on it when he looked. He waited for the motion-activated light to flicker back to sleep. When it did not, he sighed again and tapped three keys on the control board in front of him, bringing the camera feed onto the large main screen. He pressed his thumb against the joystick in front of him and jiggled it twice. The camera image shook in response, and he started to move it slowly, first completely to the right and then to the left.

The red motion light switched off.

He raised an eyebrow at the LED then scratched his stubble-filled chin, leaning back in his chair. As his mind began to wander again, he thought about shaving in the men's room before he went home. His wife had always complained that he shaved every day before going to work, and because every time he came home his face was rough and scratchy, she never got to enjoy him when it was smooth. He wondered what she would think if he came home in the morning with a baby-face.

Out of the corner of his eye, he noticed another light flicker to life, this one on the fourteenth floor. Squinting, he got up from his chair this time as he pressed the buttons on the control panel to enlarge the screen and grabbed the control stick.

The screen displayed a side-hallway of floor fourteen, mostly used for office supplies and meetings. The production floor that took calls for Shane's one-eight-hundred number was also located there (a large room with more than eighty cubicles and possibly the only place he'd ever seen more boring than his desk). He strained his eyes against the monitor as it hummed at him, trying to see any sign of movement on the low-resolution screen. He finally did, down in the bottom right, right next to the wall. A small air vent, no more than six inches squared, was flapping by the breeze created by the air conditioner.

"Fuckin' rats," he grumbled, flopping back down into his chair.

Feeling an itch growing in the center of his chest, he reached for his pack of cigarettes again and placed one, unlit, between his lips. He found that just the sensation of it in his mouth helped to calm him, as he wouldn't technically be allowed to have another for six hours. He sat there for a good ten minutes with his smoke dangling from his lips, when three lights sprang to life on floor twelve all at once.

A Shane employee had to be either security or a senior manager to gain access to level twelve. It was their research and development department and was full of files, prototypes and schematics for everything that the company planned to release onto the market for the next three years. He'd only been on that floor once, but constantly saw scientists and managers coming and going over the security monitors during the daylight hours.

"Shit," he cursed, grabbing up his flashlight and heading toward the stairwell. Behind him and outside his field of vision, the screens for floor twelve began to go dark one by one, and a second later all the red flashing lights went dead.

ʎ⟨⟩ʎ

When Wendell opened the stairwell door to floor twelve, he should have been almost blinded by the glow of the lights against the whitewashed walls. Instead, he was greeted only by the light green glow of the emergency bulbs and the dull buzz they made whenever they snapped on. It made the room glow like the spaceships in alien movies his father used to let him stay up late to watch, and that connection in his mind made him shudder.

His hand shaking, he reached for the flashlight strapped to his belt, pointing it forward and failing several times to turn it on before light finally beamed out of it in a V-shape, making a rudimentary circle where he could see more clearly. The bright light made dark shadows with the walls, making the corridor seem longer than it actually was. As he finally stepped from the doorway into the hall, Wendell almost jumped out of his skin when the stairwell door closed behind him.

Taking a deep breath and summoning all his courage, he walked up to the first door, room 1201, and touched the handle. It was locked, and even though there were dozens more doors, he still breathed a sigh of relief. Moving on to the next door he tried that handle too, with the same result.

There was less caution in his step now already, and he started walking back and forth down the hall, touching each handle quickly to make sure it was secure. Most of the doors were stark white and looked exactly alike, but some

22

of them had their own characteristics. One had a nameplate across it that read 'Arthur Shane', though he was convinced that the boss had never once used this office in his life. Another had an odd circle on it that was white and tacky, like a sticker had been pulled off it. When he shone the flashlight at it the right way, he was certain that he could see the loose outline of the biohazard symbol on it.

He had reached room 1212 and touched the doorknob. Again, it clicked and resisted as all the others had, and he turned to make his way to 1213, when he heard something shuffle about behind the door. Suddenly, that tight feeling was back in his chest, but this time it had nothing to do with smoking. His heart rate doubled from what it had been before he heard the noise, and beads of sweat began to force themselves from his pores. He stood perfectly still, listening to the darkness to see if there would be any more sounds. *One of the geeks probably left a window open,* he reasoned, trying to force his feet to walk away. But logic prevented him from moving. There were no windows on this floor, just the one stairwell entrance and the one freight elevator whose only other stops were the ground floor and the roof.

There was a sound again, and this time it was more like the tinkling of glass hitting something more solid... and a drip. There was a definite dripping sound, as if someone had left a faucet running. *If that's all this is, those nerds are gonna get reamed come morning.* He promised himself, as he reached for his key ring with an unsteady hand. As he fumbled them one by one, trying to find the one marked 1212, there were more sounds from behind the door. One of them sounded like a drawer closing. Finally, he found the right key and slid it into the lock, pressing down on the handle and opening the door.

The lab wasn't very big, at least not as big as he had expected. He had always envisioned it being large and sweeping with dozens of computers and blinking lights. Instead he saw a room not too much bigger than his living room at home. There were three computers, each parked in its own little cubicle adorned with pictures and memorabilia from the user's life. There was a large table in the middle with a few glass beakers on it—one of them very dirty—and a sink in the middle that had an extra faucet with a gas valve attached. On the far-left side of the wall was another desk, this one filled with computer parts and circuit boards of various shapes and sizes ranging from two millimeters to two feet in length. The tools lying around and the smell in the air led Wendell to believe that one of the scientists had been working on something at that desk just before he'd left for the day. On the right side of the room there were two safes, one mounted on the other... the bottom one open.

"Jeez," Wendell huffed, taking a step forward to examine it further. His foot splashed into something. When he looked down he saw that most of the floor was covered in a black, gelatinous liquid. He cursed the one word his wife hated, stepping back from the fluid again. As it ran slowly toward him, he shone his light toward the safe, spotting a canister knocked over near the open door. *Someone was here,* he thought, closing the door behind him again and hearing the snap as it locked itself automatically. *Someone was in there and tipped over that container of god-knows-what.*

He paused outside the door for a moment, listening for more sounds inside, like someone stepping out from behind the door or a closet. There was a small splash, similar to the one he had made when he stepped into the liquid. He backed away from the door a little more, and when he did he saw that the black ooze had made its way to the door and was now spreading into the hallway.

He turned and ran for the stairwell, his footfalls echoing off the white walls as he did. He slammed into the locked door, his chubby face mashing against the window for a second before he stepped back, fumbling for his key ring again. Finding the correct one, he glanced back at the eerie green glow of the hallway. The blackness was still seeping from under the doorway, and he briefly wondered just how much of it could have possibly have fit into that canister anyway. He opened the door frantically and started down the stairs, taking them two at a time as he tried to get to the security desk as quickly as possible.

It's nothing, he told himself over and over again, but did not slow his decent. *It's absolutely nothing. It was some rat or the wind or some kid getting into trouble or...*

He stopped just short of the exit onto the seventh floor. There, almost completely blocking his path, was a large puddle of black ooze.

He stared at it for a moment, and it was like staring into a muddy lake or a coffee cup. His reflection was marred and distorted, bending his facial features this way and that like a fun-house mirror. As he watched it, the strangest quote came to his mind, something a friend of his used to say when they were in college: 'if you stare into the abyss long enough, the abyss stares back'. Even though he knew it was crazy, Wendell Voters could not shake the feeling that the dark puddle was somehow examining him as much as he was examining it, and the thought sent shivers down his spine.

There was a small pit against his shoulder, and when he looked at it there was black goop running down his shirt onto his chest. He looked up and saw a great wave coming down toward him, and the last thing he heard was the sound water made when it screamed.

CHAPTER FOUR: CITY OF ANGELS

Xander threw his head back against the soft cushion of his headrest as the plane leveled off, breathing a sigh of relief. He felt his guts settle back down, no longer feeling like they were clinging to his rib cage for dear life. He closed his eyes and let the light from the lamp above his head filter in through his eyelids, watching as his flesh distorted the colors and shapes. It had been something he'd always done to try and relax himself. As the world around him seemed to shake just a little before righting itself, he realized that it wasn't going to work this time and he dug his nails into his armrest, resisting the urge to pop his claws.

"Comfortable?" Mike asked playfully, leaning in close to him from the adjacent seat. His feet were resting against the seat in front him and he was chucking complimentary peanuts into his mouth one at a time, looking more relaxed than Xander had seen him in a month.

He kept his eyes closed for a moment, swallowing back hard in an effort to make his ears pop. They did not. Taking a moment to prepare himself, he turned his head toward his friend and shot him a cold look. "You're enjoying this, aren't you?"

Mike grinned, glancing out the window and then back to his friend. "On many levels, actually."

Deep inside Xander, the womb organ twitched and shuddered and he felt a sudden surge of adrenaline course through his body, his muscles tightening and then contracting again. It was as if his entire body was hyperventilating. There was a large weight pressing down on his chest, making it feel as though his breast plate were always on the cusp of breaking, but never actually doing so. The weight sank deeper and deeper, like someone pouring thick tar around his heart. He felt like he was drowning. "I don't think I like flying," he said in a hushed voice, looking around at the coach cabin. Dozens of people were going about their business, listening to music, typing on laptops or just sitting and reading. Everyone appeared to be comfortable except him.

"First time?" Mike asked, but it was phrased more like a general statement than a question.

Xander nodded once, feeling as though any more motion than that may have caused him to re-live his dinner.

"Been a few years for me, but my parents and I used to go on vacation to Florida almost every summer. We flew the first year, and ever since then I've loved planes. Way better than being stuck in a sweaty car with my dad for eighteen hours."

Xander nodded once again, as if he hadn't heard a word of what Mike said.

"Best thing to do is try to relax. Think of something different."

Again, Xander shot him a look. "I'm several thousand feet in the air with at least one student who I know wants me dead, at least one administrator who I think wants me dead, and my best friend who seems to find all these things very amusing. You think of something different."

Mike laughed, then gave Xander a shove in the arm. Xander looked like he was about to vomit, and Mike made a note not to do that again. "I still think you've got O'Toole pegged all wrong. Maybe if you weren't so confrontational, it wouldn't seem like he was out to get you as much."

Xander paused to consider that for a moment. "Maybe," he conceded begrudgingly.

Mike's smile faded a little but did not disappear completely, as he nodded his head toward the next row of seats. "If I were you, I'd be more worried about her."

Xander furrowed his brow, turning to see what Mike was talking about.

Julie looked away the second he turned, pretending to laugh at something Tommy had said while picking up a magazine and starting to flip through it.

"What about her?"

Mike just smiled, turning back into his seat. "Nothing, man. Forget I said anything."

Xander watched Mike for a moment, then, steeling himself for motion, turned and looked between their seats at the row behind them, where Cathy was actually reading her magazine. "How you doing back there?" he asked, sticking one finger through the seat and waving to her with it.

Cathy looked up from the out-dated magazine and smiled at him. "Did you know that by the year 1999, personal computers will be small enough that one might actually fit in your home?"

Xander snorted, recalling that he'd heard that analysis somewhere before.

"I'm fine. It's not my first time flying."

"First time to L.A., though, right?"

"Yeah," she smiled, and it was a good thing to see on her face. He'd always loved her smile, and lately thinking of the future had only brought her sorrow. Maybe O'Toole had been right about this trip after all. "I've wanted to go for a long time. There's so much culture there that you just can't get anywhere else. I really want to see the Griffith Observatory and Grauman's Chinese Theater."

He shot her a look, his eyes sparkling with interest. "Seems like this is something you've put some thought into."

She blushed, and turned to look out the window as the clouds floated by, giving her brief glimpses of the ground far below.

"I think it's nice. You should get a chance to see those things, and more. I just... really didn't think of you like that before, is all."

She grinned at him mischievously and picked up her magazine again. "There happens to be a great deal about me that you don't know, Mr. Drew."

He smiled at her tease and turned back in his seat to leave her be.

Mike tapped Xander on the arm, grinning. "See what I mean? You still think this trip's such a bad idea?"

Xander felt the womb organ again rumble and jostle inside him, sending out a shiver that made even his toenails ache. "Sure of it, actually," he mumbled.

Tommy took his headphones out of his ears and laid them against his lap. The music still blared from them loud enough that he could hear almost every syllable and beat played, so he switched it off with his thumb.

He turned sideways in his chair, his long legs sticking out from under the armrest uncomfortably as he leaned out into the aisle and craned his neck until he could see the person behind him.

Julie flipped the page of her magazine, actually reading it now. Her hair had fallen into her face on either side, framing her features so that he could only see the inside half of each eye and the dimple in the center of her lips.

He smiled, a grin spreading over his entire face. It turned his cheeks into large, round balls under each eyelid, somehow defying gravity and making him beam. Eyes sparkling, he opened his mouth to speak.

"No," she said simply, not even looking up from her article.

He stopped, recoiling a little. "I didn't even say anything."

"Whatever it was, the answer is no."

"How can you be sure until you've heard it?" he drawled, that sly grin returning as he leaned forward.

She huffed, closing the magazine of her lap. "It was either to ask me if I wanted to join the Mile-High Club, or to ask if I wanted to see the cockpit. Either way, the answer is no."

The smile faded from his face and he moved to turn back around. He got halfway before he stopped, then spun back.

"No."

"Fuck," he groaned, turning around and lying back on his headrest. He picked up the headphones and brought them back to his ears, then let them fall back onto his shirt. His head lolled to the left, where Randy Owchar sat with his own set of headphones on.

Randy was tall for his age, his head almost touching the overhead compartment every time his head bobbed to the beat. His hair stuck out in dark clumps from around the edges of the tattered red baseball cap he always wore backward and there was a thin layer of stubble on his upper lip, but nowhere else.

Tommy reached toward him then stopped himself. Biting his lip, he leaned in and tapped him on the shoulder.

He jumped, turning quickly and forgetting to breathe for an instant. Chuckling, he pulled on the headphone cord, but left one in and his head continued to sway slightly to the rhythm. "Sup?"

"I got a good one for you."

Randy smiled, turning slightly to listen.

"I'm sitting on my porch the other day --"

"You don't have a porch."

"It's part of the joke."

"Whatever. You still don't have a porch. Why couldn't you have just been looking out your window?"

"You wanna hear the joke or not?" he huffed. "Anyway, I'm sitting on my porch and this guy comes walking down the street with some chicken wire in his hand, so I holler: 'Hey man, watcha doin' with the chicken wire?'

"'I'm gonna go catch me some chickens,' he says back."

"'You can't catch chickens with chicken wire, dumbfuck'

"'Believe what you want, man,' he says, then walks away. So I wait, and sure enough about an hour later he comes waltzing down the street with a dead chicken in each hand."

Randy raised an eyebrow, smiling slightly even though there was nothing to smile about yet.

"The next day, same guy comes walking down with some duct tape. So I yell: 'Watcha doin' with the duct tape, bro?'"

"'I'm gonna go catch me some ducks.'"

"'You might be able to catch chickens with chicken wire, but there is no way you can catch *ducks* with *duct tape*.'"

"'Believe what you want, man,' he says. So I wait again, and sure enough the motherfucker comes down the street about an hour later with a dead duck in each hand."

"So yesterday I'm sitting on my porch and the same guy comes walking past, only I can't quite see what he's got this time. So I yell out: 'Hey bro, watcha got this time?'"

"He looks at me, then raises his arm and says: 'This? I got me some pussy willow.'"

"So I say: 'Hold on, I'll get my hat.'"

Randy snickered then let out a full-blown laugh. Tommy did the same.

"Where'd you hear that?" he asked after a moment, his laugh fading into a chuckle.

"Sud's Dad told us once when we were out staying with him in the Cove. Said he heard it from a buddy of his he was stationed with over in Bosnia."

Randy nodded respectfully, then turned to glance out the window. Clouds moved past slowly in the distance, catching rays of light and scattering them in all directions. He couldn't see the ground, and was almost glad. "Thought they'd be going by faster," he mumbled, more to himself than to Tommy.

"Right," he said, shifting uncomfortably. "So, what'd you do to get recruited for this little adventure?"

Randy looked back at him, smiling. "Stole a bunch of smokes from that shop down the street. Didn't even get a chance to have one before the cops found me and made me bring 'em all back. What about you?"

"Couple fights, couple pranks. Was at O'Toole's memorial service, so I think that made me a de facto invitee."

"Glad I missed that one."

"Yeah, I--" He stopped as Mike pushed past him, making his way up the hall toward the front of the plane, cursing along the way. He scoffed, leaning out to throw a dirty look that would never have been seen by the intended person. Frowning, he turned back to Randy. "People."

"Hn," Randy nodded, his eyes following Mike as he went. He rolled his eyes then placed his headphone back into his ear as Tommy started to talk again.

"Need anything in there?" Mike asked, rapping twice on the bathroom door.

Xander threw up again in response, the sound of a solid, moist mass hitting the hard porcelain of the toilet bowl.

He balked, his hand in front of the door as he debated whether or not to knock again.

The door opened suddenly. Xander stood with his hands propping him up on either side of the frame, his face drenched with sweat and tiny bits of half-digested meat clinging to his lips.

"I ever come to LA again, I'm walking," he stated, urging a little as though he were going to vomit again, then stopping.

"That's three thousand miles. You may want to rethink that."

He grunted, pivoted toward the sink, and turning it on. Water spilled out into his cupped hands for just a second and he splashed it into his face then repeated the motion three more times before looking at Mike again.

"Better?"

"Much. How far are we?"

"About half way."

"Fuck," Xander moaned, stepping out of the bathroom and back into the hall. At nearly the other side of the plane he could see O'Toole looking at him, those shimmering round glasses sticking up over the seat in front of him.

"Ignore it," Mike said, offering Xander his hand.

"He'll tell me I've been drinking, next," he balked, waving the hand away. He stopped three rows down, then turned and went back into the bathroom.

Mike sighed, then turned to follow.

⋀⋁⋀

They arrived in LA after an ungodly long bus ride from Los Angeles International Airport. Everyone else had slept on the way over. Xander wasn't allowed such a luxury, for fear of slaughtering everything on the flying death trap called an airplane. He got off the bus and stretched, tilting his head upward to let the sun splash on his face. When he did not feel its warmth, he opened his eyes curiously. Although it was a warm fall day, the sun and sky seemed to have been permanently blotted out by the thick layer of smog that coated the skyline. He frowned, grumbling to himself as he turned and ducked into the porch of a small convenience store just out of the view of O'Toole and Hall, placing a cigarette between his lips and striking the flint on his lighter. He lit the cherry and took a drag, waving pleasantly to a shopkeeper that was eyeing him, who in turn flipped him off. *I think I made a friend* he thought, taking another puff.

"Hi," Mike said, stepping up beside him.

Xander nearly dropped his smoke in fright. "What the hell?!" he screamed, then calmed his voice, knowing that O'Toole was probably near. "What the hell?"

"What?" Mike frowned, shrugging.

"How did you know I was here?" he demanded, pointing down at the ground as if to explain where 'here' was.

"It was the closest dark, shady spot near the bus," Mike explained, as if it were a fact of life. "That's where you migrate to. Even at parties. I swear, if there was a table with chips and dip on it next to you, this would be Cathy's last birthday party all over again."

Xander stared at him blankly for a moment. "No way am I that predictable."

Just then, Cathy stepped up behind Mike. Her hair was still a mess from sleeping on the plane, but she looked like she was slowly making efforts to straighten it. "Hey guys," she said. Then she addressed her boyfriend specifically: "Mike, you know it's impolite to interrupt Xander when he goes into his dark corners," she scolded him, sounding much like a jaded schoolteacher. She even pretended to slap him on the wrist, to which he responded with a fake wince.

Xander narrowed his eyes, turning away from them both and noticed that Dawn Wieners were on sale for two for ninety-nine cents. That was a pretty good deal, all things considered. If his body actually needed the nutrients supplied by food, he might go for that. "Frig you both," he grumbled, taking a long drag of the cigarette, watching it light up his reflection in the pane across from him.

They both laughed at him, Cathy laughing a little harder than her boyfriend.

"Since when do you smoke?" Mike asked after a moment, motioning toward the slender white stick between Xander's fingers.

"Don't you start," he warned, aiming the cherry dead center between Mike's eyes. "I've already gotten preached at once for that, thank you very much," he glared at Cathy when he said that last bit, and she reciprocated the bitterness by sticking out her tongue at him, just a little bit.

"Seriously, man..." Mike started.

Cathy cut him off. "Don't start," she tisked, looking around her and smiling like neither of them had seen her smile in what seemed like forever.

Maybe some good will come of this, after all, Mike thought hopefully, watching his girlfriend take in the city. His own freckled face beamed as well as he saw the skyscrapers that jutted up from the skyline like weeds or fingers trying desperately to reach the sun.

"This place is beautiful," Cathy continued, her eyes darting around excitedly. "The streets are beautiful, the sights are beautiful - "

"The street vendor pretzels are beautiful," Xander interrupted. "The old homeless lady dressed in plastic Glad garbage bags peeing on herself is beautiful. Those prostitutes are beautiful... Actually, that one looks kind of like a middle-aged guy dressed in drag."

Cathy stopped then turned back to Xander, crestfallen.

"Cut it out," Mike said, low and authoritative. "Just because we can't enjoy this, doesn't mean she can't."

Xander looked as though he was about to object, then thought better of it. He finished his cigarette, threw the butt to the curb and crushed it with his toe. He stepped forward slowly, watching as more kids got off the shuttle bus, hurried along by a very impatient Warren O'Toole whose face seemed to be getting more and more red by the minute.

A sweet, thin girl with freckles stepped out, followed by a bulkier man-in-a-boy's-body.

"Did you find out anything about Julie and Tommy?" Xander asked, and his friends knew from the tone of his voice that the meaningless chat was over now. With that one, smooth motion they'd slipped into business mode.

"Julie was actually pretty excited about this trip," Cathy reported, walking over to Xander and placing and hand on his shoulder. It sent cold shivers down his spine. "She's never been real far outside of Maine, and seeing LA has always been on her 'to do' list. Just, with her parents' divorce and everything, she didn't think she'd ever get the chance."

"Hmm," Xander grunted, rubbing his upper lip as he watched her.

"Tommy's a different story," Mike piped up, "He's pissed cause Sud didn't get to come. Royally. Parents wouldn't sign the permission slips. He's been talking to Randy a lot though, and the two of them seem to be getting along fine."

"Randy?"

"You remember him, right?" Mike asked, his serious tone gone now as he fell out of character. "We used to always hang out, but when the schools merged after grade seven, our class was too big and got split into two. He went to the other class and we kinda lost touch."

"Oh, yeah," Xander remembered, his voice a little high and out of their military-game character as well. "No big deals yet, then," he mumbled.

"Let's keep it that way," Cathy chimed in, digging her nails into Xander's shoulder. It hurt, but he understood why she did it. It wasn't some moron with a vendetta they were fighting this time. There were over a million people in this town and no way to trace a monstrous murder by the time they left town. If the Black Womb got free, it'd be like a buffet table lined up solely for his enjoyment.

And Xander doubted that this time the creature would allow him to sit alone in the dark, snacking on Ruffles and dip.

"This is ridiculous."

Both Tommy and Cathy looked at Xander when he spoke, then frowned and turned back to the front of the bus as its brakes squealed it to a halt. Everyone on the bus seemed to rise as one, grabbing their book bags and knapsacks from between their legs.

Xander did not move, his body scrunched against the left window as he looked out at cars crawling by.

"Anything in particular you find so ludicrous?" O'Toole said as he stepped up behind Xander and waited for the line off the bus to move along.

"No," he smiled sarcastically in response. "Nothing in particular."

O'Toole smiled and nodded, pushing his glasses up onto his face with one jilted motion before moving on down the line.

Xander watched him go, his smile melting into a sneer.

"You're trying it now," Mike huffed, leaning forward from the seat behind Xander.

"Yes."

"That's not gonna make things any easier, you know."

"Depends on your point of view, I suppose," he said under his breath, pushing off the seat in front of him to get up. Mike followed, snatching up his own overnight bag. "Can't wait to see where they've got us holed up."

"It might be nice."

"It won't be nice."

"It might."

The line shuffled forward once again as Cathy stepped down off the stairs and onto the street, followed closely by Tommy and Randy.

"Wish I could see what was going on out there," Mike said, standing on his toes to try and get a better view through the grease-stained windows.

"You think she's going to get kidnapped thirty seconds after getting off the bus? And people call me paranoid."

Mike fell back onto his heels, shooting Xander a snide look as Julie and Warren O'Toole walked outside.

"I think maybe you need to take your own advice and learn..." he stopped, turning away from Mike as he stepped off the stairs and onto street level, looking up at the hotel.

It was a massive glass building at least thirty floors tall, tinted blue while green rays of light shone down at him as he stared up at it. Just a little to his left was a gold-trimmed revolving door that was at least twice his size, spinning to allow people in and out. Bushes and shrubs lined the base of the building on either side of the door as people walked in and out continuously, while a line of cars was waiting to pick each of them up as though they were pieces on an assembly line. Not one part of the building appeared to have a piece of dust on it.

"...Wow," Xander finished, unable to remember what quip he'd been about to make at Mike's expense.

In front of him, O'Toole tilted his head to look at Xander from over his shoulder and smiled. "Welcome to *The Bastion*, Mr. Drew."

He took one step forward, then another before finally finding his feet, continuing on through the revolving doors. There was a desk just to his left that was at least twenty feet long with odd angelic carvings etched into a surface that appeared to be marble. Cathy was smiling at one of the four receptionists behind the desk as they gave her a room key, then turned to see him and smiled.

"Not bad, huh?" she grinned, almost bouncing as she walked over to him.

"Uh... yeah," Xander said, still looking around. The main lobby was actually two floors high, and there was a restaurant at the far right that made his mouth water. The floors were shining and spotless, so much so that he almost felt guilty walking on them. Lining the wall in front of him were large glass display cases exhibiting different mementos from L.A. and the hotel. A large case featuring the front of a ship caught his eye, and he made a mental note to examine it more closely later.

Cathy smiled at him.

"What?"

"Nothing."

Mike stepped up behind Cathy carrying two room key cards, handing one of them to Xander. "We're all on the third floor. I think the school booked the whole thing."

"Hn," he hummed, gently taking the key. It was a dark gold color, and for some reason made a shiver run through his arm when he took it. Snapping back to reality after a moment, he turned toward Cathy. "Who'd you get roomed with?"

"Julie," Cathy drawled, rolling her eyes.

"Could be worse."

"Meh. I'll make the best. Always do."

Mike grinned, pulling her forward slightly and kissing her on the head.

Xander turned with a smile and started toward the elevators, spinning his key card around one finger by its chain.

⋏⟨⟩⋏

"...is based on the principles of Euclidean plane and solid geometries," the pencil-necked presenter told the students, almost giddy with excitement, completely unaware that he was putting the entire population of the field trip to sleep, save Warren O'Toole. Even Miss Hall was dozing off; her aging features slumped back against the stiff, wooden chair. Perhaps it wouldn't have been as bad if this man weren't so unbelievably boring. He could give Ben Stein a run for his money any day of the week. "So, for the next hour, you will be introduced to the basic postulates and theorems of geometry," he smiled to himself. "This is pretty exciting stuff." Half of the students began to laugh, only to realize after an annoyed glance from Warren O'Toole that the man was not joking. "You're encouraged to take these ideas and apply them to the topics of similarity, circles, area, volume, construction and proof. You kids are going to develop an understanding of these concepts, probably without realizing it..."

Xander became aware of a spot of drool working its way down his chin and wiped it away, hoping that no one else had noticed. He glanced around to make sure, then grumbled as he lost what was possibly the only half-decently comfortable position that one could accomplish while in these chairs. *At a science center, you'd think they'd know that the human anatomy was not meant to fit into something this shape.* He cursed, then looked around. Cathy and Mike appeared to be equally bored and uncomfortable, but Julie seemed to have found a startlingly good way to sit. Good looking, too, with her legs crossed before her. His gaze shifted from the girl, and up to the dinosaur models and signs pointing out sections on the genetics of human evolution. There was even an area closed off as 'COMING SOON - RENOVATIONS'. That caught his eye more than anything else. From the bit that he could see from here, there appeared to be models and presentations of different prototypes of technologies from the world over, and even a display on the possibility of anti-matter. *Then again, you'd think that they'd be showing us the interesting parts of science and math at this center, too.*

"What was that?" the presenter asked, raising an eyebrow at Xander.

Xander looked around. Everyone was staring at him, and O'Toole was giving him a particularly dirty look. Next to him, Cathy's eyes were wide with fear and amazement. He bent over to her slowly and discretely, whispering. "Did I say that out loud?"

Cathy nodded, clucking softly. "Yes. Yes, you did."

"I'm an idiot," he cursed, still whispering.

"Yes. Yes, you are."

He frowned at her, then turned back toward the presentation and pretended that nothing happened. Everyone was getting out of their seats now, and they were headed into a video Math lesson. *What joy, what bliss.*

Xander moved to get up as well, then stopped dead in his tracks.

33

Inside of him, the Womb flared up faster than it ever had before. It was a sensation that he imagined was not unlike drowning. Every piece of him filled with it all at once, and for a second he couldn't breathe and his heart would not beat. His eyes dilated so fast that they actually hurt, making him want to pop his claws right then and there to scratch them out just to make it stop. His muscles tightened and became stiff, and he felt like a statue inside his own body. He tried to call out to Cathy as the group began to move on ahead of them, but all he managed was an: "Umm-nh."

It was enough.

Cathy turned toward him, mere inches from where he had sat, seemingly paralyzed. She bit her lip as she ran over, motioning for Mike to move ahead to block them from O'Toole's view.

He complied, if reluctantly.

"What is it?" she asked, her voice heavy with concern and fear. "What?" when he did not respond again, she grabbed him by the face and forced him to look at her... with those two, soulless black eyes. Her own grew wide. Thinking quickly, she pulled him to one side, shooting an urgent glance at Mike.

He nodded once, moving off to stall O'Toole.

Cathy rushed Xander into a dark corner behind a very large statue, hiding from their fellow classmates. "What the hell are you doing?" she demanded.

"Mhn. Mhnnnugh!" he said in response.

She shot him an odd look, then realized what he was trying to say and released her hand that had been still clenching his jaw. "Sorry," she shrugged apologetically. "Now, what's up?"

Xander nearly collapsed onto the grey tile floor, trying to decide whether to clutch at his chest or his side, both of which were on fire. The Womb was trying to pump itself into his system. As it did this, it increased the pressure in his veins until they popped open at the wrists, neck, and sometimes groin, releasing itself onto the world, something Xander was currently trying very hard to circumvent. Sweat poured down his brow as he struggled for the air to speak. When he did, Cathy noticed that his mouth was bleeding steadily, from the extra set of jagged womb-teeth that were forcing their way through his gums behind his normal set. "New," he managed to spit out, his voice more womb than human.

"Huh?"

He took a deep breath, his face flushed red, and then he tried to continue. "The new exhibit. Last door to the right," he took a second and pointed. "There's something there. Something that's making the Womb act up."

Cathy made a face. "Why're you on the offensive all of a sudden?"

Xander shook his head, a motion that appeared to take a great deal out of him. "Not..." he shook again, as if forgetting he had already done it, "Not offensive," he corrected, "*defensive*. Whatever's over there, it has the True Womb freaked like nothing else. It's something its... we've... *I've* never encountered before."

Cathy turned, careening her head to see the exhibit door. There didn't seem to be anything odd about it. "You sure?" she pushed. "You haven't been getting much sleep lately, maybe it's reacting to that? Trying to wear you out so you'll have to break down and let it out?"

Xander paused, considering that possibility for a moment. "No," he said, finally, then tried to get up, leaning against the statue. "No, it's specific to that direction. All of my senses are up to eleven, and they're all pointed at that door, no matter what I do to try and pull them away. The Womb wants to know what's there, and it doesn't matter what I want."

Cathy wiped her brow, exhaling loudly. Her eyes fluttered about in her head, as if searching for a response to the question she dared not ask. "So, what are we going to do?"

"*We* are doing nothing. *I* am going into that display room to see what the Womb wants."

"Are you crazy?"

He turned to Cathy, his sharp teeth fully stretched now, making him look feral. He fought the urge to curse at her, the anger welling up inside of him with the black ooze. "If I go in there like it wants, it'll stop trying to take me over. Would you rather I 'womb-out' in front of everyone here? Kill more helpless students? That'd be fun, wouldn't it?"

She ignored his sarcasm, nodding in admission.

The anger melted from him upon seeing her looking so defeated, and he calmed slightly despite the womb's call to action. He got up and immediately collapsed onto her.

"Hey!" she yelped in a high tone, forcing him onto one shoulder. "You're not going anywhere, mister!"

"Let me be," he said grimly. He steadied himself, turned toward the door and began walking. Suddenly, he was an entirely different person. He was the man that she'd always known was inside of him. "If I'm going to die today, I'll do it standing up."

He made a beeline for the exhibit door, doing much better this time. With every step he took, it seemed that the Womb slacked off on its assault on him a little bit more. As he walked, he gained confidence. Confidence that he could handle whatever was behind that door. He'd taken down Genblade and Spider without a scratch on him. *Whatever you are, the Womb is the least of your worries. You're dealing with...*

"Alex!" came a perky voice from behind him, cutting off his own determined pep-talk. It was just as well, as he didn't really believe much of what he was telling himself, anyway.

He turned, the motion making the Womb flare up in annoyed anger, pounding at the gates of his subconscious. He could almost feel those teeth slicing down through his gums again, still sore from their last penetration. Coming straight for him was a young girl wearing a tight-fitting leather skirt that just barely qualified as a mini, showing off her long, slender legs all the way down to her knee-high boots that elevated her almost to his height. She had on a red shirt that looked more like a rag tied over the front portion of her body, the strings interloping on the back and casting the illusion of a spider web. Her brunette hair bounced and shone in the light from the fluorescent bulbs high above, her green eyes sparkling almost magically as she came toward him, a coy smile planted firmly across her rosy lips.

"Julie?" Xander mumbled softly, cursing his luck. Then he realized that he hadn't actually spoke, just meant to. He composed himself slightly then repeated "Julie!" mimicking her own constant perkiness.

She strolled up to him, stopping a mere foot in front of him and placing her hands on the back of her hips. "Hey, what're you doing hanging around back here? Going on some secret mission?" she asked jokingly, giggling a little and showing off that amazing, pearl-white smile of hers.

"What?" he said speedily, shocked visibly by her playfulness. "I'm sorry, I meant *what*?"

Julie looked confused for a moment then tilted her head forward a little. "Joke," she explained, trying not to laugh at him. "But not a very good one. Sorry."

"S'okay," he assured her, forcing a smile.

She smiled back, and laughed a little. It was the kind of laugh that young girls made when they thought a boy was interested in them: a kind of sweet, bubbling sound. It was a flattered laugh, one that his hyper-keen senses failed to pick up on. She pressed her hands against her hips a little more, as if posing for him, showing off. "Um," she began uncertainly, "It's just the way you stopped Derek after the memorial thing, y' know?" she continued, still trying to explain her apparently inappropriate quip.

"Oh?" he asked, trying to make it seem like a casual thing, to maybe diffuse the situation. "You were there?"

She seemed a little hurt. "Yeah. Um... ha... yeah. We, ah... we talked about it before."

"Did we?" he asked, stumbling over his words, "I mean, we did, didn't we?"

"Yeah. Anyway, you were, really brave."

"It was mostly *Cathy*, anyway," he said, putting extra emphasis on his friend's name.

Over behind the statue, Cathy heard and finally turned in their direction, eyes wide.

Xander struggled to stand, the Womb flaring up, hating being so close to what it wanted, and yet unfathomably far. "Cathy's the one who really stopped Derek. Actually, he almost killed me. My shoulder's still really mangled up."

"Oh?" she said, not without concern, reaching over to caress it. Her eyes bulged a little upon contact, and her smile crept upwards a little more, "Jeez, Alex. You're all muscle."

"Hmm?" Xander asked, noticing that his shirt was open a little. "I, ah, do sit-ups."

"Yeah," she said absent-mindedly, opening his shirt a little to get a look at his shoulder. "Sit-ups. But that... shoulder's not as bad as you'd think."

"I heal fast," he chuckled, the first honest words he'd spoken yet. He closed his shirt. "But, it's still tender and all."

She nodded. "Well, if it's any consolation, you look great."

"Thanks."

"So why are you over here? You couldn't take another minute of that load in there, either?" She laughed, motioning toward the mini theater where the math movie had already begun to play.

Finally, Cathy made it over to them. She took immediate notice to the proximity between the two, coughed once, and stepped between them. "Julie!" she said happily, forcing the brunette into a hug, "Long time!"

"Yea." Julie said sarcastically, rolling her eyes. "Must have been thirty seconds."

"No, silly. Since we talked!" Cathy shot a look at Xander, who nodded.

"We've never talked, Cat."

"Has it been that long?" Cathy continued, ignoring the girl completely. "We have to catch up." She started leading the younger girl back over to the shadows behind the statue, and Xander immediately turned and started back toward the exhibit.

"We should talk later," Julie called out to him, not realizing that he was gone. "Just the two of us."

Xander was less than a foot away from the door. He could feel whatever was inside. He could almost sense the shape of it, its power. He reached for the door, and he could feel vibrations coming from it into his fingers. As if somebody was playing a song with a lot of base just on the other side of the door.

"Mr. Drew!"

"Fuck!" Xander cursed loudly, clenching a fist and turning... right into the face of Warren O'Toole. His face turned white as he stammered, trying to find the words. "Um, you see, I was..."

"What were you doing back here, Mr. Drew?" he asked impatiently.

Xander looked past him to see Mike and Cathy shrugging at him apologetically. He cursed them, turning his attention back to O'Toole. "See, I was coming back from the bathroom, and the group had moved on. So, I was looking for..."

"Um-hmm." O'Toole grunted, obviously unimpressed. "Right. Well, the class is moving on to a different building now: Shane International Head-Quarters. Then we're going back to the Hotel Suite and ordering pizza, room by room. Have you and Mr. Harris decided on your toppings yet?"

"No, sir," Xander admitted, walking away from the door alongside O'Toole despite the Womb's heated objections.

Above them, unknown to Xander, a thick black liquid began to drip slowly onto the floor.

ʎʎ

Sweat poured down Greg Civil's shirtless back as he sat in his room, his jaw quivering and shaking.

His eyes were bloodshot and his nostrils burned as the stench of his own urine filled them, making him gag violently. His feet dangled over the edge of

37

the bed, just barely touching the floor and jittering back and forth against the carpet.

He tilted his head back slightly, looking at the jersey pinned just above his headboard. It was from when he'd played on the Coral Cove varsity team, the year they'd taken home the cup. Just below it was the last few remnants of a bottle of vicodin and an empty bottle of cheap wine.

His eyes squeezed shut as his hand moved up toward his head and he felt the muzzle of his gun rest against it lightly. Tears streamed out and added to the rivers of water falling onto his cheeks as he took one final, choked breath.

"Fuckers," he said with a wet voice, then his finger pressed down on the trigger.

ʎ⟨у⟩ʎ

Mike brought the pizza to his mouth, bringing his free hand up to catch the cheese that dangled off its tip. He smiled a little as the black olives over it mixed with the pepperoni to create a sweet, salty sensation that he was sure couldn't be duplicated by anything else. When he opened his eyes, he saw Xander staring straight at him from across the box, his dark hair down in his eyes. "You gonna have any?"

Xander sighed, looking from Mike to the half-eaten pizza and then back again. His stomach did a back flip and he squeezed it to try and settle it back down. "Think I'm still sick from the plane."

"Or from smoking."

"Or from the *plane*."

"Whatever." Mike shrugged, taking another bite. He didn't notice the cheese this time, and a long, greasy white tendril fell from the crust and landed on his crotch. Xander watched it fall, smirked to himself, and then looked out the window behind him.

There was an office building across the street that was made up entirely of large green windows. It took up his view of the skyline, so much so that he would've had to press his face against the glass and look up to have seen blue. Not that there was much blue to be seen in this city.

The glass shimmered and shook. He thought he could see his own reflection in it, staring back at him from the green world across the street. His stomach surged again.

"I think I'm gonna be sick," he said in a voice that sounded like his mouth was full of food. He got up and quickly scampered past Mike toward the bathroom.

Mike turned to watch him go for a second, then leaned back against the bed and took another bite of pizza. He looked down and noticed the cheese on his pants, spun his head to make sure Xander wasn't looking, then picked it up and ate it as well.

"Hur-Ruuuah," came the sound from the bathroom, followed by the unmistakable sound of vomit splashing down to water.

Mike balked before finishing off the pizza slice and throwing the crust back

38

into the box. Chewing and wiping his hands with a serviette, he noticed Xander's pack of cigarettes laying on the table a few feet away. He briefly considered tossing them out, but remembered that he'd be stuck in this room with Xander for several days and should probably avoid getting on his bad side. Instead he picked up another slice of pizza, shoving almost half of it into his mouth.

"Hur-Ruuuah."

The splash followed again, a little longer this time. It was followed by a series of light drips that he didn't want to think of. The toilet flushed.

"Hey," Mike called out between chews, "you done in there?"

There was a moment of long, still quiet.

"Hur-Ruuuah."

He rolled his eyes, tossed the pizza back into the box, then got to his feet. "Jesus Christ, man. You don't eat, how did you get so much --"

Mike opened the door and saw a large splash of blood on the floor next to the toilet. The redness spider-webbed out in all directions, forming hundreds of trails leading off from the source. There were chunks of meat in its centre that looked *raw*, the muscle the pinkish hue of rare steak and the fat a cloudy clear color.

His face turned white as he spun the corner, knowing what he would see but still being unprepared for it.

Xander was hunched over the side on the tub, facing away from him. His hair was damp with sweat. Every breath was crackled and laboured, his shoulders rising and falling painfully with each one. He spit, then sniffed, leaning in and arching his back once again.

"Hur-Ruuuah!"

Mike winced.

There was another splotch of blood against the tile wall of the tub. Instead of being splashed and spattered about, this instance had stayed in a small oblong near the faucet; slowly sliding its way down toward the drain. It was a deep, deep black.

"No!" Mike ordered, grabbing Xander by the shoulder and spinning him around.

His eyelids had receded and were almost missing now, revealing the tender muscle beneath them. The veins throbbed and pulsed and his pupils bulged, getting larger and larger with every beat of his heart. Soon they would overtake the entire iris.

Nostrils flared as blood ran from them freely, still red but on the darker end of the color wheel. His teeth were the real giveaway, though. They'd become long and sharp, growing over the originals in a sprawling maw of red.

Mike grabbed him by the shoulders and shook him. "You cannot do this, you understand? You can't do this here!"

Xander looked at him, the blackness covering almost all of his eyes now. He opened his mouth to respond, his lower lip quivering softly.

"Hur-Ruuuah!"

The blackness flowed from him now, as though someone had turned the faucet on high. It splashed down onto him and clung there, wetting down his shirt and pants until they clung to his body like a second skin.

Mike leapt backward as the black ooze got on him as well, but it just ran down his leg as though it were immune to the friction his clothes should have provided, splashing against the floor with a plop. Xander crashed to the floor in a large puddle of blood, vomit and black tar. The force of his impact seemed to make it come alive, splashing up and cascading inward instead of outward, folding back in on him until it covered him whole.

His shoulders stopped heaving, and the sound of his breath became very faint.

It lay there in a lump for what seemed like forever, so anamorphous and bulbous that it was hard to tell for sure which end was the front and which end was the back.

"No," Mike said, his voice a hoarse whisper and his back against the far wall.

Its eyes opened on the top of its head, staring straight at Mike. After a moment of glaring, they shifted down to where they should have been, staring at the floor. It turned its head upward, extending its claws to their fullest. Its scales shone in the soft sixty-watt glow of the bathroom lights as it leaned over one last time and vomited its mouth into existence.

"Hur-Ruuuah!"

When it looked back up at Mike its teeth were out again, yellow and sharp and stained with blood. It took one menacing step toward him, then another, never once taking those massive lenses away from him.

It remembered.

"Black Womb lives!"

"Fight this," Mike managed to say, his voice shaking and cracking more than it had on his first date with Cathy.

It took one last step forward, bringing them nose-to-nose. It stank like the sweat that wafts up from wet shoes, each of its powerful breaths making the odor worse and worse. It raised its claws until they were level with Mike's eyes, its almost featureless face staring at him from a million miles away even though it was only a hair's width away.

He closed his eyes, turning his head as far into the wall as he could and braced himself. He could almost feel the creature's claws even before they struck, remembering how it felt before. Remembering those quick, sharp little movements that almost felt good for the slightest moment as endorphins raced through his body. That euphoria was quickly replaced by a blinding pain that makes him wish that death would come quicker.

"Don't..." he tried to say, and wasn't sure if he did or not.

When he opened his eyes again it was gone, leaving only its stench and three massive pools of blood behind.

CHAPTER FIVE: DEVIL'S PLAYGROUND

Black.

That was the first thing Carlos Richards noticed when he stepped around the marble corner. It was a short, black dress clinging so tightly to the woman who wore it that it appeared as though she had been *poured* into it, to quote one of his father's favorite expressions. He hadn't quite understood the meaning until now.

She was young, no older than thirty-five. Her figure was thin and smooth, taking on the appearance of an hourglass. The dress she wore was strapless, held up, it seemed, by nothing more than her will. Her face was small and came down to a pointed chin, which seemed to be the only angular thing about her, and her hair was short and black, gelled down to such a degree that it almost conformed to the shape of her head.

Almost instantly, he felt all his muscles relax, save one, which seemed to tighten the more he looked at her. He coughed once, realizing that he was staring and yet unable to turn away.

She turned to look at him, her eyes almost too big to be believed and so dark a tone of hazel that they were almost black themselves. "Hello," she said, smiling brightly and showing off wonderfully white teeth behind dark lipstick. She looked gothic in nature, her skin so pale it was almost the color of ivory.

"Um, hello," he said, and his voice cracked a little in a way it had not since he was a teenager. He brought a hand up to his throat, his cheeks filling with livid red embarrassment.

Her smile grew, and it put him at ease once again. "I'm a little lost," she said, taking a step toward him and tilting her head, showing off a slender neck. "I was with a tour and got separated."

Carlos raised an eyebrow, walking over toward her, adjusting his belt discreetly as he did. "Only tour that came through here today was a bunch of high school kids... and you don't look like one."

"I'm a teacher," she replied, extending her hand forward. "My name is Leigh."

He took her hand and shook it gently. Her skin was warm and clammy, her hand delicate and soft. "You don't look old enough to be a teacher."

She smiled, looking down at the floor for a moment. If she had blushed, her skin was too pale for him to tell.

"If I'd had a teacher like you in high school... well, I would've paid a little more attention in class, if you get my drift."

She laughed a little then took a look around. When she did, Carlos could see beads of sweat on her forehead, one of them running down the side of her face. He found it odd. Although it had been a very warm day, he'd had the air conditioner on for hours. "I'm sorry, are you closed?" she asked, a worry in her tone as if she had only now noticed the dimmed lights.

He smiled warmly. "Yes, ma'am. We've been closed for about an hour now. You must have gotten very lost." They started to walk together toward the exit, and he placed his arm on her shoulder casually, a move he'd practiced many times in his youth. Her flesh was warm there, too, but instead of drawing curiosity it now filled his mind with pleasurable thoughts.

"Mmm," she smiled, taking a quick glance at his arm on her shoulder. "Yes. I was examining this exhibit and must have gotten lost in thought," she said, her voice wandering as she motioned toward the new exhibit. "One of my... students... was interested in it. Do you know when it opens?"

"Oh, a few days' time," he smiled, trying his best to sound as though he knew what he was talking about. "All of the displays are ready. I've gotten a good look at it while on night patrols... it's pretty impressive." He turned toward her, grinning, one eyebrow raised skyward. "Don't suppose you'd like the nickel tour?"

Leigh smiled coyly at him, taking a step toward the entrance to the exhibit. "I'd be... delighted," she said, her voice full of promise.

He adjusted his belt again as they both started toward the exhibit, and he held up the yellow tape that blocked it off to let her pass under.

The room was large and seemed to go on forever. Each table was a display full of dancing lights and dazzling effects. Some were more simplistic than others, with computer terminals running three-dimensional schematics. One had a virtual reality helmet attached, presumably so that the wearer could see something too large to fit on a display.

She scanned the room, and her smile faded until her face was expressionless. Her eyes darted along the exhibits, finally coming to rest on one: a computer terminal set into a dos prompt, waiting for a command line. Slowly, her grin returned, but it wasn't nearly as inviting.

Behind her, Carlos looked around, seeming more and more like a rube. His mouth gaped as he eyes the different displays, making it clear that his statement of being in here before had been a fabrication. "That's weird," he grunted, taking a step toward the north wall. "The air conditioner is off."

He stepped toward the grate on the wall that should have been churning out cold air for the rest of the night, waving his hand in front of it and not getting even a hint of a breeze. He frowned, wondering if maintenance was still on staff as he looked over the broken device, his hands on his hips. Looking down, he noticed something on the floor. He bent down to examine it, and found a small puddle of dark liquid. He pressed his finger to it, rubbing it against his thumb. It had the consistency of tar at first, but as he rubbed it the substance became loose like water, dribbling from his fingers and onto the floor.

He looked down at it, wondering what could have made the air-conditioner spit out the vile fluid. It didn't look like Freon, or anything else he'd ever seen. As he watched, the dark pool began to flow down the floor for no reason at all. His eyes followed it as it went, seemingly of its own accord, down the hall. He had never been a scientist, but even he knew that water shouldn't run like this down a flat surface. It swiveled a little as it went, like the way a snake's body slithers back and forth as it travels.

He looked up, his face turning as white as Leigh's had been. The liquid joined with her at the foot as she stood before him, still smiling. The smile was different again now. Her head was tilted down and it showed off her teeth and gums... black gums, worse than any smoker's. Her eyes were still wide and sparkling with anticipation, but now Carlos finally recognized that it wasn't the same anticipation he'd been hoping for. Sweat was coming off her in buckets now, pooling at her feet and swirling about, as if it were an extension of her body.

He gulped hard, reaching quickly for his service revolver.

His yells of terror echoed throughout the halls even after he lost consciousness.

ᛣᚤ

He ran down the corridor, his body screaming out in pain. Every one of his joints ached, begging him to stop his sprint. His heart slammed against his chest with every beat, the blood it sent throughout his body hot like fire as he finally complied with his body's demands, resting against a garbage bin while trying to catch his breath. He closed his eyes and leaned back against the foul-smelling plastic lid, letting out a long sigh that bubbled into a laugh as a smile spread over his lips.

He'd made it out.

An hour ago, Lucas Sinclair and two of his friends had been at the Normandie Casino playing Texas Hold'em poker. Jimmy had gone out first, but they'd expected that the whole time. Jimmy *always* went out first. He had a tendency to bet when he had absolutely nothing in his hand to try to scare off the competition, but it didn't work on anyone who knew him. Still, he'd done his job well. He'd divided his chips almost equally between Lucas and Malcolm; giving them something of an advantage against the five other players at the table after Jimmy had gotten up.

With almost two thousand dollars' worth of chips in his stack, Lucas had gone all in before the flop with seven-deuce off-suit. Malcolm had looked at him with a wry smile on his face, knowing full well that he hadn't had a hand but folding anyway. They were there to pool their money at the end on the night, so it made no sense to take each other out. Four of the other players had folded, but one big guy with a crew cut and a UCLA jacket on followed him, sliding his two thousand chips into the center of the table and laying down pocket aces.

Lucas' eyes had almost bulged out of his head, and Malcolm let out a little laugh, slamming his knee. Pocket Rockets.

The dealer had even chuckled a little, looking at Lucas as if to ask if he should even bother putting out the flop. Lucas had gestured casually, laying down his seven-deuce and grinning confidently in a way he'd learned years ago to fake in such situations.

43

The dealer burned one card, laying down the three of spades, the king of diamonds, and the seven of hearts.

Lucas stared blankly at the seven, glancing from his to the one on the table and then back again. The rough looking man from UCLA did the same, but not quite with the same amount of nervousness.

A deuce of clubs hit the board. Then a seven of diamonds on the river.

A full house.

Lucas had leapt skyward triumphantly, as the college-boy ran his hands through his scalp, even cursing a little under his breath as he chuckled and watched the dealer push the majority of his chips toward Lucas. Ten minutes later, Lucas, Jimmy and Malcolm had cashed in their chips and were outside the Normandie having a cigarette. They had been getting ready to light up a joint when they got back to Jimmy's old station wagon.

One minute after that, they were running for their lives from four giants wearing UCLA jackets.

Lucas laughed again, bringing a hand up to inspect the gash on his forehead. It still streamed blood down his face and onto his shirt, but he laughed heartily anyway. He could feel the weight of the bills in his pocket, and that was more than enough for him. He wanted to take them out right then and there and count them, but forced himself to wait until he got home. Laughing again, he started to sing in a low voice. "Know when to hold 'em... know when to fold 'em... know when to walk away, know when to run..."

There was a clang in the darkness at the end of the alley that made Lucas jump nearly out of his skin, the pores in his forehead forcing more sweat to run down into his open wound and sting at it fiercely. He moved to the center of the alley and stared out into the darkness, watching as a discarded can of Coke rolled its way out toward him, stopping in a puddle of gas about three feet from where he stood. He gulped back the saliva his mouth was producing in copious amounts, trying hard to steady his breathing in case he needed to run.

From the other side of the dumpster, almost wedged in between it and the wire mesh fence that blocked off the alley, a foot protruded out, lying lazily on the ground.

Swallowing hard again, Lucas stepped forward. He almost fingered a twenty in his pocket, ready to take it out if this turned out to be some poor derelict down on his luck. He'd been there before, not too long ago. As he got closer, he smelled something that he recognized from his days as a short-order cook: burning flesh. He could almost see a thin trail of smoke working its way up from the garbage and joining the smog of the city. "Are you okay?" he asked as he stepped around the corner of the dumpster, holding out a hand in aid. He still couldn't see whoever it was, but he could see their outline in the twilight now. Whoever the poor guy was, he was small and he didn't move much, and Lucas was worried for a moment that he might have stumbled upon a body.

A low growl emitted from the darkness, and Lucas stopped dead in his tracks. All at once, two aqua-colored eyes opened, glowing against the black like beacons. They had no pupils, yet somehow Lucas knew they were staring right at him.

Before he could even scream, the creature was in the air. A moment later it was upon him, the money falling out of his pockets and scattering along the ground.

CHAPTER SIX: FREE DAY

Xander stumbled in through the window of the hotel room that he and Mike shared the next morning, his body slamming against the plush, pink carpet. "Ugh," he groaned, as the over-used floor fibers ripped and burned at his back. A thin layer of blood had formed around his body, and had already begun soaking into the carpet. His shoulder burned, but he wasn't sure why. His entire left world was encompassed by searing, white light that made it impossible to see anything clearly. He squinted to get past it, until realizing that it was him, not the room. As he tried to move, his shoulder screamed at him to stop. "Fuck," he cursed softly, reaching up to it. His hand withdrew from the wounded arm covered in blood. Fresh blood. His own. He grunted once, turned, and dragged his nails across his face, peeling the thick, congealed fluid away from his naked body; slapping it onto the floor. He stayed there for a moment, briefly enjoying the ability to breathe without sucking in his own bodily secretions, then looked up.

Mike was sitting on the edge of his bed calmly, his fingers folded in front of his mouth with his elbows rested on his knees. He was using his left foot to scratch the right, bunching his socks as he did so. The room was dark in the pre-dawn hours, the sun just barely beginning to peak above the far-off skyscrapers and in through their window. He wasn't looking at Xander, but was rather basking in the soft glow of the television screen, centered in the hotel room.

Xander sighed. "Look, I know what happened last night must have been hard on you..." he began. "... it's hard on me too." A beat. "You have to understand. Even though you can't. What you saw me like last night was... was what I really am. It's the part of me that's always been waiting to come out, and now I can't stop it. I've tried... starving myself. I've tried the whole, fun insomniac thing... lord fuck, Mike, I've even tried killing myself!" He stopped, waiting for a response from his still-dormant friend, receiving none. Getting not even the slightest hint that the man was even acknowledging his words. He waited another step, then inched closer to the bed. The television was changing colors rapidly now, like a fast scene in an action movie. "And nothing works. I can't stop it and it's in me and I don't want it to hurt you, man," he forced the words out, but not without feeling. "And it's not like I'm trying to make myself out to be some kind of hero or something, with you and Cat as my sidekicks. Gawd knows you're better at being a hero than I am. You saved me from Engen, stopped that rapist and... and!... you're the one who was looking after all of us during the whole Derek thing. I..." he paused, looking down at the floor. "I keep thinking that, if you'd gotten these powers... not me... this wouldn't be happening. You'd be together, calm and cool. You'd be what I can't, a - "

"Shut up," Mike said, finally turning. He raised a finger to add punch to the order then pointed it at the glowing blue television.

Brow knitted, Xander finally walked over until the television was in full view. He placed one hand on Mike's shoulder, and another over his gaping, shocked mouth.

"- Tilby keeping you live from the Los Angeles Science Center; where the city was stunned hours ago when a local security guard reported the death of his partner over, of all things, the as-yet incomplete exhibit. Details are few, but one report has the survivor stating that he was attacked by 'darkness'. The man fell unconscious soon after, but police are investigating every angle in this brutal crime. More at ten, when David Brofield brings you 'Good Morning L.A.'..."

Mike turned his head slowly, taking in his friend's expression. He tried to think of something witty to say, but words escaped him. After a moment of searching, he simply shook his head: "...Xander..."

ʎʎ

"...is so cute," Julie reiterated, punctuating the remark with an open-palmed gesture that Cathy had thought was only used by cheerleaders in bad teen movies.

She rolled her eyes, trying to hide it from the energized young girl sitting across from her. "Yes," Cathy agreed, flopping her head down onto the fluffy bed. The covers were even still on it, and there were no other obvious signs of use. "Sure. Why not? Xander's cute. Fine. Terrific. Can we move on now?"

"So, what do you think?" Julie continued. If she had noticed Cathy's frustration, then she was paying absolutely no attention to it. "He's sweet enough, and he's got that weird, silent thing going on. You think he'd ever go for someone like me?"

Cathy's ear perked a little at hearing this. In all the long hours they'd been talking, this was the first time that Julie had gone beyond 'he's cuter than cute'. "I don't know," she started, then paused and let out a long huff. Her eyes became small and distant as she said, "Xander's not like other guys." She caught herself in a chuckle then, and it almost scared her. "He's *really* not like other guys."

Julie giggled. "Oh gawd, I know," she smiled bashfully, looking down at the bed she was sitting on, at her hands as she picked at her nails absent-mindedly. She had a starry gleam in her eyes. She tisked, as though she were punishing herself for thinking the thoughts she was. "I know. He's such a dork with the computers. I never see him at any of the big parties or... anywhere, for that matter. But, he's good... right?" she paused and squinted at Cathy, as if trying to ask herself as opposed to her roommate. "Yes, he's good. He looks at you like... I dunno. When he looks at you, it makes you feel weak. Everything starts to quiver and you don't have any control. It's like you're in one of those dreams where you want to run, but can't. And it's a little scary."

Cathy nodded. She had been in that situation with Xander before, though

46

not in the way that Julie was describing.

Julie nodded in return, taking the gesture as encouragement. "But at the same time, you get this feeling. And it makes you stronger. It's like you're better for having known him. He knows that he makes you weak, but the fact that he would never try to hurt you makes you strong. And when your body is contradicting itself like that, you stop feeling everything. Anything. You're just complete. There's no good or bad. You're just in that moment... and he's there too. You understand?"

Cathy took her words in; the bored look removed from her face. She looked at Julie in a new light, and nodded slowly. "Yeah," she said simply, smiling. "Yeah I do. I think you should go for it. I think you're what he needs right now."

Julie laughed, her hair bobbing slightly as she did so. "Oh my gawd!" she squealed with excitement. "I can't believe this. I swore when I was done with Glen, I was never going to go for another fixer-upper." She shrugged in dismissal. "But, I guess I've still got a little charity work left in me after all, hmm?"

Cathy laughed at that, now unable to wipe the smile from her lips.

Sud Windser leaned over the dust-covered counter of The Factory, giving a curt wave to Wade in the back through a porthole-sized window. The man nodded, wiping a thick line of sweat from his brow with one arm before turning his attention back to the grill. The fryer behind him was beeping wildly and threatening to boil over, but went ignored.

Sud nodded to himself, running a hand over the stubble that had formed over his scalp since earlier that morning, then started to tap his hands against the counter impatiently.

From across the room an older woman turned, looking at his hands and then at him. A wry smile perked up the corners of her lips, which were painted a light pink that had already been rubbed off onto several shot glasses. She got up out of her chair slowly, slipping just once before steadying herself and making the journey to his side of the bar. It was daunting to watch, like a toddler taking their first steps from one object to another.

He turned toward her, lifting up one eyebrow suspiciously as he looked her up and down. She was wearing a halter-top that he suspected had been swiped from her daughter's wardrobe. Most of the glitter had been washed out at some point, but some still hung on for dear life. Her face was covered with makeup and she constantly chewed on a large wad of nicotine gum, even though she carried a pack of cigarettes in her left hand.

"How you doing, sweetie?" she laughed, reaching over and touching him on the arm. Despite all outward appearances, she had a nice voice. It was sugary and pleasant, with a grittiness to it that came from many, many years of unfiltered smoking.

He smiled at her, looking up from his overhanging brow sheepishly. When he blushed, his whole head blushed, even his ears. "Hm."

She smiled. "You staying for a bit, or do I have to hurry?"

He smirked, tossing an eye at the doorway to the kitchen.

"You don't say much, do you?"

"No, ma'am," he said finally, smiling.

"That's fine... welcome change from most men I see around here. Don't be ma'aming me, though. You'll make me feel old," she laughed, leaning in and touching his arm again.

The kitchen door finally opened and Wade stepped out, practically balancing the bag of food he carried on his gut. He plopped the greasy brown bag in front of Sud. "Two cheeseburgers, three onion rings, a plate of fries and a Coke," he recited, checking a slip of paper in his hand once, then peering inside the bag. "That'll be fifteen ninety."

Sud nodded, reaching into his back pocket for his wallet.

Wade turned to the woman, looking her up and down. Without a word, he reached out his hand to her.

"What're you, looking for a handout?" she barked, laughing.

"Keys," he said, simply.

"Fuck you. I'm fine."

He stared at her a long time, little to no expression on his face. "Keys."

"Fine," she huffed, reaching into her jeans pocket and producing a massive collection of key chains with only two keys attached to it. "Beer's watered down more'n piss. Can't see how you think anyone could get drunk off it."

He snatched them away from her, laying them on the other side of the bag next to the register.

She turned to Sud as he handed Wade the money, the register opening with its tell-tale buzzing and whirring noises. "Why don't you pay him for last night while you're at it?" she laughed, turning and walking away from them both. "Friggin'... fruit cocktail fucker fucks."

Sud raised an eyebrow again, watching her walk back toward one of the pool tables and nearly impale herself on it, somehow. He shook his head, coming back to reality as Wade laid his change in his hand. "Thanks."

"No problem, man." Wade smirked, turning to glance at the woman. "Don't pay her any mind. That's Doris McFadden. She'll come in here eight times a week and pull this crap."

Sud stuck out his lower lip, nodding in acceptance, then scooped up his bag of food in one sweeping motion. Nodding once to Wade, he turned around and left the way he'd come in, the electronic buzzer in the back chiming as he opened the door.

Wade snickered, turning to watch as Doris yelled obscenities at the offending table. Wiping another dab of sweat from his forehead, he turned to grab her keys and toss them under the cash.

The counter was empty.

᚛᚜

Sud tossed the bag of food into the passenger seat of Doris' car, then got into the driver's seat. He cursed over and over to himself as he slid the key into the ignition and started it, the car revving to life beneath him.

He smiled, pushing it into drive and pulling out of the parking lot as fast as he could. He turned left toward the city limits then kept on driving.

"You're sure?" Cathy asked, shoveling scrambled eggs into her mouth as she kept an eye open for both Julie and Warren O'Toole. Despite the situation, she couldn't help but smile when she put the yellow fluff into her mouth, soaked down with homemade maple syrup. "You're sure it was you?"

Xander shot a look at her from across the table, a full plate of food in front of him.

She met his gaze for only a moment then turned back to Mike, shoving more eggs and sausage into her mouth.

"How can you eat that like that?" Mike frowned, shaking his head as he watched a huge glob of syrup run down over her eggs and onto her plate.

"What? I like syrup."

"I like syrup, too. On pancakes. Or waffles. Especially on waffles... but it's not supposed to go on eggs," he said, grimacing at the food that disgusted him, yet unable to look away.

"I beg to differ," she chimed, dipping the last of her sausage into the pool of light brown liquid and popping it into her mouth.

He shook his head, turning away as if the conversation hadn't taken place. "We're sure. When he left the room, he was pretty deep in womb-mode. I think I managed to piss it off, actually. Then, the next day, they report a murder by a dark creature..." he let his words trail off, knowing he didn't have to finish the sentence.

"That reminds me," Cathy said, raising a hand to Xander as she forced herself to swallow. "I've got to talk to you about Julie Peterson."

Xander raised an eyebrow, but did not smile. "How did this conversation remind you of that?"

"I dunno," she thought, mulling that over in her head for a moment. "It just did. Listen, I really think she's got--"

"We don't have time," he cut her off, slicing his hand through the air in front of him, as if to physically cut the conversation short. "We've gotta find out more about this. About what I did."

Mike almost laughed. "Man, this ain't Coral Beach. I don't have cop friends here, and you don't have lawyer friends here. How in the hell do you expect us to find anything out?"

Xander frowned, looking down at the eggs on his plate and began to shuffle them about with his fork.

"Actually, I've got an idea," Cathy said, smiling proudly as she finished off her breakfast.

"This is ridiculous," Xander sighed, glancing from side to side. People pushed past him in all directions as he stood on the sidewalk, looking up at the building in front of him.

It was massive and white, with great marble steps leading up to the steeple that dominated his field of vision. The building stretched out for nearly half a block on either side of him, its walls pristine and white and dotted with the most lush and wonderful trees he'd seen since coming to the city. There were black metal gates with weathered orange lights on either side of them directly in front of him, just beyond where Mike and Cathy stood waiting. Far above, the stone visages of scholars looked down upon him with a mixture of admiration and contempt in their pupil-less marble eyes.

Mike turned slightly and frowned at Xander, giving him a stern look before he squeezed Cathy's hand a little harder, then continued toward the spacious building. The words above them read simply 'LOS ANGELES PUBLIC LIBRARY' in thin, cursive font.

"Just come," Cathy said, her hair bobbing from side to side as she motioned toward the doors with her head. "It's on my list of things to see anyway."

"Fine, whatever," he continued, his voice huffy and frustrated as they all passed through the solid oak doors. "How much information do you think we can get... from a... library..."

His grumbling slowed until it was dead in its tracks as he passed through the main doors, fighting the urge to let his jaw go slack. Mountains of books were stacked on high racks, reaching a ceiling that the he could not even see from where he stood. His hands fell to his sides as he watched gaggles of people move in silence, gathering information from hard records and a long line of computers. People moved about hurriedly, and yet without a sound, regarding old newspapers, texts, and encyclopedias; all of them were completely engrossed in what they were doing. They scurried about their tasks like feverish ants, each one oblivious to the person next to them.

From the main foyer, he could see up three levels, as well as the large metal statue that cascaded up through the center of all the floors. He couldn't have counted all the books he saw if he tried. It would have been like trying to count grains of sand in an hourglass.

"Wow," he said, craning his head so that he could see the ceiling.

"Yeah," Cathy concurred, "And if you spell that backwards, you get 'wow'."

Xander gave her an odd look. "Did you just make that up?"

"I think I stole it from somewhere," she pretended to whisper, bringing a hand to her face.

Mike smirked at both of them. "Yep. They have everything in here. They probably even know why they call pants 'pants'."

Xander and Cathy exchanged a look, their features growing red.

"Come on," Mike continued, motioning over to the computer terminals. "We've got work to do."

Mike sat down at a terminal and turned on the screen, then jiggled the mouse to get the annoying screen saver to disappear. "Okay, what are we doing?" he asked, opening his palms on either side of the keyboard with a tiny shrug.

Xander sat down on the other side of Mike, taking off his thick jacket and laying it on the back of his chair. The air conditioning tickled his skin, but he didn't mind. "Log onto the LAPD site."

Mike frowned and typed in the address into the web browser at the bottom of the screen. A golden badge emblem appeared in the top left corner, with blue words inscribed into it: 'LAPD Online.Org.' Next to it was a picture of the Los Angeles cityscape on a clean, beautiful day with no fog or blimps or anything else to block the sun's rays. He wondered when such a picture possibly could have been taken. Underneath the badge was a list of choices and topics about community events, missing persons, and most-wanted lists. There was a place near the center proudly stating that violent crime was down seven percent and property crime was down two percent. There was a spotlight in the selected area when the page was fully loaded, the picture and text slowly coming into view.

"Maybe that's it?" Cathy asked, pointing to the still-rendering image.

Xander shook his head in dismay, the picture coming into full view. It was a story about the Metropolitan's Mounted Police Division. He sighed. "What kind of city are you living in when a monster attacks an industrial complex and it isn't the biggest thing you have going?"

"Not a great one," Mike agreed, hovering his mouse over the links. "What am I doing?"

Xander leaned forward, pressing his finger against one of the lower links and smudging the screen, making it shimmer with grease. "That one. Press Releases."

He clicked the icon, and a new page began to load. It was a series of neon-blue links, none of which were helpful. "What now?"

"There," Cathy spoke up, motioning her head toward a search bar at the top of the screen. "Type in 'homicide'."

Again, Mike complied with the order given to him, having to go back twice after misspelling the word. Finally, he clicked 'search'. The mouse curser changed into a small hourglass for a moment as the page loaded up on the screen. When it did, Xander bit his lip. Cathy looked as though she'd seen a ghost.

There were over three hundred and fifty links to separate homicide cases. Unsolved. *This month.*

"Dear God," Mike breathed, the words coming so naturally that he didn't even realized he spoke them, surprising himself.

"We, ah..." Xander started, then noticing a link leading to a case of the murder of three young girls and had to stop and compose himself. "We... need to narrow this down."

Mike nodded, clicking a list to restrict it to area. "It was around Foothills, right?"

"No... No, it'd be South-East," Cathy said in a monotone voice, her eyes now glued to the floor.

Mike nodded once in thanks, then clicked the link. "Here we go. Homicide last night, industrial complex, strange circumstances, C.S.I. unit investigating..." he smirked a little, turning to Xander. "We got it."

Xander stared at the screen grimly. There was silence as his two friends listened to the sound of his teeth grinding together.

The smile wiped from Mike's face. "I'm sorry, man. I know this must be difficult for you. I just didn't think that..."

Xander did not respond. Did not budge. Did not shift his gaze in the slightest. If there was any change, it was that his eyes burned with more and more ferocity with every passing second.

Finally, Cathy traced her friend's stare to the exact spot on the news statement he was staring at. "Second case," she mouthed, barely giving herself time to allow the words to register, then read on. "...'the attack on the Science Center was the second attack described in which valuable scientific equipment has been stolen in last few weeks. The first instance was...' was before you got here," She couldn't help the smile from spreading across her lips. "Somebody else did this, Xander!"

Xander remained as tight-lipped as ever.

Mike nodded, understanding. "Which means there's something else out there. That powerful whatever-it-was you sensed at the Science Center."

"Something I had the chance to stop, but didn't," Xander finished, biting each word as it came out of his mouth. He got up without another word, grabbing his jacket and heading toward the exit.

Mike and Cathy scurried up and started after their friend. "Xander?" Cathy called after him, making no attempt to hide the concern in her voice. "We've got the whole day off," she reminded him as she caught up with him, heading back out into the warm light of day. "What do you plan on doing?"

"Yeah, man," Mike agreed, placing a hand on Xander's shoulder. "We have enough trouble catching people in Coral Beach. What do expect to do here in Los Angeles?"

Xander turned to face Mike, not without his typical overdose of melodrama. "I'm going to find this bastard. I'm going to show him what a real womb can do." He turned and kept walking, slipping his jacket over his arms despite the heat, and headed back toward the hotel.

Mike scowled, making a face at Cathy. They both followed him.

Xander's pace quickened, making his friends jog to keep up. His jacket ruffled slightly, the sound cutting through the air as he brushed past people, bumping shoulders with everyone crowding the streets. His lips were kept tight, offering not even a grin in solace to the people he was passing and ignoring.

"Xander!" Cathy called out from behind him, she and Mike becoming lost in the waves of human bodies covering the streets. It was like she was being carried away by a tide, reaching out her hand for him the save her or to notice her. He didn't.

Heading nowhere in particular, he just kept walking, his heels clicking loudly against the concrete sidewalk. The noise echoed off of the brick buildings surrounding them. Street vendor pretzels assaulted his senses with grease and filth.

Sewer drains backed up and made him cringe even more. The very air around him pricked his senses, feeling like tingly needles all over his skin.

Sud opened his bedroom door drenched in sweat and peeled off his sweat-shirt, letting it fall to the floor.

He took a step forward until he was next to his bed, then looked down at his chubby, hairless torso.

There was a gun sticking out of his waistband, only the grip visible outside of the tattered denim. His breath was heavy and laboured, his cheeks flushed and deep pink as he tried desperately to catch it.

"Muh," he grunted, his voice damp. He shoved his hand down the front of his jeans and withdrew the weapon, putting it down on his end table. It lay silent and still yet, somehow, it still raged with danger, like a jungle cat stretched out in the afternoon sun.

He let out a deep sigh, taking one last look down at himself. There was a small scrape on his left bicep that had almost stopped bleeding even though it was fairly fresh, a few small slivers of crimson trickling down his am and ob-scuring the tattoo there. It was a semi-circle facing downward with two prongs on each end, and the blood dissected the center of the arch and turned it into a lowercase letter m. He unbuttoned his jeans but did not take them off, giving himself some room to move. He belly-flopped onto the bed, the weak springs squealing out for mercy and then stabbing back at him in retaliation. He barely noticed. As soon as his head hit the pillow the long hours between his visits to it caught up to him.

He was asleep within minutes, the gun on his nightstand maintaining its silent vigil over him all throughout the night.

The trio of friends walked down the hotel's main hallway together, each of them feeling so numb that they barely noticed the way the soft floor felt against the soles of their shoes. Xander turned toward he and Mike's room, motioning for Mike and Cathy to come with him.

"Naw, man," Mike said apologetically, with a slightly mischievous smile. "I think we're gonna see what's on the television."

"There's a television in our room," Xander said, staring at the ground emo-tionlessly.

Cathy wrapped an arm around Mike from behind. "Not what we want to watch," she giggled, speaking in a naughty voice that she rarely used, yet was one of her most valuable weapons.

Xander's head finally popped up and looked at them, realizing what was going on. "Oh," he said simply. "Oh! Yeah, sure. I'll be..." he motioned toward the door, "if you need me, that is."

"I think he's got it covered," Cathy chuckled, then kissed her boyfriend's neck as she opened the door to her hotel room. He followed her in like a dumbfounded puppy, an unmistakable grin spreading from ear to ear.

Xander watched the door for a second, smiling. He thought briefly of Sara, of the way she used to move. The seduction of even the simplest twists or turns of her body. The way the corners of her lips pressed together while sipping strawberry milkshake from a straw. The way she dipped each individual French fry into a small pile of ketchup at the side of her plate before eating. Right then, he'd have given anything to have what Mike and Cathy had again. He'd wanted so long for Sara to belong to him, he'd forgotten about the simplistic joys of belonging to one another, of being with each other. His two best friends had started getting their lives back on track again, after all the madness had been placed on the shelf. They were the way they were supposed to be, now. Lovers. Friends. So, where did that leave him?

They've begun to put what's happened behind them... incorporate it into their lives... how can I do that without having Sara? Without having a person to give me their strength, and help me where I fail? How am I supposed to protect people, if I'm forever in need of protection myself?

He slid his card key into the door to his hotel room and stepped inside. He took a deep breath through his nose and caught the irresistible scent of vanilla. He smiled. Sara used to wear that: vanilla and rose oil by some European designer. It was so expensive she'd ask for a bottle every Christmas and only wore it on special occasions, but she'd always put on a little when he was coming over to watch movies. Just enough so that he could smell it when she reached for the popcorn that was rested snugly between his legs. He hadn't been expecting it and it hit him off guard. He became instantly aroused, and as such thought it was his own overactive imagination when he felt a firm, delicate hand upon his shoulder. *Sara.* He thought longingly, turning just out of almost morbid curiosity to see if she would be there.

Before he knew what was happening, he felt warm, wet lips press against his. He caught a flash of brunette hair, with the tips dyed a subtle blonde. The hair whipped about him, making it hard to even see, as the True Womb surged. He caught a glimpse of red fabric as he stumbled backward, losing his sense of balance with the hundred pounds of extra weight that gripped his shoulders. He fell back onto the bed, the sudden change in altitude coupled with the jolts of erratic electricity sprouting from his lips making his mind ache with dizziness.

She broke off the kiss long enough to look at him, straddling his waist slightly, if not awkwardly. Julie Peterson looked down on him, wearing a satin, form-fitting nightgown that showed way too much cleavage for a girl her age. It rode up to her knees as she looked down at him, a playful smile spreading over her thin lips. "Sit back, Alex Drew," she said, forcing her palms onto his shoulders to hold him down. "This is your lucky day."

CHAPTER SEVEN: LADY IN RED

He felt her lips on his, and it was as if everything melted away.

There was no monster living just a few blocks away from where he slept. There wasn't a rapist on their school faculty. There wasn't a killer designed to enslave all humanity rotting in a penitentiary. And most of all, there certainly was not a man he had considered his friend stabbing him in the back and trying to kill his girlfriend. He had not helped an evil, disturbed child commit violent acts against others. None of these events had occurred. Because as far as the two of them were concerned, it was only moments like these that truly mattered. Her lips, her entire body was like a heated mould next to him. Every spot he touched conformed to his fingers, creating comfort. He felt her hand brush through his blonde hair, then felt it glide slowly back into place, sending shivers up and down his spine.

"Mike," she said, her voice soft and full. "I love you." Her fingers traced down over his neck and chest as she spoke, stopping at the places where she knew that there were scars.

His lower lip quivered, longing for her touch to be welcomed there again. His blue eyes darted up to meet her own, unsure of how to proceed.

"I understand if you can't say it back." she gulped hard, her throat bobbing a little. "I would. We've both just been through so much lately-"

"And none of it matters," he cut her off, bringing a hand around to the back of her neck and pulling her closer to him. "All that matters is right now: this moment, none before. What's happened to us, what's been done to us... this is the first day. A fresh start. And all that matters is how much I love you." He kissed her again, and they leaned back onto the bed, their hands pulling each other closer together. The only sound heard was their lips smacking together, until they heard a door slam shut.

Both of them jumped up, their eyes immediately shooting toward their own door, praying that it wasn't O'Toole. The door opened with a loud thud, and Xander poked his head in. "Hey, guys. Hope I'm not interrupting anything." he said politely, if not with some sarcastic undercurrent. "Mike." he said, addressing him friend and cocking his head to one side. "C'mere a minute."

Mike cursed and got up, walking over to the door.

"Cathy," Xander said again, cocking his head toward the confused girl on the bed. He pushed Julie out of the hall and into the bedroom. Her eyes were bloodshot and her cheeks were soaked with tears, her hands and knees trembling a little. "Deal with that."

Mike walked back into the room he shared with Xander, shaking his head a little. "Do I even wanna?" he asked, scratching the back of his head.

Xander shot him a droll look. "You really don' wanna. Gawd, I don't even wanna."

Mike laughed, turning and laying down on the bed. "So, how is she?" he asked bluntly, no longer trying to hide his amusement.

Xander's eyes went wide, his cheeks red. "Shut up," he ordered, pointing a finger. "That's... that's just... I can honestly say I don't know what that is. Really."

"You really can choose 'em, man."

"Shut up."

"The only real question is: how could you not have seen it coming?"

"I'm telling you to shut up. I don't even know why I'm telling you, I'm not even listening to you. You!"

Mike shook his head. "Julie Peterson," he frowned, taking a more serious tone. "You know you can't, right?"

Xander nodded. "Not even if I wanted to. I know, I know."

There was a long moment then when neither of them said anything.

"Hmm." Mike grunted, and Xander didn't even look up. They both knew what he was going to say. "Big-Time Super-Hero, huh?" he asked, almost rhetorically.

Xander just huffed a response through his nose. "Yeah." he added, clapping his hands together once. "Yeah."

There was another long silence. "But, Julie Peterson?"

Xander laughed, and the sound felt good in his mouth. Somehow, sitting in a cheap room across from Mike Harris and talking about girls just seemed right. Suddenly, they were just two guys, in a room, talking about girls. *Who needs to grow up, anyway?* Xander reminded himself. *No regrets, not one. And missing this stuff... that's definitely something I've been regretting... and I bet that Sara would have regretted it, too.*

Mike, still laughing, flipped on the television to a news report of several murders at Shaw Tech just a few hours before. The second-biggest technology manufacturer in Los Angeles. Both Xander and Mike stopped laughing and watched as they wheeled bodies out of Shaw Tech one after another, seemingly to no end.

"- suspect that these murders are linked to those from earlier last night. The police behavioral analysis unit advises that the suspect may be becoming increasingly desperate, and should be not be approached under any circumstances-"

Oh, yeah. Xander thought, sharing a look with Mike. *Now I remember why I'm here.*

ʎ‹ʎ

Julie Peterson sobbed into Cathy's chest, her ribs shivering and convulsing as her lungs gasped for air. She tried to speak for the fourth time, again making the tiniest possible sound, almost like a puppy's yelp heard from afar. "I - feel - so - stu - pid!" she cried, tears again streaming down already burning cheeks, as she hiccupped for air after every syllable.

"Oh, honey," Cathy soothed, stroking the younger girl's hair back, using her nails to comb it rhythmically as her own mother had done for her many times over the past few weeks. She almost rolled her eyes, then remembered the days during she and Mike's relationship when she'd done the exact same thing, and thought better of it. "You're not stupid, sweetheart, no... no, no. Shhh. You're not stupid. You just came on a little strong, that's all."

Julie broke off their embrace a little, sniffing every two-point-five seconds as she wiped off tears and mucus in the neck of her nightgown, now covered partially by her bedspread. Her eyes red and bulging, she slowly eased herself away from Cathy, but never out of arm's reach. She looked off to one side for a moment, staring off into space and sobbing once or twice, slowly gaining control over her body's spasms. "Why didn't he want me?" she asked out of the blue then sniffed, letting tears dribble down again. "Why doesn't anybody worthwhile want me? Gawd, I thought him of all people... y' know?" she sniffed for what seemed like forever then, throwing herself back into Cathy's arms. "Thought," sniff, "thought maybe, he might like me for who I am and not just my body. But he didn't, he just ignored me when I tried to talk to him. And even when I tried to just *give* my body to him... And he still didn't want me."

"Honey, I think - "

"Gawd, am I good for anything? Why doesn't he want me?" she shook violently, and Cathy held her tighter to stop it.

Way to go, Xander. She groaned to herself. *Idiot.* "I know, sweetheart. I know exactly what you mean," she paused, leaning away from Julie until there was a foot of space between them so they could talk sensibly.

"How could you?" Julie whimpered, her gaze growing hollow.

"I was there, remember?" Cathy smiled, putting a hand on Julie's knee sympathetically. "I know what Masters did to you, right? And you're right, Xander isn't like that." *In daylight.* Cathy added mentally, taking a minute to see if Julie wanted to talk about her rape and belittlement. "But I was there too, remember? Masters tried the same thing with me, and Grendel tried it just a week before. And I turned to Xander for comfort, too. And it helped in some ways... but in a lot of others, Xander just didn't clue in. And it hurt me, just like it's hurting you now."

"Why would Alex do that?" Julie asked, finally speaking without tears or sobbing.

Cathy sighed, making the choice to tell Julie. "Xander was in love, Julie. Totally, madly in love with Sara Johnson. But now that she's..." she paused, forcing the word out, "...dead, that doesn't change the fact that he loves her. And it's all he sees everywhere he looks. He's not looking at us like we're women, he's looking at us like we're people. As far as that boy is concerned, the only woman on the face of the planet died a few months back." She paused then added. "And if you really want Xander... and I think that you should try to be with him, because he needs somebody... then you have to take it slow, girl. You have to take it at his pace. And who knows? Maybe he'll see you, the way he sees Sara now."

There was a long moment as Julie absorbed all of this into her system, wrapped up snugly inside of her blanket.

ʎ⟨⟩ʎ

The glow of the television illuminated Mike and Xander's face as they watched. They saw the camera pan over to a window where a black figure glanced out of the Shane Technical Institute at the commotion outside, then slinked its head back in. The secondary Shane building was a bustle of action as everybody tried to get in to see exactly what was happening.

"- The individual who has been terrorizing the business community has been trapped. With co-operation from Arthur Shane Jr., owner of Shane Incorporated, the police planned to make this building into a trap for -"

Mike didn't even need to watch as Xander ran to his bag, rummaging inside it for a moment before producing a small, curved blade. Out of the corner of his eye, he could see the blood start to flow as the redness turned to black, then sprung to life.

"- the creature, that we now know calls itself Black Heart. As it is, Black Heart has sealed itself inside of Shane HQ, with thirty-one hostages consisting - "

The blackness enveloped Xander's entire body, and for a moment, he was only slightly visible because of the blue glow of the screen. Then, the glowing red eyes burst out of his skull, and he opened his mouth.

" - of both Shane employees and customers using the firm downstairs. Black Heart has threatened to kill all of the hostages if she does not receive safe passage out of the building within twenty minutes..."

"Black Womb lives."

CHAPTER EIGHT: BLACK HEART

Pitch black saliva oozed its way between Leigh's clenched teeth as she stared through the venetian blinds at the crowd gathered below. The people on the street blended together at this distance, their movements seen only as ripples in the human wave that surrounded the building.

Sweat was tumbling down her forehead in great grey clumps as she turned away from the window, wringing both her hands through her hair and squeezing out the water there; sending it splashing unceremoniously to the floor.

"Fuck," she cursed, pacing the tight area between the window and the wall again and again, shutting her eyes stiffly and waiting for the answer to come to her. When she opened them again, they were all looking at her.

Thirteen Shane employees with sweat and tears pouring out onto their three-piece suits, all of them with their eyes fixated on her, watched her every twitch and motion. They ranged in age, sex, and race.

One man in the second row was particularly attentive. He kept looking her up and down and sneering, as if to say: *I could take her.* He wouldn't try though, but he was judging her for doing this, she could tell.

-MEEEEEP!-

The phone started to ring for the fourth time in as many minutes. The sound sent a shock down the wooden desk that she swore she could feel in her toes. She did not turn to look at it, but felt a brief release from the intense glares of everyone in the room as they all did, if only for an instant.

-MEEEEEP!-

She reached over to the receiver without looking and picked it up, immediately slamming it back down against its cradle. The others jumped a little.

Leaning against the desk for support, she took several deep breaths and stared at the floor for several seconds. There was a telephone jack with nothing plugged into it that caught her eyes for no particular reason, only that it was in her immediate field of vision and did not have eyes with which to stare back at her. Her grey-hued cheeks puffed in and out as she pushed air back and forth between her lips, more sweat drenching its way down her face and onto her neck.

The man in the second row looked her up and down again, letting out the smallest puff of air from between his lips.

Her head shot up as soon as she heard the sound, locking eyes with him. It was the first time she'd made direct eye contact with any of them since taking the room, and she was relieved to find it empowering. He shied away almost immediately, now the only person in the room who *wasn't* looking directly at her.

"You," she said, motioning him toward her with two fingers. "Get up."

He turned to the woman next to him, as if to say *Get up.*

"No, you," she repeated, pointing at him directly this time.

Swallowing hard, all indignation gone from him now, he slowly got to his feet. He still hunched, as if the slightly lowered elevation somehow hid him amongst those around him.

"Come here," she said, gesturing toward herself again.

Closing his eyes, he stepped out over the first row of hostages until he was in front of them all, then slowly closed the distance to her.

He was an average-height man with a cheap navy suit and a haircut that belonged in an eighties rock band. His face was boney and thin, but the rest of him looked like he'd missed a few too many runs on the treadmill. Still, he had the look of someone who at least *thought* they were in decent shape; at least he had until she'd called on him.

-MEEEEEP!-

She picked up the phone, quickly bringing it to her ear. "I want out of here, okay? That's all I want. You get me out of here and you get these idiots. Every three minutes I'm still in here, I kill one of --"

The lights went out, making the small office area seem too large to comprehend. Darkness has a way of distorting perception like that, making even the closest wall seem like it could be miles and miles away.

She grabbed the man next to her around the neck, digging her nails into his soft flesh as her eyes darted aimlessly around the room, waiting desperately to adjust to the light. Slowly, the shapes of the men and women before her came back into view from the light of the window and her mouth curled back downward into a scowl.

"You think that's fucking funny, do you?" she yelled into the phone, her eyes ballooning out of her face. "You've got two minutes before I off Mr. Roboto here, so you'd better wise the fuck right up, you fuck!"

She slammed down the receiver again, this time so hard that the phone snapped in two pieces.

"Please..." the man she held gasped, his hands wanting to pry her fingers away but not doing so. "Please, don't do this."

"Shove it," she snarled, giving him a little shake as she turned back toward the window. She reached out and pried the blinds open again, staring at the ever-growing crowd of police cars and pedestrians that were gathering around the building. None of them seemed to be moving about as she expected. None of them appeared to be clearing a path for her car or helicopter or paddle bike or what-the-fuck-ever. She turned back toward the hostages, holding the man between them like a shield. Letting out a long sigh, she wrapped her free hand around him until it rested upon his abdomen. If someone were looking in and did not know what was going on, they may have thought the two were spooning.

Her touch was light and yet vicious all at the same time, like the sharp edge of a blade dragged softly across your finger, just enough to tug at the ripples in your skin. Her hands were warm and damp, soaking through his shirt after only a moment and making it stick to his stomach like a layer of sweat.

He turned his head down despite his better judgment, her nails scratching at his neck as he did, and watched her hand as it lay against his gut.

Her palm was clammy and damp, making the ashen flesh come alive with sparks of moisture. A muscle near the base of her thumb twitched uncontrollably, making the rest of the appendage shudder and echo along in time.

He felt her breath hot against the nape of his neck, becoming heavier and heavier the longer she remained wrapped around him. Her heart slammed against her chest like a battering ram, each vein reverberating as waves of blood crashed through them. As he watched, the sweat that drenched her hand started to gain a dark tinge to it as an impossible amount squeezed its way through her pores. At first, the darkness was minuscule compared to the salty pools around it, like thousands of tiny blackheads. The beads swirled and wove about in their own tiny currents, growing and spreading until the liquid that covered her hand was almost totally the darkened colour of tar.

Her fingernails were sweating, too. As impossible as it was, beads of black as dark as shoe polish had formed on each nail, dripping down from one finger to the next and becoming more the consistency of wax than sweat. Her fingerprints became shriveled and loose as though they'd been immersed in water, their ridges and whorls changing into something unrecognizable almost instantly.

As he watched in horror, sweating into his eyes, the muscle and bone of her hand began to melt and shift in a way no human's could, caving in on itself and losing shape while somehow retaining mass, flowing down and then circling back to bear like water circulating through a fountain.

She was melting.

It was clear long before he realized it. The concept was so far from reality and so foreign that his mind would not go there even when presented with clear, irrefutable truth. When their flesh touched again it was like a puddle of water had been poured slowly into the concave arc of his chest, then left to warm in the summer sun. It stayed there for almost a full minute, defying gravity without a ripple or wave, before suddenly becoming sharp.

The liquid somehow pierced his sternum, sending bursts of pain into the massive cluster of nerves it found there. Signals crossed and jumbled in spectacular disarray before shooting up his spine and blasting out the back of his skull. The pain was horrible, yet each burst was followed immediately by a blast of tingling numbness that washed its way back down over him, doubling back down the path the shock and pain had taken. Insurmountable pressure built in his chest as more and more liquid pooled there, fed by the blood that spewed its way from the ever-growing hole in his torso, like air bubbling up from a drain as water swirled down.

He screamed, all the air expelling itself from his lungs in one massive, mournful burst. When the sound died, he tried to take in air and found that he could not, the flood that was weighing him down compressing his lungs too much for him to draw a decent breath.

She squirmed inside him as he felt one long sigh on the back of his neck again, followed by the quick gasp of someone who'd held their breath long past the point they should. She took one more gasp and let it go again before sliding her hand back out of his gut, whole and solid with all five fingers wriggling and consistent. The only sign that the event had even taken place was the splash of crimson that covered her hand in a swirling, unnatural pattern. It had almost stained her, as though when the appendage had reformed itself it had mixed with the blood, creating a tattoo on her flesh.

With a sickeningly moist sound, like a knife slicing through ripe grapefruit, she removed her nails from his neck. He crumpled onto himself as he fell to the floor.

Her face was expressionless, yet exhausted. Sweat clung to every spare piece of skin, especially along her upper lip. Her formerly tight cheeks now appeared chubby as her jaw went slack, every haggard breath shaking them violently.

"Guh," she said finally, taking a step over the body and toward the crowd, getting the bleeding mass out of her line of sight. She stumbled once, her legs turning to rubber. Slowly, she forced both her body and mind back to composure as she stared at the people in front of her. "You see that?" she yelled, spitting tar. "You see what just happened?"

-MEEEEEP!-

Another phone sprang to life from across the room. She turned only slightly toward it before slashing a long nail through the air, pointing at a middle-aged blonde woman in the back row. "You, get that! Tell them what I just did! Tell them that I want out of here, free and clear, or I do it to this guy!"

-MEEEEEP!-

She swirled toward the front row, her torso turning so fast that it seemed to be independent from her hips, connected only in the loosest possible sense of the word. She grabbed the first man she found there, trembling and soaked with tears and urine, forcing him to his feet. Immediately they were at eye-level, and she could see his cheap navy suit and a haircut that belonged in an eighties metal hair band. His face was boney and thin, but the rest of him was flabby and out of shape.

It was the man she'd killed a moment ago.

Despite the already pale nature of her flesh, she managed to become even whiter. Loosening her grip on the quivering, whining man, she turned her eyes back to the crowd. Moving her eyes over her hostages slowly and carefully, she counted each one. Her lips moved slightly as she mouthed each number, taking care to make sure her eyes weren't playing tricks on her. Then she counted again, finding that no matter how many times she did, there were still thirteen. More than that, they all stared forward in absolute, unwavering fear... but for the first time in nearly an hour, it wasn't directed at her. She turned slowly, chewing on the inside of her cheek as she came around a full one hundred and eighty degrees until her eyes found the body of the man she had thought she had killed.

He was not in a small pile on the floor as she had left him. He was hunched over, as if the simple act of standing took great effort. His eyes bored holes into hers, unblinking and unwavering, only slightly hidden by the damp bangs that fell in front of them. His jaw was set and clenched, cheeks shaking with each deep breath he took, finally able to breathe again. One arm was wrapped around his mid-section, holding in his innards as blood, bile, and shit from his ruptured intestines gushed out onto his arm. The smell was magnificently putrid, all the different enzymes of the body converging into one sick witch's brew. The free hand hung by his side lazily, swaying back and forth as though it was a disconnected pendulum; yet, somehow, it seemed ready to strike as well. At the end of each finger a thin hook of bone poked through, and it took her a moment to register that the man had claws. The blood that was still flowing from his mid-section, albeit slower and slower with each passing moment, was in fact no longer red but a deep, shadowed black that rivaled even her own.

Xander took one long breath as his lungs finally finished knitting themselves together, then let it back out again. The veins in his eyes bulged a deep coal, each beat of his heart making that darkness expand more and more.

She leapt quickly, the transition from shock to defense so sudden and clean that he barely had time to move. Her motion though the air was so fluid that when she changed direction it was jarring, like watching water move about freely of its own accord, independent of gravity. He dodged to the left, the screaming wave connecting to his arm. What looked like liquid had sliced and dug down to the bone, rending the flesh into long, spiraled ribbons.

Xander screamed as his blood gushed outward and upward, splashing to the floor while his body tried desperately to heal. The sensation was uncanny, like when rain ripped around you so fast that it felt like it was stinging and slicing at your flesh, only this time it was.

"Damn it!" he hissed, spinning and backing up to get away from her, almost slamming his back into the people knelt there. He turned to them angrily. "What're you waiting for, an invitation? Get the fuck out of here!" he bellowed, cheeks livid and pulsating with each syllable.

Most of them got to their feet, one or two stayed frozen where they were for a moment before the stampede of bodies toward the doors knocked them back to reality. They were screaming now, because they finally felt safe enough to scream; emotions that had been held behind a thin dam for so long finally flooded through.

He turned back to her and immediately felt her nails rake across his cheeks. Her fingers had grown long and thin, almost like talons. All surprise had eroded from her face as she stared at him with cool poise, her lips drawn up in a small black bow. He brought his hand up to his face, screaming as he felt her pass though his cheek and into his teeth. Now that his stomach was unprotected again, she twirled and spun both arms, melting into flowing, sharp masses as she moved and opened up the wounds again.

"Stop!" he yelled, swinging wildly and making contact with her for the first time, digging his claws into her shoulder. She screamed so loudly that it seemed like it was coming from everywhere, but the only way he knew it was a scream was the drawn out expression of agony on her face. The sound itself was like gargling, thousands of bubbles popping at once, until finally, the flesh his talons were in gained the same tar-like consistency her hand had a few minutes before, and then slipped through his grasp.

She backed up a pace, again breathing hard as he did the same; his ears ringing from the horrible, horrible sound.

He turned slightly, confirming that they were alone now. He looked down at the fingers that had been immersed in her shoulder just a moment ago, confirming that the flesh was, in fact, still there. He turned back to her, standing not quite a safe distance away, her shoulders heaving up and down as she struggled to take in air. It looked for the world like tides rising and falling, the waters dark and cancerous. "What the hell are you?" he asked finally, feeling his jaw ache as it moved. His words came out slurred, the sound distorted by the extra hole in his face.

She huffed through her nose, looking him up and down and then nodding toward his talons. She opened her mouth to speak, closed it, took several more breaths, then tried again. "You're one to talk."

He did not respond, watching as her skin seemed to literally crawl. Goosebumps formed on the surface of her flesh, flowing this way and that like waves. Even her eyes seemed to swirl about like whirlpools, and he could not bring himself to look at her teeth. Black as molten glass, her teeth and gums were set as a seething maw waiting to consume anything that came near them.

She lunged forward again, slamming both hands against his shoulders and forcing him to the ground. She was surprisingly solid and heavy now, pinning him down and digging her knees into his sides. They became so sharp that they broke the skin, puncturing his small intestine and forcing it again expel its contents.

He ground his teeth together and fought back the urge to scream.

She turned her head slightly, looking down at him with a mixture of puzzlement and curiosity. Her mouth pursed tighter than he'd ever seen before, becoming a tiny sphere in the centre of her face. All at once her head lurched forward and she opened her mouth past the point that any creature should be able to, almost becoming a Glasgow smile. Putrid smelling back vomit sprayed from her as though someone had turned on a hose, drenching down over him just as he was taking in a lungful of air. "Grrallgh!" she bellowed, her neck straining and stretching forward as more and more of her mass spewed down his throat, suffocating him. She held him tightly, her fingers like vice grips that refused to let go.

He brought his talons up toward his head, slashing at her wrists.

She tumbled backward, screaming again as she cradled both her arms in front of her, staring down at them as if she were coddling a child.

Xander got to his feet quickly, regurgitating the vomit she'd poured into him. It didn't smell like blood, but it certainly tasted like it, only stronger, fiercer. He tried not to think of the implications as it dripped and drained from his mouth and nose. When most of it was gone, he looked up again, watching her as she touched her disjointed flesh tenderly. It bled, the colour a spectacular crimson red.

He almost smiled, but found the gash in his cheek prevented it. "Had to turn solid to hold me down, huh?" he said, squatting down and withdrawing the talons from his other hand.

She made an otherworldly sound that he'd heard before. It wasn't something people often did, though they were more than capable of it. It was low, haggard and full of hate, so much that it charged the air around her and made her eyes sharpen with intensity.

Despite himself, his fangs started to push down through his gums and he felt the True Womb hammering at the gates. He crouched down then leapt from all fours, connecting with her mid-section and forcing her back into a line of chairs. She splashed against them, travelling up in a wide arc and falling all around him as he passed through her, slamming into the chairs himself. One caught him in the eye, and for a moment all her could see was pristine, white light. "Rahg!" he bellowed, rising to his feet quickly and spinning to face her.

The room was empty.

He stood completely still, only his pupils moving from side to side over the room as he stood ankle deep in the blood. His pupils were huge by now, the womb feeding them with every beat of his heart until there was very little left to the white sclera of his eye.

The room was silent at first, and then a bubbling sound started to come up again, as if from nowhere. It was her scream, rising up and going everywhere.

"What the sweet holy fuck?" he whispered, bringing the talons of his right hand to the wrist of his left and applying first pressure, preparing to let the Womb out into the open air.

Suddenly his feet were taken out from under him and he slammed his head back against the hardwood floor. The puddle he'd been standing in came out from under him like a rug, arching upward and becoming a massive wave that hovered above him, ready to crash down. Her scream came to deafening levels as he looked up at the wave in horror. He took a deep breath and prepared for it to envelope him, not sure what he would do once it did.

"Amateur," said a feminine voice from behind him.

He opened his eyes and spun around in time to see her elongated talons slash into his eyes.

He woke up twenty minutes later with blood and bile oozing from most of the holes on his face.

Blackheart was gone.

Xander walked back to the hotel, hanging his head in shame. Walking hurt the soles of his feet, and when he shoved open the glass doors to enter the lobby, it felt like his hand was on fire. His entire body seemed to be in shock; nothing felt right. He took one step into the lobby and looked up. Standing there waiting for him were Mike, Tommy, Cathy, Randy, Julie... and Warren O'Toole, shaking his head. "Get upstairs, Xander. Sneaking off is definitely *not* permitted here, young man. And you can expect me to recommend that your parents to administer a drug test on you," he fumed, his face broiling red.

Randy just sat back and laughed a little with Tommy, until Julie turned and gave them both a look. "Idiots," she said simply, shutting them both up.

Xander passed them all, walking into the main lobby, where three twenty-something guys were talking, each bearing large smiles.

"No way," a red headed one said, slapping the one in the center's knee. "That did not happen, Lucas."

Lucas Sinclair grinned at them both, a bandage holding the scrape on his forehead closed. "I'm telling you guys, this thing came out of nowhere. This big, black... thing. It had these huge green eyes and it just jumped out at me."

"Then what happened?" Malcolm asked, taking a sip of his coke as he nursed the cast over his arm gingerly.

"I grabbed up this broken beer bottle and I dug it right into the thing's face. Left side, I think. Anyway, it screams... it's still got the bottle sticking out of it. I start to runnin', right? Anyway, that's when them UCLA guys found me, but when they got a look at that thing..."

Xander smiled a little at the snippet of story he'd heard, and it made him swell with just a little bit of pride as he walked past.

"So?" Cathy asked as she, Mike and Xander all hurried up the stairs. "What happened?"

With one painful gaze at each of them, he told them everything they needed to know.

Mike was the one who actually said it, his voice bitter and contemptuous. "Black Heart escaped."

CHAPTER NINE: THE RIDE

The wheels on the bus vibrated as the vehicle sped down the highway back toward Coral Beach from the airport.

This trip was going to be long and Xander sat alone, his head leaned against the window, watching the ground go by beneath them. *It's like life,* he decided, frowning as the scab over his heart itched. The sensation was dulled now, but it still took him by surprise every time his clothes touched against his skin. *The wheels keep turning, bringing us to wherever the road may take us. We take for granted that the destination is good, that we're going home at the end of the day. But I guess we have to believe that to carry on. To keep rolling. To get past all the bumps and swerves that often surround us, and try to knock us down. There's only so much we can do to stop it, and sometimes, we will fail. Sometimes we will fall. But we have to keep driving. I have to believe, that as people, we will survive.*

He stopped, looking out the window at the trees. For a second, he thought he saw Sara's face within those old oaks, but she was gone in an instant. *I have to believe that this road will take me home. That all the bumps along this trip were actually worth it.*

Cathy watched Xander from afar, the turmoil ever-present on his face. She turned to Mike, whispering something to him. He gave her a quizzical look, but she kissed him, slipping her tongue between his lips slyly, nudging him to do what she had asked. Mike turned, whispering something to Tommy, who merely shrugged and whispered to Randy Owchar. Then, all four of them huddled together and started talking, leaving poor Julie Peterson in the dark, who sat alone next to them. After a moment, and a few glances from Cathy, Julie got up and moved to another seat. Cathy smiled.

Julie walked to the back of the bus and noticed Xander, his breath steaming up the glass. "Can I sit here?" she asked shyly.

He said nothing. Did nothing. Did not even respond to her presence. He just kept forcing himself to breathe, watching the breath as it touched against the window and being thankful for it.

"I asked, can I sit here?" she repeated herself, impatiently.

This time, Xander's head swiveled toward her, waking from the deep thought he had been absorbed into. "What?" he asked, looking up at her freckled face for the first time, really noticing her for once. Her cheeks sparkled a little, complimenting her gorgeous green eyes. "Oh," he realized, moving a little closer to the window. "Sure, I guess. If you want."

She sat, looking forward for a moment as the bus went around a very sharp turn. It skidded once then went back on its way as if nothing had happened. Xander's head knocked against the window hard, making him recoil from it.

"Oh!" she hissed, hearing his skull connect with the glass pane. "Are you all right?" she asked, bringing a hand to him tenderly.

He jerked away, a little too quickly. "I'm fine."

"No, here," she insisted gently, her voice soothing. "Let me see."

He conceded, turning his head to the left so that she could see. There was a cut there that was not quite closed, left over from his fight with Black Heart. The smack had caused fresh blood to begin to leak out of it, the healing factor in his body not yet restored.

"That looks bad," she cooed, and before he could stop her, she was caressing it carefully.

Goosebumps danced over his flesh as he got an odd feeling in the pit of his stomach. Like butterflies, or stage fright. In that instant, it didn't burn anymore. The damage he'd taken had healed and he felt her touch. Only her touch. Then, without warning, he felt something *more* than her touch. He turned and looked at her. This time, he saw her the way he never had before. The sun in her hair was like a halo, her smile somehow whitening as he caught a glimpse of it, and then her smooth, soft lips formed a little 'o' shape, out of pity for his wound. In that second, he realized: *she is beautiful*. He was about to speak, when she started.

"Look," she began, sighing her smile away into a frown. "I know I came on really strong the other day. I know that I shouldn't have... well, anyway, Cathy explained it all to me. What I needed to know, anyway." She paused, just for a moment, the regret evident on her face. "Anyway, I know, I, like, shouldn't have done what I did." Her eyes locked with his, and they both fell into a deep trance. "I should have just done this," she leaned forward, her lips touching against his softly. They parted a split second after they met as they both jumped back a little, and then they both moved forward again.

Her skin felt like heaven against his. She tasted of wildberry lip gloss. She was warm and comforting, and he found himself wanting more despite himself.

Deep inside of him, that new, good feeling grew with every second of her touch. And then, pain erupted from his gut, and another feeling shot through him, dominating all the rest. The Black Womb surged, wanting him to take more of her. He withdrew too quickly, and the hurt in her eyes was clear. He was about to speak, to try and explain.

"Miss Peterson?" came an authoritative voice from the front of the bus. Both of them turned to see Warren O'Toole glaring back at them. "Why don't you come to the front of the bus?" he said, and it was clear that it was not a question.

Julie turned to him, chancing a smile at Xander, then made her way back to sit next to Cathy.

Cathy smiled at her warmly, expectantly. There was a long silence as they looked at one another, a silence which was finally broken by Cathy. "You like him, don't you?" she asked, unable to wipe the smile from her lips.

"Yeah," Julie replied absent-mindedly, staring forward and re-imagining the kiss she'd just experienced. "Yeah, I do."

CHAPTER TEN: BLACK WOMB LIVES

He doesn't know where he is, he thinks, and yet he somehow manages to keep going. That seems to be his story these days... to wander aimlessly from one disaster to the next, simply praying for a glimmer of hope. Sometimes, more often than not, it doesn't seem worth doing. It seems like a fool's life, to go on despite a total absence of promise. And yet, he keeps going.

Somewhere, he thinks, he hears thunder. But right now, there is nothing but the dream. He's running, through woods and rivers. A wooded area devoid of all life... a forest of death. There's no colour: that's how he knows he's dreaming. The trees are a weird pastel grey, and there's no sound. No sound, that is, except for the patter of some far-off storm.

He feels something wet on his face and then falls over, clutching his abdomen in pain. He screams, but no sound emerges.

"Argh!" Xander gasped, as his nose and eye landed in the muddy, rocky ground. He felt blood rise to the surface of his skin, splashing out and letting the brown liquid all around him in, stinging at his flesh. As he reached up to wipe it away, he felt droplets of rain splash against the back of his hand. He opened his eyes and looked at it, and they burned as he wiped away the thin layer of congealed blood that covered his body. Bringing a hand gingerly to the side of his face, he found that the wound had already healed itself. He cursed nonetheless.

His shirtless body shivered relentlessly against the cold that seemed to assault him from all sides, biting at him like a ravenous wolf. He gasped and his lungs heaved, trying to get in every ounce of oxygen around him. He closed his eyes as his organs ached with pain, surging and rupturing blood vessels throughout his body under the stress of the change. He wanted to speak, to cry out, but had given up on such things weeks ago. There were no words. There was nothing that could portray or explain what he was feeling. The English language didn't convey such phrases. Nobody could understand what he was feeling right now... nobody else was the Black Womb.

Xander coughed, clearing his lungs and nostrils of the leftover remnants of the black ooze that had covered his body seconds before. When he did, his senses caught the full force of the stench of disgorgement that was caked onto him and his stomach turned over. Finally, he opened his eyes. He squinted into the darkness, and a wave of confusion swept over him.

The rain poured down, weaving a wet blanket over the world. All around him were evergreen and spruce trees looking dark and ominous in the low light.

He turned to see that stretching out on either side of him was a long, narrow stretch of highway, the yellow line in the center just about worn off, made to look even more faded by the growing puddle of liquid forming across it. The wind tore through the trees and the skin of his half naked body, chilling him to the bone. The rain smashed against his bare back like tiny pellets, feeling almost hard against sensitive flesh. Something howled behind him and he spun around quickly to find nothing but the same lonely highway.

The Womb, he realized with a start, *it didn't take me home.* A bolt of fear shot through his mind as something rustled the bushes to one side of him, then subsided.

"Where am I?" he wondered aloud, as water streamed over his face.

Out of nowhere lightning illuminated the sky, making him jump, followed almost immediately by the unmistakable crack of thunder. For an instant when the light was almost blinding, his eyes adjusted to his surroundings. About ten yards away from him was a green road sign with reflective letters that read, quite clearly: 'Coral Cove: 1 Mile'.

He glared at it for a long moment, gasping for breath as he tried to understand what was going on. "What the hell is happening here?" he asked himself, but received no response from his better half.

Thrown out on the side of the road like a greasy fast food bag, he started to trudge through the rain toward Coral Cove.

ᚷ

-RING!-

"Urgh," Cathy Kennessy grunted as she rolled over in her bed. The bright red numbers on her alarm clock glared at her menacingly, screaming the time through the blackness that penetrated her room. It was quarter past five, according to the glowing crimson digits. She reached over and turned the small, black clock toward her just to make sure. "Fuck," she cursed into the darkness, slamming her hand down on the snooze button to shut it off.

-RING!-

The clock called out again, and this time she clenched her hand into a fist and slammed it down onto that device that she so hated. "Dammit. I'm sure I set you for seven. If Trina messed with it again, I'll ring her tiny frigging neck..." she hit the clock again, and still, it let out that annoying noise.

-RING!-

Irritated, she sat up in bed and started to wake up a little bit, brushing her frazzled hair out of her eyes. She looked at the clock again and saw that the alarm button was still activated, so it had not gone off yet.

-RING!-

Her eyes grew wide and she turned toward the wall next to her bed, snatching the cordless phone off its mount. *Gawd,* she pleaded desperately, closing her eyes for a second as she brought the phone to her ear. *Please, let it not be Mike. Please let him be all right.*

"H - hello?" she stammered, bringing the phone to her ear. It whined sharply, and she pulled away from the sound as it assaulted her eardrums. She brought it to her head again, her grogginess showing through the concern at this late hour. "Hello?" she repeated, moving to shield her eyes as she switched on the lamp next to her bed.

"It's me," Xander said hoarsely on the other end of the phone. His throat was soggy with rainwater, and he fought the blinding urge to regurgitate. He coughed once then held the rest back as he watched the rain beat down against the small glass phone booth he was contained in. *Superman never had it this bad,* he thought to himself, struggling to pull a soaking red jacket around his half-naked body.

"Xander?" Cathy groaned quizzically, pressing her free hand against her other ear to try and hear him better. "Xander, is that you? I can barely hear you, speak up!"

"Yeah," he said louder, despite the pain it caused his vocal cords. "Yeah, hun. It's me."

"Are you okay?" she asked, then cupped a hand over her mouth. "Is Mike okay?"

He paused for a moment, making no effort to stop her words from cutting deep into his heart.

"I'm sorry," she said hastily, realizing what she'd implied. "I just - "

"It's okay. I understand. No, nothing happened to Mike. At least, I didn't do anything to him." He stopped long enough to cough again. "It's just the rain, it's itching at my lungs. I need a smoke," he cursed inwardly, wishing he could train the Womb to take a pack and a lighter on his nightly prowls.

She lowered her eyebrows, craning her head to see out the window. "It's not raining here..." she started to say, then realization swept over her. "Where are you?"

He turned around for a moment, and was greeted with a passing truck splashing muddy water on his face. "Argh!" he grunted, gurgling up the dirty water. Disgusted, he turned back into the booth. "Um, I'm outside a Burger King."

"What? There's no... What *town* are you in?" she asked, more specifically.

"Coral Cove, I'm pretty sure," he answered honestly, turning and giving the finger to the night staff at Burger King as they gawked out the window at him. "Go blow a goat," he mumbled.

"Excuse me?" she asked in that huffy, almost prissy, offended voice she used only on Xander and Mike.

"Not you," he snapped sarcastically.

"Alexander Drew, how did you get in Coral Cove? That's gotta be thirty miles away," she replied, fully awake now.

"Thirty-six, actually," he corrected anal-retentively, trying to be annoying now, agitated by her use of his full name. "And I don't know how I got here. I woke up here; the Womb brought me. I've got one hell of a migraine, that's all I really know."

"To or from?" Cathy asked, closing her eyes and massaging the bridge of her nose in frustration.

"What?"

"Were you going to Coral Cove, or coming back from it?" she repeated, slowly so that he might understand, although she still doubted it.

"I don't know," he answered, his voice growing distant. *What was the Womb doing out this far, anyway?* he questioned himself for the first time, turning and taking a hesitant glance around the streets. With a cautious eye toward the road, he brought the receiver back to his mouth. "Cathy, can you come pick me up?"

"Xander, I can't ask my parents to go out and get you at five-thirty in the morning! Why can't your parents do it?" she shouted.

"I'm supposed to be grounded because of that stunt in L.A., remember?" he sighed. "What about Mike?"

"His parents are out of town. Business, supposedly. In other words, they wanted a hotel to themselves again," she commented, rolling her eyes as she added in her own commentary about her boyfriend's parents.

"Shit. Last resort."

"What?" Cathy asked, gripping the phone. "Who?"

"I'll tell you later," he said, hanging up suddenly. He stopped, staring at the silver, square buttons on the pay phone, sighing deeply and closing his eyes before picking up the receiver again. He dialed the first three digits of the number, then stopped, trying to remember the final four. After another two, he paused again. *I can't do this. Can't call her.*

-BEEP- the phone screamed in his ear, as the monotone, automated operator invaded the line. "Your call cannot be completed as dialed," it informed him. "Please hang up and try your call again."

He scoffed at the black plastic in his hand, slamming it back down into place as if the answering machine could be offended by it. He stood there, breathing hard, glaring at the device and haunted by its obscurity; mentally willing it to erupt into flames.

Fuck this, he decided, turning and opening the door to the booth with the screaming of rusted hinges. He started walking toward the Burger King that rose up from the ground before him, the grass of its lawn wet and cold beneath the thin soles of his shoes. The workers within were still looking at him from beneath ludicrous paper hats, sweeping floors and pretending to pay him no mind. Three lone customers sat at a corner table, hunched over their food like vultures about to devour their prey. One was wearing an old-fashioned leather jacket with 'Harley-Davidson' printed across the back. The sleeves were lined with softly coloured, clear-red stones that seemed an odd contrast to the masculine, worn leather. On the bicep of each arm was an odd looking stylistic letter 'T'. He wore gloves, just the ends of which were visible from this angle, and black jeans that hung loose on his hips that appeared to be held up by a thick belt. Except for the light, curled blond hair atop his head, he could have easily stepped right out of the movie, *Grease*.

Xander stopped, freezing dead in his tracks. What little bit of drying off he had done while sheltered within the glass walls of the phone booth was for naught now, as the mid-autumn winds that swirled around him had already drenched him in icy water. He focused in on the man wearing the leather jacket, who was probably twenty from what Xander could tell, and ignored his two casually dressed companions who appeared to be gangly, and a little nerdish. They were a little like him, actually. The older man turned slowly, just enough so that one eye could look behind his back. It found Xander instantly, glaring at him as if to say, 'I know you're there.' It locked on him, as if Xander had been caught in some testosterone-saturated staring contest.

"Argh!" Xander screamed in pain, fighting the urge to double over as his entire arm felt as if it were on fire, blazing beneath the sleeves of his coat. He heard a loud splash interrupt the rhythm of the rain, and looked down to see fresh crimson rise to the surface of the puddle. Groaning, he turned away from the Burger King and pulled back the right sleeve of his jacket. His talons had emerged, yellow-pigmented shards of bone with black tips that were usually all that emerged unbidden, but now stretched to their full length, a good seven inches from his fingertips. Near the base, they would have been nearly transparent, had tendrils of blood not stained them. "Gahh!" he hissed, pressing the thumb of his left hand into his palm and pulling down, trying to force the claws to retract by using the same method he'd heard that vets sometimes used on cats. There was an odd wet, ripping sound just a moment before pain again surged inside him, this time bringing a response from the previously dormant organ within his stomach: The True Womb. He looked at his hand again, finding that the pressure of the claws coming out had torn the skin off his fingers, and it now hung loosely at the base, like a ripped glove.

"Dammit!" he cursed loudly, clenching his teeth until they ground together. The rain felt hot against the exposed muscle on his hand, sending shivers through his nervous system. The claws had come forth with such force that they had loosened his flesh clear down to his wrist. Tears welling up, he pulled his sleeve back down and placed the mangled hand inside his jacket pocket, praying that it would heal. When he looked up again, the telephone booth was squarely in front of him, centered in his vision. Taking another quick glance back toward the fast food joint behind him, he began walking back to it.

-Do doo doo doo doo dee do doo doo dee-

The simplistic version of the tune to *Funky Town* sang out, the user's chosen ring tone loud and aggravating, begging its owner to answer the phone and grant everyone around sweet silence.

Julie loved it. She picked up the bright pink cell phone and brought it to her ear, her trademark perfect smile stretching from ear to ear. "Hello?" she said in a perky voice, plopping down into a beanbag chair that dwarfed her in size, her brown hair lifting and falling softly as she did, the motion forcing a bubbly giggle to come out of her throat.

"Hey, Jules," Xander said half-heartedly, looking down at his hand as the claws slowly retracted. It was like playing a scene from a horror film backwards, watching them slide back into place within the bones of his fingers. "Sorry to wake you," he continued honestly after the talons had disappeared.

"You didn't wake me," she laughed, as if the idea were impossible.

"Its five-thirty in the morning."

"Yeah. I got in like, two hours ago. Then I started watching television. They were interviewing this really cool guy on Conan, who I thought was a guy, but it turned out to be an impersonator of that guy, but he wasn't, like, a guy at all, it was a girl... but she looked a lot like that guy, y'know?"

Xander dropped the phone for a moment so she wouldn't hear him sigh. He paused, working up the courage not to simply hang up on her. He rubbed the bridge of his nose, chanting softly to himself. "You can do this. You've saved the planet at least once now. Sure, nothing else you've done has worked out quite right, but I'm sure you can manage this, at least."

Taking a deep breath and ignoring the headache building in the back of his skull that he'd come to dub *Peterson Syndrome*, he brought the phone back up to his lips. "What were you doing out at three-thirty, Julie?"

"Wouldn't you like to know?" she replied coyly, and the sexual undertone made him shudder.

"Not especially," he groaned.

"What?" she asked, her voice a mixture of hurt and surprise.

"Nothing," he assured her, drawing a fist to punch the glass wall beside him, then glanced back at the still lingering Burger King representatives and deciding against it. "Hey, Jules, can I ask you a really big favour?"

"Mmm," she smiled, curling her legs up into her body. "Not until the third date."

"No," he said, trying to remain patient, "I was wondering if you could give me a lift."

"I'm surprised I haven't already."

He sighed, and she laughed. It was only then that he realized that she was deliberately trying to make him uncomfortable. He almost laughed, but the pain in his hand made it nearly impossible. "No, I kinda need you to pick me up. Now, this is gonna sound weird, but I'm by the Burger King in Coral Cove."

"No problem," she said without a moment's hesitation, then there was the muffled sound of the phone against her chest as she screamed: "Mom! I need a ride to the Cove!"

Xander pulled away from the phone, startled by the loud sound.

"Hi?" Julie said, coming back to the phone.

"Uh, yeah?"

"I'll be there in twenty minutes."

-click-

Xander just stood for a minute, scratching his head in confusion.

Cathy stared down at the phone just as she had for the last five minutes, curled up in a little ball and willing it to ring. Across from her, her television was on, the volume on low, as she waited to see a news bulletin that she knew would be inevitable. Any other fifteen-year-old girl her age would be watching the TV right now with the hope that some serious snow warning had caused an itchy principal to close the school. Instead, she was waiting for a news bulletin that would tell her that one of her friends was dead. Maybe it'd be that guy who sat behind her in math who used to put tacks on her chair when she was in grade three. Maybe it was Tommy or Sud, or somebody that worked late at the Factory on Friday nights and gave her the elevator, looking her over with their eyes while they poured her a cherry Coke.

What if Mike had finally broken and tried to stop the Black Womb? He'd been getting more and more reckless, darker even, ever since all this started. There was the debacle with Phillips when he frightened that young girl into admitting that he raped her. Then there was when Genblade's trial was going on and he took on the Womb alone, on purpose no-less... what if he'd finally went after the beast and snuck off in the middle of the night now that he knew his parents wouldn't catch him? What if Xander had killed him, and that's why the Womb had been running? Because it was afraid that if Xander found out, he'd kill himself?

What if--

She got up and grabbed her coat from the doorknob where it hung and pulled it on over her arms as fast as she could. Sliding open her bedroom window, she got the brunt force of the cold fall air and paused just long enough to zip herself up before jumping from her window onto the grass below, the impact putting a weight on her heels that didn't leave until she was well on her way down the road in the direction of the Harris house.

∧✕∧

A white minivan pulled up right next to the phone booth where Xander was still huddled. Its headlights were blinding, but gave Xander enough light to check on his hand once before getting in. It had healed, mostly, except for a few barely recognizable scabs on the tips of each finger. *Thank heaven for small miracles.* He huffed, opening the door to the booth and stepping out into the rain.

The vans wipers were going as fast as they could to fight the rain, making it impossible to see the driver. Mud had splashed up along the sides, making them look dirty and crusty, as opposed to the white sheen that enveloped the rest of it. The rain again drenched him, and this time it felt like the chill sank into the bone immediately, every drop hacking away at his very life. The Womb wasn't helping with the cold this time, or maybe it was just psychological. Like the way he still got hungry every time the lunch bell rang, even though he didn't need to eat.

The back door slid open, slamming against the ends of the metal track it was on. The sudden movement startled him as he slowly walked up to the door, unable to see inside from the blinding headlights.

There sat Julie Peterson, wearing a light purple Winnie the Pooh pyjama set with small bees dotted all over it, and Pooh himself snacking on honey on her left breast. Her smile was wide, and under different circumstances it would have been contagious. Her hair tumbled over her shoulders, curled naturally from the moisture in the air. Her lips were coloured a bright, vibrant pink that drew his attention directly to them, and when she saw him get in she scrunched her nose playfully, making the freckles that dotted her cheeks dance.

"So, this is the famous Alexander Drew?" came a voice from the driver's seat as Xander sat down, trying hard not to get the mud from his shoes on the seats.

It made him jump a little, though he didn't know why. "Uh, I guess that'd be me. Though I wouldn't call myself famous. I am distantly related to Adam Sandler, though. I was offered a role in *Anger Management*, but I just couldn't seem to fit it into my schedule."

She laughed, this middle-aged woman who looked enough like Julie that they could have been twins. She was a little rounder though, and gravity was clearly her enemy at this stage in her life. "That's funny, Alex."

He forced a smile as she turned the van around in the parking lot of the burger joint, starting back onto the road toward the highway. "It's Xander," he corrected warmly. "My friends call me Xander, Mrs. Peterson."

"Call me Sam," she grinned. "And that's odd. Julie never calls you that."

"It's stupid," Julie commented, finally speaking after what had been possible the longest stretch in her life without doing so. "It sounds so fake, like a character in a science fiction show or something. Wasn't that hot guy off of *Triple X* called Xander? Yeah. Every time I say your name, I think of saying: 'You have just entered, the Xander Zone.'" She did some creepy off-brand Twilight Zone music then, wriggling her fingers before her comedically.

"How'd you get a name like that anyway?" Sam asked, glancing into the rear-view mirror.

"Yeah," Julie chuckled. "Were they, like, on crack or something?"

"The nuns gave it to me," Xander said solemnly, trying to smile. "I never knew my mother. They named us all after saints. I was St. Alexander, but there were two others already there, so I got 'Xander'."

Julie laughed.

He gave her a look. "What's so funny?"

"Nothing, it's just, y'know, 'Saint Xander'," she laughed again, and this time her belt was all that kept her from tumbling out of her seat. "So, what's a Saint doing in a community as hard as the Cove at, like, five thirty in the morning?" She turned to him, making it clear that she expected an answer.

"I..." he started, lowering his voice so that Sam couldn't hear. "Um..." he said again, scratching the back of his head and avoiding eye contact. "I don't remember?"

"You can't remember?" Julie frowned, raising an eyebrow.

"Yeah, um," he said again, his mouth twitching a little. "I was drinking."

"Drinking?" Julie questioned skeptically.

"Yeah."

"You were drinking?"

"Yes."

"Straight-as-an-arrow Saint Alexander 'Xander' Drew was out in Coral Cove drinking."

"Uh - huh."

"At five-thirty A.M.?"

"Yep," he said again, his voice quivering with the lie more and more.

She paused for a long moment then nodded. "Okay," she smiled, leaning her head down onto his shoulder and snuggling in without warning, getting comfortable and then placing a hand lightly against his inner thigh. In a voice almost a whisper, she said, "Maybe later this week we should get blitzed and fool around."

Mike walked down the stairs into the main hall of his home, grunting and trying to flatten down his bedhead before he got to the door. *Maybe I could teach myself to sleep standing up?* he thought as his slippers flapped against the hardwood floor. *Or invent a static-proof pillow. Yeah. I should put that on my agenda. I'll get to that right after I cure cancer and rid the world of hunger.* The knocking at his front door was beginning to get more erratic, and was definitely coinciding with the pounding of his skull by the time he reached it and threw the door open violently.

There she stood, the early morning sunrise captured in her long, black hair as her fingers crossed nervously by her chest. Her cheeks were wet with tears that had made damp spots on the collar of her jacket, her lower lip quivering as her eyes looked upward slightly, making contact with his.

Immediately his barriers collapsed. He didn't care about his hair or the fact that he was wearing his mother's old fuzzy slippers or anything else, only that he shared her pain, even if he didn't know what had caused it.

She bolted to him like lightning, wrapping her arms around his abdomen and uncontrollably sobbing into his shoulder.

Holding her tightly with one hand, the other instinctively reached for her hair, stroking her head and soothing her softly. "Shh" he hushed, "No more crying, now. No more tears," he said, almost begging her as every drop that fell from her eyes killed him a little.

"I thought you were gone," she said nasally, her nose clogged with moisture as her voice began to break, hacked with sobs. "I thought you left me all alone..."

He tilted her head away from his shoulder just long enough to close the door and look at her, and then wrapped her in his embrace again. "No, baby," he assured her, his voice firm. "Never, baby. I'll never leave you, baby. I promise." He broke off their embrace, leading her into the living room with one hand. "What started all this?" he asked, forcing a smile. "What time is it?"

"Six," she said, sniffing back another nose full of mucus as she tried to compose herself, using the sleeve of her jacket to wipe her eyes. "I'm sorry."

"It's okay. It's ooookay," he guaranteed her, squeezing her hand as tightly as he dared. "Now just tell me all about it."

"Xander. He, he called, and I thought maybe something might have happened..." she began to sob again, "...to you."

"Shhh," he consoled her again, trying to keep her calm. "Why'd you think it would be me? Why would the Womb attack me as opposed to every other moron with a heartbeat in this town?"

"I dunno," Cathy answered shyly, avoiding Mike's gaze for the first time since she came in.

"You're a horrible liar," he laughed, tilting her chin so that she was looking at him again. The opportunity to move in and give her a small peck on her lips was irresistible, so he took it.   "It wasn't Xander coming after you I was worried about," she said finally, an accusing edge tacked onto her still emotional voice. "It was you going after him."

"What?" he asked, moving away a little. His hand slid off hers, and he seemed visibly hurt before the pain was replaced with a small scowl. "I don't understand."

Cathy swallowed, hardening her glare before she met him again, but when she did it immediately softened. "You've changed so much, Mike," she said, and she was unable to stop it from sounding like a plea.

"We all have," he countered, letting the comment roll off his back. "We've grown up."

"No," she corrected through pursed lips. "No, Mike. This is not 'growing up'. Growing up is having these things happen to you... and *not* changing. It's realizing that the world doesn't owe you anything just because you've suffered. It's being a good person... a good man." She smiled a little, in one corner of her lips.

He sighed, crossing his fingers just below his nose and leaning on the entry table in front of them. "Are you saying you don't want to be with me anymore, Cathy? That you don't like what I've turned into because of Xander?"

"It's not his fault. Say what you want about him, but at least the only change he's made since all this started is for the better," she spat, her lip tightening as he brought her best friend into this.

"A psychotic serial killer. This is your version of better?" he snapped.

She stopped, calming and composing herself. "At least he has a reason. You fit that description all on your own."

Mike stopped, as still as the dead.

"You've gotten so dark. I remember when we used to have fun. When we used to play pool and hang out at the Factory and be stupid kids." Her hand reached for his again, and they touched softly. "Remember? I want that Michael Harris back." She paused, looking at the floor. "I lost Sara, Mike. I don't want to have to lose you, too."

With that, his gaze softened and he collapsed onto his knees before her, clutching her around the waist and pulling her in, until his head now rested on her shoulder. "It's just so hard," he admitted. "I mean, I was playing pool with Jamie, and then he left and smiled and had a smoke, and then the next day I see his picture everywhere. On the news and in the papers and he's dead and he's just not going to come back, and I don't know..." tears streamed now, hot against her breast. "I still just don't know what to do. It's like, I didn't get a chance to deal with that before Sara died, then the whole mess with Xander, the rape case went by in a minute in my mind, and the thing with Derek, and the field trip, and... ALL OF IT!" he screamed into her chest. "And all the while, I keep wondering: when is someone going to talk to me about Jamie so I can start getting over all the rest of it?" he sniffed. "Because you've changed, too. You spend all your time with Xander now, helping him with his problems. And I *hate* him for it. But, then I feel bad for hating him, cause what he's going through is so much more major than what I'm going through, but it's like I can't help it. It's automatic, or something. You used to talk to me, not him. Remember just after Jamie died, I was so fucked up?"

"Yes," she said, stroking his hair.

"Well, you asked me when it'd be okay to talk about it, and I said three days, at Grendel's party. Then everyone died at the party and nobody talked to me about him since. And I've been waiting for you, Cathy. Waiting for you to care. But then you were almost raped. And I feel so stupid bringing up all this stuff when everyone else's stuff if so amazingly bigger, it's just..."

"Shhh," she said, sobbing and feeling horrible about herself. "It's okay, Mike. It's okay." She frowned then smiled as she craned her head to look at him. "Mike, is it okay to talk about Jamie yet?" she asked, pretending not to hear anything he just said.

He grasped onto her, laughing although crying full-fledged now. "Yeah, hun," he smiled a little. "It is." He paused, adjusting himself as he sat across from her. "See, about a month before he died, he told me this story about a scorpion and a frog. I can't really remember it, but that's kinda why I feel bad. Most of the really important stuff, I just can't seem to remember... because I didn't take the time to notice it when he was here."

"Uh-huh. But that's not your fault. Keep going. And, Mike?" she broke in, pausing a moment. "It's gonna be okay, y' know."

"Yeah, Cat," he grinned stupidly, an expression she hadn't seen on his face in months. "Yeah, I know. See, the thing is, I remember at his funeral they said that he'll live forever in our memories. But if everyone slowly forgets, then..."

CHAPTER ELEVEN: SUICIDE

Coral Cove. A town dwarfed so much by Coral Beach in size that it rarely appeared on state maps. It was always grouped as being a division of its larger companion, but it had enough resources and landmarks to be considered a city, even if its population didn't embrace such a title. This place was quiet and peaceful... that's why a scream ringing out in the middle of the night should have been heard by everyone, but nobody did.

It perplexed Officer Patrick Lee more than he cared to admit, looking down at the young body that lay before him.

It helped to call it a body, or a form. Even corpse was acceptable to most people, while it made others squeamish. But the second you called it a person, the second that the thing lying before you was identified as being a young human life, it became unbearable to comprehend, impossible to withstand. Lee hadn't known this child, only known of him. In a town like this, everyone either knows someone personally, or through someone else. He'd gone to college for a term with the boy's mother, back when he thought he wanted to be a marine biologist. She'd been a sweet girl, and he was sure she'd grown up to be a sweet woman, Carolynn Danvers, mother to the now dead Ash Danvers.

Oh, gawd, he remembered, his eyes wide. *Has anyone called Carolynn yet? Somebody should call Carolynn, just to be sure she knows... but if she already knows, wouldn't it upset her more? Somebody should find out if she's been called.* He was about to turn and ask one of the lower Officers to do it, but couldn't. He couldn't take his eyes off the young boy, no more than sixteen years old, if memory served. He'd only seen the kid once before, at his niece's birthday when they were both seven. *Gawd, how will Clarice take this? They'd been friends since they were both five, I think.*

Now the lifeless *form* of Ash lay there, his hands clutching a knife that Lee knew would be covered in the boy's own prints. Blood had stopped gushing from the gaping gouges in both of his wrists since his heart stopped about two hours ago, and the thought that those jagged wounds were self-inflicted was gut wrenching. How would he tell Carolynn? He prayed somebody already had. Then it wouldn't have to be him.

Because there was a reason nobody in this quiet little town came running when they heard the death cry of an innocent young boy.

Because people don't usually scream when they commit suicide.

CHAPTER TWELVE: SHRUNK

Biology was always the worst: nobody to talk to, and plenty of people to talk about him.

A lot of people that would always see him as the wannabe nerd surrounded Xander in his last class of the day, which always seemed to stretch out the longest. This was in no small part due to Mr. Miles' long winded, anal-retentive lectures on microbiology, and a bunch of other college-level stuff that wasn't going to be on the midterm. He just seemed to think it was interesting. Nobody else did, just him and Brook Woods, who sat in the back of the class and didn't speak, just scribbled away at her notes frantically. He could hear her Bic .7mm mechanical pencil scrape against the rough paper of her notebook even above Miles' loud voice, scratching away at the very ebbs of his sanity.

"... eight, two, seven, six..." somebody said on the other side of class, and his head jolted in that direction. Cold sweat started to form from his pores as his eyes darted around the class, looking for the source. It was Randy, and he was talking to a nameless blonde with cherry lips. They were all nameless to guys like that. That was probably the sixth girl he'd been with this month. He was marking down the numbers on the palm of his hand, smiling devilishly. "Yeah, I'll call you as soon as I get home. We can hook up later tonight when I get back from Tee's place." After he turned away from the girl, he resumed his usual activity of staring out the window, lost in thought. For someone so dense, he always seemed to have a lot on his mind.

Xander sighed, burying his head so deep into his arms that the cold tiling of the desk chilled the tip of his nose. *Calm down, Xander,* he coaxed himself, having nobody else around to do it. His right hand was shaking, and when he looked at it, he discovered that last night's scars still had not completely healed over. The flesh was whiter than that around it, fresher.

"Alexander Drew," blared the service announcer as it crackled to life in a spasm of static, "Please report to Warren O'Toole's office, Alexander Drew."

When it rains, it pours, he thought, getting up and grabbing his book bag.

Mike and Cathy both looked up at the P.A. system simultaneously, then at each other. All the other eyes in their Family Living class seemed to go straight to them.

She tried hard to breathe as he squeezed her hand just a little bit tighter. "What now?" she whispered to herself, closing her eyes and wishing it all away.

Xander stared at the pane of smoked glass on the door that stood between him and Warren O'Toole's office. He could see the guidance counsellor rummaging about inside of his office, and could hear him scuffling through the mounds of files that littered his desk. Taking a deep, infuriating breath of air that made his nostrils flare, he turned the knob and opened up the door.

O'Toole cocked his head up at the boy, the fluorescent lights reflecting off his large, round glasses and straight into Xander's eyes, making the man's expression difficult to determine. He opened a drawer and brushed a gigantic pile of papers into it, slamming it shut and squashing a great deal of them. He smiled, obviously about to greet Xander, when he found himself abruptly cut off.

"What now?" Xander snapped, tossing his book bag alongside the desk and then plopping himself down lazily in the chair across from O'Toole.

"Excuse me?" O'Toole said, his voice reaching a high pitch. He looked very much like a cartoon hen that just got its feathers ruffled.

Xander raised his hands in a miniature shrug, then let them slap back down against his knees. "What now?" he repeated, his lips pursed with annoyance and anger, like someone who felt they were above what life had thrown at them. He looked smug, sinking down in the chair to relax, crossing his legs over the armrest. "Why am I here now? You gonna pick at my head some more? Try to get me to talk about 'mistakes I've made', 'my terrible childhood', or maybe," he put one hand up to his mouth in a fake gasp of shock, "it's time to talk about 'what I'm really feeling'," He smiled sarcastically, clutching at his heart.

"Noooo," O'Toole stretched out, dragging the 'oh' sound as he raised an eyebrow at the boy's insolence. "I just wanted to talk about you. You strike me as being a particularly troubled young man, and I really think that you could be helped a lot by - "

"Or maybe," Xander continued, raising a finger to shut the counsellor up as he began speaking again, as if he had not even paused, "you want to send me on another field trip, hmm? Great idea, by the way. To escape the pressures of their dangerous hometown, bring teenagers to one of the most dangerous cities in America. Brilliant strategy. What are you going to do next, send me on an outing to Afghanistan?"

"So, I've heard some rumours circulating about you and Miss Peterson," O'Toole cut in suddenly, crossing his hands on the desk in front of him the way he did when he really wanted someone to know that he meant business.

"Excuse me?" Xander said quickly, sitting straight up in his chair and motioning toward the man across from him with one finger. "What did you just say?"

"The faculty talk. I swear to you, Miss Hall and Mrs. White are like two little old ladies sometimes. Always making their own renditions on what the student body is saying about something. An hour after they hear that something might have happened, they convince themselves that it really did happen. Idiots. They should really start airing episodes of *Passions* around their work schedule... might give them something to occupy their minds." O'Toole now took a more relaxed tone, leaning back and putting both legs on his desk.

"Nothing went on," Xander scoffed, but his eyes went directly to the ground.

"Would you have liked it to?"

"No, I flat out refused her," he admitted without thinking.

"I see," O'Toole drawled, making a face and nodding slowly. "That's good. Things like that could be... dangerous. At your age, I mean."

"Hmm," Xander mused, stroking his chin a little. "Yeah, I guess."

"Still, it must stab at you. Like betrayal," O'Toole continued, getting up and starting to pace, his hands clasped tightly behind his back. "It must get hard. This is two out of two for you, now."

"What do you mean?"

"Johnson, Sara." he quoted, glancing down at a file folder. "She died. Was a friend of yours, wasn't she?"

Xander swallowed hard and glared, but did not answer.

"I thought as much. Maybe we have different views, but I believe that death is like betrayal. It's like... why couldn't she have stayed...for you?"

Xander forced a sardonic smirk. "I'm afraid I don't share your point of view, sir," he spat.

"Yes," O'Toole chuckled. "I suppose someone like you would feel that you betrayed her."

The color drained from Xander's face, and he shuffled in his chair. "I loved her," he stated as flatly as he could after a moment. "I should have protected her."

"Mmm," O'Toole smiled. "I understand. Really, I do, boy." He picked up a pencil and started tapping it against his desk. Xander glanced at it momentarily then looked away again. "Someone with such a great potential for good such as you... I imagine that these feelings of protection are starting to bleed into other places by now. Cathy and Julie when they were taken advantage of... you must feel as though you should have stopped that, too."

"I should have." Xander almost yelled, then restrained himself at the last minute. "Julie, she's just... she's so much like Sara..." he laughed, "but in all the wrong ways. When I look at her, I see the flaws in Sara that I was too naive to see while she was alive. Their weaknesses, their common mistakes."

"Do you ever think that if you could help Julie... you might be able to bring Sara back in some small way?" O'Toole ventured, tapping his pencil even more rapidly.

Xander's eye twitched with every rapping sound the pencil made, making him blink and regain focus with every beat. "No," Xander said finally, visibly uncomfortable with the notion. "No, it's not like - "

"It's okay," O'Toole smiled, dropping the pencil and reaching out to touch Xander's shoulder. "Really, it is. You did great today."

"Today?" Xander remarked, getting up quickly and grabbing his book bag. "What's that supposed to mean?"

"Oh, I didn't tell you?" O'Toole smirked, and now he looked as smug as Xander had a few scant minutes ago. "I've requested that you come in for weekly psychology sessions." He leaned in closer. "I even think that you'd be a wonderful candidate for some new techniques involving hypnosis."

Xander's eyes grew wide, as he backed away from O'Toole and bolted out of the room as fast as his legs would carry him until he felt safe again.

"*Hypnosis?*" Mike shouted as the trio of friends walked home, their heads hung low and their hands in their pockets.

Xander took a quick glance around the scenic, woodsy trail that ran parallel to the major roads in Coral Beach until he was satisfied that they were alone, then he withdrew his hand from his pocket and revealed a cigarette. Bringing it to his lips, he reached into the breast pocket of his black-buttoned shirt and withdrew a match, striking it against his finger and lighting the slender, white tube. He looked down upon himself, feeling dirty and scared and horrible all at once, then noticed that his shirt was buttoned up wrong at the bottom. He started to fumble with the buttons, his fingers still thick with scabs from the previous night. "Yeah, hypnosis. Stupid new-age mother fuck. I kinda miss the days when he would have been burned at the stake for mentioning something like that." He continued fumbling with the buttons of his shirt, trying to get it right.

After a moment of watching, Cathy huffed heavily and slapped his hands away, buttoning them up for him. "How're your fingers?"

He gave her a little look, followed by a smile. "Better. How'd you...?"

"I noticed they were bugging at you in Economics. You kept dropping your pencil. It was like it was made of butter. I think Mrs. White was getting pissed off." She grabbed his hands and flipped it to see the tips of his fingers.

"Nasty," Mike commented, squeezing his lips together to make a disgusted look. "Your claws do that?" he asked before his hand automatically went to take Cathy's, letting it be a link between the two.

"Yeah," Xander nodded, scratching at the closed wounds for a minute before taking another puff of the smoke that dangled between his lips. Cathy coughed once, violently as the smoke billowed toward her, and he removed the cigarette from his lips and threw it out into a puddle near some bushes. "Sorry," he frowned, honestly.

She smiled in response.

"So, what happened last night?" Mike asked, his voice a mix somewhere between hard, down-to-business, and genuine concern. He leaned his head in closer to his friend, a habit formed from having to talk in secret so often.

"Dunno," he admitted, making eye contact for a long second. "Same as always, I guess. Womb takes over, my consciousness just goes out the window. But, it was different this time. It didn't make it back in time for day. It almost always makes it back. This time, I just woke up in the middle of nowhere, standing in the rain, covered in blood."

"Blood?" Cathy chimed, gripping Mike's hand as tight as she could, steeling herself for bad news.

"Mine," he clarified, smiling consolingly at her.

"Well, good. I mean –" she stammered, tripping over her own words.

"It's cool. I understand. I breathe that same sigh of relief every damn morning, remember?"

"Do you know what it was doing?" Mike broke in, bringing the other two back on topic. "Was it coming or going?"

"Coming... I think," Xander replied uncertainly, crumpling his brow in disarray. "I'm not sure. I just got the feeling that it had accomplished whatever it set out to do."

Mike frowned, looking back at Cathy as she made the same face in response. "I was afraid of that."

Xander's eyes went wide, and his eyes darted back and forth between their faces. "Why? What's happened?"

"Last night... in the Cove, they found a guy dead. Stabbed by a small blade," Mike said somberly.

Xander closed his eyes, pursing his lips together and holding back the urge to hit something. "Who was it?"

"Me and Cathy stayed up all night looking online after you called... they still haven't released the name, but the police there think the guy committed suicide."

"I'll bet," Xander spat. "Small blade. Why would the police there think it was a suicide, after everything that's happened here?"

Mike stopped, placing a hand on his friend's shoulder. "Because it's the third suicide in the past few weeks. All of them young. Police are keeping the details to themselves." He paused. "There's no reason to think it was you, man. I think we all should've learned that while you were in Los Angeles. You're innocent until proven guilty, just like everyone else. There's no reason to think that the Womb did this."

Xander looked as though he were about to explode, then he started to breath slower, calming himself down. He re-opened his eyes, taking Mike's hand at his shoulder and holding it for a minute in thanks before nodding. "Whatever reason the Womb was in Coral Cove, we'll figure it out tomorrow."

"What about your appointment with O'Toole?" Cathy asked, reminding them of the problems that he could cause by going solo now that someone was watching him.

"I should skip it anyway, until I can figure out a way around the whole hypnosis thing. The last thing we need is for that idiot to put me into some deep sleep."

"Yeah," she nodded. "Knowing what happens when you go to sleep, I'd hate to see what happens if you couldn't wake back up."

CHAPTER THIRTEEN: BLOWN OFF

"Why are we doing this again?" Cathy whispered, motioning with her head to the front seat of the white minivan, still a bit muddy on the outside from two nights ago. Now that it was in the light, it was easier to see the rust spots that covered it. It didn't look as new and inviting as it had seemed to Xander the first time he had stepped in it. In the front, Julie Peterson and her mother were chatting back and forth; the only discernible word from the exchange was 'like'.

Xander leaned in, and Mike craned his head to hear the conversation as well. "We have to get to Coral Cove. We'll never be able to figure out why I was there unless we see what's going on there. The police files sure aren't going to help us. Those morons are way too vague."

"Don't blame them, man," Mike interjected. "It's a small town. Chances are everyone on the force knew these kids personally. It had to have been hard to write up reports on their bodies."

"Yeah," Cathy drawled, giving Mike a look for changing the topic. "But that still doesn't explain why we're dragging Tweedle-Dee and Tweedle-Dum along for the ride," she hissed, pointing her thumb discreetly at Julie and her mom.

Xander looked over at Julie for a moment, his face expressionless. "They're not along for the ride, Cat. They *are* the ride. Do you think your parents or mine would have agreed to us skipping school to run off to a town where there have been a string of deaths?"

"Right," Cathy responded, rolling her eyes. "Cause it's so much better in our town. We have our very own serial killer. We shouldn't try to be greedy and take theirs away from them."

Mike flopped his hands down against the seat, exasperated. "Will you two cut it out?" he snapped, giving them both a stern look. "We need them here, alright?"

"Julie's gonna get in the way," Cathy snorted.

"She is not," Xander protested.

"Sure. Right. Fine. Because when you got so distracted by her in L.A., it was because she was just showing you her lingerie collection," she huffed, leaning back as if to exit the conversation.

Xander felt a growl build in his throat, but not from the confusion. He turned to Mike. "Mental note: if I ever understand that girl, commit me into the nearest mental hospital."

"Do they still offer cash incentives for that?"

"Shut up."

"Seriously! Or did they change their policy? Maybe now it's 'commit seven friends, get a free steak-fish.'"

"Stop," Xander rephrased, but the smile was already spreading over his lips.

"I could use a good steak-fish."

"I said stop," he repeated, laughing this time.

"It's not like we have any shortage of insane friends or something."

Xander waited a minute to stop laughing, then looked long and hard at Mike. "It's good to have you back, man."

Mike smiled. "It's good to be back, dumbass."

"Hey now!" Julie's mom, (what was her name?), *Sam* said. "We don't use that kind of language in here."

Mike stared at the floor, looking sheepish.

"If you're gonna say something like that, say it right. Call him an asshole. Or a fucker. Or a son-of-a-bitch. But I don't want to hear any more dumbed down words like 'dumbass,' okay?" she joked, glancing back at them and smiling.

Mike smiled, turning back to Cathy. "I like her," he said stupidly, an idiotic expression on his face. "We should do this more often."

Cathy rolled her eyes. "Great. Like we don't investigate enough murders."

Julie turned around to face them, her hair flapping around and a broad, innocent smile on her lips. "We're almost there. Like, what have you guys been whispering about all this time?"

"Nothing!" Xander chimed happily. "Just... talking about what we're going to do when we get to the strip mall you were telling us about!"

"Oh!" Julie laughed, pulling her hair back. "Cool! Well, add plans for another, cause me and Mum decided to stop at my Aunt's and pick up my cousin Mandy so the two of them can have, like, old people time." She paused, grinning. "You'll love her! She's, like, just like me!"

Mike and Cathy's arms both sank, and they shot Xander a look. Cathy mouthed the words 'I told you so'.

Terrific.

Sitting beside the window in the small, cramped office, Dr. Warren O'Toole tapped his yellow 2B pencil against the edge of his desk, chipping away at the soft wood with each beat. He was trying to get the beat to the *Friends* theme song down, but just couldn't get it. He sighed, tossing the pencil into a small green cup holding nine more just like it. He leaned against his clenched fist, sighing heavily, his cheeks puffing out like a blowfish beneath his glasses. He looked at the two cups of coffee he'd poured nearly an hour ago. One was long since empty, the other was still full and ice cold by now.

Leaning forward, he took off his glasses and laid them on the desk. Burying his face in his hands, he peered angrily through his fingers at the clock on the wall. Xander was two hours late. *Damn that child,* he cursed inwardly, slamming a fist into the desk and cracking off the corner. He leaned over to his intercom and spoke clearly into it as he opened up a new file on his desk..

"Will Randy Owchar please report to the guidance office please? Randy Owchar to the guidance office."

He sat and waited for the second young man, huffing loudly.

"Isn't this so incredibly great?"

Julie squealed as she, Mike, Cathy, Xander, and Mandy all walked through the tiny strip mall, which seemed to be composed entirely of a GAP and an unsanitary eatery.

Mike rubbed the bridge of his nose, trying to get the headache that had been building since all of them left Coral Beach to fade. Ever since they'd picked up this new Peterson, it seemed to have mysteriously doubled in strength. "It's so great I think I'm going to down an entire bottle of Excedrin for fun. I might get some peace for the five seconds before I die," he mumbled, squeezing his face so hard that he thought he felt his nails slip through his flesh.

Xander overheard the comment and couldn't help but chuckle a little at his friend's dry wit. He turned back to Julie then, watching her bounce with a kind of giddy joy, and got lost in amazement and envy. *Here she is, this girl that went through so much... some of it partially my fault.* He smirked as he watched her hair bob and weave in sequence with her body, her jacket zipper clanging against her belt buckle. *And still, she can be happy. She can find pleasure in the simplest things and enjoy her life for what it is. And the more I look at her, the more I realize that it's not that she's a flake. It's just a remarkable ability to put the past behind her. She can't change what's happened, so she moves on.* She turned and smiled at him with those eyes and that perfect movie-star smile. *I wish I had that choice,* he mused as he smiled back.

Their hands swung in unison, side by side as they walked together, taking in every ounce of beauty that had been miraculously trapped in this stone and concrete building. It was so natural when their hands touched for a moment, then joined together the next. Neither of them realized that they had done it until a few seconds later. Julie looked down at their entwined fingers and her eyes met his, filled with joy and the simplistic peacefulness of the experience they were a part of.

"What are you guys doing?" came a voice from behind them.

Julie rolled her eyes a little, but the expression of annoyance was lost, as was her and Xander's touch, as she turned and spoke through clenched teeth: "something that has nothing to do with you, Mandy."

"Oh, come on! I hate this place. Let's hit the theater! They're doing this thing, playing the first three *Terminator* films back to back to back, and it's only three bucks and..."

Mike's ears pricked up when he heard that, and he was about to speak when Cathy pressed her nails into the palm of his hand hard, shutting him up.

Mandy Peterson pouted as her cousin ignored her, instead walking a little bit faster and encouraging Xander to do so as well with a series of small tugs and pulls. The younger girl stopped, stomping one foot in a miniature tantrum, her cheeks puffing out angrily. Her skin was smooth and flawless, save for a tiny m-shaped scar on the top of her forehead that was mostly concealed by her brown, shoulder-length hair. Her lips were thin and small like Julie's, and they also shared the same deep green eyes with an odd, eternally innocent sparkle in them. Her cheeks were almost devoid of color, as if she were a ghost, and her small body was so thin you had to question the girl's eating habits. She wore a tight red crop top with a keyhole back that would have been better described as a rag tied to her front with thin strings. The only things that the shirt really concealed successfully were her shoulders. Combined with her ultra-low jeans, it seemed that the girl went to great lengths to show off her stomach and pierced naval.

The thirteen-year-old girl kept glaring menacingly at her cousin until Mike and Cathy passed them, at which point her expression of hatred faded into a secretive smile, her eyes dancing over Mike. She seemed to light up with the devilish quality that her cousin was famous for, and then started to walk again. She came right up behind Mike, locking her arm around the side opposite of Cathy. "Would you like to go to the movies, Michael?" she asked sweetly, her eyelids batting sweetly.

"Uh..." Mike stammered, obviously shaken by the girl's forwardness. "Um..." *Dear Gawd,* he thought, as Cathy held him tighter, *it's genetic.* "Well, um, I don't usually do things... without... Xander?" he said, but it was more questioning whether the girl would buy the half-assed explanation.

"Oh," Mandy said, a little confused. "I wouldn't have thought of you for one of those guys who swings..."

"No!" Mike announced loudly, raising both hands in defense. "No, I'm not... I mean, there's nothing wrong with that, but..."

"It's okay," she smiled warmly, reaching out and touching his arm. "My Mom has a cousin whose ex-husband's girlfriend's sister dated a bisexual guy once, so I get it."

"I'm not bisexual!" Mike yelled while trying to contain his laughter. He stopped, then looked around and noticed that all of the people in the mall were staring at him uncomfortably. He sighed heavily.

"Oh!" the girl laughed again, and again she caressed Mike's biceps. "That's cool, y'know. We can always hook up whenever you want, and do... well, whatever." She smiled, and those lips turned to something like venom when she turned them on Cathy.

Cathy smiled in a fake way, and Mandy returned it eagerly.

"Well," Mandy said, clapping her hands as if to shatter the tension that filled the air. "I'm gonna go talk to Julie about something, okay? Why don't you ask Alex if he'd like to see a movie?" she chimed, turning to walk away.

Cathy lowered her eyes at the girl. "Petersons," she growled, turning back to Mike. "You don't like her, do you?"

Mike laughed a little. "Naw," he smiled, "The only girl I like is using her nails to cut off blood circulation to my arm because she's insanely jealous of a thirteen-year-old girl."

Cathy let go of her boyfriend's arm immediately, biting her lip. "Sorry."

"It's alright. Now let's go talk to Xander before Mandy catches onto us," he said, his expressionless 'business face' shadowing his good mood in an instant.

They walked up to Xander just as Mandy was pulling Julie aside.

"Hey," Xander greeted them both. "Guys, we've gotta move. Soon Sam's gonna wanna drive us back to the Beach, and this'll all have been just a fun chance to meet the Julie clone."

"Don't get me started," Mike frowned, rolling his eyes. "Is there such thing as a slut gene? 'Cause if there is, I think the Peterson's have it."

"Watch it," Xander responded quickly, pointing a finger at Mike briefly, not wanting the moment to linger on more than it had to. He stopped a moment, thinking. His ear pricked, and he turned to overhear Mandy's conversation.

'Mike is so cute.'

'I think you should go for it. Cathy's interested in someone else anyway, I think.'

'Really? I'm gonna go ask him to the movie again'

'I can get Xander to go. Stick with me, hun.'

"Okay," Xander sighed, turning back to Cathy. "They're coming back over. I want you to distract the girls long enough for me and Mike to come up with a plan to get all three of us out of here, okay?"

"Cool," Cathy nodded, followed by a quick nod from Mike. "All I have to do is bring you up and there's a three hour he's-so-cute-a-thon from Julie anyway."

"Excuse me?"

"Nothing. Hey, Julie!" Cathy said without a beat, moving to intercept the girls. She smiled at them both, masking her contempt. "The guys needed to talk about some movie or something, they wanted to be alone."

"Oh, cool," Julie shrugged.

"Has Mikey seen *Terminator 3* yet?" Mandy asked, oblivious to Cathy's thinly veiled irritation.

That girl has a one-track mind, Julie groaned, shaking her head and smiling at Cathy. "I'm not sure about the movie, actually. I'll talk it over with Alex."

Cathy barely heard Julie, glaring at Mandy: *Mikey?* she hissed evilly.

"Let's leave it to Mikey and Alex to decide," Mandy suggested, tilting her head up as if to make herself 'higher-up' than Cathy.

"*Let's,*" Cathy responded bitterly, her lip curling. She turned back to where Xander and Mike had been talking, and they weren't there. "Guys?" she called out, glancing around for them. "Guys?" she asked again, then realized: she was the plan to get them out of the mall. *Spec-tac-u-lar,* she fumed inwardly, crossing her arms and imagining what she was going to do to them when they got back.

ᚦᚹ

Dee Peterson poured herself up a drink of Jack Daniels until it overflowed just a little, and then tapped her smoke onto one of the many ashtrays that littered her kitchen, making the whole room smell stale and musty. The white walls had been tainted a sickly yellow by years of tobacco stains. She made her way over to the kitchen table where her sister sat, hacking once, then coughing twice.

"So," she said in a gruff voice, "How've you been doing?" She tapped the ashes on her cigarette again before taking a long, hard gulp of the liquor that she cradled carefully in her hand. For women like Dee, alcohol abuse meant wasting a single drop. Her grey college t-shirt was stained and full of holes, and smelled of a thousand different fragrances, none of which were appealing. Her brown hair was thinning, but she still kept it cut short, just like her daughters, and the premature wrinkles that covered her face clung to her heavily applied concealer, which, rather than freshening her complexion, made her look like a withered old clown.

"Oh, I'm fine," Sam replied, tapping her smoke as well. She stared down at the drink in her sister's hand with great longing, her lips becoming parched, calling out for the liquid. "Just fine. I had to come into town for one of Julie's friends the other day, and it reminded me how long it's been since I came in to see you."

"You still carting that kid around like a maid?" the older woman laughed, with a tinge of resentment in her voice. "When are you going to learn to let that child grow up? She's fifteen years old, for God's sake, Sam."

Sam nodded at this, but her eyes followed her sister's hand as it again brought the glass to her lips. She licked her own.

"You sure you don't want a drink?" Dee offered, motioning back to the forty ounce bottle that sat on the counter next to a pile of dirty dishes that were beginning to sprout mould around the edges.

"No, Dee," she responded, gulping. "We both got on the wagon the same day, remember? The day Jake left?"

Dee smiled, "Yeah... I still miss 'im, y' know. He wasn't that bad. The man could drink."

"He could also beat on Amanda when you were passed out, stoned and loaded on the couch," Sam responded bitterly.

"Least I got a man," Dee snapped, taking another shot of her whiskey. "I got one now, says he loves me. He loves Mandy, too," she grinned, motioning toward the other room.

Sam turned, following her sister's gesture until she saw the man sprawled out on the couch wearing a stained wife beater with his hand resting in an open pizza box.

Someone else sat in an armchair not far from him, playing a handheld game and taking sips from his drink between levels.

Sam's brow furrowed, shaking her head.

She got up and walked the short distance to the hall, stepping over a small pile of discarded clothing and a relatively clean kitty litter as she went. She frowned, passing two doors and then hanging a right into the third, entering Mandy's room.

The door was missing, having been taken off at the hinges long ago. Only an odd sequence of rust-stained circles remained to mark where it had been. She could see the room no better from inside than from the outside. It was covered from end to end with clothes that had passed the point where they could be defined as simply 'dirty'. Her dresser was home to several dirty dishes and forks that had fused together with grease and grime. The few available surfaces were caked in dust an inch thick.

Sam sighed, turning her eye to the closet. There were several bottles of vodka and gin there, each of them unopened. In her mind's eye she could see Mandy stealing her mother's liquor when she got too drunk; not to drink it herself, but simply to stop her mother from drinking it.

Dee finally met her in the hall with her drink still in hand. It followed her wherever she went. She stank of it. "Girl's always pulling some kinda shit or another."

She winced then walked back into the kitchen with her sister. "Sounds like she's giving you a hard time."

"Ugh. Damn teachers wanna see me every damn week it seems like."

Sam bit her lip then leaned in, treading carefully. "I could take her off your hands for a few days, if you need a break."

Mike stared down at the long, metal bed that had ejected from the silvery wall. The loose form of a man lay upon it, still shrouded in the ghostly white sheet it had been stored with. He was watching the way the victim's nose made an indent in the thin blue blanket, the lights above him making weird shadows on the body. He heard Xander's footsteps come down the stairs to join him as his friend made one last check on the floor above them. "Anything?" he asked, not turning to look.

"Naw," he responded, taking one last glance up the stairwell before turning to join his friend. "The cops are all trying to get hold of the victims' families. The rest are either gone or trying to keep the press at bay. Doesn't seem like anybody's gonna come down to disturb us."

Mike nodded, his eyes not having yet left the form before him. "I'll never get used to this," he said at once, sniffing and wiping his nose in his sleeve. The smell of the bodies was beginning to get to him, making him wonder how some people did it day in and day out.

Xander sighed, patting him on the back. "That's a good thing, man," he smiled. "It's what makes us human. If we lose that, then we've got nothing."

"Times like this I wish those horror movies had desensitized me, just like Mom always said they would."

"Tell me about it," Xander replied. He paused a moment, then reached over to the top of the cloth and pulled it back.

Mike turned for a second, then slowly brought his head back. "Dammit," he cursed as he looked at the body of the nineteen-year-old man. The body's mouth was hanging open loosely, a bullet hole in the side of his head still spattered with dried and frozen blood, giving it a crusty appearance he wasn't used to seeing.

"You gonna be okay?" Xander asked with care. "I could examine them all if you want... you could keep watch?"

"Naw," Mike said, steeling himself and putting on his best game face. "Naw, I can do this. You go see the other two."

"Okay. Just remember, that's the second victim. I'm gonna go see to the first and third. I'll be right here if you need me." He turned and opened two drawers behind Mike, pulling off both covers and kneeled down, getting a closer look at the bullet holes and what looked like red marks on one of the wrists of the first victim.

Mike reached out and touched the man's arm to move it and see what was on the back. When he made contact with it, he jumped back a pace. The body felt cold, and oddly swollen. All of the man's skin had become puffy, like a giant, invisible bruise covering his entire body. It had fluffed out so much that the man probably wouldn't be recognizable for his funeral. He felt a pang of sympathy for the family. It would be the last time they saw their boy before he was put to rest, and he would look like a stranger to them. Breathing deeply, he turned the boy over and looked at his back. There was nothing strange. A few scars, a mole the size of South Dakota, and a tattoo that looked to be an amateur job, at least by city standards. Here, it was probably top notch.

"Mike," Xander called out, startling his friend. "You find anything?"

"No, not really," Mike answered, turning away from the dead body only to be confronted with two more. He felt his stomach turn. "What have you got?"

"Come look at this."

Mike walked over next to Xander, where the first victim lay. He stared at the dead boy for a moment, until he felt tears start to well up in his eyes. "What?"

Xander pointed to the right temple, where the bullet had entered. The dirty, bloody hole went clear through the youth's brain. "It's on the right," Xander said simply.

"So? Maybe he was right handed."

"No," Xander sighed, pointing toward the boy's left hand. "See that? The trigger finger of his left hand is still tight, ready to pull the trigger, like he died holding the gun."

Mike frowned. "He did die holding the gun, Drew."

Xander raised a finger. "No, he didn't."

"What?"

"Look here," he motioned, getting closer to the circular wound in the person's head. "The wound tract is straight. The barrel of the gun was perfectly placed over his temple. That barrel must have been at least four inches long. It's humanly impossible to shoot yourself in the right temple with your left hand and still get the gun straight. Plus," he added, picking up the body's left hand again, "Check out the wrists. They've got these red marks..."

"Ligature," Mike corrected. "They're called ligature marks. They mean that something or someone had him held pretty tight by the wrist... wait, are we saying somebody else shot him, but forced the gun into his hand first to make it seem like a suicide?"

"Way too complex for the Womb. He prefers the old stab and twist approach."

"I remember," Mike growled a little, clenching his side. He looked down, struggling not to stare at the body's face. Instead, he looked at the shoulder. "What the hell?" he spoke aloud, getting closer. He hoisted the corpse up a little to reveal a shabby tattoo of a half circle with prongs sticking out the sides.

"It's an Omega symbol," Xander observed, kneeling as well.

"Huh?"

"Greek alphabet. You knew ligature and you don't know that?"

"I got ligature off of *C.S.I.* reruns."

"Ah."

"There was one just like this on the guy I examined."

Xander jumped up, making his way to the latest victim who 'stabbed himself' with a blunt knife. He rolled the boy over carelessly, revealing a large Omega tattoo on his left shoulder blade. He turned to exchange a look with Mike. They both turned to leave.

ᚠᚲᚤ

On the way home, the van was eerily quiet.

Xander and Mike sat next to each other, looking glum. Usually, this would have been normal, but this time it seemed worse. They looked defeated, like men who suddenly had their cause taken from them. They looked like people in old war videos, the sole survivors of their platoon after a battle.

Cathy stared at them, wondering exactly what was wrong and unable to ask, her head hung low, afraid to ask.

Julie was in the front seat pouting, apparently not speaking to any of the three now. Her silence, at least, was a change welcomed by most in the car. Sam's witty banter had faded away, and she now drove the vehicle with an element of road rage, everything agitating her. The most perplexing change since the ride there, though, and the one that nobody dared to speak of, was the addition of Mandy Peterson and three brimming suitcases.

"So, like, are you sure you guys have room for me?" the child asked, both nervous and polite at once. "I don't want to be any trouble."

"Of course, dear," Sam replied heartily, faking her smile until it was almost perfect. "I'll sleep on the couch. I usually do anyway, up late working and all that. You can have my bedroom. We'll be fine, love..." she trailed off, "...at least for a few days, until your mother can get back on her feet."

"This'll be great!" Mandy chimed giddily. "We can go out tonight! Mike, what are you doing later?"

Xander chuckled softly to himself, turning his head toward the window to avoid Mike's glare. He was taking a divine amount of pleasure in the situation, after all the ribbing that he'd gotten from his friend about Julie. He struggled to keep his low laugh from bursting into a roar, clasping his hand over the bottom part of his face. "Yes, Mike," he added out of spite, "I don't think we are doing anything later, *are we?*" he emphasized the point to make the jab at Mike, a spectacular grin on his face as he did so. *I forgot how much I enjoyed making fun of him.*

Mike squinted angrily at him, as if silently wishing for his head to explode. "*Nothing,*" he hissed through gritted teeth while still looking at Xander, and then he turned back to Mandy. "I'm going to have a quiet night alone at home."

"Alone?" Mandy gagged, a disgusted look on her face. "Who likes to be alone? How lame are you?" she laughed a little, oblivious to the fact that nobody else did.

The laughter cut through Xander's pounding head like a knife. He'd been thinking so much about what they'd discovered at the morgue that he thought his brain was going to break out of the back of his skull and crawl away. He rubbed his eyes frantically to make the pain cease.

He felt something touch him lightly on the shoulder, and he jerked in shock. His head jolted in the direction of the sensation, and he saw that Cathy was leaning in toward him. Her hair smelled like strawberries, and it dangled so dangerously close to his nose now that it was intoxicating. The hurt and worried expression in her eyes was heartbreaking... and for some reason made her also attractive. Like he felt the need to make it all better for her, so she'd never have to wear those expressions again.

"What is it?" she asked, her voice full of concern, pain, love, and so many other emotions that nobody would ever have been able to describe it in words. "What's wrong?" She touched his face, making it turn toward her. His eyes were bloodshot and his face sick with stress, and her heart automatically went out to him.

Xander groaned just a little, forcing himself to make eye contact. "I can't get this. All of these victims committed suicide, but none of them did. They were murders, Cathy. Murders painted to look like suicides. And whoever did it was so good I don't see the cops even seeing it. Not these cops, anyway," he frowned.

"The only thing I can see they have in common are these Omega symbol tattoos on their backs. I just can't wrap my head around this. What... what was it? Some insane tattoo artist, marking random people for death? I don't, I just..." he stammered, and then he felt her arm around his shoulder.

"Shhh," she soothed, leaning in until her head rested against his in solace. "It's alright. It is. You can't know everything, can't be everywhere."

Xander stopped, his expression changing. A grim realization came over him. "But he knows," he said, pointing toward his gut. "The Womb. It knows what's going on in this town. It must, or it wouldn't have brought me here in the first place. It knows, and it's doing everything to get me to figure it out... but I'm just too stupid."

"You're not stupid."

"But I am."

"But you're *not*," she reiterated, speaking firmly and putting on her 'resolve face'. She started talking with her hands, the way she always did when she thought she had something important to say. "You are not stupid. You've got so much to deal with, and you can't possibly know anything about how the Womb thinks, or even if it thinks. It probably just runs on instinct, you've got too-" she stopped, noticing Xander's face.

His eyes were wide. As if in stop-motion animation, he sat up straight and slowly turned his head to look at her. There was a malevolent sparkle in his eye, but other than that, his face was nearly devoid of all emotion. She hated it when he looked like that. "I've got a really bad idea," he said, honestly.

She thought about that for a minute, then it dawned on her, and she began to shake her head slowly, as if very afraid. "No, no, no..." she began to repeat, softly.

"I can't get inside the Womb's head, but there's one man who always could," he said firmly, and she stopped chanting. "We *need* him, Cathy. There's nobody else. It's time to get some outside help."

"We can't tell Mike," she insisted, her voice commanding.

Xander nodded, conceding to her terms. "Alright. But if we're gonna do something, it has to be soon."

"Why's that?"

Xander looked directly at her, then through her. "Because whoever's killing these people is getting better and better at it... and every time he gets better, he's going to enjoy it more, and want it more."

There was the tiniest quiver of fear in his voice.

She sipped on a slurpie, and was instantly transformed.

Up until this point, he'd thought that Xander was the only person gifted with that power, but before his eyes, his girlfriend proved him differently. As she sucked on the brightly coloured slush she'd picked up at the Factory on their way back to his place, she became the girl he'd known and loved all his youth. She became something small and precious and just for him, something that the

94

rest of the world couldn't touch. She was his Cathy again, and he felt the clear air between them that he hadn't even realized was gone, yet now wondered how he had lived without.

"What're you looking at?" she giggled, and it was infectious. She blushed, trying to hide her face behind long, silky hair.

"You," he smiled, his gaze dancing over her. "The same thing I'm always looking at." There was a pause between them then, as they looked at one another longingly. Mike stepped forward, then stopped, coughing once, changing the topic to something a little less tense. "So where are you and Xander headed off to?"

Cathy looked away, staring at her straw as she swirled it around the goop in her plastic glass. "Oh... we're just gonna hit the streets. Y'know, try to get some information on this 'omega' thing. He can't make heads or tails of it, but since the whole thing with Black Heart, that seems to be going around." The last part was honest. That was how she covered up the lie, with a thin veil of truth.

"You'd think after months of practice covering up for a friend's secret identity, you'd be a better liar," he sighed, walking over to her and calmly sitting next to her on his couch. "Come on, Cathy," he spoke, and his tone was almost pleading, "I thought we agreed earlier not to keep things hidden from each other anymore. I need to know what's happening."

"You can't know this," she said, her eyes nearly tearful. "I'm sorry Mike, but you can't. You'd freak out. You'd take it out on Xander. And this whole thing is just too big for you and him to get into another –"

"You're going to see him, huh?" he cut in, but without anger or resentment in his voice. It was just a clear understanding, a knowledge that shattered the lie between them.

Cathy paused a moment, her jaw slack. "Yeah," she said finally, nodding once.

"I thought so. Xander was all quiet, and you looked scared and excited at once, so either you were going to sleep with each other or you were going to see him."

She stopped for a second, touching his hand and taking another long gulp of her slurpie, her mouth dry like sandpaper. "I don't think of him like that, y'know," she blurted out as fast as she could, making it impossible to tell where one word ended and the next began.

He turned to her casually, his blonde hair falling gracefully as he tilted his head to the left to get a better view of her. "Think of who like what?" he laughed, smiling and mimicking the way she had said it, only a little slower. He'd never done anything that fast in his life, and he didn't think he was going to start now.

"I don't think of Xander as more than a friend," she re-stated, and it sounded like an admission to guilt. She said it with such weight, like telling him that his mother had just died. She said it as though it was the opposite of what she meant.

"I know," Mike said simply, bending over and taking a sip out of her drink.

"That is good..." he mumbled to nobody.

"Huh?"

"I know that there's nothing between you and Xander. I'm not stupid."

She blinked in disbelief, not knowing what to think. "But... you always act so weird around him."

He laughed, leaning in and kissing her. "Of all the things I'm jealous of him for, you are not one of them. I know I have you. Nothing's going to change that."

"Oh," she stopped, smiled, then it faded again. "What are you jealous of him for?"

Mike sighed, regretting his choice of words. "He has the power. He has it all. If he's the hero, then what does that make me? The bastard sidekick? Some stupid supporting character?" He scuffed his feet against the hardwood, then stared long and hard at the black mark that it had made. "I feel like he's the hero, you're the best friend, and I'm the best friend's boyfriend. It's like I'm not even worth mentioning half the time."

"No," Cathy said simply, turning his head back to her. She had a loving smile on her face as she brought his head close to hers. "No, I don't believe that's true. See, I think that we've all got our own stories. Every single person. Sure, you might just be a supporting character in Xander's, or a blip on the radar screen in somebody else's. But in your own life, you're the star... and in mine, you're the hero." She kissed him, and he smiled, laughing a little. "Besides, even if this was all about Xander, I like to think that you'd be the hero anyway."

"You think?"

"Yeah. I think."

He looked at her, smiling from ear to ear. "Thank you," he said honestly, leaning over and kissing her, softly at first, then harder. He looked at her for a moment, and his smile got brighter, like it was more real. "I love you," he said quietly, looking into her eyes.

She smiled back. "I love you, too," she replied, as he leaned in to kiss her again, laughing at the same time. "If this is your version of thank you," she said, taking a short breath. "I can't wait to see what happens when I do something really great."

⚜

Xander walked down the sidewalk in the dead of night, his finger twitching slightly as it healed. He'd managed to electrocute himself a few minutes before he'd left his house, trying to get his computer to work again. He'd bought a new hard drive, assuming that all of the old wires still worked. Turned out he was wrong. By the time he realized it, electricity was slowly fragging his *new* hard drive. Unplugging it in a hurry, he'd managed to give himself a major shock, and his hand had been spasming for at least five minutes.

He cursed the night as he walked. He had so badly wanted to get this done before daybreak. It hadn't really seemed all that plausible though, since the sun had been well on its way to disappearing behind the hills even as he had gotten

96

back home. A shiver went down his spine and his hand twitched, snapping the wrist so hard that it cracked the bone, forcing the claws on that hand to come out with an enormous burst of pain.

"Argh!" he shouted, clutching at his wounded hand as he watched the claws finish protruding. "Fuck!" he yelled at the Womb, "It's never enough with you, is it?" Blood streamed down his wrist slowly as he panted angrily at it, his expression calming into something resembling normal, accompanied with a wince or two. He raised an eyebrow, grateful for the fact that neither Mike nor Cathy had been there to see him yell at his own arm. Shoving his hand deep inside his jacket to hide the mauled flesh, he started walking again, ignoring the pins and needles that rang out from the exposed muscle. Blood soaked into the material that covered his frame as he felt the skin around his fingers stitch itself back together. He could almost imagine an invisible needle and thread patching them up. It always hurt worse closing. It was like the same cut again, only dragged out over minutes, sometimes hours.

He kept walking along the street anyway, getting increasingly pissed off as he went. His eyes were bloodshot, a lack of sleep and energy beginning to wear down upon him as he surveyed the street in front of him. It was empty and dark, just like it usually was after dusk. Most smart people wouldn't even step outside their doors in this part of town anymore, for fear of things that went bump in the night. *Things like me*, he thought awfully, wishing for his hand to heal as it continued to shoot sensations through the large lump of nerves located in the ball of his hand. Feeling it heal a little more, the bone of his wrist snapping back in place, he hoped that nobody would be around to notice it. Then, taking another glance at the streets, he chuckled. *Only a complete moron would be out on a night like this.* He laughed.

"Hey, Drew!"

He heard a voice call out from behind him and froze in his tracks. He recognized it, but still closed his eyes and prayed for it not to be who he thought it was. "Please, no," he whispered to himself as he turned and opened his eyes to make sure, then made a smile that was blatantly fake.

There were four of them, something that surprised him a little. The first, Tommy (who had called out to him with his slightly lisped speech), was usually only seen with his partner in crime, Sud. But Sud didn't seem to be anywhere in sight. There were two others that Xander couldn't name, but he was sure that he recognized them from school. They wore oddly bright neon-green and orange shirts that looked like they'd been washed in bleach more than once. They were tall and gangly, a little nerdy even, with half of one collar stuck up, thick sunglasses (at night), and mouths that hung open to reveal crooked, moronic-looking teeth. All in all, they could have been Goofy's second cousins. The last was Randy Owchar, a kid from his Biology class, a real ladies' man, but never one for social events. Xander had never seen him at the few parties he used to go to, or even at memorials. He wasn't even at Grendel's party a few months back, the 'social event of the season'... luckily for him.

"Hey, Tom," Xander responded dryly as they caught up to him, shoving his free hand into his pocket. "Where's your better half?"

Tommy stared blankly for a moment, not quite realizing that he had been insulted.

"Sud, moron," he explained, rolling his eyes.

"Oh! He didn't wanna go out or nuthin'. Weird, huh? Says people he knows have been dying. I say, 'When aren't they?'" he laughed a little, jabbing Xander playfully. "So, hey, man, me and the guys saw you and was wonderin' if we could bum a smoke off you?"

Xander frowned, looking from one face to the next, then turned and glanced across the terrace to the street that led to Mike's house. Weighing his options, he decided that staying and having a smoke with them would probably be quicker and easier than trying to leave and having them follow him all the way into Mike's. Then he'd have a whole new set of problems... He reached into his pocket, careful not to use his damaged hand, and withdrew five cigarettes from his pack. Each person took one of the four, leaving Xander to put the last one in his mouth.

"Thanks, man." Randy smiled, lighting his smoke and then offering the flame to Xander, who took it eagerly, having just wondered how he was going to light his cig without exposing his mangled wrist. "You're not as bad as I thought."

Xander half smiled. "Thanks. I think."

"See?" Tommy grinned, stretching one arm around Xander in exuberant theatrical play, the smoke trailing from his fingers in circles around them both. "I told you Xander was all right. He's a good guy to have around in a jam."

Xander turned to Tom as he took a long puff, blowing it in the boy's face. "Again... Thanks," he murmured, continuously looking over his shoulder atthe terrace, then turning back to Randy and the others, not paying them much mind. Randy was wearing a coat a little like his, but more stylized. It looked good on him, suited him. He was going to mention it for conversation, but decided against it. These were male high school students. Their response to any compliment from a member of the same sex was almost always an accusation of latent homosexuality.

"So, what're you doing now?" Tommy asked, to make conversation.

Xander became rigid, visibly defensive. "Just out for a walk."

Randy nodded. "Be careful, man. These streets aren't safe anymore. You never know what's going to pop out of the shadows at you."

Xander held back a laugh, taking the advice as an honest good gesture. "Thanks, man. I'll try to keep that in mind."

Randy smiled. "We'd walk with you, but we're all heading home too. Lost track of time. Didn't mean to stay out past dark."

"Yeah," Tommy agreed, "Besides, I never miss *The OC*. That show's like *Dawson's Creek* on crack, man."

They all looked at him for a moment.

He took his hand out from around Xander, throwing his cigarette butt to the ground and stomping on it. "The tail on that show is gear, all I'm saying," he mumbled quietly, then his voice picked up. "So, are you going far, Xand? I mean, we could walk you if it's not far..."

"Naw," Xander refused, dropping his own cigarette to the ground. "I don't think so. I think I'm gonna head into Mike's, actually. Call my parents from there, get the old man to come pick me up."

Both Tommy and Randy nodded.

"Well," Tommy smiled, starting off, "I'm gone. I'll catch up with you guys later."

"Yeah, us too," Randy reciprocated, heading off in the opposite direction, his two friends in tow. "Thanks for the smoke, Drew," he said politely, giving Xander a friendly wave good-bye.

"No problem," he replied warmly, "And call me Xander."

Randy smirked once more, then turned his back and left, walking away.

After watching them disappear around a corner, Xander exhaled for the first time in what seemed like forever, grunting as he glanced at his watch. "Goddammit." he cursed, turning toward the road that ran adjacent to the terrace. "I'm gonna be so fucking late..."

As he ran off into the night toward Mike's house, a small, shadowy figure emerged from the brush that surrounded the terrace. Just as the figure was putting on a jacket, the streetlight allowed for a glimpse of their shoulder, which sported a carefully marked Omega tattoo. The figure then started walking casually down the road, in the same direction that Xander had taken toward Mike's house, a sly grin slowly making its way over a thin face.

ʎʎ

The knocks came suddenly at Mike's front door, interrupting the kiss that he and Cathy were still taking part in on his couch. They were rapid and refused to stop, so Mike tore his lips away from his girlfriend and made his way quickly to the door. When he opened it, Xander was leaning against the frame, looking extremely out of breath.

Mike smirked a little, letting the door prop him up. "Can I help you with something?"

"Sorry I'm... late," Xander panted, his tongue hanging out. "Got distracted, had to run."

"Are you trying to sell me something? Cause if you are, I can tell you right now I'm not interested."

Xander looked up, glaring at the grin on his friend's face as Cathy fixed her hair in the hall mirror and put her jacket on, both arms at once. "I'll be selling you your ass as a hat if you don't let me in to sit down," Xander shot, stepping in and plopping himself down on the couch.

Mike laughed a little as Cathy ignored them both, trying to find her shoes. "What happened to you?" he asked, sitting down next to the exhausted youth.

Xander turned toward him, squinting. "I just had a 'friendly' conversation with Tommy. *Nobody* has suffered like I have suffered."

"I feel your pain."

"You would mock the dead?"

"Sorry. You poor dear," he said, each sentence dripped with more joyful sarcasm than the last.

"Let us never speak of this again."

"Agreed," Mike finished, slapping his palms against his knees to help himself up, then offering a hand to Xander for the same purpose. Without even thinking about it, Xander offered his friend his right hand.

Mike took it, then flipped it over, showing the blood spatter on it, then raised an eyebrow. "That's what I thought," he frowned, catching Xander's eye. "Has our little appointment gotten you all worked up, bud?" His tone was deadly serious.

Xander gave Cathy a look, who then searched for her shoes ever more quickly. "Well?"

"No," Xander winced under Mike's grip of the damaged soft tissue as he stood up. "Electric shock. Made the claws pop. Nothing more."

"Nothing more?"

"Nothing."

Mike patted Xander on the back, his voice friendly again. "Make sure it stays that way. Bringing yourself on this little errand is one thing. Bringing her is quite another."

Xander nodded. "Don't worry. I've got this one covered. He'll never know what hit him."

Xander turned then to meet Cathy in the porch, instinctively taking her by one arm. "Come on, girly girl," he said nonchalantly, as if they were doing nothing. "Let's go visiting."

The door closed behind them, leaving Mike Harris to stare at it. He sat on his couch and waited for the next knock to come: the one that would tell him that his love had come home.

ʎ⟨⟩ʎ

"You had to tell him, didn't you?" Xander smirked, turning down his collar as he and Cathy started to walk down the street away from Mike's.

"Didn't," she chirped, rolling up her sleeves.

"Bullshit," he laughed, jogging for a pace or two to catch up to her. "If you didn't tell, then how did he know?"

"Don't know, don't care," she smiled. "He's smarter then he seems, you know."

"Well he'd have to be."

She clicked her tongue, slapping him across the arm.

Three men stood underneath the streetlight not far ahead, the glow turning them into silhouettes.

Cathy walked a little slower, allowing Xander to close this distance between them. She stepped slightly to the right until their arms were touching, staying as close to him as possible as they approached the trio.

One of them turned toward them, a bright white smile shining through the shadow.

Xander smiled. "Relax. We know them."

"That's supposed to make me relax how?"

"We also like them."

"Speak for yourself."

Xander frowned. As they got a little closer, Randy, Char and Duncan came into full view.

"What's goin' on?" Randy called out, still smiling from ear to ear. "Sneaking off with Harris' woman?"

"Something like that," Xander smirked.

"*Nothing* like that," Cathy corrected, giving Xander a look. "Enough people at school think I'm a tramp as it is."

Xander laughed then turned to Randy. "Thought you were heading out."

"Was." Randy said after a momentary pause. "Still am, kinda. Just seems like too nice a night to waste, you know?"

Xander laughed then felt Cathy next to him again. He turned to her, the smile fading from his face. "Anyway, we gotta be going... I'm just walking Cat home, anyway. You know what they say, can't be too careful."

"Sure you can," Duncan said, smiling. "Just they don't talk about it afterward."

Xander raised an eyebrow as Randy shot him a look. "Right. Well, like I said... best be going."

"Thanks again for the smoke," Randy drawled, tapping Duncan against the chest with the back of his hand as the three started to walk in the opposite direction.

When they turned the corner, Cathy leaned into him with her voice hushed. "What the hell was that about?"

"Nothing. I lent them a smoke earlier," he shrugged, reaching into his pockets and producing a tattered cigarette. "Speaking of."

"Don't start. God, if that's the kind of company smoking attracts you, cancer's the least of your worries."

"I've never had a problem with Randy."

"Me neither. It's the other two."

He paused then nodded. "Well, I think I'd rather be stuck with both of them on their worst day as opposed to where we're going."

Cathy snorted in agreement.

Xander lit his smoke then took a long drag.

Pouting, Cathy batted it from his hand. It fell to the pavement and bounced twice before finding its way into a storm drain.

He sighed, then stuck his hands into his pockets and kept walking.

Mike sat patiently, his right knee tapping up and down and his fingers playing the beat to *Play that Funky Music White Boy* against the arm of his chair. He stared down at the hardwood beneath him, and at the black rubber mark that was still there. Pursing his lips, he began to wish again that none of this was happening. Slowly, mechanically, he bent down onto his knees, leaned against the couch, folded his hands in front of him, and began to pray.

"God," he started, his voice small and moist. "I don't even know if you're there anymore. I used to believe it so completely, but after everything that's happened, I just don't know anymore. Anyway, I'm sure you know about that. I'm here to ask you for something: don't make it any worse. This thing, Xander... this whole town, could you not make things any worse, or any more complicated? You can help if you want, but if you can't... then just try to stay out of it, huh?" he sniffed once. "And please, if you do anything, just bring my girl back to me, please. I-"

The loud, rapid pounding on the door broke him from his prayer, as his head shot directly toward it. For a moment, he dared to hope. He smiled like he never had before as he jumped to his feet and rushed for the knob. When he turned it and opened the door, it almost disappeared. He felt his body sink, his shoulders slumping in with disappointment. But at the same time, he fought to maintain his smile, as the expression of shock had not yet left his face.

Leaning in a promiscuous pose against his door frame was Mandy Peterson, her lips painted a dark, seductive red to match the dress that came half way between her hips and her knees; her torso was covered by a warm-looking jacket. Her eyes had been painted the way that most thirteen-year-old girls did, applying just a little too much of the wrong colours to make them look gaudy. Her hair was done up nicely in a bun that spiraled off into several smaller buns, and Mike couldn't help but think that Julie was behind at least that much. "Hey, you," she said, a little giggle escaping from her throat.

"H- Hi," Mike stammered, floored by her sudden appearance at his door. He took a step back from her, and she took that as an invitation to enter. He scratched the back of his head as he watched her look around the house, her heels making her look taller than she was, closer to Cathy's height. "Um," he began, unsure of how to proceed. "Don't take this the wrong way, but what are you doing here?"

She turned, smiling at him. "You said that you were going to spend the night alone. Then I thought, 'that's not right'. So, I'm, like, here to keep you company. Julie was being boring anyway, she was talking about hitting a rave downtown..."

"We have raves?" Mike asked, shocked.

"She was going to do something... I dunno. It sounded boring to me," she dismissed with an elegant flick of her hand.

"We have a downtown?" Mike questioned again, trying to get his mind off her and how dressed up she was.

She sat down at the couch, motioning for him to join her. She smiled softly as he walked over to her uncertainly, putting his hands firmly against his knees and sitting as far as possible from her. She corrected his mistake by shuffling over toward him, placing a hand upon his.

His skin crawled with goose bumps, and he was left completely speechless for the first time in recent memory. "Um..." he started, but then found nothing with which to continue the sentence.

"Can I ask you a question as a friend, Mike?" she said, and her voice had an extremely sexy undertone to it as she leaned her head in toward his casually while she spoke, reaching up and letting her hair down. It flopped down around her cheeks in one smooth motion, making her even more attractive, and Mike felt his body rise to her motions, despite his objections.

"Sure," he said quickly to stop himself from stuttering.

She smirked as she took off her jacket and tossed it carelessly onto the floor, revealing long, smooth arms and the top of a shirt which plunged down so low he thought he might be able to see her naval. Instead, he accidentally saw other things. He bit his lip, but she smiled, moving her hand to his inner thigh and then kept going slowly, delicately biting her lip devilishly as she did so. "Do you find me... attractive?"

Before he could respond, she jumped on him, putting the weight of her tiny, slim body against his and her hand moved to where it wanted to be, as the other started running through his hair as she locked their lips in a kiss.

His eyes were wide, but all he could see was her bare shoulder. All he could do was flail a little and try not to hurt the girl. As he tried to push her off , he caught a glimpse of her right shoulder, where an Omega tattoo was printed in black and red ink, moving rhythmically as her body ground against his. When he saw it, his eyes bulged.

God, he thought again, chancing a glance upwards. *I could have sworn I just asked you not to make this any more complicated.*

CHAPTER FOURTEEN: SHAKE

Sam Peterson sat hunched over her dining room table, the pale green surface dully reflecting her tired face. She looked around the room, seeing the beaten and scratched furniture that surrounded her, as well as the chair she was sitting on, made from an old box. Sighing again, she hung her head low, and the papers stared right back up at her.

They were custody papers for Mandy, and Sam's hand quivered next to the dotted line that she had to sign before sending it off to her sister. Papers that would declare Dee unfit to be a parent, and give Sam sole custody of Amanda.

She buried her hands over her face, sighing. Then, using one hand to cover her eyes, she used the other to sign the papers and put them in the large document folder laying across from her, ready to be posted the next morning.

CHAPTER FIFTEEN: ALPHA - OMEGA

Mike felt Mandy's lips pull at the tender, tight skin of his neck, bringing trace amounts of blood to just under the surface. He heard her giggle as he moved his hands down over the sides of her body, then grabbed her by the hips and turning her off of him, forcing her onto the floor.

She landed on the hardwood with a solid thump, and a tiny yelp escaped from her mouth as she felt her tailbone bruise.

"I'm sorry!" he said immediately, almost before she hit the ground, as he wiped his mouth with the sleeve of his shirt.

"Ow!" she yelled at him, more out of anger than pain, glowering at him as she got up. Her fists were clenched. "What the hell is the matter with you?"

"Me?" he boomed, getting up and grabbing her by the shoulders, spinning her around until her back faced him. He jabbed one finger into her back, pointing to where the tattoo was engraved. She let out another tiny yelp. "What's the matter with you? Where the hell did you get this?"

Mandy turned around swiftly, slapping his arm away from her. "That is none of your business!" she screamed. "You have no right to throw me onto the floor and then question what *I've* done with *my* body!"

Mike took a step backward, the accusation hitting him like a blow to the face. "I'm sorry," he sighed, then approached her again, softer this time. "Where did you get the tattoo?"

She rolled her eyes, starting toward the door.

"Hey!" Mike called out, rushing ahead of her of placing a firm hand against the exit, holding it closed. "I asked you a question."

Mandy looked up at him, her eyes full of fury and spite as she pursed her lips, looking about ready to let out a long string of words that a girl her age should not even know. "It's nothing. Like, half the people in my school have them. Most of the older people do. They just think it looks cool. I thought it would be too." she frowned, glancing at her feet.

Mike stood perfectly still, taking in everything the she'd just said. "Who at your school has them?" he asked after a second's thought, his hand still pressed against the door.

Mandy huffed, giving him a look. "I dunno, you freak. Mostly seniors. They all hang out, and most of them have cars." She had a smug look as she stepped up to him, standing high on her heels in a vain attempt to make eye contact with the much taller boy. "I bet you don't even have a license," she spat, as if it were extremely insulting.

He rolled him eyes. "No, Mandy. I don't," he admitted, feigning shame. "So, I'm afraid I can't give you a ride. You'll just have to walk *straight to hell.*"

"Urgh!" she grunted in defeat, throwing her arms up in the air. "What the hell is the matter with you?"

"Me?!"

She stopped, smiling a little. "I get it," she nodded, laughing patronizingly. "I understand. It's the girlfriend isn't it?"

He swallowed, squinting at her as he forced his fists not to grip.

"You don't even know, do you?" she giggled, poking him on the chest with a sharp nail, "She doesn't love you. She's not even happy with you. She's leaving you, dumbass. I've only been here a day, and even I can see it."

He took a deep breath. "Way I see it is, you're such a stuck-up brat that you've only been here a day and you already think you know everything," he scoffed, looking her up and down with disgust. "I knew slut ran in your family, but now I think stupidity does, too."

Her eyes went wide, and her hand automatically went to cover up her mouth.

Immediately he felt remorse. "Hey," he started, putting a hand on her shoulder. "I'm sorry. I just... I - I get used to trading blows like that with Xander, I forget sometimes how much it can hurt people."

"Because you think it doesn't hurt him?" she asked, tilting her head into an offensive position again, displaying a fine streak of defiance... a Peterson trait that Mike had obviously underestimated. "You really don't know *anything*, do you?" she growled. "Julie talks. She talks all about you. You think the people they locked up are monsters? Why don't you take a good look in the mirror-"

He pulled an arm back to slap her across the mouth but stopped himself, his hand quivering.

She looked shocked, but still stood her ground. "Go ahead," she goaded, not flinching. "I'm used to it."

He lowered his voice, calming himself. "If you know so much, then how come you didn't know that there was no way you could just walk in here and have me? That when it comes down to it, I'd rather be in a relationship that I know will break my heart..." his tongue whipped out of his mouth a little, his voice like poison as he finished, "...than be with someone like *you*."

She bit her lip as it began to tremble, then reached for the doorknob. This time, he made no effort to stop her from opening it. She walked out onto the porch in such a hurry that she forgot her coat. She turned after she was out the door, pointing at him to make one final jab. "What the hell is the matter with you? I walk in and jump you and you push me away? How gay are you?" she scoffed, turning and giving him the finger from behind. "Total queer," she mumbled, as she walked over his lawn and back onto the street.

Mike turned to close the door then slammed it. *This is so the opposite of what I need*, he groaned to himself, turning and flopping down onto his couch. He picked up her jacket, catching the strong scent of perfume on it. *Maybe I was a little hard on her.* He frowned, hating himself and his temper. *She's just a kid... she seems like she's had a hard life, probably has no idea how to treat men, like Julie.*

He stopped, scratching the back of his head, thinking back to the Omega tattoo that the young girl wore. *If it's just something that the 'cool kids' are doing, maybe we've been on the wrong track all along. If all these kids are getting them, then it could be just a coincidence.* He huffed angrily, throwing her jacket to the floor. *I hope Cathy and Xander are able to get something better. If not, the square we're in will start to resemble one.*

⋏⟨⋏

Xander picked up the phone that hung against the wall, glaring through the thick, bulletproof glass a few inches in front of his face. He could see his reflection in it vaguely. It was transparent, like a ghost. His features were so contorted with hatred that he almost didn't recognize himself.

He felt a soft touch of his shoulder. He turned to see Cathy smiling glumly at him on the chair next to him, and his face relaxed. But then the person on the other side of the glass picked up his phone, and Xander's face resumed its glowering posture.

"Hello, Alexander," Adam Genblade smirked, showing off his jagged teeth, sharpened almost to a needlepoint. It made him look like a wolverine trapped in a man's body, only the teeth showing. The scruffy, out of place hair didn't help either, and it looked as though the man hadn't seen a real shower in a month. His beady eyes dissected Xander at once, studying the boy's every gesture and movement for flaws and weaknesses to exploit. He found none. Content, he sucked in his already thin cheeks and made a popping sound into the phone before speaking again. "You don't call, you don't write... but you finally came to visit your old friend Genblade, hmm?" he snickered, turning toward Cathy and licking his lips grotesquely. "And I see you've brought me dinner."

The warden stepped up from behind Genblade, raising his nightstick, until Xander waved him off.

"That's enough, Adam," Xander snapped authoritatively, wiping the smirk of the killer's face.

Genblade shuffled in his orange penitentiary jumpsuit, the chains that bound his arms and legs rattling over the receiver as he did. He chuckled a little, smudging his index finger against the glass in front of him. "Okay, Alexander. We'll play it your way," he turned to Cathy. "I'm sorry, dear. I don't believe we've ever had the privilege."

"Is that what you call it?" Cathy snarled, her upper lip curling.

"Ha!" Genblade laughed heartily, a good, honest belly laugh. "That's a good one. I like her, Xander, she's got spunk. You got yourself a good one." He stopped laughing, leaning in to press his nose right against the glass, whispering, "She's got more meat on her than your last little fuck-er-ie, Womb. I might take her for a spin before I gut her. I think my knife might actually have to go through a couple of times to puncture all the fat on her, though..."

"Shut up," Xander demanded again, keeping his voice even as the True Womb flared up inside of him. He restrained it, taking several deep, long breaths before making eye contact with the killer again.

Genblade rippled his muscles, winking at Cathy once as he did, making cold

106

shivers run up and down her spine. She never broke eye contact. He coughed once then took a different tone. "To what do I owe the pleasure, then? If you haven't brought this lovely teen to me for a conjugal visit, then what the hell are you here for?"

Xander swallowed hard. "People. You killed or helped kill a lot of them."

Genblade raised an eyebrow, leaning back a little, intrigued now. "I did," he nodded flatly.

"You and that disabled moron Alpha spent months investigating this town, looking for me and the right way to get at me... along with that little playmate of yours, right?"

Before Genblade could respond, Cathy slapped Xander.

"Ow!" Xander yelped, shocked. "What the hell was that for?"

Cathy glared at him. "That was the most despicable thing I've ever heard!" she yelled at him, snatching the phone from his hand. "Just because he hurt you, that's no reason to talk about someone he loved like that!" She raised the phone, conking him over the skull with it, to Genblade's amusement. She put the phone to her ear and smiled politely through the glass as Xander got up, moving to lean at the wall behind her. He crossed his arms and started to grumble. "I'm very sorry about that, Mr. Genblade," she said coyly, faking a smile at him.

Genblade snuffed, smiling at her, and trying hard to hide his teeth. He crossed one arm and leaned forward a little. "That's all right, love," he said politely, as Xander rolled his eyes and turned away. Genblade watched Xander's discomfort with great pleasure. "He's always doing stuff like that, trying to hurt my feelings."

Cathy turned to glower at Xander, and then turned back. "That's awful."

"Yeah," Genblade groaned, his eyes turning down toward the floor, "I'm really just a sensitive guy at heart, y'know. Being in prison and all, you have to be tough, or they'll walk all over you."

"I know, sweetie, I know," she soothed, rubbing one finger against the glass seductively.

He smiled wide then forced it away. "I have managed to make some friends, though. Maybe you know him?"

"I don't think -"

"Name's Derek Smith." He smirked, his grin dripping of hate as he stared at Xander, watching as the hairs on the boy's neck stood on end. "He talks about you a lot. But I don't know what he's talking about..." he trailed off, making eye contact with Cathy, "...raping you isn't going to be the *first* thing I do when I get out of here," he finished, licking his front teeth and cutting his tongue on them, laughing.

"That's nice to hear," Cathy smiled.

Genblade's smile gave way in shock, his face growing pale as his remarks bounced off the girl's skin. "What?"

"I know you're just saying this to upset Xander," she smiled. "He can be so mean sometimes. Just the other day he said I was a carpenter's dream!"

He leaned in, taking a protective tone of voice over this young teen. "He said that to you?" he said, pursing his lips then turning to Xander. "For that, I'm gonna turn your flesh into splinters, maggot!" he threatened, yelling so that Xander could hear.

Xander laughed a little, simply giving Genblade the finger in response.

"Fuck you!" Genblade cursed, trying to stand as his hand gripped around the phone so tight that Cathy could hear the plastic crack on her end.

"Don't mind him," Cathy shrugged, waving it off. "He's just grouchy cause we can't seem to get our heads around this new murder thing... say, Mr. Genblade, do you think you could help us out with that?"

Genblade smiled, and Xander looked disgusted. "Sure," the killer sneered, "But please, call me Adam."

"Okay... Adam!" she giggled wildly.

"So, what's up? Is it another organ grinder like Alpha, or somethin' diff'rent?" he asked casually, as though he were talking to a co-worker.

"No," she said quickly, shaking her head. "See, it's out in Coral Cove. All these people committed suicide, only they didn't."

"Huh?"

"They were killed, made to look like suicides."

"Classic. Like somethin' out of *Murder She Wrote*."

"You watch that?"

"Yeah, they got me the Déjà View channel. Love that show," he grinned. "Angela Lansbury kicks ass. You could be like her when you grow up, couldn't you?

"I dunno about that..." she blushed, turning away shyly for a moment as Genblade stroked his chin. "Anyway, the only thing all these victims have in common is a tattoo of an Omega on their..."

Genblade nodded, chuckling. "On their backs... right. You found any with the letter 'T' on the back of their head yet?"

Cathy looked confused, shaking her head. "No."

"You will, don't worry," he smirked, gazing at her eyes, her eyelashes thick with mascara.

"What do you know?" Xander demanded from the background, looking up from the floor.

"I wasn't talking to you!" Genblade screamed, "Didn't your mom ever tell you it's impolite to eavesdrop? Oh wait, she's dead. I'm sorry, I forgot... you stupid little inbred bastard!" He snarled, then turned back toward Cathy, calming immediately. "I'm awful sorry about that, luv, what were we talking about before the womb-shit interrupted?"

"Suicides," she said quickly in explanation, looking him up and down carefully. "Something about a letter T?"

"Oh, yeah. Heh. You know, it's a pity your boy Xander over there wasn't with Engen for the genetics war a decade back. We could have used a fighter like him. We lost a few good men in that one, it was terrible. Captures and kills, terrible tragedies on both sides. Not only because they were people, but because they were genetically engineered people. Works of art that scientists spent years of their lives on. Devastating, really," he said with sincere mourning, shaking his head.

"Are you saying that there's some kind of rival to Engen involved with this?" Cathy asked, wide-eyed and astonished.

"No! No..." he chuckled, waving his hand in dismissal until his chain caught it. "I'm not saying that they're not playing their part, I wouldn't really know from in here, anyway. The point is, Xander's just not used to war, like he should be."

Cathy turned pale as the pure white background behind her. "War?" she gasped, trying to regain the ability to speak. "Are you saying we're in the middle of a war? How is that possible? Wouldn't we have heard..."

"You're thinking too big, darlin'," Genblade soothed, bringing color back to her flesh. "Wars can happen on domestic scales, too. See, the Omegas, they're not that bright. The Coral Cove crowd never was, they got way too much hick in their genes, if you know what I mean. That's why it didn't take us very long to figure out that the Womb was here, not there," he glanced at Xander, then continued. "But the Tees over on this side of the fence, they're relentless. Right around the time I caught up with Drew, they were settling into a new leader. Big guys, lots of brains. Older, too, with military training. Served in Bosnia 'til they kicked him out for being high as a kite in the field. Got a few of his comrades killed. Stupid thing to do, you ask me."

Xander's brow was furrowed as he stepped closer. "Are you saying that this is all over some moronic bad blood between our two towns?" he asked, not quite believing the words even as they came out of his mouth. "That normal people, *teens*, did this?"

"'Fraid so, buddy boy," Genblade sighed, expressing a genuine sympathy for their situation. "There are no sadistic teenagers or genetic mutations in your future, son. Just real pain." He smirked. "But that's where your power lies, isn't it?"

Xander took a step back, blood draining from his face, but did not respond as the Womb organ screamed for carnal release.

"You really are an idiot," Cathy snarled, speaking again, finally. She snarled with hatred at Genblade, digging her nails into the phone.

"Excuse me?" Genblade yelled, shocked at her tone.

She smiled a little, victorious. "I never thought *you'd* be stupid enough to fall for Xander's plan, but I guess I overestimated you."

"What are you - ?"

"He knew you wouldn't give any new information to him, especially after the court case." She grinned, her voice confident and triumphant. "So he had me dress my hair like that Spider girl to get you all hot and bothered so you'd let your guard down," she hung up the phone and blew him a kiss. He couldn't hear her, but he knew what she said: "See ya soon."

He gripped the phone until it broke, crumbling in his hands and falling to the floor. His face grew infuriatingly red as he locked eyes with Xander, who gave him a quick wave as he walked away.

Genblade screamed as the warden signaled two guards to drag him back to his cell.

The warden exited to call booth and walked up to Xander, who was walking out with the brunette girl quickly. "Alexander!" he called out, and Xander almost didn't respond, taking a minute to recognize the extended form of his name. The warden slowed as Xander turned, placing a hand on the boy's shoulder.

"What is it, Warden?" he asked softly, "Did I do something wrong?"

"No," the warden huffed, staring into the child's eyes with pity. "Nothing at all. I know why you keep coming back here. What that monster must have done to you..." he trailed off for a moment, taking a glance around to make sure nobody was listening. "I know you need to look him in the eye. If you ever need to do it without the glass, it can be arranged. I feel for you, son," he assured Xander, slapping him on the back.

Xander smiled slyly. "Thank you," he said, a hint of mischievousness in his voice, "Thank you very much."

He and Cathy turned to walk away then.

"Come on," Cathy said grimly. "We've got to get to Mike. That word Genblade said... Tee?... I know where I've heard it before."

"Me too. I don't think we have time to get Mike. You see to him; I gotta explore a different angle," he growled.

As soon as they were clear of the prison, Cathy leaned into Xander's arms, shuddering.

"Woah!" Xander grunted, caught off guard by the drop in her bravado. "Hard sell?"

Cathy's brow furrowed as she looked up at him. "Just a tad," she sighed, watching as the city's residential zone grew closer with every step.

Mandy Peterson huffed angrily as she walked home. Her heels clicked against the pavement with every step she took, ringing sharply through the early morning air. It was a beautiful, cool fall night, but she did little to appreciate it as she stormed down the street, visibly displaying her anger as if Mike could still see it. Her fists swung back and forth violently, whipping through the air like two miniature wrecking balls, making sure that anyone who happened past would know exactly what would happen if they got in her way tonight.

Morons! she glared at every person that stared at her through tinted windows as they drove by, or poked their drapes just a tad to see if there was anything gossip-worthy about her. *Idiots, all of them. Frigging country inbred hicks, probably wouldn't know what a real girl was if she slapped them in face. I don't see what's got all the guys in this town so hung up on Cathy Kennessy anyway. Is everybody here fucking retarded or something? Geezus, I don't know why I came out here anyway. I should have just stayed in th' Cove with Mom. Things would've been fine, but Julie and Aunt Sam had to come and-*

She stopped at the corner of Barrett and Lundrigan and looked up at the dim, fading streetlight, and it seemed to look right back at her. It bathed her in a kind of ghostly light, like something streaming down from heaven to shine only for her. It blinked and was diminishing fast, but while it was there it provided her with some sustenance, some sign that maybe things weren't so terrible all the time. She smiled, and it was truly a wonderful thing to behold, or would have been if anyone had been around to see it. For the first time in months, she wasn't smiling seductively, or smiling to get what she wanted, or smiling because her mother's boyfriend told her to, she was just... smiling. It came to her under that streetlight, surrounded by darkness, that everything was going to be all right. And if any of the gossipy old ladies that populated Lundrigan Street had bothered to open their windows a tad, they would have told you that it was like God raining down heaven upon the Earth for just one angelic little girl.

Sadly, only three people happened to see the closest thing that Coral Beach had had to a miracle in nearly thirty years.

And those three didn't appreciate it, at least not for what it really was.

"Hey!" came a friendly voice from the darkness. Even though it sounded benevolent enough, it still made her jump.

Her eyes darted out toward the darkness that surrounded her little shield of light, unable to focus on anything outside of it. "Hello?" she called out, squinting, trying to force herself to see.

Randy Owchar stepped out of the darkness and into the light, casting his face into long, stretched shadows. He looked sinister, like something from a noir film from the 30s. Everything except his smile screamed 'bad guy', with the black sequined jacket sparkling as he moved in the light, bringing the triangular points to a shimmering glow. It was worse when his two friends popped their heads out from behind each of his shoulders, giving the young girl the impression that she was surrounded.

Mandy backed up a pace, one ankle bent and ready to run at a moment's notice. She looked around, realizing that in her rage she had no idea where she had gone. No clue what part of town she'd placed herself in. None of the houses looked familiar, and all the drapes were closed tightly by people who didn't want to know, or just plain didn't care about, what happened outside of their own homes. "Do I know you?" she asked the large man in front, trying to reciprocate his smile.

"Sorry!" Randy laughed, showing off more of that great, big grin beneath his curly locks of blonde hair. He looked a little like a greaser from the old fifties movies and his face was like Patrick Swayze's in *Dirty Dancing*, before he got older and leatherier. "I thought you were somebody else!" He looked at one of his friends, who clearly also noticed the resemblance. "Say, you wouldn't happen to be related to Julie Peterson, would you?"

"Yeah..." Mandy started, easing herself a little, her shoulders relaxing. "Yeah, I am. I'm her cousin, Mandy, from Coral Cove. You know her?"

"Sure we do, from school," Randy answered immediately, almost before the question was even finished. He removed his hand from his pocket and extended it to her, the sweat coating his palm glistening a silvery sheen.

She took it, shaking it softly as he squeezed just a little too tight. "And you are?" she asked finally, raising an eyebrow to each of them.

"I'm Randy," he replied, pointing to his own chest, then turning to his tall companion in the neon orange t-shirt. "This is Combs, and my friend in the dorky wind-catcher over here is Ian." He smiled, a little weirder this time, giving his friends a look. "Where did you say you were from again?"

"Coral Cove," she smiled, leaning against the lamppost now, scraping her shoe against the gravel that scattered across the sidewalk.

"Have you been in the Beach long?" Ian spoke up, and it startled her a little. Up until this point, the other two had been like mimes, always there but never talking, just mimicking Randy's actions.

"No..." she replied slowly, turning to look at Ian. She glanced at his wind-catcher, noting that it was in fact quite dorky. She shivered, rubbing her bare arms and finally realizing that she'd left her jacket at Mike's house. Her thumb touched her shoulders, wincing as she touched the spots on the Omega tattoo where Mike had poked her. They would bruise soon, she thought, but that wouldn't really be a new look for her anyway.

"Would you like us to show you around?" Combs piped up, sticking his thin, cartoon-like head over Randy's shoulder as he tried to hide the fact that he was wiping his nose in that tacky orange shirt.

"No," she answered simply, "No, I'm okay. Really."

"You look lost," Randy ventured, his voice full of concern. Whether that concern was real or imagined was another matter entirely. "Can we help?"

"I dunno..." she sighed, taking another glance around and reminding herself that she had no idea where she was. "Well, I'm trying to get back to Templeridge Drive; do either of you know where that is?"

"Sure!" Randy grinned, stepping up next to her. "You must be staying at Julie's. I'm a good friend of hers, see her all the time. I can take you right home."

"Then you must know Mike Harris?" she asked, looking up at him expectantly.

"Sure, I know Mike. Nice guy."

"He's a jerk," she stated factually.

"Why?" Randy asked, laughing at her directness. "What's wrong with Mike Harris?"

She chuckled. "Try Cathy Kennessy, in a one-track I'm-a-love-sick-puppy-dog-with-no-mind-of-my-own kind of way..."

Randy laughed loudly at the girl's choice of words as the four of them walked off into the darkness.

⋏⋏

Tommy pulled on his checkered plaid pajama pants, stretching the elastic waistband so that it didn't snap too hard against his stomach. He smiled comfortably as he lay down on his bed, the thermostat cranked up on high so that he didn't have to use his covers, allowing him to just lie there atop the cottony sheets and fall asleep watching *The Late Show*.

His room was filled with pictures taken on class field trips and different

112

nights at the Factory, just hanging out with friends. Most of them were dead now, and there were some pictures that he couldn't even keep posted up anymore, like some that he'd taken at Grendel's party a few months ago. Too many people had died that night, and sometimes it seemed like the dying hadn't stopped since.

In one picture, Derek Smith smiled out of the photograph at him, those pale blue eyes piercing that glossy paper it was printed on. It seemed like he was watching you, like he could leap out of the picture any time he wanted and start to kill everything again. That was why Tommy couldn't take that picture down. In the back of his mind, he was afraid that if he did... it would make Derek angry. And he wasn't the type of person that you wanted to get angry.

-tonk!-

The sound came from his bedroom window, sending a quick convulsion over his flesh. His eyes darted around the room frantically, finally settling on the window. Breathing heavily, he stared at it for a long moment, waiting for something to happen. For the glass to fly in at him and start to rend his flesh into rivets and slivers. But it did not, and he sighed at his own crazed paranoia. *Just the house settling,* he reminded himself, leaning back on his pillow and aiming his remote at the television screen.

-tonk!-

"Who's there?!?" Tommy yelled, jumping from his bed before the sound was even done being made, accidentally tossing his remote into a corner, along with some dirty shirts and a moldy sock that had been there for about three years.

His breathing was so shallow and quick that he was in definite danger of hyperventilating. He looked under the bed, peering into every darkened corner of his room to make sure that there was nothing about. He walked over to the wall and flicked on the light switch. When he did, he noticed the picture of Derek pinned next to the switch, staring at him with those cold, unfeeling eyes.

-tonk!-

Again, that rapping at the window, like when Sud used to throw rocks at it to wake him up. They had gone together to bug Cathy and Melissa late at night, making wolf noises outside their bedroom windows and listening to them talk about how scared they were in school the next day.

Slowly, carefully, he walked over to the window and peered out at the ground below. Nothing. Not a soul in sight. He turned away, grinned at his own paranoia, and headed back to bed.

-tonk!-

He turned quickly, throwing open the window and shoving his head out, trying to catch whoever was throwing stones at his window before they had a chance to duck behind a shrub.

Again, nothing.

He heard something now, though. A drawn-out cracking sound, like when you hung off a tree limb just to listen to the slow creek and moan as the wood slowly gave way. Something tickled the back of his neck, and he reached up to scratch it. When his hand came back, there were wood and paint chips beneath his fingernails. *What the hell?* He wondered, turning his head to look up.

"Granah!" the creature yelled ferociously, grabbing Tommy by the collar as he screamed frantically, pulling him the rest of the way out the window and letting his feet dangle in mid air a good fifteen feet from the ground.

It was all black, and Tommy could hear its claws ripping through the collar of his shirt, poking out just enough to scratch against his skin.

The teen screamed, as the monster continued to spout off gibberish, grunts, and bellows from deep within its throat, behind those enormous, yellow teeth and triangular red eyes. Its skin looked smooth, but it didn't feel that way: the small portions of the animal that rubbed against Tommy's skin felt rough and sharp and scaly. It felt like Sud's old pet iguana had, before they'd forgotten it in the yard and a hawk had taken it for a meal. *This was it,* Tommy realized, his wide eyes staring straight into the creature's opaque lenses. *This is the thing that attacked me and Sud at Sara's house. I didn't imagine it, it's real. It's real and it's going to kill me.* "Please, man! I don't wanna die!" the boy pleaded, tears already running down his face.

"Then talk," the Womb threatened, shaking Tommy and then letting go with one hand, digging those claws into the wall of the house for further support. "About Randy Owchar..."

Black Womb ran toward the old youth center on Moony Road, the one that all the older kids had played in when Xander was a kid, before the Factory opened. They'd closed it down about a year ago because of vandalism and graffiti. Now he knew why. His lungs heaved, and his muscles cried out in frustration as the creature's body pushed itself beyond the limitations of its natural speed, making the migraine in the back of his head grow with every footfall.

Inside the thin black skin, Xander Drew cursed himself angrily. *Idiot!* He made a mental note to slap himself on the forehead when he had the time. *Why didn't I see it before?*

"What are you doing tonight, anyway?" Tommy asked, tapping Randy on the shoulder to get his attention. *"Wanna get loaded?"*

"Naw," Randy shrugged, *"I gotta go see Tee."* His voice became hushed. *"Hey, did you hear about Julie and Xander..."*

Three lone customers sat at a corner table, hunched over it like vultures about to devour their prey. One was wearing an old-fashioned leather jacket with Harley Davidson stitched across the back. The sleeves were lined with softly coloured clear red stones that seemed an odd contrast to the masculine, worn leather. On the bicep of each arm was an odd looking stylistic letter 'T'. He wore gloves, just the ends of which were visible from this angle, and black jeans that hung loose on his hips and appeared to be held up by a thick belt. Except for the light, curled blonde hair atop his head, he could have easily

stepped right out of Grease. Xander stopped, freezing dead in his tracks. What little bit of drying off he had done while sheltered within the glass walls of the phone booth was for naught now, as the mid-autumn winds that swirled around him had already drenched him in icy water. He focused in on the man wearing the leather jacket, who was probably twenty from what he could tell, and ignored his two casually dressed compatriots that appeared to be gangly, and a little nerdish.

ᚠᚹᚳ

"Well," Tommy smiled, starting off, "I'm gone. I'll catch up with you guys later."
"Yeah, us too," Randy reciprocated, heading off in the opposite direction, his two friends in tow, "Thanks for the smoke, Drew," he said politely, giving Xander a friendly wave good-bye.
"No problem," he replied warmly, "And call me Xander."
Randy smirked once more, then turned his back and walked away.

ᚠᚹᚳ

On their way down the street a few blocks down from Mike's, Xander and Cathy walked past Randy and his two friends (Xander thought maybe their names were Char and Duncan, but he wasn't sure enough to call them by it), heading in the opposite direction. He smiled and waved to them, and they waved back. Then he was stuck with recounting his entire conversation with them to her, as he struck up another smoke.

ᚠᚹᚳ

The Tee on his jacket, Xander cursed, I've noticed it a thousand different times, lots of ways. I've heard him mention that idiot leader of his more than once... and every time the Womb flares up. Even earlier tonight, when he came up to me and asked me for a smoke, the Womb flared up, making my claws pop. And every time, I pushed it back. I ignored what it was trying to make plain. I blocked myself from seeing the truth. From seeing why it brought me out to Coral Cove to begin with. To save them...

ᚠᚹᚳ

Five of them stood around her, each of them laughing. Not a maniacal, super-villain laughter that you hear on the movies, just a regular, heart-felt belly laugh, like someone had told a sick joke that she wasn't in on, and that made it even more sickening. Like this was nothing to them, other than a cruel gag, or something to do for fun when there was nothing good on television. The arm had been ripped from the shirt she spent forty minutes picking out that evening, displaying a hefty number of bruises and the tattoo that was stamped on her shoulder.

Not long ago the light had seemed so inviting. Now it just singled her out, forcing her to bare her secrets.

Mandy Peterson lay on the floor, the mascara that she'd applied so carefully streaking down over her soft cheeks, marring them. Her carefully-placed hair had been grabbed and pulled until it looked like a bird's nest, large clumps missing and showing her scalp, red from the roots being ripped out. She sobbed, curling up to cover her breasts with her legs as she dropped her head and covered it with her arms, trying to wish it all away. Her little body shook like a leaf in fear, her shadow convulsing and quivering across the cold concrete floor of what had once been the basket ball court of Coral Beach's Youth Center, where kids her age had gone to be safe.

The irony was lost on her, as she tried to hide from their faces.

They were still laughing at their joke, but one wasn't laughing quite so hard. Randy Owchar looked at her with the same pity he had felt when he found her beneath the streetlight a few blocks away, her Omega tattoo standing out like a sore thumb against her pale skin. He shuffled uncomfortably in his leather Tee's jacket, blushing a little as he glanced into the faces of all those that stood around him.

Ian Char smiled devilishly at the girl. His eyes sparkled with desire in the hot light, dancing all over her body. He was wearing tight jeans, making his excitement sickeningly visible.

Duncan Combs was silent and had a face like a statue, just watching her as if he expected her to do something. To put on a show like at the circus, to make him laugh again, the way she had when she'd first started to cry. Maybe she could beg. That'd be funny, he guessed.

Quinton Travers, a fat older man who'd been in the gang the longest, smacked his lips hungrily at the teen, passing a gun from hand to hand as if trying to decide which one to kill her with. He laughed like a hyena and wouldn't stop. Randy didn't even think the man knew what he was laughing at.

Then there was the leader. He stood in front of her, his head partially obscured by the darkness, his massive arms crossed in front of his chest. He wore a leather jacket like Randy's, except it had a large, stylized letter T emblazoned across the entire back. He wore a long gold chain with the same letter at the end of it, and his face had been painted white, with a third letter T in red paint across his large forehead and down the center of his face, disappearing beneath his collar. His knuckles were adorned with chipped, sharp brass that gleamed in the light, shining into Randy's eyes and making the boy squint. Beneath the painted face, the large man smirked. "Tonight is a good night," he said in a loud, booming voice that commanded attention. Everyone stopped laughing and talking except for Travers, who continued his hyena laugh a few moments after the rest of them had fallen silent.

The leader smiled widely, patting Randy on the back. "Today, our newest brother, Randy, has brought us an Omega, proving that they have been infiltrating us! Proving that it was these scumbags that have been killing us, causing our numbers to dwindle for months now!"

"But, I'm not -" Mandy began to plead, looking up helplessly at her attackers. "I don't know anything about-"

"Quiet!" the leader boomed, lashing out and kicking her in the side with a steel-toed boot, making her crumple into a ball. The men smiled and winked at one another. He grabbed her up by a large clump of hair, lifting her until she dangled just above the ground, putting her body on display like a trophy. "The

Omega says that she knows nothing, and I agree!" He paused, glancing into the eyes of his fellow gang members, as though he were giving a speech. "She knows nothing of pain, and she knows nothing of death! All of that has been an exclusively Tee experience lately, those of us who have suffered needlessly over the past two months, screaming in the dark like cowards when we should have been yelling in the light like warriors!"

He threw Mandy to the ground, kicking her back three times, then spitting on her.

"But we will teach her, my brothers! Just as we have taught others, we will teach her! We will instruct her in the matters of death and pain!" He reached for Travers, grabbing the twitchy man's gun and aiming it at the child.

She was crying, trying not to look at what was pointed at her. "Please, no..." she sobbed, feeling blood leak out from inside of her in places she preferred not to think of. He'd kicked her so hard she could still feel it inside, when she realized she was peeing the blood. "God, no..."

"Go, Roulette!" The three men surrounding her chanted, raising fists in the air. "Go, Roulette, go! Go, Roulette, go!"

Roulette smiled beneath his painted face, aiming the gun at Mandy's head sadistically. "This will be a great day for us all, gentlemen of the Tee," he announced, turning away for a moment. He looked at Randy, motioning for the boy to step forward. "Today, my boy, you will become a part of the greatest organization in the history of mankind. A God among insects," he grinned, slapping the gun down into the boy's hand. "And all you have to do is kill the Omega."

Randy swallowed hard, narrowing his eyes.

Mandy curled into a ball as she felt her body being hoisted up to a sitting position again, the tiny pebbles on the floor poking at her behind. One of the hands that had moved her had gripped her breast, but she did nothing to stop it, merely cried louder, hoping that some shred of decency would flare up inside of them.

That was when she felt the cool barrel of the handgun next to her temple.

"Go, Roulette! Go!"

CHAPTER SIXTEEN: SNUFF

Randy's gloved hand quivered as he held the gun, his finger hovering just in front of the trigger. His arm was blocking most of the girl's body and face, but he could see enough of her to know that she was shivering in fear, shaking and convulsing and trying her best not to touch the wounds that littered her body. He could hear her crying for her Aunt to come and save her, for God to rescue her and forgive her for whatever she'd done wrong to deserve this. Worst of all was the smell. Aside from the cheap fragrance of perfume that the girl wore, he could smell sweat beading off of her from the lights above. He could smell the salty tears that steamed down her cheeks and fell onto her exposed gut, as well as the stink of ammonia that wafted out from between her legs as the puddle of urine around her expanded.

He could *smell* her fear.

"Come, brother Randy," Roulette soothed, bringing his face close to the boy's ear. "It's alright. She is nothing, while we are everything. Join us with this final act and be what we all became long ago. You have witnessed these sacrifices for months now, all that is left is to take part in them..." As he trailed off, his voice lost its preacher-like qualities, becoming hard and commanding. "...Now, off the fucking Omega-bitch."

Randy swallowed hard as Mandy turned and looked up at him, her eyes pleading.

"Please, don't," she begged, her hands clasping together in prayer. "My name is Amanda Grace Peterson. I was raised by my mommy in Coral Cove, and just yesterday my Aunt Sam took me here. My cousin's name is Julie, you go to school with her. You sit next to her at lunch sometimes, and you said you eat those little tea biscuits you like and share them with her sometimes," she sobbed, closing her eyes so tightly that colours started to dance in front of her eyelids. "Please don't kill me."

"He won't," Roulette laughed, patronizingly reassuring the child. He reached out and took the gun from Randy with a broad smile. Then the smile melted again, the movements of his face distorting the paintings on it as he shoved the gun into Mandy's hand. Something in her finger cracked hard as he grabbed it, forcing it around the trigger. "You will."

Roulette motioned for Randy to step forward and take the gun, and he did.

Randy held the girl's finger in place as the both of them shivered. His face contorted with anger and fear as he fought back tears. "I'm sorry," he whispered, so softly that even she may not have heard it.

But someone did.

"If you were really sorry," Black Womb growled, drawing the attention of everyone in the room to the light above the main entrance, all the way across the gymnasium. He stood there like a marionette, arms folded across his chest in the shape of an x, his hands protruding above the shoulders with claws already sprung, gleaming along with his scaled body in the light. He looked like someone had cut the shape of a man out of the shadows and pasted him into the light, until he opened his eyes. Those big, red, sparkling eyes that saw everything, even in the blackest night. "You wouldn't be killing her."

Roulette stepped forward, crossing his arms in front of his chest. He remained stoically silent in front of the newcomer, not once flinching. There was no fear in him, nor shock or surprise. He didn't scream. Like a marble statue, he did not bend when the winds pushed against it.

"Who the hell are you?" Travers spoke up, even as the two teenagers backed into the shadows that surrounded them, already covering up the Tee tattoos branded on their arms. You could smell the stench of fear on all three of them.

The Womb stood there, unwavering, not moving an inch. Its eyes, unseen to everyone else in the room, darted back and forth between Mandy, Randy, and Roulette.

"Get out of here," Roulette growled, taking one menacing step forward. His footfall shook the ground all the way to Xander from sheer weight and muscle, the man's thighs rippling from the feedback. "This is none of your concern."

"Some days," Xander chuckled through the Womb's face, a sound that was disturbing on more than just a superficial level, "I honestly wish it wasn't. But see, I made a promise once, to someone I loved. If you're innocent, you're hurt, or you're scared... I'll be there." He motioned with just one finger to all of them, then Mandy. "Of everyone here, who do you think that best describes?"

"Please, help me..." Mandy pleaded, opening her eyes and stretching an arm out toward the Womb, fingers open as if he could just reach out from that distance and grab her, then fly her off to safety like Superman.

"Shut up!" Roulette yelled, losing his cool for a second as he turned, raising a fist to Mandy, spitting with anger and frustration as he spoke. "Now, you little snot-" he started to demand as he turned back to face the Womb.

There was nobody there, just the soft motion of the overhead light swaying back and forth.

Roulette raised his eyebrows, or he would have, had they not have been shaved off, his jaw hanging for just a moment, then he sneered. "You see my brothers?" he bellowed, raising his arms high and turning toward his fellow gang members triumphantly. "Not even fools dressed as vigilantes can even hope to withstand the power of the Tee brotherhood!"

He turned back to Randy, who still held the gun in Mandy's hand, shaking with fear.

Roulette smiled sinisterly, grabbing the child's face between his massive thumb and forefingers, turning it toward him. "Such a pity to waste you..." he said, almost as if it were a come-on. "...I'm sure you and I could have had fun *before* I had you killed, if you hadn't been one of the Omega's broads." He pushed her face away violently, and she felt the cartilage in her neck pop, the sound ringing in her ears for a few seconds afterwards. "Travers!" Roulette screamed, holding out his hand. "Pass me the silencer! Where there is one Omega, there may always be others!"

There was a long, dead silence then. All that could be heard was Mandy's fast, laboured breathing.

Roulette turned angrily, his teeth and fists clenched as he looked ready to strike. "Travers!" he bellowed again, but the man was not there. His annoying hyena laugh no longer penetrated the darkness that enveloped the rest of them. Roulette looked confused, his eyes searching the shadows where his underling had been. "Travers?" he said again, weaker this time, a touch of dread in his voice.

"Holy crap," Ian whispered fearfully, bringing a hand to his mouth. The teen's eyes scattered about the blackness around him, finding nothing to catch on. No movement, no light reflecting off a scaly stomach, no sound of stressed muscles expanding and contracting. The boy turned quickly back to Roulette.

"Holy fucking crap, man!"

"Calm yourself," Roulette murmured, waving the boy's behaviour aside. "It's probably nothing. Travers is a drunk. Probably went out for a piss."

Duncan shook his head, pursing his lip together. "Naw, Rou, man, it's that *thing*. It's here to get us." He shook, convulsing with fear. His hands moved so fast that they were practically invisible in the low light, just a blur attached to the bottom of his arms.

"Listen, boy. You haven't been here very long, so let me explain-" Roulette began, turning to the young man.

"Can we get this over with?" Randy asked, his voice wavering as he spoke, holding the gun at Mandy's temple. His voice was herald to no response.

"No!" Ian shouted back at Roulette, pointing a finger at him, "No, you listen! You listen and admit that you don't know shit about what's happening here for once!"

"Please," Mandy begged again.

"Quiet!!" Roulette yelled as loud as he could at the frightened child. He turned, grabbing Ian by the scruff of his neck and dragging him completely into the light, throwing him down in front of Mandy, ripping at the young man's shirt. "Listen, boy," he said, his cheeks glowing with ire. "If I hear one more word about things that go bump in the night from either of you morons, the police will find a *double* suicide, do I make myself clear?"

"Yes, sir," Ian gulped, looking down at the dark shadow he cast on the concrete floor.

"Good!" he cried, turning and pointing an accusing finger at Duncan. "And as for you!" He stopped, a perplexed look again flushing over his face, this time staying for longer. The makeup that concealed his features seemed to get considerably paler. He took one step into the darkness but stepped back, as if thinking better of it.

"I told you," Ian chuckled softly, still lying on the floor near Mandy, his face red from Roulette's assault as he pulled a shred of fabric from his ripped shirt up over his arm. He got up slowly, wincing in pain as he moved his sore back. "I told you this would happen."

"Shut up."

"They've been talking about it on the streets for weeks now."

"Shut *up*," Roulette demanded, turning to face the Ian this time.

"You know what it is, don't you? You've heard it too."

"*Shut up*," the fanatic stressed, his flabby cheeks vibrating and his eyes bulging.

"You've heard the whispers. Seen the marks where they killed Dawkins. Saw the way the cops thought it was us at first."

"*Shut up!!*" he demanded, screaming so long and so loud that even his white face turned red. Mandy flinched once, until the gun pointed at her moved, then she sat perfectly still again, her hand beginning to get cramped in the same position for so long. "It is not the Black Womb!" Roulette swore, stomping his foot again.

Randy chuckled a little.

"What are *you* laughing at, pledge?" Roulette screamed at his newest member, sweat running down his forehead.

Randy turned his head just a little, enough to see the skinhead leader out of the corner of his eye. "Are you trying to convince us, or yourself?"

"Insolent little shit!" the painted man screamed, stepping up quickly and drawing back an arm to backhand Randy. "I'll have your balls for th-" he stopped, a sly smile playing over his face. "Kill the girl," he demanded of Randy.

"What?" both Randy and Ian yelled simultaneously, shocked expressions assaulting Roulette.

"You're not thinking clearly, R," Ian scowled, waving his hands as if to call foul. "If we gotta fight that thing, whatever it is, we really don't wanna piss it off first." He grimaced, touching his shoulder tenderly. "I say we exchange hostages... her for us, man! Tell that bastard that if we let the girl go, he lets us go."

"No," Roulette said stubbornly, yet calmly. "She is an Omega."

"Did you happen to see the photos of what the Womb did to that Dawkins guy?" Ian yelled, pleading now. "There wasn't enough left of that kid to fill a shoe box! And now you're talking about making him mad, then taking him on?" He shook his head wide and expressively. "Well fuck that, man. Fuck that shit all over."

"You have no say," he reminded Ian, then turned back to Randy. "Will you kill her for me, son?" he asked, placing a hand on the boy's shoulder. "Do it... for me?"

"I'll try..." Randy replied softly, squeezing back tears. "For you."

"There, you see?" Roulette boasted, turning back to Ian.

Who was gone.

"What?" Roulette gasped, shaking a little. "He was here just a moment ago, I -" his eyes searched through the darkness until they eventually met with light.

There, under the light that marked the entrance, it stood in the exact same position it had moments ago. Its arms crossed its chest in a giant letter x. Its claws stretched out as far as they could at either side of his head, its eyes blazed with lust and vengeance. The only difference was that now blood dripped from the claws, making tiny sounds against the grey floor. Its breathing was heavy, excited. Somewhere in the dark skin of the creature's face, a smile formed. Its mouth opened, and the words that it spoke were both simple and terrifying:

"Black Womb lives."

Roulette stammered once, then regained his footing, composing himself enough to stare down the creature. The room was like spotlights on a stage, one directed at Randy and Mandy, the other at the Womb, Roulette interacting with both. "Come here, where I can kill you," Roulette demanded of the Womb, pointing down at the ground at his humongous feet.

The Womb slowly stepped toward the gang leader, one foot in front of the other as if on a balance beam, closing his eyes. The second he was outside the embrace of the light, he disappeared again.

Roulette began to look scared, an emotion that had overcome Randy Owchar long before. His eyes darted about, searching for the creature, until he felt a blinding pain snap across both his shins as his legs were kicked out from under him. He fell backward, his skull cracking against the hard floor, something inside his body snapping violently. He'd heard the sound many times before, but never from within himself. Roulette tasted blood in the back of his throat and groaned, first out of pain, then allowed it to grow into hate. When he opened his eyes next, he could see the Black Womb looking down at him, crouching next to his body with claws extended and ready to slice the flesh off of his bones.

He breathed heavily, lying with his back against the floor, tiny pebbles sticking into the small of his back and neck. He glared up at the thing in front of him. They both remained perfectly still for a long moment, caught in some twisted game to see who would blink first, to see who would make the first move in their petty standstill.

Finally, the Womb reached back, getting ready to hack away with the tiny knives on the tip of each of its fingers.

Roulette rolled away onto his stomach, pushing both palms against the floor as hard as he could to help propel him back to his feet. He turned swiftly to face the demon, both fists clenched so tight that his knuckles turned as white as the paint on his face. The Womb was already up, crouching now with its arms extended at its sides, talons scraping against the floor and making tiny gouges. There was another long moment when the two just looked at each other, weighing each other's strengths and weaknesses. It was as if the battle itself was not being fought with their hands, but with their wills. Slowly, Roulette reached for his belt, revealing a knife that he kept hidden there, forcing a tight grip around its black rubber handle.

He lunged quickly, swinging the knife high, the light from behind him sparkling off it.

The Womb stepped to one side easily, and both the blade and the man kept going.

"Grah!" he screamed, his voice loud and commanding, but it wavered in tone. It spoke more of his uncertainty, rather than his anger.

Without even looking, the Womb kicked one heel backward, connecting with the back of Roulette's left knee and snapping the cap into three distinguishable pieces.

"Argh!" the man cried, dropping the knife to let both hands clasp the fractured bone before toppling to the floor again. "Fuck!" he screamed loudly, echoing off the hidden walls of the gymnasium.

Black Womb calmly walked over to where Roulette lay in a pain-wracked slump, until The Womb was only a hair's breadth away. The Womb knelt down, blinking its big, red eyes once as its taut muscles relaxed a little. Placing one palm against the floor for balance, it reached out with the other to tilt Roulette's head forward just a little. It watched silently as the man's facial muscles bulged and conveyed the pain that he felt reverberating from his lower half, looking upon the man in pain with childlike fascination.

Inside, Xander felt the True Womb fill his form, wanting to be unleashed, to finish it, to kill. He swallowed it back, forcing himself to stay in control.

It watched calmly as tears streamed down the man's face... and then, the creature smiled. Right then, it'd won. It turned his head slowly toward Randy, who had watched all this with unblinking eyes, afraid to so much as twitch. He was still holding the gun in Mandy's hand. "Let her go," he ordered softly, those three simple words holding more weight than all of Roulette's previous yammering.

Slowly, Randy allowed Mandy's hand to slip away before lowering the weapon to the ground.

"No!" came the scream from the blackness, as Roulette lunged a hand from the ground, plunging his knife deep into the Womb's neck.

Xander fell, feeling the handle of the blade press against one side of his throat while the tip tried to prod through the thick skin on the other side. Black blood forced itself out from around the dagger, feeling like a million tiny throbs of pressure, making the boy's head want to explode. He tried to scream, but couldn't, as he felt the womb's healing factor try to repair vocal chords and air passages *around* the steel, incorporating it into his system.

His mouth wide in a feverish scream that made no sound, he slowly reached up with talons that were already on their way to retracting back into the marrow of his fingers and sunk them deep into his own neck. He ripped and shredded at the flesh, tearing at it like a wolf gnawing at a limb that had become ensnared by a hunter's trap until his fingers could finally wrap around the blade.

Gripping it so hard that his hands slit open, he pulled the miniature sword from the veins, then fell onto all fours. Gasping, he watched as the blood slowly stopped pouring down onto the ground.

-click-

He looked up slowly, seeing Roulette standing above him, a gun pointed directly at his head.

"Stop," came a voice from behind Roulette.

The man's gleeful sneer turned sour. As he looked behind him, Randy Owchar came into full view... pointing his own gun at Roulette.

"Don't shoot him," he said loudly, with all the authority that Roulette had once possessed. There was a long pause in which, if a bullet had been fired, it may not have punctured the tension that hung in the air. "If you shoot him, you won't kill him."

Roulette looked hurt then, giving Randy a look of betrayal, an expression that he had not used with the other members of his gang.

"Get out of here," Randy told him, motioning with the gun toward the exit.

Roulette paused a moment, looking from Mandy to Randy, then finally to the Womb, who stood slowly and crossed his arms across his chest, as though he had never even been wounded. He sighed, wiped something from his eye, and took off for the door. He slammed it shut behind him, the makeup on his face streaking down his cheeks.

Black Womb turned to Randy, who shoved the handgun he was holding into his jeans.

"Look," the boy started, his eyes glued to the floor.

"Run," the Womb stated blatantly, then watched as the boy took off for the exit as well.

The creature stood there for a moment, staring like a statue down at Mandy Peterson as she slowly got up. She did nothing to hide herself.

She felt safe.

Although she was cut and bruised, bleeding in some spots... she was beautiful, like a work of art, a strange and tragic tribute to strength.

"Go home," he ordered, before taking one step backward, fading into shadow.

Looking around cautiously, she gathered her bearings and then ran for the door.

As soon as he heard it shut, the naked form of Xander Drew dropped to the center of the light, coughing up blood similar to that which covered his entire body in thin layers as bile gushed forth from the still bleeding scratch across his neck. He lay on his back, staring up at the light as if looking at heaven from the vantage point of a soul trapped in hell, letting all the rocks and tiny pieces of glass burrow into his skin...

...and began to laugh, the smile on his face undeniable.

I won, he thought triumphantly, closing his eyes for the briefest of moments, and actually relaxing.

CHAPTER SEVENTEEN: SECRETS AND LIES

"So, it's over?" Cathy asked, biting into an apple as the three of them sat on the picnic table in the back of the school. She smiled a little, as if she had been waiting to hear those words for a long time.

"Seems that way," Xander nodded, staring off into the sky blankly as he finished his cigarette. He threw it to the ground, letting the cherry burn itself out. "The cops still don't know who Roulette is, and they're having a bit of trouble rounding up the Tees, but yeah. Yeah, it's over. They won't be making any pit stops at the Cove anymore."

"That's great," Mike chimed in, honestly congratulating his friend. "Good work, man."

"What about Randy?" Cathy asked, inching a little closer to Xander.

Xander looked beyond the fence that boxed in the playground, out into the school bus parking lot, where Randy Owchar sat alone. His face was buried in his hands, his body wracked with sobs. "I think he's suffering enough for now."

"Mandy's staying," Mike said, breaking conversation.

"What?" Cathy said, almost laughing. "No way."

"Way," Xander nodded. "All Julie could talk about on the way to school. Apparently, her mother's not right or something, and now she's staying here."

"Even after?"

"Even after."

"Ugh," Cathy groaned, rolling her eyes and getting up, throwing her book bag over her back. She jumped off the table and started to walk back to school. "That's all this town needs: another Peterson."

Xander chuckled a little as both men watched her hips sway while she disappeared into the school.

"Nobody like my Cat," Mike sighed happily.

"No sir, there is not," Xander agreed, never taking his eyes off the spot where she disappeared.

Mike stopped, looking up at Xander. There was a long pause as the boy clicked his tongue against the roof of his mouth, deliberating whether to ask the question that was poised on his lips. "What happened to you?"

Xander turned, feeling the scar tissue on his neck that had not quite healed over yet. "What? This? Just a scratch."

"No," Mike whispered, shaking his head. "At Engen."

Xander stared in silence then shook his head. "It means a lot that you're ready to ask me about that, man," he said glumly, getting up from the table, "but I'm not ready to answer it. Not yet." He walked away, waving with the back of his hand. "I got somewhere to be."

"Well, things are looking great," Warren O'Toole beamed, as he and Xander finished their first session, late coming as it was. "It's nice to know that you don't plan on skipping out on all our conversations, Mr. Drew."

"Yeah, well..." Xander groaned as the class bell rang and he sprung up from his chair, heading toward the door. "Don't let it go to your head, Doc."

"Have you given any thought to the hypnosis treatment?"

Xander did not respond to that, just opened the door to O'Toole's office violently, stopping dead in his tracks when he saw who O'Toole's next appointment was.

Mandy Peterson.

Without a word, she pushed past Xander and walked over to sit in the chair. Xander took a step out into the hall as the door slowly closed on its own, O'Toole and Mandy disappearing from view.

"So, Miss Peterson," O'Toole started, tapping his files against his desk to straighten them. "Tell me more about this black angel you've been dreaming about. You say you know who..."

The door clicked shut, leaving Xander wide-mouthed in the hall, staring at O' Toole's name printed on the plate glass.

EPILOGUE

The crosshairs dissected the skull of Adam Genblade as he glared down the barrel of the gun, raising one eyebrow in suspicion, a wry grin spreading across his lips.

He shuffled slightly inside his brightly coloured orange prison jumpsuit, the numbers 00876 marked in black across the left breast. He glanced behind him at the back of the old, flimsy wooden chair that he'd been seated upon, the thick steel chains that bound his arms and legs to it. Twitching slightly from the itch on his nose, he looked back at the barrel of the gun that was staring down at him, the hammer pulled back and ready to fire.

"What the hell is this?" he asked finally, an annoyed undertone in his voice as he shuffled within his restraints.

Xander smiled, one eye closed as he aimed the gun with the other, pointing it directly between Genblade's eyes. His face was emotionless, expressionless as he held the gun, standing just under the disengaged security camera at the front of the plain, white criminal conference room.

"This?" he replied, motioning toward the weapon with his head, "This is a .38 caliber revolver. They're manufactured in Hartford, Connecticut."

Genblade sighed, the hot fluorescent lights making his sweat and distorting his facial features, making it look as though there were large, circular shadows beneath each of his eyes. "I know what it is. You know damn well that's not what I - "

"It's currently the most popular handgun in America. Thirty-eight million registered," Xander continued, as if Genblade had never spoken.

"Womb, what's this..."

Xander raised a finger for silence, and got it. "There is a reason that this is the most popular handgun in America," he sighed, as he raised the barrel to the side of his head, then let go of the hammer.

-click-

"It kills people," he finished with a groan, taking down the gun and holding it at his waist, staring at it sadly.

Adam stopped, examining him. He was shocked at first, but that faded away. He resumed staring at his enemy with what would have been perfect composure, had his hair not been matted and greasy, strands of it falling in front of his eyes as he tried to blow them away in vain. The silence resumed until finally he decided to speak. "Great theatrics. Really, I'm impressed. Mind explaining why you're in here, disturbing me?"

"Oh, Genblade," Xander smiled, chuckling a little. "You were disturbed long before we crossed paths. But I'm here because your warden offered me the chance to... 'look you in the eye', I think was the way he put it. To maybe put what went on at Engen behind me, once and for all. I thought it'd be rude not to take him up on the offer."

Genblade nodded to the side, taking that in and reminding himself to take a pound of flesh out of the warden at the next appropriate opportunity. "Well, that covers the *how* of why you're here, but I asked for the *why*."

Xander turned, pointing the gun at Genblade's head again, lining the crosshairs in the sight perfectly with Genblade's right eye.

"Why, Genblade?" He asked mockingly, taking a step forward just to remind the killer who was free to move about in the oblong room. "We're here to play a little game of roulette." He laughed sinisterly, like so many of the men he'd fought had. "But not the kind you play at Vegas, dummy. No. This roulette is played with one gun, one bullet, and two idiots," he explained, using the gun to motion back and forth between them. "See, in roulette, it's a game of luck. The lucky idiot wins, the unlucky one gets dead." He re-aimed his gun for the third time, carefully marking Adam's skull.

-click-

Genblade winced slightly at the sound, but did well enough to hide it. He glared at Xander with his soulful blue eyes, trying to figure the boy out. *More complex than a Rubik's cube,* he thought bitterly. "Why are you here? What set this off?" he asked finally, already tired of the game that they'd been playing, wondering what the point of it would be.

"Why don't you tell me?" Xander yelled, thrusting an accusing finger at Genblade. "As far as I'm concerned, you started our game the second you killed Sara. That's what our lives have been since, hasn't it? A game of roulette, testing ourselves until one of us is dead." He paused, staring down at the gleam that came off the gun. "Sud died yesterday." He sniffed then snorted a little.

"Did you do it?"

Xander did not respond to that, just kept speaking as if Adam never had. "You know, I didn't even realize his real name was Frederick until after he was dead? Frederick Windser..." he paused, stopping to look at his enemy. "I never really knew him. I guess now, I never will..."

Xander exited Dr. Warren O' Toole's office and walked down the hall to meet up with Cathy for Economics, feeling the same emotional distance he always did when he came out of one of O' Toole's sessions. He walked down over the slippery stairs and waved politely to Mr. Larkin as the old guy mopped, who responded with a tip of his hat.

The main hall was crowded. Beautiful fall light streaming in from the skylight above, bathing all the people there with a glow only broken when a stray cloud happened to pass by.

"Hey!" Xander called out, reaching up as high as he could to get Cathy's attention from across the hall.

"Hey!" Cathy replied, motioning for him to join her.

He started wrestling his way through the crowds of people, mumbling something about this being worse than rush hour. He hoped that he'd bump into Julie, that they'd get a chance to talk today.

All of a sudden, there was a wave that went throughout the crowd. It was just a slight movement, but the emotive fear that ran through people was tangible. Xander turned and looked as Tommy tried to pull Sud away from the fight that was going on between him... and Randy Owchar.

Xander's eyes grew wide as he started pushing people aside, trying to get to them in time. Trying to put some distance between Sud and Randy, trying to stop what he knew was going to happen. Just... trying.

Both Randy and Sud reached for their waistbands at the same time, pushing aside their coats. Randy pulled out the handgun as fast as he could, aimed, and fired three times.

For a moment that lasted forever, there was no sound. It was like the world had just gone deaf. Then Frederick Windser's body hit the floor in what already seemed like a liter of blood, and the screaming started...

Xander sighed, closing his eyes tightly. "So, yeah, Genblade," he answered finally, "Yeah, it was my fault."

"What?" Genblade yelled stupidly, "What the fuck are you talking about? That was no more your fault than it was Cathy's. It was a stupid teenager out to Columbine his school. That's the trend these days, kid. Ask me, it's your school's fault for not having metal detectors put in, in this day and age."

Xander took that in. "You may be right," he agreed. "But on the other hand, Randy Owchar was a Tee. A gang member that hunts down and kills people from Coral Cove, called Omegas."

"I know, Drew," Genblade heaved, rolling his eyes. "I told you this, remember?"

"Frederick Windser was an Omega."

"That I did not know," Genblade snapped, surprised.

"Me neither, until paramedics cut away his shirt, showing off the huge tat the guy had on his chest." He raised his voice, pointing to his own chest for punctuation. "I let Randy go, thinking that he'd be alright. Thinking that if I gave this kid a second chance, he'd prove himself. Now, there's a dead fifteen-year-old, and another on the run with the rest of his gang." He looked off to the side, lowering his voice. "I guess he finally got to be a full member." He turned back, raising the gun to the side of his head. "So, it is my fault, for being so careless. For not taking the promise I made to Sara seriously enough, even after I preached it into the Tee's heads."

-click-

Genblade sighed, his shoulders falling as much as his restraints would allow. "Not that I care if you off yourself or something, but I'd hate to see your brains splatter against the wall for something so pointless. You couldn't have known."

"But I should have."

"But you *couldn't* have," Genblade insisted, leaning forward a little. "Couldn't. Could-Not. Look it up."

"Anyway," Xander huffed, waving the gun as if to shoot away Genblade's insult. "The funeral was worse, because it's always worse..."

ʎⴹⴸ

The coffin lowered into the large rectangle hole in the ground with a loud -thunk- that made everyone in the crowd jolt and Sud's mother cry even louder. She was lucky that she didn't have Xander's sense of hearing. He was the only person who could hear the poor boy's body bounce around inside of it, between the pillow and the barrage of teddy bears and flowers that had been buried with him.

Cathy pulled her head even further into Xander's chest, sobbing uncontrollably, convulsing in his arms as her tears stained the fabric of his only good dress shirt. He'd gotten to wear that shirt a lot more lately, as he and Cathy went to more and more funerals.

Not Mike, though.

Ever since Sara, Mike hadn't come to a funeral. Hadn't been able to bear it, some said. As for Xander, he assumed Mike felt the same way he did: that they were too young to have to bury as many friends as they had.

The numbers 358 were engraved into the front of the casket as the family started to bury it with mounds of dirt and soil. 358 had been Sud's locker number. It seemed a horrible way to be remembered, but somehow fitting, as the boy did die at school.

Xander turned away as Cathy cried on him and he walked her back toward his parents' car, where his mother waited to pick them up. As his eyes drifted upward to the top of the hill where Sara's grave rested, he saw one lone figure that had not moved since the ceremony began: Tommy.

ʎⴹⴸ

"...broke my heart to see him like that," Xander groaned. "You know that expression 'you look like you've lost your best friend'? Well, it's stupid. Because there is no situation when anyone can look so sad as they do when they lose their best friend... except that one."

Genblade's head went down immediately, his own pain making the words resonate within him. "You're right."

"Yeah," he said quickly, sucking in air before snapping the gun into place, aimed at Genblade's head again. He'd aimed it so many times that he didn't even need to check the sight to know where the bullet was going this time. "That's when I remembered something else, Genblade." he smiled, and the grin was sickening. Like an evil clown. "I remembered that it was all your fault."

"What?"

"Let me explain. About, I dunno, ten years ago...

ʎⴹⴸ

Randy and Xander played together, their plastic Stone Soldier figures smacking off of each other, their swords and sais clanging for the fate of the world, in their minds.

"Boys!" came the booming voice of Randy's father as the floor boards shook beneath the two five-year-olds, making their toys fall over when the mountain of a man came into the room. He was fat, and when he spoke, his cheeks shook. But you didn't laugh,

129

because he spoke to scare you. "What are you doing playing with those sissy dolls?" he demanded, slamming a fist against a coffee table.

Both children stopped, looking up at the man with wide eyes. "Saving the world?" little Randy hazarded.

Mr. Owchar let out a long, loud chuckle, stroking his beard. "Well," he smiled devilishly, "I guess this world could use savin'... but that's not how you do it." He turned, motioning for them to follow. "C'mere. I'll show you how to save the world."

He took the boys into his room. Standing on a chair in the closet, he pulled down a ratty old shoe box. It opened with a cloud of dust. He reached in and pulled out a pistol, stroking its barrel as if it were a beloved pet or child. "In this world, this is the only type of security you can have. This is what keeps your family safe...your world..."

Both Xander and Randy stared at him, watching as he felt the weight of the gun in his hand. He smiled, the reflection off the barrel sparkling against his teeth. He turned and looked at the boys as if he'd forgotten they were still there, then frowned. "You two go on and play. G'wan."

Randy nodded, tapping Xander on the shoulder as he turned to head back into the living room.

Owchar looked down at the gun again for a moment, before carefully placing it back into the box and onto the closet shelf.

From across the room, Randy watched his father intently as Xander started to play. Smiling, he turned toward Xander and said: "When I grow up, I'm gonna be just like my dad."

ᚹᚤᚹ

"Don't get me wrong," Xander explained, "I have nothing against the boy looking up to his father... it's *why* he was looking up to him that bothered me."

"Don't blame you," Genblade agreed, "The old man sounds like a farm-fresh Alabama hick to me."

-click-

"Christ!" Genblade screamed, as Xander clicked off another round. "The least you could do is warn me!"

"Four out of six." Xander smiled, looking down at the gun, "We're both lucky so far, Genblade. But how long can our luck really last? Two shots left, after all," he sneered, glowering.

"What happened after the funeral?" Genblade asked, seemingly interested, but probably just buying time.

"Well," Xander resumed, giving the other man a look. "After the funeral I went back to the school, thinking I could be alone. I was wrong. I was punching the bag around, when my hearing picked up on a familiar voice..."

ᚹᚤᚹ

"Where is he?" Mike yelled, slamming Duncan Combs against the wall of the locker room, making the metal doors rattle and shake. "Where is Roulette? Where's Owchar?"

"I dunno, man!" Combs yelped, trying to squirm away to no avail. "I been tellin' ya, I dunno!"

"Where?" Mike yelled again, drawing back and punching him right in the mouth,

130

splattering blood all over the lockers.

"The corner of Tam and Prewer!" the crook spat finally, tears running down his face. "It's a small place. Looks like a cabin!"

Mike lashed out once more, punching Combs in the side of the face to put him down for the count.

He walked outside the school building and started across the lawn. Halfway across, he stopped dead in his tracks, sighing with defeat. "What are you doing here?" he groaned, turning to face the Black Womb.

"What does it look like?" it asked rhetorically, raising an eyebrow. "I'm stopping you."

"This is bullshit!" Mike exclaimed, clenching a fist and taking one menacing step toward his best friend, tears running down his shirt. "I have to stop them, or they'll do it again, just like they did with Jamie."

"Leave that to me..."

ʎ↑ʎ

"And did you?" Genblade asked, licking his lips with the promise of a battle now.

"Oh, yeah," Xander said softly, frowning. "I did. I walked right into that place and sliced and clawed my way through every Tee. Roulette wasn't there, but that was fine. The person I really wanted was. I grabbed hold of Randy and held him up high. He was already unconscious, so his body was hanging there, limp in my grip as I drew back my talons and aimed for his jugular..."

He stopped, bringing the gun to his head. He closed his eyes tightly and squeezed the trigger.

-click-

"Five out of six, Genblade." He smiled, pointing the gun at his nemesis. "The last one's yours. But, I guess I might as well finish the story first."

"Did you kill him?" Genblade asked frantically, sweat pouring over his brow, now.

"No," Xander said sadly, carefully aiming the pistol. "I wanted to," he sighed, looking at the gun he was aiming. "This isn't that gun, by the way. Not the one that killed Sud. This was my father's. The one that shot Derek, and that I almost used to kill myself. I guess I still haven't dealt with that yet. I'll have to, eventually."

Genblade smirked. "I didn't know you tried to- "

"I didn't tell you!" Xander responded, snapping. He walked toward Genblade until the gun was less than an inch in front of Genblade's forehead, right between the madman's eyes. "You know why I couldn't kill him, Genblade? Because in the end, it wasn't Randy Owchar's fault. See, both he and Sud pulled guns that day. Randy's just the one who shot faster, better. He was saving his own life. If things had been different, it would have been Owchar's blood all over the hall at school, and I'd have been slamming Frederick Windser into the wall, looking for revenge. No, the blame doesn't fall on either of them. There's a reason they brought guns to school, after all."

He paused, making eye contact with his prey as he lifted the hammer of the

131

gun one last time.

"Us. We maimed and killed so many of that school's population, I'm surprised that they're not all carting guns around. They're scared of us. We started this."

He put first pressure on the trigger, and Genblade began to sweat more.

"They think they're being heroes. Like their dads taught them to be. That's why we're playing this game, Genblade. We're both at fault, so I'm letting the gun decide who takes the blame. Was Randy Owchar pretending to be fighting me when he killed Sud? Or you? Or Derek? Or Phillips? Who's to say? All that matters is: we started this."

He sneered, a final gesture of hatred toward his enemy.

"The problem is this: it's the same reason I couldn't stop Roulette when he was going to kill Mandy Peterson. The same reason I couldn't kill Owchar, even though he deserved it. The same reason I can't stop evil. Because even when I have it right in my sights... even when there's no way I can miss you..."

-click!-

He threw the revolver aside as Genblade took a breath for the first time in minutes.

He turned and walked out the door of the white conference room. "We're stuck with each other, Genblade."

BOOK FIVE

GHOSTS OF THE PAST

WEDNESDAY, DAY TWENTY-TWO

You never know when your life is going to change, Xander thought as a glob of blood traveled down his throat.

He had to swallow at least once every few seconds, or the red fluid spraying from the artery in the roof of his mouth would start to flow out past his lips. His eyes were foggy, and he tried desperately to hold his guts inside of him, his throbbing intestines threatening to spill out onto the floor.

Blackness was melting off of him and dripping onto the dull concrete floor. Blood flowed by his feet, rushing to a drain in the center of the room.

His head weaved back and forth from exhaustion and dizziness, but he managed to hazard a glance toward the officers that lay around him. Some were missing limbs. The rest were missing heads. He felt their blood wash past his feet, and as he did, his eyes went to another victim.

Adam Genblade lay on the floor. A long, slender pipe had been shoved into his gut, and his face was covered with so many bruises and cuts that it was nearly unrecognizable. His orange jumpsuit was tainted red and stuck tightly to his skin, making it easy to see that he was not breathing. *You never know when fate is going to jump up and bite you in the ass and say: "I can't believe you didn't see that one coming." Because that's the worst part of sitting here... I really should have seen it coming.*

As his vision began to fail and he could feel himself slipping away, he looked up at the hulking figure that had done all of this, and his eyes filled with fresh terror at the renewed sight of the squirming form of black flesh and teeth and claws. Its mouth alone was bigger than Xander's entire body.

Uttering one last attempt at breath, Xander fell, his body crashing to the floor and his eyes rolling back into his head. His last thought was wondering how he'd let this sneak up on him. How he'd let his entire world come crashing down around his ears, when he'd had so long to stop it...

CHAPTER ONE: THERAPY

TWENTY-ONE DAYS EARLIER
Wednesday, Day One
Three thick file folders slapped down onto Robert Snyder's desk. He jumped

with fright and his hand jolted against the paperwork he'd been absorbed in, making the pen bump and scratch his name. He stared at the files for a moment, his eyes scanning over their pastel yellow covers, as if he was unsure of where they had come from as he woke up from his trace-like state. He turned his head to look to the person who had thrown them there, the lights above him reflecting off of his bald, egg-shaped crown and illuminating the backs of his ears, making him appear cartoonish. "Is there something I can help you with?" he asked calmly, but his voice was small and curt. He spoke down to people out of nature now, barely even realizing that he was doing it.

Warren O'Toole looked down at him, his arms crossed and his mouth taut with determination. His typically pleasant smile and demeanor were gone now, replaced by a grim, single-minded man's scowl. His black hair was matted and misplaced. The light coming in from a big bay window reflected off his glasses, which might as well have been telescopes that made his eyes impossible to see.

"Have a look," O'Toole said finally, gesturing one hand toward the files before taking his arms out of their crossed position and leaning both palms against the desk. He stared Snyder down. "Go ahead. Have a look and try to tell me that I didn't tell you so."

Snyder kept his cool, twining his fingers together as he straightened himself in his seat. A bone cracked somewhere in the center of his back, giving the troll-like man a momentary sense of relaxation. "Why don't you save me the trouble and tell me what's in them?" he responded coyly, sticking out his tongue a little as he spoke like a cobra hissing at a small mouse. "Something tells me I'm going to hear it anyway."

O'Toole's nostrils flared and he fought to keep his face from turning red with anger. He looked down at the files and flipped the top one open. A harsh black and white picture jumped out at the principal, making him balk.

It was a picture of Frederick Windser, taken shortly after he'd been shot a few days ago in the halls of the school by another student, Randy Owchar. Both of them once belonged to rival gangs, the Tees and the Omegas, respectively. Randy was still loose on the streets, and Frederick was buried in the ground, far too deep, it seemed, for anyone to remember.

"This is a police file on the murder of Windser," O'Toole stated, flipping through the pages methodically, slowly exposing close-up shots of different areas of the young man's body to Snyder's increasingly disgusted face, like a sick slide show.

"I can see that!" the principal snapped, rising slightly in his chair as the skin on the back of his hands became rough with goosebumps.

"Good for you," O'Toole quipped, shooting him a look. "Beneath it are two of my own folders on both Windser and Owchar, along with the information on them compiled by Phillips, the previous counselor," he informed Snyder as he continued flipping through the grotesque photos of the dead teenager. He'd made it as far as the morgue photos now. The boy had been sliced open from chest to pubic bone and spread wide with clamps to get at the bullet that had killed him, lodged just to the right of his spine.

Snyder's hand snapped forward with one quick motion, slapping the folder shut. "Is there a point to all this?" he yelled, saliva squirting from the gap between his two front teeth and making small, round water spots on the papers he'd been signing.

"I believe the point is that a young boy is dead, Principal Snyder," O'Toole responded coldly.

"I know that!" the smaller man protested, throwing his hands up a little, his face becoming one of pleading. "Don't you think I know that? All I've been doing for the last four days is sign papers and sheets and legal documents and ward off lawsuits and try to explain to lawyers that our board does not *believe* in metal detectors and..." he huffed, burying his nearly hairless head in his hands. "I know all that, Warren," he sighed, his voice sounded defeated. "Just tell me why you're in my office, reminding me of it all, when I've just spent the last four days trying to forget."

O'Toole frowned, his features softening for the first time since entering the office as he watched the man plead. He relaxed himself, then sat in the chair across from the principal. When he spoke, he hesitated to first make sure that his voice was even and fair, and in no way as accusatory as it had been at first. "I'm here because it could have been prevented," he explained, his voice a near whisper as he reached out and opened the file on Randy Owchar, pointing to a long list of dates and times. "I've called that boy into my office once every day since I got here, sir. Look," he motioned, pointing to another column, this time actually gaining Snyder's attention. "His grades had been slipping, his attendance record was almost nonexistent... This kid was textbook. He was another Derek Smith, and we all should have seen it. I asked you *thirteen times* to force him into regular therapy appointments. And before me, Phillips asked you ten times."

"I told you. It violates board policy. Besides, what if we hadn't gotten parental consent? You've never met that boy's parents, Warren. I have. Believe me, the last thing they'd want is a teacher telling them what went on inside their son's head."

"But we could have stopped it," O'Toole sighed, reaching down and holding up a large stack of files that he'd concealed beneath his chair when he came in.

"What's that?"

"This?" O'Toole responded in mock surprise, pointing at the stack of no less than twenty folders. "These are the folders of each of the other students who have either been refusing therapy, or have been attending but show signs of snapping."

Snyder turned white.

"Three more have been added to this pile since Fred Windser was killed, and I expect a few more by the end of the week," he said, flipping through the folders.

Snyder sighed heavily, his eyes darting back down to the paper he'd been signing to deny the school's responsibility. Now he wasn't so sure if he wanted his name on it. "What must be done?"

Warren smiled a little, his eyes shrinking a little as his cheeks pushed up. "I need to be able to force the students with probable cause to commit violent acts into counseling."

"Force?" Snyder repeated, his voice speaking volumes of his distaste for the word and its placement here.

Warren raised his hands in defense. "What I mean is, order them to come to me on a regular basis under penalty of suspension or expulsion, regardless of parental consent."

"That'd be difficult."

"So is cleaning blood stains off the hall tile."

Snyder closed his eyes and took a few long, deep breaths. He sighed. "Do whatever you have to," he said calmly, shaking his head in disbelief of his own words. When he opened his eyes again, they stared menacingly at Warren. "But so help me, keep it within reason, or you'll be the one who needs help."

O'Toole ignored the comment, the smile on his face wide as he scooped up all of his files and turned to walk out the door. As soon as he was outside the office and in the vacant halls of the school, he flipped through his folders eagerly, finding a thick one and holding it up, beaming at it.

Across the top, in bright red letters, read: Drew, Alexander.

CHAPTER TWO: LINES IN THE SAND

"Yes!" Xander announced, letting a laugh slip through his lips as he finished keying in the start-up codes for his computer. He spun around in his chair and clapped his hands high in the air as his computer started to boot-up without major errors for the first time in three months.

It had taken a new hard drive, a new fan, a new motherboard and the replacement of every circuit wire in the entire box, but it was finally finished. The browser appeared on his screen with the tiny blue and white animation on the bottom telling him that everything was going fine. When his desktop finally loaded, it showed the bare minimum. All of his files were gone, all of his hacking programs, all of his games. Even some higher-up functions weren't operating and would have to be loaded from the system CD, but he had a computer, he had Internet, and everything else was fine, as far as he was concerned.

Slipping into his old habits, he pushed back his shaggy, dark brown hair, and dragged the mouse pointer down to the bottom right corner and clicked on the (miraculously) still-operating messenger service. A blue screen popped up with a small blinking red circle in one corner to tell him that he was online. Instinctively, he opened up his contacts list. His screen name started to bounce back and forth along the top of the screen, and the others slowly came into view as the computer checked them.

One stood out among the rest.

The screen name was 'baby_gurl'; it had been Sara Johnson's online tag from the time she was twelve years old until the day of her death. He stared at it long and hard, focusing on it until it seemed to pop out of the screen at him.

He turned to the left, gazing out of his bedroom window.

Her house was there; her bedroom window almost directly across from his. The lights were off, but if he tried hard enough he could imagine the soft glow of her monitor, which meant she would be online. Maybe she'd even notice him and give him a little wave. Then she'd sit down at her computer and pop a fresh piece of gum into her mouth. A few seconds later, he would hear a chime coming from his computer as she sent him a message, probably making fun of him for something he'd done in school that day. Or who she had a crush on now, and how it wasn't him. Or how crappy everything in their lives was. Or how she couldn't wait till tomorrow, so she could live another day of her crappy, little life.

He closed his eyes, forcing his gaze away from the window and back to the screen. When he opened his eyes again, her screen name was beckoning to him. He half expected to hear a rhythmic chime as she messaged him. But, of course, she didn't.

Huffing, he brought the pointer up to her name and double-clicked it. A 'send message to' window came into view, overlapping the one that was already there. Frowning at himself, he felt the palms of his hands rest comfortably against the edges of his desk, his long fingers outstretched over the keyboard, like settling into an old chair after a long time to find that it was still grooved to fit your form. He took one deep breath, then started to type:

HEY SARA, I HAVEN'T SEEN YOU
IN A WHILE. JUST WANTED TO
WRITE AND ASK IF EVERYTHING WAS-

He stopped, then backspaced the entire passage, grunting to himself before starting again:

DEAR SARA, ITS BEEN TOO LONG
SINCE I'VE SEEN YOUR FACE. I MISS
YOU SO MUCH THAT IT KILLS ME
EVERY DAY, THINKING ABOUT
WHAT I ALMOST HAD, AND NOW
HAVE TO LIVE WITHOUT. JULIE
HAS BEEN-

He stopped, pushing the keyboard away in frustration, this time closing the dialog box. "Idiot," he chided.

-RING!-

He started in his chair as the phone rang downstairs. He then took a deep breath and composed himself after a moment, laughing. He brought the white mouse arrow up to Sara's screen name and right clicked it, moving down a long list of options until he reached *delete contact*. Hesitating just for a second, he pressed it, and she disappeared from the screen.

He stared at it for a moment, as if not understanding what he'd done.

His eyes darted over the screen, fluttering about and waiting for it to somehow magically reappear, but it did not.

His head dropped and he turned off the screen, then stood up and moved to the bed.

"Xander?" his mother called up from downstairs.

He sighed, rolling his eyes. "Yeah, Mom?"

"That was someone from your school on the phone. They said that you have to go into the school therapist's office instead of Technology tomorrow morning."

Xander sat up at the side of his bed, staring off into the darkness for a minute, feeling it around him. "Great," he said, then laughed a little. "Why would I need a therapist?"

ᚥ

Mike Harris lay with his head on the soft pillow of his bed, his short blonde hair messy from a long night's sleep. Despite the early hour, he felt his eyes shutting as if they were weighed down by anchors, resistant to his efforts to keep them open. The soft light of early evening beamed in through the creases in his window blinds, providing just enough light for him to see the small girl using his chest for a pillow, the beating of his heart having lulled her to sleep.

Her name was Cathy Kennessy, and he had no doubt that she was the love of his life. As her dark, almost black hair tickled his nose and dared him to sneeze, she sighed gracefully in her sleep, a magical smile spreading across her lips. Her cheek was squished into his body, and she looked irresistibly cute. The top of her head was incredibly kissable, so he kissed it. In that moment she stirred, and he cursed himself a thousand times in his mind. Her dark eyes fluttered open in the pale blue light that softened her face and body, and she looked up at him, her eyes filled with beauty and peace.

"Hi," she said. The sound almost did not emerge, and when it did, it was small and fragile, like a mouse.

He smiled back at her, the arm that had been holding her tight to his body as she slept, squeezing her just a little tighter now in a lover's grasp. As if trying to hold onto love, to create a tangible something from that which is forever intangible. "Hi," he responded, beaming.

"Ugh," she groaned, laughing a little as her free hand reached up to pat down frizzy hair -- her vanity showing for only a moment. "How bad is it? Do I have crow's nest hair?"

He chuckled, making her still tired head bounce upon his chest as it heaved. "No," he assured her warmly, although her head looked like a mullet from those cheesy 80s hair bands where the singers didn't so much sing as scream. "You look amazing."

She rolled her eyes. "Yeah, I'm so..." she stopped, rethinking her sarcastic response in the spirit of the moment. "Okay, sure," she smiled to one side of her mouth, shrugging and re-nuzzling her head against his shoulder. "Amazing it is."

He stroked his hand through her long, flowing hair and watched as trace

140

amounts of light got caught in it, trapped by this young woman's sweetness. The world stood still, and the only sound in the universe was their slow breathing in unison.

There was a long pause between them that said everything in the world. It spoke of the bond between them that could been seen for miles by blind men. Of the pain that they crawled through and still came out pure and whole on the other side. Of the love that bonded them and would continue to bond them no matter how many miles apart they were from each other. In their minds and their hearts, they would always be one, lying alone in the twilight, hearing nothing but one another's heartbeat.

"You know what tomorrow is, right?" he asked glumly, the words escaping him in the form of a deep-throated sigh.

"Yeah," she said, playing with his chest with one finger, dragging it along and scraping at the skin lightly with her nail. "I know."

"Are you okay?"

She smiled, moving her head to look up at him. "Yes," she said definitively, as though commanding it to be true. "Yeah, I'll be fine."

"How do you think he'll be?"

She paused, frowning. "I'm not quite sure. You never can be with him. I think it's safe to say it won't be good. He still hasn't gotten over it."

Mike shook his head, correcting her. "Yes, he has," he argued, stroking the side of her face until she quickly kissed him playfully. "As much as a man can, anyway."

"Now," Warren O'Toole said in an authoritative voice, "pay attention to what I'm telling you to do."

All traces of the man's kindness were gone. The walls that he'd built to deal with stupid, immature children had vanished, and he was now more like a drill sergeant. He no longer had to coax the young man in front of him to do anything. He had the authority, and he chose to use it.

Xander lay on the long, oblong couch that had been clumsily shoved up against the far wall of O'Toole's office, his hands folded at his chest, mocking the position he'd seen in so many movies. "Oh, come on now," he smirked. "Is that how Robin Williams got Will to open up?"

"This isn't *Good Will Hunting*, Mr. Drew," O'Toole reminded him curtly, as he fiddled loudly with things outside of Xander's view. "And even if that were the case, you are neither a closet genius nor a beaten adolescent," he drawled, walking over to Xander and sitting on the cheap chair next to the couch. It was flimsy and threatened to give out under the thin man's weight. He looked at Xander for a long moment, appearing tired and worn out. He looked like a man who hadn't slept in weeks.

Xander sighed. "So, how do we do this?" he said, trying desperately not to make it sound like a groan.

O'Toole smiled at Xander's compliance, although it had to be forced out of him. He reached into the breast pocket of his faded blue shirt, pulling out a gold pocket watch. "I'll be placing you into a hypnotic state, Mr. Drew. While in that - "

"With that?" Xander said, raising an eyebrow and pointing at the pocket watch. It spun on the end of its chain, but an engraving could still be made out: *To Warren, for many years of loyal service.*

"Excuse me?" O'Toole stuttered, trying to find his words after being interrupted.

"You're seriously going to try and hypnotize me... with a pocket watch?" Xander laughed skeptically.

Warren smiled, dangling the golden chain confidently. "Why, yes, actually."

Xander laughed, covering his mouth with one hand. "Okay, enough. That's funny. What, am I on Candid Camera or something?"

O'Toole frowned, rubbing his free hand through his hair and grabbing it. "No, Mr. Drew. You're not on Candid Camera. Although I'm starting to think that this seems more and more like that kind of situation, don't you?"

Xander squinted his eyes at the older man. "You're really serious, aren't you?"

"That's what I've been telling you."

The younger man clicked his tongue against the roof of his mouth a couple of times, letting saliva slosh in and out of the gap between his two front teeth. "Can I see it first?"

O'Toole smiled wide, handing him the trinket.

Xander held it in the palm of his hand, watching as the light from the desk lamp gleamed off of its gold-plated surface. He bit his lip as he saw his own reflection in it, and could almost picture himself transforming. He could almost feel the beast inside of him breaking down barriers, clawing at the doors of his consciousness, waiting, wanting. Wanting the blood. As Xander stared at the watch, he thought he could hear O'Toole's heartbeat get louder and louder until it was all he could hear; like a soft drink machine with 'drink me' scrawled across it.

"I'd like to have that back now," O'Toole coughed, reaching out and grabbing the watch by its chain. "Is there anything else before we begin?"

Xander stared forward, his eyes still glued to the gold that was swinging before his eyes. He nodded despite himself, sweat starting to bead on the top of his forehead. "What kinds of things are you going to ask me?" he said suddenly, as the doctor leaned into place.

O'Toole ignored the young man, and began dangling the watch in front of his face. Already, Xander's eyes were getting heavy, his pulse slowing. "Watch only the watch," O'Toole instructed him, his voice forcibly monotone and flat. "Listen only to my voice."

Xander closed his eyes reluctantly. After a moment, his breathing became steady as he drifted into a deep, heavy sleep...

Julie Peterson watched with vibrant green eyes as the clock on the classroom wall slowly ticked away, each second feeling like an hour. She tried to distract herself from the long winded teacher as she went on to no end about logarithmic functions and how they might actually have some use in the real world, and they weren't just invented to make students fail eighth grade math. Julie filtered everything out until the chatter of students, the droning of the teacher, and the shuffling of desks and chairs all melded together to form a hum that she was apart from; beyond, even. And in the instant that she transcended the classroom, all she could think about was him.

Dr. Darren Phillips.

Posing as a guidance counselor, Phillips used his position to figure out which young girls were emotionally unstable and prey upon them with two of his friends.

They chose her first.

While on her way home from school one day, they slowed down next to her in their car, jumped out and shoved her into the alleyway that her bedroom window looked out on. They punched her, kicked her, tore off her clothes and left them around her, like shreds of her sanity blowing around in the wind. Each of them took a turn and climbed on, one by one. They killed a part of her, emotionally and physically. Physically, they demolished the part of her that would allow her to carry on. The part of her that could better herself, and give a new and beautiful life to the world. With their feral, carnal rage plunging in and out of her, they destroyed any hope for her future of having children.

One boy helped put Phillips away where the sun would never be able to touch his face again. To a place so far away that she could feel safe and secure and not be afraid to look out her bedroom window and wonder if he was still there, watching and waiting: Xander Drew.

Now, she knew he was in the hands of the latest guidance counselor. He was under the older man's influence, and she couldn't help but to be terrified by that thought. The thought that something so terrible might happen to him, like it did to her. Because, despite what everyone said, and despite what her own head was telling her, she found herself falling in love with Alexander Drew a little more every day.

She took a deep breath and looked down at the notepad in front of her, only now realizing that she had been subconsciously etching Xander's name into the brittle lined paper. She turned the page quickly, but it was still there. She'd pressed so hard that the imprint of his name was left on the next sheet, just like he'd been imprinted upon all of her thoughts.

I hate this place. She thought suddenly, looking around at the student body that surrounded her. *I hate what it's done to Xander, to me... to Mandy.*

Mandy Peterson; Julie's thirteen-year-old cousin. On her first day living with Julie and her mother, Mandy had been captured in the night by a group of fanatics calling themselves the Tees. Something had saved her... she wouldn't say what - just made up a wild story about a 'black angel' that had taken hold of her and made everything all right. *There isn't a person in this town that hasn't been hurt or scared in some way... but they all pretend like it doesn't happen. And by doing so, they make you pretend. They give you this look when you try to speak out, like you're insane. They don't want you to shatter their fantasy about what their town is like. And I hate them for it. And I wonder...* she thought, rubbing a hand through her shoulder length brown hair in frustration as she began to scratch his name in blue onto her pad again. *What terrible thing is it that Alexander Drew is hiding from everyone, and when will it come out?*

It sat in the woods just north of the more populated areas of town, fidgeting and twitching a little. It was covered in blood and saliva, the latter its own, the former not. Its great lungs heaved in and out as its body struggled for air, winded from the exertion and near sexual pleasure of the hunt. In one of its great hands it held what remained of a young golden lab, its tiny form still hot from the blood that streamed from the gaping gash in its shoulder and back. The creature raised its treat to its lips again. Massive jaws spread so wide that there was a snapping sound as they dislocated. It revealed three rows of long, razor sharp teeth that sparkled in the light that escaped between the oak branches enveloping the beast, concealing it from the world outside. It took the head and upper body of the infant dog this time, its strong mouth snapping the tiny bones of the pup's spine and rib cage, squirting more blood and spinal fluid into the killer's mouth. As it chewed briefly and then swallowed, its large, red eyes began to dissect the wilderness around it, instinctively searching out something new.

It was hungry.

Xander woke, his sinuses filled with a throbbing pain that seemed to grow bigger and more frustrating with every beat of his heart. Everything was dark, and he couldn't see one foot in front of his face, save for a thick mist that seemed to cover everything. It was like being inside steam, and to his horror, there didn't seem to be any discernible floor for him to stand upon either. It was like being gas, his body as weightless as a feather frolicking in the summer wind. He turned his head quickly, and when he did, his features seemed to distort and skew. Everything was blurry. When he moved his hands, it looked like he had eighteen fingers. He could feel the blood coursing through his body, and each beat of his heart brought pain.

"No..." he said softly, biting his lip as he craned his head, trying to find some small source of light to fixate on, to let his eyes gain focus. He turned, and came face to face with himself.

The other version of himself was dripping blood from his nose and mouth, and stared blankly at his reflection. The beaten, bloodied version of him seemed to fade backward until Xander could see the full scene of what was happening. Then he knew exactly where he was. He was staring at himself upon a crucifix.

Blood was flowing from the sacrificed one's veins onto a barely lit panel of metal floor, and the entire scene seemed to hang there in the darkness. His eyes were rolling up into the back of his head, and the parts that were white had thick, prudent red vines developing at the base. His hands and feet were twitching violently under the enormous pressure of the three metal spikes that had been shoved through his legs and both wrists. It was a constant battle for the crucified young man to keep his head up, one that he was losing. His entire torso was covered in scars and bruises, and each one was like a memory: a painful, repressed memory that one only visited when forced to.

He picked Xander up, propping him up against the wall. He took out a small, sharp blade and jammed it into Black Womb's right side. A soft -shink- sound indicated that it went clean through the wall. Genblade let go of Womb, letting the blade prop him. "There's a few things you should know, Womb. Number one..."

Shunk. *Genblade stabbed Xander in the arm.*

Xander winced in real time, the recollection of that feeling coming back to him. But more than that, he fell over. When he looked at his arm, blood was erupting from his arteries like a fountain.

"... *your right side is your weak spot. It's where your true self... the real Black Womb... resides. But you probably figured that out. Number two...*"

Shunk. *He stabbed him through his other arm.*

Xander opened his mouth to scream, but no words would come out. He gripped the new wounds at once, his mind torn as to which gaping hole to clutch, which arm felt like it needed to be torn off more.

"... *that healing factor of yours will only go so far. If you tax it too much... or if I do... it'll simply cut out. Number three...*"

Shunk. *He stabbed him through both feet, pinning them to each other and to the wall.*

Xander fell now, into the blackness. For a moment, he thought that he might plunge into the shadows forever, an eternity of awaiting death at the end of some bottomless pit. Then his head slammed into concrete, followed by the rest of his body. He impacted the ground like a bag of stones, and his entire body ached for a long time; he wasn't sure how long.

"... *nobody. I repeat, NOBODY, escapes death.*"

Genblade stepped back and admired his work. Black Womb hung there, his body pinned into a cross position. Black Womb's mind reeled. He couldn't focus on anything, his vision was blurry, and black around the edges. He felt the healing factor cut out. He lifted his head to face his attacker.

"A crucifixion," Genblade sneered. "It'd almost be poetic, if it wasn't so damn funny."

When Xander decided to move, he pushed off of the floor with all the force he could muster, which was just enough to roll himself over. His chest rose and fell violently as his lungs struggled for oxygen. Blood bubbled to the surface of the blunt force stab wounds that were scattered over his body -- each stab surrounded by a ring of contusions. As he lay on his back, struggling for air, the lights came on. He didn't need them to, they just did. He didn't need to see the dome-shaped metallic ceiling, or the flat, square fluorescent lights, or the observation window that the people in charge used to look down upon experiments. He didn't even need to see the creases of the nearly hidden doorway that would soon be his exit. As soon as he'd seen himself on the cross, he knew there was only one place on earth that he could be.

Engen.

"No..." he said again, and in his mind, both words were spoken simultaneously. But as the growing puddle of blood around him would testify, he'd been there for at least an hour, perhaps more. He shook his head in rebellion, pouting his lower lip. He closed his eyes tightly and wished for it not to be true, but when he opened them, he was still there. "No, not here again!" he screamed, begging the walls that did nothing except echo back at him. He groaned. "Not death again. I've been here once before... and escaped. I don't want to be here. I shouldn't be here. I have... places to be..."

The watch dangled in front of his face, reflecting light and blinding him.

He blinked hard, and it was gone. It was just him, all alone, again. Clutching his head tightly to keep it from throbbing, he slowly sat up and rubbed the back of his head. He turned to look at himself, or rather what appeared to be a representation of himself, hanging a few feet from the floor, all of the blood draining from his body. He reached out and touched the steady stream of the blood of his past that ran toward the drain in the center of the sloped floor.

His hand passed through it, but more importantly, it passed through his hand.

The red liquid did not change its course to avoid his flesh, it simply passed right through it. "I don't know how I got here this time," Xander spoke, running the scenario through his head over and over again, trying to recall how he had gotten there. He rubbed his thumb and forefinger together, verifying that there was no trace of blood there. He looked over at his crucified self, frowning with pity as though he were looking upon an old friend that he no longer remembered. "But, I sure as hell know how he got here."

He reached out and almost touched the bleeding, sagging form of himself, who didn't even seem to recognize his presence there. The body twitched as it neared unconsciousness, making Xander's arm recoil in fear as he regarded the bleeding man with a strange pathos.

"It was months ago now. Maybe longer, maybe shorter. Who knows, really. When the story of your life reads like mine, dates and times tend to fade into the background

so far that they become void. Everything was going great... even though I didn't realize it at the time. Back then, I thought my life was crap. Less than crap. My life gave crap a bad name. Got beat up all the time at school, Sara was my best friend and that was never going to change, and even Mike and Cathy wouldn't publicly admit to having been my friends. Yeah, everything was terrible... but I'd have given anything to have it all back again. Because then the day came that everything changed. The day that Jamie Dawkins died.

"Then again, 'died' is a pretty loose term for what happened to Jamie. He was found eviscerated in an alley just after he and Sara were supposed to hook up. Every major organ aside from his tar-ridden lungs had been snatched. After that, everything started to read like a horror novel.

"Looking back, it seems like everything was counting down to that one moment when everything exploded. Like my life was a ticking time bomb, and the shockwave took out everyone and everything closest to me. The big boom: Julian Grendel's party-of-the-century. So, as the bodies kept piling up and Mike and Cathy were added to the critical list, everyone else pretended that the world was normal... even me. At Grendel's party, the moment I'd been waiting almost fifteen years for happened: Sara kissed me. Well, almost. I got called off to help with a computer problem, being the resident nerd and all. Sara waited outside for me... but somebody else had been waiting too.

"Ten minutes later, Grendel tried to rape Cathy, Mike had been beaten into unconsciousness, and I was at the bottom of the stairs, victim to a mob who thought I was the person killing all of their friends. And Sara... Sara was hanging from a ceiling fan, her entrails falling out of her violated body onto the blood-spattered hardwood floor.

"When I woke up, I was here. At Engen. This is where I met the man who changed my life: Adam Genblade. He told me the truth, or at least his edited version of it. I'd been the one killing the students in my school; I attacked Mike and Cathy -- everything. It had been me. All because when I was still inside my mother's womb, Engen geneticists had implanted me with a darkness. A blackness that had the potential for the worst power known to man. They'd given me the Black Womb.

"But there was something wrong. My personality had fractured and splintered, leaving me as two people living in one body. When I slept, Black Womb woke. It ripped itself out of my veins, pouring black ooze all over my body until it covered me with a scaly second skin. This thing was acting on my deepest desires, like an impressionable child wanting to impress mommy and daddy.

"Engen wanted me back. They wanted their living weapon. But they didn't want me. They knew that I would never work for them, not after they helped me put Sara in the ground. They wanted the organ. He wanted it. Alpha, one of the worst minds ever to have existed. He needed the Womb's healing factor to make himself whole again. To use my incredible power to rain down fire upon the world."

Xander looked at his reflection, and his heart sank.

"Given the chance, I'd take my old life back in a minute, compared to this."

Suddenly, his reflection looked up, making eye contact with him. It spat out a bit of blood before sneering at Xander. "Oh, shut the fuck up," it drawled, pulling its arms and legs free of the spikes that pinned it to the wall, landing gracefully upon the cold metal floor. It rose up, staring Xander right in the eye. "Do you always whine this much? I don't remember ever hearing somebody yammer on so self-indulgently before."

Xander stepped back, shocked. He raised his hand to strike, but then let it hang in midair, awaiting answers. "What the hell are you?"

"Don't you recognize me?" the other Xander smiled evilly, using one nail to scrape a bit of dried blood from his lips. *"Here,"* he smirked, stepping forward and grabbing Xander's hand, *"maybe this'll help."* He pulled Xander's clenched fist to his gut, and Xander was horrified to watch the tip of a sword punch out the other side, spraying blood and shards of human flesh against the wall. When he looked down, he saw that the hand his ghost had forced was now holding the grip of a sword. The spider-sword, to be exact, encrusted with gold and rubies to shape a deadly blood-red spider.

"This didn't happen," Xander whispered, confused.

The second Xander pushed the first, sending him flying to the floor, bumping his tail bone violently. *"You're a Womb, kid. You gotta stop living in the past. This is the now,"* he said, but his voice had adopted a soothing, feminine quality to it. It was like spring time. The Ghost-Xander took the sword out of himself, twirling it around majestically as black ooze erupted from the gaping hole going right through him, transforming him. But as he transformed, his flesh re-imagined itself, not into the red-eyed, over-bitten Black Womb, but into a small, muscular feminine body. Almond eyes formed, and a sly pair of black lips that were locked in a sinister smile appeared. She was scantily clothed in red silk; a gust of wind in either direction would have exposed her voluptuous form.

"Spider lives," she said sarcastically, turning and pointing the sword at Xander's throat. *"Your life is so horrible... well, at least you're alive. The part of the story that you seem to like leaving out was when you killed me, stuck me through and through with my own blade."*

"It was in self-defense," Xander protested.

"Semantics. I was just following orders."

"You enjoyed it."

Spider paused, her smile spreading further. *"Yeah, I did,"* she chuckled. *"But you have no reason to bitch anymore. You know it wasn't you that killed all of your friends now... just one or two of them."* Her skin morphed, and she became a male again, with scruffy brown hair. Her voice stayed the same, but she was still Derek Smith. *"It wasn't Genblade either. It was your own friend who killed all your little buddies: Derek. So, why are you still blaming us? Why are you still saying that we're responsible for everything?"*

"Because you are. You started this, you woke it up," Xander snarled, his shock having transformed into anger as Spider transformed into Smith.

"We didn't start it, sweetie," Spider grinned, resuming her own form. *"And if it wasn't for us, I guess you wouldn't have had the opportunity to stop all the evil around you, anyway. You shouldn't be cursing us... you should be thanking us."*

"I'm not cursing you -- you cursed me."

"Yeah," she snarled sarcastically before changing again, this time into a young female: Julie Peterson, tiny freckles and all. *"And I suppose you would've been able to save your little girlfriend from the perverted guidance counselor if Engen hadn't given you your power, hmm? And Derek, and Blackheart, and Roulette... you think we've caused death by creating you? Your 'evil' Womb has done more good in a few short months than*

you did in fifteen years hunched over your computer. So, why don't you think before you start throwing around..."

"Get out!" Xander barked at Spider, getting up off of the floor and brushing himself off.

"Excuse me?" Spider-as-Julie said, raising an eyebrow. "You're the one who came here, remember? Don't tell me to leave."

The watch dangled in front of his face, reflecting light and blinding him.

"Get out of that body," Xander exclaimed, taking one menacing step toward Spider.

Spider hummed happily, amused at the torment she was instilling. She began rubbing her hands all over Julie's body, changing the clothes as she went until she was wearing the little red night gown that Julie had once used in an attempt to seduce Xander prematurely. "What's the matter, Alex?" she said, her voice sounding like Julie's now. "Don't you want me? Aren't I good enough for you? Why can't you love me?" She broke out into an infectious giggle, Spider's giggle. "And you said your life had petty problems before. All you've done for weeks now is swoon over the first sweet young thing to jump you in a hotel room. Yeah, you've matured so much. You're practically an adult."

"Get out of that body," Xander repeated, ordering her in a tone of voice so forceful it surprised even him.

Spider smiled at him with Julie's lips. "Have it your way," she said, transforming again. "Maybe I was wrong. Maybe there's a different stupid teenager you've got the hots for."

She grew short blonde hair, and the freckles and scars disappeared to reveal perfect, flawless skin and a ruby smile.

It was Sara.

Xander began to tremble, his form losing its edges. His lower lip began to quiver, and he fell to his knees on the ground before his love, the tears beginning to roll down his face.

"There, there, lover," Sara soothed in her musical voice, crouching next to him and pulling his head into her breast, stroking the hair on the back of his head. "Calm down. I'm right here, Xander. You must have had a terrible dream, sweetheart. It's okay now."

She closed her eyes, kissed him once on the forehead, then laid him back onto the cold floor and started to sing him to sleep.

"Tora Lora Lora, tora Lora lye.

Tora Lora Lora, hush now don't you cry.

Tora Lora Lora, tora Lora lye.

That's an Irish lullaby."

He smiled, then turned to face her, his eyes sparkling the way they hadn't in months. When he looked, he was lying next to Spider.

She stabbed him with her sword once in the gut, then shoved him away with more force than the assassin had ever wielded in life, sending him skidding across the floor. "Is that how you think it is?" she laughed, standing above Xander and pushing the tip of her blade toward him until his chest bled from its wound. "She won't choose you, you know," she grinned, kneeling down to get closer to him. "None of them will, in the end. Because the only person you've ever picked for your lover is death. The only people that will ever take you in are the angels, boy. The angels in the darkness with their wings of

149

blood and feathers of fire, mount their horses, the four of them will... the other two can fly, you see."

"What are you rambling about, now?" Xander spat, masking his obvious pain with annoyance.

She raised a hand to her face, and was about to speak, when Xander cut her off.

"Let me guess," he said, raising his hand to interject. "Scar tissue, right?"

"It'll heal, lover."

"Do you have to insist on calling me that?"

"But sweetheart..." she laughed, leaning in and giving him a kiss. "I was your first."

Xander looked confused, bewildered. "Um, but we've never..."

She drew back and slapped him with an open palm across the face. "Not sex, stupid. Kill. I was your first kill. The first that you did all on your own, without any help from your precious little Black Womb. You did me all on your own... the first of many."

"I've never killed anyone since you. The Womb's committed all the murders I've done since Engen."

"But you will, my love," she cooed softly, straddling his waist. "You'll kill more than Alpha, Genblade, and me combined. Because you have something we don't. Something you share with Derek and all the others."

"What's that?"

"You, my boy, have the capability for real evil. Even before you were a Womb, you sat at home at night and fantasized about killing every red blooded male on the earth so that your magnificent Sara might actually have you... although, it's more likely she would have gone gay rather than date you. Engen may have created the Womb, boy... but you gave birth to it."

"Argh!" Xander yelled, flipping Spider off of him and jumping up into a fighting stance, ready for an attack.

She merely sat on the floor and laughed, her legs spread toward him. "And just as I was your first, you'll be his first. His One. The first angel in the dark..."

"Shut up!" he yelled, clutching the sides of his head as if it were going to explode. "'Pain is my power,' 'angels in the dark,' will you stop talking in riddles. Just tell me what you're going to tell me and be done with it! I'm sick of all the mind games with you and your twisted little boyfriend Genblade!"

Spider looked solemn, then. Her eyes cast downward. "Adam," she whispered, her gaze becoming watery. "I fear that he will join me all too soon. Before his time."

Xander squinted, relaxing his stance to look at Spider, until his eyes grew wide with understanding. "Genblade?" he demanded, "Are you saying that something's going to happen to Genblade? Is he what's coming?"

Spider turned her head into the darkness that surrounded the both of them, and an image formed there. It was Adam Genblade, his eyes locked open as blood poured from every crevice in his body, and a few newly ripped ones. His face was covered in so many contusions that he was only identifiable by the orange prison jumpsuit that he wore. There was a pipe sticking out of his side, and blood was running out of it as if on tap. Judging by the amount of blood surrounding him, he was past the point of saving.

"No..." Xander gasped, walking toward the image until he touched it, and it vanished like fog. He closed his eyes tightly, clenching his fists. He frowned in determination. "So, Adam's gonna die, huh?" he said, hiding his own pain. "Wow, I'm hurting. Really, that's painful. I think I might have a moment."

Spider smiled through her tears, wiping them away. "You cannot hide yourself from me, Womb. We're siblings, you and I. But even if you could let Adam fade to black... it would do you no good in the battle to come."

Xander squinted. "What battle?"

"Your greatest battle yet, and possibly ever. The battle that has been coming ever since you were given life and ripped from your mother's teat. You're going to lose everything, Womb: no family, no friends... not even Genblade to save you. And when it comes, you'll have nobody to blame but yourself. Somebody has let it out. And it's going to kill the world, Xander. It's going to make it bleed."

"Who?" Xander demanded, punching the air for effect. "What? Tell me what's coming!"

Spider looked sad, giving the Womb absolute grief. "You are."

ʎＸʎ

Xander's eyes snapped open as the small, golden pocket watch was taken away. O'Toole rubbed it with a small cloth for a moment, then tucked it back into his left breast pocket. He looked up to see that Xander was still laying there, blinking over and over again, as if to try and awaken himself.

"That was an excellent session," O'Toole beamed, almost patronizingly. He took off his glasses, revealing tiny, beady eyes, and used his handkerchief to wipe the lenses. "I think your unconscious mind reached many revelations about itself."

"Revelations?" Xander repeated, sitting up, his expression one of bewilderment as he rubbed an ache on the back of his neck.

"Yes, you seemed very calm. I used a few relaxation techniques on you that should prove helpful toward alleviating the stress that most males your age enact upon their body and mind, even unconsciously," he explained, tucking away the rag and perching his glasses back upon his nose.

"Relaxation?"

"Mmm-hmm. I would have kept going, but I have another appointment that I'm eager to get underway. Can I expect to see you again soon?"

"You're forcing me into this."

"I know. I was just being polite. But, if you insist on being curt, I *will* see you again soon."

Xander frowned, getting up and stretching out a crick in his back until he heard it snap, then walked toward the door. When he opened it, Mandy Peterson was standing outside.

Her skin was flawless, devoid of any mark or blemish, except for one tiny m-shaped scar that was mostly hidden by her hairline. She could often be found in the girls' locker room applying makeup to the small bit of damaged tissue, complaining about its refusal to go away. The only thing really defining about the girl's face was its absence of color, making her look like she was wasting away. She had dark brown hair that came to her shoulders, and accented her deep green eyes. Her lips were small and delicate, and right now they were giving Xander her trademark infectious, toothy smile. She was wearing a tight tube top with a kitten in the center of the breasts and words that read: *Watch out, I bite*, along with bell-bottom jeans that were just a little too short for her, exhibiting a bit of leg.

"Hi, Alex!" she beamed, calling Xander by his given name. It was a quirk that she'd picked up from her cousin, Julie, and now it seemed like a full time job just to explain to the both of them that he hated to be called that.

He forced a laugh, but it sounded mechanical. The gears in his head were beginning to turn about what Spider had been talking about in his vision. "Hey, Mandy," he smiled, "is your cousin around?"

"Julie? No, she was in class, then she stopped going to class and went for a smoke, then she came back from her smoke and went to another class, but I saw her in the hall and she said that she thought that the class was, like, boring, so she went out walking. First she went to the girl's room, but Snyder caught her in there, so then she left, and now I don't know where she is. Maybe she's in class. Or having a smoke. Or in the girl's room," Mandy took a breath after the long-winded speech, resuming her open-mouthed smile.

Xander stared at her, wide eyed, for a moment, then looked at the clock, and then at Warren O'Toole. "Right. One hour on the clock she's gonna be talking," Xander chuckled, almost feeling sorry for the counselor. "Have fun with your handful, buddy." He walked out, closing the door behind him.

"That reminds me!" Mandy's high-pitched voice said from behind the doorway. "I had another dream about that Black Angel guy last night, and it was so weird, but he kept speaking like someone I know..."

Xander stopped, stared at O'Toole's name on the door, then sighed and walked away.

CHAPTER THREE: LOVER'S WALK

She danced in her backyard before dinner, her long, curly black hair waving about in the light of the low sun.

She wore a small, dark blue dress that seemed to catch even the most minute traces of wind, chilling her legs and making her shiver, even though she didn't really notice. Little Kerri Walker was no more than seven years old. She still didn't talk much, but the doctors had told her parents time and time again that there was nothing wrong with her. She'd just talk when she felt like talking, and that was all. When she did speak, her missing two front teeth caused her to have a lisp that all of the boys in her grade made fun of, even when the teachers yelled at them for it.

Her shoes were red and sparkly, something she had insisted upon after watching the *Wizard of Oz* for the thirtieth time. Every time she got mud on them, she'd scrape them through the wet grass repeatedly to clean them until the sparkles shone like diamonds, then tapped her heels together three times, repeating 'there's no place like home' with every tap. Her sea-green eyes regarded everything with interest, the freshness of seeing everything for the first time and finding wonder in it. Every time the trees outside of her house blew in the wind, she watched the leaves and branches in their fluid motion, brushing against each other and making a rustling sound like when her teacher crumpled up paper to throw in the garbage. Sometimes, leaves would escape from their branches in a strong breeze and float along on the wind a few minutes before touching the ground or getting stuck in the shrubs that her father tended to meticulously -- not out of enjoyment, but in competition with the neighbors and their gaudy lawn ornaments. She'd chase the leaves, jumping and clapping her hands together in an attempt to catch them, always missing, but never quitting. When they eventually met the ground tenderly, like daddy's lips on mommy's cheek, she'd pick them up and carefully place them in the sandbox, decorating it for just a little while until the wind grasped it again, or mom came out to clean up.

The wind whipped forward, blowing the trees again, this time swooping upward and revealing bits and pieces of the underbrush. For a moment, she thought she saw something red. Red and sparkling with life, just like her shoes. She smiled her little missing-tooth smile, walked over to the edge of the brush and peered in, pulling back branches to see what was sparkly. Her eyes were filled with that innocence and wonder of a child seeing something for the first time, never once dawning upon her that whatever it was might want to hurt her. Never thinking that anything bad could happen. She'd never been hurt before, and the very notion was so foreign to her it might as well have been in Oz.

She gazed around, but all she could see was blackness, even though the sun was still in the sky, illuminating the forest. Kerri jumped and grabbed a high evergreen branch, pulling it down. Two red, curved, triangular eyes peered out at her, having been watching her the entire time. She stared at it for a moment.

Its breathing was heavy, all of its long, sharp teeth tucked inside of its mouth. With one movement it grabbed her and pulled her into the cover of the brush outside of her home, time enough for only the tiniest yelp to escape from her mouth.

As it dragged her into the forest, it was all she could do to tap her shoes together between screams and whisper, "there's no place like home... there's no place like home... there's no place like home."

It was a simple slab of stone in a garden where mounds of carved rock seemed to sprout up like live trees that were fed by the dead and strangled sunlight from the living. The letters engraved upon it were still etched perfectly, as sharp and as definitive as they had been months ago when they were put there.

"I'm not really sure what to do here," Mike coughed, squeezing Cathy's hand as they both stared down at the grave of Sara Johnson. The debris of Fall passed by them on the same breeze that caught hold of Cathy's hair and did not seem to want to let go. "Is it always this noisy?"

"It's noisy?" Cathy said, her voice distant at first, then perking up with sarcasm as she raised an eyebrow in his direction. She turned away from the grave with a puzzled look on her face. "There isn't a sound here, Mike. It's a grave-yard."

"Well, yeah," he admitted, shuffling around a little, looking at the ground on which he tread while making small circles with his feet in an odd, oval shaped pattern. "But, it's a talkative silence. It's like you can hear everything that all of these people *aren't* saying. All the things they could never say, but always wanted to. It's a noisy silence." He continued shuffling his feet until he realized he was messing up the soil atop his friend's grave, then quickly retracted his feet into a militaristic position.

Cathy stopped, her eyes slowly panning over the headstones that sprang up out of the ground like weeds in a garden. The names faded into the black-ness just before dusk on even the brightest nights, casting sinister silhouettes and making the entire landscape look like nothing but crosses and angels. For a moment, she wondered if this was what heaven looked like, just as the sun set. "You're right," she agreed, nodding once before turning back to him. "It is noisy in here. You just have to figure out which voice is Sara's, then talk to her."

Mike made a guttural, scratchy sound deep in his throat. "That's the stu-pidest thing I've ever heard," he scoffed, pulling away from Cathy just a little. His eyes refused to even glance in the direction of his lost friend's grave. "She can't hear us, Cathy. She's dead! They killed her, then they buried her, and now she's a rotting corpse whose ears probably aren't even attached to her head!" he screamed, punching the air in front of him as he bellowed at the graves at the bottom of the hill.

Cathy just stood back and watched, both her index fingers pressed against her mouth, waiting for the time when he needed her to speak.

Chest heaving, he turned back to her, revealing a face full of molten-hot tears. He took a step forward, then collapsed onto Sara's grave. Open palms grabbed great handfuls of dirt, wishing that it were the smooth flesh of her shoulders as he held her in a tight embrace. The mud got under his nails and stained his hands as water from his body fed the earth, helping to give it the life he wished he could provide to his friend. "Why?' he said, softly at first, his voice cracking from tears. He pushed himself up on his knees, heaving the mounds of muck at the headstone, making huge splotches. "Why!" he screamed as loud as he could, eyes filled with hate. "I needed you, Sara! I needed you and you went away. You could have done anything else but that, and I would have stood by you, but do not expect me to forgive you for this!" he yelled, burying his face in his palms and covering it with dirt, not that he cared.

Cathy slowly walked up behind him, placing her hand on his shoulder at first, then wrapping her arms around his neck and squeezing him so hard that she thought her ribs might collapse, but she didn't care. "She loved you, you know," she assured him, kissing his neck lightly with every word she spoke.

Mike sniffed back the mucus in his nose, nodded, then wiped his eyes in her jacket. "I know," he said, pulling her even closer to him. Taking comfort in the smell of her skin, the way her long hair itched his nose when he got too close to it, and the way her slender neck looked up close, blurry and somehow sensual.

"*I* love you, too, you know," she said, her voice shaking like one of the leaves that blew around the churchyard, getting caught in the wire mesh fence that surrounded it.

It was kind of like her, thought Mike. *I built so many fences just to try and keep her out, to keep everybody out, so that I wouldn't have to deal with anything. So that I could keep myself separate from everything. But she manages to get herself into every part of my life, manages to touch it and make it better just for having been there, even if she never ventures back again. And if I put up a fence, she becomes a leaf and gets stuck in it, until that fence is just a wall made of her love... protecting me, instead of holding me in.* "I love you more," he said finally leaning in to give her a kiss.

"Believe me, that's not possible," she whispered, laughing a little.

"Oh, yes it is," he chuckled in return. "Just look up 'love' in the dictionary. You'll see a picture of us there, and I'll have a little plus sign above my head, indicating who loves who more."

"Funny," she smirked, giving him a look. "Do you have to be competitive about everything?"

He smiled warmly, gently brushing an eyelash away from her face. "Only you," he responded, turning to look at Sara's grave. "Yeah, Sar," he chuckled, "I know."

Cathy hugged him again. The chilled wind left them alone now. It knew it couldn't touch them anyway. "Come on," she coaxed, cocking her head toward the trail back to the road, "let's go for a walk. It's a nice night, shame to waste it."

The two of them got up and started walking back down the hill hand in hand, until Mike stopped. "Oh!" he exclaimed, giving himself a tap on the head. "Didn't you want to talk to Sara?"

Cathy smiled, shaking her head. "That's okay. She already knows what I was going to say."

⋀⋏⋀

"Kerri!" called Macy Walker, her voice loud and shrill, probably waking all of the neighbors as she screamed out her back door from the small kitchen where she was mixing the batter for low fat muffins. More batter was on her than in the bowl, with splotches all over her face. She huffed and put down the mixing bowl, scrunching her forehead. "Kerri, it's time to get washed up and go to bed, you filthy little girl!" she yelled again, purposely stomping as she walked around the corner to the patio door to let her daughter know that she was serious.

As she turned the corner, she could see the backyard through the door window, and she slowed a little. The low light of evening turned the green paint on the wall odd colors, making them eerie. Picture frames and open closet doors cast long shadows, making dark corners that seemed to taunt Macy, as if the darkness knew something that she did not.

Her face went completely white as she peered out into the peacefulness out-

155

side. It was calm and tranquil. The only sound was that of the breeze, and the only movement was that of the swaying, flapping grass.

She didn't have to look to be sure, but she did anyway. Deep in the pit of her gut, she knew before she'd even called out her child's name. But she opened the door and looked outside, and heard the most horrifying sound she'd ever heard: nothing. No sound of her child laughing, or playing in the mud, or chasing leaves. Not a giggle, or a whine, or even a scream.

She ran out into the yard, and started to look around, tiny pebbles digging into the soles of her feet and drawing blood, not that she cared. She pushed back the tree leaves, hoping to find something. Any trace of her little angel, but there was nothing. Just trees so old that they creaked, their branches hanging low, as if in sorrow.

"George!" Macy called, spinning around and running back into the house. "George, it's Kerri!"

〤〢

Mike and Cathy walked down Lee Street hand in hand. As late evening hit, the stars sparkled dimly in the sky, just waiting for the sun to go to bed so that they could play.

The sidewalk was well-lit by the street lamps that loomed above the lovers on huge, towering poles. The city had put more and more of them up lately, trying to keep the streets as illuminated as possible. They said it was to make people feel safe, but they knew full well that they were only doing it to appease the journalists and the little old ladies who had rioted for something to be done. Electricity for bulbs is cheaper than a competent police force, after all.

More leaves had gathered, mobbing the streets and throwing themselves against anyone who dared walk by, as if they'd taken over. The leaves added a voice to the wind. The cold chill could no longer sneak up on you and send shivers down your spine, making you flinch. Now you could see it coming because of the leaves it wore, and zip your jacket up to near-strangling levels before it caught you. Sometimes, the gusts would even turn away if they knew you saw them, spinning around in tiny tornados filled with grit and sand, until flying off in another direction.

In any event, the walk of the two lovers was not quelled by the winds, only propelled by them. As they stepped over the leaves, they made crunching sounds like potato chips until they were kicked away by their heels, forced back onto the wind again.

The sky was a tapestry of blues and purples and yellows. If they thought it was strange that the sun made its most glorious appearances just before it went to sleep, Mike and Cathy were appreciating it too much to pay it heed.

Somewhere, somebody played music far too loudly, but here it was just a soft whisper; a beat for the two to walk to. Their strides were so unified, so in tune with one another, that a casual onlooker would have thought they were dancing, their bodies swaying to beats and chimes that only they could hear.

The scent of overcooked steaks wafted toward them, tickling their tastebuds while, unbeknownst to them, a middle-aged man cursed loudly as he tried in vain to put out the fire that had erupted from his barbeque.

His hands felt warm inside of hers, and although the freezing air had taken the rest of his body to sub-zero temperatures, Mike could not do anything to suppress the growing smile on his face. Nor did he want to, because the warmth from her hand had somehow made its way to his heart, and he found himself greeting everyone he passed with a smile and a nod. He looked at her, smiling as he never had, and found it was reciprocated in kind, if not better. "How do you do?" he said in a muddled British accent, making an over-exaggerated bow at an elderly woman. The old biddy stopped and looked him up and down, no doubt wondering how he managed to hide his eighteen other heads under that shirt, then clutched her purse and scuttled away.

Cathy tried to contain her laughter, but found that it was like trying to contain a dam by plugging it with a finger. Soon it flowed out of her, and she slapped Mike playfully on the arm to get him to stop. "You're awful!" she proclaimed, still laughing.

"And you love me," Mike shot back, tapping her lightly on the nose to annunciate his point.

"True," Cathy admitted without pause.

"You loooove me!" Mike sang, thrusting his hands into the air and making a long 'o' sound, like an opera singer.

"Yes, I do," Cathy whispered.

"*You,*" Mike gasped, grabbing her quickly by the waist and pulling her into him and tilting his chin down until he looked like an old man with thirteen chins, "*love* me."

"Incredibly," she assured him, giving him a wide-eyed stare that meant she knew people were watching. "Now can we stop it, please, now, stop it?" she begged, tapping him on both shoulders to signal him to let her go.

"Somebody, stop me!" he yelled, doing an impression of Jim Carrey in *The Mask* while waving one arm around gracefully and holding her hand with the other, spinning her toward him as though they were waltzing. "It had to be you..." he started to sing, softly at first and then raising his voice so that anyone could hear them. "It had to be youuuu..."

"Okay, Mike, you have to stop now."

"Looking around, finally found..."

"Really, you can give it up."

He dipped her suddenly, kissing her passionately, his tongue slipping against hers for the briefest of moments. "Somebody whoooo..."

"You sound like an owl," she remarked dryly.

He hoisted her back onto her feet in an instant, sending her spinning until he grabbed her hand, snapping them both back into place. "I'm sorry, I know you were talking, but I was distracted. All I could think about is that fact that..." he ran at her, leaping into her arms until they both fell down on the grass behind them. "...You love me."

"More than anything," she laughed, kissing him on the nose. "But why are you acting like this?"

"Hmm," Mike hummed. He looked thoughtful, or at least pretended to, bringing a finger to his head and scratching it methodically. "Why am I acting this way? Hmmm, that's a tough one, you know? I wonder…" He turned, looking into a restaurant across the road from them, where a bearded, overweight man sat down and ate. "Let's ask this guy."

"Mike, no!" Cathy squealed, trying to grab his arm, but he shrugged her off joyfully and just walked on in. She ran after him.

"You!" Mike yelled menacingly, pointing to the man just as he stuffed his mouth full of sandwich. "I wanna ask you something, and you better pray you get the answer right..." he glared as the man swallowed hard, looking up with fear. "Why am I acting this way?"

The man gulped down the rest of his food. "I dunno, man!" he yelled incoherently, peppers falling out of his mouth and rolling down his shirt, staining it.

"See?" Mike yelled, throwing his hands into the air as he rushed Cathy back out the door. "He doesn't know either! Maybe it's because there's a full moon out tonight. Maybe it's because I can see it reflecting off of your eyes as the grass and leaves dance around you but never touch you. Maybe because of the way your hair catches in the wind and then falls perfectly back into place like nothing happened." He smiled, caressing her face. "Maybe it's because of the way your skin feels or the way your cheeks move when you're happy. Maybe it's because you argue with me, even when you know I'm right. Maybe it's because you hit me and think it'll hurt, or because you always feel so bad and kiss it better when it does. Maybe it's because of the way you smell, or the way you taste, or the way your laugh sounds when I've told a really stupid joke and you're the only one who's laughing. Maybe it's because of the way we fight, then promise never to again, then do it again. Maybe it's because you dance in your seat when a good song comes on over the car radio. Maybe it's because you ask me trick questions, ones you know I can't answer. Maybe it's because you think you're fat, when we both know I think you're the most wonderful creature on the face of the planet." He went to her, wrapping his arms around her. "Or maybe it's because you fit perfectly in my arms every time." He kissed her again, passionately, for just a moment, leaving her longing for more.

"Mike," she said after a moment, waiting for the fog that always seemed to cloud her mind when he kissed her to clear, "you're acting crazy."

"Yeah," he agreed, nodding, "that's how people in love act." He kissed her again, then took her hand and started to walk with her. "Come on, it's not much farther."

"Where are we going?"

He smiled. "Shall we ask that guy again?"

"Kerri!" called a Search and Rescue officer off in the distance, as he pushed a mound of shrub aside with such force that it broke at the root.

Every able man in town had come out with George Walker to help search for his little girl in the forest with, while the women stayed home with Macy and the police asked lots of questions. Old man Harper from two houses down had heeded the call so fast that he was only in his long-johns. His wife's striped, flowery slippers flip-flopped on his feet as he ran past trees, his legs getting sliced by branches and thorns.

Terrence's eyes searched back and forth, and even up and down. He was panicking, looking in places that the child could never have set a foot, even turning over medium-sized rocks to make sure she wasn't under them and pushing apart small shrubs. Sweat poured down his brow as he thought of how he'd seen the child play by the road or in the mud, the last bit of innocence left in this town. The last hope for something better to come. "Kerri Walker!" he yelled, climbing a few feet into a tree, trying to see over the undergrowth, trying to see some glimpse of her, just playing in the grass by some clearing.

Chad's face scrunched up as he took off his glasses, trying to see through the darkness a little better. Many of them, like Chad, did not have flashlights, and didn't care. If they got lost, it would only give them an excuse to keep looking; keep searching for the child -- keep searching for hope. Suddenly, a woeful scream sliced through the darkness, and Chad turned abruptly, his long blonde hair discarding the twigs that had become caught in it as he rushed over a stone pile to where the anguished sound had come from.

There, George Walker knelt in a small pile of oddly colored muck. It was only when one got very close that one realized that the mud had been mixed with blood. Not much, but enough to change the color. There, the father of the missing child wept uncontrollably, stopping only long enough to let another wail pass through his lips, as he clutched one small, red, sparkly shoe. It was dimmed only a little by the blood.

In that instant, all men present, no matter what religion they believed in—if any—took off their hats and bowed their heads in prayer, left with a hollow understanding that their prayers might not be answered.

"Oh, Mike," Cathy gasped, as he dramatically opened the front door to a tiny deli on the corner of Fifth Street, motioning for her to enter first. She bowed back to him, feeling silly, as she got into the spirit that he was trying to portray.

"Do you remember?" Mike asked, smiling from ear to ear.

She turned, raising an eyebrow at him. "I couldn't forget if I wanted to."

"Do you?"

"Only when I'm with my other boyfriend."

"Huh?" he spat quickly, his face going white.

She giggled at him, and then he began to laugh a little too, remembering every laugh they'd had through the years.

"Where are they?" Cathy said impatiently, blowing a strand of hair out of her face.

Mike sat across from her, wondering the same thing. "I don't know," he admitted. "I hope they show up soon."

Cathy huffed. "They better."

Mike raised an eyebrow. "But it wouldn't be so bad if it were just the two of us... would it?"

Cathy glanced from her salad to Mike. He was looking straight into her eyes. She'd never seen him look at her that way before. But, to be fair, she couldn't recall ever looking at him that way before either. They both leaned in and kissed. The second their lips met, they both pulled back, a little afraid. They leaned in again, and held it longer this time.

ʌᐯʌ

"It was Sara's, wasn't it?" Cathy asked, trying hard to remember as they sat down in the same booth they had a lifetime ago.

Mike nodded, "Yep. She told you to be here, and she got Xander to tell me the same."

"Remember how we thought at first that maybe they'd gotten together, and that's why they hadn't shown?"

He laughed as he poured himself a coffee and took a sip. "Yeah, wishful thinking, huh?"

"I dunno. I like to think that if they'd had more time..."

"Me too," Mike agreed, nodding. "And I'll always be grateful that we didn't wait until it was too late, like poor Xander."

"I know, this has got to be killing him."

"It is," Mike responded, sighing. "He won't say it, but I know. It's obvious. How could it not be? Today is the three month anniversary of Sara's death, for gawd's sake."

"It's the three month anniversary of a lot of things," Cathy mumbled glumly, pressing a hand against her pelvis gently.

Mike frowned, deciding to change the subject. "Remember the time Sara hooked up with that Canadian kid, Keenan, on a dare?"

Suddenly she erupted with laughter, her woes from a moment ago fading away. "How could he not have realized? The kid was like, three feet tall, and if he'd popped all of his zits then he would have lost half of his face!"

"One thing about Sara, she never backed down from anything. She always did what she wanted, when she wanted," Mike added.

"Yeah," Cathy smirked, "She really used the expression 'seize the moment' to death, didn't she?"

Mike shrugged. "I dunno. I like to think that she did everything she wanted to before she died. She definitely wouldn't have had any regrets. Sometimes I wish I could be like that, especially now that--"

"Hey hey!" came a high-pitched, annoying voice from the entrance to the deli, the small bell above it ringing loudly as the Peterson girls walked in, their smiles wide and stupid enough not to realize the moment that they'd interrupted.

Julie wore a short black skirt with a black leather jacket, completely inappro-

160

priate for this or any other time of year. Her lips had been painted a dark red that was almost black, her eyelids a dark blue. Her face was covered in makeup to hide the freckles that she despised with a passion, giving her skin a milky quality. Her brown hair was messed up from the wind, making her look as wild as she often felt. Her emerald eyes sparkled and shone, looking at Mike and Cathy from behind her toothy grin.

Mandy walked in behind her, without the wide smile. Her short brown hair was tied up in a stubby ponytail, revealing the small, m-shaped scar on her forehead. Her face looked different than usual, and it took Mike and Cathy a moment to realize that she wasn't wearing any makeup, not even lipstick. She wore a sweater that was far too big for her, a plain dark-blue in color, except for her name across the sleeve in white. She wore denim overalls, the top part of which were covered by the sweater, making the bottom look baggy. They were paint-splattered. Her eyes were mostly glued to the ground, careful to make contact with neither Mike nor Cathy. Especially not Cathy.

"Hi guys, how are you doing?" Julie said, dancing across the floor and plopping down next to Mike, grabbing his coffee and taking a sip, then spitting it back into the cup. "Ew, who drinks black? What are you, some kinda caffeine addict or something? Ugh. Anyway, what's up?"

"We're having some time *alone*," Mike stressed, nudging Julie away from him.

"Well, that's over, now. We'll stay with you."

Mandy still stood by the door, not speaking, and looking very much like a wall flower.

Cathy frowned at her, knowingly.

"What are you doing here, Julie?" Mike asked finally, sighing heavily.

"Just out looking for Xander. Do you know where he is?"

"Probably at the cemetery," Cathy breathed.

"Why would he go somewhere like that?"

"To pay his respects. It was three months ago today that Sara died."

Julie's face went even whiter, and for once it seemed as though she had nothing to say. "Come on, Mandy," she said, grabbing the girl by the sleeve. "I'm taking you home."

Before she was hauled out the door, Mandy shot a look at Mike. A smile, and then a wink, followed finally by a nod.

Both Mike and Cathy sighed, then chuckled a little.

"They certainly do make life interesting, don't they?" Mike coughed, lying back against the booth.

"Never a dull moment," Cathy responded coyly, giving him a mischievous smile as she slid from her side of the booth over to where he sat, placing a hand on the inside of his leg and rubbing it slowly, tenderly. She leaned in and started kissing his neck, causing him to laugh nervously.

"What are you doing?" he asked, trying to say it in a way as to not discourage her from the act.

She smiled, gazing deeply into his eyes. "Seizing the moment," she whispered, leaning in to kiss him gently on the lips.

"They have no idea where she is," Officer Moony cursed, turning toward Constable Lyle as they both stared into the wooded area behind the Walkers' house, scratching their heads. "They found a shoe and some blood. We can give it to the dogs with some clothes and try to get her back here as soon as possible. Did you call the dogs?"

"For the third time, I called the dogs," Lyle responded, frowning. "They're coming as fast as they can."

"That might not be fast enough. Every second this girl is gone is another second the kidnapper has with her: not something I'm overly comfortable with."

"I know. The parents are hick morons. Didn't even thin out the forest and put up a fence. That kid could have been murdered ten feet from their back door and they wouldn't have seen it."

"Don't say that word. It won't be long before the media gets hold of this, and you don't wanna slip up like that and send the mother to the loony bin."

"The media here are stupid. I wish White were still here. He'd have this solved by now."

"Tell me about it."

"You gotta wonder, though. Town like this, how does someone justify leaving their kids unattended?"

"They've lived in that house for ten years, without incident. Not even a yell late at night. People think that if something doesn't happen for long enough that it never will."

There was a long silence between the both of them then, their swollen stomachs growling for food even as they forced down egg salad sandwiches.

"Do you think she's alive?" Moony asked, his ears wanting to hear something he knew he wouldn't.

Lyle sighed. "I don't know. I don't believe in miracles."

The graveyard was a still, lonely place in the first few hours of night, with nothing but a constant, slow howl to let you know that you haven't gone completely deaf. It was an atmosphere that Xander was used to. The cold chill of nightfall had become like a second home to him. It was the only time he knew real peace.

All around him were the graves of his friends, the nearest and dearest to his heart. But the one at the top of the hill, the one he stood at now, was closer than all the rest of them combined. Her name, in life, had been Sara Johnson, the greatest love he'd ever known in his short time on this earth, until she was taken from him. Ripped. Pulled away from him by a monster the likes of which the world had never known.

"Remember your funeral, Sara?" he asked shyly with an embittered lip as he stared down the headstone, cracking his knuckles before reaching into his breast pocket, pulling out a smoke and then lighting it, taking a long drag. "Right before I made the vow to protect and all that? It was a nice day. I thought it was gonna rain. It always rains in comic books when they have funerals, y'know? You used to hate it when I read comics... not as much as you hated it when I read school books, though, huh?" He laughed, resting the cigarette between his lips. "Anyway, remember I was supposed to read your eulogy, but I couldn't? Well, it's taken a few months, but I think I finally figured out what I needed to say." He took a deep breath, his chest heaving. He began to read, his voice uneven and unnatural as he read his own words.

"I don't understand. I don't understand this world, and they keep telling me that I have to. They keep throwing these things at me, like I'm supposed to save the world or something, when really it's all I can do to keep from crying from minute to minute, and I want to know how you did it. How did you crawl through the dirt and the grime and come out clean on the other side? How did you stay so pure? Out of everything, that's the one thing I can't manage without you, Sara. The loneliness I can handle. Even the pain, most of the time, but I need you to finish telling me how to live without you. How to live this life that you helped me make..."

Tears started rolling down his cheeks, but he sucked them back, trying to keep his composure.

"Every night, I try to make you proud of me. I try to make the world a better place, but there's always a price. It can never be a complete win. I put Derek away after he went on a killing spree under my nose for a month. I put Phillips away after he scarred Cathy. I defeated Genblade after he killed an innocent lawyer. I defeated a gang of Tee's only to have one of them shoot Sud. The only exception to the rule is Blackheart, and that's just because she beat me completely. And you, Sara... why is it I'm never the one who pays the price for my failures?"

ʎ〈〉ʎ

Kerri cried more as she lost her second shoe, the branches scraping at exposed flesh.

ʎ〈〉ʎ

"Why is it that it's always those closest to me, or worse yet, complete innocents, that get hurt when I can't cut it?"

ʎ〈〉ʎ

The sounds of the demon's grunts overwhelmed her, drowning out the low whimper that had been emanating from her throat since the creature had snatched her from her peaceful backyard.

ʎ〈〉ʎ

Xander knelt down before the grave, feeling the cold earth through his black jeans. "But most of all, I have to know why it was you. Why you had to leave me here. It's like you took all of the air out of my world, and now I'm stuck suffocat-

163

ing in this vacuum. . Is that my life, now? Spending every waking moment just waiting for death so I might be with you again?" He frowned, shaking his head. "I'm sorry Sara, but I can't live like that. I can't. I have to hope that tomorrow will be better, but I also have to know that it won't be. That it can't be. Because you're not going to crawl out of all that dirt and soil and be pure again for me, are you?"

He frowned, caressing the grass and pretending it was her hair.

"I've met someone," he blurted, then turned red with embarrassment. "There, I said it. I wasn't hiding it from you, just myself, really. She's not really my type... but then, I guess since I've never had a girlfriend I don't really have a *type*," he laughed, tossing his smoke away and curling his fingers into the dirt nervously. "Just like when you were alive, I have to admit things to you before I can admit them to myself. She's not you, though. She could never be you. She's a little like you, though. She's definitely got your forwardness with men, not that I ever saw any of that from you. She's not as kind as you," he smiled, "and she has all the grace and tact of a water buffalo with a hernia, but she's good to me. And she cares about me. And... I think I'm ready to start caring about her." He laughed a little. "This wasn't much of a eulogy. But, I think it was mostly about putting you to rest, and it was long overdue. I've been keeping you alive in my heart for so long... this is the first time it's occurred to me that maybe you wanted some sleep." He bowed his head for a moment in prayer. He stayed there for a long time, just feeling the wind and listening to the sounds around him.

"Can I help you with something?" he asked the person who approached him from behind. He had known who it was just from the scent, and the way she stomped of leaves making her way up the gentle slope of the hill. He grinned a little. "Hello, Julie."

"Am I interrupting something?" she panted slightly, catching her breath and trying to get her wind-ruffled hair out of her face.

"Not really. I just wanted to be alone," he replied, turning back toward the grave.

"Oh," Julie sighed, turning to look back down the hill. "And, away we go again..." she said, rolling her eyes as she started back down the hill.

"No, that's all right," Xander chuckled, motioning her to come stand next to him. "I can be alone with you here."

She smiled, stepping up to stand next to him. He stared down at the grave, not moving or speaking. She tried to have the same amount of focus on the slab of stone. She licked her lips, then smacked them together. Then she did it again. She waved her hands back and forth, looking around at the other graves. "Depressing," she mumbled.

"Hmm?" Xander hummed, giving her a look. He was so absorbed in his thoughts, that he almost forgot she was there.

"All the headstones," she elaborated, motioning to the long line of graves. "I dunno. It's probably dumb, but when I die, I want something funny to be put on my urn."

"Urn?"

"Getting cremated," she explained with a smile. "There is way too much, like, prime real estate being taken up by graveyards. I mean, there are, like, so many homeless in New York, couldn't all that land be used for, like, cheap housing or something?"

Sticking his lower lip out, he tilted his head to one side for a second, then nodded. "I guess that's true."

"Damn right."

"Maybe I'll be cremated," he stopped, brushing some dust off the side of his jacket. "Hey, did you just make a good point?"

"I was overdue," she shrugged comically, rolling her eyes. She looked at him, then knocked on his forehead with one fist. "Doof-head."

"You went from intelligent conversation about homeless shelters to calling me a doof-head."

"Uh-huh!" she chimed, giving him a big smile and flapping her arms against her sides.

"So... you're insane."

"Uh-huh!"

"But you're still Julie?" he asked, quieter now. Almost romantically.

"Uh-huh," she breathed, looking at his lips.

"Good. I can deal with that."

She closed her eyes, leaning in to kiss him. At the last moment, he turned to face the grave, his demeanor solid as stone, as though the conversation had never happened. She sighed, scuffing her feet against the grass and looking around at the different last names on the graves, paying close attention to old friends and people she didn't know with her own last name. She stayed silent for a long time, just observing him as he stood. He looked like a living, breathing painting. *A painting named 'The unmoving man who never ever moved, not even to pee,'* she decided on the spur of the moment, nodding silently at the excellent name.

"So," she said finally, after a great time where nothing had been said. Verbally, anyway. "Anniversary, huh? I get that. A lot of my friends died that night, too. It also makes me think of Derek, and Grendel's party... those entire few weeks of my life. It's not just the date they died, it's like, it's the date that who we were died, y'know? It's like the woolly mammoth. He's just chillin' out one day (pardon the pun), when... BAM!... he's extinct. I doubt he even saw it coming, stupid elephant wannabe. Anyway, that's what it was like. It was like something hit this town, and it was, like, evolve or die. So, some of us died, but some of us had to change to survive. We had to adapt. To, like, evolve. Or, something like that. I think that's what I thought."

All the time that she had been speaking, Xander had not moved or even flinched. It was only because of her close proximity to him that she knew he was actually breathing. Then, suddenly, he raised an eyebrow and turned to look at her. "What?" he asked loudly, completely perplexed.

"Sorry," she apologized, genuinely. "I rambled. I was talking about this being the three-month anniversary of Sara's death and all."

"Hmm," Xander huffed, then turned back to the grave.

165

"What? Did I do something wrong again?" she pleaded, grabbing him by the arm and turning him toward her.

"No," he shrugged. "I just hadn't realized this was the anniversary."

"Then why are you here?"

He turned back to the grave, hands at his sides. "I do this every night."

She stood there with him for another thirty minutes. The wind picked up, and her hand started to get cold. It lingered near his hand, so she took it without question or pause. She clasped his hand so tightly that she made impressions in his skin, and he enjoyed every second of it.

He smiled, nodding down at Sara's grave. "Yeah, yeah," he said sarcastically. "I know. She's great, isn't she?"

ʌ⋎ʌ

He felt the heat coming off of her skin, even as he looked into her eyes. They sparkled in the dim moonlight, alive with fear and excitement all at the same time. Their skin twitched and tugged as they touched, feeling the warmth emanating from each other.

They kissed, and if there was any uncertainty, neither of them thought to notice.

The skin on her stomach was smooth and milky white, without wrinkle or blemish. There were stretch lines around her waist and breasts, which he noticed as her shirt fell to the floor a few moments ago.

For a moment, he was on top of her.

Uncertain, she withdrew.

"..ure?

"You sure?"

They both nodded. They had both asked.

He stroked her cheek with his thumb as he kissed her, her tongue moving quickly inside of his mouth. Every taste,

every sensation,

a new surprise.

Every touch, every time she felt his body close to hers, she would pull away from shock, then immediately go looking for the same spot again, only to find something better.

His hand drifted down from her cheek, down her neck. He stopped at her breasts, tracing the red marks that came with her age and their growth. She laughed, but was embarrassed.

She is beautiful, he thought.

She *is* beautiful.

His lips followed his hands, caressing her. He breathed deeply as the taste excited him further, pulling their bodies closer.

She stiffened, uncertain, but never wanting him to

stop.

He looked up every few seconds, unsure himself. Making sure that she was okay, and briefly kissing her lips before continuing his descent.

166

He was tracing her naval with one finger.

Am I fat?

She is beautiful, he thought, unable to think anything else.

She *is* beautiful.

His fingers went down then, and electricity surged through her body.

Twitch.

Her leg twitched, and again, she was embarrassed.

The embarrassment was still not enough to get it to

stop.

twitching.

Again, his tongue followed his fingers, as they went even lower still.

Soft.

There was the pressure of resistance, a sudden rush of pain, and then it was a rush again.

Like sour limes.

Her body welcomed him, wrapping her legs around him,

Tender.

pulling him in further.

Moist.

Beautiful, he thought, the word screaming at him everywhere he looked.

Wet.

Beautiful.

lime.

he was on her again, but this time she made no effort to

stop.

Him, wrapping her legs around and kissing his passionately as he sank into her, for his first time. Her first time. Their first time.

His head flew back so hard that he thought it might snap his neck, his brain exploding with pleasure from mere contact.

He melted into her.

Sank into her.

Soft

Lime

Tender

Moist

Wet

Her back arched, and he went deeper still.

Suddenly, it was okay for her to move. It came naturally. She did not want to

stop.

energy built up inside her and everything started to get faster more alert things stopped making sense as the world began to spin around her making her dizzy at first then the feeling began to build it was almost like she needed to pee but she did not she felt herself filling up creating pressure wanted to release it wanting it to come out come out went harder tried to make it slow down no rush but she wanted it to come to come so badly she could almost taste it

lime

suddenly the feeling spread traveling from the soft lime tender moist wet warm and going up her spine in tremendous leaps and bounds

"Don't."

stop.

The en-er-gy kept build-ing and get-ting more pow-er-ful with ev-er-y step it took then it ex-plo-ded out of the back of her skull like fire-works and mist-ed down over her body, a calmed and relaxed feeling spreading over her. She smiled.

His eyes grew wide as he went faster, harder... then

stopped, exploding himself. It felt like she was pulling back as he became soft and small, humbled by what they had accomplished.

Slowly, as one, their breathing became normal again. The world stopped spinning out of control, and they relaxed in one another's arms.

"I love you, Cathy."

"I love you, Mike."

They kissed passionately.

lime.

stop.

Alone at home, Mandy watched *The Late Show* on her tiny, fuzzy television, waiting for the host to say something funny. He did not, but everyone seemed to laugh anyway. She looked at her watch, wondering how long it would be until one of those other late-night shows with the stupid stories and the really bad, naked actors would come on. It would be at least another half hour, a million light-years away for one with an attention span so small.

She sighed, looking around her room for something to do.

It was bare, and just a little bit dark. Everything looked different now. The light from the television was all that kept the room from being pitch black, and even its glow had its limits. She could not see the corners of her small, claus-trophobic attic room, and the television made cruel shadows that moved and whispered in the dark.

A shiver ran down her spine that had nothing to do with the cold.

She had left all her things with her mother in Coral Cove when Auntie Sam made her move out here with Julie. All her friends and everything she had was back in that town, but she was here in this one.

Keeping both eyes on the darkness to make sure nothing jumped out at her, she reached under her bed and pulled out a small, furry notebook with a lock that always had its key in it. She turned the elaborately designed key and opened the diary. Notes that she had passed back and forth between friends tumbled out from between pages, and she tucked them away behind the back cover before flipping through to find her place.

June - Mom's drunk again. I tried to talk to her about a boy at school, but she just yelled about Dad...

July - I went all the way with Tom, then yesterday I heard him telling his friends how easy I was... saw him kissing Anna Speads.

September - Why does he have to hurt me when he

October - I don't deserve to live... stupid h...

November - I know something. Something so weird and awful that it could probably get me killed. I've never been more scared, or excited.

She stopped, pulling out the pen she'd won at one of those dime-a-dozen amusement parks that travel around the interstate and continued the passage, a sly smirk on her face.

Bad men took me. They took me away. I didn't think this place was any better than home, but then he came. He's so smart, and so strong. He stopped all of the bad men, dragged them off into the darkness. I thought he killed them, but he didn't. He saved me, though. Saved me from all of them, like a guardian angel.

He was black -- not African-American black, real black. Shadow black -- with red eyes. They were gentle, though. I didn't think red eyes could be gentle, but he looked at me, and then they were. Big, red eyes... that were kinda pointy. They were round, but they turned up. Like a cat's eyes, a little.

He had so many muscles, and he just threw the bad guys around like they were nothing. It was great.

He had claws. Claws like a bird. An eagle. Angels have bird wings, so why not claws, I guess? He needed something to save me, so I guess he grew them.

I think he had wings, but I'm not sure. They could have been folded back. I think he had wings.

My own guardian angel. A black angel sent to make everything better.

I've got a secret.

I know who the Black Angel really is...

Mandy giggled to herself, smiling as she continued to write.

She'd stopped crying.

She still wanted to, it was just that the tears wouldn't come anymore. Still, Kerri Walker sat in a field about twenty kilometers from her house, deep inside the forest. The air stung at the cuts and bruises all over her. She thought about running, but every time she did, she noticed the bones of a small dog lying near her, and decided not to.

Blood vessels had ruptured in her right eye, making her perfect face look torn, like a used piece of paper. Where smiles had once been, now there was only a blank expression. She had stopped crying after the first few hours, when neither the creature nor anyone else had paid much attention to it. Her clothes were muddy and dirty, with twigs stuck in them and rips everywhere.

Once, while the beast was dragging her away, she thought she heard her mother cry out to her, but she couldn't summon her voice to call back.

Now, the monster was hunched into a ball about ten feet from where she sat, using its massive, knife-like claws to dig at the soil, shredding grass and placing it into a small pile that was beginning to look like the bed her hamster used to

169

make for herself before she went to hamster heaven.

Kerri felt the tears begin again as she thought of her mom and her dad. A small whimper escaped from her lips, and the tears rolled down her cheeks.

The creature looked up, stiff but alert, like a horse that had heard a strange noise. It sniffed the air twice, then turned toward her suddenly, as if only just noticing that she was there. It growled deep in its throat.

It leapt toward her, using one of its massive hands to pin her to the ground, digging its claws into the ground to keep her there. Slivers branched off of its body, moving about it like tentacles. Teeth-like spikes sprouted at the end of each, and they reached out toward her, ripping and shredding at her.

It climbed onto her.

She screamed in pain at first, just as her body found its tears. The creature clawed her across the face savagely, and her screams immediately stopped, quieting to a low whimper.

The whimper would have been heard long into the night, had anyone been around to hear it.

CHAPTER FOUR: GHOSTS

Friday, Day Three

"So, what do you think about this young Kerri girl?" asked O'Toole, clicking the top of his retractable pen and writing the date across the top of his notepad, which was completely hidden behind the flaps of Xander's folder.

Xander glared at O'Toole, biting his tongue. He avoided the doctor's gaze, instead looking all around the room at the various university degrees and souvenirs that lined the walls and shelves around the office. He pointed one out, smiling. "Hey, you never told me you met President Bush."

O'Toole smiled, leaning over to glance at his own photo. "Yes. Remarkable man, really."

"That's kind of ironic."

"Oh?"

"Yeah," Xander said, his smile wiping away to become deadly serious. "Because, you know, you've got all the tact of carpet bombing."

O'Toole sighed, putting down the pen. He looked down, then brought his face back up. For the first time, the man was showing the stress he must feel every day, making Xander pity him. The doctor got out from behind his desk, leaving the file, and came over to sit next to him. "Sorry," he said honestly, resting the heel of one foot against the knee of the other leg. "Tell you what? No more recording everything you say. We'll just... talk."

Xander squinted, slowly nodding.

By this time, everyone in town knew about what had happened to Kerri Walker. Snatched from her own home. The child had never even been outside of the town limits, and rarely out of her parents' sight. Xander couldn't help think of how terrified she must be, how alone she must feel.

He was also barely able to keep his claws from unsheathing as he thought about what he'd do when he found the sick bastard that had done this.

"Really, Alexander," O'Toole said, snapping Drew out of his murderous fantasy. He took off one shoe and started to casually rub his own foot, wearing a facial expression that greatly resembled ecstasy. "What are you thinking about right now?"

"Killing a person."

Silence.

O'Toole swallowed hard, taking a glance back at his pen and paper and fighting the urge to dive at it. "Really? Who?"

"I dunno. Could be anyone."

"I s-see..." he stammered, again wishing for his notepad.

"I just want to find the bastard who did this to a little girl and claw their eyes out," he grunted, pretending to strangle an invisible foe.

O'Toole sighed in relief. "Oh. Yes, Alexander, I'm sure we all feel like that. But what can we really do about it?"

"I dunno. Anything's better than this. I should be helping."

"What do you think you can do to help?"

Xander was about to answer, then stopped himself. "I dunno."

"How have you been sleeping?" O'Toole asked suddenly, pulling a one-eighty on their topic.

Xander stared for a minute, leaning back, stroking his upper lip before pointing at the doctor. "Do you hear voices?"

"Now, what makes that question so hard to answer?"

"No, seriously. Cause, I'm kinda hungry, and I'm really broke. I figure if I turn you in, I can get myself fifty bucks and a fruit basket. Wadda-ya say? Gonna help a guy out?"

"Okay, I think that's taking it a bit far. But, now that you mention it, I'm a bit peckish, too," O'Toole added.

"You can eat my ass."

"Eat your ass?" O'Toole exclaimed, eyes wide. He pointed a finger at the boy. "Listen here, you..."

"Jeez, what is it with you people and molesting your patients?" Xander laughed, shrugging and looking around at the fake studio audience that he was sure would have been in stitches by now. "First you talk about sleeping with me, now you're ordering me to eat your ass. Explain yourself!"

O'Toole sighed, laying his head against his desk and looking catatonic for a moment. "Just answer the question, dammit."

"Language."

"Shut up."

"Why do you want to know how I'm sleeping?" Xander asked finally, raising an eyebrow. "To complete your mental fantasy?"

"No," Warren replied, regaining his composure. "It's part of my study. People under hypnosis tend to change their sleep patterns sporadically. I don't want an upset sleep pattern to upset your day-to-day routine."

"Oh," Xander huffed, puffing put his cheeks and thinking, trying to recall the night before. "No, I slept all right," Xander smiled, realizing that he actually had.

"Good."

"Yeah."

"So, getting back on subject, did you have anything to do with the disappearance of Kerri Walker?" Warren said calmly, all in one breath as to get it out as soon as possible.

Xander felt the smile fade from his face, and his claws were ready to pop again. Another instant and he might have transformed right then and there.

"Did you kidnap her to fulfill some sexual or psychological need you might have?"

The boy's nostrils flared, and he thought he might soon discover that he also had the power to breathe fire. "Excuse me?"

"Did you do it to prove yourself to the gang that was responsible for the recent deaths of youth in town?"

"The Tees."

"Yes, the Tees," O'Toole nodded. "Sorry, I couldn't recall without my notes."

"I have nothing to do with them, aside from the fact that I would burn each of them alive if they had something to do with this."

"Really? Thomas Drake thought you were involved with them," O'Toole pointed out, putting his show back on. "Carl Dent too. I'd sure like to ask them what their thoughts are on all this... but they're dead."

"That's not my fault," Xander stressed between gritted teeth.

"Did she feel good, Xander?"

"Shut up!" Xander yelled, his voice completely that of the womb, a low, guttural sound. He pulled back, trying to restrain himself, although part of him did not want to. He got up and grabbed his book bag, heading toward the door. "See ya around, Tool."

"I'm sorry, Xander," Warren said sincerely.

Xander turned and looked at the man. His head was down and his shoulders slumped to the floor, bringing the tall man down a peg or two.

"I truly am. But, if I find out that you or any other of my patients were involved in this... doctor-patient privilege be damned. I will hang you myself."

Xander nodded, turning back to the exit and closing the door behind him.

When the door snapped shut, Warren O'Toole smirked to himself, reaching into his pocket and pulling out a miniature tape recorder, pressing a button to make it stop recording. He scurried back to his desk to begin transcribing, pressing play.

"Shut up!" Xander's voice rang out, filled with static on the recorder. O'Toole raised an eyebrow, then began playing the clip over and over again.

172

Xander stormed down the hallway, his book bag slung over his back carelessly. He was walking like an army cadet, or a storm trooper, like he had some purpose. He stopped at his locker, turning the dial to 19 - 08 - 04, then opened it, throwing his bag in with a clang. He slammed the door with such force that it bounced back and nudged him, so he punched it as hard as he could, screamed angrily, then turned and started walking again.

Immediately, he bumped into Julie.

"Hi!" she chimed, waving as if to get his attention, even though they were the only two people in the hallway. "Yeah, I hate those lockers too. This school is so cheap, they really should get new ones. So, about last night, I'm sorry if I was, like, bugging you or something," she pulled back her hair and avoided making eye contact, "but, like, if you enjoyed yourself as much as I did, then I'm not sorry, because I, like, really enjoyed myself and stuff, and I was wondering..."

Xander rolled his eyes, turning to look directly at her. "Julie," he snapped, rudely flicking her on the forehead with one finger.

"Ow," she whined, rubbing it for a second, then smiling at him again. "Yeah?"

"I don't have time," he grunted, bumping past her as though she wasn't even there.

As he turned the corner to walk away from her, her lower lip stuck out. She sat on the floor, leaning up against his locker. Anyone that saw her was reminded of the agonized cries of another little girl in Coral Beach right now, and they shook their heads in dismay.

Chad stopped for a moment when he reached a large field, resting against the great stick he'd been using to help prop himself up. Sweat was pouring down his brow now, and his lungs ached. He needed a cigar, but he smoked his last one about three hours before.

It was starting to get cold out now, and beads of sweat were freezing onto his forehead, making him wish that he hadn't abandoned his trench coat along the trail a few miles back.

Letting out a long, hard breath, he scanned the field. It was starting to get dark, and he was miles from the nearest road. This would be his second day not showing up at the office, but since his supervisor was out searching too, he doubted that anyone would mind. His eyes darted over the horizon. It looked almost peaceful, like a Da Vinci landscape, with golden rays from the sun caught in the tall yellow grass.

Then, something caught his eye: a blue piece of fabric caught in an alder branch near the center of the field. Letting his stick fall to the ground, he walked over to it and carefully picked it up.

"Oh, no," he frowned, as he held little Kerri's dress, ripped and stained with blood. Next to it were the bones of a small dog, picked clean of all meat, the eyes rotting in its tiny skull. "Please," he pleaded, gripping the tattered clothing. "Please, God, no."

CHAPTER FIVE: RETURN

-pit-

-pit pit-

Xander grunted, refusing to open his eyes as he felt the water drip onto his cheek.

His other cheek was already soaked, along with that side of his head, and he had the overpowering taste of dirt in his mouth. Something was wriggling dangerously close to one eye, so he opened it to see what it was.

Immediately, his open eye stung so much that it nearly blinded him. "Argh!" he bellowed as he sat up, realizing that he had been half submerged in a mud puddle. He spat twice, and fair sized rocks came out, along with one tooth from the back of his mouth, followed by some coppery-tasting blood that, mixed with the grime, made him want to vomit.

-pit-

Drops of condensation from the leaves of an overhead tree landed on his clay-matted hair, making it run down into his eye. Blood vessels were opened in both eye sockets, and pebbles stuck into them, making it impossible to see anything straight. He reached up to get them out, promptly screaming in pain.

His claws had still been out, and the action had only served to further gouge his eyes.

"What the fuck?!" he yelled, grabbing a handful of cloudy water and splashing it into his eye, trying to get it to work right again. He opened the other eye, using it to search his surroundings. It was foggy, and he was in the forest. He strained his ears to try and hear which direction traffic was in to get his bearings. He found he heard none at all, meaning he was further out than the womb would have brought him frivolously.

His breathing was labored, and when he looked down there was a large branch sticking out of him, with blood-soaked leaves still hanging on one end. His eyes went wide, and suddenly he could taste the sap on his breath, filtering up from his lungs. Forcing both eyes open despite the pain, which seemed minimal now, he checked himself over.

His kneecap was missing. There was a large steel bolt sticking out of one hip, and all of his ribs had been either bruised, cracked, broken, or in some cases, all three. His heartbeat was erratic, meaning there was likely something wrong there, too. He spat again, and a large chunk from the top of his jaw detached from inside his mouth, plopping onto the ground.

"Fuck," he cursed, but it came out muddled. He leaned out over the puddle he'd nearly drowned in. Half his face was covered in mud, but it stung so hard that the muscle might as well have been bare. He began to wash himself off, and the stinging became more and more unbearable the more pressure he put on himself. When he looked back, he realized why. The muscle *was* bare. Whatever had done this to him had taken the flesh off of half his face.

There was something sticking out of his cheek, and when he reached up to pull it out, he saw that chunks were missing out of his arms: bite marks like a dog would make, only bigger. Broader. He pulled the foreign object from his face and examined it.

It was a tooth.

A long, sharp, tooth.

"What the hell is going on here?" he wondered, looking around to try and get his bearings. There was no noise except for the rustle of curious woodland creatures, but would still not get close. A squirrel, maybe even a chipmunk or two. Definitely a wolf, by the smell of it. But there was another smell, one besides the pine and dung. One that didn't belong.

He felt the pull of the true womb organ as it tried to divert all of its power to Xander's olfactory senses, telling him that he was on the right track. He took a big whiff, and his eyes opened wide. "Concrete, oil... phosphorous?" he frowned, furrowing his brow. "What would that be doing all the way out here?"

He stopped, turning to look around, suddenly realizing where he was. It was all too familiar now. He staggered to his feet, moving to a nearby tree and pushing its great branches aside. There, looming high above him, was the Engen complex.

A fortress of steel and concrete, it was here that he'd first battled Genblade. Where he'd been crucified and tortured. Where he'd begged for death time and time again. *Why would the womb bring me here?* He thought to himself, as he limped slowly toward the entrance.

The building had been blown apart by his final battle with Alpha, the mad-scientist that had woken up his Other three months ago. The concrete inside was crumbling everywhere, and Xander had to watch every step he took for fear that the floor might cave in under him. The levels went down further than they went up. If he fell, he'd be falling for a long time.

Paint had been chipped off the walls. Steel girders lined the halls, making it so that you could see into the ceiling and beyond in some spots. There was mold everywhere, and the smell of old, wet books in a library had sunk into everything. Animals both large and small had begun using this place for their home, their feces and nests littering the concrete, yet bringing life to the inanimate stone building.

To his far left, just behind a fallen pillar and some slabs of rock, was a large glass window. It was shattered, but not broken; still clear for the most part, simply spider-webbed in many places. A chipmunk scurried about next to it, barely noticing that Xander was even there.

"Hi, Bob," Xander snickered playfully, picking up a small acorn and tossing it toward the creature.

It looked shocked and offended, then grabbed the acorn and scurried through a hole in the glass into the area below.

Xander's eyes followed it into the pile of rubble and sand below the window. Whatever had been in the large, semi-circular room had received the brunt of the damage from the explosion, demolishing the walls and turning most of the ceiling's steel girders into mulch, which was now the home of a small family of birds.

Only after a moment did he realize what this place was.

He turned around slowly, getting a good look at Alpha's control room. The room below him was the arena, the sick place of torture where he'd battled Genblade, been crucified, and been forced to kill Spider.

The control room was more spacious than he imagined it, even more so now that there were holes blasted in it. Even so, he always pictured it being a little snugger. Like a musty old den where Alpha could smoke a pipe, twirl his mustache and practice laughing evilly while watching *Masterpiece Theater*.

Not that he ever had a mustache.

Or an upper lip, for that matter.

Xander turned around, looking at where a bookcase had been. Most of the books were completely burned to a crisp, but a few were only half burned. *Moby Dick*, *The Many Adventures of Robin Hood*, *The Bible*... he stopped at one, taking it off the self, smirking a little. It was *The Strange Tale of Dr. Jekyll and Mr. Hyde*, a first edition, nearly destroyed.

Irony, thy name is evil, he mused, placing the book against the side of the shelf.

Immediately, the wood crumbled and turned to dust, and the rest of the case fell down around Xander's ears with a large crash, the books disintegrating into ash and soot.

He winced, closing his eyes as he waited for the dust to settle, his teeth grinding together. "Uh," he started, opening one eye to take a look around, "I didn't do it?"

Then he stopped, opening his other eye and realizing what stood in front of him. The fire damage was worse on the wall where the bookcase had stood. The walls were blackened by flame, except for one perfect square, which was still shiny and metallic and perfect. Raising an eyebrow curiously, even though it stung the exposed flesh of his face, Xander limped toward the square.

Grunting furiously as blood once again forced its way out through his mouth, he leaned against the untouched metal and pushed. Slowly, it went back into the wall inch by inch, then finally he heard a snap and pulled back. The door reached its springs and jolted to one side, revealing a room dimly lit by red light. The loud buzz of a generator was evident now, and it was clear by the numbers that flashed over the computers that there was still a power supply in this section of the complex.

He turned one monitor toward him. It said the words: 'Subject Health Report' across the top, and was updated every three or four seconds. There was an outline of a human body there, with red splotched on its knees, face, lungs, and all over its body. "It's me," he realized after a moment. He raised a talon and made a small scratch on his right arm, then watching a red splotch appear on the mockup's arm. "Must track me the second I come into range," Xander smirked, amused, until he saw the words at the bottom of the screen. "Situation critical. Cease harm on Womb. Near... death?" He looked down at his gut, which could barely contain his intestines beneath a slight layer of translucent skin.

The room kept going. There were more screens, with an outline of both Genblade and Spider. Genblade's was waiting for a signal, while Spider's was permanently an aqua hue. "Red bad, aqua worse," he chuckled. "I knew I should've gotten a patent on that."

He turned to a fourth screen, one that was also waiting for its subject to return to transmission distance. Leaning in and squinting, Xander couldn't help but crack a smile. "Zakron?" He shook his head. "What kind of a name is Zakron for a genetic experiment? Who is this thing anyway? Maybe they made soup. Genetically enhanced soup, and it ran away or something."

"Yes, because that's likely."

Xander turned, thinking that he'd heard a voice. A voice like springtime. When he looked, there was a long row of cylinders. Looking much like clear, round coffins, each one was made of green glass and an odd viscous fluid pooled around it; fluid that did not seem to want to evaporate.

Carefully, Xander bent down and touched the fluid. It was gooey at first, then it soaked into his hand. Immediately, the cuts and scrapes on his arm began to heal. "Sweet," he said, pumping his arm once in celebration. He turned to the steel-grated clear caskets, all lined up in a row. The glass was broken on all of them, each one long ago smashed by the looks of it. Close to twenty years ago, by the looks of the way the fluids around the glass had softened their edges.

He reached over and dusted off a control switchboard which had a locking mechanism for each door. The words 'Darkness Containment Cells' were engraved on top.

He turned back to the cells with new-found appreciation and horror. "This is where they kept the test subjects before and after me. This was destroyed when... when my mother escaped from Engen." He looked down at the fluid again, taking some and rubbing it on his stomach and then watching it heal. "This is the same gunk that kept Alpha alive for all those years after the explosion."

"Can't get anything past you, can we?"

Stepping up, Xander started to walk past the different coffin cells. As he read the names engraved on each one, he could not help but smile vibrantly, as his past became a little clearer for the first time. Red Falcon, Zero, Abel... these had been his father's: those who had come before him so that he could be what he is today.

He stopped, staring for a moment at the next cell. It read Eve, the first name of the woman who would become Spider. It only now dawned upon him that she was killed less than a thirty second walk from where she had been born. These walls were probably all she'd ever known.

He stiffened, becoming aware of what was happening. He turned around, and he was standing face-to-face with Eve Spider.

Instinctively he lashed out, clawing at the visage. Instead of connecting with flesh, he simply slipped through the air and skidded across the floor, which would have hurt if he hadn't landed in the clear goo. He turned quickly. "How?" he demanded frantically, watching her statically fragmented movements as she jumped across the floor. Her motions were not whole... like watching a movie reel with parts missing. One minute she'd be crouching for a leap, the next she landed. The in between was missing. "How are you here?"

"What do you mean, Womb?" Spider asked, giggling a little in her lovely voice. The voice that could not have originally belonged to someone so cruel, Xander decided. It must have been taken from a sweet, innocent child and placed within her by Alpha, to put off her enemies.

"You know what I mean!" he accused, rising to his feet and twisting to follow her as she danced around him, while her swords were sheathed behind her back. "You're not real! You're some fever dream I had when O'Toole knocked me under! How are you here now?"

"Hypnotic suggestion maybe?" she laughed, shooting him a look. "Have you heard nothing I've said?"

"Yeah, I remember," he scoffed. "'Those that are allies today will betray me tomorrow,' right? You were talking about Derek, then. So what now? Why are you here? To warn me of the big bad that's coming?"

"I am here because you need me to be here," Spider assured him, unsheathing a sword and swinging it toward him. To his shock, it cut deep into his cheek.

"What the fuck?" Xander yelled, grabbing at his face as blood streamed down it. "I didn't think you were real."

"You think many things, Womb, but few are correct. And few are incorrect. All that matters is that you assume all, and that is when it will strike. When you assume that you are safe and snug in your bed with the pretty flowers that dance like rainbows and headphones."

Xander gave her a quizzical look, tilting his head to one side. "I can't put my finger on it, but I think you lost me somewhere. Oh, maybe when you started talking crazy. Just a thought."

"You think you know all, but you don't know him," she accused, pointing her sword at him. "And you don't know her. The one who will start it, with the blonde hair and the blue eyes... She'll sing for you, she will. She'll make you dance and shout, but she whispers the truth to me when she's with her children, she does. She whispers that she won't choose you to be her One and only. She'll choose the child instead, and that's when they'll all turn on you."

Xander took a step forward, then nearly collapsed onto the floor. Getting up and literally holding his legs together, he finished the movement. "Ignoring all the other cryptic crap, what do you mean I don't know him? Who him?"

"The one that did this to you, and the one that will do worse to my dear Adam," she said, her voice becoming a wail when she said her lover's voice. "He'll make him like a faucet, hot and cold running blood. And you will not know, for you do not know yourself."

"Wait, what?" Xander jolted, becoming alert. "What was that last bit? What does it matter whether I know myself or not?"

"Because you are fighting yourself, my boy. Because that's all you've ever done. And even with the traitor helping you, you still cannot fight it. And now yourself is coming, along with the traitor and all his little tin men."

"Traitor? What traitor?"

She pushed him, and he landed on his back. She flipped skillfully, and when she landed she was sitting on his chest, smirking at him. "You know what I like best about you genetically altered guys? You're always good for a ride... or maybe that's just your lover's parts down there talking, hmm? Maybe she wants to be scratched again?"

"What traitor?" Xander yelled, grabbing Spider by the arms and flipping her over, with his body nestled snugly between her legs. The effort made the tender flesh on his gut split, and the blood went right through Spider, and then he did too, slamming his nose against the concrete.

For a second, while they were translucent, their bodies were one. "I always wanted you inside me," she giggled, and it was Julie's giggle. "But, very well. You think you know who the traitor is. You said so only moments ago. But when I warned you of him, it was not a singular incident I was speaking of."

"You mean..." he gasped, trying to think of some other way to interpret what she was saying. "You mean that another friend is going to betray me?"

She smiled, but did not answer. "All good things come to those who wait, Womb. For right now, try and make it to the end of the month, hmm? Because what happens every month, will not happen this month. And you will lose everything, Womb. And then it will destroy you."

"Just show me what you mean!" he screamed, punching the floor and splitting his knuckles.

Behind him, the screen that had previously been blank flickered to life for one second, then dropped out again, the words 'waiting for signal' re-appearing on the screen.

Spider grimaced, then frowned. She turned and pointed, then faded away into the nothing again until only her voice remained. "It's everything you are, but it was made to hunt you down, Womb. Made to hunt us down. It is an Anti-Womb."

Xander looked toward where she was pointing. Another containment cell was there. This one was larger than the others, though... broader. As if someone with really thick shoulders were trying to fit inside. As he looked closer, he realized that this cell wasn't broken. The metal and glass on it were too wide for that. This one was just hanging open. Whatever had been inside it had escaped. He stepped closer and closed the lid, and the word engraved across its cover suddenly wasn't funny anymore.

It said Zakron.

CHAPTER SIX: HUNT

Sunday, Day Five
Tommy pushed back the underbrush of the grounds as sweat poured off of

him, slowly trickling down his back. His breathing was hard, and he wished that he had taken his mother's advice and brought a bottle of water along with him. He was deathly thirsty, and he could feel his blood sugar level drop with each passing second.

Right now, he couldn't care less. He could have dropped into a coma where he stood, and he still would have fought to keep moving. "Kerri!" he yelled at the top of his lungs, cupping his hands over his mouth. His voice was dry and crackling from the dehydration, so it didn't carry very far.

He stopped for a moment, holding his ear to the wind and praying for some kind of response. Anything that might let him think that he was on the right track, that he might be able to save the child, or help someone else save her. There was no response, only his echo and the sounds of other rescue workers calling out the same name.

Somewhere, Tommy realized, the girl's father was out there. And her friends. Her young friends at school would be wondering where she was. He wondered what their parents would tell them. How do you tell a child that their friend is gone, and that you'll try everything to get her back, but it might never happen? Or, worse yet, how do you tell someone that young that their friend is dead?

If you do it like Tommy's parents, you don't. You don't speak of it. And you make fun of him when you catch him crying in his room just a few weeks after seeing his friend murdered.

What do we tell our children? Do we give evil a name? Do we give it a face and a title, and show it to them so that they will run if they see it in the streets? No. They will have nightmares enough with their friends littering the ground.

No, we tell them that we will try harder. That we will protect them. That our love will keep them safe and warm. That nothing can hurt them.

And then when they are stolen in the night, Tommy scoffed, taking out a small piece of red tape and tying it around a tree. It was an approach that the rescue workers had begun to use to mark an area as searched. *Then we will cry ourselves to sleep and realize that we were lying to ourselves more than we were lying to them.*

Grunting to himself, Tommy pledged on into the night, trying to think more positively. He started working on the speech he'd give when he found and saved the girl.

ʎ✗ʎ

Cathy sat in the padded chairs of the Turismo 3000 racing game at the Factory. She watched the animation as it played over and over again, a blank expression on her face. It was early morning, but classes had been unofficially cancelled. Most teachers were out helping with the search.

Her face was as white as a ghost, her eyes wobbly, unable to focus. The screen seemed blurry as the car on it turned this way and that to avoid other cars and road blocks, flipping over, then starting again looking like new. Her head started to tilt from side to side, following the car as it moved around the screen. She looked to be in some kind of trace, like she was caught in a cobra's eyes.

From across the room, Mike looked up from his shot at the seven ball, watching as she swayed back and forth.

"Again today?" Xander frowned, following his friend's gaze as he leaned against his pool cue.

Mike nodded, then turned back to his shot. He'd connected too far to the left and the cue missed the seven completely, scratching into the corner pocket instead. He sighed, slamming his fist lightly against the green matting.

Xander's eyebrows jumped as he waited for the cue ball to emerge from the hole on the side of the table. He took the ball in hand and placed it in the center of the table, firing at the seven and sinking it. He turned to shoot at the eight, then stopped, turning to Mike. "At the expense of my pool game, I'm gonna have to ask you what's on your mind."

Mike was still staring at Cathy from across the room, a girl who had slowly gone from white to green in the past few seconds. "She's been like that all day," Mike admitted, leaning against the table.

"Maybe she's upset. Didn't her sister used to babysit for Kerri? Maybe she knew the kid," he added, holding his gut as the true Womb churned.

Mike shook his head, "Naw. It's more than that. She's sick. She's sick and she won't let me help."

"What kind of sick?" Xander asked, joining Mike against the table, holding the cue stick against himself.

"When I picked her up at her house today, she was throwing up. Throwing up bad."

"What did you do?"

"Nothing. Couldn't. She was locked up in the bathroom. She tried to tell me she wasn't sick, but I could hear her gagging. Now look at her."

Xander frowned, turning back to the game and taking his shot at the eight. It connected, but the eight did not go in, it merely lingered by the hole. "This is so the worst time ever for this."

"Why's that?" Mike asked, turning to take his shot.

"Because of what's coming. Whatever this thing is, man, it took out the Womb and I don't think I hurt it."

"Things are taking you out all the time," Mike almost smiled, sinking the eight and lining up his shot at the nine.

"Yeah, but not the true Womb. This thing took out my worse half without a sweat. And then the dream with Spider... I know you don't buy into that, not sure I do, either... But she called it an Anti-Womb. Like maybe its equal and opposite force. Remember? From physics?"

Mike nodded curtly. "Whatever it is, it had better come soon. I don't know how much longer I can deal with this waiting." He took the shot, sinking the nine into the side pocket, then they both turned to watch Cathy again as she stared blankly at the cars driving across the game screen.

ʎᏇᏗ

Tuesday, Day Seven
Xander landed against the thick branch of an evergreen tree, digging his

claws into the bark to steady himself. The branch swayed a little beneath the added weight as he peered into the black of night that covered the forest. It was nearly eleven, and the chilled air was nipping at his skin like a tiny mutt with sharp teeth.

With a sound like ketchup being squirted out of a bottle, his eyes became cloudy and black, until they were a pure, reflective ebony. Suddenly, the forest was like day to him. He could see every nook and cranny of the trees, every bug on the leaves that were sparsely growing on low shrubs.

He breathed hard. He was about ten kilometers from the nearest house, and thirteen from where Kerri Walker had been abducted. He'd bolted here as fast as he could the second he heard his parents go to sleep, swinging from tree to tree to save time. Raising his nose into the air, he felt the womb-organ shudder and spurt as it diverted extra power into his sense of smell. He took a long sniff, then crouched on the branch like an acrobat, staring straight down at the ground.

He smelled fresh feces, dog hair mixed in it, telling him which species had made it. Nearby, another dog had sprayed its mark onto a shrub. But there was nothing ahead. This was the spot where the dog had stopped.

Carefully, Xander spun around the branch, letting go when his feet were parallel to the ground and landing safely, crouching beneath the foliage.

The dogs stopped here. This is where they got confused, Xander thought, scratching at the dirt a little and bringing some to his mouth, tasting it, then spitting it back out. *The police had given them Kerri's clothes, trying to get the hounds to find her. Here, the dogs kept running around in circles, not knowing where to go next.*

He bent down, putting his nose to the ground and sniffing hard, his eyes widening. *Her scent is strong here... but it keeps going, off to the west. Deeper into the woods. And there's something else...*

He popped all of the claws on both hands, crawling into the muck with his nose to the ground, licking out his tongue quickly every few seconds, just enough to taste the dirt. Suddenly, he stopped, sniffed twice, then pulled back dramatically. A deep growl formed in the back of his throat, as the Womb became excited.

Blood... he realized, and started slashing at the ground with his great talons, forcing the dirt out between his legs into a small pile, like a canine. About two feet down he stopped.

In the past few short months he had seen some of the most frightening, disturbing things that mankind had ever dreamed up, and he had faced them head on, but there in the woods, Xander Drew fell down on his hands and knees and began to cry. He cried in long, agonized howls, mucus streaming from his nose and mingling with the tears on the ground.

In the hole was the severed arm of a child, the scent of which belonged to Kerri Walker.

Harry Ford's stomach lurched again, as even more vomit spewed from his lips out into the toilet bowl with a sickening splash. Tears ran from his eyes as the stomach acids burned his esophagus, giving them access into his blood stream. He grabbed a roll of toilet paper from a nearby roll and used it to wipe his lips, then tossed it into the bowl and flushed, regaining his composure.

He walked out to where his partner, Lance Berkshire, stood, staring down at the object in front of them.

Lance looked at his friend, placing a hand on his back. "You can go home, you know. I can do this on my own."

Harry shook his head, holding his hand to his mouth to keep from regurgitating again. "No. We have to find out everything we can. Besides, you shouldn't be alone."

Lance nodded, setting the timer on his tape recorder to zero and then pressing record. "Lance Berkshire and Harry Ford, Coral Beach Precinct Morgue. DNA results back, confirm identity of appendage as that of Kerri Walker, age seven."

Harry grimaced at the mention of the child's name.

"Arm was severed by what looks to have been sharp, jagged teeth from a side angle, slicing clean through muscles, tissue, and arteries. Possibly a member of the large canine or feline family. Definitely not human. Severing occurred just above elbow. Extreme bruising on back of arm and hand indicate a struggle at some point."

Harry stepped in, turning over the arm so that it was palm up. "More bruising on the palm, as well as cuts with some pebbles in them. Some nails missing, others with grit and grass beneath them, backing up the struggle theory. Blood capillaries ruptured beneath one nail," he stopped, moving his head so that he could see where the limb had been severed. "Clean cut, from sharp teeth. Foreign substance found within one of the bite marks... Lance, any word back from trace on what that was?"

"Yes," Lance stammered, now having to hold himself up against the cold, metal desk as he looked at the sheet of paper before him.

"Well, what is it?"

"Vaginal fluid. Her own," he gulped, laying down the paper.

"So the killer..."

"Yes."

"And then he..."

"Yes."

"Gawd..." Harry groaned, his eyes tearing up as he turned back toward the arm, looking at the skin around the bite. The flesh had turned black and blue, with some capillary action making crow's feet down the limb. He looked up, closing his eyes. "Oh, no."

"What?" Lance asked, rising to his feet.

"There's bruising around the bite."

Lance stopped, burying his face into his hands. "My god, Lance... she was alive when it did this to her. She might still be alive now."

Harry turned, bolting back to the bathroom to throw up again.

Thursday, Day Nine

Adam Genblade sat cross-legged facing a bare concrete wall, striped from the shadows made by the iron bars of his cell.

His bed was a springless mattress bolted to the floor. He was allowed absolutely no sheets and his mattress had no thread binding it together since he could use either to strangle a guard. His bathroom was a hole in the middle of the floor, and he was washed with a hose once a day. There was a sewage pipe running down one corner of his cell, protected by iron bars meshed so tightly that he could not get his hands into them. His meals were soft, mushy food usually consisting of mashed potatoes and turnip. His was permitted neither utensils, nor a plate, and was fed with a ten foot aluminum pole. Therefore, he had to eat, sleep, use the bathroom and take showers all on the same floor. Sanitation issues had been brought up many times since his incarceration, but they had always been overruled by the safety issues of the guards assigned to his care.

His auburn hair had become visibly darker since his imprisonment—it was no longer naturally lightened by the light of the sun—because his cell had only one small window which the sun never faced. His face had a cut across it: an accident with the aluminum pole while he was being fed the day before. His face was taut as beads of sweat formed on his head while he tried to concentrate, to relax himself despite his surroundings.

News of the little girl's disappearance had reached him today, along with the discovery of the child's arm. Silently, although he would never let anyone know, he prayed that the child would be alive. That Xander would find her safe and sound.

Suddenly, his eyes shot open, and he turned toward his barred window. His mouth dropped in shock, his pupils dilating in fear as he heard a slow scratch just outside it, which was overpowered by a maniacal growl. "Oh, fuck, no," Genblade cursed, unable to take his eyes off of the window.

Suddenly the scraping sound stopped, and there was a shuffling in the bushes, then it started again, fainter this time.

"...checking defenses..." Genblade mumbled, rubbing his temple as he tried to remember. "...locate structural weaknesses..."

He looked up, as the scratching again moved further down the wall, until now he could barely hear it. *Please, Xander*, he silently prayed, *figure it out soon.*

Chad walked down the dimly lit corridor, looking around frantically each time he turned a corner. About halfway down the long, tiled stretch, a knob protruded from the wall and he took off his duster and hung it there, unbuttoning the sleeves of his dress shirt. His jeans were tattered and worn, with dirt and grass stains all over them. He tracked it in, but the foot prints were barely visible in the low light.

Reaching the end of the hall, he pushed open the unlatched door that was waiting there for him, slowly rolling up his sleeve to reveal the red T that had been tattooed there.

Chad was a member of the Tees, a group of youth led by older men in Coral Beach and Glover Island that waged a minor war with the surrounding communities, with much major casualties. At the moment, they were in the middle of a feud between themselves and Coral Cove, the main headquarters of the Omega gang. A few weeks ago, many of their members had been injured by some kind of black demon calling itself a womb. A few days later, their newest member had shot a young man in the high school, making the cops search them out. They'd been forced to scatter. But now that the police had their hands full searching for the Walker child, which allowed the Tees to assemble again.

"Has she been found?" came a voice from the darkness, deep and scratchy.

"No," Chad frowned, his eyes glued to the floor. "But the police believe she's still alive."

"It does not matter anymore. We keep looking until the kidnapper is found and brought to justice. There is no need for acts *this* vile."

"Yes, master," Chad said, bowing a little.

Roulette stepped out of the shadows and lit a cigarette, the fire illuminating his face, painted white with a large T marked in red down the center. "See that whoever is responsible for this is found. We will conduct a proper search when our numbers are full."

"Yes, Roulette."

༞〈〉༞

Saturday, Day Eleven

Mike pushed trees out of the way, wiping the sweat from his brow as the warm sun beat down on him.

Xander, hanging from a nearby tree and using the height advantage to look around, flipped down next to his friend, sniffed the ground twice, then shook his head. "Nothing."

"Then we keep going," Mike said, cocking his head to one side and tying a marker onto a nearby shrub.

Xander nodded curtly in response, crouching down then leaping into the nearest tree, disappearing into its branches for a moment before jumping to the next. He poked his head out through the top of the branches, stuck out his tongue to taste the air, then crawled downward to speak to Mike again. "We head east," he said simply.

"East it is," Mike said, patting Xander on the back.

The pair started east until they reached a steep slope covered with rocks and unearthed trees.

Again, Xander landed next to Mike. "You can stop here if you want, bro. That might be hard for you to get back up."

Mike gave him a look.

Xander sighed, and they both started down the hill. "How's Cathy?" he grunted as a pointed rock drove into his knee, only to be forced out again by the healing factor.

"Wish I knew," Mike sighed honestly, gritting his teeth as he slid down the slope, the seat of his pants becoming dusty. "She hasn't talked to me since that day in the Factory. I went to her house, but her mother just gave me this look."

"What - ow - what look?"

"Like the ones Sara's mom used to give you."

Xander raised his eyebrows. "Oh. *That* look."

"Uh-huh," Mike said, as he propped himself up against a sideways-growing tree for support, taking a breather as he got ready to continue his trek down the hill. As he stared at the trunk, his eyes grew wide. "Xander!" he called out to his friend, who was a little further down the hill.

Xander turned, popping all of his claws and using them to help clamor his way back up the slope, until he sat alongside Mike. "What? What is it?" he gasped, fighting for breath.

"Just look," Mike said simply, motioning toward the tree.

There, carved into the tree, were three huge claw marks. Slowly, Xander took the claw he'd pulled from his face a week ago and placed it into the gouge. It fit perfectly.

"East," Mike said, his voice filled with more resolve than ever.

"East," Xander nodded, through gritted teeth.

Richard Ortega had abandoned his shirt twenty minutes ago, and now the red T tattoo was visible to the other four men that were trudging through the wilderness with them. They were so far out that their cell phones would not even work, yet they kept going. Everyone seemed to avoid the man with the tattoo, but not from fear. They left it alone because the man was helping.

Because it didn't matter anymore. Background, ethnic origin, money... even gang relation didn't seem to matter now.

All that mattered was finding the girl.

They'd become aware, one by one, that they were no longer even searching for the girl; they were searching for her body, but even that fact didn't seem to matter.

All that mattered was the girl.

The girl.

Monday, Day Thirteen

Officer Moony walked along the grass, leaves crunching underneath his feet. He stared out into the dimly lit woods nearby.

You were here, weren't you? he asked himself mentally, crouching down to a child's height. *No...* he remembered, scrunching over a few centimeters to the left, until he was at eye-level with a hole in the underbrush. *She saw you through the brush, pulled back the leaves, and then you took her, didn't you?*

Why? What was the big deal about her? What made her so special?

186

George Walker looked out his back window and watched as Moony bent down and prayed, his hands folded before him. Kerri's father stood, grim-faced, his frown twitching at the corners as he sipped on his steaming coffee.

He brought the phone back up to his ear, placing the coffee cup back onto his kitchen table. "Naw, naw. It's just the cop in charge a lookin' for Kerri, s'all. Now, lemme tell you somethin', I don't care what you've gotta do, just get them out there, all right? I want my little girl found, and I want her found now, you understand me?" he screamed, as he slammed the phone back down onto its receiver.

He chugged another gulp of his java down, the T on his shoulder standing out, like bright red soul-fire against the drab, white background of his kitchen.

⋏⋏

His breaths were hard and labored, few and far between. He huddled in the corner of his cell late at night as the rain beat down outside.

All anyone could hear that night was the thunder and the rain, but Adam Genblade knew better. His ears picked up on more.

He could hear the unearthly shuffling just below his cell. The grunts and growls like only an animal could make. The sounds of talons and tendrils scraping against the moist concrete walls of his cell. The hisses. They were the worst. It only hissed when it was really mad. When it knew you were there. Like a snake right before it killed its prey.

"Look out!" Spider yelled, even as the Anti-Womb's massive talons ripped open Genblade's gut, exposing his organs for all to see in one massive spray of flesh and bile.

Genblade winced at the memory, lifting up his orange prison jumpsuit just enough to see the scar that the Zakron creature had left on him nearly four years ago.

Spider leapt to her lover's aid, tossing Genblade aside as she took out both of her swords, each one sparkling with ruby-encrusted arachnids. She smiled a little, blood oozing from the cut on her forehead down into her eye, making her blink.

It was all the thing needed. Tendrils spawned off of both its sides, going right through both of her wrists and lifting her up by them, making it impossible for her to get any leverage. The world's most elite acrobat, as incapacitated as a child.

Genblade tried to rise, but his intestines spilled out onto the ground. Everything went black and spotty, as the trees around him began to blend with the sky and ground.

Adam opened his eyes, sweat dripping down his brow as he recalled his encounter with the Anti-Womb. The beast had violated Spider in that battle and left her a quivering, broken mess for months. It had taken him three weeks to recover from the injuries he'd sustained. By the time he'd gotten out of the infirmary, Alpha had already captured Zakron again. It was back in its cell, where it would stay until they needed it.

It was our failsafe, he thought, remembering the word his former master had used. *It hunts and kills whatever it can, whatever's in sight. It was meant to be dropped on an area where a Womb had gotten out of control. Something that could stop it, stop anything...* he stopped, looking up at the window. For a second, he thought he saw two red eyes peering back at him, but there was a flash of lightning and they were gone. He shuddered. *I've got to get out of here. There's no way Drew'll be able to handle this on his own. That thing... it'll kill him. It'll kill everything. That little girl... she should consider herself lucky. They have no idea what this thing is capable of.*

Wednesday, Day Fifteen

Cathy walked down the hall of Coral Beach High school, hugging her books tightly against her chest as if they were armor that would protect her. She felt dizzy and disoriented; her face as white as a ghost. The halls themselves seemed to fight with her, leaning in toward her in her skewed vision. The lockers wobbled and shone, the stickers and graffiti on them turning shapes and making demons. Her salvation was at the end of the tunnel.

Mike was just closing his locker door when he noticed her, and his smile was undeniable. There was no hiding his feelings for her, as he lay down his math book and walked toward her. "How are you today?" he asked softly, taking her gently by the shoulders and pulling her close to him.

Their bodies touched, and she pulled away. "I'm fine," she snapped, running a hand through her hair to make sure it was still okay. "Why?"

He was taken aback by her response. He'd asked her the same thing every day for as long as he could remember. "I dunno..." he stammered, shifting his backpack onto both shoulders. "I, uh, called your house last night and there was no answer..."

"Well, maybe I didn't want to talk to anyone, you ever think of that?" she huffed in frustration, grabbing her hair as if ready to pull it out before fiddling with the button on her tight jeans. "Do ever even think about anything, period?"

"Yeah, I think period is the operative word here," Mike grumbled, frowning.

"What?!" Cathy screamed, pushing Mike against his locker with as much force as she was able to muster, attracting the attention of surrounding students and teachers. "What did you just say?"

"I just... nothing!" he started, raising his hands in defense before turning to walk away. "I'll see ya later," he drawled, adjusting his backpack again.

Her eyes watered and her lower lip began to quiver as she watched him go until he turned the corner, then she collapsed in tears against his locker.

Reverend Robert Gallagher sat in the halls of The Apostle Church, his robes dancing along the stained hardwood floors. The pews were empty tonight, as they had been every night for weeks, and yet he had never seen the people of Coral Beach pray or look to the clouds for hope more.

It was ironic, he thought, that the first time everyone else in town turned to God at once was the only time that Gallagher himself had lost faith.

At the head of the church, rows upon rows of candles lay unlit, save for one.

One candle burned brightly against the wind drifting in through the open windows of the cathedral, fighting against all odds to stay lit.

Walking toward it, he placed his hand over the flame, feeling its warmth for just a moment before licking his thumb and forefinger and snuffing it out with a sickening hiss. He crossed himself once, taking his collar from his neck and letting it fall to the ground, glad that nobody was around to see it.

"God, help me..." he whispered, as he prayed long into the night.

Friday, Day Seventeen

Black Womb touched down against the top of a high rock that almost peeked above the tree line, his chest heaving for air as his body melted into the shadows, becoming almost invisible to anyone who might think to look. In that moment he almost collapsed; he had to hold himself up against the stone beneath him. He had been searching for over one hundred hours straight, longer and harder than he'd ever pushed his powers, body, or mind before, searching for a scent, a shred of cloth, or anything that might even suggest that Kerri was still alive. That she still might be able to be rescued, if not saved. Even if they only found her for the sake of burying her, it was still that much more closure for her grieving parents.

But there had been nothing for days now, not a sight nor sound. Every few hours, someone would pass near him with a radio long enough for him to hear that the statistics of Kerri even being found dead were now less than ten percent.

There was also no sign of Zakron, the Anti-Womb. And yet, he was everywhere. As Xander's sleep-deprived mind began to rattle him, he saw the demon in every corner, under every stone. *I will find you,* he silently vowed to the killer, as he watched a lone man toting a shotgun patrol the trees below him, the low light of evening gleaming off the barrel. *I will find you because some things are unforgivable. Undeniable. Children should not have to be afraid to play in their yards, to go to school in peace, to walk down the street without fear of pain and murder. I will not stand for it. I am here, and I will keep being here, because this is not right.*

He turned, watching as a cadre of men both young and old stomped through the brush. He'd noticed them a few times, but never up close. They were quick and formidable, scouring the woods like a fine-toothed comb. There were thirty or so of them, some he recognized, some he didn't. But the symbol on their arms he recognized all too well.

They were Tees.

The Tees were searching the forests of Coral Beach, trying desperately to find the missing girl. *Because even those we thought were our enemies are here,* he realized, straightening up behind a tree to make sure he was not seen as he watched them pass, like silent military guerillas searching out their target, organized and elite, *because some things surpass rivalries and borders. Because the one and only thing all men have in common is a voice that screams in pain when it sees something as wrong as this. Tonight, we are not enemies. We are brothers.*

Randy Owchar looked up from his place at the back of the line of Tees, seeing the Black Womb as it stood perfectly straight upon its stone perch. Randy nodded once, and the Womb returned the sentiment of respect, as both men continued in their search.

Cathy Kennessy sat with her mother on the cold, hard doctor's table. She wore only a small paper night gown, the kind with no back, and it made her very self-conscious to be so exposed. She tried to limit her time without her back to a wall, but right now she was sitting in the middle of the room.

"Okay," said the doctor cheerily as she snapped on the second glove. "Let's see... Cathy, is it? Right, well, we might as well get started, shall we?"

When it was done the doctor frowned, then nodded at Cathy's mother.

Sunday, Day Nineteen

"Let me out of here!" Genblade screamed in panic for the hundredth time, so much so that his throat was raw and bloody. "Don't you idiots realize what's happening?"

"Fire!" ordered Constable Lyle, as his men pumped Genblade full of tranquilizer darts, making the killer fade off to sleep.

"Idiots..." Genblade smiled, laughing slightly, before passing out on the concrete floor.

Cathy sat on Xander's bed as he fiddled with the internals of his computer, sending sparks flying every few minutes as he tried to ground himself from frying his hard drive with static electricity. "Damn carpeted floors..." he mumbled, fumbling with his tiny screw driver.

Sweat was pouring down the girl's brow almost as much as the rain outside was beating against Xander's window. "Rain keeping you in?" she asked, almost absent-mindedly, not really caring about the response.

"The rain alone wouldn't, no," Xander grunted, kissing a burn on his finger. "But I tired the Womb out by forcing it to keep going for, oh, six or seven days. So, if I go out there right now, I'd probably freeze to death or die of hypothermia or something."

She nodded, although she had no clue what he had just said. She could hear little else outside of the rain pouring down. "What are you doing?" she sighed, as another spark flew toward her.

"Trying to get my sound card up and running, not that it'll ever actually happen. Fuck," he cursed, as an electrode snapped beneath his nail. "There goes another one," the Womb growled, stretching inside him, wanting to get out. It seemed the closer he got to Cathy, the more excited it became. He furrowed his brow, confused by the way it had been acting around her lately. He looked at her

190

for the first time in over an hour. Her face had become white again, and she kept twitching and shuffling her hips, as if nervous or in pain. "Is something wrong with you?" he blurted, bluntly.

She turned to him, breaking her staring contest with the window. "Excuse me?!" she yelled angrily. "Rude much or what?"

"Sorry. I wouldn't have asked, but the Womb's acting up when I'm around you lately, and I just saw it as being kinda weird, is all."

She squinted at him, then tears began to fall down her cheeks. She collapsed onto Xander's pillow, and he immediately rushed to her side, trying his best to hold her. The Womb screamed. He ignored it.

"I'm sorry!" he exclaimed repeatedly, slapping himself upside the head. "There's nothing wrong with you! There's something wrong with me! I have someone living in my gut, seriously, can you believe anything I say?"

"Yes, there's something wrong with me..." she screamed, her face already red from tears and anger.

"No, sweetheart..."

"There is! I'm stupid, and ugly and..."

"No, honey, you're not... you're adorable and loveable and..."

"Pregnant!" she yelled, burying her face into his arms, her tears drenching his shirt.

You never know when your life is going to change, he thought, as he held her close, unable to speak from pure, unadulterated shock.

Thursday, Day Twenty-One

Tommy and Xander pushed back a set of leaves, making the branches creak until they broke and splintered. The two of them had met up a quarter mile back and had worked together since, trudging through the damp, marshy woods after the rain. They had yet to speak to each other, as both men considered speech to be a waste of energy that could be better-spent searching.

"Stop," Xander said, putting an arm out in front of Tommy, who came to an abrupt halt.

"Who made you boss, Serial?" Tommy scoffed, slapping Xander's arm away.

"Shut up," Xander groaned, looking down solemnly.

"Why should I?"

Xander didn't respond, and it took Tommy a moment to notice him crying, his tears joining the rainwater on the ground.

Raising an eyebrow, Tommy solemnly pulled back the brush a few feet in front of Xander, even though he knew what he'd find there.

Laying in a puddle of reddish mud and leaves was the beaten, broken and naked body of Kerri Walker, her arm missing and her bowels ripped open, exposing her insides.

"Gawd..." Tommy choked, as he and Xander collapsed into one another's arms and cried. "... I really thought we'd save her..."

CHAPTER SEVEN: THE END OF A GOLDEN AGE

Wednesday, Day Twenty-Two

The city wept.

Everywhere you looked, people were collapsing in the middle of the sidewalk as their grief overcame them. Some had not heard the news yet. When they were told, the wail that escaped from their lips was recognizable by all who heard it. It was the sound of innocence being lost, never to return. Stripped away, killed and raped in a dark forest.

Mike and Cathy held each other as they wept. Of everyone in the town, they had cause to -- more than anyone. It was not a good time to learn that he was going to bring life into this world, on a day when everyone was wondering if this earth was any place to raise a child.

Everyone was at school for a change. Xander, Julie, Tommy, Mike, Cathy... everyone. For once, there was nowhere better to go. There was no place where you could run to escape the pain, the sense that something beautiful had been stolen away from you. The knowledge that evil won out over good again. Not a word was spoken in the halls, only tears were shed and glances exchanged. Strangers patted each other on the back, trying their best to console each other and themselves, as Principal Snyder and Dr. Warren O'Toole patrolled the hallways, trying to help the student body in any way they could. No detention slips were given for punching lockers, fighting, or even graffiti. They all understood that these people were just taking it harder than others. That maybe they'd known the girl, or known someone who had.

Even the Tees cried. They stood in a circle, twenty men from all walks of life, bowing their heads in hours-long silent prayer for the soul of Kerri Walker. Their warehouse was again darkened, but candles erupted through the darkness now, as they fought to remain hopeful. Maybe, just maybe, they would get their shot at whoever committed this horrible act. Because vengeance is not just a word. It is a living, breathing thing that will not go unfed. It will–

Three straight lines were torn in the wall of the Tees' hideout, and they all gasped and shook as they turned to look. Daylight poured in, interrupted only by the movement of their attacker, just beyond their sight.

The wall was opened into a rough sphere, enough for it to step through, to the horror of all those within.

It hunched over on all fours. Completely black and shimmering, its inhumanly large muscles flexing erratically, its great chest inhaled and exhaled with massive bursts of oxygen, enough even that its breath could be mistaken for a strong gale by someone who did not know the difference. It had just three fingers on each hand, if they could be called that. They were more like jointed claws that sprung off of his palms, the inside track of which was even edged like a razor. Tentacles danced around its body in every direction, some even looked to be fighting with each other as they snapped about, like a lizard's tongue tasting the air for fresh scent. Its eyes were blood red and so dark that they were almost impossible to distinguish from its skin. The teeth were the worst, though. Protruding from where its lips should be, it had both a massive over-bite and under-bite, making the entire lower portion of its face nothing but row upon row of teeth.

It sniffed the air twice, then looked at all of them cowering and afraid to move. It began to growl.

"It's the Womb..." someone whispered in a hushed voice.

The creature sniffed again. There was a scent here that it had been following, the scent of another creature like itself. The other one had been here, weeks ago, but to its nostrils it was like yesterday. Its eyes darted from side to side, taking in every terror-filled face before it, and regarding each with as much dignity as a normal man would the food at an all-you-can-eat buffet.

Chad slowly pulled a gun from his leather duster, and a slow smirk slid over his dry, cracked lips. He wanted this. From the moment he'd heard about the body yesterday, he'd wanted this. The chance to kill something. Anything. To watch its blood bubble up to meet air and quietly trickle to the ground before coagulating and becoming hard, like a plug. He'd watched three people die in his life; the first was on his very first night as a Tee, when he was fifteen. But none of them would ever look or smell as good as this one.

Others knew better. Ian Char had faced the thing, which was now staring at them and sizing each one of the Tees up for dinner, before. He had lived to tell about it, to add to the hushed whispers in the alleys and side-streets, and contribute to the fearful tales of those who'd seen the darkness before. He touched the scar on the side of his face, still pink from over a month ago. The Womb had dragged him into the darkness, stopping him from killing a young girl, and ripped at his flesh to make him bleed. There hadn't even been time to scream or to see what was coming. There was only the sureness of death, and the sickening, hollow pain that came when he did not die. People who've had near-death experiences and claimed to be better for it were full of crap, Ian knew. In reality, you spend every day like a walking, talking corpse, waiting for death to find you. With a shaken gulp, Ian closed his eyes and waited, knowing that his wait was finally over.

The majority of them, however, felt the way Quinton Travers did, as he pulled out a long dagger, grasping it tightly in his hand and rubbing his thumb over the edge of the blade. Quinton felt vindicated, as if this thing had been brought here for a reason. The fear melted away as quickly as it came, and all that was left was the overwhelming need for vengeance. For themselves, for Kerri, for everything. He smiled devilishly, locking eyes with the beast and licking his lips. "Come on, boys," he said, his southern accent abundant. "We got us some killin' to do."

As if on cue, the beast attacked them, leaping with all the power contained within its hind legs, as if catapulted into the sky by some invisible force. They all watched as the thing silently flew through the air, their heads circling to see where it would land, like an audience watching a man being shot from a cannon at the circus. It landed in the center of the circle they had formed, and for the briefest of moments, some of them rejoiced, thinking that they had it surrounded.

With inhuman speed it lashed out, jumping again the second it hit the ground. It leapt straight up, grabbing onto either side of one man's hips and digging his claws in deep, breaking three ribs and puncturing the liver, both kidneys, and the appendix. Blood started to fill all four organs immediately, and soon it would be spilling over into others and onto the floor. The man screamed as the others around him backed away and nearly jumped out of their skins. The monster roared, and as it did, slobber escaped from its mouth and splashed onto its victim's face.

Behind the demon, Travers snarled. "Shoot him, you morons!" he yelled, waving at Chad and the others.

Three of them pulled out handguns and started to fire, emptying round after round into the thing's back. It did not flinch, even as chunks of its flesh spray-painted the wall behind it a sickly black. It ignored the bullets as if they were not even there. Instead, it opened its mouth wide. For a moment, nothing seemed to happen. More Tees fired, but still nothing happened, and the sound of gunfire made everyone's ears ring, so it was like there wasn't even any sound. It was like watching a silent movie, and that made it even scarier. There was no sound to evoke emotion, to tell you how to feel about what you saw. Only the raw, true sickness of life. With that, the demon's jaw bone popped out of place with two hard snaps, like a baseball bat connecting with a ball for the first time, and buckling a little under the strain. A small amount of black liquid mixed with its drool as its broken jaw lowered, expanding as it went, like an elastic with a weight on one end. Within moments, it was half the length of an average man's body. The demon lunged forward, as its victim silently screamed, forcing half of the victim's body into its mouth. It raised its head, and like a humanoid anaconda, let the body slide down its throat. It stopped just below the pelvis, biting hard and letting each leg topple uselessly to the ground. Its jaw returned to its normal size, shrinking back like the monster was winding it in from behind. Then it licked its lips with a long, slobbering, forked tongue, and turned to face the rest of them.

As one, the remaining Tees turned to run for the back exit. Anyone who had glanced back in time to see would swear that they saw the creature smile.

It let out another massive leap, landing on the back of one man and driving him into the ground, his face smashing against the concrete as the monster's toe-claws burrowed into the back of his skull, then retracted, leaving brain matter on the bottom of its foot. It reached out to one side and grabbed another, pulling him close and biting off his head before the boy could even manage a scream. Blood squirted upward as his heart continued to pump in the still-twitching body. Tentacles lashed out, whipping at another two Tees' feet, cutting off all four feet with the sharpened ends and leaving them to scream and try to crawl for the exit, not realizing that they would bleed out long before they reached it.

The rest of them got out the back way, slamming the door shut behind them as if that would slow it down. Calmly, it sliced through the door and stepped out through. One man had tripped and fallen and was trying to clamber his way back up when he turned and saw the beast looming over him. He closed his eyes and waited for it. It lingered for a moment, then bent down. Suddenly, it stopped. It sniffed the air twice, then turned its head to the east.

Off in the distance, almost beyond sight, was Coral Beach High School.

It pivoted on a dime and started sprinting in a bee-line straight for it on all fours, kicking up dirt as it bolted across the road, disappearing between two buildings, leaving the fallen Tee to scramble to his feet and take off in a mad dash for safety.

⋏⟨⟩⋏

"Xander?" she called out, her voice tiny and weak.

He smiled at the mere sound of it, though he did not understand why. He turned to see Julie, her hands clasped together at her pelvis, head down, looking like a child waiting to be scolded. And yet, she had a smile on her face, as she always did, somehow. She was wearing a plaid shirt and matching skirt, with high stockings and white gloves. Dressing as a Catholic school girl was probably the most polar-opposite thing she could have worn considering her personality and yet he found it looked good on her. Amazing, actually. He scratched his head, trying to recall the last time he'd noticed what a girl was wearing and had actually cared. "Hey, Julie. How are you?"

She bit her lip, tilting her head to one side, then the other, as if weighing out her life to decide how to respond. "Pretty good, all things considered," she said, finally. "I'm kinda freaked, though. I mean, I know this sounds awful, but it's not even the fact that all these things happened to this poor girl, y'know?"

Xander nodded, reached out and stroking the side of her arm. "I know. It's not awful."

"All I can think about is, like, what if that had been Mandy or Cathy or someone?" she continued, as they both moved over to the wall and sat against it.

"Or you?" he furthered, smiling at her.

"Is that selfish?" she admitted, gritting her teeth for what she expected would be a mean, and therefore truthful, response.

"Not at all. In fact, that was pretty much all I could think of at the time too."

"Worried about Cathy? She is going through a lot."

"No," he frowned, shaking his head. "I was more worried about you."

She looked at him, her face unsure of whether to be happy or puzzled, but settling on both.

"Even when I found that body, I couldn't help but think of everything that's been done to you. Phillips, Derek, everything. I guess... I guess when I was out there, looking, I had time to think about all that. Time I didn't have before. And I guess I realized how much of a big deal it is that you trust anyone, let alone

195

me," he looked down, clenching his fists. "You wanna talk selfish? I didn't even care about that girl, or whether I found her alive or not. It was more about saving you, or Cathy, or..."

"Sara," she nodded, taking his hand and making it relax instantly.

"Yeah. And now I gotta wonder if that's why she died. I already blame myself so much, now I have to deal with the fact that maybe, subconsciously, because I didn't care enough, because my mind wasn't in the game, I didn't stop this on purpose. Maybe I should've been out looking for her killer, maybe I should have just stayed home and helped you and Cathy..."

"Shh," she soothed, wrapping her arms around his head and pulling it to her chest, stroking the back of his neck. "I'm safe. Cathy's safe. It's all gonna be okay."

Suddenly, Xander's body lunged, shaking in Julie's arms. The true womb fired up, screaming one undeniable instinct into his brain and burning it there in letters ten feet high: hide. Not fight, not run...just hide. The urge was so great that it took all his strength of will just to keep himself from transforming right there in her arms. "No," he gulped, swallowing back blood, bile, and blackness that was rising in his throat. "Nothing's ever going to be okay again."

ʎ⟨ʎ

Cathy and Mike were both still crying, holding each other in their arms. Everyone that passed them was ignoring them. They knew that their grief was different, that there was more, but there was no use to trying to help. "How could this have happened?" Mike choked, swallowing hard. "I mean, we used protection... didn't we?... We used a condom..."

She frowned, nodding, the tears shaking from her chin. "They're not one hundred percent, remember? What Miss Hall used to say? Only abstinence is one hundred percent."

"Don't lecture me," he snapped, biting his lip.

"I didn't... at least, I didn't mean to," she pleaded, her face turning the same red as her cheeks.

"I don't need this. I don't. And how long have you known?"

"Days. Mom knew first, though. I just didn't know how to tell you. I was even going to try and get Xander to do it."

"Xander knew!?" he yelled, clenching a fist , then letting it go as fast as it had. He stopped, calming himself, then looked her squarely in the eye, his voice almost malicious. "Am I the father?"

"What?" she squealed, her voice barely human through her tears.

"Am I the father?"

"How can you even ask me that? Who else would it be?"

"Oh, I dunno," he shrugged sarcastically, rolling his eyes at her, demeaning her. "He's short, stupid, a super-hero, and his last name is the past tense of 'draw.' Who do you think? He's got all these powers, maybe one of them is super-sperm?" he curled his lip, giving her a look of pure disgust. "Or maybe you didn't even make him wear one, hmm? Can't get enough of that dark and mysterious skin, right?"

"You are the only person I've ever been with!" she pleaded, grabbing him by the pant leg and practically begging at his feet now. "You're the only person I ever loved!"

"Is this how you treated Grendel?" Mike yelled, not even turning to face her as he stormed off toward the stairs in rage, "because if you did, let's give the poor guy the good boyfriend of the year medal."

"Michael!" she screamed, getting up and running after him frantically.

Suddenly, the wall beside her was gone.

There was no warning, no screams, no sounds of cracking plaster for five minutes beforehand like in the movies, just the crash and the sudden feeling of debris smashing against her head and body, forcing her to the ground, then the sounds of screams as everyone ran.

Mike turned, sweat already pouring down his face. He could see nothing at first, then the dust began to settle. At first, all he saw was Cathy, the love of his life, barely breathing under a cover of plaster and concrete.

Then he saw what stood over her.

It took a step forward, and the ground shook, cracks forming in the floor. Its teeth were disproportionately massive, even compared to its huge body, with muscles that normal anatomy books hadn't even discovered yet. The claws on its feet tapped against the ground it stood on, like a normal person tapping his fingers as he decided what to order at a restaurant. It sniffed the air twice, despite the fact that it had no nose. All in all, the thing looked like Black Womb on steroids, a notion that made Mike shiver in fear. "Zakron," he whispered, and the name wasn't funny. It was terrifying. Looking up at this monster, Mike suddenly felt a great swell of pity for any criminal that ever had to look up and see Xander come at them.

The creature turned toward Mike suddenly, like a dog whose name had just been called. It leapt, pushing both hands and feet against Mike's body and forcing him against a locker. The metal door bent in and broke, leaving the shards to dig into the boy's back, drawing blood immediately.

"Argh!" he screamed.

As soon as he did, Cathy moved, as if his cry had given her new life. She slowly pushed the debris off her back and stood, stumbling a little as she limped toward the beast. "Leave him alone!" she ordered, but her voice shook almost as violently as her body as she struggled to hold her own arm in place.

Zakron looked at her for a moment, its eyes dancing over her. Again it sniffed twice, then grunted, stepping back a pace, almost as though it was afraid. For a split second, Cathy thought that maybe simply standing her ground would scare it off, like a dog with more bark than bite.

Then it lashed out, slapping her across the mid-section with one violent blow, sending her sailing through the air. She landed on her side in the middle of the stairwell, her body cracking loudly and going limp. She bounced once, like a ball, then rolled the rest of the way to the bottom of the stairs, hitting the far wall and not moving again.

"Murderer!" Mike yelled from behind the killer.

It turned just in time for Mike's fist to connect with its face.

Again, the creature did not even flinch.

Mike pulled back to punch again, his face livid with anger.

This time, Zakron caught the fist in mid air. The beast twisted it sharply, forcing Mike's elbow to pop out of place, then held him up by it, exposing the boy's side. One swift motion with his other hand opened him up, spilling blood onto the floor.

It sniffed the air again, turning to the south and growling, then leapt out the hole it had created in the wall.

Mike lay there a long moment, not knowing whether he should try to move or not. Cathy was dead, he was sure of it. He'd seen a lot of people hurt and killed in his short life, and by this time he knew what a person looked like when they were just unconscious and when they were dead. The subtle differences in how they fell and rolled, the way their eyes looked. Even the color of their skin changes. It alters in tint just a little. Blood gushed out of his mouth and his side, his wounds stinging from the urine that was escaping him, as he lay there and wished for death.

"Mike!" Xander yelled, and it sounded like he was underwater. "Mike, what happened!?" he demanded, kneeling next to his friend and turning him over, only then noticing the slice going up his side. "Oh my god."

"Dead..." Mike mumbled, blood gurgling out of his throat until he feared he might choke on it. He prayed that coppery tang would not be the last sensation he experience before death.

"You're not dead, Mike," Xander frowned, snapping his fingers before his friend's eyes. "Now, tell me what happened here!"

"Cathy's dead..."

Xander's eyes grew wide as he looked past Mike, and saw Cathy's limp body crumpled at the bottom of the stairs, not breathing. Not moving. He turned toward the gaping hole in the wall just inside to see Zakron disappear into the woods that led to the penitentiary. "Oh no you don't," he snarled as he pulled out a knife and sliced open his own wrist, letting darkness seep out and work its way over his entire body.

"Black Womb lives."

CHAPTER EIGHT: ANTI-WOMB

"No, no, no, no..." Genblade repeated over and over again, as he paced back and forth in his cell, scratching at the rash that had formed around the flesh where the tranquilizer darts had dug into him. "This is how it starts. You take one. When they find it, they'll grieve. They'll go to old habits. He's watched them. He knows what they'll do, where they'll go, where they'll be, that's how he'll take them out. Womb doesn't know. Why hasn't he come? Why not ask for help? Moron. Moron! Doesn't he understand what this is? What it'll do to him and everyone else around him? He should kill them all now and save them the pain. Hell, even I'd do that much," he wiped the sweat from his brow, then looked up at his window suddenly, then turned back toward the hall. "You're here, aren't you?"

Adam Genblade stayed silent then, positioning his feet and hands into a fighting stance, determined not to go down without a fight.

He heard it then, far away. It seemed like miles off, like some battle being fought on the distant horizon that was no worry to him. He heard the gunshots and the pounding of the steel doors followed by the slow creak as they buckled. He heard screams. Horrible, blood-curdling screams, the kind that he used to inflict on a daily basis. He recognized the tactics... the forwardness of it. There was no emotion to it, no stopping to gloat or even speak. It was efficiency, nothing more, nothing less. The Anti-Womb was a far more effective killing machine than he, Spider, or even Black Womb. Or all of them combined, really.

A guard squashed up against the bars of his cell, sending spurts of red liquid from his mouth and ears before bouncing to the floor. He'd been thrown; he was dead before he even hit the bars. Genblade didn't move, did not so much as twitch even as Zakron stepped forward, breathing heavily from the lust of the kill.

"Always knew I'd go down in a good brawl," Genblade laughed, smiling a little with his toothy grin.

Black Womb rounded the curb, the penitentiary finally coming into sight. His black, scaled muscles tensed and relaxed with every step, shimmering brightly in the morning sun. His eyes were bright and red, darting from side to side at all times, marking everything around him and instinctively taking note of it. His claws were out, ready to strike at any moment. He was about to transform into the Xander Drew guise when he saw the two front doors ripped apart and realized how unnecessary it was. Before he even reached the entrance of shredded metal, he knew every guard inside was dead.

He stepped inside and the stench was overwhelming: the smell of bowels and bladders spilling their contents in the seconds after death. There were ten of them in the main hall alone, some were missing arms, others missing heads. It looked like something out of a Stephen King novel, the way they were arranged like the way a hamster arranges the things in its cage. The entire floor was a puddle of blood and urine that was almost a centimeter deep, but it may as well have been ten feet high, because within his second skin, Xander felt like he was bathing in it. *All this time... almost a month now, I could have stopped this... and didn't. And look who's paying the price. Cathy, Mike, and all these cops... this ends here, my idiot little cousin. You think you can stop me by growling and flashing your claws? You're up against the Reality TV generation, man. Time to play rough.*

He turned the corner to go down the hall toward the holding cells and almost smiled. Genblade's cell was wide open, ripped off of its hinges. *I'd like to see you beat me and Adam, freak. You're in for it now.*

Black Womb entered Genblade's cell just in time to see Zakron rip the copper pipe from the wall of the room, and swing it so fast that neither man could see it, let alone react to it. As water spilled everywhere, drenching all three of them, the pipe dug into Genblade's gut, forcing its way in. Immediately, blood started pouring out of him, the pipe keeping the wound perfectly round and open. It was like seeing blood put on tap. A normal person would be dead within seconds. He gave Genblade ten minutes, at most.

Genblade turned toward Xander, mouthing something indiscernible, then hit the floor with a splash.

The water came down like rain, like tiny explosions upon them both. For a moment, they just stood there. Each of them looked at the other, like seeing a fun house reflection of themselves. Polar opposite, yet with so much in common. So different that they were the same.

Suddenly, Xander felt a pang in his gut. He looked down to see that Zakron's hand was inside of him. He could feel the monster's claws wrapping around his intestines, swirling them around its claws before yanking hard, pulling them into view. "Arrh!" the Womb yelled, his entire body spraying in all directions. He hadn't even seen the blow coming, hadn't noticed the lunge. Nothing was that fast. It wasn't possible.

He felt an impact against his head, and opened his eyes in time to see the concrete wall coming at him. Again, he felt the trauma as his brain rattled back and forth inside his skull, and everything was black except for a few stars that shone brightly in the corners of his eyes. He felt something snap inside his mouth, and he swallowed one of his massive, sharp teeth. Deep inside him, he felt the womb push hard, then again... then finally give up, relaxing. As the black ooze started to melt off of him, and the face of Xander Drew started to become visible, he turned to look at Genblade, who was as good as dead on the floor. Then he looked at Zakron, standing there and waiting for its prey to fall while it remained untouched. *We didn't even get one blow in.* He almost laughed, defeated, as his knees gave out and he hit the ground, his eyes rolling back into his head.

Xander swallowed hard, a large glob of blood traveling down his throat.

He had to swallow at least once every few seconds, or the red fluid spraying from the artery in the roof of his mouth would start to flow out past his lips. His eyes were foggy and he tried desperately to hold his guts inside of him, his throbbing intestine threatening to spill out onto the floor.

Blackness was melting off of him, dripping onto the dull concrete floor. Blood flowed by his feet, hurrying to a drain in the center of the room.

His head weaving back and forth from exhaustion and dizziness, he managed to hazard a glance toward the officers that lay around him. Some were missing limbs. The rest were missing heads. He felt their blood wash past his feet, and as he did, his eyes went to another victim.

As he felt himself slipping away, he looked up at the hulking mass of flesh which had done all of this, and his eyes filled with a new terror at the renewed sight of the squirming form of black flesh and teeth and claws.

Uttering one last attempt at breath, Xander fell, his body crashing to the floor and his eyes rolling back into his head. His last thought was wondering how he'd let this sneak up on him. How he'd let his entire world come crashing down around his ears, when he'd had so long to stop it...

No!

No!

"No!" he screamed, pushing against the cold, wet floor with both hands, flipping himself upward as he willed the ooze to wrap back around his skull. He jumped back to his feet, twirling once and kicking Zakron square in the mid-section, sending the beast back a step. It grunted, staring at him as if he'd done something wrong. "I do not go out like this!" he screamed, lashing out with his claws and raking them against his enemy's face. To his relief, he drew blood. But it was gone in a moment, as the wounds healed over even faster than he had made them, the blood soaking into the creature's flesh and reintegrating itself into its form.

I drew blood, Xander thought, wanting to throw a parade for himself on that fact alone. *You can be hurt, which means you can be killed. All I need is the time to figure out how.*

He flipped backward, kicking Zakron in the chin with both feet. He landed on his hands and then flipped again, until he was out in the hall. "Hey, Zach!" he yelled tauntingly, cupping his hands over his mouth for effect. "Your mother was Molly!"

The Anti-Womb's brow slanted. It did not comprehend the words, but their meaning was all too clear. Even an animal knows when it's being mocked. It took a step forward, then another, quicker, and leapt at Xander with its teeth and claws outstretched.

Quickly, Xander pulled the broken door to Genblade's cell in front of him. Zakron slammed against it, breaking off three of its teeth. It snarled as it tried to force its way through, its slobbering tongue seeping through the bars, trying to get at him. Just to get a taste.

There was a groan of metal, and the Womb's red eyes became wide with fear until they were almost spherical. The iron bars were giving way under the power of Zakron's great jaws. Its teeth were cutting through the metal.

Plan B! Xander thought promptly, forcing his feet against the cage and pushing back with all his strength, sending both Zakron and the cell door flying backward into the wall.

"Zaaa-Kroan!" the creature bellowed, so loud that the walls seemed to shake. It batted the door away as if it were a fly, getting to its feet and looking around to see if it could find Xander. It turned left, then right, but the boy was nowhere in sight. It growled and shuffled, sniffing at the air. The water still pouring down from the broken pipe made it impossible for it to get a good lead on the scent of its prey. It turned its head up and barked twice, its Adam's apple bobbing rhythmically as it tried to use its incredible ears like a bat's sonar.

Again, nothing.

It grunted, bending down until it was almost on all fours again, scratching at the ground with its massive claws.

"Hey, numb-nuts," came a scratchy, deep-throated voice from behind. It turned, and as soon as it did, it felt an enormous pressure on its mouth and throat, followed by the taste of metal and another taste it did not recognize. The Womb smiled, savoring the moment before turning the valve to the fire hose.

Immediately, hundreds of tons of water pressure forced its way down Zakron's throat, forcing him back against the far wall.

It won't kill him, Xander had to remind himself, to keep him from getting too ahead of himself. *I can survive without breathing through my nose and mouth, it's a safe bet he can too. But it might slow him down for a-*

Zakron reached up with one blurred motion, cutting the fire hose just below the valve, then swallowed the nozzle and whatever else was in his mouth at the time, letting out a loud burp. Urine trickled down its leg and it got up, shaking, spraying everything around it with water, like a wet canine.

Plan C... Xander thought, as the creature charged at him again, as silent as ever. He ducked, diving out of his adversary's path, and rolling along the ground, coming up on his feet and breaking into an immediate run. *Gawd, what I wouldn't give for a plan 'C' right about now.* He turned to look over his shoulder, only to see Zakron right behind him, and gaining fast. *Can't stay in here... he's too big. He's got too much room on me in such an enclosed area. I've gotta get him outside.*

He turned the corner on his heel, Zakron nipping at his ankles as he leapt for the exit, rolling against the dirt and gravel outside, smudging it against his shimmering hide. People turned, awestruck, unable to move as the two monsters squared off, turning to look at each other like gunslingers in some old western. *This is it. This isn't an enemy that can be reasoned with. Only one of us is coming out of this alive... but so help me, if I go down, you'll choke on me and die yourself, you sadistic bastard. No way are you living, not after what you did to that girl...*

Zakron leapt high, but this time Xander made no effort to dodge the attack. Instead, as the public watched in horror, he leapt as well, and the two equal and opposite forces met head on.

Paramedics arrived at Coral Beach High school as students huddled together, trying to make sure their friends were okay. Nobody paid much attention as Julie and Mike cried, looming over but afraid to touch the broken, beaten body of Catherine Kennessy.

"Get out of the way!" one paramedic screamed, waving for both of them to move. Julie jumped up right away, but Mike stayed there, still as a marble statue and looking down at the woman he loved as blood poured from his body, but he paid it no mind. It was of no consequence to him.

He was pushed out of the way and backed up a few steps silently, as two men laid a stretcher out between him and his love. They hoisted her up onto it, and immediately the clean, white sheet turned to dark red. Blood seeped out from between her legs, and she did not move. Never once did she move. He reached out and touched her hand, and it was chilled, her lips blue.

Soft

Lime
Tender
Moist
Wet

          stop.

"She's so cold," he said in a hollow voice, as he watched them wheel her away into the back of an ambulance. Julie slowly walked up behind him, reaching out and grasping his hand, then wrapping both arms around him, bawling into his shirt. He turned to her, surprised that she was there, having not noticed her before. He stroked the back of her head, his stare falling past her to the rubble at their feet. "Should we get her a blanket?"

CHAPTER NINE: ZAKRON

Black Womb hit the pavement, which buckled up and folded beneath his weight. Blood shot out of his mouth through the artery that had ripped itself open moments ago, splashing against a nearby car windshield. His head knocked back, and he felt the blinding pain of his neck breaking, then immediately healing itself again. It was like feeling it break twice, and as splotches of light dotted his vision and he lost control of his limbs, he momentarily cursed his healing factor for letting him live. Glass protruded from his right eye as his healing factor slowly worked it out. Strangely, he could still see out of that eye, but it was like looking through a prism. It looked like there were ten enemies, ten Zakrons. For a moment, the notion petrified him. *Nothing's ever hit me that hard*, he realized as he tried to move, but found that his body didn't want to obey him yet. His leg twitched once, and that was the most he got. *Not Genblade, not Blackheart... nothing. Not even the explosion that leveled the Engen building hit me that hard.* "Hey, ass-wipe..." he coughed, gurgling blood, "Is that the best you... got? |..."

And for the first time since my mother made the mistake of teaching me to talk, I'm speechless. It's just standing there, waiting for me to attack. Waiting for me to strike again, so it can knock me on my ass again. It's not even trying to kill me, it's just batting me around, like a cat with a mouse.

So what do I do when some big bastard sits there and waits for me to hit him?

Oblige.

The Womb pushed off of the ground, leaping to his feet again, then crouching down until his body was like a coiled spring, letting go and zipping through the air like a bullet with his claws extended. He connected with Zakron's face, sending both creatures sprawling backward into a roll. Xander dug his talons deep into his enemy's skull, pulling as hard as he could, trying to rip the behemoth's face off. They rolled more, and Xander shut his eyes, screaming with effort as he tried to tear off a chunk of flesh. When he opened them, Zakron was on top of him, smirking.

Oh... fuck.

It raised a giant arm, slamming it down on Xander's skull, driving it into the ground.

-SLAM!-

-SLAM!-

-SLAM!-

Again and again, it beat on him, forcing its weight upon him, until it grabbed him around the neck and slung him to one side. His body smashed through the windshield of a car and landed in the front seat, bouncing against the comfortable leather. "No, that's all right everyone. No need to thank me," he groaned in a small, whiney voice. "What's that Jenna Jameson? You have a twin sister? Well, if you think she'd like to join, I won't object..."

He tilted his head up, looking around. Slowly, a wry grin spread over his lips as he saw the keys dangling in the ignition, jingling against the steering wheel. *About time I got a little luck,* he thought, sitting up in the driver's side of the Beetle and revving the engine, shifting gears into drive. *I've thrown everything I've got, and you've kept coming. Now, I'll throw everything I can find.*

Slamming his foot to the accelerator, the car sputtered to life and started forward, bouncing over detritus material and wasted lamp posts, aiming straight for Zakron. "Now, you son of a bitch!" the Womb yelled, slapping the steering wheel. "Reap the whirlwind!"

Zakron reached up, coming down upon the car with a giant claw, slicing into the hood and right down through the frame. The car continued forward under its momentum, being sliced right down the middle like a tin can, splitting on either side so that neither half even touched its intended target. When the dust cleared, Zakron was standing exactly where he had been, except now he was holding Black Womb by the neck, slowly squeezing it, forcing pressure into his skull until eventually his head would pop like a grape. It growled, and the sound was almost like the purr of a cat. As Xander choked on his own blood, he realized that this thing was happy.

Xander grunted, shifting within the creature's massive grip, pulling at its fingers with his claws, swinging back and kicking it in the chest. "Hey, precious," he whistled, fighting for the creature's very limited attention. "Wanna see a trick?" He opened his mouth wide, biting down on Zakron's thumb with all the power in his jaw, snapping it off. The creature howled, loosening its grip until Xander fell to the ground, spitting out the appendage. "Yeah!" he screamed triumphantly, turning and walking a few steps away to where a broken street light lay. "You like that, huh? Is that the way it felt for her, I wonder? Are you even feeling a fraction of the fear that she felt, you half-wit? Lemme tell you somethin'," he chuckled, straining a little as he picked up the long, metal pole. "Your pain is just beginning. I'm gonna give you everything you've dealt out in spades, baby!" He turned with a sick grin, holding up the lamp like a baseball bat, ready to connect it with Zakron's head.

Zakron's claw connected with his gut, sinking deep inside, squirming around inside of him again, jiggling at his internals. He dropped the lamp-post to the ground with a sharp clang, the agony steaming out of every pore on his face, his every muscle becoming as tense and strained as stone.

"If you can't fight fair..." the Womb gagged, blood running from his lips.

Quickly, he reached down, his claws digging into the demon's groin and pulling up, slicing straight to its chest.

"Argbda!" it yelled, tossing Xander again and smashing him into the side of the glass office building behind them.

"I'll bet you say that to all the girls, you handsome devil, you," Xander hacked, glass falling out of his body as he again picked up the lamp post. Swinging it high above his head, he brought it down across Zakron's back, knocking it to the ground with a thump. *He hit the ground!* Xander screamed inside his own head, as he drew back and hit the creature again, this time across the face, shattering the lamp bulb into its cheek and sending it onto its back. In his head, audiences were applauding him, like a runner sliding into home base at the bottom of the ninth. He drew back again, his smirk a mile long. Suddenly, tentacles grew out of its back, eight of them stretching up and catching the pole in mid-air. "Oh, come on..."

It lifted the pole high, taking Xander with it on the opposite end, then slammed it into the glass wall of the office building, sending millions of shards of broken glass deep into Xander's body, puncturing a lung and his heart all at once. Glass hit the ground with the slow, steady twinkling of raindrops, followed by the slump of Xander's beaten body.

Moaning, he forced himself to his feet, turning slowly to see Zakron calmly walking toward him, untouched. Unharmed. *Fuck this,* Xander thought as the Womb burned the word 'hide' into his skull again. Only this time, he listened. He scrambled to his feet and started to run for home, the glass digging further and further into his feet with every step, but he didn't care. *I've got to get away. This is insanity. I'm no good to anyone dead, and it's not going to bring Cathy or Mike or Genblade back to life if I get myself killed. There's got to be a better way than this. It's like this thing knows me, knows my every move, my every instinct...*

From behind him, Xander heard a woman's scream. He turned to see Zakron, standing right where he'd left him, holding up a girl no more than fifteen. It smiled wickedly with that big, toothy grin of his. *And so help me, it knows exactly what to do to reel me back in.*

"Hey!" the Womb yelled, jumping onto the hood of a car and using its momentum to force him onto the side of a nearby building, ricocheting off of it toward the ground, until he was again within ten feet of the Anti-Womb, looking straight into the eyes of death. "Our first date isn't even over, and already you're cheating. I knew mother was right about you..."

Zakron grunted passively, throwing the girl into the air.

"No!" Xander yelled, as the girl flew toward the sharp, metal wreckage of the Beetle he'd tried to drive. He leapt forward, diving out with both arms, retracting his claws as fast as he could, closing his eyes in fear. He felt an impact on both forearms, and opened his eyes long enough to see the girl in his arms before he slammed back-first into the wreck.

"Thank you..." the girl stammered, recoiling in fear of her savior.

"Just get out of here!" he yelled at her, sprouting his claws again. He turned, watching as Zakron slowly walked toward him with a macho strut, almost gloating. Xander laughed as he felt something trickle by his feet, an odd smell filling the air and making him want to vomit even more than he already did. *I wish he'd talk*, Xander thought, squinting and sizing up his enemy as the distance between them lessened, *I wish he'd gloat or call me names or something. The silence is deafening.* "This is where you get off," he said simply, striking his claw against what was left of the car's metal frame, creating a spark that traveled slowly to the pavement, igniting the gasoline that was pooled in a small pot-hole there.

Black Womb's head was lodged against the remains of a street sign, his body broken and sprawled in several different directions, like a bent compass. He opened his eyes, and the light burned him almost as bad as the flame that had churned up around him, igniting his flesh. The blackness was melting off of him, and no amount of will power was going to bring it back now. After a beating like that, he wondered if it would ever come back again. "I got you," he breathed harshly, his throat raw from inhaling smoke and fire. "I got you..."

He chuckled, slowly sitting up to look around. There was fire everywhere. After he'd lit the gas, there had been at least two more explosions from nearby cars, slinging his body in one direction after another. But the pain would heal. His bones would knit. All that mattered now, was that he'd-

"No," he whispered in shock, as a form stepped through the smoke in front of him, walking over the flame as if it were nothing. Again, Zakron was looking down at him, unscathed. "It's not possible."

"Zaaa-Kroan!" it bellowed, opening its monolithic jowls.

"Right, then," Xander nodded, getting to his feet as the last bit of blackness dripped from his naked, bloody body. Scrapes and glass freckled his face and shoulders, and his left eye was swollen shut. Great patches of his hair and eyebrows were missing, having been burned off. His brain felt like it was boiling inside his skull, and he couldn't breathe. "Let's finish this, bitch. If you think you got what it takes."

All at once, he couldn't hear anything anymore. The flames around him started to dance and scatter away, until they were snuffed out completely. Xander looked around in confusion as a wind came from nowhere, swirling about with the force of a tornado. Zakron looked even more confused, batting debris that swirled around it as if they were its enemy. The sound like a rhythmic beating filled the air, as Xander recognized it, looking upwards just in time to see the clouds part, and a huge military helicopter descend from the sky. It hovered about twenty feet above the ground, and three cords came out of a hole in its underside. Three men, all of them wearing what resembled forest green scuba gear, slid down the ropes and landed gracefully on the ground. All three opened fire at Zakron, shooting darts into the demon's backside, and it went down in a slump. After nearly a half hour of battling it, Xander watched the thing go down with three darts.

"Obtain! Obtain!" yelled the lead scuba-man. There were yellow stripes on the side of his right arm. They all wore air tanks and dark goggles, showing none of their skin. They were muscular, but human in their movements and mannerisms.

"Hey!" Xander yelled, running up to the leader. "What the hell is going on here?"

"Classified, son," the commander nodded, putting an arm on Xander's shoulder. "Circe business. None of your concern. Thanks for keeping him in one place long enough for us to get a bead on him, though," he said gratefully, turning away to grab the rope and climb up as the other two loaded Zakron into the chopper.

"Hey!" Xander yelled again, grabbing the man by the arm and pulling him back down to earth. "Where do you think you're going? I've got a lot of questions, and I know you've got answers!"

"Sorry, kid," the man shrugged honestly, turning and firing a dart into Xander's gut. "Classified."

Xander fell to the ground, remaining there for a moment, unable to move. He was only able to watch the chopper pull back into the clouds and away from sight.

As soon as he could move again, he ran into the penitentiary and grabbed up the body of Adam Genblade, taking off for the nearest hospital.

CHAPTER TEN: FATHERHOOD

Xander watched, wrapped up in a blanket he'd been handed by a nurse as the doctors removed the last few slivers of pipe from Genblade's side.

He was in a coma, they said.

Extensive head trauma, his skull had been crushed. They said there was so much brain damage the man had little to no hope of ever waking up again. They said it was a fitting punishment, living death like that. He hadn't formed an opinion yet.

Shaking his head, he turned and walked into the next room where Cathy lay weakened on her hospital bed, as Mike spoon-fed her oddly colored Jell-O.

"The doctor says you should try to eat," Mike reminded her for the fifth time as she refused to so much as open her eyes, let alone her mouth.

"If the doctor says eat, then eat, Cat," Xander said flatly, trying not to show what he was feeling. Trying not to break down and cry. She was eating for one again, but she was all right, thank God. A few cracked ribs, a twisted ankle and a sprained wrist, but all things considered, they said she got off lucky.

They obviously never looked up the definition of the word.

The force of Zakron's throw had killed the young life inside her. Tears ran down her cheeks as she refused to eat, refused to move. She just sat there, clutching her gut, her face turning colors as the grief overcame her. Her mother and sister came in and told the boys to leave. They did.

Outside, Mike collapsed into Xander's arms as his spirit died, along with all the hopes and dreams of a young father.

EPILOGUE: THURSDAY, DAY TWENTY-THREE

The five of them sat in silence, nobody sure of what to say or how to react.

Cathy still sat in her hospital bed, her pillow soaked with tears and her sheets tinged with the blood of her child that was still leaking its way out from between her legs. She twitched. She hadn't spoken a word since it had happened, not even to her own mother. Her sister had yelled at her for overreacting, saying she should be glad to be rid of it anyway, that she should be thankful. Thankful that her child was dead before it had even gotten a chance to live, that she had nothing to remember it by, not even a picture or an ultrasound, nothing. In the last four months, Cathy had been raped, beaten, molested, assaulted, and tortured. But this was the first time, she thought, she'd ever known real pain.

Mike sat next to her, his hands laying on the bed, waiting for the moment when she would take them. When she would turn to him for comfort and love. The moment did not come, instead all he got were cool stares that put him in his place every few moments, that let him know where he stood and made him feel the same way she did inside. It was like his guts were about to turn over, and every second he was trying to stop himself from throwing up. All he wanted to do was cry, but he couldn't. He had to be strong – he had to fight this.

Julie was on Cathy's other side, stroking her hair soothingly, surprisingly silent. She knew that nothing she could say would make it better, nothing would take the pain away. She turned to look at Xander every few seconds, brooding in the corner, shooting him a pitiful smile. They both knew it was fake, its only purpose to try and get him to reciprocate it, which he never did.

Mandy sat in a chair and tried not to get noticed, her hood pulled over her head until it was almost invisible.

Why is it that no matter what happens, no matter how much good is done, there's always something horrible waiting to beat it down? Xander wondered, as he leaned against the corner, his arms crossed against his chest. *Cathy had just fought her way back from the abyss that Grendel and Phillips and the rest of them had tried to plunge her into. She'd just made herself strong, taken her first steps into her real life, her first love... only to have her feet kicked out from beneath her, by something that hurt her because my scent was on her. Four Tees are dead, a girl, thirteen civilians, and one unborn child. That brings the death toll for one event to nineteen. Personally, I don't want to stick around for round two. I'm sick of it.*

Is that the lesson? That no matter how hard I try to do good, it'll be those I love the most who pay the price? Sara died because I couldn't save her. I loved her more than anything, more than I ever will love anything again. I can still feel her touch, hear her laugh... and I can see so much of her in Julie. Is this the life that I'm promising her? Death, mayhem and destruction? Pain? When ghosts of the past can't even stay buried long enough to forget them, and only the pain remains to keep you warm at night?

I thought this part of it was over. I thought things were getting better. But now, Cathy and Mike have been hurt more than Sara or Julie ever could be. Their child is gone, and it's my fault, he thought, tears welling up in his eyes. *It's all-*

"...Mike's fault," he heard Mandy mumble, almost too low for even him to hear, with his enhanced sense of hearing.

Xander raised an eyebrow, stepping over to the girl discreetly. He scratched his head for a moment, then stroked his chin. "What was that?" he whispered, touching her gently on the shoulder.

She turned to him, frowning. "Nothing."

He smiled, giving her a playful tap on the cheek. "Come on, you can tell me."

She shook her head, shooting him an annoyed look. "It's all Mike's fault," she grumbled, glaring at the blond man weeping at his lover's feet.

Xander almost laughed, although it wasn't funny at all. "And how did you reach that conclusion?"

"That thing was after him. It wanted him, and it hurt Cathy to get to him. If Mike had just been normal, none of this would have happened."

"What are you talking about?"

She scoffed at him, curling her lip in disgust. "Don't play dumb with me," she accused, slapping him, "I know Mike's the Black Angel thing. I saw it."

Now, Xander did laugh, lightly. "I can tell you this, Mandy, Mike is not that Black monster."

"Yes he is!" she protested, a little too loud, through gritted teeth. "I saw it! I'm sure!"

There was a knock at the door and Xander sighed, getting up from his conversation with the girl to answer it.

"Hey," Tommy said, greeting Xander with a nod as he held up a bouquet of flowers. "I know you guys probably wanna be alone with her, so I figured I'd just drop these..."

"Come in, Tom," Xander smiled, opening the door and patting him on the back as he walked past.

Cathy looked up, seeing the arrangement of roses and daisies, two of her favorites. She still didn't speak, but for the first time in days, she smiled. The grin brought tears to Julie's eyes, and she turned and walked outside the room, feeling that nobody needed to see her break down.

Xander followed her, shutting the door behind them. Julie sat on the floor, her back against the wall, her eyes red and puffy.

"They all must think I'm so stupid," she sniffed, wiping her nose in her sleeve. "Cathy always hated me, we're not even friends, but look at me."

"Nobody thinks you're stupid," Xander sighed, sitting down next to her, his hand automatically clasping hers while his other wiped her tears away even as more came.

She sniffed hard, her body shaking from tears. "It's just hard to see anyone like that, you know? I mean, that could have been me, and I can't imagine."

"I know. Shh," he soothed, bringing her head to his shoulder and kissing the top of it lightly, stroking the side of her face.

"And then she smiled, and I couldn't take it anymore. It just means so much that she could even smile after something like that. I can barely smile thinking about it... and... mine... are... all... fake... and..." she stuttered, her throat raked with tears, then she sniffed and started again, "and when I smile it's still fake but hers was real and she's so amazing. How can she?"

He smiled, kissing her head again. "I'll never know," he responded honestly. "She's truly the strongest person I know. The best of all of us."

Julie nodded, wiping her tears in his collar. Her nostrils cleared a little, and she smelled his aftershave, smiling at the musty odor. "I get it now," she whispered to him as she calmed down.

"Hmm?" he asked, pulling her close and squeezing her, despite the pain it caused his cracked and bruised ribs. "Get what?"

"What you were talking about before. At Sara's grave, and before that thing came to the school. When you were talking about all the stuff that happened, and how you were worried about the people you love and everyone that died. I get it now, I understand. I know why you have to try and help, why you need to save everyone. It's not some stupid macho trip or anything, it's... it's Cathy's smile. When Tommy brought in those flowers, he was the hero. Because even though all that awful stuff happened to her, he made her smile. And it was the most beautiful thing I've ever seen. It was amazing."

Xander was silent for a moment, still stoking the side of her face, "Wow," he said after a moment.

"What?" she asked, jumping out of his arms a little. "Am I wrong? If I am, I'm so sorry..."

"No," he laughed, pulling her back toward his body. "It's just... I've spent the last four months trying to figure that out, and then you go and get it right in a few sentences."

She smiled. "Well, that's the thing about talking all the time: eventually, something smart is bound to come out. It's the law of averages," she said matter-of-factly, giving him a curt nod.

"You get me more than anyone ever has and you don't even try, do you?" he asked softly as he tilted her chin up.

Her lower lip started to quiver as he drew closer. Their lips met, moist and wet as he pulled her closer to him, feeling her arms wrap around him. She tasted like raspberries.

And all of the pain, the suffering, and the sorrow that their lives had become, turned into ghosts of the past, fading away like a feather on the wind.

And they became each other's heroes.

BOOK SIX

IGNORANCE IS BLISS

CHAPTER ONE: YOUTH

"Is that what you're wearing to the dance?" Julie Peterson snapped sardonically. She peered up from her vanity long enough to glare at the younger girl, giving her a once over. She turned back toward the mirror and finished applying her scarlet lipstick, smacked her lips together once, then pressed them against a napkin to remove the excess.

The younger girl, Mandy Peterson, spread her arms and looked down at herself, then stretched to look at her own backside. She was wearing a dark blue sweater she'd picked up at the Gap, which wasn't hard to tell, as there were big bold letters across the front that read 'GAP.' Her jeans were baggy and loose, and needed the aid of a rather large belt with a buckle in the shape of Texas to help hold them up. "What's wrong with this?"

Julie rolled her eyes, bunched up the napkin and then tossed it into a nearby trash can. It was blue with hearts printed all over it. She was wearing a loose, red sleeveless shirt with a high slit in one side that came up to meet her underarms.

An older generation would have said that it looked like rags on her. Only Julie could make rags look so good.

With it she wore tight black pants with silver leopard spots that she'd painted on herself. They shimmered in the right light. They hung low on her hips, so much so that her pink lace thong was showing.

"There's nothing wrong with it." she admitted with a sigh, smiling over her shoulder at her cousin. "I just think that you're overdoing the whole beggar theme, is all."

Mandy turned away and crossed her arms. "I think you're overdoing the whole 'slut without a cause' theme."

"What?" Julie snapped, turning just in time to see the girl walk out her bedroom door.

"Nothing." Mandy waved as she disappeared into her room to change again.

Julie frowned, then turned back to her mirror.

Mandy shuffled through the boxes of clothes in her closet, sifting through them to try and find anything she could wear. She held up an elegant red dress, mulled over it for a minute, then shoved it back into the box and moved on.

"What are you getting so dressed up for, anyway?" she called out across the hall, poking her head out of her closet just long enough to make sure Julie was still there. She was, carefully applying mascara to her lashes. "Is Xander going to be there?"

Julie smiled with one side of her face, her lips curling at the end like a 40s villain's mustache. "He'd better be. And I swear, if he wears that ratty old Transformers tee-shirt again, I'll wring his puny neck."

Mandy was holding a large turquoise gown with puffy frills across the chest.

"Not that one, hun. The blue, maybe?" Julie suggested, trying to find a nice way of disapproving her relative's taste in clothing lately.

"So, are you two, like, dating now, or something?" Mandy asked, trying to make the question sound uninvolved and casual as she searched to find the shirt Julie was talking about.

"Or something." Julie huffed with a laugh, putting her makeup away and walking across the hall to Mandy's room. She poked her head into the closet. "Not that blue one. Don't wanna show that much skin."

"What I was thinking," Mandy agreed, giving the blue tank top a curt nod of disapproval before shoving it into the dark reaches of her closet. "What were you saying about Xander?"

"Alex," Julie corrected, giving Mandy a tap on the head. "His name is Alex."

Mandy turned quizzically. "He doesn't like being called Xander?"

"No... I don't. It sounds stupid. Nobody's name begins with an X."

"Xander's does," Mandy pointed out cheerily.

Julie growled, then picked up a Cherry Coke that had been resting atop Mandy's dresser and took a sip through the slender dual straws. Tilting her head to make her brunette hair fall away from her face, she reminded herself to do something else with it.

Mandy made the same motion with her own auburn hair but chose to leave it the way it was. She eyed the foundation and lipstick on her dresser, pouting out one of her thin, delicate lips so that she could see it if she strained.

"Scarlet does the trick really well." Julie laughed as she handed Mandy the Coke. "Or Strawberry Rouge, but stay away from pink and anything resembling flesh tones... they'll make your lips disappear completely."

Mandy smiled.

Julie walked over to the dresser, selected the strawberry, then tossed it over to her. "And there's nothing going on with me and Xander Drew."

"Bull!" Mandy giggled, taking the top off of the lipstick and applying it without the aid of a mirror. "I saw you two looking all chummy in school the other day. He couldn't keep his eyes off you."

Julie said nothing, then slowly turned, smiling. "He was into me, wasn't he?"

"Like a magnet!" the younger girl agreed. "I don't know how he can keep his hands off you!"

"Oh, believe me, he manages," Julie frowned. "But, it's nothing big... yet.

We're still at the 'friends with benefits' stage right now, and I've got no clue how to get it forward. Everything I've ever learned about men I have to forget when I'm around Alex. He plays by a whole different set of rules."

Mandy paused, nodding silently as she took that in. Finally, she smiled. "What kind of benefits?"

Julie laughed, picking up a shirt and tossing it at her.

That's Julie, all over and covered in whipped cream, thought Mandy as she scribbled into her notebook with a pink feathered pen. She dotted all her I's with carefully crafted little happy faces, then coloured them in with the yellow highlighter that lay on the bed at her side. She sighed every time she did so, as if it were necessary to the process. *She tries so hard to be, like, deep or something. To not kiss and tell and to not drag the boys into the dark closets, but it doesn't take much pushing to get her to break. It's not her fault. It's not even a bad thing, really. It's just who she is.*

Her relationship with Xander... sorry, **Alexander,** *is, at best, terminal. To-be-historic. Dead in the water. He's a Leo and she's a Capricorn. Seriously, need I say more? Well, he's all stoic and broody. He likes to curl up in his bat-cave and grumble a lot and stuff like that. She's more open. She wants to be out in the daylight where everyone can see her... probably doing something that should not be seen by anyone else. They're so, like, wrong for each other, that it's a miracle they never got together before. 'Cause you know that's the way it always happens. We all end up with the totally wrong person for us.*

Just look at Mike Harris and Cathy Kennessy.

"I think yesterday's storm fried a few transistors in here," Mike offered, taking a sip of his Pepsi as he pushed aside some wiring inside Xander's computer to get a better look at the RAM chips. "Extra toasty by the looks of things."

"That's great. Terrific. Your opinion is duly noted. I have noted it, tagged it, and filed it away in my brain under 'advice my idiot friends give me on subjects they know nothing about.' Believe me, I will soon take it into consideration. Whoo-boy, you don't wanna be around when I take this into consideration. It'll be a big-ol' consideration party. Considerate people will come from miles in every direction. They'll eat considerate chips and drink considerate beer and they'll considerably consider considering the information that you so considerably gave to me," Xander said, all in one breath, never once looking up as he used a small blade to slice the ends off of some computer wire.

"You know, a man can overdose on sarcasm," Mike drawled, stroking his statically fluffed blonde hair. He was topless, having taken off his sweater a few moments ago before examining the computer's internals. There was an old scar on his right side with dots all around it, indicating where stitches had been.

Xander chuckled, nodding before looking up at his friend. "Hey!" he yelled, raising an arm to quickly point at his friend's Pepsi. "No drinks near the computer!"

"But it's thirsty."

"You're an idiot. You'll drink near it, and yet you'll take off your shirt to avoid static. Unbelievable."

"Maybe I just wanted to take my shirt off," he grinned mischievously.

Xander shot him a look. "That's funny. Thanks anyway, but I happen to have a date tonight."

"Who's the lucky fella?" Mike laughed, ignoring Xander's previous order and taking another sip of his cola, making sure that he saw.

Again, Xander glared at him, even as he reconnected the computer wire to the newly installed RAM chips, letting the machine hum to life. "Success," he smiled happily. "And, for your information, it is a girl, dumbass."

"Gee, he looks like Xander," Mike said to an imaginary person next to him. "But he talks in a funny, non-Xander-speak kind of way."

Xander turned on the screen. In the same motion he picked up a can of cologne and spritzed himself with it, ignoring Mike's commentary on the subject.

"How is Julie?" Mike asked finally, taking the hint. "She doing all right?"

Xander started unbuttoning the grease stained green shirt that he always used when he was working on electronics. Several of the buttons were ripped out, but he still did the motion of undoing them anyway, like a preprogrammed action. He whipped the smelly shirt off of his back and tossed it into the corner, revealing a back covered in scars.

Every time he saw them, they served to remind Mike that nothing was as it should be. That nothing was safe, not really.

"She's fine, I guess," Xander answered, spreading some deodorant underneath his arms, wincing as unclosed wounds got stretched to the point that the tender flesh began to rip.

"You guess?" Mike scoffed, waving a finger at Xander. "Come on, we both know better than that. Every time I say her name, you get all glossy-eyed... plus, those pants are tight. You don't need to be jumping off the walls for me to know you're excited."

Xander squirted blue gel out of a slender round bottle, slowly turning and raising an eyebrow at Mike. "You're weird," he informed his friend coolly.

"And you're homophobic," Mike chipped in, taking a squirt of gel himself and ruffling it through his golden bangs, giving him that straight-from-the-shower look that he was sure would go over well with the ladies.

"That's great. Terrific. Your opinion is duly noted. I have noted it, tagged it, and filed it away in my brain under 'advice my idiot friends - '"

"Okay! I get it." Mike snapped, giving his friend a little shove. "Jesus, I never met anyone so frigging hooked on the same few gags. I swear by all that's holy, Leno changes his act more than you do."

"Funny."

"I try."

Xander finished gelling his hair, turning it from being simply dark to pitch black. Now it was nearly down in front of his eyes, hiding his bushy eyebrows.

Someone had once told him that he had the eyebrows of a Sasquatch, although he couldn't quite recall who at the moment. Probably that Canadian kid.

Mike took a moist towelette off the dresser and started using it to scrub the sleep from underneath his eyes, along with the rest of his big-cheeked, freckled face. Still shirtless, he was left vulnerable when Xander reached over casually and pinched him on the arm. "Ow!"

"Wimp."

"Pinching. The last defense of a loser."

"I thought that was screaming?"

"Fine then. The second last defense of a loser."

"Where do crotch shots go in the grand scheme of things?"

"You may now shut up."

"Oh, then I guess I shall, Master." Xander bowed, using the same motion to pick up a burgundy shirt with Chinese symbols on it off the floor. "What do you think of this?"

Mike gave the shirt a once over, and then Xander. "Dude... you're a woman."

"Sexist pig."

"Yeah, what of it?" Mike retorted, grabbing the shirt and putting it on. He was bigger than Xander, so the shirt was tighter on him, and he couldn't button it up as far. He grinned at his reflection in Xander's small, cracked mirror.

"How come when I wear it I'm a woman, but you think you can pull it off?"

"Because I'm secure enough in my masculinity to look man-pretty no matter what I have on. You, on the other hand, should stick to black."

"Why black?"

"It's your colour."

"It's not even a colour."

"Sure it is."

"It's the absence of colour."

"Fine. Then it's your absence of colour."

"Wish you were absent," Xander grumbled, picking up a black shirt and pulling it on over his head. The result was a slim, stream-lined Xander. Everything about him, his clothes, hair, eyes... all jet black. It made his skin look extra pale, but worked well on him. "When you're right, you're right, though," he agreed, grabbing a smoke off his computer table and resting it between his lips, lighting it.

"You smoke in the house now?" Mike frowned, stepping away as the disgusting scent of nicotine reached him.

"Mom found out. Doesn't care. They smoke, too, so we just end up bummin' off one another anyway."

"One big, happy, cancerous family."

"I've never wanted to live forever anyway." Xander smirked, taking a long drag and inhaling deeply, holding it in for ten seconds, then slowly exhaling. "Heaven."

217

"You're dumb."

"I so do not care right now. Besides, you're starting to sound like Cathy."

There was a pause then, as both men took in what was said and let it register.

"How is she?" Xander asked, sighing as he avoided eye contact by searching for socks.

"Better. She's talking to me, a little anyway. We're going to the dance together tonight, at least."

"I feel like it's my fault."

"No way," Mike protested, standing up. "There was no way you could have known. No way you could have stopped what was happening. It was my fault. If I'd been more careful, she never would have been in that situation."

Xander paused, looking at his friend. Tears were welling up in the man's eyes, making their blue shimmer and shake. When Xander finally spoke, he chose his words very carefully.

"That's the way I used to talk about it," he started, taking a deep breath. "'It happens.' 'She never would have.' Always keeping myself out of the story just enough that I wouldn't have to realize that it happened to me."

He paused, taking another puff of his cigarette and letting the smoke from it curl around his head.

"But it did happen to me. Just like this new thing happened to you. It seems really long ago, doesn't it? Like it didn't even happen. Like it's a story you tell, not even real. But it was real. It happened."

"Tell me," Mike pleaded, grabbing Xander's arm to stop him from turning away.

Xander looked him up and down, then nodded. "You know most of it. Back when me, you, Sara and Cathy thought we had it rough. When we thought that the world was against us. Really, we were just kids. I guess someone a lot older and smarter than me might say that all teens are supposed to feel that way, but it doesn't change the fact."

He doused his cigarette, immediately grabbing another from the pack and placing it between his lips, struck a match, and lit it.

"We were idiots. We should have enjoyed what we had, but we weren't even bright enough to realize we had it. Then, one day, we lost our whole world."

"The day Jamie died," Mike finished softly, looking down for a moment. Jamie Dawkins had been his best friend for years, and the first victim in a long and violent string of murders that swept through their quiet eastern Maine town.

"That was the day we lost one thing, and one thing only: the illusion. The thought that everything was alright. We tell ourselves that it was the loss of our friend, but it wasn't. It was the realization that life wouldn't always be the same. That we weren't safe, and never had been.

"Sara took it hardest, Jamie's death drove her right into my arms... right where I wanted her to be, coincidentally. She and I came closer to being together than we had in the fifteen years before it in those few days. Forged bonds that'll never break.

"That was why she was the next to go. Genblade took her, when everything caved in. When Grendel tried to rape Cathy. When Julie told Derek about how she'd been taken advantage of... everything happened in those few moments. That was why nobody was looking, when Adam Genblade slid his blade deep into her gut."

"I know all this," Mike said impatiently. "What happened afterward? What happened at Engen?"

Xander took a long drag of his smoke, weighing out the pros and cons of finishing the story. "I met a man named Abner Jenkins. He was the commander of the Alpha Strike Force, the first and most deadly wave of Engen's elite guardsmen back in the day. Until my mother escaped trying to rescue me. I was a part of operation: Black Womb. The project to create the world's first post-human child.

"I was a failure. I didn't carry what they called the Darkness, or so they thought. My mother rescued me, and it cost her life... but it took Jenkins' as well.

"He was a walking corpse. Had been bathed in chemical residue from all the containment pods in Engen. He'd stayed alive all those years, under the tutelage of the founders of the company, learning, creating genetic soldiers."

"Genblade and Spider," Mike breathed, rubbing the flesh between his eyes.

"The genetic Adam and Eve. But they were unstable internally, much like Jenkins himself. All three needed human organs to survive. Adam and Spider could take them, they were engineered for such processes, but Abner..."

"He needed a catalyst."

"...me. Or, the part of me that was thought a failure. The Womb, lying dormant deep inside me for all these years. They woke it up, used it to help them kill all my friends, family, Sara... everything. And then, he offered to take it from me, to keep him alive and to keep me from killing."

"You had the chance to give it up?"

"And I did. Freely, willingly. But Abner lied. He was going to use the darkness to survive the coming Armageddon... a nuclear apocalypse he himself would start. I had to stop him. So, I fought my way through. Killed Spider, stopped Genblade... and took back what was mine from Jenkins."

"To save everything," Mike sighed, shaking his head.

"But even after that, the Womb still kept killing. It's only the last few weeks I've been able to manage any level of control. And that's what I would tell myself, just like you are now: it kept killing. Like this thing is separate from me. It's as much me as any other part. I was born with it, I'll probably die with it. I killed those people. I'm responsible for Sara's death. It's only now that I can say it. So, Mike, what are you detaching yourself from?"

Mike stopped, taken aback. He looked at Xander with betrayed disgust, which he returned with a stone cold face, awaiting response. His lower lip quivered, as tears returned to his eyes. "My child died. I was going to have a child..." Tears began to fall down his face, and he collapsed to his knees.

Xander took hold of the back of his friend's head, pulling him into his chest and holding his close, letting wave after wave a grim realization find the man he considered a brother.

"Gawd, it was my child..." he gasped, drowning on his sorrow as his lungs fought for breath.

"My child..."

Mike's cute, but he's got definite issues. There's no doubt he's got a dark side. People think I don't get that, but really, I get it more than anyone. I've seen it, up close and personal, and it isn't pretty... but doesn't every man have a little beast inside of him?

Cathy and Mike are still going through the rough spot to end all rough spots. They think it's, like, world ending, but I've seen this same thing a hundred times before and they're just being stupid about it. Cathy got pregnant. No big surprise there, I just wonder if it was Mike's. Someone should tell her that if you're going to give it up so easy, you have to wear a rubber. Or at least have some kind of protection. Maybe I'm giving the her too much credit. But I thought Mike would know better, somehow.

Anyway, so Cathy's pregnant, but then she's just not. She has a miscarriage, like, right in the middle of school, like some kind of spaz. But, anyway, now she's not pregnant.

Suddenly, it's all 'poor Mike, poor Cathy' when they're not even, like, together anymore as far as anyone can tell. I guess they're still an item, but how long can that really last? They should just break up and get it over with.

Xander, he's another story.

Nobody really knows what's up with him, but he seems to know what's going on with everybody else. It's seriously creepy sometimes, the way that it happens. Sometimes, he'll just know things. It's like he goes home at night and spends all his time calling everyone in town to find out everything that's going on. But most times, the stuff he knows is stuff nobody would tell. Like when him and Mike helped take down that guy that hurt Julie, Xander just knew stuff. He knew where to be to help Cathy... as if she wasn't just giving it up anyway.

But what's really creepy is when you tell him stuff. You tell him secrets you shouldn't tell anyone, things that could get you killed. I don't know why, but every time I have something big happening, I always tell him first. I always check in with him, just to let him know that everything's fine. I dunno, it's stupid, he's a total social reject... but sometimes he's the best one of us. Sometimes you have to tell him things, because he's the guy that always wants to hear it, always wants to help.

I've been around a lot of guys, and they always look at me like I'm nothing. Which fits, because that's what I am. Why else would those guys down the block have got it in their head? But even when he's with girls like me and Julie and Cathy, he doesn't look at us like he wants us. Doesn't look at me like I'm a slut. He just... looks at me, and I tell him everything, and then everything is all right.

There aren't many guys like that.

The room was large, easily twice the size of the room of the average kid in his class. It was lined with pictures of his life. That had always been a yearly ritual of Tommy's. Every year, he'd change all of the pictures on his wall to those he'd taken the year before. His family had always called him shutterbug for it back when they paid any attention to him at all.

The past year was documented on those walls, each frame glistening in the beam from the pull-string light hanging from his ceiling, a testament to how old the house really was.

Cameras, film, frames... That's what most people gave him for gifts. Not that he minded. It was his one real hobby, and he loved it. Last year, someone had been smart enough to give him a bulk film loader, cutting his costs drastically. Over in the corner was his closet, converted into a makeshift darkroom. There were always clothes on his floor with nowhere to hang them.

The photos on the wall told the story of the most interesting parts of his life. This year, when everything is supposed to change for young men and women, everything changed. Only for them, it was different.

He pulled on an old tee-shirt and turned to face one of the photos. It had been taken in the Factory, a place that had died off in the few months since. It was like he was the only person who had time for it anymore. In the picture was Cathy, Mike, and Jamie all leaning against a pool table. Mike and Jamie had their arms crossed, trying to look tough, while Cathy tried her best to hide her face from the camera.

There was another picture of Sud, Jamie, Derek, Mike and himself taken just a few months later. Grendel had taken it, he thought. There they were: the Avengers, the Squadron Supreme, the Teen Titans. It had always been the five of them, ever since they were kids. Xander had never fit into it. Most of his photos of Xander were lone shots. He was always either talking to Sara or watching gay porn on the internet or something.

There was a picture of Sara and Grendel kissing, back when the two of them had been an item. They both looked so happy, her hair was so gorgeous...

There was another picture of a long line of headstones. Their headstones were front and center, Julian Grendel and Sara Johnson, buried very near to one another. He always thought it was poetic that the two of them had died on the same day. It should be that way, when two people are meant for each other like that. It was beautiful. Sure, at the time, Grendel had been with Cathy and Sara had been going after Jamie, but that didn't change the fact that they would have gotten together. He liked to think that they were together now.

Then there was the picture that was flipped around, facing the wall. That was the one he wanted so badly to take down, but was afraid to. It was a head shot of Derek Smith, his steel blue eyes staring right into the camera, making them look like they focused on you no matter where you were in the room. Eyes that made Tommy wonder how they'd ever thought Derek was okay. How they hadn't known that he was a murderer. The eyes... they made him look as though he would jump out of the page and start ripping into you if he could. Maybe he'd use that knife he carried around, the one they used to teased him about, saying that he'd never used it. That he looked stupid. That was why the picture was flipped over. He was too afraid to take it down, too afraid it would piss Derek off.

There were other pictures, too. Ones that would never come down. Pictures of Jamie, Grendel, Sud, Sara... all of them dead. All of them killed senselessly, violently. Ripped open for all to see.

He pulled on some black jeans, then sprayed himself with a bottle of cheap aerosol cologne to mask any of the excess funk.

Now he was the only one left. Sometimes he thought the loneliness would kill him. Other times he hoped it would. Maybe then he'd see them again, maybe then he'd find peace.

He turned to his mirror and checked his hair once again to make sure that the gel was holding every spike in place perfectly. Rubbing a hand over his recently shaven face, he smiled brightly at the mirror, choosing to not be lonely anymore tonight. He turned and looked at his newest picture, one of Julie, Mandy, Mike, Cathy and Xander, and smiled warmly at it. If the world he lived in was changing, then maybe it was time for him to change with it.

Tommy's kinda like the Lone Ranger now. He's got nobody, and I feel bad for him. First Jamie dies, then Grendel, then Sud dies and all his other friends try stuff with me, and now they're all on the run, so if he does see them, it's in a poorly lit alley.

Maybe that's where he met Cathy. Seems like the type of place she'd hang out.

Ever since that thing in the hospital a week ago when Julie and Xander hooked up (finally), things have been stressed between everyone else. Mike and Cathy are still together, even though they're never in the same room. So now, everybody's waiting for me and Tommy to either get together or pair off with different people ourselves. Suddenly it's like, not okay to be single and loving it anymore. Now we gotta talk to people between make out sessions.

It blows entirely.

It wouldn't even be so bad if Mike and Cat would just hurry up and end it or whatever.

Cathy winced as she poked a faux-diamond earring through the hole in her ear, gritting her teeth a little as she did so.

It had been months since she had had any reason to wear earrings, or jewelry of any kind for that matter (although from time to time she was prone to slipping on her mother's pearl necklace to go to school, just for the sake of showing off a little bit). In her season-long period of social hibernation, she didn't realize that the flesh had folded and grown over the punctures in each lobe, which she had had since before she was old enough to walk.

Now she hissed as pain shot through the side of her head, staring at her reflection in her bathroom mirror and trying desperately to keep her hair out of her line of sight. As her teeth clenched together, she cursed on herself for being so weak. After all she'd been through, this should be nothing. This *was* nothing. After all the pain and sorrow and heartache… after all of the times that she thought agony would keep bleeding from her heart until she was dead, a small piece of metal through each earlobe shouldn't have even fazed her.

And yet she squinted her eyes until they were shut and bit her lip with two paper-white teeth, trying to plunge the earring through the tender skin. Anguish jolted through her system and forced her to pull back at the last second, unable to take it any longer.

"Fuck," she said, glancing in the mirror and wanting to strike out at what she saw there, even going so far as to clench a tight little fist.

Instead her knuckles loosened. She pulled back her neatly combed black hair, revealing the tiniest dribbles of blood, pushed out through the dent in her head by the pressure from her heart.

"Argh!" she huffed as quietly as possible, mindful of her parents and sister downstairs. She ran her fingers through her hair and dug her long nails into her scalp until she thought it might bleed as well.

She bent over and picked up the earring, her lower back aching from weeks of restless nights and uncomfortable, lonely trips to the doctor's office. Calcium popped in her hip, making her blink once in surprise before coming back up to stand, the earring pinched between her thumb and forefinger.

Holding it up to the row of incandescent light bulbs that surrounded her bathroom mirror, she noticed a small, swirling splotch of blood on the cubic zirconia. It made the light that reflected off of it a sickly, dark red. Her free hand automatically went to her ear, returning with the smallest possible dot of blood on it.

She remembered those commercials. *A diamond is forever*, they always said at the end, while the two shadows were kissing happily and holding one another. She wondered who those people were. Were they really happy? Or was there something else going on there?

Maybe the shadow-couple had been having problems lately, bad ones. The guy was an idiot and would rather talk to his idiot friends about his problems, leaving the girl at home all alone. Then, of course, the guy would come back home drunk at four in the morning expecting to get lucky, but no, the girl doesn't want to obviously. So, he goes for the easy fix. Instead of talking the problems out, he saves up and buys her a diamond ring. She is filled with fleeting, momentary gratification and the false impression that their problems are solved, they make love, go maybe a week without incident, and are finally back where they started.

The commercial should say: 'A Diamond: it'll open her knees,' she thought.

But still, before her was a tiny piece of treated glass with a swirling puddle of red in it. She stared at it intently, at the way the light spun out of it like a spider web, or that CD cover from that one old British band about bricks and drugs. If she looked hard enough, the redness seemed to dance for her, painting a macabre tapestry of what she had to look forward to in her life. She reached out without looking, without thinking, and turned on the bathroom sink. She shoved the earring under it, watching as the swirls of red melted off, danced around against the white of the sink for a moment, then disappeared down the drain.

When she returned the small trinket to her sight, she could still see the red. It wasn't there, she knew it couldn't be, but she was convinced that she could see it. She stuck it underneath the running water again, the cold of it nipping at her slender fingers, sending tiny shocks up her arm. She felt the blood pump to the chilled appendages, and the pores in her flesh became visible as some of her recently applied nail polish traveled down the sink as well. She pulled back the earring again, looked at it only a second, then put it back beneath the flow.

This was not the first time in the past week that Cathy had been forced to wash out tiny droplets of blood. They had been found decorating the inside of silk undergarments of late, along with bed sheets, jeans, and the occasional pair of pajamas. It wasn't her cycle, she knew that much. They were too irregular. Wrong time for it too, even though recent events might have thrown her off course.

She knew what it was. It was her child still inside of her, screaming for something she could not hear. She could picture it, wriggling about within her, wanting food or water and getting nothing, her bleeding from the inside out the only indication of her unborn child's anguish.

And so, Cathy Kennessy had become accustomed to a schedule which included the late night to early morning washing of sheets and scrubbing of mattresses, and the feeling of cold water freezing the tips of her fingers as redness washed down the drain.

Out, out, damn spot.

She withdrew the earring again. It was almost clean now, only the slightest hint of pink where the blood had been. Pink was a colour that she was more readily prepared to contend with. She poked the freezing cold metal through her ear now without hesitation, then the other, and mechanically flipped open her makeup kit and started to apply foundation.

The dance tonight is like the sudden rush of air after you've been holding your breath underwater for a really long time. You wait for it, you ache for it, and even though you know it's going to hurt just a little, it's outweighed by feeling so good. The people around here though, they don't seem to think so.

Coral Beach is weirder than any place I've ever been to, even though nobody seems to realize it. Everyone in this town feels like they're, like, waiting for the other Wal-Mart reject shoe to suddenly drop.

Social gatherings are the worst.

Apparently a while back some dude went all Freddy at a party around here, all hack-and-slash and stuff. Since then, everyone's got cabin fever, and not the cool kind from Muppet Treasure Island, either. The kind that makes everyone turn into social lepers and stay inside all the time, like there's something in the dark that's going to jump out and bite them.

Xander was really interested in going. He saw the poster up in school when he was walking around with Julie and had been all: 'Hell - yes.' He actually smiled, a serious rarity, but it's becoming more common than a lot of people realize.

The teachers weren't so happy 'cause they have to chaperone. Apparently the students aren't the only people with house-rat syndrome. The only one that jumped at the chance was Principal Schneider, and the rest of them had to be bullied into it. I don't think Mr. Miles was all too pleased about it, he said something in that Boston accent of his about today's music sounding like the musicians played their guitars with rabid cats.

Julie didn't want to go at first, which is the opposite of everything she's been since she was eight. But the second she saw that Xander... sorry! Alexander... wanted to go, she was all over it (and him), which is more like the Julie we all know and tolerate.

Cathy didn't want to go. She still doesn't, I think. She's just dragging herself along to make an appearance. She'll show up long enough to be like, 'Hey, look everyone, Mike's still my boyfriend,' then she'll go home with the first piece of raw meat she can find and won't be seen for a few days.

Mike wanted to go really bad. Him and Xander were practically dancing around like little girls when they saw the poster. But, as usual, one look from Cathy took the smile right off his face and buried it next to Alicia Silverstone's career. He was brought right back down to the dumps, and when he went to her, she turned away and left. Poor her. Wah. I so totally feel her pain. Right.

But still, most of the other kids scoffed at the poster. It's like it's not in style to have fun in this town anymore. They need to get out and relax. I mean, sure, after what happened with the Tee's I dress a little more conservative, but I still go out. You can be careful without being a reject.

Nothing's going to happen tonight anyway.

CHAPTER TWO: NOTHING WRONG

He sat in the bushes.

In his mind, that was all he was doing, and there was nothing wrong with that.

Just off of where Morrison Drive intersected with Quesada Way, he was sitting in the bushes, peering out between windswept late fall branches at the street before him, following the odd leaf that the wind blew into his line of sight.

His hand was on his crotch, massaging it rhythmically, and he bit his lip as he felt himself near climax.

Don't do that, Malcolm.

Someone told him in a stern voice deep within his subconscious. He squinted his eyes, forcing the voice out. He couldn't recall who the voice was, only that he hated it, shrill and loud. It made his ears hurt. His vision became spotty momentarily as he felt pleasure build inside him, coupled with just the right amount of pain to make it last. Make it interesting. He bent forward, opening his mouth to speak and then shut it, afraid of who would hear, afraid of the voice that was telling him to stop.

Don't do that, Malcolm.

"Shut up, bitch," he whispered to himself, and the voice continued to speak, fading now. He was confronted by the image of a shovel, but it passed as quickly as it came.

He leaned forward again, brushing against the orange and yellow leaves, so good against his face.

"Mmm."

He loved this time of year, loved the chill that the air brought with it. Colours were everywhere, leaves were randomly different shades and textures, as though someone had taken out a box of crayons and coloured them without rhyme or reason.

He'd rented a dirty movie from the corner store earlier and paid the overweight man at the counter five dollars for it. The old, used paper bill had felt like leaves in his palm as he handed it over, tucking the porno under his arm and smiling at the woman who walked in through the front door, shying her children away from him. He'd smiled at the children too and they'd waved at him. He waved back.

The movie had not been overly satisfying. It was ripe with the plotting efforts of a bad writer unable to accept the reality of his place in life, that people who rent pornography are not in the least bit interested in what the characters are feeling, unless what they are feeling is something long and nasty. He had only attempted masturbating to it for a moment, until the voice had said, *Don't do that, Malcolm.*

"Shut up."

But the flick wasn't good enough. There were no blondes in it, and he couldn't get himself into it enough that the voice would stop. So he'd stopped and taken a walk into the woods outside his house, wrapping a scarf around his neck so that he wouldn't get cold. He'd been walking for about a half hour when he peered out from between the branches and saw a young couple walking. The girl had blonde hair that fell all the way down to the swell of her buttocks, and the boyfriend's hand had been upon it.

Malcolm felt himself rise in a way that the porno had not produced and knelt down in the mulch and dying grass, the dampness at his knees feeling surprisingly good. Then the voice said,

Don't do that, Malcolm.

But he told the bitch to shut up and it went away as quickly as it had come, so he decided to stay. Maybe the wind was drowning her out and that was why he couldn't hear her. In any event, he hadn't planned this, he wasn't like that, so there was nothing wrong with it.

He wiped sweat off of his balding head with his free hand, pumping more fiercely to increase the pressure and the pleasure, hoping that climax would come before nightfall. He watched another girl go by, a redhead (not as good as a blonde, but still better than brunettes). She had a rather large chest, and it bounced as she walked. She stopped a few feet to the left of his vision, looking around to assure herself that there was nobody about then reached into the back of her jeans and fixed her cotton thong.

"Mmm," he said, and there was nothing wrong with that, as he watched her bend over to tie her shoe lace, showing off her full, grab-worthy backside just for him, then walked on.

She knew that he was there, he decided. Some of the others that walked down Morrison didn't know, but she definitely did. She didn't want to have sex with him, he had no delusions of that, but she wanted to show off for him. To aid in his pleasure without having the guilt that comes to young girls that sleep with older men. So she showed him what she wanted to and had moved on, and later, when night fell and her parents were asleep, she would slide her hands below her red covers and think of the man in the bushes, stroking himself to her short peep show, and there was nothing wrong with that.

Don't do that, Malcolm.

"Shut up!" he whispered again, closing his eyes tight and gritting his teeth. When he opened them again he saw a teenage blonde finish her escape from his vision. She had been wearing a skirt, and possibly could have bent over. The voice had made him miss it.

Maybe he could go through the woods a little ways, get in front of her. Maybe she would have an itch and need to bend again and want him to see, like the other

Don't do that, Malcolm.

"Quiet, bitch!" he said, releasing his grip and punching a tree to show that he was serious. "I said shut up and now you're going to shut up. So shut up!"

He waited in the approaching twilight for the voice to come back. It did not. He smiled a little, then reached down again... to feel only softness.

Not the smooth, hard thing that the redhead with the thong wanted to dream about late at night. He sneered, tucking it away and rising to his feet above the bushes, then turned to walk back home.

"What ya doin'?" came the sound, small and tender, with just a touch of childish spite.

Malcolm turned and saw him, walking down Morrison Street toward Quesada Way. The child was no more than ten, probably nine, and only stood as tall as Malcolm's waist. And there was nothing wrong with that.

He wore a black and red tee-shirt with a stain on it, and jeans bought at the local market by his mother.

And his hair.

It was short with small curls at the tips that said mother had tried to get out, so blond that it was nearly white.

"What ya doing?" the child repeated.

Malcolm smiled warmly, as he finished zipping himself up. "I'm just out for a walk."

"You walk in the woods?"

"Yes. It's fun."

"Oh," the child responded. "Okay."

"What are you doing?" Malcolm asked.

The child looked hesitant. "Mom sent me down to the store to get some bread, and a candy for me."

Malcolm thought of the obese man at the store that had sold him the badly written porno. He would not appreciate such a magnificent child.

"I have bread at home I can give you," he said politely. "And lots of candy, not just one."

"Is your house in the woods?"

"No, but that's how we'll get there."

"Mom says I'm not allowed in the woods."

"But your mom wants you to get bread, and I have the bread. So she wouldn't mind."

The child considered that for a moment, thoughts of candy flying through his young mind. "Okay."

He reached out and took the child's small hand, leading him past the brush and into the woods. "I'm Malcolm, what's your name?"

"Charles. Charles Frank."

"Hello, Charles Frank."

"Hello, Malcolm."

Don't do that, Malcolm.

"Shut up."

"What?"

"Nothing."

He led the boy away from the road and deep into the woods toward his home. He hadn't planned on this, and the boy wanted to come.

There was nothing wrong with it.

CHAPTER THREE: THE DANCE

Julie and Mandy Peterson walked into the gym of Coral Beach High, both wishing immediately that the dance had been held at The Factory or some location where the school losers were not always in charge of decoration.

Fall-coloured orange, red, and yellow streamers stretched across the ceiling. At some point they had run out of orange and had started using bright purple instead, making something already gaudy into a design nightmare. Other 'fall' decorations including pumpkins, scarecrows and witches left over from the canceled Halloween dance, even though Halloween was a month ago.

There was a disco ball... yes, a disco ball positioned to hang from the middle of the gym, with orange, red and blue lights aimed at it, bouncing their reflection in all directions. The beams of light shimmered off of the body paint that spotted Julie's tight black pants and raggedy, red sleeveless shirt, and did nothing but create unflattering shadows on Mandy's sweater.

"I still can't believe you wore that," Julie scoffed between her teeth, her eyes still scanning the crowd.

"Would you drop it?" Mandy said passively as she scanned the crowd herself, her eyes darting this way and that. "I bought this just last week. It looks alright. You look just weird, dressing like that when it's this cold out."

Julie balked, looking at her cousin for just a moment. She opened her mouth to speak, then closed it and turned away to ignore her again. She decided that she actually would drop it, for now.

Across the gym Xander stood up, his black leather coat unbunching as he rose. His hands were concealed by sleeves too long for them, making his arms appear shorter than they actually were. He smiled warmly and checked his red shirt and blue jeans (he had decided against Mike's choice of black on black) to make sure there was nothing on them, then started to walk forward. He gave a little wave, then turned to Mike (who was sitting beside him) and motioned for him to rise as well.

Mike did so, reluctantly, and the two navigated the mingling teenagers on the dance floor.

"Here they come," Julie smiled, turning to Mandy. "Try not to be a spaz around Mike, okay?"

Mandy gave a fake, condescending grin in return. "Try to wait until you're out of public view to accidentally lose your shirt, okay?"

Julie frowned, then turned back toward the oncoming boys. "Hey guys," she said sheepishly to both of them, although it was clear that the plural was only for politeness and that she was only talking to Xander.

"Hey," Xander replied, reaching out and pulling her into a little hug, leaving Mike and Mandy to simply nod courteously at one another. Mandy gave a smile, and Mike returned it. "You're a little late."

Julie grinned devilishly, relishing in the fact that her arms were wrapped around his neck. "You have a lot to learn about women, Mr. Drew. Don't you know that it's fashionable to arrive at least ten minutes later than you're supposed to?"

"Silly me," he chuckled, slowly releasing his hold on her hips, sliding his hands across her exposed skin and sending shivers up and down her spine that passed on to him. "I thought maybe you just liked to see me squirm."

She giggled, and it sounded odd. Usually with her it was an all out laugh, not the cute, kitteny sound that now bubbled from her vocal cords. "That too," she replied.

Mike forced a little smile as he turned and glanced around, trying not to notice their exchange. "Maybe that's what Cathy's doing. If so, it's really working."

"Maybe she's not coming." Mandy shrugged, smiling in an effort to make the comment sound innocent.

Mike turned, his brow furrowed.

"What?" he asked, not angry but shocked.

"Well, that, like, wouldn't totally break with her character lately...really."

Mike's eyes lost what little glow they had left, and he turned toward the tiled floor, which was painted for its use in basketball.

"No," he reluctantly agreed. "I guess it wouldn't."

Xander turned to his friend and smiled. "And it certainly wouldn't break with her character to show up looking astonishing just as you started to doubt her."

"What?"

Xander motioned behind Mike to the rear doors.

He turned and Cathy was there, her hair straight and shining, with sparkling earrings on and her mother's pearl necklace draped around her slender neck. She wore a faded, tight yellow tee-shirt and a long, slinky orange skirt. She matched the fall theme so perfectly that it seemed like the dance had been designed for her.

"See?" Julie whispered, nudging Mandy. "There's a girl who knows how to dress for the occasion."

𝄈𝄈

Tommy danced in traditional teenage guy fashion, shuffling his feet a little from side to side and pumping a fist in the air when the people around him started to. Not too far from him, Mike, Xander, and the girls sat the dance out.

Cathy was one empty chair away from Mike, a distance that felt like miles rather than inches.

"So, how's the Coral Beach nightlife treating you?" Xander asked, turning toward Mandy and giving her a grin.

She turned to him, surprised at the sudden sound of his voice above the roaring thump of the music. The look faded into a grin not that different from his own, her natural features showing how beautiful she could be when there wasn't a pound of makeup weighing her down. "This is all right," she mumbled, fumbling her feet beneath her chair.

"What?" Xander asked, raising a hand to his ear as Julie squeezed the other one on his leg possessively.

"I said, this is all right," Mandy repeated, her voice raised above the bump of the bass.

Xander gave her a thumbs up, proving that nonverbal communication worked best at a dance. "How come you didn't bring a date? I hear that Evan guy in your class likes you."

Mandy scrunched up her nose and giggled a little. Her feet came back from beneath her chair as she loosened up. "Evan? He's such a little freakazoid. Yesterday in Family Living class, he totally weirded out when the teacher started talking all sex ed."

Xander frowned. "I can relate to the guy. Getting lectured on sex by a forty-year-old virgin isn't the most relaxing thing in the world. Has she shown you the pictures of the STI's yet?"

Mandy's eyes grew wide. "Um, no."

"Skip class tomorrow," he advised in a sage tone, patting her on the shoulder.

"No problem," she assured him, nodding readily, eyes still wide.

Xander smiled. She was cute, in a youthful way. She reminded him of someone right at that moment, but he couldn't quite put his finger on who. Julie squeezed his hand again, and he turned toward her, giving Mandy one last little smile.

"That was nice," Julie smiled honestly, taking both his hands in hers now. He didn't even realize she had done it, it felt so natural.

"What?"

"You talking to her like that. I haven't seen her loosen up like that since we brought her home."

"All I did was talk with her. You don't mind, do you?"

Julie laughed. "Not at all. It's cute. It's nice that you're nice to her."

"Nicely said."

"Nice of you to say so."

He laughed, unable to think of another way to use the word 'nice', thereby losing their verbal match. She pointed at him, calling him on it, and he produced a defeated look in acknowledgment.

She laughed again, and the orange rays reflecting off the disco ball got caught in her hair, making her glimmer with life and youth, her eyes sparkling with happiness.

Mandy watched them for a moment, wondering if Xander would turn back to talk to her. It wasn't that she felt left out, just that she didn't want to be otherwise engaged if the conversation had not been over. After a minute, she turned toward Mike on the other side of her. "So, what's up with the empty chair? Waiting for someone?"

Mike turned to her, as if just noticing that she was there. "Huh? No... just being comfortable. Me and Cat both appreciate our leg room."

She shot him a skeptical look.

"You get into those things when you've been with someone long enough. It's instinct," he assured her, although it was clear that she was anything but assured.

"Uh-huh," she said in a chipper voice, then nudged herself a little closer to him.

Mike looked down at the shrinking distance between them, then back at her. "What are you doing?"

"Nothing," she said truthfully, her legs ducking back between her chair. "You make me feel, like, safer, is all."

He nodded slowly, feeling like a heel for calling the younger girl out on her obvious crush.

"Oh," he said. "That's okay, then."

Someone went up to the DJ, and the music slowly changed pace. Apparently someone else was sick of hearing the same two words in a successive beat for twenty minutes every song.

The twang of an electric guitar slowly being played was followed by the coos of girls all over the gymnasium as they realized what song it was, each of them either grabbing their boyfriends or the nearest available guy.

"Tears in Heaven!" Julie said longingly, turning to Xander. "I really love this song."

Xander turned, observing the dance floor. "Apparently a lot of people do. Don't you think it's a bit crowded?"

She smiled, stroking the end of his chin lightly. "I only see you."

With that he rose, taking her by the hand and leading her to a spot on the dance floor where not too many people were and placed his hands low around her hips, latching together around her backside as she did the same around his neck. They looked into each other's eyes as they moved, glancing away only long enough to smile politely at people they knew who danced near them.

Mike turned to Cathy, a grin pushing one freckled cheek up.

"You wanna dance?" he asked softly, looking at her like she was the most radiant thing the world had ever seen.

She frowned, her eyes falling across the dance floor at Xander and Julie, then at everyone else as the lyrics began. She turned back to her lover and shook her head slowly. "Not really."

"Come on," he coaxed, reaching out and touching her arm softly.

She jerked away as she felt his fingers, a panicked look coming over her. She tried to force it away as she settled back into her position, but he had caught it, along with half the room.

"What the hell?" he breathed, as low as he could. "Cathy, what's going on? You haven't even let me touch you since - "

"Don't," she barked, raising a hand to him. "Don't even try it. I'm not in the mood for this tonight."

"Then what are you in the mood for?" he asked, stretching his arms in question. "'Cause you sure as hell don't ever tell me."

She pursed her lips, then turned away from him. "I just want to be left alone and enjoy the music. Is that okay with you?"

Defeated, he shook his head. "Sure. Listen, I..."

"I don't want to hear it," she snapped, turning away.

He turned away as well, seeing Mandy still beside him, looking at him intently. "Were you just...?"

"No, I wasn't listening," she assured him, backing off a little. "I mean, I heard, but I wasn't..."

"It's okay," he apologized, lifting a hand to wave the accusation away. "Half the gym probably heard that."

There was a long pause, then. Mandy looked around and took off her sweater, revealing a top with a puppy face printed on the chest, then closed the distance between her and Mike yet again. "That wasn't your fault, y'know."

He frowned. "Well, it wasn't hers."

She gave him a disapproving look, but said, "No, I guess not. But you weren't out of line or anything. It's just like you said: it's instinct to do one thing. But your, like, situation's changed a little now, and your instincts tell you to do the wrong things."

He looked up from the floor and smiled at her. "You know... you're brighter than you seem."

She giggled a little. "Come on, I'd have to be."

He laughed at that, and was suddenly at ease again.

"Julie dragged Xander off," she complained, cocking her head toward the pair.

Would you know my name... if I saw you in Heaven?...

"Yeah, he didn't seem too hesitant," Mike chuckled. "Some friends we got, huh?"

"Oh, yeah," she huffed sarcastically. "They really know how to stand by you. Really far to the left, but still technically by you."

Mike huffed. "That's going around lately."

"Ever since I came."

He patted her on the leg, and she shivered. "No. It just seemed that way... truth told, it's been happening for a long time. You're just the first person obser-vant enough to point it out."

She grinned, looked down, took a breath, then turned her head up quickly. "Do you want to dance?"

There was a pause and Mike smiled at the floor. "Mandy, Mandy, Mandy..." he trailed off. "I would be very lucky to dance with you, believe me. But my heart is telling me no..."

He looked at her again, seeing the depressed look on her face as she began to eye the sweater again.

"But you're right," Mike continued. "Sometimes things change, and you have to do things a new way."

He rose to his feet and extended a hand to her.

She looked up in surprise and wonder. She accepted his hand and stood.

Cathy glared at them, watching them move across the dance floor to a spot opposite Xander and Julie. They put their arms loosely around one another, with about a half foot of distance between.

"Well, that was kinda cold," came a voice from beside Cathy.

She wasn't startled. She didn't even bother to turn her head. "Mike Harris can do what he pleases, Tommy, and so can I."

Tommy shrugged. "I know. It's cool... it just seemed like such a brush off. And Mandy's so into him... it seems like he's just using her to get back at you."

"Maybe you should keep your mouth shut," she suggested, trying hard to lose herself in the music.

He paused a moment, then smiled. "Do you want to dance?"

"What?" she asked, turning to face him again. "You must be crazy. Just be-cause Mike replaced me with a Peterson, that does not mean I'm going to - "

"There's that word."

Cathy sighed. "That's not what I meant."

"You said it, not me. *Replaced.*"

Cathy sighed, then smiled.

"You're going through something, I get that. I wasn't trying to be all in-your-face. If you need a fresh set of ears, I'm here. I know I'm not your friend... but you're mine. One of the only living ones I have left, in fact."

Cathy took his hand and squeezed it. She rolled her eyes, then led him onto the dance floor as the song's beat quickened slightly for the second chorus.

ᚨᚷᚨ

Xander and Julie had gotten steadily closer as the song progressed, and now the two were like spoons, their bodies fitting naturally right next to one another. Julie leaned in, put her head on his shoulder and closed her eyes, letting out a long awaited sigh of complete relaxation. "It's been a long time since I felt like this," she admitted softly, so that only he could hear.

"Is it a good feeling?" he asked, smirking.

"Definitely," she said. He could feel her tiny mouth smile against his red denim shirt.

He was smiling too, he realized. The first true smile he'd experienced in months. Months when nobody, not even his dearest friends, had been this close to him when it wasn't to cry or to shout. To just hold and to be held... he'd almost forgotten what it was like.

"It's like all these doors are opening up to me, to things I haven't let myself feel for so long... does that sound stupid?" she asked, rising from his shoulder to look at him and make sure he wasn't laughing at her secretly.

"No, not at all," he assured her, reaching up and stroking the hair on the back of her head, soft as summer grass between his fingers. "I was just thinking the same thing."

He put gentle pressure on her head, pulling it forward slowly as he leaned in himself, each of their lips quivering with anticipation until they met. They shared each other's warmth in a slow, smooth kiss that felt more right than anything had in a long time. Her lips were silky against his, and his bit of teenage stubble that he refused to shave scratched at her cheeks until they parted, both of them wanting more.

From across the room, Mike watched approvingly from over Mandy's shoulder.

"I'm sorry," Xander said, gasping for breath that had been stolen away. "I'm..."

She leaned in quickly and kissed him again, squeezing his body tight against her own until he began to squeeze too, both of them still faintly aware of the music that played all around them, surrounding them. Consuming them.

"Alex..."

ᚨᚷᚨ

Cathy turned to the beat of the music with Tommy, more joke dancing than anything else. He clasped both of her hands and separated from her slightly, doing a few quick swing dance moves to the Eric Clapton song, getting annoyed and surprised glances from people around them.

She tried to hold it in, then let out a tremendous laugh, letting go of his

234

hands and buckling over.

"See?" he said, breaking into a little disco stance, one hand pointing upward at a fifty-degree angle. "I knew you had one in you somewhere."

She forced herself to stand as she smiled. "You're awful."

"I am. A total scoundrel."

She squinted at him. "No... I thought you would be, but you aren't."

"Oh, gee," he said, pushing out his lower lip and pretending to be hurt. "Thanks a lot."

"I'm serious," she said, tweaking his nose as they began to pretend to waltz, him stepping on her toes every few moves. "This is fun."

"Thank you, ma chère," he said with a cheesy French accent, clenching his teeth as though there was a rose between them. "Now, come back with me to Cuba... we will make beautiful music together, Bay Bee."

She started to laugh again, tapping him on the chest to stop, but he continued.

"In Cuba, you no ride de horse. De horse, my friend, it rides you."

Her laughter was heard all throughout the auditorium, but neither of the pair were anywhere close to caring as it became infectious, consuming him as well.

⋌⋋⋎⋌⋌

Mike held Mandy at a distance, and she made no attempt to get closer.

"So, what's on your mind?" she asked passively, smiling at Evan as he glared with the other boys her age on the other side of the gym.

"Absolutely nothing."

She smirked. "Is that why you keep looking at Xander and Jules every time you think I'm not paying any attention?"

"Hey..." Mike smiled. "That's... that's just cheating."

"And we can't forget your looks at Cathy, the girl who didn't feel like dancing."

"Mmm," he agreed. "Good thing she wanted to feel the music, huh?"

"Really."

"Re-ally."

"Re-all-y."

They both started to laugh, and he held her a little tighter. Taking a big chance, she bit her lip and leaned her head forward, resting it on his broad shoulders. He leaned his head against hers, giving her the smallest of pecks on the top of her head as they continued to dance.

He opened his eyes to look around as the music slowed down. "Did you see where Xander and Julie went?"

⋌⋋⋎⋌⋌

Beneath the bleachers, in the moonlight that reflected off the football score-board, their lips were locked together as if magnetized. Their eyes closed, Julie reached up blindly and pulled his leather jacket off of him, trickling her fingers over his shoulders and chest, smiling in mid-kiss as she did so.

He giggled a little, a sound that seemed foreign coming from him. He pulled her closer by the hips, and she sunk down a little. He followed her until he was almost on top of her, and then they went back up, smiling. Her hair was all around him, like his arms her. Their hearts beat harder and louder than the fast dying Clapton song.

"The music's gone," she said between kisses, as he brought his lips to the curve of her neck playfully.

He stopped, looking so deep into her eyes that he thought he might drown. "I still hear it."

They kissed again, and continued to do so long into the night, until it was almost time for the dance to end. By the time they got back, almost everyone was gone, and the floor was theirs for one long, amazing dance.

That's the really weird thing about life in Coral Beach.

Mandy wrote as she let down her hair, lying down on her bed when she got back from the dance.

It doesn't matter how bad it gets, there are always going to be places that you can go and know that everything is going to be alright. Like to Xander or Mike, or to a lesser extent, Tommy. They're people who understand what is happening and why, and they have a way of simplifying it and making you believe that life isn't as weird as people make it out to be after all.

CHAPTER FOUR: THE BOW BREAKS

Los Angeles, California.

She slid through the inch-wide crack in the hardwood floor beneath a stone desk, the black liquid that made up her body bubbling up like boiling, frothy milk. It spread out over the floor and started to spurt up and take shape until curves formed around her hips and breasts, and a sleek, pointed chin came into view. Cute, tiny lips emerged, along with big black eyes that gleamed with childish delight.

Seconds later, Leigh Blackheart was lying in the middle of the floor. Quickly, she stretched her slender neck and peered around the corner of the desk into the long hallway beyond, found it to be vacant, then stood up.

She stretched, took a few deep breaths and wiped the sweat from her brow, then smoothed down her short black hair until it was tight to her scalp. She took a whiff of the air, curled her nose, then looked up at the sign that hung from the ceiling.

Museum of Natural History: The Past is the Way to the Future.

"I just hope the future doesn't smell this bad," she said, her west coast accent apparent. She turned quickly, scanning the room until she found what she was looking for. In the adjacent room was a tall glass case, inside of which was a blue gem, shimmering in the bright fluorescent lights aimed at it.

Confidently, she walked out into the room and took it in, the smell of old things still following her. She bent over the glass case with an air of sexuality, knowing that she was going to be watched by middle-aged men on security tapes when the deed was done. She read the inscription and smiled coyly to herself.

"The Gem of Aberdean... well, if that isn't a mouthful."

She reached into her pocket and pulled out a glass cutter attached to a large suction cup. She stuck it carefully to the glass, slowly twirling the blade around until a circle had been cut. Softly, she removed the device and tapped the inside of the circle.

Nothing happened.

Sighing, she tapped it again, a little harder.

Again, nothing happened.

"Oh, fuck this," she huffed, reaching back an arm and punching through the glass, shattering the entire case and grabbing the gem as alarms began to sound all around her.

Closing her eyes tightly, her feet began to melt. Her face filled with anguish as the rest of her body followed, and she again disappeared into the floor.

She reemerged a moment later outside the museum, drenched in sweat. Looking down at the brilliant blue stone in her hand, she smiled devilishly.

"So, you're what everyone's talking about?" she smiled, turning briefly back toward the museum. "Sorry guys. When I collect the five mil for this baby, I'll be sure to send you an air freshener."

Suddenly, she screamed, dropping the gem to the grass.

Her body began to shimmer and shake, blobs boiling off of her everywhere. Even her eyes became as large as dinner plates, then as small as needle-points, as she morphed uncontrollably and fell to the ground.

She turned onto her back, an action that seemed to take all of her energy, and faced her attacker.

There stood a tall, white man with dark brown hair that came down in two long streaks on either side of his face. His face was sharp, almost to the point of being triangular, and his mouth was small and curled up in a holier-than-thou sneer. He wore a strip of cloth across his forehead, which featured a tiny green gem in its center. His eyes were a piercing cobalt blue. The strangest thing about him was his attire. Dressed in long black robes from head to toe that covered his feet and made him look like he was floating, along with patterned pieces of ribbon that twirled about his body, engraved in gold thread with runes and Egyptian symbols. He pointed a long cane at her, and energy crackled from its tip.

If this had been a hundred years ago, she would have said that he was a nobleman.

"Who the fuck are you?" she spat, still twitching, a mixture of blood and sweat seeping from her pores.

"I, am Sebastian LeGaea," he said, making it sound royal and important with his strong Scandinavian accent. "You, are Leigh Blackheart. Formerly Leigh Draco."

He pulled back a leg and kicked her. To her shock, it actually connected.

"You are an idiot. And yet... you have accomplished something I could not, the retrieval of the gem."

"How the hell did you know I was going to be here?"

He looked down at her, raising his cane. "I hired you, you twit. I hate to inform you, but the gem is worth nothing... putting it right on par with your pathetic life."

He brought the cane down against her head, causing her to black out into a dreamless slumber.

CHAPTER FIVE: INNOCENCE

He looked at her, seeing the fear in her eyes and loving it.

Ian Char had always reveled in that fear, and found his home in it. Found comfort, even, the way most people find comfort in curling up next to a lover on a cold winter's night.

He had not known the touch of a lover in many years, but that was not to say he had not known the touch of a woman. Indeed, he had known the touch of many as their fists beat against his chest, begging for him to get off as he held their legs apart, before he eventually shot them, stabbed them, or otherwise made sure they would never tell a living soul what he had done.

This girl was older than the ones he usually picked, but she would do just fine. Most of the young ones were at the teen dance, and after everything that had happened in this town lately, they had taken to walking home in what could only be described as small packs.

He rolled up his sleeve with the hand that was not holding a knife, revealing the red letter T tattooed on his upper arm. He smirked a little as the woman's eyes filled with even more fear, were that even possible. She recognized the symbol. That was always good. It meant that he wouldn't have to kill her, or deal with the body. It meant that she wouldn't tell a soul, anyway. The benefit of gang warfare.

"Please, don't," she begged, her groceries scattering the ground around her as she raised her arms to try and protect herself. "I won't tell anyone, I swear."

"I know you won't," Ian responded coldly, twirling the knife around in his hands. "You won't tell a single soul. You know that even if I went down, they'd come find you."

"Please," she whispered, as she realized her back was against the wall.

"Come on. Beg," he coaxed her, passing the blade playfully from hand to hand. "I love it when they beg."

The woman began to cry in heaping, helpless sobs.

"Why are you crying?" he said, sounding almost sympathetic. "It won't hurt..."

"Wrong," came a low, scratchy voice from behind him.

He turned, seeing the thing from his nightmares leaning against the far wall of the alleyway behind him, arms folded across its chest. Its skin was oily and thick. It was all black except for the eyes, which shone like twin red flames, burning with a passion for its work.

"It's going to hurt a lot, Ian."

"You!" Ian yelled, turning away from the woman and getting a better grip on his knife. "Why don't you go back where you came from? Things were great before you came!"

"And they say one person can't make a difference," the Womb barked, pushing off of the wall and into a relaxed fighting stance, fists at the ready.

Ian lunged forward with his blade, slashing at the beast. "Why can't you leave us alone?"

The Womb dodged, let the knife hit off the wall, then brought its knee up squarely into Ian's mid-section. "Why can't you stop raping women? Why does the world turn? Why is the sky blue? All these answers and more next time on Discovery Planet."

It drew back, releasing its claws with a sickening sound of bone ripping through flesh, and clawed Ian across the face. It reopened the wounds it had inflicted on the man weeks ago. The Womb leapt away from the bleeding mugger, then looked the woman up and down.

"Run!" it yelled, wondering why they always had to be told.

She took off, not bothering to pick up her groceries as she bolted down the block.

The Womb turned back toward Ian, only to find himself alone in the alley, catching a glimpse of the man as he took off into the night.

"Coward," he muttered as the blackness melted off him, revealing a thin layer of congealed blood covering his flesh. "You'd think this was the first time I whooped his ass."

He reached up and peeled the blood off of his body, then walked over to the dark corner where he'd left a white plastic shopping bag. He opened it, checked its contents, then started on his way again out of the alley and back toward the Peterson house.

They're getting brave again, Xander thought to himself, pulling his collar tight. *I thought the Tees had scattered after the last thrashing I gave them, but lately I've been seeing the signs again. People running away from shadows and not saying what. Rape victims that mysteriously drop charges against their attackers... and the cops. The cops aren't around this part of town as much, which means the cash flow from the Tees to the police has started again... with interest, I'd wager.*

I could figure out where they're hiding now... they're stupid enough to use that same warehouse off Laird, I'm betting. But maybe not. That leader of theirs... Roulette... he's not as dumb as he lets on. He's managed to get away with this crap for the last decade or more, so he must be doing something right.

At least the Tees are all that's on the streets, now that Genblade's in a coma and Derek's rotting in jail.

He turned into Julie's driveway, then skipped up the steps to her front door and opened it without knocking. It opened directly into the living room / kitchen / dining room / hallway, and Julie turned around in her spotted, torn couch to face him.

"What took you?" she asked innocently, glancing at the clock to make sure she wasn't being overzealous. "The store is, like, thirty seconds away."

"I ran into a friend on the way back," he smiled, leaning over from behind her and greeting her with a short kiss on the lips. "Had a chat with him for a minute."

"Anyone I know?"

"I hope not," he mumbled, plopping the bag down in front of the couch then hopping over it himself, landing next to her. The tightly coiled springs pushed into his rear.

"What?"

"Nothing."

Her eyes went directly for the bag, and she licked her lips a little. "Did you get it?"

"Get what?"

There was a moment then when they just looked at one another. He tried very hard to keep his face stalwart and stern, but a stupid grin was already starting to trickle along the sides of his mouth. She just looked at him, mouth partly open and eyes wide, waiting to see if he'd crack. Trying to figure him out.

"Don't tease," she decided finally, smiling contentedly as she turned toward the television. It was a thirteen-inch and sat on a box a few feet in front of the couch.

"I'm not. Was I supposed to get something?" His smirk was adamant now. He was only lying to himself by thinking that she didn't see through his flimsy ruse.

She sighed, letting him know that there was only so long that she'd put up with this game. "I said don't tease. I wouldn't mind if you were good at it, but you're a horrible liar."

"Is that so?"

She giggled. "'Tis so. 'Tis so indeed."

This time he really did have to ward off laughter. He felt his ribs ache with it, wanting to roll around on the floor at the joke that she hadn't even realized she'd made. Still, he kept it in, letting it pass with a quick cough aimed to one side, then returned her to his line of sight. "Well, I don't know that you're a good gauge for truth anyway."

"Yes. Right. Noted," she said impatiently, folding her arms in a cute, mock-pouting fashion. "Now, tell me that you got it."

He noted the change from *Did you get it* to *tell me you got it*, and decided to end the charade quickly before someone got hurt. Namely, him.

Rolling his eyes, he reached into the bag and pulled out a battered old VHS case.

"Yes," he said, defeated. "Yes, I got it."

She snatched it up and squealed with glee. She hugged the video cassette to her chest as if it were a small stuffed animal, leaning forward and giving him a quick peck on the lips.

The kiss took him aback and he fumbled a little on the chair, that stupid grin returning to his face. After a moment he shook it off, but his eyes still looked partially glazed over with pure, unadulterated schoolboy amazement at the feeling of her soft, silky lips.

"Hamina," he said, then shook his head to clear out the cobwebs she'd so easily placed there. "If that's what I get for the first one, I should have got the whole trilogy."

Julie smiled, getting up and bringing the tape over to the VCR. She bent over in an overtly sexualized manner and popped in the tape, somehow making that sexual as well.

He realized that she wasn't the only person completely comfortable with what was happening... he was, too. He remembered someone that he used to feel this comfortable with. Someone that he used to cuddle up on the couch with and watch cheesy movies, but even that was a far cry from this because she felt the same way now. She was reeling him in, and he felt no pain as the hook went into his mouth.

"I'm just glad you knew what I meant when I said 'The First One,'" she said slyly as she plopped down next to him, the springs digging at her. "When you took so long, I was starting to worry that you'd picked up Episode One."

"The Phantom Boredom?" he asked, cocking an eyebrow at her. "You think I'd waste five bucks on that piece of garbage?"

"I think you'd do just about anything I asked if you thought it might get you a little further," she smirked, her mouth moist and barely opening. Her eyes were half closed and fluttering over his body as she leaned in and gave him one slow, short kiss that rattled his entire frame. His every pore screamed for her to continue.

He smiled a true smile. A smile that he didn't even realize was there, it felt so normal. "I'm happy with where we are."

She gave him a quirked grin. "I know," she told him in a patronizing voice. "I was teasing. See? That's why I'm good at it."

He raised his arm. She snuggled into the spot he made for her, fitting as though she had been made for it, and he placed it comfortably around her, giving her one prolonged squeeze.

"Thank you," he said suddenly.

"For what?" she laughed, not taking her eyes off the screen as the decades old coming attractions came up, the tracking on the old tape jumping just enough to be annoying.

"For being a Warsie."

"A *what*?"

"A *Star Wars* fan. Apparently not enough that you know the terminology, though."

"Why is that such a big deal?"

"Do you have any idea how hard it is to find a girl that will request *Star Wars* for a movie?"

"As long as it's not Episode One," she chimed, shooting a finger dramatically into the air.

"As long as it's not Episode One," he agreed, nodding curtly.

"Jar Jar Binks must die."

"Too true."

Julie stopped for a moment. "Thank you."

"For what?" he asked, wondering if the conversation were about to repeat itself.

"For being the kind of guy you can watch movies with."

"There's another kind?"

She laughed at that, and it was just a little condescending. It was the laugh of someone with far more dating experience than he. "Yes. There are. There are guys that say they're going to watch the movie, put their arm around you, and then think you don't realize when they're trying to get your shirt off."

"I see," he coughed, not enjoying that mental picture in the least.

"No, you don't," she said, this time without the slightest hint of patronization. "That's what's great about you. You don't see how some people can be like that, and it's the best part of you. Not only are you not a jerk, but you can't get your head around how other guys can be jerks."

He huffed a little at that. "I've known my fair share of jerks."

"But none of them tried to get your clothes off."

He paused, a slight smile creeping onto his face. "There was one... but she turned out to be all right after all."

Julie blushed a little at that, burying her face in the crook of his arm. After a moment she poked her eyes up just enough to see if he was watching her. It was astonishingly cute. "I hoped you'd never mention that again."

"Abandon that hope," he chuckled, tickling her just a little with the arm that was wrapped around her.

She yelped at his surprise touch, jumping back up into her previous position.

He squeezed her again, then they both turned toward the screen in nearly perfect unison as the operatic instrumental started, and golden words began to scroll up onto the screen.

He held her close, and she him, and were as comfortable as they could be on a couch with springs poking out of it.

"I want to go home," Charles whined, stomping his foot, just to show that he knew what he was saying. Kids had a way of dramatizing simple things like that; it was part of their appeal. They could get away with so much that adults never could.

The whine cut through Malcolm's skull like a knife, slowly sawing at what he thought were the last remaining strands of his sanity. In fact, those strands had long since been sliced away. "Not yet. There's more candy. And you haven't even gotten the bread for your mother yet."

"I think I should go home." Tears were welling in the child's eyes now, his bottom lip quivering.

Malcolm sighed, not knowing what to do. The boy had wanted to come, had approached him. Surely they'd understand. What was he to do, send the child to that perverted obese man who looked like a country bumpkin inbred hick? No, he couldn't have that. The fat man would have abused the boy, taken advantage of him. Malcolm had fallen in love with the boy's golden locks. He would never hurt the child. Never.

Unless the boy wanted him to. Not hurt him, of course. He was not delusional. He knew that no child wished to be hurt. But if he was gentle... all kids these days knew about *it* (Malcolm blamed MTV). Charles, although sweet and innocent, was no different. He had wanted to follow Malcolm into the woods. Did he see what Malcolm had been doing there, hidden behind the shrub? Maybe the boy had wanted to be taken into the woods, his clothes hung on a tree.

He wouldn't hurt him. He'd be gentle, so gentle.

The boy might want it. Maybe that was why he was crying. Crying because he didn't feel he was beautiful, thought Malcolm. Maybe he did not like the golden curls his mother had tried to rid him of.

Suddenly, Malcolm had the image of holding the boy's head down where Malcolm's hand had been earlier, and running his fingers through those golden curls.

Don't do that, Malcolm.

"Shh," he hissed quietly, not wanting to alert the child to the others about. They might try to hurt him, and Malcolm never would.

"I want -"

"I was just talking to your mommy," he said suddenly. He said the words before he even really thought them. "She said it was dark out and that you shouldn't walk home. Isn't that what Mommy tells you?"

Slowly, Charles nodded.

"Your Mommy said you should stay here tonight. She'll see you tomorrow. If you want?"

Again, the child slowly nodded.

See, thought Malcolm, I knew he wanted to.

Don't do that, Malcolm.

"Shh."

CHAPTER SIX: SOUND COUNCIL

Dr. Warren O'Toole walked through the hallway of Coral Beach High, waving to students who never waved back as he passed. Over the past month they'd come to regard him as the boogeyman, and the children that were regulars in his office had taken on a dubious reputation of their own. Not one to be outdone, when he caught the teens mocking his patients, he'd use the authority that Principal Shnieder had reluctantly given him to bring the bullies into therapy, hoping that eventually he and his patients would be viewed as just as normal as anyone else.

This day, on the other hand, his courteous waves were just a charade. In fact, he was having what could only be described as the world's worst day.

He'd picked out his favorite blue dress shirt to wear to work that morning. He was only inside the front doors of the building for thirty seconds when an overly energetic seventh grader had shoved past him, making him spill hot coffee all over himself.

That thought in mind, he reminded himself again to call the boy's parents and suggest Ritalin to them.

When he made it to his office his tie had gotten caught in his door as he closed it, ripping down the middle. Now only the top half of Mickey Mouse's head was visible, making him feel like an Indian to Mickey's cowboy from one of those old forties Disney flicks gone horribly wrong.

Then, he stubbed his toe on the edge of his desk. Normally not an overly painful experience, but he happened to have a hangnail on that exact appendage. The pinky, of all things.

Around this point in time, he was beginning to feel like an unwitting victim on *Candid Camera*.

Then, Shnieder came into his office, looking more weaselish than ever, and informed him that a young girl in grade eight named Tracy Hoder was pregnant, and she did not know who the father was, so she was being sent to him on a weekly basis to help deal with her oncoming emotional difficulties.

So he was already having a bad day when his two o'clock appointment didn't show up.

If this had been any other child, he would have written a detention slip and relished in the hour of relaxation, but, of course, this student was Alexander Drew.

O'Toole called Xander's teachers. Yes, he was in school today. No, none of them knew where he was. They thought he was supposed to be with him.

He wondered if Shnieder would eventually crack and allow him to start writing detention slips for teachers. He ran his hands through his thick black hair, taking off his tinted glasses every five minutes to make sure that they weren't dirty, and waved politely to people as he scoured the halls looking for his lost patient.

He poked his head into the lunch room, getting an annoyed glance from a small group of senior students sitting in a semi-circle and pretending to study. He raised a hand in apology, then quickly backed out of the room again.

Where is that kid? he growled inwardly, trying to keep himself calm as he felt his blood pressure rise past normally acceptable levels. *Maybe I should bring Xander in to meet my physician,* he thought whimsically as he darted in and out of classrooms. He even poked his head in through the men's room, finding nothing but more annoyed teenagers. *Maybe he'd up his Xanax dosage...*

He passed by the locker room, at first seeing nothing but a row of sickly green lockers. As he was ducking out again, a slight motion caught his eye. He turned back swiftly, seeing it for what it was: the female form pressed against the male form. Teenagers making out in the locker room.

With a wry smile, he turned away and continued on his search.

He was ten steps down the hall before he stopped.

Turning on his heel, he stomped back toward the locker room, fists clenched into tight little balls of repressed rage. He came back to the entrance of the room and stood in the doorway, getting another good look at what he saw there.

After he was done his double-take, his blood pressure was higher than it ever had been in the months since Xander had come under his care.

"Xander!" he yelled, and Julie leapt from his arms, no longer pinning him against the lockers in unbridled passion.

"Mr. O'Toole..." she stammered, fighting to catch her breath after the fright and the exhilaration of the kiss. "I mean, ah, Dr. Warren... Mr. Warren..."

"Dr. O'Toole?" he volunteered, through clenched teeth.

"That's it," she agreed, nodding and trying to hide her smile through pursed lips. "You know, Alexander and I were just talking about you."

Xander just stood with his back against the wall, looking totally dumbfounded. He still wore that silly smile he'd had on last night, the one all teenage boys get after kissing beautiful young girls.

"Really?" O'Toole ventured sarcastically, giving Xander a look.

"Oh, yeah," she assured him, trying her best to appear innocent. "I was just giving him a kiss for luck. He really wanted to impress you with his, um, thoughts on what he's been... feeling lately."

"Has he been not been feeling well?" Warren asked, his voice laced think with mock concern.

Julie could not suppress her smile any longer. "No, actually. He feels quite well."

"I'm sure," he barked, then turned to Xander. "And what about you? Where's your usual dry wit when I'm finally in the mood for it, hmm? Cat got your tongue?"

Xander shook his head without opening his mouth, looking rather sheepish.

"What then?"

He reached into his mouth, pulling out a small, metallic loop.

"Earring," he said simply, with an awful smile pasted across his lips.

Julie's hand immediately went up to her right ear in shock. She grabbed the jewelry back and started to place it back inside her lobe. "About that, Dr. O'Toole... it's a good luck thing... my family's French you see, and - "

"Really?" O'Toole interrupted, taking one menacing step forward. "My family's French, and I never heard of that particular tradition before. What part of France did you say your family was from?"

"Well," she stammered, her tongue feeling like it was doing cartoon loops inside her mouth. "You see - "

"Go to Shnieder's office, young lady," he ordered, waving to dismiss her.

"Yes, sir," she said, skittering away as quickly as she could.

He took a step toward Xander, shaking his head in dismay. "We had an appointment, young man."

Xander said nothing, but met the older man's gaze head on. Now that Julie was gone they'd both taken off all masks of civility. They'd been playing this same game for far too long to bother with it, and found it more efficient to skip the pleasantries.

"You never learn, do you?" he asked, throwing his hands into the air. "I try, and I try to get it through that thick skull of yours that I'm trying to help you, but you don't listen. You don't get it. You never will, either. You'd rather just run around acting stupid, shirking your responsibilities this way and that to go off with some girl."

"Watch it," Xander said bluntly, curling his upper lip.

O'Toole froze for a moment, then slowly lowered his hands and stood up perfectly straight. The only indication of his altering mood was that his eyebrows had sunken down below his glasses to become hidden. "Excuse me?" he said finally, after giving Xander a moment to alter his confrontational tone.

"You heard me," Xander said again, cocking his head at the counselor. "Don't pretend to know about my responsibilities, or what I feel responsible for. You have no sweet clue..."

"Okay, listen," Warren started, putting his hands in the air.

"No," Xander barked, shaking his head. "You listen. I've been listening to you yammer on and on for two months now, and I gotta say, I'm bloody sick of it. A few weeks ago, a little girl was kidnapped. I was out every night until at least four in the morning, searching for her through mud and grime and brush -"

"All right, I -"

"When I'm done, you can speak," Xander demanded, shutting the older man up quickly. "I found that little girl's arm. Her *arm*. It was buried under a foot of soil. You know who else was out searching? Gang members. Jerks, criminals, and psychos. You know who wasn't?" He paused, giving the words a second to sink in. "You, Warren. You didn't step foot outside your office, and now you're consoling the people close to her as if you have any idea what you're talking about, and then you're surprised when it doesn't work."

"I only meant that -"

"I'm not finished. If I want to blow off one of your insipid lectures to relax a little, to pretend for five seconds that I have a normal life, I will. So, tell you what, when the next kid goes missing? You look," he snarled, looking the man up and down with an expression of utter disgust. "'Cause I'm on vacation."

Xander moved to brush past O'Toole, feeling more than a little proud of himself.

"And what about Julie?" O'Toole asked, turning again toward Xander, the fluorescent lights gleaming sinisterly off his glasses.

"Fuck you," Xander shot, continuing to walk past.

246

O'Toole lunged out, pressing his palms against Xander's shoulders and shoving him.

Hard.

Xander went back against the lockers, denting them upon impact, to the sound of grinding metal as the hinges ached and strained.

"Hey!" Xander screamed, rubbing his shoulder.

"You're right, Drew!" O'Toole shouted, pointing a finger in Xander's face, all but pinning him against the lockers as the older man's face turned livid with anger. "Maybe you do deserve a normal life. But that girl does, too. She's been through more than you, even if you're too self-absorbed to admit it. She's been raped. She's been beaten. Worst of all, she's been denied... the latter of which by you. Now that you need a break, you decide you like her? Huh? What happens when you want to go back to the way things were? Are you going to just throw her aside again?"

"Maybe I don't want to go back to the way I was. Maybe I'm sick of digging up arms."

"If we had a choice about what fate wanted for us, I wouldn't be in a locker room that smells like shit lecturing a child whose father should have given him a couple hard smacks. But we don't have a choice, and eventually, you're either going to hurt her, or they'll be digging up her arm in a field."

Xander paused, shaking his head. "I'm not going to let Julie get hurt."

"Like Sara?" O'Toole snapped, again shoving Xander's back against the locker.

Xander's eyes bulged with anger, his heart sending boiling blood throughout his veins. Then, without warning, the true-womb organ began to twitch. Slowly coming to life, it started pumping blackness throughout his body, filling it until it felt ready to burst, taking over.

When he realized what was happening he stopped, the anger fading from his face and falling into desperation. O'Toole, although he couldn't possibly know it, was right. Emotion was a major trigger of the Black Womb. If he almost transformed out of anger... there was nothing saying that strong emotions caused by Julie couldn't do it too. Slowly, he nodded.

"You're right," he agreed, forcing his voice to be its normal, human self, despite the growing frog in his throat.

O'Toole relaxed a little then, motioning back toward the door. "It's time for another hypnosis session," he said, smirking. "And if kissing a girl is the worst thing you do at age fifteen, believe me, I shouldn't be saying anything to you."

Xander forced a smile as he followed the man back to his office.

Warren O'Toole has an attitude problem. I think maybe he didn't get enough attention as a child. Or maybe too much... don't ask me, I don't know anything about this kind of stuff. But, like, neither does he.

Mandy Peterson sat in class, her Geography textbook stood up in front of her on her desk, hiding the fact that she was writing in her notebook instead of paying attention to whatever the teacher was rambling about.

The desk she was sitting at was riddled with graffiti pledging allegiance to popular musicians, sexual commentary, and information for those who wanted to know who was easy in the class. She had taken care to erase her name from the list every day, and every day it appeared again, like some phantom was floating around late at night with a pencil, intent on making her life miserable.

He's, like, totally a herb. A troll. Beyond help of any kind. He thinks that he's doing us a favor by making us dredge up all these things from our pasts, confronting old ghosts and all that psycho-babble bull. Really all he's doing is reminding us how horrible everything is, not letting us forget.

Like Xander.

He's totally the school sweetheart. No doubt about it, that's why he's the outcast. Everyone knows they'll never be what comes so easily to him, no matter how hard they try. The sad thing about him (and the reason that I'll never understand what Julie sees in him), is that nobody will ever convince him that he's there.

He wants to be some kind of saint. I think it's because of Mike, because of everything Mike does to make this town a better place, to help people. It's jealousy. But he's there. He's right up there with Mike and the rest of the big-time superheroes, but he'll never understand that. No matter how many times you tell him he's there, he'll look at you and say, like: "You're wrong. I'm almost there, I just need this one last step."

In his mind, he'll always need to go that one step farther.

That's why these sessions with O'Toole are bad for all of us. It makes us think that we have to accomplish something to be at peace, that we have to face these demons to be free. Really, to be at peace and be free... just, like, do it. Say: I am at peace, I am free; and then believe it. There. Done. Mission accomplished. No psycho-babble or twenty minute hypnosis needed. Just do it, like the sign says.

Mike's a different story. He's a guy who should be saying that he's just one step away. Him and Cathy have been terminal for a while... last night at the dance only proved that. I felt the way he held me, the way we laughed at stuff we never would have even talked about with other people. But he thinks everything's okay, peachy. He doesn't even realize how fast it'll all come crashing down.

And I don't really want to be around when it does.

Because the only thing worse than Cathy's cold stares is the look in Mike's eyes when he's really mad. He doesn't even look like himself anymore. He changes, I don't know how or why, but he becomes someone different when he's mad.

He becomes the Black Womb.

He became it to save me from the Tee's last month, first when I moved here from Coral Cove. They were going to kill me, and he came in. Xander says it wasn't him, but I know it was. Is Xander lying... or does he not know what Mike is?

I hope he does, because there's only one thing Mike looks at worse than he did the Tee's, and that's guys that try for Cathy.

And there's only one person Xander looks at more than Julie, and that's Cathy.

No matter what way the bread gets sliced, Xander's the one who's going to be bleeding.

Xander Drew.

Mike Harris.

Tommy Irons.

"Keith Richardson?" Mr. Miles called out across the room. A hand was raised unceremoniously by Keith, letting the old Boston teacher know that he was present.

The names were scrawled on Cathy's desk in dark red ink, splotching involuntarily at times, turning it just a little darker and making it look like blood.

"Pamela Walsh?"

There were more names there, though. People that she had never seen, and yet she had come to know very well in the past month.

Cora.

Gwen.

Alexandra.

Amora.

Sarah.

Cora was after the town, Coral Beach. Although it had done so much to her, she still loved it more than any other place on earth. It was where her family had their first home. It was where she'd met her childhood friends and where most of them were buried, each gravestone like a place in her past to be visited periodically.

Gwen was after a character on Xander's favorite show growing up. She'd never watched it herself, but had heard it in that background a few times and couldn't help noticing it. The name, for some reason, had stuck in her mind as a symbol of beauty and grace.

Alexandra was an obvious spin on Xander's name, the recipient of it maybe even being referred to lovingly as Xandra (pronounced 'Sandra'). She had thought of it once while Xander was recounting the way he got his name. He had told her that the nuns at his orphanage had named the children for saints, like Saint Alexander. Since there was an Alexander and an Alex already, he got saddled with the name Xander. She thought about a fourth combination from the name, and its feminine version came to mind after only a few moments of thought.

"Leonard Kirby? Leona - ah, there."

Amora. In Norse mythology, which her father had always had an obscure fixation with, Amora was the goddess of love. It seemed a very fitting name, both in reference to her father's hobby and the emotion itself. She pictured the recipient being eyed by boys, whose name they loved to roll off their tongues.

And Sarah.

That one was too obvious, named for her dead best friend Sara Johnson. But she'd never liked the idea of naming directly. She didn't want this new person to be 'Sara the second,' so a letter 'h' was added for clarity.

There was another list of names too, albeit not quite as long.

Darrell.

Duncan.

Mike.

Darrell had been her grandfather's name, and was also her father's middle name. It was important, she thought, to keep some of that alive, especially since it was perhaps the one good reason that her father had wanted to have boys.

Duncan, after her Uncle Duncan Ross (on her mother's side), who had died of cancer two years previous.

Mike... Mike, after the father.

The names were those never chosen, never needing to be chosen, for the child she never had. The child robbed of her. Taken by a monster as well as monstrous events. It had been inside of her. She had felt it as much as she had felt the father's presence within her for the all too brief time he had been there. And now it was gone. But unlike most mothers, who got to hold their babies when their time carrying it was through, Cathy only got empty arms and a gaping hole where her heart had been to match.

It was like when her child had left her in tiny seeps of blood, it had grabbed onto her insides to try and stay, accidentally taking something with it. Now there was just that void, and no knowledge of how to fill it.

The names could be matched, of course. Middle names and all.

There was Sarah Alexandra Harris... that seemed right, to put those two together in a way their counterparts never got a chance to be. Poetic, almost.

Darrel Michael, which just sounded right.

However, she never considered Cora Amora. That just seemed like it would be a lapse in good judgement, or the mark of a truly cruel parent.

"Calla McFadden?"

Not far down from that list was another, far longer than any of the others.

It was a list of her dead.

Jamie Dawkins.

Liz Tyler.

Kerri Walker.

Sara Johnson.

Roxanne Carpenter.

- -

Her pen tapped nervously upon the space at the end. The emptiness from it seemed to glare up at her, ordering her to put something there. There was another name to be added to the list, it needed to be there to commemorate such a tragic loss of life. But the person she wanted to remember never had a name, just a short list of potential names.

So the space remained.

And with nothing to hang onto, no graves, no scribbling on a beaten old desk, no spot in her memory to visit whenever she needed to, the gap just floated there in the back of her mind at all times, calling out for attention like a child in the mid-summer night.

"Cathy Kennessy?" Miles called, pointing a pen across the room slowly as he tried to find her.

Cathy's head popped up, shaking her from her trance.

"Here," she said sheepishly, then lowered her head and entered that hollow area inside herself again. The next thing to bring her out was the bell to end class.

CHAPTER SEVEN: SPYDER SPYDER

Coral Beach Penitentiary.

Home to some of the most vile and disgusting criminal minds ever to come out of New England, its extremely underfunded budget had recently come under scrutiny by the state legal commission.

Sexual sadists shared the same walls as mass murderers, both from the town and the surrounding areas. It had been transformed from a simple court holding facility to a full-fledged prison in the early seventies, when an upsurge of criminal activity had plagued the township. It currently housed seventy-three inmates.

One of them was sleeping so deep that the compounds modest medical staff has predicted that he would never wake up inside his lifetime.

That inmate was named Adam Genblade.

Genblade had lived his life within concrete walls, first at the Engen facility where he was born, and now at the prison. He had only been outside such walls twice, both within the last five months.

He will die here, spilling out the remains of his bowels and bladder into the bedpan that now rests partially beneath him, one final insult to the town that he reaped so much chaos on.

An oxygen mask covered the lower half of his face, a mechanical ventilator barely a foot away pumping air into his massive lungs for him. Intravenous needles punctured his cast arms in multiple places, providing him the drugs and nutrients he needed to stay alive and to heal his body, if not his mind. A chart at the foot of the bed kept logs of his brainwave activity, of which there was none. Scabs and scars littered his bare chest, memories of battles both recent and historic. His eye was swollen beyond comprehension.

Although it was difficult to see, several of his filed-down back teeth had been broken and now lay somewhere inside his colon. Soon he would pass them, leaving a nasty surprise of blood and enamel in his bedpan for the nurse.

The door to his room opened and two nurses entered, one wheeling in a cart with a fresh IV bag for the patient. The other went to the computer readout that had monitored his heart rate, brain activity and respiratory pace for the last twenty-four hours.

"Let's see what you're trying to tell us today, Mr. Genblade," Nurse Reilly said, making a few quick clicks on the keyboard to bring up that day's report. "Anything interesting going on in that head of yours?"

The other nurse, an African American woman named Nurse Porter, un-hooked the old, shrunken IV bag and prepared a full one.

"While you're over there," Reilly chimed, glancing over her shoulder as she continued to type. "Don't forget to check the pan for surprises."

Porter stopped what she was doing, put her hands on her hips, and glow-ered. "I checked it yesterday. Cleaned it, too."

"I'm pretty sure I did it yesterday."

"I'm sure you didn't."

"Just do your job."

"I think we need a calendar for this. To keep track."

"Stop whining. Did you catch Leno last night?"

"Naw. He sucks, I'd rather watch Kimmel, and that's saying -'"

Nurse Porter stopped what she was doing, jumping just a little as her heart began to flutter. Reilly turned as well, not taking her eyes off the object of her fright. There, standing in the doorway, was a tall man dressed completely in robes, holding what looked to be an elaborate cane.

His face and chin were slender and free of blemishes, making him look like he could have been a member of a boy band in his younger years. His hair, which came down around either one of his nearly clear blue eyes in great streaks, was coal black and shone under the fluorescent lights. His lips were small and tight, and he wore a lace bandana across his head with a gemstone in its center, just up from being directly between his eyes. A second stone was on another piece of cloth, wrapped around his right hand so that the stone was flat against his palm.

He regarded the nurses with very little fascination.

"Who are you?" Reilly finally got up the nerve to ask.

"I am Sebastian LeGaea," he said with such magnitude, importance, and imperialism that he made it seem like he was saying 'I am Jesus Christ.' He had a thick Scandinavian accent.

"You're really not allowed in here. This is a secure facility," Reilly informed him, crossing her arms.

He let out a very dry laugh, which to anyone else would have sounded fake, but on him was just right. A regal laugh, of someone being amused by the actions of those beneath him. "Secure. Yes, very. I walked in through the front entrance while the man out front was reading a vulgar monthly publication featuring an-orexic, nude teenage girls. The definition of security has changed, hasn't it?"

Reilly looked stunned, gave Porter a look, then turned back to LeGaea. "I guess... so? Anyway, I don't care how you got in, I'm telling you that you have to leave. This is a very dangerous man."

Again, laughter. LeGaea surveyed Genblade, giving him a brief once over. "Again, I feel the definition of the word has changed since I first used it."

"The patient is not to be seen," she spat in finalization, using words that she was sure he could not mock or bounce back at her in his pretty-boy accent again. "Leave."

LeGaea stood a moment, watching her with an expressionless face, the small

252

twitches near the corners of his tiny lips probably the closest he ever came to a smile. "I'm afraid I cannot do that yet. You see, this man has chanced upon something I need. A part of the Tri-Ok'Force. Useless on its own, but with the other two... not so useless."

"Well," Porter said, finally finding her voice. "Like the song says: two out of three ain't bad. Scram."

LeGaea, again without the slightest hint of change to his face, regarded the woman as if he had only just realized she was there. "If only that were true. However, in this instance, it is not so. Please discontinue swaying me from my path, or I will strike one of you in the left temple and the other in the jaw, rendering you both unconsciousness, neither of which I wish to do unless otherwise compelled."

"That's it," Reilly growled, moving quickly to the wall and reaching for the direct line to security. "I've had just about enough of you, Prince Charles."

As she reached out to pick up the phone, LeGaea took one menacing step toward her. His robes billowed behind him, flapping like flags in the wind, the symbols on its lining seeming to move of their own accord.

Reilly reached up to block her face from his attack, her mouth agape, but was too late. He bent his elbow high and shot it forward, cracking her in the left temple with it. As she fell in a heap to the ground, Porter's eyes went wide and she opened her mouth to scream.

LeGaea turned, whipped his cane forward and threw it. It spun once before meeting its target, the grip connecting with Porter's jaw and shattering it, sending teeth scattering to the floor. The cane bounced back toward him, and he bent over and picked it up, its simple black wooden handle again resting in his palm.

Porter hit the floor, and did not get back up.

"I told you, you did not listen. That is the problem with American women," he admonished, stepping over Reilly's body, his heels clicking against the tile floor. He turned to look at Genblade, as helpless as a newborn kitten in a sack at the pier. There were even still open wounds from biopsies all over his once magnificent, but now broken, form. Sebastian balked, leaning over and spitting ceremoniously, the saliva hitting Genblade on the forehead. He then continued to a locked steel cage on the other side of the room, guarded by a computerized keypad. Casually, he raised the end of his cane to it and shocked it with electric blue energy. He was temporarily bathed in sinister shadows, then reached out and simply opened the door.

He walked down the long hallway, past row upon row of lockers and safes, along with bags of contraband and cocaine he could smell from the hallway. Near the end was a locker on which a placard read: Genblade, A.

He opened the unlocked cabinet, revealing two identical items inside: the Spider-Swords. Gifts from the Engen higher-ups to their greatest weapon, Eve Spider, Adam's dead wife. After her murder, they had become Genblade's. Now, it seemed, they belonged to LeGaea.

He carefully lay his cane against the lockers, and slowly began to unwrap the cloth around his hand, which held the gem of Aberdean in place. When it came loose, he held it in the palm of his hand, bringing it to touch the gem on his forehead. With his free hand, he reached out and touched one of the swords, then the other. He picked up the second, feeling its weight in his hand. He twirled it once, admiring the way it moved. His mouth again twitched in what might have passed for a grin as he reached out and removed the ruby that made up the glimmering torso of the spider decorating the handle of the blade, holding it to his head as well.

A big, broad smile spread across his lips. He took the gems down, then wrapped the Spider-Gem in cloth around his left hand, and Aberdean around his right.

The smile faded confidently from his lips until he was back to his formal postulate. He picked up his cane and walked toward the exit, his robes billowing behind him.

CHAPTER EIGHT: IGNORANCE

Xander awoke with a start, and for a moment he just laid there with his eyes roaming back and forth across the stucco ceiling, unsure of his surroundings. He felt sweaty and uncomfortable in his clothes, like they were a little too loose on him. His mouth was dry and the bright fluorescent lights shining down on him stung his pupils.

For a brief moment, he thought he was back at Engen.

Then, a familiar voice snapped him away from that thought.

"Well, that was a good session," Dr. O'Toole said cheerily, tucking his pocket watch into his front pocket, then used a handkerchief to quickly wipe his hands. The watch glimmered for a moment before disappearing into the tall man's pocket completely.

Xander sat up slowly. His back ached horribly and his head was pounding to the beat of a Jamaican drum. He got a head rush as he moved, multi-coloured spots splotching his vision, each one representing a different kind of pain. "Ugh."

"Something the matter?" O'Toole asked, with something very close to actual concern, as he turned his back to Xander and poured himself a cup of coffee from the little One-Cup on his bookshelf.

"My head hurts a little," he answered, rubbing the bridge of his nose.

"You probably just sat up too fast. Coffee?"

Xander raised an eyebrow to the man, glancing at the coffee maker. "Thanks, but I'll pass."

"Also, your smoking could be causing your headache," O'Toole offered, giving him the *you should quit* look, but not actually saying it. "It's probably nothing, but I could prescribe some pain killers if it keeps up..."

"No," Xander replied, waving his hand in dismissal. "No, I'll be fine."

Warren shrugged, then nodded. "All right, then. Would you like to talk about your therapy now?"

Xander shot him a look. "No, but by order of Shnieder, I have to, don't I?"

"Glad to see you're so cooperative," the counselor said sarcastically. "I'll keep it quick, though. I'm sure you want to go see Miss Peterson."

Xander got a little quiet then. "Yeah, I guess... yes, let's make it quick."

"Your progress is coming along nicely. It seems like every time you go under, you have less and less stress than the previous times. It's really quite wonderful. Have you been feeling the effects yourself?"

Xander paused, letting the question bounce around in his head for a moment. "A little, I guess. I can't say I have any less stress, but it has been easier to relax lately."

O'Toole nodded, smiling. "That's because the stress these sessions help relieve you of was putting pressure on your subconscious. You won't wake up after being hypnotized and all your homework be done, your girl having forgiven you, and your parents having raised your allowance."

"If it were like that, I wouldn't be so reluctant." Xander pointed out with a whimsical smile.

"Hah. Yes. But seriously, what the work we do here means is that when the homework is done, the girlfriend is happy, and the money is spent... it'll be easier for you to wind down because there aren't a thousand things eating at you that you aren't even aware of."

Xander frowned. "That makes sense, I guess."

"So, can I expect you to be on time next week?"

Xander smiled devilishly. "Depends on whether or not I get distracted. Either way, you know where to find me."

Xander closed the door to O'Toole's office, a smile on his face that he could not suppress. Even his sessions with O'Toole were getting easier. The guy seemed to actually be developing a personality, which was a bonus. Life as the Womb was getting easier to handle; he wasn't transforming at night when he went to sleep half as often as he did just a few months ago... he wasn't even transforming a third as much as he had the first few weeks he got his powers. Even when he did transform, it was much easier to control the Womb now, no aqua-eyes in sight. Even though things between Mike and Cathy were rough, things between he and each of them separately hadn't been better in months. Mandy was being a real cutie lately, and things with Julie were making his life happier than ever. All and all, things were going great.

He turned the corner around the office, and saw Mike leaning against the wall waiting for him. Mike frowned, looking up from the floor.

"We've gotta talk," he said hoarsely, his throat raw from fresh tears.

Xander stared at the tiled floor before him, his own vision steadily becoming blurry and wet. His lower lip quivered violently, and he could not bear to lift his head.

"How old is he?" he managed finally, turning to Mike. His friend was already crying again, rubbing the knuckles, which were sore from punching the walls of the school while he had waited for Xander.

"About nine, give or take. I could call a few and ask, but..."

"It's not important," Xander finished, placing a hand on his friend's shoulder. "I know."

The cafeteria they sat in was vacant, not even the workers were there. The echoes all around them were steady and haunting, like voices crying out at them from just beyond their sight.

"Those neighborhood watch people that have been popping up since... well, since the last time this happened? They're out in full force now. I don't think there's any way we'll even be able to make it onto the street without bumping into them."

"So using the Womb to track him isn't an option," Xander sighed, leaning back in his chair as his brain began to ache from trying to work out the situation.

There was a long pause, then Mike finally looked up, his voice accusatory. "Is it possible that this is Zakron?"

Xander's eyes went wide as he considered that, reliving his last few moments with the twisted fun-house-mirror version of himself.

"No," he answered finally, shaking his head. "No, this isn't him."

Mike threw his head back, breathing a sigh of relief. "Thank you, God." When his head came back around, his expression was a form of joy, but more than anything, a sickening guilt. "I know that shouldn't make a difference. There's still a kid out there... but it just makes it-"

"I know," Xander nodded, raising his hand to allow his friend to stop explaining himself. "You have every right to feel that way. I do too. But if we're dealing with a human here, then the chances are even slimmer that this kid is going to be found in one piece."

"How's that?"

"At least with Zakron we could predict him. He was an animal, he followed instinct. Whoever this is is a *person*, and that's a way sicker animal. If the police or the neighborhood watch handle this the wrong way, this kid is going to wish he was Kerri Walker."

"All right, all right," Mike said, waving his arms for his friend to stop talking. "What can we do?"

"With underprivileged soccer-moms roaming the streets? Not so much. You know I hate to say this... but I think we might just have to call it a night on this one, at least for now."

"What?" he said, jumping out of his chair.

"*For now*," Xander reiterated, easing his friend to calm down. "We can't do anything. With Zakron, if he caught me behind him one night, he wouldn't even realize I was looking for the kid. If this creep even feels you or the Black Womb looking down his back, he'll murder that kid and use his blood to paint a giant 'Helter Skelter' across Coral Beach, you catch my drift?"

Mike shook his head in defiance, his eyes now glued to the floor. "So, what are we going to do?"

The bell rang, startling Mike, but Xander just sat in the same position.

"We're going to go outside. I'm going to smoke, you're going to ask for a draw to calm your nerves, and we're going to eat our lunches with the girls because it's been a long day."

Mike sighed and started walking toward the door, Xander tagging along close behind. "You don't have to come. You should, but you don't have to. But you can't stop me from looking for that kid."

Xander frowned, squeezing his friend's shoulder. "You keep believing that, man."

⋏⟨⟩⋏

Macy Walker looked out her back window, staring at one spot in the ground: a fading patch of green grass, dulling in the longing fall months, until soon there would be hardly any colour left to it at all.

That was the last place where she had seen her daughter, playing with the leaves, her long, curly black hair streaming behind her. She was wearing a dark blue dress and sparkly red shoes that looked like they had come right out of the Wizard of Oz, which she had watched nearly seventy times, always with a new sense of wonder in those big, amazing brown eyes of hers.

Macy had sent her out to play because Kerri was always a bug while she was doing the dishes, pulling on her pant leg, wanting to help, wanting to get up in her arms, wanting to play... just wanting attention, really. What did a child that age care if the dishes got done or not? She'd probably just as soon buy paper plates to eat off all the time, then throw them away.

She had seen her daughter once since then, but at the same time, had not seen her.

She had gone with the child's father, George, to identify their baby's body at the city morgue. Her arm was missing, and the rest of her tiny body was beaten and ravaged almost beyond recognition. She remembered shaking her head yes when they asked her: "Is this your daughter?"

But it wasn't.

Her daughter didn't look like that. Her daughter had eyes that glistened in the moonlight while she read bedtime stories about Lions and Witches living within a magical wardrobe. No, that hadn't been her daughter. Somewhere, she was sure, her daughter was still playing in the grass, chasing leaves and following butterflies all around. Somewhere, in a world far better than this one, she was safe. Macy was sure of it.

She turned briefly from the scummy dishes and the kitchen window, looking at the rest of the small house that seemed entirely too big now that it was just she and her husband living in it.

The living room was a jumble of papers and old editions of the Beach News

257

Daily, along with posters that the neighborhood watch people had given them. Each was a large piece of bristle-board with Kerri's face printed on it, followed by two bolded words: Never Again.

Never Again.

Who were they to make such a ridiculous promise?

Her child's killer had never even been caught. He was still out there somewhere, smirking about what he'd done to her little body, how he'd crushed her tiny soul beneath the weight of him. She could picture him. Sometimes, she thought that maybe she saw him in the supermarket, or in the mall. Those people that gave her polite nods of respect and fake smiles... there was always someone whose smile did not seem all that fake.

And now there was another child missing. A young boy, not much older than Kerri had been. How long would it be before some punk teenager found his arm in a ditch? Next there would be signs up all around town with his face on it saying Never Again and everyone would forget about Kerri. Everyone except for her.

Never Again? It had been a little over a week, and already people had found something new. How could they stop this from happening to another child when the demon that did it was still out there?

Over at the Town Office, they'd started up a memorial: a giant wall for all the people that had been murdered in this town. She and George had wanted Kerri's name up there... but they wouldn't allow it. Kerri had not been born in Coral Beach, George had moved them back to his hometown a little after she turned one. By that stupid bureaucracy, they would have to pay a fee of two hundred and fifty dollars to get her name on the wall.

George was down at the Daily arguing the point now, but it would make no difference. The people at the town office were adamant. George had been laid off a few months ago, and they could not afford the money.

So with nothing to remember her little girl by, not even a body that looked like her, Macy Walker took her only comfort in the words Never Again... words that she not only disbelieved, but had already been proven wrong.

ʎ〈ʎ

Xander took a puff of his cigarette, tapping it twice and watching the ashes fall toward the butt-littered ground around the side of the school. Just a few yards down was the new patch of temporary building, there because of the Zakron's attack when it came to search out the Black Womb. That part of the building would be fully rebuilt in the spring, but right now it had just been closed off for repairs until after the snow melted.

He kept one eye trained on Julie, who was sitting across the fenced-in field alongside the school. She was sitting on the picnic table that faced the south entrance, as she usually did, eating her bag of chips and sipping on the Pepsi she'd gotten from the cafeteria. She glanced over at him for a moment, throwing him a friendly, nearly seductive wave as she turned back to Cathy and Mandy, talking about some unknown subject that girls were wont to do when men could not hear.

"God, that girl is beautiful," he said wistfully, taking another long drag.

"Aren't you supposed to be quitting that?" Mike scoffed, waving the smoke Xander was exhaling away from his face, although the steady breeze seemed determined to keep it there.

"Naw, I tend to like it. I don't need to eat now, so I need something stupid to spend all of my money on. This works. Plus, healing factor. Don't have to worry about cancer."

"Your teeth could still turn yellow."

"Crest whitening, man. Duh."

"Fine. Do what you want. See if I care."

There was a moment then, as Xander turned and waved at Julie again.

"All right," Xander said, finally. "Cathy's not looking."

"Finally!" Mike frowned, throwing an accusatory glare at his friend as he took the smoke. He took quick, steady puffs and inhaled them back as fast as he could while Xander kept an eye on their respective girlfriends.

"So, what's the deal with Mandy?" Xander asked.

"What deal? There's no deal." Mike said quickly, between hauls.

Xander turned, smirking at his friend. "He protesteth too much, me-thinks?"

"Shut up."

He chuckled, taking the smoke back from Mike to savor the last few draws. "I only meant that even though she hasn't told us about what happened to her, we know. I think it's cool that you're not freaking out about her asking you to dance and stuff, just be sure you know the line between being nice and leading her on."

"Thanks," Mike nodded appreciatively, smirking. "And I do know the line. Dancing and talking is the line, the occasional hug when there's nobody around to give it. That's all this is going to be."

"That's great, man." Xander said, impressed with his friend's turnaround. "Now, I think we gotta head back over to the girls."

Xander walked right up to Julie and gave her a kiss, a smile spreading across his lips as he pulled away. She wrapped her hand around the back of his neck and pulled him back in gently for a longer one, not satisfied with what he'd provided.

"We still on for tonight?" he asked her between smacks.

She did not even bother to part her lips to respond, merely shook her head in agreement.

Mandy rolled her eyes. "P.D.A at twelve o'clock," she groaned, turning to Mike. "Totally unnecessary."

"Yeah," Mike agreed, tapping Xander on the back for him to stop.

They did not.

Mike sighed, then turned to Cathy. "You thirsty?"

She did nothing at first, then turned to glare at him. "No," she said finally, when he seemed oblivious to the meaning of her icy looks.

"You sure? I could run in and get you a Coke..."

"I'm fine."

"Okay, well, if you want anything..."

"I won't."

Mandy rolled her eyes again. "P.D.A." she said under her breath.

"What?" Mike asked, somewhere between annoyed and intrigued.

Mandy blushed a little when she realized she'd been heard. "Public Display of Aggression."

He laughed. "Yeah, I guess so. I was thinking more along the lines of Periodic Display of Assumption. I keep assuming that things are all right between me and her."

Mandy sighed, touched his arm gracefully, and sent shivers up his spine. "It's not."

"Hey, girls!" Tommy said loudly, breaking up the individual conversations (as well as Xander and Julie's kiss) as he entered the circle around the picnic table. "Whoa, Drew! Didn't mean to interrupt. If I'd had known, I would have brought popcorn."

"Hi, Tommy." Xander breathed, choosing to ignore the previous statement. "How are you?"

"Better now that I'm here," he said, giving Cathy the once over with his eyes, then spotting Mike alongside her. "Three guys, three girls... that spells orgy in my book."

"Well, like, it spells 'Threeguysthreegirls' in mine," Mandy smirked.

Tommy smiled, moving away from Cathy and Mike and over to Mandy. "Yeah," he agreed, nodding slowly. "Yeah, I guess that's true."

Mike stiffened.

Xander shot his friend a look, before turning to Tommy. "Hey, man. Did you take notes in History? That's where O'Toole's session fell this week and I need to make it up."

"No problem," Tommy agreed without even giving Xander so much as a glance, his gaze trained on Mandy. "So, what do you do all evening?" he asked her, his voice low and thick. He did not seem to notice that for every step he took toward her, Mandy was backing away two.

"Just homework, I write in my journal," she answered honestly, still stepping backward until she was against the table with nowhere to go.

"Do you ever write about me?"

"Sometimes."

"How about I come over sometime and give you something to write about." It wasn't phrased as a question, more like a demand.

"I don't think so," she said, laughing a little, although it was clear from the frantic look in her eyes and the beading sweat on her forehead that she didn't find the situation very funny at all.

"Why not?" he chided, stepping forward again, until now they were nose-to-nose. "I bet me and you could have some real fun..."

"Me too," Mike said, grabbing Tommy by the shoulder and pulling him away. He purposely put too much force behind it, sending the taller boy toppling to the damp grass, soaking the seat of his pants. "But you were right, you were interrupting something. Can me and Mandy finish our conversation now?"

Tommy looked up, his face a mixture of the hatred he felt toward Mike for ruining his moment, and shock that things had not gone as he'd planned; he wasn't fitting in after all, it seemed. "Sure," he said sarcastically, fixing the shirt collar that Mike had ruffled up. "No problem."

"Thanks," Mike replied, patting Tommy on the back and sending him on his way, then walking over to continue talking to Mandy.

Cathy glared at both of them as they started to talk again, her eyes turning bloodshot and teary.

"So," Tommy said, stepping up to her. "How about you? Did you enjoy yourself last night?"

"Go to hell, dirt-bag," she said simply, barely acknowledging his presence before she walked back toward the school.

Julie pulled Xander back in for another kiss. As she closed her eyes, he left his open for a moment, watching Mike and Mandy talk, Cathy walk away, and Tommy just sit there looking stupid.

Crossed the line, man, he sighed inwardly, wondering what his friend had gone and done now.

CHAPTER NINE: BAD LATIN

Malcolm woke up on his couch around four.

He had let little Charles Frank take his bed, for obvious reasons. The child was magnificent, and deserved more than a night of late-night TV and butter-stained cushions.

He had not touched the child. Not last night. It hadn't been the right time. The child was too busy sucking on his candy to have wanted to suck on anything else, and Malcolm had enjoyed just chatting with the boy, finding out everything there was to know about him.

They'd both sat on Malcolm's bed talking until twelve when the boy had finally drifted off to sleep. Malcolm had carefully taken off the boy's clothes, leaving the underwear of course, that would be wrong. He folded the boy's tee-shirt and jeans and placed them on a nearby chair, as carefully as possible.

He did nothing else, but oh, he had wanted to.

He had felt himself grow and become hard in a way he could not remember having done in years as he pulled off the child's pants, revealing the wonder of his flawless, smooth body. Not a scar, not a scab. The boy was perfect, and soon would be perfect.

Malcolm had gone out to the couch and taken off all of his clothes, jumping under the dirty blanket he always left there. Slowly, he slid his hand underneath the covers and gripped what he found there, hard. He started to think of the boy, merely feet away. And the redhead that had so wanted him to see her, so that she could run home and do the same thing that he was doing now, if not better.

There was nothing wrong with that.

Maybe, after he was done being inside of the boy, either in the room or the woods, or maybe even against the couch, maybe he would take the boy out for a walk afterwards and the redhead would see them, and then the both of them could come home with him. Maybe she would show Malcolm her beautiful, silky body in exchange for seeing the boy's.

But she could not have him. There *would* be something wrong with that. The boy was only for him, his lips only for Malcolm's body, not some smutty teenager that wasn't even a blonde. No, she could not have him. But she could feast her eyes upon his naked form as he watched them. Yes, the boy would watch, naked for the girl, as Malcolm bent her over a chair, her dirty clothes in shreds on the floor.

That was the way it would have to be then. That was the way the boy wanted it. Charles not only wanted to have Malcolm, but to watch Malcolm conquer others. Wanted to watch as their useless, naked bodies tried to give Malcolm pleasure and failed. Then, as they watched and wished it were them, he would take the boy and then make them leave, touching the boy. Touching his privates gently, oh, so gently. Unless he wanted it to be rough.

Yes.

Maybe he wanted it to be rough. To play the game little boys played, when they said no and meant yes.

He waited, but the voice said nothing.

Finally, he burst, and he let out a long, pleasured howl of ecstasy, looking at the door where the boy would still be fast asleep.

CHAPTER TEN: THE SLEEP

Xander clicked on the web browser at the top half of his screen, and to his surprise, it actually opened up.

"All right," he smirked, clapping once in celebration of himself. "Got my browser working, always a plus. That's all the operating system stuff stuff."

He opened a CD case that stood next to his monitor and began to flip through the shimmering disks one by one. "Now I just need to reinstall my games, redownload all my music and videos, and reestablish my entire web-cracking library. It only took me five years the first time."

He groaned, wanting to bash in his screen but deciding not to, as it had taken him almost two months to save for a new one from the last time his machine had frazzled on him.

A short beep came from his tower then, like a worker threatening his boss that he could strike again at any time. Xander responded as most employers would, by swiftly kicking the machine. It teetered once, then came back, resuming the pleasant humming sound it usually made.

"Still haven't fixed the problem of shutting you off..." he murmured to himself, as he grabbed a potato chip from a bag that had been open on his table for weeks and popped it into his face. He made a disgusted look, then moved the rest of the bag into the trash bin. "...every time I try start you up you go into safe mode. Why do you do that? I hate having to reroute every time, you stupid thing. Ugh."

He typed a command that opened his control panel and personal settings, fidgeting around with commands there.

"Can't be the Engen Virus... you're basically a completely new system. I flattened that hard drive, unless it was some kind of super-advanced trojan horse... no... why do you keep starting in safe mode?"

Because it can, he thought to himself, frowning as he continued to type away. *And you wish you could, too. Every time something goes wrong with the computer, every time it feels threatened in any way, it goes in to its safe mode and next to nothing can hurt it. It's protected... shielded, almost. I think it's one of the things computers do that we humans really admire. If we could do that, maybe our children wouldn't be as vulnerable. Maybe we'd be able to protect ourselves against the viruses out there. Maybe we'd actually have a clear shot at heaven.*

But I doubt it.

The computer made an odd groaning noise, and Xander glared at it.

"Quiet," he commanded, pointing at it dramatically. It continued making the noise, and Xander held the pose for a moment, feeling very stupid even though nobody could see him.

As if in deliberate defiance, the buzzing got louder.

"Judas," he said sardonically, shutting off the computer and reaching for his screwdriver. "I bet it's that damn CD Rom drive that Randy sold me that time. That son of a bitch..."

There was a knock at his bedroom door, and it gave Xander such a start that he dropped the screwdriver. He turned, then smiled a little as he realized who it was. He glanced over at his clock, realizing that it was six. She was early. That was a good sign, he assumed.

He walked to the door and unlocked it quickly, opening it wide. "Hey, Julie, you're..."

He stopped, giving Cathy an odd look as she gazed at him, holding her hands together in front of her waist. She was wearing the same pink sweater that she had been in class today, and the same loose jeans, even though they were considerably more wet. Her hair was soaked, and he guessed that she had gotten a shower and just decided that her old clothes would do. But her eyes were wet, too, smearing the make-up that looked like it had been applied in a hurry.

"You're not Julie." he said, but he was still smiling honestly. "Come on in, though. You were my second choice, I assure you."

She stepped in, taking a glance at the computer without a top cover on its tower. "I'm sorry if I disturbed you. Your Mom let me in," she said quietly, her voice harsh like she had a throat infection.

"It's no problem," he said, tilting his head at her.

She just stood there, looking down at the floor, standing perfectly still, one arm holding the other. Her black hair was even blacker now that it was damp, and the water weighed it down enough that it was pulled straight on either side of her face like twin lines, a stray hair curling wildly every now and again.

She kept staring at the floor, and he followed her gaze to try and figure out what she was staring at. The only thing he could find in her line of sight was a sock he'd missed when he cleaned up earlier, one that he thought might have gone missing from the last wash load. He made a mental check to pick it up before Julie arrived.

"Is something wrong?" he asked finally, craning his head down so that he could see her face, hidden by her hair.

As if on cue, tears started to fall from her eyes again and her arms came up to her face, shielding it from all the world. A pain-filled moan escaped from her lips, and nothing had ever hurt Xander quite as much.

"Oh, come here," he said softly, pulling her into his arms. Her face immediately found its home nuzzled under his chin as he wrapped his arms around her, holding her tight.

She still covered her face with her hands, not hugging back, just wanting to be held. Her entire body began to convulse as the tears overcame her, and when he knees began to wobble he led her over to the bed and sat her down.

"You're shivering," he noticed, wondering how he had not before. He grabbed the blankets off his bed and wrapped them around her, bundling her up as best he could. "Did you walk over here like that after a shower or something? Cathy, you'll catch your death of cold."

She spat something then, a word he didn't quite recognize.

"What was that?"

"Good," she repeated, a little louder this time.

He frowned, looking at her. He reached up, took her hair and pulled it behind her ear, caressing her face as he did so. "No, that would not be good," he informed her politely, even a little patronizingly. "Because you, you Cathy, you are my very favorite person of everyone I know. And that's saying something, because I'm a popular guy lately."

She smiled a little, but it wasn't a real one, and she was only fooling herself if she thought he bought it. "I guess," she said finally.

He moved closer to her and put an arm around her, letting her rest on his shoulder.

"What's wrong, Cathy?" he asked, his voice suddenly wiser despite his youth.

"It's Mike..." she started, sobbing a little as she said his name. "But it's not. It's me. It's everything about me. Why does it have to be this way? Why can't it all just go away? Why can't I be happy, Xander?"

He took a breath, letting out a respectful chuckle.

"That is a lot of questions," he said, giving her a little squeeze with his arm. "And the answer is... I really don't know. I wish I did, I really do. As near as I can figure, you're the person who gets punished when I mess up. I didn't notice Grendel, he hurt you. I didn't notice Phillips, he hurt you. Derek, he hurt you. I couldn't stop the Anti-Womb, and it hurt you. It seems like you're the thing that God punishes to tell me, 'You're not fighting for yourself, y'know. Nobody that gets real power gets any choice'. I wish you didn't have to be. I wish I could do a better job of protecting you."

"You shouldn't have to!" she said, forcing the words out through involuntary whines made by a throat racked by tears. "But you still do. You do everything and still try to protect me. Mike's supposed to protect me, but he's too busy saving Mandy from someone asking her out on a date!"

"To be fair, Tommy was asking for..."

"I don't care!" she screamed, but not at him. "I want a boyfriend who'll protect me. Who'll never push and will be there when I need him and that I can go to anytime and feel safe in his arms! I want someone who will love me and hold me, and..." she sobbed, and her shoulder convulsed. She buried both her head and arms in his lap, letting out a painful wail that, if you were paying attention, had in it the words, "...and I want my baby!"

He shut his eyes tight when he heard that, several tears running down his cheeks. They dripped from his chin slowly and landed on her head.

She noticed them and sat up.

His lower lip quivered, but he wiped away the tears before she could see.

"Oh, Cathy," he said, looking at her red, puffy eyes and sniffing back moisture. "I am so sorry I can't make any of those things happen for you."

She started to cry again. "Yes, you can, I know you can."

"Honey, I wish I could..."

"You can," she said, almost a whisper. She moved forward, her lips found his.

She smelled like spring rain, that crispness in the air that followed a light shower, everything in nature clean and sharp. Her lips felt like silk on his and he leaned forward, opening his mouth to get more. His head screamed more, yelled at him to see how much of the silky feeling of her lips he could find with his own. Her tongue tasted tangy, like limes. He could hear her breathing and he felt that breath against his cheek.

Suddenly, he pulled back. "Um... Ju..." he stammered, raising a finger to stop her as she started to come forward again.

She smiled, and began to lean in again.

"Julie," he said finally, finding his wits. He sat up firmly and she sat up too, leaning back away from him. "Cathy, I'm with Julie. You're with Mike. He's my *best friend*."

"Yeah, right," she sighed, nodding. "Sure. Why not?"

"If it wasn't for that..."

"Got it," she said quickly, cutting him off as she stood up and started for the door.

"Cathy, you don't have to go," he said, rising and stepping between her and the exit.

"No, actually, I really do," she said finally, stepping around him. "Because both you and Mike have Peterson on the brain and I can't even... I thought you of all people... I love you so... and Mike, he..." she started to cry, turning from him and heading out the door without another word.

And for once, he let her go. He turned quickly and kicked his computer, slamming it against the wall. It immediately started in safe mode.

"Lucky bastard," he cursed, closing his door and rubbing his hands through his hair as he sat on the edge of his bed.

Julie's gone out to meet Xander. Second night in a row they had a late-night date. Good for them, I guess. The sooner they get into dating, the sooner they can go at it. The sooner they go at it, the sooner they can break up.

Mandy had just gotten out of the shower, her hair still damp and pulled up into twin pig-tails on either side of her little face. She had switched from her pink, feathery pen to a more traditional Bic blue. It wasn't nearly as fancy, but she found it was easier to use. No feathers to tickle her nose, either.

That's the way these things happen, isn't it? Guy meets girl, they go at it, he leaves? I know that's not always the way it happens... but really, it is. Someone always leaves, someone always dies or divorces you. Better for it to happen sooner than later, as far as I'm concerned.

What's really unhealthy is what's going on between Mike and Cathy. It's bad enough when couples that are happy don't break up before they become, like, inevitably miserable, but they're already post-historic. Why do they keep up this dog-and-pony show when all they ever do is fight and make people uncomfortable?

Mike stood up to Tommy for me today, and it was great. He's such a sweet guy, and he deserves so much better than Cathy. He deserves better than me, too, but that won't stop me from trying. No way will that stop me from trying. He told me I looked pretty. And that he liked the way I danced. He told me that last night I looked like a little angel. A princess. Then he said I looked like the angel of a princess, and I laughed. He laughed too, because it was kinda funny. I guess you'd, like, have to have been there... or something.

Another kid went missing last night. That's two in two months, which is really creepy. The town is, like, talking about putting the curfew in again, which would be great. Really. But the kid was taken in broad daylight. What? Is curfew going to start at noon?

Nothing makes sense anymore. These past few days, it's like we've all just been floating around. Eventually, one of us is going to bump into another. I'm just going to make sure that, at the end of the day, I'm the one on top.

Xander lay on his bed, staring up at the plain white ceiling he'd had ever since he could remember. Every big moment in his life was marked by a scar somewhere on the face of that room, a place that had seen the worst of his anger during times of trial.

He thought that those walls were very lucky, because they got to keep their scars.

He wasn't so lucky. He couldn't just look to a patch of white skin on his elbow and say, 'remember when I scraped that on my bike,' and then not look at it or think of it for months. No, his scars would heal. But with nothing to reference from, they came back to him over and over again, without rhyme or reason.

Cathy must feel the same way, he thought. *That must be why she acts the way she does, does the things she does. She's like me, she doesn't have the benefit of scars to go along with what she feels on the inside, because all of her damage is on the inside.*

There was a very faint knock at the door. Xander leapt to his feet, turned the knob and opened it swiftly. It swung even faster than he had meant it to, and there she was, standing with both her hands holding her purse in front of her, looking like a top prize. She was wearing a loose navy sweatshirt that had a very wide neck, which she wore down over one shoulder, revealing a great deal of her upper arm. The shirt was cut off half way, showing off her navel and slender form before reaching the hip-hugger jeans that looked like they would have fit Mandy two years ago they were so tight. Her hair was in two identical downward pointing pigtails, drawing her hair back from her beautiful face. Foundation covered up most of her freckles, but a scattered few shone through beneath her soft, green eyes.

"Wow," Xander said, tearing his eyes from her long enough to look down at his plain black shirt and jeans. "Suddenly, I feel under-dressed."

She gave him a coy smile that he recognized all too well.

"You look great," she said honestly. "But, just for the record, I'd prefer you undressed to underdressed every day of the week and twice on Sundays."

Xander raised an eyebrow. "Every day of the week and twice on Sundays, huh? Can I get that in writing, maybe? Written contract, declaration of intentions..."

"Most of my intentions for you are illegal in forty-eight states," she responded, and she didn't look like she was joking, although she had always been good at making him squirm at just the right moment.

"What are the other two?" he asked, the sexual-undertone lost from his voice now, replaced by a genuine interest as he stepped closer to her.

"Alaska and Hawaii... the freak states," she laughed, wrapping her arms around his neck. "They'll let you do just about anything there."

"I see, I see," he replied, taking a deep, calming breath as he wrapped his hands around her waist. He pulled her body close to his until he could smell her perfume all around him and feel those pigtails caress his chin and chest. "So, how was your day?"

"All right. I thought I saw a raccoon outside my window, but it was just a really weird spotted cat."

"That's great."

She smiled, drawing her lips so close to his that they were a hair's width away from touching. "So, I think that's enough small talk for today, don't you?"

"Absolutely," he nodded, kissing her passionately as she pulled him onto the floor of his bedroom, their lips and hands dancing over each other wildly. They let themselves go like never before, neither of them afraid, neither of them worried, and both of them understanding.

They lay on his bed and watched *Mallrats*.

They'd already gone through *Clerks*, during all ninety-one minutes of which Julie had wondered why anyone would film a movie in black and white now that there was colour, unless it was set in World War Two. She also wondered what she'd done to Xander to make him angry enough at her to force her to watch a movie based on convenience store clerks and junkies.

"It's a cult classic," he told her again, smiling in disbelief that she really had not enjoyed the film.

"Apparently 'cult classic' means: 'nobody but idiots and obese people from New Jersey will like this film'."

"Hey," he started, waving a finger. Then he stopped himself, considered it, and lowered the finger. "Actually, for the most part, yeah, that's true. But *Mallrats* is good."

"The case says there's mild nudity in it," she said, reading the back of the neon green case. "And it had Jason Lee in it. He ruled in *Almost Famous*."

"Indeed he did," Xander said. He had no qualms about any film that could combine romance with rock and roll.

"How come none of the movies you like to watch have excessive nudity, or even, any nudity on the back? Seriously, would it kill you to rent a good porno to get me in the mood?"

He almost burst a gut at that, slapping his hand against the floor. "I think you and I both know that we're not trying to get each other 'on the go'. Wasn't the last hour rolling around on my floor playing and making out touchy-feely enough for you?"

She smiled devilishly and turned around from where she lay, giving him a kiss. "Not nearly."

He fought his cheek's urge to turn blazing red with embarrassment.

"Aww, look at the boy blush," she teased, reaching up and squeezing his cheek. "Isn't he cute?"

He smiled. "Yeah, yeah. Flattery will get you nowhere."

"Got me this far. And honestly, I don't want to be any farther, yet."

"Me neither."

"I'm glad," she smiled, again leaning back on him.

There was a pause then as Ben Affleck punched some guy in the ribs and made a rude comment about his girlfriend, then Xander interjected. "Then what was with all the talk about porn?"

He felt her grin, although he couldn't see it. "Girl's gotta get her rocks off somehow, don't'cha know."

Mike ran down the stairs as the knocking continued, more frantic than ever now, like the pounding of soccer balls against his front door.

"I'm coming!" he yelled, trying desperately to finish getting his shirt on as he ran. "At six am, this had better be..."

He opened the door. Cathy stared back at him, soaked to the bone, her lower lip quivering. She stared at him, and him right back at her for a long moment, until she stepped inside.

"We need to talk."

CHAPTER ELEVEN: BLISS

He woke up first.

As his eyes blinked open, it took him a moment to process exactly why that had been his first waking thought of the new day. When he opened them completely, the answer was all too clear.

Julie was next to him, asleep with one of his arms still wrapped around her slender body, which had been stripped down to her undergarments late the night before. She promised him that she'd only wanted to sleep for a few minutes, a promise that the both of them had had every intention of keeping.

Xander had fallen asleep to the gentle sound of her breathing, the smell of her hair and the feeling of the silky skin of her body against his. She was quite possibly the most gorgeous thing he had ever seen right then, as he saw her from the other side of the morning light that came streaming in through his bedroom window.

The colour slowly drained from his face and he became haggard as he leaned closer to make sure she was still breathing. Putting a hand near her nose, he waited for what seemed like forever until she exhaled gently onto his palm, then breathed a sigh of relief.

What was I thinking? he cursed himself, slapping his forehead with his free hand. *Falling asleep with her next to me? If I had transformed, she would have been the first thing the Womb would have ripped into. She would have been lucky if she'd even gotten the chance to wake up.* He shuddered, trying to force that mental picture away. It lingered, hanging there at the base of his skull and haunting him.

It would have looked at her with those cold, aquatic eyes and it would have opened its mouth, hungry for her blood after all this time watching her from within Xander's consciousness. It would have gently rolled her over, gazed upon her supple breasts through that white, almost transparent bra she was wearing, and lapped out its tongue out to tickle her all the way down to her stomach. She would have started to wake then, giggling just a little. She may have even woken enough to playfully ask him to stop.

And it would.

It would have opened its mouth all the way, then dug into her with those great, sharp fangs, spraying her blood into its mouth as her eyes jolted open in

269

pain and shock. She would have been so scared she wouldn't even have realized what was happening until she was very close to death. She'd have looked around for Xander and wouldn't find him, called out to him and he wouldn't come...

Argh! he yelled at himself inwardly. He slapped his head again, as if to knock the wicked thought from his skull and turned to look at her.

The makeup she had so carefully applied was smudged now, most of it having rubbed off onto his pillows or his shirt at some point during the night. Her freckles were all showing now, each one a slightly different size and shade than the one before it. They were snowflakes, each one of them unique.

He leaned over and kissed her carefully on the cheek, gentle enough not to wake her. She smiled warmly, and it made him feel good. Even her dreams were undisturbed by him. He hadn't so much as twitched. The Womb hadn't so much as twitched.

He thought back to the raspy words of Adam Genblade, when he'd first been told about the nature of The Womb.

"Because," came the voice from the darkness. "It's true. The Black Womb's consciousness resides within you. You have remarkable skills, my boy, but not even you can control it twenty-four hours a day. These past few months while you sleep, it escapes. It's easy to identify. When you call him, when you have his body surrounding yours and you still remain in control, your eyes have a reddish tint to them. But Black Womb's consciousness is let out when you stop thinking rationally, when you get extremely emotional, or when you sleep..."

When he realized what was happening he stopped, the anger fading from his face. O'Toole, although he couldn't possibly know it, was right. Emotion was a major trigger of the Black Womb. If he almost transformed out of anger... there was nothing saying that strong emotions caused by Julie couldn't do it too. Slowly, he nodded. "You're right."

when you get extremely emotional
Emotion was a major trigger of the Black Womb.

Xander looked at Julie again and it was different than the happiness he had felt first when he had woken next to her. He didn't feel the fear and anger when he had realized what he could have done. What he felt was sadness. He wanted to be so sad that his eyes welled up and glossed over tears, but they didn't. His eyes remained dry, if ever sorrowful, as he looked upon her beautiful face.

"The Womb never stirred," he whispered to himself, slowly sliding his arm out from under her body and sitting up, all of the blood draining from his face. "Didn't twitch, didn't even flinch. It just..." he fought it, trying to think.

Maybe it had happened. Maybe he had transformed, and he just hadn't realized, and the Womb had not killed Julie, maybe--

"No," he said, arguing with the part of his mind that was trying frantically to come up with explanations. "No, there's no blood. I don't have the layer of blood on me. It wasn't there, always was before. So, I couldn't have transformed."

He sighed as he turned back toward her, then reached out and caressed her naked arm, so smooth and delicate.

"I couldn't have transformed," he repeated softly, almost like an apology.

If I had transformed, I would have killed her, he reminded himself, but that feeling of dread still would not go away. *But emotion is one of the best, most effective ways to get me to turn Womb. If I didn't feel enough kissing her... sleeping next to her... waking up with her... to even make it twitch, then I feel nothing for her. No love, no bliss... not even happiness, not really.*

He turned away from her, again wanting to cry. But he simply wasn't that sad about it, about knowing that he couldn't love her... no matter how hard he wanted to. No matter what way he tried to look at it, the emotion wasn't strong enough to make him twitch, let alone transform.

He brought both his hands up to his eyes, pressing against them until he saw spots.

So, he thought to himself. *To summarize, by sleeping next to her I was either going to kill her (proving that I loved her), or not kill her (proving that I can't love her).*

He frowned, burying his head in his hands and wishing to sob, but couldn't. He forced a fake one out, just for his own peace of mind. It didn't help.

"Xander?" came the soft voice, like the coo of a dove as it greeted the morning dew on the leaves around it.

He turned around to see her sitting there, the blankets pulled up around her to cover herself. Her hair had been taken down out of its pigtails long ago, and now dangled in front of her face in loose strands. She looked chubbier than usual, but definitely not unattractive. It was just a trick of light, but it made her look cute. She looked at him in near-nude innocence, her eyes half asking if anything had happened and half begging for something to happen. She had never looked so beautiful in all the months he'd known her, since he first spotted her at the party.

And still, he felt nothing.

"What time is it?" she asked, her voice scratchy with that mid-morning film one got when they hadn't brushed their teeth the night before. She glanced back at his door to make sure that it was locked, then stood up on his floor and let the blankets fall, casually walking around in her bra and underpants, perfectly comfortable with him.

"Um," he grunted, shaking the cobwebs out of his head as he turned toward his clock. "Quarter to nine."

"Did I stay here all night?" she asked, turning toward him and smirking.

"Yea, sorry about that." he apologized, scratching the back of his head and avoiding eye contact.

"Don't be," she said flatly, without any trace of sarcasm or taunting. She turned and walked toward him, still half-naked.

He gulped back hard, knowing what must be coming.

"I've never... it's been a long time since I woke up without being scared, without having to worry... I've never felt so safe, not even in my own bed, in my

271

own house, with all my doors locked shut, as I did in your arms last night."

He forced a smile. "I... liked it too," he managed, his voice wavering with each syllable as his eyes darted from hers, on down to the rest of her slender, exposed body.

She smirked. "If it's all the same to you, though, do you think I could get dressed now?"

"Yeah," he said simply, getting up. "I will too."

She gave him the once over with her eyes, forcing him to look down at himself and realize that he had not gotten undressed when he had crawled into bed with her last night.

"Look at that," he said with obvious mock-cheerfulness. "Done already. What's taking you?"

"Very funny," she said, turning to pick up her pants. She slapped her hip playfully, giving him a look from between her legs as she bent over.

He turned away and found a point on his wall to stare at while she got ready.   •

She pulled on her jeans, looking up at him as she hopped into them. Her eyes became confused, squinting and tilting up as they met with his. She raised an eyebrow at him.

He tried to ignore her, but she pressed the matter. "What's wrong?" she asked. She closed the few steps between them as she pulled on her sweatshirt and touched her palm against his face. "Is something the matter?"

"No," he said hoarsely, turning toward the door. "I just don't want to be late for school."

"Since when?" she asked, folding her arms and almost giggling.

"Look, really, it's nothing. I just..."

"Oh," she laughed, "I know."

He turned white as he faced her, his posture sinking. "You do?"

"Yeah, Alex." she smiled, leaning in and kissing him lightly on the lips. "I know you, remember? You're all into the emotional side of things..."

His eyes went wide. He could see where this was going. "Oh, no. See, that's not it."

"You don't have to lie to me, Mr. Drew. I wouldn't ever lie to you. I feel better with you than anyone else, and last night was the best night of my entire life. Nothing else has ever come close."

"Julie, please..."

"I love you, Alex," she said, gazing deep into his eyes, happily serious. Her eyes shone big and bright, sparkling in anticipation of his response.

There was a long pause as he met her gaze. She waited.

Hoped.

Prayed.

And with each passing second the light left her eyes a little more until there was barely any left, but she still met his stare until he broke it, turning away.

"I..." he started, hoping that the words would do something. But still, even at this moment, the True Womb refused to budge. For once, it refused to even answer his desperate call. "I can't."

It was like a bomb had been dropped on her soul as the last of the light vanished from her eyes, only to be replaced by a new sparkle: the sparkle of tears being held back as they filled her vision. "Right," she said, grabbing her purse and motioning for him to join her down the stairs as they started off to school.

"Julie, I'm really sorry," he pleaded, reaching out for her.

She moved to avoid his grip, turning back to him. "No, really. It's cool. I... I don't either. I was just saying it so that you'd feel better. I'm sorry, I just..." she trailed off, her voice becoming very wavering. When it returned it had a firm resolve he hadn't heard from her in weeks. "...I just thought it was what you'd want to hear." She sniffed once, then turned toward the door. "Come on, we gotta get going."

He nodded, then followed her down his stairs and out the door, begging the entire time for his heart to break.

But it didn't.

⋏⋌⋏

"Are you okay?" he asked her for the third time.

This time she looked up, only now noticing him.

"Oh, yeah. Sure, I guess," she said. She pulled the blanket he had given her closer around her, trying to keep what little body heat she had in.

"Would you like some more covers? There's plenty up on my bed." Mike offered, motioning up the stairs and even starting to get up to go grab them for her.

"No thanks," Cathy murmured. She reached out from between the covers and picked up the hot tea he'd just poured up for her and brought it to her lips. "And I remember, by the way."

He sighed, his shoulders slumping.

Then, suddenly, he chuckled.

"Yeah," he responded, sitting down next to her as he twirled the spoon in his own tea. "Yeah, I guess you would, huh?"

"Not the kind of thing you forget," she half-grinned, her eyes meeting his for a second.

There was a long pause as they both played with their tea.

"I'm really sorry," he said finally, dropping the spoon with a clang.

"About what?" she asked, not as a surprised question but more as a test to make sure he wasn't just saying it.

"For everything," he responded painfully, taking her off guard. "For the way I reacted, for the things I said when you told me you were pregnant... for the way I've been behaving ever since..." he groaned. "For breaking us so soon after we finally got ourselves fixed. For not trying to fix this sooner. For waiting for you to make the first move, when I should have been on your doorstep the next day with chocolates and flowers and, and, and a new car."

"I can't drive."

"Neither can a lot of people in our class, but they still do."

273

She chuckled.

"Thank you," she said honestly, meeting his gaze for more than a second for the first time since she'd arrived.

There was a long pause and Mike resisted the impulse to pick up his spoon and start playing with it again. There was already a growing puddle of tea around his cup and he hadn't taken so much as a sip yet.

"And just for the record," she said, sighing deeply. "It took the both of us to break this relationship, and it took both of us to keep the other from taking that first step."

He thought about that for a moment, then nodded. "You know," he said carefully, praying that he wasn't pushing things. "As first steps go, I'd say this isn't too shabby."

She grinned at him. "Not too shabby at all."

Both sets of eyes went back to the tea.

"About what happened... I should have been there for you," he said.

Slowly, carefully, she reached out to him and touched his hand. "We should have been there for each other. Since it died, I've just felt like everything is wrong. Tainted, somehow."

"I know that feeling. I've been having it all month."

She sighed. "I know it might seem that long... gawd, it does to me too, but it hasn't been..."

"I've been feeling it ever since you cut me out. Ever since we made love, and you just shut me out. You didn't let me talk to you, you didn't call, you avoided me... what was I supposed to think?"

"Shh..." she soothed, rubbing his hands. She nodded quickly, over and over again. "I know, I know, baby. We both made mistakes. But... it can be better now, can't it?"

He swallowed hard, choking on unshed salt water.

"I don't know," he answered finally, looking away from her.

Her mouth dropped, and she looked as though she could not breathe. "Oh."

"It's not that I don't want to," he said hastily, his eyes filled with panic. "But there's been so much pain, so much hurt done to us and done by us... how can we ever make it right again?" He laughed then, and she gave him a quizzical look. "You wanna know something stupid?"

She shook her head. "I'm sure it won't be stupid."

"I've been naming it."

Her eyes went wide. "What?"

"It. Our baby."

"I know, but what do - "

"Girl names, boy names... doing lists. Trying to have something to pin my grief to, y'know? Trying to..."

"Trying to give it a home so you can visit it, instead of just keeping it in the front of your mind at all times."

He looked at her, perplexed.

"I do it, too," she said, stepping off her chair and kneeling down close to him. "Oh, gawd, I do it every other minute."

Mike sniffed, the tears flowing freely now, as he drove his head into her breast. "And that story in the Daily about how the Walker parents can't afford to put Kerri's name up on the wall, and now this little boy has been missing for days and... oh, my god, Cathy... what kind of a world is this to bring a child into anyway?"

She nodded, her eyes growing wide. "I know, baby. I know. It's terrible."

"But we can do it," he sniffed, coughing.

"What do you mean?"

"We can fix it," he said, taking his head from out of her shirt and lacing their fingers together. A lover's grip that she did not fight. "We can make it better. We can make the world better, make it a place fit to bring a child into. And then, someday, we can do that, too."

She took him into her arms and kissed him. Tears streamed from their eyes as hot as any passion ever felt, and they were never more sure of where they belonged or of who they belonged to.

She chuckled a little while they held one another on his dining room floor, as their tea got cold.

"What?" he asked, kissing her neck briefly.

"I just wish I'd come to you first," she laughed, returning the favor and kissing him on the neck.

"Why?" he smiled, moving back so that he could look into her amazing eyes once more. "Who did you go to first?"

CHAPTER TWELVE: GRUDGE

The boy had asked to go home again, playing the game where he pretended not to like it here. Pretended not to want Malcolm, saying no when he meant yes. He had told him no, that he could not go home just yet. To wait a little while longer, or his mother would get mad.

The boy was hungry; he could see that.

"Would you like some cereal?" Malcolm asked, smiling at the boy. "I have Frosted Flakes."

The boy nodded, wiping his eyes and smiling at his new friend. Malcolm smiled back, winking at the child. See, there? He wanted to stay, he just wanted something for it, like any young boy.

Malcolm led the boy to the table and turned on the porno that the obese man at the store had rented him, telling the boy to watch it. He went into the kitchen and opened the cupboard, taking out the Frosted Flakes and milk, as well as and a bottle of extra strength Aspirin. He dumped the remainder of the bottle into the bowl and poured the milk in, stirring it until the pills had dissolved completely.

This was the way the boy wanted it. He wanted to wake up and know what had happened, and then he would want it again.

There was nothing wrong with that.

Xander sat by the brick wall at the far side of the school, puffing on his cigarette. The smoke was stale and hurt his throat, but he ignored it. Although his body did not want it right now, his mind was craving the satisfaction of holding it in his hand and watching the smoke swirl up from it into the air all around.

How did everything get so messed up? he wondered to himself, as he watched each strand of smoke until it disappeared in the fall air. *I thought everything was going perfect. Everything was all right. What happened? Maybe it wasn't okay to begin with. Maybe I just didn't let myself see what was wrong, so that I might actually have a shot at being happy or knowing some peace.*

I guess what they say is true. Ignorance is bliss.

He took another puff, closing his eyes to enjoy it as the smoke traveled down into his lungs, ripped away at flesh as it went. It burned at his insides until the desired reaction was reached and his craving ceased.

Suddenly, pain erupted from the left side of his head, and he felt himself lift briefly from the ground only to meet it again, face first. Gravel stuck into his cheek and old cigarette butts crammed into his mouth, his smoke flying into the grass. The moist greens smoked a little before the cherry extinguished itself.

He growled a little, deep inside his throat. He turned his blood and grime-soaked face to see who had assaulted him just in time to see the sneaker come at him again. This attack would have driven a normal person's nose into their brain, killing them instantly, but on Xander it only felt that way. Blood gushed immediately from both nostrils, making the stench of smoke that had irritated them before seem as sweet as roses as his senses were overwhelmed by the coppery taste and stench of blood. The healing factor sputtered to life deep within his gut, taking a moment to gather itself, as if it, too, had been taken by surprise.

"What the hell?!" Xander screamed. His vision slowly returned to him as he tried to get to his feet. He raised his hands this time before turning in his aggressor's direction, afraid to pop his claws for fear that it was some punk kid like Tommy or Randy.

When his vision cleared, Mike was standing before him. His shoulders were hunched and his fists were clenched.

Xander wiped the blood from his lower jaw, rising to his feet to meet his friend's eye. "Mike? What the fuck is the matter with you, man?"

Mike drew back and slammed his fist into Xander's right cheek, sending saliva spattering against the wall of the school, followed by Xander.

Xander slid to the ground, his gums ripped to shreds by the brick.

Mike drew back his foot again and connected it as hard as he could with Xander's side.

There was a wet snap as Xander felt his ribs part, followed by an even sicker, longer moist crack as the healing factor pushed it back into place before it could puncture an organ. "Mike, why are you -"

Mike picked up a large rock in his right palm and slammed it against his friend's head, driving the pointed granite deep into the base of his neck.

Xander screamed, long and loud, having to bite down on his lip until it bled to stop himself. His eyes bruised almost instantly, darkening from the continuing grievances being slammed against it.

"What did I do?" he bellowed. Mike responded only by pummeling him with the rock, which now felt more like a small boulder. It landed in roughly the same spot he had the first time, forcing Xander flat against his belly.

Mike stepped onto his friend's back, curling his lip in hatred and disgust. He knelt down to his shivering, bleeding compatriot and grabbed a clump of hair, pulling back and stretching the neck until he heard the calcium within it pop. Then Mike gave one last, hard tug before bringing back his leg again, kicking him at the point where the skull met the neck, driving Xander back down into the gravel.

He stood there, breathing heavily on his friend's back for a moment, his fists clenched so tightly that they were turning white and stinging. His breathing got heavier, showing no sign of calming down.

There was almost as much blood as there was mud on the ground now; the resulting colour was sickening, like a mix of everything that you didn't want coming out of your body at once.

Mike kicked him in the side, making Xander's body jolt.

"Argh!" Xander bellowed.

Mike kicked again, this time getting the desired result as Xander rolling over onto his back. He bent over and forced his knees into Xander's ribs, bending them inward until he heard the snap. He grabbed Xander by the collar and pulled him up, his head hanging against the back of his shirt.

Mike drew back his arm and punched, slamming as much force as he could into Xander's jaw. Then he did it again. And again. The third time, he let go of the collar, letting Xander fall to the ground. He leaned over, grabbed his friend around the throat and pushed both of his thumbs into his adam's apple as hard as he could, smiling as he felt them sink in deep.

Xander's hands shot up as quick as mercury, grabbing Mike around both wrists. His eyes opened, revealing that the black his pupils had finally taken over, rendering them an opaque ebony that reflected Mike's face back at him.

"That's about enough," he said, grunting as his vocal cords were pressed even tighter. With four sickening sequential -thunks!-, he impaled all eight of his finger-bound talons into his friend's arms, sending tiny spurts of blood from both of them as the razor sharp implements sliced through both sets of flesh.

"Ah!" Mike grunted, gritting his teeth together before mentally bundling the pain into a tiny ball and throwing it into the back of his stomach where it belonged. He tried to pull away, loosening his grip on Xander's throat, but the claws were still inside him, dangerously close to vital veins. Pursing his lips and puffing out his cheeks, he took one long, frustrated breath then pulled away, making the claws rip the remainder of the way down his arms and out through his palms.

Xander's heart pumped faster, aching within his chest, and the true womb began to bleat and churn, rolling over like a sea-sick gut.

"You..." Mike snarled, holding both of his arms against his chest in a vain effort to stop them from hemorrhaging. "You of all people. I *trusted* you, and you did *that*."

The Womb sprang to life, flowing into Xander's veins, traveling through his entire body in the span of a few seconds and increasing his blood pressure until it felt as though he were going to suffer a heart attack and an aneurism all at the same time.

"I don't know what you're talking about!" Xander pleaded, his voice corrupting into a more feral, bestial growl.

"Cathy!" Mike screamed at him, thrusting his hands outward as he gave into the rage pumping through him. His blood spilled against the walls and ground as he swung wildly at his friend, without any of the calculated hits he'd been performing before.

The pressure inside his body was finally too much, as both of Xander's wrists burst in tiny, red and black explosions, followed by an eruption on the left side of his neck. Spouts of blood splashed down over his body like a living thing, swirling about as though the liquid had an agenda all its own, covering every inch of Xander's form. Xander's mouth opened wide in a silent scream as the black ooze traveled upward, taking over his head and face.

For a long moment he stood there, like a statue of a dark shadow. Three curved, red lines appeared on his face, each opening to reveal strangely shaped eyes and a mouth full of razor sharp teeth that protruded from everywhere in his stained, putrid gums.

"Black Womb lives!" the creature bellowed so loudly that everyone inside the school must have heard.

Mike grinned, regarding the thing that nightmares were made of with an odd, detached chuckle. "I was beginning to wonder when you'd show up," he smiled, wiping a bit of blood from his face onto his sleeve. "Now the party can really start."

Black Womb stood stalwart and still, waiting for Mike's attack.

It came without a moment's notice, as Mike picked up a hunk of gravel and butts and hurled it into the Womb's large, scarlet eyes.

"Argh!" the Womb yelled, bringing Its hands up to Its eyes, accidentally sticking the claws in as It did so, drawing blood and impairing his vision. The healing factor took a moment to snap to attention, as if caught with its pants down.

When it opened its eyes, Mike's fist was less than an inch in front of It.

The blow struck hard, avoiding where the nose would be and taking advantage of the creature's sloped facial structure, hitting It between the eyes on a downward angle. The blow forced The Womb's yellow top teeth through their gums. A moment later the healing factor pushed the teeth back out, the action bringing the pain back anew.

"What the hell?" Xander screamed through the Womb's form, unsure of which part of his face to clutch in pain first.

"Don't look so shocked," Mike snarled, drawing back a heel, this time connecting with the soft patch of skin where he knew there were missing ribs from months earlier, connecting with the weakened true womb organ. He smiled as It howled in pain in three separate voices. "We've done this dance before, you and me... this has been coming since the first time you made googly eyes at my girlfriend."

From the ground, the Womb's head turned up and smiled, a sickening look on the beast. "Just so you know, she was the one who started with the googly eyes thing. I just wanted to be friends, scouts honor. But you know Cathy..."

Mike yelled, hurling his right fist through the air.

But this time Xander was ready for it, catching it in front of his face and digging the claws into each of Mike's tight, white knuckles, drawing blood and scratching bone with a sound like nails on a dry chalk board.

"Screw..." Mike started, but Xander squeezed harder, cutting off the snide remark.

Xander pulled back on his arm, forcing Mike's entire body forward, his head butting into the Black Womb's as hard as possible. There was a suckling sound as both their skulls ached under the pressure, and only the Womb's healed right away. Mike was left clutching his forehead.

"You!" Mike finished, kicking one of his legs from behind him and connecting with the Womb's calves, sending it toppling to the ground with rocks driving into its shoulders. "You knew what she meant to me! How could you?!"

"I didn't!" Xander coughed as he got up, black liquid foaming around his mouth. "I swear! She came to me, you idiot! Because you went and pushed the line too far with Mandy, she had to come to me! She was confused!" he sprang to his feet, punching Mike in the left cheek, sending his friend back against the brick wall.

"I hate you..."

"She couldn't go to you, and you couldn't help her, because you were both being stupid! So, yeah, she came to me. And, guess what? I turned her down!"

He lashed out, all the pain and frustration of the past few hours leaking out through his fists, slamming Mike in the teeth as he tried to talk, chipping one in the back.

"I didn't want to! I would have given anything just a month ago! But it's different now. Everything's different! I didn't say no because of me, or because of Julie, and certainly not because of Cathy... it was you, you idiot! You stay with her even when you two aren't together, but no other guy is allowed to even LOOK! Not me, not Tommy, nobody!"

He attacked again, this time swiping his claws so close they ripped Mike's shirt in three places.

"Well, guess what, pal, it's time to pick a station or get off the train, cause I'm sick of this bullshit from you."

He slacked off then, letting his arms go limp at his sides.

Mike started to get up, this time raising an open palm in surrender... which quickly closed into a fist that jutted directly at the Womb's solar plexus, knocking It back at least a foot.

"It's not just Cathy, you moron!" he bellowed as the Womb fought Its way to Its feet. "You've been so wrapped up in your little life, you forget what's going on out there! Peterson on the brain? You think I crossed the line with Mandy?" The confidence that had dominated his voice while he had been hurling insults had ebbed, a shake to each word replacing it. "While you're cuddling it up with Julie, there's a boy out there being kidnapped by some pervert two blocks from your house! What were you doing then, huh? Playing doctor with O'Toole, or trying to cop a feel from Peterson? Or was it the other way around?"

The Womb's claws shot forward, this time connecting with flesh as both parties staggered backward. "I've tried, dammit! I can't be everywhere, and I'll fucking try to kill myself again soon if this keeps up! I can't do everything, can't know everything! I'd give anything to be ignorant, don't you get that?"

Darkness fell over them then, as a man came down from above, landing with the grace of a ballet dancer directly between them.

The man stood up with his hair still perfectly placed despite the fall, in two perfectly straight lines on either side of his face. He wore black robes accented by ribbons, highlighting patterns that looked like Egyptian symbols. His milky facial skin was all that was seen of him, and even that was partially covered by linen bands that lapped his forehead, a small crystal caught in its center. Two more like it were found on similar bands, ceremoniously wrapped around each wrist.

"I don't," he said simply, as if the answer the Womb's question.

The man turned swiftly, raising a cane from beneath his cloak and whipping it into Mike's face, sending him to the ground with a face full of dirt and grime.

He turned then to the Black Womb, preparing to execute the same maneuver. He stopped and tilted his head slightly to the left, examining the creature.

"A darkness," he said casually, leaning the cane against the wall. "Interesting."

He brought both of his palms up to his forehead until the three gems were in line, and the blue one at the fore front sparkled for a moment before he brought them back down.

The Womb lunged and the man looked up, as if only now taking interest.

He smiled, a look that seemed odd on his colourless lips, reaching out and grabbing the Womb by both shoulders and spinning him in midair until his back was facing him. He brought his thumb and forefinger up to and pitched a muscle between the Womb's right shoulder.

All at once, faster than it ever had, the Womb splashed off of Xander's body as if it had the consistency of water rather than tar. There wasn't even a layer of blood covering his skin, and Xander was left with the bizarre feeling of disorientation, his world spinning before him. He wanted very much to vomit, then realized that the layer of blood had somehow retracted into his stomach.

"What did you do?" Xander gasped, coughing violently.

"A simple nerve pinch," the man responded, again picking up his cane. He drew it back, cracking Xander over the head with it. "You will be able to utilize your darkness again in a few scant hours. In the meantime..." he turned, again beating Mike across the face with his cane, who had been sneaking up behind him.

"Who are you?" Mike flouted, wiping blood from his eye.

"I, am Sebastian LeGaea," he said matter-of-factly, sticking his cane into the ground dramatically and striking a pose. His Scandinavian accent shone through thick when he said his own name, making it sound proud and majestic.

"And that means what to me?" Mike almost chuckled, nursing his broken cheek.

LeGaea's eyes narrowed, turning to really look at the boy for the first time since he had arrived. "It would mean a great deal, I assure you, were you not an ignorant pup pining over some teenage female."

"He's got a point, Mike," Xander murmured from the other side of their attacker.

"Shut up," Mike retorted, making a face.

"Enough. I grow sick of the both of you," LeGaea announced, as though it was God's decree then that they stop talking.

"Yeah, that oughta do it. Don't deal with teenagers much, do ya, Sebby?"

"Infidel," LeGaea cursed, turning and taking a step toward Mike now, a touch of vibrant red added to his pale cheeks.

As he spoke, Xander, still hazy, squinted at the gem on the man's right hand. It was large and red, and in any other place would have looked like one of the gaudy pieces of jewelry that Mandy wore. And yet, it looked almost familiar. "Is that..."

The Spider-Gem. The one and only. He could never not recognize it, now that it was in plain, unobstructed view. That was it. That gem was taken from Spider's sword, a woman Xander had killed in the heat of battle, which started the blood feud between he and Adam Genblade.

"If I were not in a rush, I would take the time to tear your eyes out and - "

"Guess what?" Xander asked.

When LeGaea turned, the boy was directly behind him.

"I'm feeling better."

He lashed out, punching LeGaea clear across the face. At the same moment, Mike kicked out both his feet, striking the robed man in both knee caps at once. He went down with a hard thump, followed by the rustling of settling fabrics.

Xander reached out and grabbed the Spider-Gem from LeGaea's outstretched palm, ripping the linen cloth as he did so.

"No!" Sebastian wailed, his eyes suddenly becoming bloodshot, like a junkie relieved of his last fix. "That's mine!"

Xander raised an eyebrow. "Have you looked up the definition lately?"

LeGaea lunged at Xander with both arms, trying the retrieve the gem.

Xander pulled back, but the man caught it with his left hand, maneuvering his head to try and yank it away. For the briefest of moments, all three gems touched.

"Run!" Mike yelled, as he forced Cathy ahead of him. The creature landed on all fours on the sidewalk. His glossy eyes studied their movements, how they ran. He found their weak spot at the sides. They'd both been damaged there. It moved like a jaguar, leaping to the sidewalk and then onto two legs to pursue them.

"Keep... going..." Mike encouraged Cathy, holding his side. They were almost to her house. But they'd both danced this dance before. He wasn't about to make the same mistakes twice. He cut through an old alley, hoping to run across the backyard of the complex until reaching her back door. They could see the house now.

"Mike..." Cathy pleaded, grasping at her side. "It hurts."

Images of three girls crying, of a blonde woman holding her child, covered with blood. Tears are streaming down her face. I try to reach out to her, but my hands... they're knives. I keep trying to reach out, to help her... hold her... but I just keep cutting her. Stabbing at her until, eventually, they both die. A brunette, a blonde and a baby, dead in a pool of blood at my feet, and all I can do about it is keep reaching out...

Tom Petty blaring on a loud speaker. Too loud. Burning air. Pop tarts. Red. Blood red. Red. Red hair. Hurt. Pain. Hurt pain. Scream: too loud! Shattered. To ground. Look up. Smell of cream. Touch. Hair. Cheek. Grinding teeth. Death. Death! DEATH!

The blond boy's shirt came off with ease, tugging just a little at the end, around the fingertips. His body was plump and perfect, just as it had been imagined. Death. Tiny nipples. Freckles, lots of freckles. Something happening outside, no matter. The door. The door!

Sara's lips twitched as they turned blue, her body struggling to suck in air as she fought for life. An inaudible word passed through her lips. She cringed. Her body went limp as Genblade breathed her in. His jagged teeth rattled as he brought his lips to her face, his breath smelling like the sole of an old shoe.

"You taste like strawberries," he said finally, letting her fall to the floor.

She was crouching over him in a way a woman wearing a dress like hers typically didn't. It was a red dress with long slits up either leg, the fabric draping down and hanging in the arc she'd formed between her legs. She wasn't wearing shoes, he realized with an odd fixation, staring at manicured toes that stood atop jagged, sloping rock. Her hair, long and blonde, fell down over her shoulders in tumbling curls, just as it had on the *security footage he had twice seen her on now.*

There were children close to her, so close they made him uncomfortable. They were clothed in shirts too small for them and dotted in filth, and each of them had visible scabs: the sort that lingered and kept getting reopened and became a puss-filled gangrenous sore by the time it was dealt with. She turned from him and walked to the nearest group of children, a group of four that looked to have a mean age of ten, and one larger boy who seemed much older.

She brought her nails to him and ran them over his skin, then up through his hair, in a way that looked similar to that which Cathy had touched Mike, but was different – it was one of those rare human interactions where intent shone through, and in this the intent was possession. In one fluid motion she had told him everything he needed to know about her relationship to these children.

When she laughed, it shook him even into the coldest reaches of his soul.

LeGaea looked up at Xander, shocked.

Equally shocked, Xander stood in bewilderment for a moment, then shook it off as sweat began to pour across his brow, making it silky and smooth. As he came to his senses, he ripped the Spider-Gem away from Sebastian, drawing back a foot and kicking him under the chin. LeGaea flew into the air and crashed to the ground back-first, grunting uncharacteristically as he did so.

Mike swerved to miss him, then turned and eyed the second gem, the gem of Aberdean, strapped to the villain's left hand. He raised his sneaker high, bringing it down on the crystal and cracking it, right down the middle.

"No!" LeGaea cried in shock, blood gushing suddenly from his nose and mouth. "I am Sebastian LeGaea!"

"And I'm Mike Harris," he smirked. "Deal with it."

He kicked again, connecting with the bleeding man's face.

LeGaea hit the ground, this time getting up quickly, running toward the fence and leaping over it with ease. He took off down the street and into the alley behind Clarke's convenience.

"Dammit!" Mike cursed, trying to keep a visual bead on their attacker. "Where the hell did he go? We have to follow him!"

"No," Xander said, and the word sounded like a gasp.

Mike turned to see Xander, propping himself against the wall on the school, one hand holding the Spider-Gem and the over clutching his ribs, fighting for air. "Are you okay?"

"I'll be fine in a minute," Xander assured him, trying to convince himself more than Mike. "But we gotta go."

"Go?" Mike asked quizzically, throwing up his arms. "Go where, exactly?"

Xander looked up, and his eyes were filled with anger and hatred.

The blonde boy's shirt came off with ease, tugging just a little at the end, around the fingertips. His body was plump and perfect, just as it had been imagined. Death. Tiny nipples. Freckles, lots of freckles. Something happening outside, no matter. The door. The door!

"I know where he is."

CHAPTER THIRTEEN: THE WORST THING

The boy had gone out like a light. It hadn't even taken as long as he thought. For a moment, Malcolm wondered if he had given him too much. That maybe his boy prince would expire, and not know the sublime pleasure of waking up next to Malcolm, knowing that he had been inside him and feeling happy for the first time in his young life.

The boy probably didn't have a father, he had decided at some point while watching young Charles Frank gobble down his special Frosted Flakes.

He reached out to the space near the boy's upper lip, waiting to feel the air come forth. After a moment it did, and Malcolm breathed a sigh of relief. He let his hand glide down an inch, finally getting to touch his finger against the boy's soft, silky lips. They were so smooth and fragile, not even that snobby teenager had lips like these, he decided.

Charles had enjoyed the dirty video that Malcolm had gotten from the obese man at the store even though there weren't any blondes in it. But there was nothing wrong with that. Charles was blonde enough.

Don't do that, Malcolm.

The voice said. It had returned an hour ago, as Charles had been eating his cereal. He had ignored it previously, but now he yelled, "Shut up, you bitch!"

The child did not stir, and Malcolm smiled as the voice ceased.

The child liked the movie, so he decided that he would bring the teenager over... maybe tomorrow, after Charles had woken up. Maybe after the boy let Malcolm play with his dirty parts for a little while, moaning the way Malcolm had the previous night while thinking of Charles. Yes, the boy wanted it. And the boy was letting Malcolm take his perfect body, so Malcolm would repay him with the girl, whether she wanted to or not.

He had to, to please the boy.

There was something happening outside, but it didn't matter.

He grabbed the boy's tee-shirt gently, pulling it over his head. It came off easily, except right at the end, when the boy's fingers got wrapped around the cloth. Even then, it took only a minute.

The boy's body was perfect and beautiful in its simplicity. It was splendid, and yet delicate.

There was a creaking sound, but he ignored it. The boy was all that mattered now.

His navel was an in, and that was something he was thankful for.

Don't do it, Malcolm.

Shut up, he thought, pushing the voice into the back of his mind where she belonged.

There were freckles on his body, and they seemed to make shapes like in the stars. What were they called? Constellations. The boy's freckles made tiny constellations across his body: of lions and tigers... and one of Malcolm, he was certain.

That decided it. The boy was made for him.

Don't do it, Malcolm, the voice chided.

Then he heard the noise again, somewhere near, but far away.

"Shut up, all of you."

He undid the button of the boy's jeans, preparing to remove them as well.

DON'T DO IT, MALCOLM!

"Shut up, slut!" he yelled again, thrusting his head up toward the ceiling. "I'll do whatever I want, you understand me?"

"Believe me, you won't."

Malcolm turned just time to feel Xander's fist ram square into his nose.

Mike ran around them and scooped up the boy, taking off for the door, regardless of the blood still leaking slowly from his arms.

Malcolm hit the floor hard, slamming his head on the coffee table. What remained of Charles' Frosted Flakes spilled onto the floor from the impact.

Malcolm passed out there, wedged between the couch and the coffee table, blood leaking from his nose.

One punch.

Squinting angrily, Xander leaned over and grabbed him, wailing his fist once more into the unconscious man's head just for good measure, then backing up twice and running to join Mike outside and bring the boy to the hospital.

Malcolm did not get up again until the police dragged him away, telling him to watch his head the officer put him into the back of the car. He turned, wanting very much to bite the officer.

Don't do that, Malcolm.

"Shut up, bitch."

CHAPTER FOURTEEN: IN THE FUTURE

Mike took a deep breath as he followed Xander through the large, gray doors that led to Adam Genblade's bedside cell. Entering the room, the first thing he noticed was the smell: the peculiar odor that always accompanied unnaturally sterile rooms. It was somewhere between the smell of bleach and sugar water.

The walls, floor, and ceiling were all glimmering white, not an item out of place. It was like an exhibit at a museum, the ones that always looked too neat. Nobody lived like that, not in real life.

It took him a moment to notice the figure laying in a bed against one wall.

The sheets were just as white as the room, devoid of stains or any sign of human life whatsoever. The man lying on the bed was barely visible through the mass of pipes and wires and needles poking out of him. His face was almost completely covered by a clear blue mask that allowed him to breathe through the thick plastic tubes shoved down his throat. The only movement in the room was the man's chest, rising and falling with a machine's calculated rhythm.

If it had been anyone else but Adam Genblade, Mike would have felt a great swell of pity for the man. In this case, it was only the slightest touch of pity that slanted his heart, making it so cold that he had to shiver.

"You sure you want to do this?" he asked, reaching out and touching Xander's shoulder. "You don't have to, you know."

Xander turned his head just enough to see his friend in his peripheral vision, then back to Genblade again. "Yes, I do."

He reached into his pocket and pulled out the Spider-Gem, held it up to his eye, and examined its gleam one last time.

"What is that thing, anyway?" Mike murmured, motioning toward the ruby.

"A hunk of glass," Xander responded in a condescending tone.

Mike shot him a look. "You know what I mean."

"And you know what I said. I really think it's nothing but a hunk of glass now."

"What made it so special, anyway? Why did LeGaea want it so bad?"

Xander frowned, taking another look at Genblade and then stepping toward the room adjacent to it, followed closely by Mike. "The three gems, when they touched or whatever... I saw glimpses, thoughts, feelings..." He turned to Mike, his eyes filled with a unique pain that his friend had yet to see on him. "I think it was my future."

Mike's eyebrows shot up. "What was it like?"

Tom Petty blaring on a loud speaker. Too loud. Burning air. Pop tarts. Red. Blood red. Red. Red hair. Hurt. Pain. Hurt pain. Scream: too loud! Shattered. To ground. Look up. Smell of cream. Touch. Hair. Cheek. Grinding teeth. Death. Death! DEATH!

"I don't remember," Xander said dismissively, starting down the long row of lockers leading to the one that contained Genblade's belongings. "But it showed me where the boy was and what was going to happen to him if we didn't get there."

"That's kinda freaky," Mike said, motioning to the gem in Xander's hand again. "In that case, are you sure that we should be giving it up,?"

Xander tossed the stone into the air, catching it in his palm again. "Naw. The way LeGaea freaked, I think that you need all three for the mojo to work. Even if he hadn't run off, you smashed one of them pretty good. Like I said, this is just a hunk of glass now."

Mike sighed, letting his eyes get caught up in the gleam of the ruby for a moment. "Still, heck of a thing to just give up."

Xander shook his head. "I think it's overrated. I think that's been the point of all this... it's true what they say, man. Ignorance is bliss. There's no way that knowing too much about who we are or where we're going can lead to anything good."

Reluctantly, he nodded. "What was up with that LeGaea guy anyway?"

"Don't know. He wasn't after us, I think. There's been no sign of him since, and he left a pretty clear path of destruction wherever he went. Still, if he could see the future, you'd think he would have avoided us." He shrugged, opening Genblade's locker and taking out the Spider-Sword. Its sheen was magnificent, even after all those months of being locked away without use. The light reflected off it like a shimmering star burning brightly against the dull, colourless atmosphere of the locker room.

"Maybe the future's written. Maybe he couldn't avoid it."

"Run!" Mike yelled, as he forced Cathy ahead of him. The creature landed on all fours on the sidewalk. His glossy eyes studied their movements, how they ran. He found their weak spot at the sides. They'd both been damaged there. It moved like a jaguar, leaping to the sidewalk and then onto two legs to pursue them.

"Keep... going..." Mike encouraged Cathy, holding his side. They were almost to her house. But they'd both danced this dance before. He wasn't about to make the same mistakes twice. He cut through an old alley, hoping to run across the backyards of the complex until reaching her back door.

They could see the house now.

"Mike..." Cathy pleaded, grasping at her side. "It hurts."

"Now that's a scary thought," Xander mumbled, mostly to himself. He brought the gem up to its rightful spot on the sword's handle, and it clicked into place. The sword looked like a complete work of art now, restored to its natural significance.

"Still don't see why you had to do that," Mike ventured, gazing at the blade in fascination.

Xander frowned, putting it back inside the locker and closing the door. "Genblade killed the first woman I ever loved... but I killed his, you can't forget that. Taking this from him, it'd be like someone taking my last picture of Sara from me... it'd be wrong. Not even Genblade deserves to suffer like that. Nobody does." He started walking back toward the exit, and Mike followed. "Plus, Genblade's helped us out a lot since. In a weird way, I feel like I owe him."

They opened the doors, and both of them walked past the living corpse of Adam Genblade without so much as glancing at it.

"I don't feel that way anymore," Xander continued. "And if he ever wakes up from that coma, there won't be anything holding me back. It'll be just the two of us."

"I guess so," Mike nodded, stepping up to walk side-by-side with Xander. "Yeah."

"Besides, I had to try and get something positive out of this whole mess."

Mike gave him a quizzical look. "What do you mean? Me and Cathy are back on track, we defeated LeGaea, we saved that kid, returned the gem, and now that Malcolm creep is going to spend eternity times two rotting in Coral Beach Pen. And I didn't kill you. All in all, I don't consider that a bad day's work."

"I dunno," Xander breathed, glancing at the ground. "I feel like I lost this one. I wanted so much to be normal. To be like everyone else and have a girl-friend, and for the only thing on my mind to be a stupid school dance... but I guess I can't have that. Never will. I mean, fuck, why me?"

Mike took a moment to absorb that, then reached back and slapped his friend in that back of the head.

"Ow!" Xander cried out, though not really hurt. "What the hell was that for?"

"For being an idiot," Mike said simply as the two continued to walk out of the police building. "You know what I think every time you say 'Why me'?"

Xander frowned, then shrugged.

"I think: why not you? Seriously, why not? For all your whining and bitch-ing... and for all the times I've kicked you to the curb, you're doing all right. I can't think of one single person who would do better at what we're doing here. Someone's got to do it, so it might as well be you. And we'll figure it out eventu-ally. I know we will. Me, you and Cat. And while we're figuring it out, we'll save some kids. Hell, I can think of worse ways to spend the day."

Xander smirked. "I guess so."

"Yeah," Mike laughed, patting his friend on the back. "We good?"

"Yeah." Xander responded, forcing a smile. "Yeah, we're good."

Cathy walked up to the Walker house and took a long, deep breath. She knocked on the front door and Macy Walker answered, her eyes soaked with tears.

"What do you want?" Macy asked, without resentment.

Cathy smiled, her hand on her purse. "Can I come in, Mrs. Walker? There's something we need to talk about."

Three days later, a name was added to the Coral Beach Memorial Wall:
Kerri Walker - Kennessy.

Xander sat at the bar, took a puff of his smoke and flicked the ash into a nearby tray. His black shirt conformed perfectly to his body, making it look as though it had been tailored for him. He took another long drag, then extin-guished the cigarette.

Just as he did, a woman walked in and sat next to him, taking off her coat and shaking off the late fall cold before motioning to the bartender to get her a drink. He nodded before moving to a different part of the bar to prepare the drink.

She wore a navy-blue blazer with white pin-stripes, matching slacks, and an off-white scarf around her neck that made her look professional. Her dark red hair was perfectly groomed, and her pale white skin was offset by blazing red lips. She looked powerful, in control of everything and every man in the room... except, of course, for the one she happened to be sitting next to.

"Megan Greene. What are the odds of finding you here?" Xander asked without looking at her, a wry smile spread across his lips. He motioned for the bartender to bring him a beer when he was done mixing Megan's drink.

Megan turned to him suddenly, as if not even realizing he was there before, but her look of shock quickly melted into a warm smile. "Xander. Long time, no see. How'd you know I was going to be here?"

Xander smirked. "You mean besides the fact that you come here every Saturday, order two absolute vodkas but only drink one and a half, then drive around downtown for a half hour to kill time before a date with Tony?" He glanced at her for the first time since the conversation began. "Just luck, I guess."

Megan slowly raised an eyebrow at him, even as the bartender handed her the drink. "Do I have a stalker now?"

Xander chuckled. "No. When you spend enough time in this town... you get to know things."

"I'll keep that in mind."

He looked her up and down, taking notice of her more expensive attire and the shape of a slimming body. "You seem to be doing well for yourself."

"Yeah. I'm high profile now thanks to you and your friend Adam Genblade," she smiled, taking a sip of her drink and fiddling with the olive in it.

"I wouldn't call him a friend."

"It was meant to be humorous," she said bluntly. "So, what brings you by here? Come to warn me of impending doom?"

"No," he laughed, accepting his beer and paying for it, then lighting up another smoke. "Just needed to see a friendly face is all. How are things?"

Megan rolled her eyes. "Terrific. I got rights groups breathing down my neck one way, and angry mothers the next over the Genblade thing."

"How's that?"

"Well, you remember those people who wanted him executed? The ones who didn't want their tax dollars going toward feeding a murdering sociopath?"

"Yeah?"

"Imagine how they feel now that their tax dollars are helping keep him breathing."

"Ah," he mused, taking a long puff, then blowing it out. "Not too pleased, I take it."

"They're demanding they pull the plug. Bunch of savages, I tell you," she turned toward him, getting more involved in the unexpected conversation. "What about you? I see you've been keeping busy."

He shot her a confused look.

"That Malcolm guy. I heard about that. Good work, by the way. Top notch stuff."

"Could've gone better."

"You couldn't have caught him sooner, Xander."

"No," he scoffed. "The guy went down with one punch. I would have greatly preferred to have been able to wail on him for at least a few minutes."

"The nerve of some people," she drawled, rolling her eyes.

"Really. Do you think they'll have any trouble putting him away?"

Megan almost laughed. "Not likely. They found his mother's corpse propped up on the upstairs toilet, been there for at least a month. Guy said she was still talking to him, yelling at him."

"Yikes."

"Can you imagine someone being so loony as to talk to dead people?"

Xander paused, coughed once, then took a sip of his beer.

Megan observed the silence for a moment, then chose to disregard the topic. "So, what about you? How's life outside murder and mayhem treating you?"

Xander snorted. "I only just now found out I can't have one."

"Who says?" Megan nearly yelled, waving a hand at him dismissively. "I thought that way once, before Tony came along. You gotta make these things work, they won't just fall into your lap, y'know. What's the problem, anyway?"

Xander smirked. "It's a girl."

Her eyes widened, and she nodded smoothly, taking a knowing sip of her drink. "Gotcha."

"No, it's not like that..."

"What's it like then?"

"It's special. It's... something I never felt before, not even with Sara. It's a weird sense of belonging, like everything falls into place when I'm around her."

Megan nodded, encouraging him to continue.

"When she's around, everything else falls away. It's like: Julie! There could be a million other things going through my head, but when she's in the room, it's: Julie! And it's not like I'm ignoring everything else... no, when she's around, everything seems to work out for the best anyway. It's magic. She makes even my life simple, and every simple moment I have with her is just a gift... each one completely new and different from the one before."

"That sounds great," Megan smiled.

"Yeah..." he said, trailing off, wishing he could cry. "It was."

"Was? Why can't it be now?"

"Because," he hissed, taking back the rest of his beer. "I can't love her. Even if I could, I'd only hurt her."

Megan laughed. "Oh, sweetie."

"What?"

She leaned closer, adopting a motherly tone. "You know all that stuff you described?"

"Yeah?"

"That's love, babe. And even if it isn't, all those things are the best way to get to love. Believe me, I know. And as for that 'if you love her you'll hurt her' stuff... baby, that's par for course with any love. And that's not your choice to make. You need to let her decide if the risk is worth taking. Stop worrying about her and just... look inside your heart."

A light flashed in Xander's eyes, and he turned to her. He leaned in, kissed her on the cheek, then extinguished what remained of his cigarette. "I gotta go. Thank you so much."

"Anytime. Next time you gotta tell me how a kid your age gets in here anyway."

He turned and smirked at her as he headed out the door. "I keep telling you... I have my ways."

She watched him leave, laughing gently to herself as she motioned for the bartender to bring her a second drink.

⚡

Julie walked out to the front door and opened it, wanting only for the nonstop banging to end. She swung it open, a hard glare ready on her face for whoever was there.

"Xander," she said simply, watching him as he doubled over and tried to catch his breath.

"Julie!" he gasped, his lungs aching for oxygen.

"What are you doing here?"

"I had to tell you, I figured it out!" he blurted, taking another deep breath. "I know what it means now, I got it. Well, Megan got it, but I'm here now and you're here and that's all that really matters, right?"

She looked at him, and a smile spread across her lips as she held onto the door.

He smiled back, the first honest smile he'd worn in days.

"Xander," she started, her voice calm and even.

"Yes?"

"I've got a hell of a lot of thinking to do about us," she said bluntly, then slammed the door in his face.

EPILOGUE

It's like a dance. Mandy wrote in her journal as Xander walked alone down the front steps and out onto the sidewalk. He was holding back the tears he had wished for days ago, and was now sorry he had. *Nobody really knows the beat or the moves... or really even what song we're all grooving to, but we all keep dancing anyway, because we can't bear to sit one moment out... even if sometimes we end up looking stupid, like, doing the Macarena or something. But in the end, that's all life is: a dance.*

Mike and Cathy are back together, and by the looks of Mike, that's for the best. He's so happy now, happier than I've seen him in a long time, and me and him really get along now. Me and Cathy, too, as weird as it sounds to, like, write that down, or even say. I'm just glad he's okay. I wasn't sure for a minute there.

Cathy got over the whole pregnancy thing. Well, probably not over it, I'm sure, but she's doing a lot better, and that's always good. She put a name to her pain, and that's always the way to do it. I guess you can't just let things like that linger around, or when you turn your back on it, it'll kill you.

Julie's been crying a lot. I don't think her and Xander did it... but I think maybe it was something worse. Like, maybe something worse than sex can happen with a boy. I

291

know that... falling in love is probably the worst pain ever. There's no end to it, but we still crave it more.

Like black licorice.

She didn't come out of her room all weekend after Xander left, not even to tell me to turn my music down, even though I only had it turned up that loud so she would finally come out. No matter how loud the music got, though, I could still hear her crying.

Xander hasn't been talking a lot. He's back to his same old routine, letting life pass him by again, keeping to the shadows, skulking a lot. He's still super nice to everyone, even me, but it's different now. Tommy says he's seen him like it before, right after some girl named Sara died. Said he's gone back to that place again, the dark place where everyone has to go at some point in their lives, but where Xander seems to live. Hopefully he'll get out of it again soon, I liked him better when he was all right.

And me... nothing really changed with me. I guess if someone else was writing this, they'd tell you that I sat this dance out, that I didn't do anything. That I was standing still. But really, I danced with everyone. They just didn't realize it. They all think I'm a loser, that I'm not even important.

ʎ×ʎ

Dr. Warren O'Toole sat on his chair in his office, one leg crossed over the other. He scribbled handwriting only he could understand on his notepad, which was placed uncomfortably on his lap. With his free hand, he waved his pocket watch back and forth in front of Mandy's unconscious face, holding her in her deep, hypnotic trance. "What did you say, Mandy?"

"The Black Angel came... the Black Womb... he came and saved everyone... he always does... he looks so awful, but he's really sweet and kind... he's my friend... Mike's my friend..."

"You still believe Mike Harris to be the Black Womb, Mandy?" O'Toole asked, scribbling away.

"Oh, yes... I saw him... he saved me... he's so nice..."

O'Toole flicked back through his notes, then continued writing, stopping once to adjust his glasses. "Does the Black Womb have strange eyes or fingers?"

"Yes... his eyes are red, and his fingers have claws...not all the time, though, not when he's Mike... and the claws can go away, he touched me and didn't even hurt me... saved me..."

"Does it look anything like the creature that attacked the school earlier this month?"

"No... yes... it looks different... strange... it was different..." the girl's brow furrowed.

"Tell me more about him, Mandy." O'Toole pressed. He put down the pad and leaned forward, smiling.

They all think I'm a loser, that I'm not even important.

Boy, are they in for a surprise.

292

BOOK SEVEN

BECOMING

BECOMING: CHAPTER ONE

He felt cold.

Unnaturally cold, the type of chill that starts from your heart and pumps its way through your entire body. Cold that freezes you slowly, starting with your blood, then moves to your muscle tendons, your flesh, and your hair. Your eyes are the last to go, still skittering about in their sockets, watching all of the paralyzed parts of you that your brain orders to move fail to do so until you're a living statue of ice.

All around him was dark and black and death; everything was filled with that death. That weight that pulls you down into the shadows and won't let go until it has you forever. Where you can't even see the knife in your own hand before you stab yourself just so you can stop feeling the cold.

He felt his arm twitch, but without the benefit of seeing he wondered if it had only been his imagination. The only thing he knew for certain was that there was blood somewhere. He could smell it. After all this time being absorbed in it, drowned in it, its scent had become more familiar than any he had ever known. That red coppery tang was more familiar to him than the smell of an oven-baked apple pie to most.

It was home.

He ran his hands over himself, rummaging about in the darkness to make sure the red fluid was not coming from him and that he wasn't dying. His touch was freezing and not his own, as though he were poking at himself with thick gloves.

Somewhere there was a steady hissing noise, but it was faint enough to ignore for now. He blocked it out and continued to pat down his flesh to see if it was wet with redness and death. There was none, but he now realized that he was naked. Naked and cold in the dark, black room, with nothing but soft, mechanical hissing to keep him company.

"Ugh."

His head shot up, making his hair bounce and several strands fall into his eyes. He stared into the darkness, waiting for the sound to happen again, not sure if he was looking in the right direction or if his nose was two feet from a solid wall.

"Ah."

He heard it again. A moan, but not of pleasure. It was agonized, filled with pain. It sounded almost moist, if sounds were capable of such texture, as though the person speaking were drowning. He noticed that each syllable was accompanied by a clicking noise, the long scrape of metal against metal.

There was harsh, labored breathing now, both from him and whomever was out there in the darkness calling out in pain. It was definitely coming from the direction he was facing now. There was no wall, he was sure of it.

"...help..."

She was small and tender, and he recognized her somehow. He recognized her cry for aid as if he'd heard it a thousand times before.

He tried to get up but found that he couldn't, the fatty tissue of his calf sticking to the freezing cold floor. There was a deep, sick tearing sound that got worse each time he tried, but he felt no pain and kept rocking back and forth until he was free, leaving behind a tattered maw of flesh.

He held his hands under his armpits to try and keep them from freezing and stumbled forward, almost falling after the first step but somehow pressing on. His teeth chattered. He felt the urge to urinate come to him then leave again at a rapid pace as the chill reached his bladder. He tried to call out to find out where the voice was coming from, but he could not.

"...please..."

It came again, and he felt a deep pang within his chest, in a place that he had gone to great lengths to hide from a cruel world that had beaten and tortured his very soul into submission. It was his heart, he realized, as grim determination set in to counteract the cold. The pangs he felt were a lover's pain, the longing to help and to be helped, to love and to be loved. His heart wanted to find this girl and preserve the feeling she brought as long as possible.

He tripped and fell to the ground which had been so soft before and now was as hard and unforgiving as stone. His knees scraped its ragged surface, rending flesh and drawing out blood. He gritted his teeth to howl as something penetrated his knee cap, but again, no sound would come. His voice was afraid to be heard in the darkness, he wondered why.

Something moved in the dark.

He turned toward it, terrorized sweat running down his brow as he squinted, trying to find the source of the motion. But still, all he could see was the black. The black that seemed to both go on forever and to end right in front of his face. Something slithered there just beyond his senses, snaking about in the dark, brought forth by the smell of the blood that was already freezing to his skin.

With a grunt he forced himself to his feet again, limping his way into the hollow that stretched out before him.

"...love..."

Love? Was that why he kept going, refusing to lay down and die? To stop the madness that had enveloped his darkness, threatening to swallow him whole? Somewhere inside he screamed yes and wanted to be heard. He wanted to tell her that he was here, that he was coming, that she need not fear. And yet he did not, for fear itself had its plump fingers wrapped around his neck.

"Ah."

He stopped. The voice no longer came from in front of him. He looked around, searching it out, trying in vain to regain his bearings when there had been none to begin with. His lip quivered as he searched, his teeth clenching to stop the chatter until his gums bled from pressure and point.

Something skittered before him, coming from above and below. Left and right. It was

296

everywhere. It was as if the darkness itself was what was attacking him, frightening him, keeping him from the person that he wanted so desperately to help. The skittering stopped for a moment, as if the thing had only just noticed him. He got the distinct impression that he was being watched, like great eyes were upon him. He felt like now that he was in their sights, they would never let go. Like his life would be spent forever running away.

A new cool came over him, far more bitter than the last. It was the chill of fear: that harsh, tingly numbness that comes with being stalked, being observed, being forlorn.

"...please..."

He turned around completely, too shocked and frustrated by the new direction of the sound to care about the attacker now. It wasn't about him; the only thing that mattered was her.

Her.

She lay in the center of a pale stream of light that had not been there before, and he wondered how he had missed it. Her body was sprawled out like a star. She lay there, unmoving, unwavering. Her long raven hair was all around her, drawn in a misshapen circle with the pale skin of her cheeks and the whites of her eyes in its center. Her lips were as red as the very mouth of the fire burning brightly in the dark and igniting flames within him as he limped forward. Her eyes were as dark and hollow as the air that surrounded him, but he felt as though he could look into them forever without dread or regret. Life would not pass him by looking into those eyes, for his life was contained within them. Her breast rose and fell peacefully, if rapidly, and her slender neck and collar moved in unison, throbbing each time she swallowed. She was draped in a red cloth that did little to cover her slender, smooth white legs, she looked like an angel wrapped in the clothes of the devil.

She was beautiful.

"Eve?" he whispered, so low that she could barely hear. She turned toward him as he knelt next to her, reaching for her hand and clasping it tightly inside both of his.

A smile spread over his lips as their fingers met and he could no longer feel the cold.

"Adam..." she gasped, though she was not surprised. Her every breath was labored. It was as if she had to fight to find her voice, and he had to fight to hear it. Her eyes welled up, tears beginning to flow from their corners. "You came."

"Of course," Adam said gently, caressing the side of her face as he bent down and kissed her hand, softly. He ran a finger through her hair, and it was as smooth and silky as it looked.

"I'm sorry..." she said sadly, her lower lip trembling. "I'm sorry I had to go."

Her voice whined at the end involuntarily, the unshed tears in her throat distorting her voice.

"You don't have to go anywhere," he hushed her and kissed her forehead desperately. The salt water dribbling down his cheeks made a liar of him. He raised his hand to run it through his hair, then stopped, and looked at it. The fingers were stained with red, so red that it was almost black. When he looked back at her, he saw that the red cloth was not as long as he had thought. He saw that it was not cloth that covered at all: it was red liquid that seeped into the patch of light surrounding her.

"Honey, I have to," she sobbed, staring into his soul and shattering it forevermore.

"Then I'll come with you." he gasped, bending over her body as the sobs raked through him, making his body quiver and shake. "I can, I will... I'll come with you..."

"No, baby..." she chided, using all the energy she had to bring a finger to his lip, calming him. "No, you have to stay. You can't follow me where I'm going, honey. You mustn't."

"Please, please..." he sobbed, tears seemingly coming from his nose and mouth as well as his eyes now, coming from any place they could, just needing to get out. "Please, don't leave me. Don't leave me here all alone, please...I'll do anything. I'll be better, I will. I promise I will. Please...just please, don't leave me..."

His body shook and convulsed as hers stopped. He paused after a moment and realized that he was talking to himself, and that she was gone. Still crying, he leaned in slowly, kissing her lightly on the lips and then turning away, unable to watch as his heart of hearts broke.

When he opened his eyes again, a second stream of light had appeared, spotlighting someone new.

"Adam," the deep, scratchy voice bellowed, as it stood proud in the spotlight, its back arched. It was made of the darkness, tiny scales of shadow linked together to make a form that only vaguely resembled human. It was sleek and smooth, its skin almost like that of a seal's, oily in its purity. Its red eyes were slanted triangles, the tips pointing into curves, forming half-spirals. It was muscular, but not overly so. Lean. At the tip of each long, slender finger was a talon about four inches in length, gleaming in the pale light. It growled at all times, even when it spoke.

"Black Womb," Adam sneered, standing up. He no longer cared that he was naked in the dark, that he was cold, or that he was afraid. All that mattered was the red smear on his hand, and the despicable creature which had caused it.

"Black Womb lives!" it yelled, leaping forward at Adam. It crossed the distance between them in two great bounds. When it sprang it did so claws first, plunging their serrated edges deep into Adam's chest.

"Argh!" Adam cried, lashing out with his sword and digging it deep into the Womb's shoulder.

Had there been a sword before?

The creature grabbed Adam by both shoulders and pulled him forward, forcing the blade deeper into its own flesh. Smiling a wicked, toothy grin, it brought both feet up and dug its toe-talons into Adam's chest, locking the naked man in. It bent over quickly as if to touch its toes, lashing out into Adam's face with its claws.

"She made me!" it yelled frantically, pleading even as it ravaged Adam's cheeks and lips savagely. "I had no choice! She made it for me, don't you get that, you murdering freak?"

"So, I'm the freak?" Adam sneered, grabbing it by the neck and pushing so hard its back slammed into the floor. The sword scraped into the metal tiling, effectively stapling the Womb to it. "Take a look in the mirror lately?"

"Rahh!" the Womb roared, pushing out with his legs and flipping Adam over onto his stomach. It reached up and pulled the blood-soaked sword from its central plexus as if it were nothing. It stood up and spun the blade between its fingers. "You think it's so tragic, what happened to Eve, but what about what happened to me? What about what you did to me?"

The Womb plunged the sword down through Adam's back, severing his spinal cord and pinning him there with his face pressed against the floor. Sneering, the creature drew back a foot and kicked Adam in the head again and again, sending blood and saliva squirting into the darkness in V-shaped spurts.

The Womb stopped as Adam struggled for breath, forcing himself to look up at his attacker. The creature sneered.

"Look at what you're making me do now," *it chuckled, before raising its foot high once more...*

Xander woke with a start, his nose freezing.

He tried hard to open his eyes, finding that it was almost impossible. It was like they had been sealed shut, and when he did finally manage to open them, it was accompanied by a tearing sound. He wiped them with the backs of his hands, discovering that they'd been covered in a hard yellow crust so thick that it came off in one great layer.

"Gah," he gasped, taking a deep breath as sweat dribbled down his face and chin. The salty putrid stench of perspiration was all he could smell. His underarms were bathed in it. It stung at the cracks in his lips and made his irises sore. His hair, damp with it, clung to his head.

Everything around him was white, even his hands. Smooth, silky white covered everything that he was. As his eyes adjusted and his vision came into focus, he discovered that his hands were actually a disturbing purple colour, with veins popping out their backs. His entire form was shivering now, quaking like a leaf on the wind as fresh mucus clung to his nose like tiny icicles while freezing his mouth shut.

He raised his hands slowly. It took considerable effort. They were numb beyond the telling of the word and it felt as though he were carrying weights attached to each finger. His palms were red, every pore in them open, full and tinged with tiny black flecks. He could look into them as if they were black holes. He put his hands back down into the white, silky cold that surrounded him and scooped it up into a tiny ball, mashing it with his right hand.

It was snow.

He tilted his head up to watch it fall. Thousands of snowflakes glittered in the air, each one different from the next, or so people said. Each one traveled gently, carefully down until finally resting with the others, settling in as if it belonged there. Undisturbed, snow was nature at its very best.

The flakes fell between the trees, some of them sticking to hefty branches and weighing them down, making them look sad and droopy. The trees hung above him, leaning in as if to surround him, leaving him no alternative but to stay in his little clearing, freezing and naked.

It's night, he realized. It was the first thought his addled brain produced. He still didn't quite know why that was so important. With all of his senses screaming how cold it was at once, all wanting a warm bath and a smoke at once, it was nearly impossible to think. There was a hard throb an inch above his right eye that was pounding at him, and he felt like that part of his brain was actually trying to escape.

For an instant, he was confronted with the horrible mental picture that his brain was actually a baby that was kicking the inside of his skull the way a normal child would kick at the inside of its mother's womb.

He got a flash of the child breaking free finally, its chubby fat leg pushing out through his forehead, sending brain matter and bits of bone spewing down into the white of the snow.

"Guh."

He tried to concentrate, but he had what could only have been described as brain freeze on mushrooms, slowing his thoughts down to a crawl.

Closing his eyes and willing himself to move, he stood up. He clenched and unclenched his fists a few times to try and get the blood circulating to them again, then moved his legs and wriggled his toes to make sure he still could. He could not feel them, and had to bend over to see if they were moving.

The Womb never wakes me up at night.

The thought came to him from nowhere, and it came from a voice that was not his own. He'd read stories about people able to pick up transmissions before... radio stations on high-end frequencies being heard by war vets with plates in their heads. Glasses that picked up the signal from baby-monitors when filled to just the right depth. Teeth fillings that made an electric hum when brought too close to a microphone. He'd always thought they were bullshit, but sometimes the thoughts in his head were so strange to him that he couldn't help but remember tabloid headlines like: *My son gets broadcasts from Outer Space!*

He squinted as he looked around, scanning between the trees for any sign of movement. There was a squirrel perched on a branch ten feet away, looking at Xander and the snow with equal amazement.

"Hello, Bob," Xander chuckled.

Satisfied that he was alone, he began to examine himself.

There was no blood on him.

In the past four months, Xander had learned a small set of rules for dealing with situations like this. There were things that happened when he was taken over by his Mr. Hyde persona and things that did not. One was the eye colour. It was an odd physical marker that went along with the personality shifts and one that he hadn't been able to explain yet, but whenever he was the consciousness in charge of his other form he had stark red eyes. Whenever the Womb was in control, it had putrid green eyes.

Another thing was the blood.

Whenever the Womb left him and the second skin fell away like a snake's, there was a thin layer of blood left behind. He'd come to understand it to some degree: that it acted in much the same way a normal person's blood-brain barrier worked. It was supposed to separate them, to protect them from things the immune system simply wasn't equipped to handle.

It was a disgusting and awkward treat that was left behind whenever the

Womb was forced back inside. If it wasn't present now, then the Womb hadn't retreated under normal circumstances.

"It wanted to bring me here," Xander deduced, looking around with new eyes, searching for some reason that his other half would be so specific as to bring him here on the first snow of winter.

The trees all had faces, great massive noses and sagging mouths that gaped, looking ravenous and insatiable. The moonlight bounced off of the virgin snow and reflected it in all directions, creating eerie illumination that made the faces move to speak or to eat, their great jaws chomping away at the winter night like ravenous wolves hungering for their prey.

"Look at what you're making me do now..."

Xander shuddered at the memory.

Something brushed past him, sharp against his shoulder blade. The hairs on his back stood on end and he turned around quickly, his fists clenched before him like a boxer's.

There was nothing there, and the feeling of cold, boney fingers gripping his shoulders was still upon him, digging in even deeper now.

When he looked west he could see lights. He knew then that he was no more than a few yards from his house, and even closer to where Sara used to live. He sighed deeply, bending down again to get a better look through the branches and into town. He placed his hand down in the snow for leverage, then immediately yanked it back and gasped.

Blood poured from a long slice going down his palm, dripping into the cold snow and staining it red. He looked into the snow where it had been, but there was nothing there. Nothing sharp enough that it would cut him, except for the snow. Everything was colder here, harder, sharper than it was any other day. Even the snow could slice you open, rip you inside out. Feed on you. He'd felt this way before, just not in real life. Not in a place that he knew so well, where he had climbed trees and caught apples and gotten stung by bees.

This was death.

Cold, hard and sharp. He was sure of it now, as sure as he had ever been of anything. No more than twenty feet out the back door of his house, and he was in the presence of death.

The fingers on his shoulders gripped him harder.

He began to walk toward home.

BECOMING: CHAPTER TWO

-BEEP-
-BEEP-
-BEEP-
"Did you check the pan?"
"I am right now, checking the pan."

301

"Good, because I really didn't want to have to have that fight with you again."

"Would you shut up?"

"I'm just saying..."

"You keep throwing that back in my face. One time I didn't check the pan. One time."

"Hey, I just don't want to come in tomorrow and find a big - "

"One! Time!"

"All right, all right. Sheesh, just check it already, and stop talking about it."

"I told you, I'm checking the pan."

"And?"

"And as sick as this guy was when he was awake, the stuff I find in the pan brings new meaning to the word."

"That's why you check the pan, and I check the heart monitor."

"How is he today, anyway?"

- -

"How is his heart rate?"

- -

"Hello? Crazy lady? I asked you a question. What is his heart rate like to-day?"

"Hmm? Oh... it's spiking. Every few minutes."

"Spiking?"

"Yeah... looks like little Adam Genblade is having nightmares."

"Huh."

"I wonder what it takes to scare a sick fuck like him anyway."

She giggled, her nose crinkling just a little as she did, in the cutest possible way. Just like the way that she did everything else, it was all just about as wonderfully peaceful as it could be.

The sun was shining. It was a beautiful summer day, and there were warm rays against their backs.

The picnic basket lay neatly on the red and white checkered tablecloth, spread out against the greenest grass God ever put on this earth. Ants crawled around the plates, their feelers twitching at the scent of apple pie and boxes of cranberry juice.

"More strawberries?" Adam asked, quickly reaching up a hand to make sure that his hair was all right. It was, perfectly molded and quaffed by half a pound of extra-hold gel. He had wanted it to look perfect for her, but now he worried that it looked like a dirty blond hard hat sitting on his scalp.

Eve giggled at him again, a bubbly sound, like fresh water from a spring well.

"I saw that," she taunted, scolding him playfully by waving a finger at him. "What are you all dressed up for today, anyway?"

"Oh, I don't know," he smiled, leaning a little closer to her. His nostrils flared to pick up more of the divine perfume she was wearing. He could not pin down what it smelled like, but he knew that it was good. "I guess I just felt the need to be half as pretty

as you are for a change."

"Aww," she cooed, tapping him playfully on the face. *"You're so sweet."*

He winked at her.

She rolled her eyes, then took one of the strawberries from the bowl near him and put it past her pearly white teeth and her soft, red lips. She bit down, sucking on what remained.

He felt the hairs on the back of his neck stand on end. It always amazed him how she could be so sensual in everyday things... in everything she did, really. How she could turn him on with just a look, or the way that her raven hair fell across her breasts a certain way... or the way she could say his name when he wasn't feeling good and make all of the bad things in his life melt away.

The wind picked up and the trees all around them swayed with the breeze.

"How was the casserole?" he asked, looking down as he played with the last bit of mashed potato on his plate with the end of his plastic knife.

"It was great, baby," she assured him, motioning toward her empty plate as proof. She ate whatever he cooked anyway, even if it tasted like garbage, as it almost always did. *"I loved it."*

She smiled, plucking the stem off a strawberry before holding the rest out to him.

He leaned in and took it into his mouth, keeping his eyes on hers the entire time, watching them light up as he kissed her fingers before he started chewing the strawberry.

"These are really fresh," she commented, picking up another and plucking the stem off of it, running the pointed side along her lips before putting it in her mouth. *"Where did you get them, the deli?"*

"Picked them myself. I put a few of them in the fruit salad, too..."

"I noticed. It made it sweeter. Probably your best yet, hun."

Adam looked down, his cheeks turning a little red.

"No need to blush, lover," she cooed, reaching out and tilting his chin up. *"This was perfect. It was just what I needed."*

He smiled, blushing even more now that he knew that she had noticed it. *"I know that work's been tough on you lately..."*

"Work has been a nightmare." she giggled, lying back on the tablecloth. *"Anderson pulled some strings and got his cousin out of the mail room (where he belongs) and up into the editing suite. I swear, there were at least fifty mistakes in last night's run, and who gets fired? Lorraine, that's who."*

"He really fired Lorraine?"

"Yeah."

"That's awful."

"So, his little knob cousin gets her position, and..."

"Wait, he messes up, someone else gets fired, and he gets a promotion?"

"Uh-huh."

"That's insane."

"That's television, babe."

"I honestly don't know how you can handle working with those vultures. I would've fed Anderson through the tape deck long ago."

"It's simple," she said slyly, crawling over the plates to get closer to him. "I've got you to come home to, big guy."

He grinned as she leaned in to kiss him, making no motion forward as she did. Their lips met, and the sweet taste of strawberries rubbed off onto his tongue as her own came into his mouth, hot and fast, making his body tingle all over.

Suddenly her eyes shot open and her nails dug into his side.

He opened his eyes and looked at her, seeing her panic and fear. Their lips parted, but hers still moved, trying to tell him something, trying to let him know. He drew back the hand that had been wrapped around her waist, and found that it was covered in blood. Silky, red blood that dribbled down his arm to his rolled up sleeves. It soaked into the shirt he'd taken so long to pick out and expanded, soaking ever outward until it was drenched in her.

Her body slumped against the tablecloth, staining the white checkers red until the cloth wasn't checkered at all anymore. It was just red. Her face landed in what was left of his mashed potatoes.

He wondered if she had even liked the potatoes, really.

He looked up.

A young man stood just on the edge of the cloth, dressed completely in black. A cigarette hung loosely between his lips as he took small puffs, blowing them out through his nose. In his hand was a small blood-stained dagger with a handle that was etched into the shape of a dragon. He couldn't have been any older than sixteen, but his face was worn and scarred, the face of a young man who had seen too many fights in his life. His jaw was steadfast and unwavering despite the horrible thing he had just done. His eyes were black, covering his entire eye like one great pupil.

"What have you done?" Adam screamed, looking from his fallen lover to the madman that stood before him, cold and uncaring. There must have been some mistake. She was everything to him, all that he lived for. Rolling over and seeing her was his sole reason for opening his eyes every morning, and knowing that he could do it again the next day was his reason for closing them at night. She was his rock. His peace. His everything.

"Why would you do this to her?" he sobbed, tears streaming down his face. "What could she have possibly done?"

The boy snarled, spitting the burning cigarette out of his mouth. It landed in Eve's hair and singed it, filling the air with the rank stench of burning hair and starch. He raised his blade and brought it down swiftly, slicing down Adam's cheek and drawing blood.

Adam stumbled backward onto the tablecloth. He felt it soak into his arms and lower back as though it wasn't even a cloth at all anymore... it was a shallow pool of Eve's blood, somehow suspended in a perfect square in the center of the grassy knoll. He threw his free arm back to try and catch himself, but only succeeded in twisting his wrist in. Pain shot through his arm as he stared at the boy, who met his gaze head on as he opened his mouth to speak.

"Black Womb sends his regards."

Adam's eyes went wide as the killer took one threatening step forward, twirling the blade between his fingers. For the first time, his stony face showed an emotion... and it

304

could only be described as utter glee. He'd seen it on Eve's face a thousand times, and never would again.

"Why are you doing this?!" Adam screamed.

The killer said nothing, just took another calm step forward, followed by another.

Adam turned, scrambling to his feet and taking off toward the park. There would be someone there who could help him. Policemen patrolled the park all the time on bikes, and they'd help him.

He ran as fast as his feet would carry him. The trees around began to blur together until all he saw was a deep green tunnel curving up on either side of him as he ran. His heart slammed in his chest and he felt like he was going on forever, pounding mercilessly through the endless cave of evergreen.

He stepped on the shards of a broken beer bottle, and only then realized that he hadn't been wearing shoes. He'd taken them off sometime while he was eating his fruit salad.

Pain erupted through his leg and he fell, tumbling end over end down an embankment he hadn't seen a moment ago.

There were rocks pressed into his face. Mud and pine needles stuck all through his hair and made him look wild, like a man of the forest itself. He tasted blood in the back of his throat and wasn't sure if it was his own or not. His breath was so heavy that it stung at his chest. Everything hurt. The skin of his cheek had been ripped off by an errant branch at some point during the fall.

The boy stood at the top of the hill, only a shadowy black outline visible against the clear spring sky.

Adam stared at him, unable to do anything but take those heavy, labored breaths. He could not take his eyes off of him.

A wry, toothy grin spread over the boy's face, starkly white against his black silhouette. He hopped down onto the incline of dirt and moss and began to skid his way down the embankment.

Adam cursed, pushing himself up off the ground and running again. There was glass sticking out of his foot and a rock caught between one eye and its lid, but he kept running. Eve would want him to keep running.

The grass that had felt so nice before now sunk beneath his heavy feet as he tried desperately to get away, to be anywhere but here. He left small pools of dark red behind him in each footprint, the glass working its way in and out with every impact.

The killer walked calmly, one foot in front of the other, still twirling the blade as he went. He juggled it between his hands like some deranged circus clown, complete with a painted grin. He wasn't running, or even walking fast, but somehow he was still gaining on Adam. It was like Adam was running in place.

Adam turned to face forward, seeing nothing but the haze of trees and moss again.

Hadn't there been a path here?

Sweat poured down his brow as he realized that he had made a wrong turn somewhere, that he wasn't heading for the police or the park or anything else. Glancing around quickly, he grabbed up a large stick, pulled it free of its branch, and tried his best to look menacing through his blinding fear.

He turned around.

Nothing.

No killer, no knives, and no dead lover. Just evergreens and furs and a scant few maples looking back at him, their trunks like long faces, ready to devour him at a moment's notice.

It was suddenly very cold.

The sun was gone now, hidden behind some rather ominous looking clouds that had come out of nowhere. Twigs from the branch cut into his palms, but he dared not let it go. He smacked his lips together, trying to bring some moisture to their stale, arid surface. They still tasted like strawberries.

"Oh, god..." he cried softly, tears welling up in his eyes. "Oh, god no..."

"Don't bother asking God for help," came a voice from behind him.

He turned quickly, only to find himself face to face with the killer.

"You'll be seeing him soon enough."

Adam's lower lip quivered as he raised his stick high.

The killer lashed out with the blade, driving it into the branch Adam was holding. It dissected it easily, the blade pierced it right to the hilt.

Adam yelped.

The boy twisted then pulled back hard, breaking the branch apart and turning it to splinters within Adam's grasp. Some drove into his palm and he screamed. It was almost as bad as the glass had been, the sticky sap stinging at the wound and making his flesh swell and pound.

"Why are you doing this?" Adam wailed. "Why would you hurt her?"

"She made me do it, Adam," the killer snarled, becoming visibly enraged by the question. "She made me kill her. You and her, you made me. You made the Black Womb."

"I don't know anything about any Black Womb, I swear," Adam pleaded. "Just tell him that he's got the wrong people, I'm sure he'll understand..."

"Why don't you tell him yourself?!" the killer screamed, as his skin began to turn a charred black. It came from him like a tidal wave, a giant mouth crashing down onto Adam with thousands of tiny teeth ripping into his flesh, sucking the marrow from his bones and the blood from his veins.

It swirled and spun around him, ripping at his flesh and tearing at him, as though he were caught in the center of a tornado made of knives. He tried to scream but couldn't, his voice lost in the maelstrom.

The wave of blackness crashed upon the trees and crashed back onto itself, filling the space the killer had occupied until he was whole and solid once again.

All that was left to Adam was a pile of bones too thick to be devoured.

Calmly, the killer reached into his pocket, drew out a smoke, lit it, and took a deep drag.

After holding his breath for several, long moments, he blew out a trail of smoke from each nostril.

He smirked, looked down at the bones, then chuckled to himself a little. "Black Womb lives."

ʌʑʌ

Genblade's heart raced, his body convulsing inside of the restraints that kept him pinned to his hospital bed, thrusting uncontrollably.

"Nurse Reilly!" Porter called, her hairnet flying as she bent over to pin Genblade down. "Reilly, get in here!"

Reilly ran around the corner from the adjacent room, immediately rushing to Genblade's side and helping Porter pin him down. "Press the button for the orderlies! We have to get him restrained! He'll break his own neck if he keeps this up!"

Porter turned and slammed a red button next to the bed, buzzing for reinforcements, then returned to her position atop Genblade's arm. "He needs sedatives! His heart rate is off the scale, I think he's having an attack!"

Suddenly Genblade stopped, laying lifelessly in his bed again.

Reilly pushed a strand of hair back behind her ear. "What the hell was that?"

"I dunno. Whatever it is, if it keeps up, it's going to kill him."

"Wouldn't that be a shame," Reilly growled, turning to the cabinet to prepare an injection.

BECOMING: CHAPTER THREE

"The first snow of winter brings out the kid in everyone," Cathy Kennessy observed, taking a careful sip of her hot chocolate. Her dark hair was mostly hidden behind the hood of her fluffy blue winter jacket, poking out in defiance here and there and refusing to be contained. Her face looked rounder in it, and unmistakably cute, with her button nose and chubby cheeks both beet red from the chill in the air. Tiny snowflakes dotted her eyelashes. She watched Tommy and Mike fling snowballs at each other from behind trees as she sat on a small, but sheltered, bench at the bus stop.

"Why are we waiting here again?" Xander asked, watching the steam rise up from her hot beverage intently, his mouth watering as his nostrils flared to take in every bit of the glorious scent that he could.

"We're waiting for the bus." She smiled, her eyes never leaving her playful lover as he carefully dipped a freshly made snowball into a nearby puddle and waited for it to freeze so that it would impact upon Tommy with the maximum amount of damage.

Xander rolled up his sleeve for a moment and looked at his arm, only to find that it was bare. Sighing, he reached out and gently took Cathy's arm, pulling her sleeve up to examine the time on her watch. "It's 8:45. The bus left, like, fifteen minutes ago."

"In that case, we're watching my man pummel the other man with cold balls of half-frozen liquid," she admitted, taking another sip of her drink then licking the excess foam from her warm, dark lips.

"Just as long as we're being honest about our total lack of punctuality regarding our academic obligations."

"Is using big words like that some lame attempt at a penis extension for you?" she blurted suddenly, turning from watching Mike to looking at him.

He stopped, giving her a droll look and holding it until she finally cracked a smile.

"Sorry," she chuckled, turning back to the boys. "I couldn't resist."

"Exactly how long have you been waiting to say that?"

"Ever since Laird Street. You said something about a gargantuan essay you had to write, I thought maybe you said words like 'gargantuan' to make up for something that is the very opposite of 'gargantuan.' But by that time you and Mike had moved on to a different subject, so I buried it away and figured it wouldn't be too long before I got the chance to use it again."

"You put that much thought into burning me?" he smirked, raising an eyebrow in her direction.

"Sometimes hours of planning," she nodded, taking some more of the hot liquid and glancing at him, finally noticing the hungered look he got on his face every time she brought it to her lips. Rolling her eyes, she took another small sip and then passed it to him without looking.

He smiled widely in anticipation, bringing the paper cup to his lips and letting the brown foam glop down his throat until it was almost gone.

"Thank you," he gasped as he came out of the cup for some air, then quickly downed the rest. He turned toward a nearby garbage can, jumped, and threw the cup while still in midair. He missed his target completely, the cup landing in the snow next to it and sinking down about an inch.

He stopped and stared at it for a moment, his shoulders slumping in defeat as he turned back around to where Cathy stared at him, shaking her head.

"You're hopeless," she mumbled, patting him once on the head. "Even with super-human abilities, you just can't seem to sink one free throw, can you?"

"Hey! Give me a sword and I'll make paper dolls out of a house! But that... that..." he huffed. "It was only a paper cup anyway. It has no mass. The wind took it."

Cathy stuck her finger into her mouth and held it up in the air. "What wind, exactly, would that be?"

"My body's blocking it from you now."

"Then move."

"I... don't want to?"

"You suck."

"I do. I really, really do."

"And it's the fact that you know that which redeems you."

"Really?" he smiled, looking up.

"Nah," she spat, brushing the notion away. "I just wanted to see your hopes get up. That shoulder slumping thing you do is just too cute."

Even as she said it, his shoulders were doing just that.

She turned back to her boyfriend playing in the snow, laughed a little, then waved at him with only her fingers. He waved back, giving Tommy the opportunity to pelt him with a custom-made ice ball, right in the side of the face.

"Blonds," she mumbled softly to herself as she watched Mike prepare to take his revenge.

Mike shook the chill off his face, then tucked what remained of his hair beneath his black and white toque. A grim, determined look came over him as he scooped up an armful of snow, winked at his girlfriend, then silently plotted his revenge against Tommy.

Tommy was behind a nearby bush, waiting for the angered Mike to come to him and his pile of balled-up death.

"So why aren't you over there playing with the moron twins?" Cathy asked, motioning to the large pile of snow at Xander's feet. "I'm sure you could make balls so big and heavy that the wind wouldn't take them."

"No thanks, I already got two like that. Besides, I kinda wanted to talk to you about something."

"Oh," Cathy sighed, frowning for the first time today. "I think I know what it is."

"You do?"

"Yeah, and I'm really sorry about what happened the other day. I know you're with Julie now, and I swear I never went over there with the intention of kissing you, I really didn't. And I really didn't mean for Mike to go after you like that. I know that things are okay between you and him now, but I still want you to know that all of this was my fault, and that it'll never happen again. I was just so hurt, and I thought you... I don't know what I thought, but it wasn't right either way. I love you, Xander, and I really don't want to do anything to jeopardize that, ever. I'm so mad at myself for some of the choices I've been making lately, you have no idea. It's like I'm not even--"

"Cathy," Xander interjected, raising a finger as if to poke it in the middle of her train of thought. "That's all very nice and all, but that's not what I wanted to talk about."

"Oh," she said, blushing and looking down a little. "Forget I said anything then."

He reached over and tilted her head upward, feeling the softness of her face. "And just for the record, it was my fault. If I'd made my feelings about the possibility of us clear, you never would have gotten so confused."

"But, I --"

He cut her off, raising the finger again.

She smiled, then reached up and pulled the finger down, clasping his hand tightly for only a moment. She mouthed a simple thank you, knowing full well that he would stop her if she tried to actually say it. "So, what's up then?"

"It's my relationship with Jules," he said glumly.

"I always thought it was unhealthy, the amount of time you spent in the science fiction section of the library," she scoffed with mock contempt, putting one hand on her hip and waving the other finger at him menacingly.

"Huh?"

"Jules Verne," she explained.

"Ah." He nodded, understanding. "That's lame, even for you."

"I didn't have time to prepare, and I thought a joke about your family jewels would be a little below the belt."

"Yeah, well I -"

"Jewels? Below the belt? Come on..."

He frowned, and she finally stopped.

"Sorry," she said, shuffling over on the cold, wooden bench so that he could sit next to her. "What's going on? Are you two having a fight?"

"I wish," Xander replied. "If we were having a fight, at least she'd be talking to me from time to time."

"Ew, silent treatment?"

"Like you wouldn't believe. I've never seen Julie go this long without talking... ever."

"She does have the gift of gab, there's no denying that."

"How bad is this?" Xander asked, grimacing as he did, knowing what the answer would be.

"Remember when I gave Mike the silent treatment?"

"That bad?"

"No," she said. Then she paused. "No, that would be how bad it would be with a normal girl. With a jabber-mouth like Julie Peterson... well, she's probably so mad right now that you should count your lucky stars she's not talking. What did you do, anyway?"

"Me?" he turned, almost snapping. "What makes you think any of this is my fault?"

She gave him a look.

He sighed. "Oh, all I did was lead her to believe that I wanted a very serious, loving relationship (which she has never had, by the way). Then, when she finally comes around and decides that she does too and tells me that she loves me, I don't say it back."

"Ouch. Her first time saying it?"

"Dunno. But it was her first time meaning it, anyway."

"Double ouch. That girl's got a lot to think about."

"That's what she said!" he blurted, waving his hands excitedly. "How do women do that?"

"Oh, it's called having a brain," she retorted. "You might want to try it sometime. Idiot."

Xander buried his head between his legs and covered it up with his arms until he had almost vanished from the neck up, cursing himself internally. His bones ached from the night before, the cold still coming out of them despite the protection his body was supposed to offer him.

Mike bounded over to them cheerfully, a silly grin plastered all over his face. "Hey guys, what's up?" he said loudly, his nose red and sniffling.

"Oh, my, god." Cathy said slowly, looking his snow-covered body up and down. "How did you manage to lose that badly?" she asked, giving him a little slap on the arm.

"What are you talking about?" he retorted, a distinct chill in his voice. "I won this fight."

Xander turned to see Tommy hobbling toward them, his face full of snow and just the tiniest dribbles of blood seeping from his nose. "So you did."

Mike stared at Cathy, unable to stop smiling.

"What?" she asked finally, unable to understand what was happening.

He lunged at her with both arms spread wide, enveloping her in a hug that covered her little body with snow from head to foot.

"No!" she squealed, half laughing and half whining. "It's cold! It's cold! Stop!"

Tommy and Xander shot each other a look, then decided not to mimic their friend's behavior, instead turning to walk toward the school.

Tommy looked at his watch. "We've officially missed the free breakfast at the cafeteria."

"Mmm, stale hash browns that McDick's would have turned away. Be still my beating taste buds. I don't like the morning lunch lady anyway, she looks at me like she wants to get in my pants."

"Hey, that's my aunt!"

"It's a hard truth, Tommy. Deal with it." Xander sighed with fake empathy, patting his friend on the shoulder.

"What's a hard truth?" Mike asked breathlessly, as he and Cathy finally caught up.

"Is Tommy coming out of the closet again?" chimed Cathy, taking her place next to Mike.

"What?" Tommy interjected, eyes wide.

"Yeah, we've been talking about it a lot Tommy," Xander added, nodding.

"And we think it's pretty obvious," Cathy finished.

"Bastards," Tommy chuckled a little, sticking his hands in his pockets and looking down at the sidewalk. "You guys are fucking bastards."

"Oh, I'm hurt," Mike grumbled.

Cathy turned to Xander, then, whose eyes kept darting from the sidewalk to the road ahead. Forward, then down. Forward, then down. She frowned, then leaned in close to Mike and whispered something to him.

He nodded, then continued to berate Tommy.

BECOMING: CHAPTER FOUR

George Walker sat in a car outside the Big Eight motel on Reservoir Boulevard. It was a rental with rust dotting the wheel wells, bought on the fly from one of those we-don't-ask-questions places out by the airstrip. It was a busted old Buick that stank of Cheesies and spermicide. The man who gave it to him had smiled with all thirty-two of his pearly white teeth when he passed over the keys. He'd been wearing a blue and pink checkered shirt and a straw hat held tight to his forehead by a purple ribbon, and looked like he's stepped right out of a Don Bluth movie, with his bowtie and deep, sunken eyes.

"The tank is full," the man had said while holding either side of his checkered coat. "The tank is full, and she'll get you wherever you need to go. I'd stake my reputation on it."

George hadn't responded to the words. Hadn't even really heard them, he just kept nodding until the man stopped talking and then he took the keys to the parking lot. He remembered the words now and thought of telling the man that they didn't increase the value of the purchase. Talk was cheap, after all.

He'd always been quick-witted in hindsight.

George was pushing fifty and had very thin hair that was still quite black and allowed him to fool himself about his age. His cheeks were chubby and shook whenever he moved. As the years wore on, George began to develop a bit of a gut that tended to hang over the waist of his jeans and pull at the buttons of his shirts. His shoulders were wide, and his arms spoke to a history of physical labour, bear hugs, and strong-arming; though, the firmness of muscle was softening with age and atrophy, leaving droopy pockets of flesh where his triceps used to be. He wasn't as fast as he used to be, nor was he as agile. All told, George considered himself still very fit for his age, even though he never had the opportunity to prove it.

His fingers strummed along the hard rubber of the unfamiliar steering wheel. He had turned off the radio almost twenty minutes ago, but the last song was still stuck in his head. "Panama, by Metallica," the DJ had said, though it was really by Van Halen.

When he reached the end of the song, he slammed his palms against the wheel so hard that it left a swelled red mark across them. He gripped the wheel and looked across the long parking lot of the motel that stretched before him. There was a door with a letter on it, and then a large bay window with the curtains closed. Then a door, with a letter on it, and a large bay window with the curtains closed. After that was a door, a letter on it. Next to that was a large bay window. It had curtains. They were closed. Doors, doors, doors, windows, windows, windows, curtains, curtains, curtains. He couldn't see its end, and it seemed like it would go on forever. They all looked the same, and he wondered which one he was supposed to be looking at.

He turned from the motel to the Jeep that was parked next to him. It was large, towering over his rented Buick like a bully. The passenger door encompassed nearly all the view out of his driver's side window. It shone in the sun like it was new, and was that greenish-gray, baby-shit green colour that all jeeps seemed to be. It had halogen lights The tires were spotless, all smooth and rubber and black on big, shimmering rims.

The jeep was already there when he'd arrived. He'd hoped to get here before it, but this might be better. At least now there would be no lying when he found out for sure. At least now he would know.

He let out a long breath and leaned his forehead against the steering wheel. Closing his eyes, he let his thoughts spread over him and tried to clear his mind, tried to clear his head. His father had always told him that he did too much thinking with his gut, and lord if he hadn't been right. Too much thinking with his gut had lost him his daughter, had gotten him in trouble with the town council, and now... this.

I don't know what I'm doing here, he thought. His hands fell away from the wheel and came to rest sadly on his lap. The sun outside beat down hard and not even the fall breeze or the air conditioner fought it well, baking his exposed forearms and coating them with sweat.

"Now I don't want to hear any of that from you," said the frail old man in the passenger seat next to him.

George turned and looked at him as though just now realizing he was there, his head never leaving the wheel as he moved it.

The man had a big red nose and wore a tweed cap slanted to one side. His smile was so big it made his ears wiggle. His eyes were pale blue, so pale they looked ghostly. His name was Richard Walker, and he was George's father. "You're here because you want to be here."

"That's not true," George whispered, shaking his head just a little. "I don't want this. I don't want any of this."

Richard snorted, then turned away from him and stared out the side window. They sat in silence for six full minutes, according to the dash clock, before he finally spoke again:

"Giant eighty-foot water slide," he said, with the firm and authoritative voice of a circus showman.

George cocked his eyebrow and turned, slowly, to look at the old man.

Richard smiled that ear-wiggle smile at him again, then turned back toward the window. "Lasik eye surgery, only $499. Well, you can keep it."

George laid his forehead on the steering wheel.

"Latex condoms," Richard said, still in that same booming voice. He turned around and tapped his son on the arm. "Hey, why didn't you put me up in one of those instead of shoving me away in that goddamn home?"

George chuckled. "No, Dad, a condom is a -"

"Oh, I know," Richard scoffed, waving his hand dismissively. "Christ fuck, I can't even have any fun with you anymore. If I wanted to sit in a car with a stick-in-the-mud I would've driven out to the Cove with your mother again."

George smiled, then went right back to leaning on the steering wheel. He threw an occasional glance into his rearview mirror but said nothing.

"Hey, you remember that summer I met Macy?" Richard giggled hoarsely, tapping him on the arm again.

George looked up, his brow so furrowed that there were deep torrents gouged in it. After a moment they loosened, and he smiled. "Oh, yeah. Yeah, of course."

"You were twenty-one and I told you not to make the same mistake I did. You were supposed to be damn near thirty before you brought anyone home and asked me what I thought of her."

"You liked her, though."

"She was eighteen. I liked her caboose."

"Dad!"

"What? I married your mom because she had an ass that wouldn't quit!"

"And?"

"It did," he grumbled, then played with the non-functioning power locks for a moment. "Anyway, she stood there in her jeans and her little black top and held her purse out in front of her like she was scared out of her mind."

"She was."

"And what did she have to be scared of, huh? What'd you go telling that girl to make her scared of meeting little old me?"

"Nothing but the truth, I swear," George laughed, finally falling back onto the chair. Several of the springs felt like they were about to dig into his back.

Richard looked thoughtful for a moment, staring out the windshield with a blank expression. "Man, she was beautiful though, wasn't she? Sweet too. Brought those presents for Charlotte and your sister. Except you didn't label which one was which and you said -"

"Said I didn't need to, hun, because you taught me how to tell them apart."

"The bigger one was for your sister, because she was the bigger one!" Richard finished, slapping himself on his boney knees. "Woo, did her face turn red! She didn't even say nothin', just sat there as red as a beet while we all had a good laugh at her."

"I think she figured you'd all hate her after that."

"Naw, she should've known better. She was a peach, always has been. Made you happy enough."

George was quiet again. He closed his eyes and felt the cushion of the seat against the back of his head and took a long, deep breath.

Richard watched him like that for a minute, then turned back toward his window. "Bargain Dentistry, walk-ins accepted," he mumbled after a moment.

George turned away from him, rolling his forehead along the steering wheel. It was beginning to leave a colourful smear across his head just under where his hair started, part red from the friction and part black from the shoe polish that had been used to make the wheel look presentable.

He stared at the smooth, green panel of the jeep beside him. Slowly, he raised his right hand and brought it up to where the keys dangled in the ignition. At first he didn't recognize the feel of them. They didn't have the surfboard keychain that Macy and Kerri had picked out for him at a truck stop while driving across Texas on his birthday several years before, nor were they weighed down with gas tabs, house keys, bike lock keys, padlock keys, the keys to the business, or the keys to every vehicle George had ever owned whether it was in running order or not. These weren't his keys, these were the rental keys. All that was on them was the one key which would both open the doors and start the ignition, as well as a leather ornament that said PADDLECOTT USED CARS AND RENTALS. Below it was a simple drawing of the bowtie the salesman had been wearing, polka-dots and all.

He took the key out of the ignition and clasped it in his hand, his index finger riding the smooth edge of it and turning it into a serrated claw. He held it like that for a moment, feeling the pressure of it and liking it, then opened his door and stepped out of the car.

Richard leaned down to watch him, his wrinkled old eyes barely visible under the brim of his cap. He said nothing.

The sun was hot and the air was cool. George turned around and looked at the Big Eight's parking lot, seeing only the gleaming tops of the cars parked there. There was nobody in sight, and they were far enough off the main drag that cars were few and far between. The check-in for the motel was in sight, but the clerk behind the counter was not. If he couldn't see the clerk, the clerk couldn't see him, as his father had always said.

"Never once did I say that," Richard mumbled.

There were no security cameras. Bad for business at a place like this, but good for George. Yes, very good indeed.

Satisfied that there were no eyes (human or electronic) watching him, he turned his attention back to the smooth green panel of the truck's passenger-side door. It shimmered and shone like a twisted funhouse mirror. He could see his reflection in it, distorted and malformed but him all the same. His hair was receding and there were lines under his eyes, not to mention a big black streak across his forehead. *Is that me?* he thought, turning from his reflection to the reflection of the Buick. The rental looked even smaller in the green-gray hue of the Jeep, like the dinkies he'd played with as a child. Vroom vroom vroom, time to get the car washed! Watch out for the suds! Vroom vroom vroom, now it's time to gas up! Don't forget to pay! Vroom vroom vroom!

Kerri had loved to play that with him. Macy had watched while washing dishes and smiled, only slightly.

The hand holding the key shook as he locked eyes with his gray-green reflection again. It was him, he decided. His mirror self, other self, dark self, whatever self. It had been a long time since he let it out to play but now it was time to do a little mischief. It had been years, but it wasn't like he forgot how. He swallowed hard, brought the key up, and pressed its glossy steel surface against the car.

He paused. A world of possibilities scattered over the surface of his mind like jacks over pavement, each one a fresh idea of what he could write. Bitch. Slut. Skank. Whore. Tramp. Or the always gratifying, simple squiggly line.

He pressed in on the key and felt as the jeep's panel bent it slightly until the pressure, distorting that demon-image of himself into weird greenish-gray swirls. His mouth was wet with anticipation. His heart pounded against his chest so hard that he could hear it in his ears. It was, in fact, all he could hear. If someone had seen him and snuck up from behind, he wouldn't have heard them until their hand was on his shoulder.

With that thought in mind he glanced over his shoulder out onto the parking lot. It was still empty.

Licking his lips, he gripped the key so tight that he felt its pattern press itself into the palm of his hand... then paused, the tension leaving his arm. His smile faded into a sad frown as his arm went limp and hit his side, keys clasped in it loosely.

He stared down at the mark he'd made, a white dot so tiny that he wasn't even sure if he could see it. He gawked at it madly, shifting focus from it to his reflection and then back again.

He put the key into his pocket, opened the door to the rented Buick, and got in with a sigh.

"You fucking pussy," came a gruff voice from the back, so full of anger that it startled George. "That was the most ridiculous thing I've ever seen."

George looked in the rearview mirror and saw Terrence Owchar sitting in the back seat. He was a massive bald man who took up the majority of the space in the back, his head scraping along the dirty plush roof of the car. He did not have eyebrows. What he had instead was a scowl that made his forehead come out like a caveman's, turning his eyes into beady pearls of white in a sea of black shadow. On either side of his mouth were the long ditches of frowns that had been worn not for days or months but for years. His face looked like a Thwomp from Super Mario Bros.

He stared at George from his reflection in the mirror, his gaze as unmoving as a stone.

"Oh, don't listen to him," Richard scoffed, waving a hand toward Terrence dismissively. "He was always trying to goad you into trouble. I'm proud of you. You're too old for that kind of rubbish."

"Bullshit you are. Fucking bullshit," Terrence snapped. "You remember that summer after Kerri was born? I know you do."

He did. He'd just been thinking about it.

They'd had a mutual friend named Roland who always had a bit of a crush on Macy. George had always thought it would go away once he and Macy had been together a while. Then he thought it would go away once they got married, then once they had Kerri... but it never did. One day around Christmas after a few drinks and a little pot, Roland had tried to kiss Macy. He hadn't gotten very far before she backed up and hit her head off the cabinet doing it.

"You didn't need me to goad you that night," Terrence said, snickering out of one side of his mouth. George could see his gums in the rearview, bright and pink at the bottom but blackened and dark around the edges of each tooth.

There was a sound from one of the motel rooms, he wasn't sure which, that made him look up. It had been like a scream. When he examined the doors again, they were still just doors and windows and curtains. Nothing had changed.

"That was different," Richard said matter-of-factly. His voice had become hoarse and he did not look at Terrence when he spoke, merely turned slightly in his direction. "Men do things when they're hurting like that... things that they'd never do normally. That's the thing to remember here, George, that she's hurting too."

"Whose side are you on, anyway?" Terrence urged, glaring at the old man.

It shut him up, at least for the moment.

"You still remember that night though, don't you? And not just the memory... the feeling. It felt so good. Better than anything else you've ever done, almost."

It was true. At the time, George pretended to laugh it off at first and had continued drinking until he could tell from Roland's expression that he had forgotten about it. The lot of them had gone out for a smoke around then, and slowly the others peeled away until it was just George and Roland left.

"What the fuck did you think you were doing?" George demanded, both his fists clenched. "Are you fucking retarded or something? What in Christ's name were you thinking?"

Roland tried a few times to explain, but it kept sounding stupid. The only thing that wouldn't sound stupid was the truth, and he wasn't about to say that.

Roland had had a bad knee for about a year at that point. He had fucked it up while working in a mine up in Kannibus and spent about three months walking with a cane and another four besides walking with a limp. George kicked it with everything he had and sent him scuttling to the ground in a twitching, yelling mess. Then, George started in on him. He'd mostly worked on the kidneys and the liver, but there were a few face shots too. Those were the ones he remembered best.

When he went back inside, Macy was waiting with a cold beer.

"For me?" he asked, smiling.

"For your hand," she frowned, placing the glass to his palm.

She was right. The cool condensation coming off the beer bottle soothed the hot, swelling digits of his hand. He could feel the muscles relaxing.

"You're not supposed to hit with a closed fist," she said, kissing him on the cheek.

"Heard that." He had smirked, flexing his fingers. "But it is at times hysterical."

In the front seat of the Buick, George laughed at the memory, his hand flexing against his calf the same way it had that night. He barely even realized he was doing it. The laugh felt strange and foreign to him, but still good. He held it as long as he could, not caring for the moment that his eyes were closed when he was supposed to be keeping watch.

"You see?" Richard said, piping up again after remaining quiet the whole way through the story. He turned around to look at Terrence and then back to George, his smile so large that it made his ears wiggle again. He slapped his knee. "You see what I was saying?"

The laughter was winding down now, and George wiped the smallest peck of moisture from his eye.

"She stood by you. You've done that and worse over the years and she stood by you. Maybe you should spend a little less time thinking about what she's done wrong and spend a little more time thinking about what you've done wrong."

George stopped and took a deep breath, then lay his head against the steering wheel again. He felt as though he were going to cry, but didn't. *Wanted* to cry even, but couldn't. Something in the back of his head kept stopping him and forcing the tears back. He thought about what a wonderful experience it would be to cry... a cathartic episode that might allow him to get through this. To weep out some of his horror and frustration and then leave it drying in the ripped seats of this condemnable rental car alongside the semen stains and soda splotches.

He opened his eyes and looked through the middle of the wheel at the motel again. There was a door with a letter on it, and then a large bay window with the curtains closed. They all still stood there in a row, completely unchanged, going on forever until they disappeared behind the greenish-gray jeep. The sun shone on them and shimmered all the metal doorknobs, creating a straight line of stars three feet above the cracked concrete walkway.

There was a door with a letter on it, and then a large bay window with the curtains closed.

He sighed, then shoved his hand into his pocket and withdrew it with the key and leather ornament again. He shoved it into the ignition and turned, holding it in place for a second until the engine roared to life.

Frowning, he slammed the car into reverse and took a deep breath.

He stopped.

There was a door with a letter on it, and then a large bay window with the curtains closed.

The door was opening.

He shoved the car back into park immediately and cut the engine, then ducked down below the steering wheel.

The door to room 1C seemed to open of its own accord.

He held his breath without even realizing it, his face turning red.

Macy stepped out, her hair up in a bun with thin spidery locks coming down from it in all directions, framing her pale, beautiful face. He'd always loved when she wore her hair like that. It was very similar to the way she'd worn it on their wedding day.

She was wearing a pink dress that came down halfway to her knees and clung to her so tightly it was like she had been sewn into it, except around the breasts. It was loose on them, tottering this way and that against the tiny swells of her bosom. She carried a small black purse in one hand and had a gray jacket on over her shoulders, which she was just now pulling on.

She fixed her shoes. The heels hadn't been in the straps right.

She fixed her dress. It had bunched when she'd put it on.

She glowed in a way he hadn't seen in years.

A man came out of the room next. He was large, at least a foot over George who stood at a paltry five eight. He had a full head of hair that was swept to one side perfectly, even after the day's activities. He wore a nice suit that had to have been tailored, and shoes that looked to have cost more than the beaten-up Buick George was driving.

Macy started walking toward the jeep.

George ducked, making sure he was concealed by the dashboard.

The man stopped her, placing a gentle hand in the crook of her arm. He pulled her close to him and she fell into a kiss, holding it for a few seconds. She had to stand on her tip-toes to reach his lips.

They both smiled.

Their lips parted but their mouths stayed close, hers moving and saying something as her hand danced across his chest. She pushed it playfully.

George couldn't hear what she was saying, but knew it all the same.

Stop it, she had said, though she didn't want him to. She laughed coyly and sensually when she said it, patting him on the chest and using it as an excuse to touch the firm flesh. She'd done the same while they were dating, when he kissed her on her parent's couch with her father in the next room. She'd been both excited and scared by the possibility of getting caught.

The man smiled at her, and then the both of them made their way to the jeep. They sat in it for a moment, then the engine roared to life and they backed out.

George got out of the car again when they were pulling out of the parking lot and watched them as the pulled out onto the street. They did not look back and notice him.

He let out a deep sigh and got back in his empty car, then drove home alone.

BECOMING: CHAPTER FIVE

The morning light shone through his bedroom window, reflecting off one of the cans of cheap orange soda in the case a few feet from his bed. It glimmered brightly in his eye, making him groan and roll over, only to find that she was right next to him. She looked as alert and beautiful and perfect as she always did, her big, dark eyes studying him with unmistakable interest.

"Good morning, sleepy head," Eve said lovingly. She wrapped her hands around his neck loosely, then moved in and gave him a quick peck on the lips.

"Is it morning already?" Adam groaned, glancing over his shoulder at the sun. "Fuck. How long were we up last night?"

"You've been asleep about five minutes," she admitted, tracing her fingers over the imperfections along his back. "I'm sorry if I woke you up, but I just couldn't get to sleep after all that... well, I'm sure you remember."

"How could I forget?" he chuckled, rolling over until he was on top of her, the covers and blankets twisting around their naked bodies.

She felt so smooth beneath him, her every touch setting fires on his skin and making it scream for more of her. It was impossible to ever get enough. Just impossible. Her skin was so silky, her lips so sweet...

"Baby!" she cried in pleasant surprise. "Again, already?"

He smiled, leaning in and kissing her.

Their lips met, and the sweet taste of strawberries rubbed off onto his tongue as her own came into his mouth, hot and fast, making his body tingle all over.

Suddenly, her eyes shot open and her nails dug into his side.

He opened his eyes and looked at her, saw the panic, and the fear. Their lips parted, but hers still moved trying to tell him something, trying to let him know. He drew back the hand that had been wrapped around her waist, and found that it was covered in blood.

Silky, red blood that dribbled down his arm to his rolled-up sleeves.

"Aaah!" he screamed, pushing away from her.

"What?" she yelled, her eyes darting around the room in confusion. "What's wrong?"

"You..." he started, tears running down the sides of his face. "Eve, you were dead..."

She smiled, drawing his head down onto her breast and brushing her fingers through his short, dark hair. "Oh, sweetie... sweetie, no. It was just a dream."

"No, no it's not. It's not a dream, you're dead. You're not really here."

"Shh, shh, just listen." she told him, forcing him to keep his head on her chest as his hot tears spilled out onto her breasts.

He obeyed, stopping to listen to her.

But she said nothing.

"Honey?" he asked, confused.

"Shh," she chided him, pushing his head back into place.

He sighed, and for a minute there was nothing. Then, out of nowhere, he heard it, wondering how he hadn't before.

Bump-Bump.

Bump-Bump.

Bump-Bump.

It was her heart, beating for him, just for him, pumping the love that she felt for him through her entire body.

"Hear that?" she asked.

He nodded.

"See, I'm alive. I'm okay. Really, Adam, I'm fine."

"It just seemed so real."

"But it wasn't."

"I love you."

She smiled at him, bringing him back up to give her a kiss. "I love you, too... but are you ever going to take this out?"

He looked down.

The end of a blade was sticking out of Eve's chest, blood pumping out onto their sheets and mattress. The point protruded from between her breasts so far that he didn't know how he hadn't felt it or been impaled on it as they'd rolled around between the sheets. The bed around her was filled with blood.

"Oh my God!" he yelled, even as the blade thrust forward, stabbing into him as well and stapling the both of them together. He screamed.

"I love you," his lover mouthed, and he as well. As the both of them kissed and embraced once more, the bed itself became a massive set of lips and teeth, closing over them and swallowing.

Big, red eyes opened as its tongue whipped out and licked its lips.

"Just like mother used to make," the creature chuckled, laughing at his own little joke.

320

In his hospital bed, somewhere in his subconscious, Adam Genblade heard the shrill beat of his heart monitor.

Beep, beep.

Beep, beep.

Beep, beep.

Somewhere, deep inside his heart of hearts, the sound brought him some sense of peace.

BECOMING: CHAPTER SIX

Xander brought his lighter to his lips to light his cigarette, only to realize that he already had a lit one in his mouth. Huffing at his own stupidity, he placed the unused smoke carefully into his pack, then took a long haul off of his current one.

"I thought you were quitting," Mike said, strolling up to him from across the school yard. Mike knew exactly where to find Xander doing exactly what he was doing now, by the large brick wall that faced Eastman street. The of the road was blocked by a high chain link fence and a collection of alder trees that were bare of leaves this time of year. It had become the undisputed smoking section of Coral Beach high.

"Shut up," Xander responded, blowing smoke in his friend's face.

"Fine," Mike conceded, raising his hands in defeat. "But just because you've got a healing factor, doesn't mean you have to poison the rest of us, you know."

"Nut nust necause nou not na nealing nactor... blah blah blah," Xander mimicked, extinguishing his smoke in the ground next to him. He sat for a minute, a determined look on his face, as though he were bracing himself. Suddenly, he threw his head back, slamming it against the wall as hard as he could.

"Ow! Fuck!" he cursed. He brought his hands up to the already expanding welt on the back of his head, hissing as his touch brought new pain to it. "Fuck fuck fuck."

"Feel better?" Mike asked calmly.

"A little," he said, rubbing the back of his skull. "You know, for a second."

"How many times have you done that?" he asked, leaning over to examine the blood smear against the wall.

"Oh, fifty or sixty. It starts to take my mind off things after about ten tries, but then I start to bleed and the healing factor kicks in, so I have to start all over again."

"Dude... you need help," Mike chuckled, finding a morbid humor in his friend's words.

"No," Xander corrected, shaking his finger. "What I need is for life to stop slapping me when I'm not looking. At least when it's the wall, I know when it's coming. But standing around like a doof waiting for something bad to happen...

that makes you crazy."

"No, the fact that you actually used the word doof in a sentence makes you crazy."

Xander did not smile, instead opting to reach for his cigarette pack and pull out another smoke. He lit it quickly, snapping the lighter shut again to douse the flame and then pocketing both it and the half empty pack.

"Didn't you just finish one?" Mike asked, giving the paper cylinder a disgusted look.

"No, I just started one. Pay attention," he drawled, taking a few short puffs to make sure that it was lit. His eyes glazed in relaxation as the smoke traveled down his throat and into his lungs, and he held it in as long as he could stand before exhaling again.

"Fine then, be that way. All I wanted to do was talk."

"No, Cathy told you to come out and talk to me the first chance you had to get me alone," he snapped, turning to glare at his friend for the first time in the entire conversation.

"How did you-?"

"Super. Human. Senses."

"Right," Mike nodded. "Sorry. Didn't mean to patronize you or anything."

"No harm. No foul."

"Seriously, though. You wanna tell me what's on your mind?"

"Nothing," Xander said quickly, giving his head a little shake.

Mike leaned forward, looking around to the other side of Xander, where there was a pile of no less than ten cigarette butts and growing. "You maybe wanna try that one again?"

Xander exhaled through both nostrils.

"Look," Mike started, sitting down next to Xander and folding his large hands together. "I know that this thing with Julie is rough. And that it sucks. But, if there's one thing I learned from that massive fight Cathy and I had, it's that -"

"It's not Julie," Xander interjected, waving his smoke in dismissal, sending tiny tendrils of smoke into the air.

"What, then?"

Xander sighed, leaning his head back against the wall and staring forward into the gray sky. "I think... I think I was in Genblade's dream last night."

There was a long pause as Mike glanced back and forth. "You mean... you had a dream about Genblade."

"No, I mean Genblade was having a nightmare and I was there somehow," he explained in an 'isn't-it-obvious' kind of tone that made him sound even more insane.

"Ooookaaay..." Mike stretched, his eyes widening. "I'm trying to follow you here, buddy, but you're going to have to help me out. Let's just say for argument's sake that that's actually possible. How exactly would you know this was Genblade's dream? Did you take a wrong turn, end up walking out his ear and go: 'Hey, this isn't my head'?"

322

Xander laughed, coughing up smoke. "No. No, I know it was Genblade's dream because I was the bad guy. It was from his point of view. It was all about me killing Spider for no apparent reason, which is, I'm sure, the way he sees it."

"All right," Mike interrupted so that Xander would be quiet. "Again, assuming that were possible... Genblade's comatose, man. He is experiencing no brain activity. It's not like he's asleep or something, so the guy is not waking up. The doctors said so."

"Have you met the doctors in this town?"

"In any case, Adam Genblade is *brain dead*, okay?"

"What about the brain stem? There's no way of knowing how all of the chemicals and crap in Genblade's system affect him. His consciousness may somehow be buried in his..."

Mike gave Xander a look.

"I'm reaching a bit far, aren't I?"

"Yes," Mike said bluntly. Then he continued, more softly. "But then, a week ago I was about to kill you when I was interrupted by some freak that used crystal gems to tell the future. So, we'll be giving you the benefit of the doubt on this one."

Xander smiled, placing the butt of his smoke between his thumb and forefinger and flicking it over the nearby wire mesh fence. "It wasn't even so much the dream, really," Xander began, his words jumbling together as he got more and more worked up. "I woke up from it easily enough. But in the middle of the night. With no blood, it just..."

"The Womb's an animal, and animals don't just change their behavior like that for no good reason," Mike nodded.

"Right!" Xander breathed, glad that someone was articulate enough to voice what he had been thinking. "Exactly right!"

Mike was thoughtful for a moment. "It could be the snow. You never know, the Womb might behave differently in winter."

Xander shot him a look. "Every time we make excuses for my other half acting all wonky..."

"Somebody dies. I know." Mike groaned. "Besides, I feel it too. I woke up a couple of times last night. Once I even fell out of bed. Cathy was saying the same thing. We can all feel it. It's a... a..."

"A change in the wind," Xander finished.

"Yeah."

"Like the weather felt it too, and thought it was time to snow, but really it was just something coming. Something big. Something drastic."

"I'm sure it's nothing."

"I'm sure it's not," Xander grumbled sarcastically, lighting another smoke.

Mike snatched it away and was about to break it in half when he brought it to his own lips instead, taking a long drag.

Xander stared at him, then pulled out another cigarette and lit it.

"What do you think's going to happen?" Mike asked, taking short but relaxing drags.

"I don't know," Xander admitted somberly. "But I think we've both been down this road too many times to expect something good."

BECOMING: CHAPTER SEVEN

Mandy Peterson awoke suddenly, her eyelids clicking softly as they snapped open. At first, she wasn't quite sure where she was as she looked up at an off-white stucco ceiling. Her heart rate raced so quickly that she could hear it pounding in her ears.

"That was a good session," said Dr. Warren O'Toole from where he sat perched on his chair across the room. He was still scribbling notes on the sheet of paper attached to his clipboard, his hand going a mile a minute.

"It seems like I just closed my eyes," she said groggily as she sat up and put her hair back in a ponytail, pushing it away from her cute, plump face. Her cheeks were perfect and smooth, except for a few teenage blemishes and a small M-shaped scar on her forehead that she'd had since birth. Her sweater kept her warm on this chilly day, so big on her that it only stopped halfway between her hips and her knees. It made her look innocent and sweet, two words that anyone who really knew her would probably not use to describe her.

"You always say that," he grinned from behind his large round glasses, pushing the bangs of his black hair back and shoving his pocket watch into his breast pocket. His hand was covered by a red and white handkerchief. He stood up, revealing himself to be a tall, lanky man, his arms straggly yet strong. "It's the truest sign of a good session."

"And you always say that," she pointed out, smiling at him just a little.

She used to despise these hypnosis psychology sessions but had begun to find them quite relaxing. She even looked forward to them from time to time.

"So, when will you need to see me again?" she asked, stretching wide and then sighing happily.

"Hmm?" O'Toole hummed, lost in some stray thought. "Oh, yes. I'm sorry... um, let's say next week sometime. Contact me on Friday and we'll see when's a good time for you, okay?"

She shrugged the way only a fourteen year old can.

"Whatever," she chirped, then turned toward the door.

Warren watched her leave, then collapsed back into his chair, visibly exhausted.

"Oh, God..." he mumbled as reached behind his desk and pulled out a bottle of Jack Daniels and a short, wide glass. Throwing his clipboard into the nearest open cabinet, he poured himself a drink.

"Once more into the breach, my friends..." he murmured, downing the contents of the glass as fast as he could. "We few... we happy few."

Julie Peterson walked through the halls of Coral Beach High School, well aware of the fact that she was being watched. Stared at. Some even gawked, but mostly just those who rode the little bus to school and simply didn't know better, in her opinion.

She didn't mind either way.

She was more than used to being looked at, talked about, and secretly sworn upon. It had been happening to her for her entire life, and today was no exception. Except for the fact that today, they all had a good reason to stare.

Her shirt was loose on her and not at all appropriate for the weather outside. It was bright purple and came down across her arms in long, open sleeves. The neck was ruffled and bunched so much that it looked like she had a scarf on with it, although the material was so airy it wouldn't have provided any insulation. It was much more conservative than her usual attire, and she'd almost decided to not wear it several times that morning. In the end, the choice had come down to one simple fact:

It was one of his favorites.

The rest of her ensemble, her makeup, even her jewelry had been chosen on similar merits, right down to the choice not to conceal the freckles that dotted her cheeks. He'd always said he thought they were cute.

She stormed down the halls, her eyes filled with a grim determination and a spite that had become her trademark. Coming into the lobby, she took a long look around at who was standing around in the pre-class crowd. After just a moment, she spotted her prey.

Xander Drew sat in one corner, his eyes far off and distant. Mike Harris, Cathy Kennessy, Tommy Irons and Julie's her cousin, Mandy Peterson, all stood near him, talking about something stupid no doubt. He seemed oblivious to the rest of them.

She walked right up to them.

Cathy noticed her first, her eyes growing wide.

Julie tapped Xander twice on the shoulder.

Slowly, Xander turned around to face his girlfriend. He knew it was her before he even saw her just by the smell of her perfume and that feeling he got in the pit of his stomach when she was close by. He smiled at her. She had sparkling green eyes and freckles that ran across her cheeks and the bridge of her nose no matter how much lemon juice she applied to them. Her hair was never the same way twice, always highlighted differently so that she was always fresh, always new, always beautiful.

"Hi," he said simply when he realized that he was staring at her.

She smiled, then leaned in and opened her mouth. She kissed him in front of everyone, her tongue going in and out of their view as it darted between his mouth and her own, her hands traveling a mile a minute as they danced everywhere over him, squeezing him closer, grabbing at his muscular arms and abdomen. Her lips were soft, so soft, and yet the way she used them was so hard and powerful that it made his head swim, hard to think.

She broke off the kiss and stepped back, leaving him and every other person around awestruck. She smiled at him, tilting her head to one side and letting her hair fall over her shoulder in a way he'd always found adorable.

"Xander..." she said softly, soothingly. "... It's over."

With that she spun on her heels and started to walk away toward the front doors.

"Julie!" Xander called, shaking off the effects of her kiss and taking off after her. He almost tripped once, still lightheaded.

Cathy cringed as she watched the event, wanting to close her eyes and yet completely unable to, like the way people stopped to watch car wrecks. Even though you'd have nightmares for a week, you just couldn't miss it. Mike squeezed her hand tight, frowning. She did the same.

Mandy shook her head and sighed, looking as though her eyes might soon well up with tears.

Tommy just stood there, dumbfounded. After a moment, he elbowed Mike. "Did you see that kiss?"

Mike rolled his eyes.

"Julie, wait!" Xander called again, catching up to her as she neared the exit and taking her by the arm.

"Get your fucking hands off me!" she screamed loudly, whirling around and drawing the attention of anyone who wasn't already watching.

Warren O'Toole stopped talking to Principal Schneider, turning around and cocking an eyebrow at the scene.

Xander obeyed, letting her go immediately. "I'm sorry, I just... what was that, Julie?"

"That was a break up," she said matter-of-factly. "A damn good one, if you ask me. Just ask any girl here outside of Cathy and Mandy, and I'm sure they'll agree."

"Can't we talk about this?" Xander whispered between clenched teeth, very aware of the crowd.

"I've done all the talking I was going to do, Xander, but if you wanna talk... fine! Let's talk!" she yelled, shoving him back a pace. "Let's talk about the way you started off by rejecting me time and time again, making me feel like crap! Huh? Or, would you rather talk about all the ways I tried to be everything you wanted, and every time I did, you changed what you wanted! Or maybe..." she snarled, pointing toward Cathy. "Maybe we can talk about your little crush on her, hmm? Come on... everybody else is!"

The crowds gaze shifted momentarily from Julie to Cathy, who tried her best not to lock eyes with any one of them. Mike smiled at her, and suddenly she didn't care what they thought.

"Julie, please," Xander pleaded, his eyes filled with hurt. "Julie, don't do this. I thought you said you -"

"Yeah? Well, I don't. Guess you're not the only one here who can change their mind, huh?"

She snarled at him, then turned to walk away. This time he made no effort to stop her, just watching her hips swing from side to side in a triumph, even if that triumph was over him.

She reached out to open the door, when suddenly it swung open hard and fast, catching her in the nose. Blood spewed forth from it as she fell back, hitting the tiled floor like a ton of bricks, scraping her hand as she did so.

The door cracked against the wall, shattering the plaster there and sending small chips to the floor.

Ian Char and Duncan Combs stepped into the school, their big, black hiking boots making long streaks on the floor. Ian looked down at the bleeding Julie and smacked his lips at her, giving her a quick double kiss before reaching into the front of his pants and pulling out a gun. Duncan followed suit, pulling two similar handguns from behind him, aiming at nobody in particular but causing everyone in the room to scream nonetheless. On each of their right arms was a bright red tattoo of the letter T, their sleeves ripped off to accent it, hiding it from no one anymore.

"What the hell?" Mike swallowed, taking a long step forward. Cathy pulled him back. Taking note of the guns, he nodded.

Xander clenched his fists. The Womb organ swelled up inside him, the beast banging at the doors, ready to explode from his veins and take them down.

He suppressed it.

There were too many people around who would see, and Julie might get hurt if there was a firefight. He took a step forward, leaning down to pull on Julie's shoulder.

From between Ian and Duncan, Randy Owchar stepped into the school, brandishing a shotgun and his very own Tee tattoo.

Xander quickly got Julie to her feet and back into the crowd, where Tommy's teeth could be heard clenching above the screaming and yelling. Randy had killed Tommy's best friend, Sud, in order to gain entry into the Tees. He'd shot him in cold blood in this very hall.

Randy noticed Xander and aimed his gun directly at him.

"Hold it!" he bellowed, although his voice didn't really suit his attitude. Not deep enough. Not that anyone was going to argue the point with him while he was brandishing a sawed-off shotgun.

Xander froze immediately, raising his hands in the air. *I might... might be able to survive a blast at this range, depending on where it hit, but there was no guarantee that nobody else would get hit either.*

"Turn around," Randy ordered.

Xander complied, biting his lip because he knew he could take down that son of a bitch child-killer in ten seconds flat.

"Well, well, well," Randy smiled, shaking his head at Xander. He lowered his voice considerably, so that only he and Xander could hear. "If it isn't the Black Womb."

Slowly, Xander's eyes went wide, as he started to realize what that feeling he'd had was all about...

BECOMING: CHAPTER EIGHT

Alone in the dark, Adam Genblade scuttled around, looking, waiting, watching. There were voices in the dark, he would swear on it. He thought that he recognized them, but he just couldn't pin them down. He knew... he knew that he had to find them though. Something very bad would happen if he didn't. He was warm, but there was a cold breeze. There were sticky things stuck to him all over, but he couldn't see what they were.

"Honey?" Eve said, and Adam opened his eyes quickly.

"What?" he blurted, turning away from the road just long enough to look at her. "What is it, sweetie?"

She gave him a look that was both angered and disappointed.

"You're falling asleep," she huffed, crossing her arms.

"I am not!" he protested.

"I was just watching you. You were falling asleep!"

"I was just resting my eyes!"

"That's the same god damn thing!" She almost smiled at how feebly he was arguing, but tried to resist it. She couldn't smile, that would only encourage him.

He caught the grin, smiling back. "We'll stop at the next gas bar and get something to eat, I'll rest up a bit, and then we'll grab some coffee and get on the road again, okay?"

"Yeah. There's a McDonald's only a mile away."

"I didn't see that sign."

"Maybe because you were asleep."

"Yes, dear."

"Oh, don't you yes dear me..."

The highway McDonald's was cleaner than most, most likely due to the frequent hungry businessmen and travelers that came through. You never can tell when someone important enough to know the head health inspector in the country would just walk in and order a Big Mac.

Eve walked over to a booth seat and sat down, shooting a smile at Adam. "You know what I want, right?"

His eyes went up into his head as he regurgitated the order that she'd always made for the last seven years. "A quarter pounder with cheese, no mayo, no onions. Large fries. Side order of six-piece nuggets and one fajita. And a Coke."

"Diet Coke." she corrected.

"I knew that," he said, waving a finger at her lovingly.

"You did not."

"I did," he repeated, blowing her a kiss as he stepped up to order.

At the desk was a cute little blonde number with hips that were shaped like an hour-

328

glass and large breasts. He didn't mean to notice that she had breasts, but found he couldn't help it. He didn't think she was wearing a bra. Her name tag, which he read aloud to cover up the fact that he had been gawking at this young girl's tits, said 'Sara'.

She looked him up and down, tilted her hips to one side and licked her lips. "May I take your order, please?"

"Uh..." Adam stuttered, trapped in the girl's big, blue eyes. He realized that she could not possibly be one day over sixteen. "Um... I'll have a... a double Big Mac meal, please. With Coke."

"Would you like that super-sized? I know I would," she said, winking playfully at him.

"Um... no, thanks," he gulped.

"Will there be anything else?"

"No. Yes! My... my wife, she'll have a quarter pounder with cheese, no mayo, no onions. Large fries. Side order of six-piece nuggets and one fajita. And a Coke."

"By the looks of her, she should be getting a Diet Coke," Sara muttered under her breath.

"Yes!" Adam realized, almost yelling. "Yes, she'll have a Diet Coke!"

Sara smiled at him, again looking him up and down. "That'll be fifteen eighty eight, please."

He reached into his pocket and pulled out a twenty, unfolded it, then handed it to her. As she took it, she rubbed her finger against his thumb. He jerked away fast, and she smiled, passing him his change.

The meal went without incident. Eve gobbled up her quarter pounder like there was no tomorrow, then slowly ate her fajita and nuggets, like always. He was done everything before she even started eating the fries, so he decided that he would step outside for a cigarette. Giving his wife a kiss, he left the building and headed out back.

He pulled a smoke out of his jacket pocket and brought it to his lips, then began patting himself to find his lighter.

"Here," came a voice from behind him.

He turned quickly to see Sara sitting against the brick wall behind him, halfway through a smoke of her own, handing a butane lighter to him. The top three buttons of her shirt were undone, showing off an insane amount of cleavage. Her breasts were so large, and smooth... and now Adam realized that not only was there no bra, but no tan line either.

"Uh, thank you," he said, his hand shaking as he took the lighter.

Again, she looked him up and down. She got up, stepping toward him.

"Excuse me..." he started, but didn't finish, unsure of how to act as she continued to back him up until his back was against the wall.

She unbuttoned her pants quickly, grabbed his wrist and forced his hand onto her crotch. She was strong, stronger than she looked, and Adam could not pull away. Her other hand reached down and grabbed him between the legs, squeezing it tightly, longingly, the way Eve had not since they were teenagers. Before Adam knew what was happening, she was kissing him passionately on the lips, despite his very real efforts to stop her. She forced his hand down inside her pink panties with the rose in front and he felt her warmth, smooth and wet. He felt the warmth melt away his ability to resist, and he found his fingers doing things that he wished they would not.

329

"Sara!" came an angry voice from behind them, and the girl quickly turned around. There, standing with the sun against his back making him appear to be aflame with anger, was Xander Drew. "What the fuck are you doing slutting around again? How many times do I have to tell you, you're my girlfriend?"

"I'm not your girlfriend!" Sara screamed, tears flowing down her cheeks even as he descended upon her. "I never was!"

"Oh, you are and you will be!" Xander bellowed, grabbed her by the arm and pulling her forward into a kiss.

She bit his lip, drawing blood.

"Bitch!" he screamed, drawing back and punching her as hard as he could between her legs.

"Ahh!" she screamed, blood soaking through her pants as she bent over in pain.

It was only now that Adam noticed that the boy had a concealed knife in his hand. He had just stabbed the young woman in the privates.

"Oh my God!" Adam yelped, backing himself against the wall again.

Xander turned from Sara, her body raked with sobs and screams, as if only just now noticing Adam. "What the fuck do you want, pops? What were you doing with my girl anyway?"

"Please, I'm a tourist. I'm from Texas. Really, I... I really don't understand what's going on here, sir."

"Shut up, hick," Xander scoffed. "Fucking Texas hick."

"Please, I -"

"Adam?" came a voice like springtime. Both men turned to see Eve standing by the corner, her last chicken nugget in her hand. "Adam, what's going on?"

"Eve, for god's sake, go inside!" Adam barked.

"No, no," Xander smiled. "You got to have a go with my woman... only fair that I get to have a go with yours..."

"What's he talking about, Adam?" Eve asked, hurt in her voice. Then she noticed Sara, clinging to life against the wall as blood soaked her jeans right down to her knees. "Oh my God..."

"Don't worry, baby." Xander smiled evilly, holding up his blade. "It'll hurt, but it probably won't hurt that much if you're good."

"No!" Eve screamed, turning to run.

Adam lunged for Xander, who slashed out with the blade, slicing through Eve's tender flesh. She went down, hitting her head off the sidewalk and breaking her nose.

"No!" Adam yelled, crying himself by now.

"Fucker!" Xander yelled, kicking Adam in the ribs as he got to his feet. "That's two of my good fucks you've ruined in ten god damn minutes."

Adam coughed, trying desperately to get his breath.

Xander smiled. "That's okay, though. I'm in the mood to eat something else, now..."

Adam turned around. In one horrifying instant, he realized he was no longer standing next to Xander Drew, but the thing from his nightmare back in the car. The Darkness. The Black Womb. A massive, hulking creature made of black ooze that clung to him with hate and loathing. The demon's claws twitched, ready to rip off flesh for it to eat. Its *mouth dislocated like a snake's, to fit more of Adam past those big, filed teeth of his.*

"Black Womb lives!" the creature snarled as it leapt down upon Adam, biting into his jugular and ripping it away. As he died, out of the corner of his eye, he saw Eve twitch with life.

"Don't worry, man," the Womb assured him. "She'll be joining you as soon as I'm done with her..."

Adam blacked out then, hearing only the beginning of his wife's scream before he passed out.

BECOMING: CHAPTER NINE

Xander stared at Randy Owchar, their gazes equal in their rage and ferocity, neither of them moving for a full minute. His heart was beating a mile a second, a thousand thoughts going through his head at once, but only one loud enough for him to actually hear:

How does he know who I am?

Xander's left eye twitched with unreleased anger, his tongue moving as if to say words that he knew he could not in a mouth as dry as a desert.

Randy smiled. He'd shaved his head since Xander had last seen him, in an obvious attempt to look more like the leader of the Tees, Roulette. Roulette, a murdering, child-molesting skinhead that sucked in young boys and turned them into killers with the coldness and effectiveness of a factory, and one of the Womb's greatest enemies. And Randy's idol. And now Randy knew who the Black Womb was.

Randy moved forward, his leather vest ruffling. There were two handguns shoved into the front of his ripped jeans and a red bandanna sticking out of one pocket. He looked as though he was trying to grow a beard, the effect of which was a very patchy five o'clock shadow. His eyes were still blue, but they seemed beadier now, narrower since he'd killed Sud.

He pointed the gun directly at Xander's head.

He motioned to Ian, Duncan, and eight other Tees that had gathered in behind them, each of them sporting a Tee tattoo. He recognized one of them as George Walker, the father of Kerri Walker. Kerri had been killed by Zakron, the Anti-Womb, along with God only knew how many other people.

I guess now we know why the Tees wanted to help find Kerri so much, thought Mike from back in the corner. As he slowly took a step forward, Tommy followed his lead. Cathy pulled Mandy back.

"Find the Omega-Slut," Randy demanded, and Duncan and Ian immediately started searching through the crowd, their guns pointing at everyone they passed. "The rest of you, get on crowd control. I don't want any stragglers."

Cathy's eyes went wide as she realized who they were talking about. Mandy had been living in Coral Cove until a few months ago, where she'd dated a member of a rival gang called the Omegas. He'd branded her as one of 'their' girls, which caused serious trouble when she'd first moved to Coral Beach. Randy had tried to kill her to gain entry into the Tees.

"We have to get out of here," she whispered harshly to Mandy.

"No!" Mandy protested, pulling away from the older girl. "We have to stay here with Mike! He'll look after us!"

"What are you talking about?"

"Stop pretending you don't know what I'm talking about!" Mandy demanded, a little too loudly.

Randy smirked at Xander, now that it was just the two of them near. "All these months, it's been you... hasn't it? Ever since that first Tee got the crap beat out of him by the Black Shadow back in September when he was trying to get some action... that was you, wasn't it?"

Xander stood tight lipped, squinting his eyes.

"Now that I know it, I can't see how I didn't see it. It's in the eyes... even though they're so different, you can see all that anger in your eyes, Womb."

"And what do you see right now, asshole?" Xander whispered, speaking for the first time since the whole ordeal started.

Randy chuckled. "Fear. Because you know what's happening here. And you know you can't stop it. Just like you couldn't stop me from pumping eighty-seven cents worth of hot lead into Sud."

"You're going to die, Randy," Xander promised, his nails digging into his own palms so hard they drew blood. "I'll find you. I'll hunt you down. After having you this close, and me this mad, you think I'll ever forget your scent? The only chance you got at living is if you start running, right now, and never stop."

Randy smiled, quickly pointing his gun to the side and firing, blowing both barrels in a seventh grade girl's face. She flew back onto the floor, her flesh, blood, and brain matter spread across the wall in a large V-shape.

Everyone screamed, and Xander's eyes went wide with shock. He turned to lunge at Randy, onto to discover he had the gun pointed at another girl.

"I'll kill one of them for every threat you make, little man," Randy assured him politely, a childish glint of glee in his eyes.

Xander said nothing, keeping unbroken eye contact with the killer.

"Good boy," Randy chimed approvingly.

A young blond boy that Mike recognized as Dwayne Piercey stepped between him and Tommy. The kid had light brown eyes that betrayed how scared and determined he was, a dangerous combination in someone holding a gun. He had a scar on his upper lip and wore a backward baseball cap. His tattoo looked fresh... earlier that day fresh. Mike gave Tommy a look and a wink, who nodded.

"Hey!" came Ian's voice, from the back.

Mike's eyes darted in that direction as he realized that the bastard had found them.

"I got her!" Ian yelled, pulling Cathy out of the crowd and throwing her to the floor. An Omega tattoo stood out in bright red on her arm.

Randy raised an eyebrow, throwing a glance at Duncan.

"That's not her!" Duncan screamed, slapping Ian alongside his head. He picked up Cathy and threw her against the blood spattered wall, her red pen falling out of her jeans pocket onto the floor with a clack.

Cathy smirked devilishly, licking her thumb and bringing it to the tat, wiping the corner of it off. "Gotcha."

"Bitch!" Ian screamed, raising his gun to her.

At that moment, Mike and Tommy both turned on Dwayne, each of them kicking his feet out from underneath him. Mike drew back and kicked Dwayne's wrist, sending the gun skidding across the floor, lost in the crowd of horrified onlookers.

Duncan turned to where Ian had discovered Cathy just in time to see Mandy take off toward the rear exits.

"Fuck," he whispered. He raised both his handguns toward the crowd, who immediately parted to get out of the line of fire, inadvertently giving him a clear shot at Mandy.

Cathy kicked Duncan in the kneecap, and the shot shattered the trophy case instead of hitting Mandy.

"Slut!" Duncan cursed, turning the barrel toward Cathy, his teeth gritting as he seethed.

"Watch it!" Tommy said, slamming him over the back of the head with both fists. "Or somebody might get the impression that you're a woman-hating murderer."

Cathy smiled up at him as he helped her up.

Randy's eyes went wide as he saw the scene that was playing out before him. Most of his Tees were either frozen stiff or engaged with unarmed children. Grunting, he stepped forward and took aim at Mandy with the shotgun.

Spurt!

He opened both eyes and looked down, seeing Xander's hand pressed against his arm, but couldn't figure out why it hurt so bad... until Xander withdrew, revealing that there had been four claws at the end of each finger, each one now covered in his blood. In his other hand, Xander held a small, curved dagger with a hilt that had been carved into the shape of a dragon.

"Now who's scared?" Xander quipped. He jumped backward, ducked, then propelled himself forward into Randy, tackling his legs as they both went down.

George Walker squinted, watching as Tommy, Cathy, and Mike all engaged various Tees, while Xander was trying to wrestle Randy's gun away from him without success as the two of them rolled around on the floor. He turned, catching something out of the corner of his eye, then smiled to himself and raised his gun.

Mike punched Ian in the face, sitting atop his chest and wailing on him relentlessly, throwing off the Tees that were trying to pull him off of their compatriot.

"Son of a bitch!" he bellowed, spittle flying from his lips. "Think you can come in here and pull this shit? I'll rip your face off!"

Sven Douglas, a small, middle-aged balding Tee with buck teeth, pointed a gun at Mike.

Mike immediately got up as if to surrender, then backhanded the gun away, lashing out with a strong punch with his other hand.

"It's not nice to point," he whispered, turning back and kicking Ian again before turning to another Tee.

Cathy was kicking Duncan in the ribs repeatedly, trying to make sure he stayed down, swearing at him and his mother with every blow, sweat pouring off her brow as she worked off months of anger and frustration aimed at her oppressors.

Tommy took on a Tee he knew from grade school named Justin Langley, who had beaten him up once in grade three. He found it gave him a remarkable sense of closure, a justified smile across his lips.

"Gimmie *your* lunch money!" he yelled at the confused man as he pounded another blow into his skull.

Xander pinned both of Randy's arms to the floor, inches away from the pre-teenage girl that Randy had so callously murdered just moments before, her blood sticking to his leather vest.

"Killer!" he spat angrily, digging his claws into Owchar's hand. "I should give you death! You deserve death!"

His eyes began to darken as his pupils expanded, the true Womb organ in his gut pumping fiercely against Xander's will, trying with all its might to burst free.

"You should talk!" Randy retorted, kneeing Xander in the gut.

Xander let go in shock, allowing Randy to kick him off.

"I should have killed you when I had the chance!" he bellowed in the Womb's voice, echoing off the lobby walls.

Randy scrambled with his weapon and pointed it at Xander, who batted it away and slashed at the killer with the blade in his opposite hand. Randy reached for one of the guns held in his pants, drawing and pointing it directly at Xander.

Xander grabbed him by the wrist, digging his claws in deep and pulling forward. He dropped the dragon blade and snatched up the gun, turning it on its owner.

For the first time, Randy's eyes were filled with fear instead of hatred as Xander pulled back the hammer on the gun and placed first pressure on the trigger.

"Everybody stop!"

All parties turned in the direction of the voice.

Xander's resolve melted in an instant as his eyes found Julie's.

Her arm was held tightly by George Walker, the tip of his gun pressed forcefully against her dimpled cheek.

BECOMING: CHAPTER TEN

Walker smiled, taking a deep whiff of Julie's hair as she cringed away, blood still streaming from her nose.

"She seems nice, Xander," he said soothingly, turning toward the boy. "Put down your weapon, or I'll kill her."

Xander stared at Julie for a long moment, and she back at him. A blood vessel had broken in her left eye, but she still looked so beautiful. So fragile. Letting out a deep breath, he dropped the gun to the floor with a clang that momentarily shattered the silence that Walker had created in the room.

Randy picked up the weapon quickly and aimed it at Xander's head.

"Put up your hands," Walker demanded, pushing the gun tighter against Julie.

She yelped when the metal touched her temple, just loud enough to be heard.

Xander took but a second to retract his claws, then complied with Walker's demands as the blackness drained from his eyes.

"Now tell your friends to do the same."

He shot a sorrowful glance at Mike. He, Cathy, and Tommy all reluctantly raised their hands.

"Fuck," Mike groaned as Ian sprung to life, taking one of Duncan's guns and aiming at his ear.

Xander grimaced at Walker. "If only your daughter could see you now," he whispered, shaking his head.

"Watch it," Walker snapped, pulling back the hammer on the gun. "Or they'll have a plastic bag for each one of your bitch's brain cells. What would that be, two?"

"Xander, please..." Julie pleaded, tears mixing with the blood on her face.

Xander bit his lip, and did not respond to Walker's taunts.

"Good." Walker smiled. "Now, Omega-Slut!" he called out to the crowd, turning to face them. "I know you're still here! I can smell a cover from a mile away!"

From the crowd, there was nothing.

"You don't show yourself, I'll make paper-maché out of her skull!" he threatened, squeezing Julie's arm until she made a painful sound.

"No, no, no, no..." Cathy repeated to herself, her eyes darting over the crowd.

"All right," Walker sighed, putting his finger on the trigger.

"Wait!"

Xander closed his eyes and cursed to himself. When he opened them, Mandy Peterson was stepping slowly out of the crowd.

"Don't do this," he whispered to Randy without daring to turn and face him. "It doesn't have to be this way. I've got friends - Tim White, in the FBI - I can get you a deal if you end this now, Randy."

"Shut up," Randy sneered.

"I know you aren't a bad person..."

"Shut up!" Randy yelled, firing a shot past Xander's head and striking someone in the arm. He didn't see who it was, but they fell into the crowd and disappeared. His screams rang out across the hall though.

Again, Xander bit his lip, this time so hard that it bled.

"You can't trick me again," he warned, the gun shaking. "You can't."

Ian and Duncan stepped up, each of them grabbing one of Mandy's arms. Ian pulled up Mandy's sleeve and examined the Omega tattoo on her right shoulder blade, trying to rub it off. "It's her, boss."

Boss? Xander thought, his eyes darting briefly in Randy's direction. *What kind of mistake have I made here?*

"Good," Randy said.

"Kill the hero," Duncan said, smiling so wide it showed off his sickly yellow teeth.

Randy paused, looking down the barrel of the gun at Xander. "No," he said finally. "That was part of the deal. We were given the Omega, we gotta let him go, for now." He turned to Walker. "Stay here with her."

Xander watched as Randy turned back to him, sneering contemptuously at him as he addressed the crowd.

"If any of you so much as breathe wrong for ten minutes, the girl dies. Everybody out!"

With that, all of the Tees started scrambling for the exits.

Duncan and Ian dragged Mandy, kicking, screaming, and crying for Mike's help.

Mike watched her go, blood dripping from his hands onto the floor.

"You got lucky today," Randy said, only to Xander. "Soon as that sun sets, you're fair game. I'm gonna take pleasure in killing you in your sleep."

"Right back at you," Xander said under his breath, not moving an inch for fear of Julie's life.

Randy laughed, then backed up triumphantly until he was against the doors. He turned, then left.

"Dammit."

BECOMING: CHAPTER ELEVEN

Walker glared at Xander from over the gun with a sick smile on his face. His eyes were wide and bulging with beads of sweat pouring down off his forehead every few seconds. He glanced at Julie, then turned back to Xander again.

"She's cute, man. I'd like to have a go with her, if you wouldn't mind. Wait, what am I saying?" he laughed. "Didn't she just dump you? Man you are getting shit on all over today, ain'tcha?"

"It's gonna look like sunshine and roses compared to what I'm gonna do to you," Xander said, allowing himself a smirk at the thought.

"Haven't you been paying attention?" Walker snarled. "You. Lose. Is it that hard to get through your skull? Kids today."

"Speaking of kids," Xander interjected. "Would you like to know how your daughter died?"

"Watch it!" Walker yelled.

"...Xander..." Julie moaned.

"That thing... it grabbed her right out of your backyard. Jeez, you can't have been watching her very good, could you?"

"Shut! Up!"

"I bet that hurts. I bet you blame yourself for what he did to her, your little girl. When he bit off her arm and ate some of it. I think he had some kind of paralysis venom in his saliva or something, because she just kept on living, even after that."

"Quiet!" he yelled, putting more pressure on the trigger.

"I'm sorry, did you not know that? I knew that. I can show you the coroner's reports if you want, they're on file. I found her arm, you know."

"That's it! She dies!" screamed Walker, ready to pull the trigger.

Mike slammed Walker over the back of the head with a collapsible chair and he slammed into the floor face first.

The students broke apart like roaches when the kitchen light was turned on, scattering in all directions and making their way toward the exits.

Julie bolted straight for Xander's arms and he clasped her tightly, stroking the back of her head. For a brief, wonderful moment, he was at peace. When he opened his eyes again, they were almost black.

"Okay, guys!" he yelled, motioning to Mike and Cathy. "We gotta move fast! I didn't hear any cars so they're on foot, but they still could've gone in any direction once they got outside. We have to find her, now! Their trail gets colder every second we stand here!"

"Right." Mike nodded, as all three turned toward the front entrance.

"I wanna help," Tommy said grimly, standing where Sud had been killed.

"Me too," Julie added, wiping the blood from her nose.

"Fine, good," Xander snarled as they walked toward the doors. "But Owchar is mine. Anyone disputes that, they become the enemy as far as I'm concerned."

"Hold it!" came an authoritative voice from behind them, grabbing Xander by the shoulder and pulling him back with amazing force.

Xander spun around and was almost blinded by the glint off the taller man's glasses.

"None of you are going after them!" O'Toole demanded. "This is a matter for the police to handle!"

Xander shot a look at Mike.

"Run!" Mike yelled, and the four of them took off out the doors.

"South on Laird!" Xander bellowed after them, praying that they'd heard it.

"Cute," O'Toole spat. He sighed, then grabbed Xander by the collar and shoved him into the wall with surprising strength, rattling the Womb within his gut.

"Argh!" Xander screamed, looking around for help to find that there was nobody there. Still, there seemed like there was. He heard something, smelled something. The Womb flared.

O'Toole sighed, turning to drag Xander into the hall.

"I never dreamed..." he mumbled, rubbing the bridge of his nose with his free hand. "...in a million years..."

"Let me go, you freak!" Xander protested, wrestling out of his grip. "What the hell is wrong with you? Were you asleep during all of that?"

There was a sound to his right and he turned, only to find nothing there. He squinted, then shook his head and turned back to O'Toole.

"Let me go, you piece of shit!"

O'Toole lashed out, punching Xander across the face with one of his small fists.

"I am sick of your attitude, you little snot!" he screamed, kicking Xander in the gut hard enough to hurt the Womb. "You've already caused enough trouble for yourself, you fucking idiot, now what did you tell that girl?"

"What are you talking about?" Xander gasped, his mouth filling with blood.

"Does Mandy Peterson know you're the Black Womb?!" O'Toole demanded, slapping Xander across the face with his palm, sending blood against the wall.

Xander stood, stunned for a moment, then turned to face the empty corridor, then back to O'Toole.

"How did you?" he demanded, popping his claws. His eyes went from resolute to confused then back again all in the span of a few seconds. He turned around again, looking around the vacant hallway and finding nothing. "There's someone else here, isn't there?"

"Rasputin." O'Toole sighed softly, taking off his glasses and dropping them to the floor. "I believe we're past the point of discretion here, sir."

The air in front of Xander seemed to get thicker. Gradually it got worse and worse, until it was wavering like the air above hot pavement on a hot summer's day.

Out of that mist, a shape started to appear.

"I don't think that was your choice to make, Agent O'Toole."

Agent?

"I'm sorry, General, I think we've run out of options..."

General?

He watched her as she ate.

She giggled, her nose crinkling just a little as she did, in the cutest possible fashion. Just like the way that she did everything else, it was all just about as wonderfully peaceful as it could be.

The sun was shining. It was a beautiful summer day, and there were warm rays against their backs.

It all seemed familiar, so familiar... but then, this wasn't the first picnic they'd gone on.

The picnic basket was laid neatly against the red and white checkered tablecloth, spread out against the greenest grass God ever put on this earth. Ants crawled around the plates, their feelers twitching at the scent of apple pie and small cardboard boxes of cranberry juice.

"More strawberries?" Adam asked, reaching up a hand quickly to make sure that his hair was all right. It was, perfectly molded and quaffed by a half pound of extra-hold gel. He had wanted it to look perfect for her, and now was worried that it looked like a dirty blond hard hat sitting atop his scalp.

She's going to ask me why I'm all dressed up.

Eve giggled at him again, a bubbly sound, like fresh water from a spring well.

"I saw that," she taunted, scolding him playfully by waving a finger at him. "What are you all dressed up for today anyway?"

So familiar.

"Oh, I don't know." He smiled, leaning a little closer to her. His nostrils flared to pick up more of the divine perfume that she was wearing."I guess I just felt the need to be half as pretty as you are all the time for a change."

I'm so sweet.

"Aww," she cooed, tapping him playfully on the face. "You're so sweet."

He winked at her.

She rolled her eyes, then took one of the offered strawberries from the bowl next to his chest and pushed it past her pearly white teeth and her soft, red lips. She bit down, sucking on the tip of what remained.

He felt the hairs on the back of his neck stand on end. It always amazed him how she could be so sensual in everyday things... in everything she did, really. How she could turn him on with just a look, or the way that her raven hair fell across her breasts a certain way... or the way she could say his name when he wasn't feeling good and make all of the bad things in his life melt away.

The wind picked up and the trees all around them swayed with the breeze.

"How was the casserole?" he asked, looking down as he played with the last bit of mashed potato on his plate with the end of his plastic knife.

"It was great, baby," she assured him, motioning toward her empty plate as if to offer it as proof. She ate whatever he cooked anyway, even if it tasted like garbage, as it almost always did. "I loved it."

She smiled, plucking the stem off of the berry before holding the rest out to him.

So familiar, it seems like I've done all of this before...

He leaned in and took it into his mouth, keeping his eyes on hers the entire time, watching them light up as he kissed her fingers before he started chewing the strawberry.

"These are really fresh," she commented, picking up another and plucking the stem off of it, running the pointed side along her lips before putting it in her mouth. "Where did you get them, the deli?"

"Picked them myself. I put a few of them in the fruit salad too..."

"I noticed. It made it sweeter. Probably your best yet, hun."

Adam looked down, his cheeks turning a little red.

"No need to blush, lover," she cooed, reaching out and tilting his chin up. "This was perfect. It was just what I needed."

He smiled, blushing even more now that he knew that she had noticed it. "I know that work's been tough on you lately..."

"Work has been a nightmare." She giggled, lying back on the tablecloth. "Anderson pulled some strings and got his cousin out of the mail room (where he belongs) and up into the editing suite. I swear, there were at least fifty mistakes in last night's run, and who gets fired? Sara, that's who."

Wasn't it Lorraine?

"He really fired Lorraine?"

"No, Sara."

"Oh. That's awful."

So sure it was going to be Lorraine...

"So, his little knob cousin gets her position, and..."

"Wait, he messes up, someone else gets fired and he gets a promotion?"

"Uh-huh."

"That's insane."

"That's television, babe."

"I honestly don't know how you can handle working with those vultures. I'd have fed Anderson through the tape deck long ago."

"Simple," she said slyly, crawling over the plates to get closer to him. "I've got you to come home to, big guy."

He grinned as she leaned in to kiss him, making no motion forward as she did. Their lips met, and the sweet taste of strawberries rubbed off onto his tongue as her own came into his mouth, hot and fast, making his body tingle all over.

Suddenly, her eyes shot open and her nails dug into his side.

He opened his eyes and looked at her, saw the panic, and the fear. Their lips parted, but hers still moved trying to tell him something, trying to let him know. He drew back the hand that had been wrapped around her waist, and found that it was covered in blood. Silky, red blood dribbled down his arm to his rolled up sleeves. It soaked into the shirt he'd taken so long to pick out and expanded, soaking ever outward until it was drenched in her.

Her body slumped against the tablecloth, staining the white checkers red. The red ones remained the same, until the cloth wasn't checkered at all anymore. It was just red. Her face landed in what was left of his mashed potatoes, smearing into her hair so deep that they ingrained themselves into her scalp.

He wondered if she had even liked the potatoes, really.

He looked up.

A young man stood just on the edge of the cloth, dressed completely in black. A cigarette hung loosely between his lips as he took small puffs, blowing them out through his nose. In his hand was a small blood-stained dagger with a handle that was etched into the shape of a dragon. He couldn't have been any older than sixteen, but his face was worn and scarred, the face of a young man who had seen too many fights in his life. His jaw was steadfast and unwavering despite the horrible thing he had just done. His eyes were black... not dark brown but black, covering his entire eye, like one great pupil.

"What have you done?" Adam screamed, looking from his fallen lover to the madman that stood before him, cold and uncaring. There must have been some mistake. She was everything to him, all that he lived for. Rolling over and seeing her was his sole reason for opening his eyes every morning, and knowing that he could do it again the next day was his reason for closing them at night. She was his rock. His peace. His everything.

"Why would you do this to her?" he sobbed, tears streaming down his face. "What could she have possibly done?"

"She knew you," he said coldly, taking a step toward him.

Adam fell backward, turning as Xander continued to press toward him, running for the park. He passed through a knoll of trees, coming out of the other side to find himself in a graveyard. At night.

"What?" he spat, turning to see that the killer was still following him.

"You can't run," the killer taunted. "I always find you..."

He was right, Adam remembered. He does find me. He kills me.

The boy snarled, spitting his still lit smoke out of his mouth. "Black Womb sends his regards."

Adam's eyes went wide as the killer took one threatening step forward, twirling the blade between his fingers. For the first time, his stony face showed an emotion... and it could only be described as utter glee. He'd seen it on Eve's face a thousand times, and never would again.

"Why are you doing this?!" Adam screamed.

The killer said nothing, just took another calm step forward, followed by another.

Adam continued running, dodging between graves. He turned around to see how close the murderer was getting, only to find there was nobody there. Facing forward again, he came to an abrupt halt, almost falling into an open grave. He turned back around, coming face to face with Xander Drew.

"Why?" Adam begged, tears streaming down his face.

Xander actually laughed at that, driving his blade deep into Adam's gut, then pushing him into the open grave.

"Black Womb lives," he chuckled softly, spinning on his heels and stopping to light a smoke.

In his hospital bed, Genblade's heart rate slowed, slowed even more...

"He's going to go into arrest," said Porter.

"What? That's impossible!" Reilly exclaimed, rushing forward. She took one look at the charts and then backed away a step. "I'll go get the doctor!"

Xander Drew stood by the new grave of Adam Genblade, puffing away on his victory cigarette.

Suddenly, a powerful hand grabbed his heel.

He looked down, seeing Adam reaching up from out of his grave, pulling him down.

"No!" Xander screamed. "You can't beat me!"

Genblade's heart rate spiked back up to being that of a marathon runner in the bat of an eye, startling Porter as she prepared the paddles.

Adam dragged Xander down into the grave, Xander's nails forming long treads in the grass as he tried to stay above ground.

"No!!" Xander screamed as he was finally forced to let go.

Several long moments passed.

Finally, a black-clad hand slammed into the dirt above the grave, pulling himself up. Adam Genblade emerged in full costume, his black jump suit with white spikes at the joints not even tarnished by the mud and grime he had just climbed out of.

Genblade's eyes shot open.

Genblade's eyes shot open.

Porter jumped back.

"Reilly!" she tried to scream, but barely got the R sound out.

He was on his feet almost immediately, looping one arm around her and bringing his IV cord tight across her neck. The hard plastic dug deep into her throat and she coughed, her hands jolting up and grabbing at it.

He took a deep breath, in through his nose and out through his jagged, clenched teeth. Her hair smelled like mint and citrus. After over a month of unconsciousness the smell was overwhelming, as though it was the first he'd ever taken in.

There was a dry, hacking sound as Porter struggled for breath and got none.

He wrapped the ends of the cord around his fingers and pulled them tight into a fist. The cord drew tighter, wearing through the skin until it produced blood.

Her plump fingers scraped at the plastic, slipping on it over and over again as her neat, well-groomed nails failed to find a hold on its surface. The grooves of her fingertips found a hold on them once or twice, but it wasn't enough to pull it free.

She gagged again. Her eyes bulged.

"Shhh..." he soothed, leaning in until his salty lips were caressing the supple flesh of her earlobe. He smiled, giving her a small peck on her cheek. "It'll be alright."

He felt her pulse slow, and then eventually stop, her face pale white and her lips a sickly shade of blue. Her eyes were dull already as her hands fell to her sides and he let go of the cord, watching as she fell into his night stand without reacting at all.

He got up off the bed, wriggling his bare feet against the cold tile floor.

"Thanks for all your concern," he mumbled, without so much as looking at where Porter had landed. He looked down at himself and sneered at the salmon coloured paper gown he was wearing. He grabbed the stiff fabric with both

342

hands and watched the way it bent and pushed between his fingers. He pulled it free with one quick tug, feeling the string snap against the back of his neck. It fell to the floor and he was naked in the cool, air conditioned room.

There was a needle sticking out of the crook of his left arm. His fingers grasped at it hungrily, so fast that its metal end worked itself in his veins and shredded one of the walls. He didn't care. He barely even noticed. Finally getting a good grip on it, he pulled it out, sending tiny squirts of his blood spurting against the walls.

There was an open doorway in front of him that he knew led out into the hall. He pressed his tongue along the sharpened contours of his teeth and turned instead to the door to his left.

There was a black card swipe on the wall next to it.

He reached over and grabbed the thin white strap that hung around Nurse Porter's neck and pulled, snapping the string and holding up a card key with her picture on it. It dangled in front of him and he watched it for a moment, the way it spun and played tricks with the light on its laminated surface.

He slid the key through the swipe and the light on it turned green. Pushing the door open, he entered a long hallway lined with lockers.

This room was cooler than his had been, and he felt gooseflesh ripple out all over his nude body. He stopped for a moment at a locker marked MARX in big, bold letters. He pushed in open and started pulling its contents out onto the floor. A small pair of shoes, a paperback novel, an old pair of reading glasses...

He huffed, then opened the next locker. Then the next. Then the next. Each time he reached in and grabbed a handful of its contents and pulled them out, scattering them onto the floor.

He opened his seventh and was about to reach in when he stopped and smiled.

Glimmering there in the green tinge of the fluorescent lights were the Spider-Swords.

Dual blades that had belonged to Eve when she had been alive and working for Engen. They'd been a gift from their master to her for being their greatest weapon in battle.

"It's good to be home," he sighed, picking up one of the swords.

It felt good in his hand, the weight of it. Like the citrus mint smell before, it was like holding it for the first time. It felt new and yet familiar all at once.

He looked and saw a battered black corduroy shirt on the floor and picked it up. He tilted his head to one side as if to examine it, then slid it on over his head. It was a size too small and clung to him tightly.

In his mind, it was the jumpsuit he'd last worn inside the Engen building.

He opened the locker next to his and found a ragged pair of jeans, the type that most people would have called work pants. He grabbed them and pulled them out, taking several medical textbooks with it and sending them crashing to the floor.

He smiled brazenly.

Outside Genblade's hospital room, Nurse Reilly whispered into her cell phone while poking her head around the corner, keeping an eye out for Genblade.

"Yes..." she repeated. "Yes, that's right, sir... it's finally happened."

"He did say south on Laird, right?" Cathy said between short, huffy breaths as the four of them ran down the street as fast as they could. They were exhausted enough from the fight, but the last ten minutes spent sprinting down the slow incline of the street was really starting to bog them down.

"I thought he said west on Eastman," groaned Julie, her eyes sharp and darting in all directions for any sign of her younger cousin.

"No, I said that," corrected Mike. "That's where the old Tee hideout is. If we don't catch them... we'll end up there going this way, where Laird meets Eastman."

"We're going to catch them," Tommy added, the first words he'd spoken since they'd left the school. "We have to. I won't let them hurt Mandy."

"Great. Vengeance vendettas," Cathy mumbled too low for anyone but Mike to hear. "'Cause that's exactly what a suicide mission needs."

"This isn't a suicide mission," Mike pressed, reaching out between strides and touching her shoulder. "We've made it through worse before."

"With Xander!" she snapped harshly. "Without him, we're just four kids with no knives, no guns, and no hope of beating the entire Tee gang."

Mike shot her a look to keep it down, motioning to Tommy and Julie, who were watching the roads for any sign of movement or activity.

"We're not gonna find her!" Julie wailed hopelessly, fresh blood spilling from her nose.

"Yes, we will," Tommy reiterated. "We're going to."

"We'll get there," Mike assured them. "Even without Xander here, he told us what we needed to do. We've got to stick together."

"What makes you so sure Xander's right, anyway?" Tommy said finally, looking down a side road. "I think they went this way!"

Mike turned, shooting him a look.

Tommy looked downward, dejected.

"You asked to come," Mike reminded him, addressing Julie as well. "Xander said you could. That's more than I would have done, but until he's here to tell us different, we're looking for her going south down Laird."

Cathy turned, smiling at him briefly.

Xander, she called out mentally, wishing that there were some way he could hear her; *Xander, please hurry.*

BECOMING: CHAPTER TWELVE

Xander stood wide-eyed as a middle-aged black man materialized into view. He had a goatee and some fluffy graying hair around the sides of his head, but aside from that he was completely bald. He was dressed in a black blazer and slacks with a dark gray turtleneck underneath that made him appear almost warm... but his eyes squashed that thought immediately. They were cold, and of a clear blue that was so rare for his race.

As he finished coming into view, it was like the rest of Xander's senses jump-started as well. Suddenly he was so aware of him that he didn't know how he hadn't been a few seconds ago. His cologne stank unnaturally, the cheap kind that didn't smell like any one thing but left a coppery tang in the back of your nose. The smooth fabric of his blazer rustled against the coarse fibers of his turtleneck and created a sound that seemed almost deafening compared to the silence that had been there before. His jaw clicked. And there was that hum, that dull electronic hum of white noise that always made Xander want to scream.

"General?" came a shrill voice from nowhere.

Xander looked around again, half expecting to see more invisible people coming into view.

The General brought a hand to his ear. "Reilly, I told you not to use this frequency. Switch to the private line."

There was high-pitched sound that Xander was sure only he could hear as the General kept his hand to his ear.

"I understand. This was to be expected when I showed up on the scene," he said finally, then turned back to Xander. "Now, young man, what do you have to say for yourself?"

O'Toole got a worried look on his face then, shaking his head feverishly from behind Xander.

Xander stood and stared at this new man for a moment in utter disbelief, then finally shook his head.

"Excuse me?" he said finally, furrowing his brow.

"Uh..." the General stammered, noticing O'Toole's warnings too late.

"I've had a very... very bad day." Xander informed him. "And now, we have you. Just you being here pisses me off, Mr..."

"I'm the General," he said, sticking out his chest a little with pride as he did.

"Yeah, that's not gonna happen."

"What?"

"There's no way I'm ever going to call you that with a straight look on my face, so you can drop the macho crap right... about... nnnnnow," he said sarcastically, a serious edge on his voice.

"My name is Hale," the man said, throwing Xander a well-polished smile.

"Well then, Mr. Hale, it's been very nice meeting you," Xander said, brushing past him and flashing him his middle finger. "Please enter the nearest classroom on the left and go fuck yourself. Or O'Toole. Whatever floats your boat. I have misplaced anger to redirect."

"Womb," Hale stated, grabbing the boy by the shoulder. "Stay."

Xander eyed him for a long moment, then turned back to O'Toole, who would not meet his gaze. "Does nobody understand that I am trying to conceal a secret identity here? How do you people know who I am?"

"Xander..." O'Toole started, looking sheepish.

"Agent!" Hale snapped, as if it meant shut up. He turned back around and gave Xander that movie-star smile of his again. "Kid, I know it may not seem like it right now, but we are here to help you."

"We? Is that the royal we, or..." he sighed, looking around. "There aren't more invisible people, are there?"

Hale chuckled at that, loosening his grip on the boy. "No. No, not at all. And just because you couldn't see me doesn't mean that I was invisible. Assumptions will get you in trouble in this racket, son."

Xander paused, turning to O'Toole. "You --"

"That particular hypnotic suggestion could certainly use some work though, eh? You knew I was here from the second I walked in. Almost bumped into me a few times."

Xander squinted.

All at once, he couldn't hear anything anymore, as the flames around him started to dance and scatter away, until they went out completely. Xander looked around in confusion as a wind came from nowhere, swirling about with the force of a tornado. Zakron looked even more confused than he did, batting a debris that swirled around it as if they were its enemy. The sound like a rhythmic beating filled the air, as Xander recognized it, looking upwards just in time to see the clouds part, and a huge military helicopter descend from the sky. It hovered about twenty feet above the ground, and three cords came out of a hole in its underside. Three men, all of them wearing what resembled forest green scuba gear, slid down the ropes and landed gracefully on the ground. All three opened fire at Zakron, shooting darts into the demon's backside, and it went down in a slump. After nearly a half hour of battling it, Xander watched the thing go down with three darts.

"Obtain! Obtain!" yelled the lead scuba-man, with yellow stripes on the side of his right arm. They wore air tanks and dark goggles, showing none of their skin. They were muscular, but human in their movements and mannerisms.

"Hey!" Xander yelled, running up to the leader. "What the hell is going on here?"

"Classified, son." The commander nodded, putting an arm on Xander's shoulder. "Circe business. None of your concern. Thanks for keeping him in one place long enough for us to get a bead on him, though," he said truthfully, turning away to grab the rope and climb up as the other two loaded Zakron into the chopper.

"Hey!" Xander yelled again, grabbing the man by the arm and pulling him back down to earth. "Where do you think you're going? I've got a lot of questions, and I know you've got answers!"

"Sorry, kid." The man shrugged honestly, turning and firing a dart into Xander's gut. "Classified."

Xander fell to earth, remaining there for a moment, unable to move, just to watch the chopper pull back into the clouds, and away from sight.

"You're the Circe, aren't you?" Xander blurted.

Hale looked at him with genuine shock. "Impressive, my boy, I didn't think you-"

Xander drew back and punched Hale square in the jaw, sending him back against the lockers. "Bastards! You could have helped me, you could have saved

346

her!"

"It was only O'Toole here!" Hale assured him. "He called us in the second it all started, but by the time I got here they'd cleared the building. I'm truly sorry, Womb."

"Stop calling me that!" Xander demanded, angered beyond imagination. "My name is Xander."

"Actually, your name is Adam. Adam Evensong. But, you knew that."

Xander stopped dead in his tracks, eyes wide.

"Been a while since you heard it though, hasn't it? Engen, Alpha Quadrant, Experimentation number 08267, if I remember correctly."

"08276, sir," O'Toole corrected, finally speaking.

"Thank you, Agent."

Xander stood, dumbfounded. "How do you people know who I am?"

Hale smiled. "We raided Engen a while back. Agent O'Toole here found the location through one of your hypnosis sessions, and he went out and got all the files pertaining to you. Truth be told, it was only then that we knew for sure that it was really you. Accounts from others indicated that it was another -"

"Harris," O'Toole interjected. "Mike Harris, another student at the school that was of the correct gender and age."

"Yes, right," Hale continued.

"Mandy..." Xander murmured.

"Yes, exactly. Smart lad."

"I have to find Mandy."

"We can't let you do that," Warren said, in his smoothest possible voice.

"Why not?" Xander demanded, spitting at Warren, his pupils getting wide.

"We have been watching you, through Agent O'Toole, for many months," Hale revealed.

"Yeah, I kinda figured that out," Xander said, rolling his eyes. "Their scent is getting cold. I have to go find..."

"You learned through Genblade that he and Engen were involved in an... in a Genetics War with us before you were called into the game, correct?"

"Yes. Fine. Whoopie. I have to go," he said quickly, attempting to rush the older man's conversation.

"We've come to recruit you for our side. Fight with us against Engen."

Xander snorted. "Check your sources pal, I destroyed Engen. Some super-spy you are."

"You destroyed Alpha Quadrant, kid," Hale said flatly.

All of the colour drained from Xander's face. "Excuse me?"

"There are more section heads in Engen than I'd care to count, each with their own lab. Alpha was just a crazed, ex-employee that got taken under a head's wing and got even more crazed. You haven't even met Engen yet, kid. And you're not ready to, not that that'll stop them."

"What are you talking about?" Xander asked, frantically. "What's going on?"

"The devil is on your doorstep, kid. That call? The reason you can't go? You're my protection. Adam Genblade just woke up, and the only person he hates more than you on this planet is me. You're not going anywhere until you've detained or destroyed that demented half-brother of yours, kid."

"I don't understand any of this," Xander said harshly, glaring at O'Toole. "I don't..."

"Kid, there isn't much time," Hale pressed. "It's time to stop playing hero, and time to start becoming one."

Xander stopped, not saying anything for a long moment as he looked at the floor.

"Otlexmndlktn," he mumbled finally.

"What was that?" Hale asked. "What did you just say?"

"O'Toole examined the location," Xander repeated, recalling what Hale had said.

"What?" Hale asked, his voice wavering.

O'Toole looked scared and wouldn't stay still. Xander noticed.

"He was at the Engen facility. The part with the computers and the caskets... where the Anti-Womb first came from." He turned, glaring evilly at Warren, who refused to meet his gaze. "You let Zakron out, didn't you, you little troll?!?" he screamed, lunging at Warren and pinning him up against the lockers, his eyes completely black now.

"I... I - "

"No more lies!" Xander demanded. "No more Circe-approved stories! I want the truth, Warren! What's really going on here?"

Warren looked past Xander at Hale, then shook his head. "As mad as you are," he said stubbornly. "You won't kill me. He will. It's not a hard choice to make."

"We'll see," Xander spat, as he let O'Toole go and turned to walk away. This time, Hale made no move to stop him.

"Genblade is coming," he said, calling after the boy.

Again, Xander merely raised his middle finger in defiance. He marched alone out into the lobby, then stopped, looking around the blood spattered room.

"Where's Walker?" he asked himself, realizing that the killer had disappeared.

BECOMING: CHAPTER THIRTEEN

Mike stopped, taking a quick look around as the rest of the group caught up. His sides ached and his lungs felt as though their strain for oxygen would soon crack his already bruised ribs. He didn't care. At that moment, a single thought coursed through his head, pumping into every crevice of his mind:

She thought I was the Womb.

Mandy Peterson had had a crush on Mike since the first day she had arrived in Coral Beach, going as far to approach him physically one of the first days that they had known each other. Since then, although her feelings for him hadn't changed, Mandy had become sweet and caring... a nice young girl, and someone that he'd come to know and care for himself, in a different way than she had initially hoped.

She'd also been through more in this life than many of the people that he knew, and for him, that was saying something. The Tees had gotten hold of her before, beating her and almost killing her. It was the Black Womb that had saved her, so of course, she had assumed that it was him. Black Womb equals White Knight in the girl's minds, he supposed.

He bent down, hands on his knees as he tried to catch his breath. The others were far behind him. How fast had he been running?

Sweat stung at his eyes as he scanned the road for any sign of movement, any hint that they'd gotten close. There was none. Coral Beach could seem like a ghost town sometimes, with enough trouble in it to keep most people off the streets. And with enough people off the street that trouble could happen. It was a vicious cycle that everyone recognized, but only a scant few were willing to step outside.

The breeze picked up and the trees next to him rustled, violently shaking as though they'd been chilled by the wind.

"This is getting useless," Tommy called out to him, limping along as he did. He'd twisted his ankle somewhere around Vietch Street and had been walking like that ever since, but he wasn't the last in line by far, so Mike had to give him credit.

Tommy was here partly for revenge, partly for another reason, Mike knew. He had feelings for Mandy, if only ones that were just beginning to spark. It must have been killing him, to first have lost his best friend to these sadists and now to be faced with the possibility of losing her.

"It's not useless," Mike returned, after a moment's lapse. He turned from the street and the trees to Tommy, and something twisted in his gut as he did so.

"Look, I'm not saying we should give up," Tommy explained, coming up next to Mike and putting his hands on his knees to relax as well. "All I'm saying is that we try something different. Sure, I didn't hear a car either, but they could've had one waiting a block back and gone in any direction after that."

Mike nodded, his feet feeling like they were freezing to the ground. "I know," he admitted finally. "I do. I realize that what you're saying is right. But I can't think of any other options."

Tommy smiled. "How about we take the fight to Randy's doorstep?"

"What do you mean?" Julie asked, as she and Cathy came up behind them.

Tommy shot her a look. "I wasn't being cute. I mean let's go to his house and knock on his door, for Christ's sake! Come on, if you were an idiot like Owchar, wouldn't you take her to your house, thinking you'd be safe there?"

"I don't know," Cathy said, not paying attention to the three of them. "If I were Owchar, I think I'd have known that Xander would figure out a way to follow me and have left a load of Tees to dispose of us."

The trees shook again, and this time Mike jerked his head over his shoulder to see what was happening.

The face of a large man stuck out from between the branches. His eyes were wide and his face chalky white and for a moment he didn't look real, like one of the totem pole faces adventurers always seemed to stumble upon in the treasure hunt movies his father had always watched with him.

Mike shot back up as the man stepped out of the brush, revealing himself not to be made of wood but rather large, commanding muscles.

As Mike clenched his fists and set his jaw, the leaves just to the side of the pale man started to rustle as well and a second Tee came out, his red tattoo so bright and vibrant that he didn't know how he could have missed it through the green of the leaves.

Cathy backed up a pace as men seemed to come out of the trails from everywhere. There were five in total but they seemed like a hundred, like they could just keep coming out of the trees until they overwhelmed them.

"Right," Mike said as he readied himself to fight, willing his joints not to ache anymore. "Because I forgot what kind of day this was going to be."

BECOMING: CHAPTER FOURTEEN

The door to the dimly lit room squealed open slowly, projecting a beacon of light over its musty, gray floor. Randy Owchar stepped inside, taking a look around with his flashlight until he was perfectly satisfied that there was nothing waiting for him in the darkness except for what he had planned. He sneered wickedly, turning back toward the door and motioning forward.

Ian and Duncan entered, each grasping Mandy under one of her arms, and hurled her to the floor. Somewhere along the way they had stopped long enough to bind her hands behind her back and tie a blindfold around her head. Her knees and face scraped along the rocks and pebbles on the ground of the exposed basement as she rolled to a grinding halt, fresh tears soaking her mask. She sobbed violently, struggling to her knees and looking around the room for any trace of light that might shine through her mask and give her some sense of where she was.

"Please..." she pleaded, her lower lip shriveled and quivering from the tears she had shed and the tears she knew she was going to shed. "Please, I'll do anything... I won't tell anyone! Please, just don't kill me..."

Randy smiled at her, reaching deep into his pocket and pulling out Xander's dragon blade. It glinted in the damp light from the doorway, and had just a hint of blood still on it. His own blood, he thought, recalling the slash Xander had planted across his side. Slowly, he brought it down and touched the side of it, gently, to Mandy's cheek.

She froze, only the sound of her frantic breathing heard in the room as she tried to maintain her precarious balance, aware only of the cold, folded steel pressed against her face. He leaned in until he was almost touching her, running his eyes over every inch of her.

She couldn't see him, but she could feel him, and it made her shudder. More tears came.

With his free hand he reached out and pinched the fabric of her sweater, rubbing it between his thumb and forefinger.

"You dress different than you used to," he said coldly, letting go of the piece and trickling his hand over her helpless, quivering body, taking pleasure in how she trembled. He turned swiftly, seeing Duncan and Ian still standing in the doorway, watching him intently. "Close the door."

"But boss..." Ian protested, actual concern flashing in his eyes for but a brief moment.

"I said get out," Randy ordered, not even twitching in their direction this time, instead following a tear as it slowly dribbled down Mandy's smooth, freckled cheeks.

Duncan sighed, then reached out and closed the door with a loud clang, leaving the two of them alone in the dark.

She whimpered softly. Even though there had been no light before, it was more obvious now. Like how even in a blackened room you can tell when your electricity has been cut off. A sixth sense. She felt him remove the blade from the side of her face, then heard it click softly against the pavement floor as he laid it down. Feeling it was okay for her to speak again, she whimpered, managing to get out a hollow "please..."

"What?" Randy whispered, with a lover's softness.

"Please..." she said again, without hardly realizing it. "Please, I didn't tell anyone last time, I didn't. I won't tell anyone this time, I swear..."

Randy chuckled a little. "You like keeping secrets, don't you?"

"What?" she asked the darkness, her brow furrowed and confused.

"I know anyway, you don't have to hide it. Just tell me who the Womb is. I know. I also know that you know, so just tell me. I wanna hear you say it..." he spoke softly, then lashed out, smacking her across the face.

She hit the ground hard on her back, and before she could scream she felt the weight of his body crouching on her abdomen, crushing her.

"You were my first, you god damn Coral Cove slut! You! And then you betrayed me to that black freak? Tell me who he is! I want to hear you betray him, like you did to me!"

Blood seeped from her mouth as she lay, her cheek against the pavement. She was still conscious, she just didn't want to turn to face him.

"No..." she said finally, and it came out as a sob.

"Excuse me?" he spat, slamming both palms into her shoulders, bringing both her collar bones to the breaking limit at once. "I told you to do something!"

She said nothing for a moment, opened her mouth, then closed it again.

"No." she whispered, sniffling.

He sucked his lip back angrily, then picked up the blade again with a long scrape of metal that made her wince. Slowly, he scuttled downward until he was sitting on her legs, still stopping her from moving away from him. Bending down, he kissed her jeans in little, intimate pecks, making her cry even more.

"Shhh..." he cooed her, as he carefully slid the knife up between her tender stomach flesh and her sweater, then brought it up tight against the fabric. "This'll only hurt a lot."

The fabric gave way as he moved the blade upward slowly, revealing her smooth belly and naval. Her skin was so pale in the dim light that somehow found its way even here. When he was done, he pulled back the remains of her sweater, revealing her slim figure and her tiny, tea-cup sized breasts.

There were scars on them that he recognized. He'd given them to her months ago. He traced his finger along them now, feeling the raised edges of the new flesh.

He put down the knife and laid both hands on her belly and slowly moved them upward, feeling every crevice in her, remembering the way that it had felt that night not so long ago. She felt just the way that he recalled, smooth and perky against his cool touch.

She found that she had no tears left in her, only dry heaves that felt like flames burning upward from deep inside her.

"Please don't do this..." she whispered, not specifically to him.

"It's okay, Mandy," he said.

When he said her name for the first time she felt like throwing up, and had to battle the urge to do so. Her body quivered with sickness that he must have taken as encouragement, as he squeezed at her harder than before. She bit her lip, not wanting to give him the satisfaction of hearing her cries anymore.

Smiling, he bent down and brought his lips to her newly exposed flesh, soaking it with hungered saliva. She felt his breath, hard and eager. The first time a man had touched her like that she had been ten years old. She'd spent a very long time forgetting that, but now it all came rushing back and it was like he was here, too. Like they were both pawing at her at the same time.

Her mother had left her alone in the toy department at the mall again, using the Barbie's and Teddy Bears as a cheap excuse for a baby sitter while she had been going about her business. A man, someone that worked there based on her memory of what he'd been wearing, had promised her that there was a room with lots more toys, and there had been. She recalled how he had fumbled with the keys, excited. He unlocked the storage department and led her inside, where there were rows and rows of boxes. He brought her to a place far in the back, where there were lots of boxes of toys.

Randy pressed the cold steel of the knife against her skin, feeling the goose-flesh that it created with his free hand. He laughed a little. Turning the blade so that the sharp side faced her stomach, he asked her again. "Who is he? Who is the Black Womb?"

"I won't tell you." she sobbed, her voice small and far away, but still containing so much strength.

Grunting, he drew the blade across her stomach quickly.

"Ahh!" she screamed, as she felt warmth flowed from the open wound, trickling down her body with each pump of her heart. It was a shallow cut and didn't bleed much, but it stung. She thought she was going to die.

She drove her teeth deep into her bottom lip as his mouth found the nape of her neck again. His breath stank of alcohol and cigarettes and Zesty Doritos chips. The feeling of him on her made her wish she were unconscious.

"I knew you were sweet." he said playfully, running his hands over the wound and grabbing at her stomach, the pressure making it hurt even more.

From somewhere deep inside, her body found the moisture to produce tears again.

"Let's see if you taste that sweet all over!" he yelled, excited now. He unbuttoned her pants and pulled them down quickly until they were around her ankles.

"No!" she screamed.

He reached up and grabbed her between the legs, squeezing as hard as he could.

"No!" she screamed, and continued to scream, as he used his body to force her legs apart and sunk deep inside of her, holding her squirming body down as he thrust within her again and again, faster and faster. It felt like he was ripping her apart inside, every pulse and pump full of friction and pain, like the knife that had sliced through her skin, only warmer. Sickly warm, excited. Like blood.

He started barging into her madly, losing all concept of self control or reservation as the feeling overcame him, the need to be as far and as deep in with every disgusting push as he could be.

She felt him building already, to the point when she could tell that it was going to be over very soon. There was a sticky, slapping sound as his gut smacked against her own, adhering to the blood that covered her torso and making a snapping sound when it broke free before happening again. She turned her head to the side and gazed into the darkness, away from the silhouetted movement of his body.

Mike... she thought, somewhere within the reaches of her mind. *Why aren't you saving me?*

He exploded, and she felt him fill her with rage and hatred. He pumped twice after that as his already small appendage shrunk even more, then finally withdrew.

He smiled, his breathing slowing as he pulled his jeans back up and walked toward the door. He opened it, letting Ian and Duncan in.

"All right." he said, smiling from ear to ear. "Let's see if you two can get her to talk."

Beneath her blindfold, her eyes widened as more tears came forth.

BECOMING: CHAPTER FIFTEEN

The body of George Walker hit the floor before Xander was even done asking where it had gone. He turned suddenly, spinning in a way that seemed foreign to him here. He was used to fighting in one instance, it one skin even, and being himself in another. Now, today, all that had changed. He found himself opting into a fighting stance as soon as his body finished turning, and the world of the Black Womb invaded his home, the school of Xander Drew.

Walker's half naked body slumped onto an already expanding pool of blood, his jugular slit so well that it looked like a single thin line a few inches under his chin. The rest of his body left more to be desired, bruises and slash marks tattering his flesh. There were bones and muscles showing in many areas. The man's spleen had been ripped out.

Standing over him was Adam Genblade, the very sight of which sent chills quivering down Xander's spine and goosebumps over his arms and legs. The last time he'd seen Genblade he had been lying in a hospital bed, and the doctors told him that the killer would never wake up. He should have known better. There was already blood slathered across his black shirt in several different patterns, indicating that he and his sword had already been more than a little busy. The sword itself was long a sleek, two gems on the handle forming the head and body of a spider, the handle stretching out in four different directions to make the legs. He held one in both hands, the bloodstained surface reflecting the flourescent lights into Xander's eyes and making him wince. His hair was spiked with a reddish tint, held up with dried blood that had become matted there. His thin, preened eyebrows narrowed as he looked Xander up and down with his beady black eyes, the corners of his lips curling with disgust and a disturbing smile all at once.

Xander reached for his blade, only to find that it wasn't there. His eyes darted around the floor in front of him, but to no avail. He was weaponless.

"Hey, buddy." Genblade smiled, bringing one of the blades to his lips and licking the blood from it. "How have you been?"

Xander thought about that for a moment. Open-ended questions from Adam Genblade usually ended in blood being spilt, typically his own, and the Womb wasn't even twitching, so he decided to tell the truth. "I've had better days."

"Really?" the killer asked, leaning back against the wall, as if they were two old friends just having a chat.

"Yeah, it's been kinda rough."

"Did you go into a coma?"

Xander looked from side to side, wondering if that gun was still around somewhere. "No..." he answered slowly, shaking his head from side to side and trying not to be offensive.

"Then I guess I win this one." Genblade snarled, reaching behind him and pulling out a handgun, aiming at Xander's head and firing quickly.

Xander dove forward as soon as he saw the gun. The shot traveled over his head as he rolled along the blood spattered ground, then ricocheted off the steel front entrance and broke the window that led into Schneider's office into a thousand tiny shards.

Genblade leaped to his feet, sheathing one sword so that he could carry one and the gun, pointing the barrel at Xander again.

"Because you didn't spend the last fucking month or so watching the woman you loved get murdered!"

He shot again, this time catching Xander square in the knee cap. The bone shattered, and he screamed as he fell to the floor.

"By you!" he finished, firing another shot into the fat of the same leg. Xander screamed.

"Adam!" he bellowed, gripping the dual gunshot wounds and trying in vain to stop the flow of blood. "Adam, please! Don't do this, not now!"

"Oh, I'm sorry!" Genblade screamed, buckling over in ferocity. "When exactly would be a good time for you to be killed? Hmm? Tuesday at six good? I'll have my people call your people to confirm!"

He kicked Xander in the back brutally, with everything he had, sending him vaulting across the room and into the wall. Xander's back cracked off the brick corner, then he bounced into the pile of broken glass the first bullet had left.

Genblade walked over to him and stepped on his back, then bent over and shoved the gun barrel into the back of Xander's head.

"I like the way I play roulette better, by the way." he sneered, then pulled the trigger.

BECOMING: CHAPTER SIXTEEN

-click-

Adam's eyes filled with surprise. His face contorted in anger as he turned, heaving the gun at the wall.

"Fucking guns!" he cursed at the thing as it bounced across the floor and found its place in the corner.

"Don't blame the tools."

Genblade turned just in time to see Xander bring a long, jagged shard of glass to his wrist and rip away at the flesh and veins beneath it.

"No!" Genblade bellowed, even as blackness poured out of Xander's forearm. Instead of falling to the floor it clung to his arm, each pump bringing more and more of it up until it stretched over his arm and took on a life all its own, slithering down across his body. His head was the last to go, Xander's smile visible until the very end, until he looked like a three dimensional shadow. Three curved, red slits formed in his face, opening at once to become feline eyes and a mouth filled with dual rows of sharpened yellow teeth. He dropped the glass to the floor, where it broke again with a tiny -tink!-.

"Black Womb lives!"

The scream echoed throughout the walls of the school, coming back at Genblade from all directions.

"Argh!" he screamed, bringing his hands to his ears as the declaration attacked him. Bringing out his second sword again, he stood to face the creature in front of him, the same one that had haunted his nightmares for months on end.

"I'll kill you!" he screamed, lunging forward.

Xander leapt to the side, avoiding Adam's blades and ducking into a roll, coming up on the opposite side of the lobby with his hands clenching then extending, forcing the claws to pop from each finger to their furthest extension.

Adam turned, foam bubbling to the surface at the corners of his mouth. "You killed her! I won't let you get away from me that easily, you took her away to where I can't follow, and I'm going to destroy you for it, do you hear me?"

Xander said nothing from inside the Womb, just watched as the madman thrashed about, turning finally to face him.

All of this, all at once! he thought as he leapt away from another attack by Genblade, slashing with his claws as he did. They connected with Genblade's side, taking a large chunk of flesh with it. *What are the chances that this would happen all at once? The Tees, Circe, and now Genblade. They're all here, and I've never been so vulnerable before.*

"Genblade, listen to me!" he blurted, ducking as Genblade carried a lunge over him. He thrust his arms up, sending his claws up into Genblade's gut, then used his own momentum to fling him face first into a wall. His pointed, jagged teeth mashed into his gums, slicing them open.

"Adam, I don't want to fight you!" he pleaded, even though his words seemed to fall upon deaf ears.

"Kill you!" Genblade screamed again, driving both swords forward.

They both sunk into Xander's flesh on either side of his chest and through the other side, pinning him to the wall.

"Argh!" the Womb roared, its massive mouth opening wide and its tongue flailing about wildly. His arms tried to move but his limbs lay there, twitching and useless.

Genblade hissed, getting right up in the Xander's face until their noses touched at the tips. "Here!" he screamed, twisting both blades in opposite directions, spreading his breast plate apart.

"Fuck!" Xander screamed, to Genblade's pleasure.

"This is what it feels like to lose, Womb!" Genblade taunted, turning the blades again. "This is what it feels like to have everything you love stripped away! This is what it feels like to be dead!"

"Genblade!" Xander bellowed, forcing eye contact with his enemy. "This is not about you and me! This is bigger than the two of us, don't you get that?"

Genblade squinted, his teeth still clenched, but it was clear that he was listening. Xander had somehow managed to get his attention.

"I know I killed Eve. I could give you a million excuses-" he started, Genblade's eyes filling with rage. "-but I won't. And I don't expect any from you for what happened to Sara. But there's someone else now, a girl that has nothing to do with either of us that I can save if you let me go, now, do you understand? We can do it together; we can make what happened right!"

The rage and the hatred slowly began to melt from Genblade's eyes, as he loosened his grip on the swords.

"Impressive." Hale said from the hall entrance behind them. "All the time I fought you, my boy, I never once thought of whispering sweet nothings in your ear."

Genblade turned to see Hale and O'Toole, along with a dozen other men in head-to-toe green jump suits and goggles that made them look like scuba divers. They were Circe men, Xander recognized them instantly.

"Tricked me!" Adam screamed, turning back and punching Xander once in the face with everything he had before ripping both of the swords out through his sides, taking a half foot of flesh with each blade. He turned to face the Circe, whose operatives raised their guns to him quickly and started pumping off rounds.

〽

Xander hit the floor and gasped, a sound that was monstrous coming out of the Womb's mouth. There were large pieces of his chest missing under each of his arms and he wrenched in pain no other person could know while the Womb worked to repair it. It was as though something had taken two giant bites out of him and then put him away for later.

Gunfire turned the floor around him into a barrage of dust and debris. He fell to his side away from it, curling his hands up into a fetal position. His heightened senses made the crack of the guns thunderous. He thought his ears were going to start bleeding.

He opened his eyes and saw the doorway to Schneider's office was open. Cursing himself, he reached out and dug his claws deep into the tile floor and pulled himself toward it.

〽

"Remember, men, this isn't Zakron or the Womb," Hale reminded them, reaching into his pocket and withdrawing a cigar and a pipe lighter. "If you aren't using lethal ordinance, you'd better switch now."

Several of the men switched clips, while the others made sure that Genblade got nowhere close to them, continuing to fire.

Genblade ran from one doorway to another, dodging gunfire and deflecting some off of his blades as he slowly made his way closer to Hale and O'Toole. Every time he got too close the agents would change their pattern and force him back, growling all the way.

"Still impressive." Hale smiled, motioning to him. "I don't think his downtime hurt him any. If anything, he's refreshed. Marvelous what those Engen boys could do, hmm?"

Across the room, Xander slumped to the floor, a trail of blood streaming down the wall in his wake. He was barely able to move, and most of his thoughts revolved around either thanking or encouraging his healing factor for healing head wounds first as blood hemorrhaged into his cerebellum.

"Sir," O'Toole said, stepping up next to Hale as the two of them watched Genblade flip around, avoiding the hot chunks of lead coming at him from all angles. "What about Drew?" he asked, motioning toward the boy.

"What about him?" Hale asked, turning a puffing a long trail of smoke into Warren's face. "If he can't even get up after that, he's no use to us anyway. Besides, the situation is under control."

"Hale!" Genblade yelled the word as if it were a curse, finally grabbing one the gunmen and turning him around, using his body as a human shield as bullets ripped into it, killing him. After nearly a full minute of this Genblade finally reached up and snapped his neck and tossed him to the ground. "I want you, Hale! You're just as much to blame for all of this as he is!" he yelled, pointing at Xander without even looking.

"Even more so." Hale chuckled, more to himself than anyone else, as the other operatives continued their assault on Genblade.

"Sir, are you sure it's wise to taunt him?" O'Toole asked, watching Genblade's movements intently as the blood of the downed Circe employee spilled out onto the already drenched floor.

"Oh, yes, my boy." Hale assured him, passing O'Toole a cigar. "Trust me, everything's going to plan."

BECOMING: CHAPTER SEVENTEEN

Cathy lashed out, raking her nails across the face of Elliot Matthews.

A short man with a big nose and fuzzy brown hair, Elliot was about the same height as Cathy, and the two matched each other blow for blow as he tried in vain to get his shotgun into a position where he could actually use it, but she kept him close, never allowing him to back up far enough that he could aim the massive weapon.

"Come on, big man!" she yelled at him, possibly for the tenth time, slashing at him with open palms, catching blood and flesh beneath her fingernails.

Another Tee, George McGyver, tried to grab her from behind. She shoved an elbow back, meaning to nail him in the face but connecting with his gut, turning to see a man easily twice her size with white hair and a broad chest clutching his stomach as he toppled over in pain.

Tommy was being held on from behind by Mark Clevet, a scrawny youth with a buzz cut and scruff to match it, another Tee trying to look like their leader, Roulette.

"What's the matter?" Mark bellowed into Tommy's ear as Justin Langley, a kid that looked like he came straight out of that painting *The Scream* punched him as hard as he could first to the face and then to the upper torso. "Can't you take a little fun?"

Tommy's head wobbled around like a bobble head, and he began to lose consciousness.

Mike threw Dwayne Piercey to the ground for the third time, mashing his face into snow which was now turning red. Mike was bleeding from slash marks that ornamented his arms and chest, but he found that they did not bother him too much, as the satisfaction of slamming his foot into the back of Dwayne's head took over. When he relinquished, he realized that Dwayne was unconscious and bleeding from both a split in the roof of his mouth and a broken nose. He smiled, then turned his attention toward Ryan Crocker, a bald man wearing a sweater who was aiming a gun across the fight at Cathy.

"Come on, guys!" he yelled in encouragement. "You can do this!"

Sven Douglas slammed his fist into Julie's face, smiling with those idiotic buck teeth as he did so, her blood covering his knuckles. He laughed a little, a disgusting sound, as she raised her arms in a weak attempt to block his attack. He took the opportunity to punch her in the gut, hard, knocking the wind out of her as she fell backward into the snow.

He stepped closer.

"Now, bitch!" he laughed, backhanding her across the face and then reaching for his gun.

Her head jerked to the side, traveling with his blow. As it did she caught a glimpse of Tommy, blood streaming from his nose and mouth as Langley continued to slam into him. Turning back, she brought back a leg and kicked him as hard as she could, squatting his finger and making him retract the hand that was going for his weapon.

"Mike!" she screamed, cocking her chin at Tommy.

Mike turned to her, laying a finishing blow on Crocker and sending him down for the count, then followed her gaze to where Tommy stood. Thinking quickly, he reached down and scooped up a handful of snow, packed it as tightly as he could, and ran toward the two Tees. He stopped only for a moment, letting the fist-sized ball of ice sail though the air as fast as he could. It slammed into the back of Langley's head with an explosion of white. When the large man turned, he had just enough time to see Mike's fist coming toward his face.

"Hey!" Clevet yelled, loosening his grip on Tommy just long enough. Tommy shot back an elbow, knocking the wind out of his captor, turning to plant a fist clear across his face.

"Hey yourself." he grumbled, kicking the Tee in the head.

Cathy grabbed Elliot by the hair and slammed him into a tree, breaking the young man's nose and sending him to the snow, out cold.

"Hey!" she squealed happily. "I got one!"

Just as she spoke George got up again and launched himself into her, slamming her to the ground and pinning her there.

"Slut!" he yelled, drawing back and punching her in the jaw. "You've fucked

359

everything up! I'll teach you some manners!"

He punched her in the chest.

She coughed hard, trying to catch her breath and get him off of her at the same time, succeeding with neither.

"Grendel, please..." she pleaded. He already had her shirt off, and now he had her jeans unbuttoned. "Please, just stop."

George grabbed at Cathy and punched her across the face, smiling devilishly as he did.

The tears ran down her soft, freckled cheeks. She sobbed. He stopped for a moment and looked up at her, then starting to pull down her jeans.

She brought her knee up fast, catching George in the groin but seeing Grendel.

He stumbled backward, clutching his privates with both hands.

"You fucking bitch..." he whined, his eyes bulging with pain.

Tight lipped, she got up. She drew back and nailed him in the jaw as hard as she could.

"You'd better believe it," she spat down at him.

Sven had managed to get his handgun out, and Julie was now wrestling with him for control of it, the both of them rolling around in the snow, biting and punching at one another for control over the weapon.

Tommy laid in a final punch to Steve, sending him down for the count, then turned to help Mike with Langley, who currently had Mike held by the throat.

BANG!

All heads turned, wondering where the shot had come from.

Sven turned, the gun now visible in his hand, as well as the fountain of blood streaming out of the gaping maw in Julie's chest.

"No!" Tommy screamed.

Mike slammed Langley into the frozen ground and they both ran toward her. Cathy turned the corner and saw what was happening, and all three of them bolted toward Sven, who dropped the gun in fright as both men pounced on him. Cathy went to Julie's side.

"Julie!" Cathy screamed, pulling the girl's hair out of her face and being very careful not to touch the wound. "Julie, are you all right?"

"Don't..." she tried to say, as blood gurgled up from her throat. "Don't stop. You have to find her."

"We will. And we'll save you, too. We will." she assured her, taking the girl's hand and rubbing it. She turned to Mike and Tommy, who were both wailing on Sven's face. "Will you two stop fucking around over there and come help me?"

Tommy took the words to heart immediately, bolting toward Julie. Mike lay one final blow into Sven, making sure he was down.

"Oh my God." Tommy gasped, his hands instantly covered in red liquid.

"There's blood everywhere."

"We have to get her to a hospital." Mike said firmly.

"No..." Julie protested, losing consciousness.

"She wants us to find Mandy." Cathy tisked. "What are the chances of that now, anyway?"

Tommy grunted. "Where's the hospital?"

Mike stopped, looking around for a moment. "Three blocks down, one over... why?"

"I'll take her, you guys go on ahead!"

Mike stopped, considering this for a moment. "Where did you say Randy lived?"

"What?" Cathy exclaimed, as Mike helped Julie onto Tommy's back.

"Fifty-six Roberto," Tommy said, grunting with the added weight. "It's the white one."

"Got it," Mike said, putting a hand on Tommy's shoulder and giving it a squeeze.

Tommy nodded, then took off with Julie, as gently as possible.

"This is insanity!" Cathy screamed, running her blood soaked fingers through her hair. "There's no way that he's going to make it in time!"

"Yes, they will!" Mike said loudly, without yelling, as though trying to convince himself. "Now come on. I've got more scum-punching in me today."

BECOMING: CHAPTER EIGHTEEN

Genblade grabbed a Circe agent and sliced him across the gut with his sword, spilling blood and bladder onto the floor as he did so.

"General, this is insanity!" O'Toole yelled.

Many of the men dropped their ammo-less weapons and picked up tasers and knives from their belts, slashing them about, the tasers crackling with energy.

"Genblade is going to kill us all, do you realize that?"

Hale just smiled, watching the fight with a childish glee.

O'Toole grunted, turning away from his commanding officer and toward the battle, running between wet works agents over to where the Black Womb lay bleeding.

"Drew!" he yelled, grabbing the boy by the shoulders and shaking him violently. "Drew, are you okay?"

The Womb reacted quickly, reaching up and grabbing Warren by the wrists and digging his claws in deep.

"Better, now that you're here," he said sharply, his monstrous mouth contorting into a sick smile. He spun Warren around, slamming him into the wall where he had been. "Now, you're gonna tell me what's going on here, and you're going to be as quick as possible about it, or I'm gonna show you what you've been playing at for months!"

"Okay!" Warren yelled, squirming as blood trickled down him arm.

There was a frenzied scream in the background as Genblade took out another operative, his sword biting at the main vein of the man's leg. Arterial blood splashed up at Genblade, soaking the lower half of his face and mouth.

"Circe and Engen were rivals, right? Have been for decades. It started with them trying to outbid each other for government rights to the programs like the one that created you, but when the U.S. and Canada lost interest, it just turned into a Cold War!"

"Why me? Why am I a part of this?" he demanded, grabbing Warren by the collar and shaking him.

"Engen had Genblade and Eve and Zero and all the rest... even the Anti-Womb! And this had been going on for years, with the Circe scientists coming up with squat to compete. We even started hiring out of other labs making genetic freaks, just to defend ourselves. So, when we heard that Alpha had tried to tap you... we were as shocked as you were. Hale sent me here, after Phillips got canned. Sent me to find out which one of you kids was the Womb."

"And Zakron?" the Womb bellowed, shaking the frightened man again. "Why would you let Engen's deadliest weapon out?"

"To draw you out!" Warren screamed, clutching at his throat and trying to get more air. His lips began to turn a pale blue, becoming paler every time Xander shook him.

"What do you mean 'draw me out'?" the Womb demanded, loosening his grip slightly.

"I was sure it was you, from the moment I laid eyes on you." Warren blurted, gasping for air. "But Hale needed convincing. Needed to see you transform. We'd been wrong too many times before. Xander, there's something you have to know..."

"*Obtain! Obtain!*" *yelled the lead scuba-man, with yellow stripes on the side of his right arm. They wore air tanks and dark goggles, showing none of their skin. They were muscular, but human in their movements and mannerisms.*

"*Hey!*" *Xander yelled, running up to the leader,* "*What the hell is going on here?*"

"*Classified, son.*" *the commander nodded, putting an arm on Xander's shoulder,* "*Circe business. None of your concern. Thanks for keeping him in one place long enough for us to get a bead on him, though.*" *he said truthfully, turning away to grab the rope and climb up as the other two loaded Zakron into the chopper.*

"*Hey!*" *Drew yelled again, grabbing the man by the arm and pulling him back down to earth,* "*Where do you think you're going? I've got a lot of questions, and I know you've got answers!*"

"*Sorry, kid.*" *the man shrugged honestly, turning and firing a dart into Xander's gut,* "*Classified.*"

Xander fell to earth, remaining there for a moment, unable to move, just to watch the chopper pull back into the clouds, and away from sight.

Xander froze immediately, raising his hands in the air. He might... might be able to survive a blast at this range, depending on where it hit, but there was no guarantee that nobody else would get hit either.

"Turn around," Randy ordered.

Again, Xander complied, biting his lip about the fact that he knew he could take down that son of a bitch child-killer in ten seconds flat.

"Well, well, well," Randy smiled, shaking his head at Xander. He lowered his voice considerably, so that only he and Xander could hear. "If it isn't the Black Womb."

ʎʎʎ

"Kill the hero," Duncan said, smiling so wide it showed off his sickly yellow teeth.

Randy paused, looking down the barrel of the gun at Xander. "No," he said finally. "That was part of the deal. We were given the Omega, we gotta let him go, for now." He turned to Walker. "Stay here with her."

Xander watched as Randy turned back to him, sneering contemptuously at him as he addressed the crowd.

"If any of you so much as breathe wrong for ten minutes, the girl dies. Everybody out!"

Xander turned and slashed his claws across Warren's face, then allowed him to topple to the floor.

"Bastard!" he screamed, spitting out the last of the blood in his mouth. "You did this, didn't you? You fucking fed Mandy to the Tees just to draw me the fuck out, you sick bastard!"

"Xander," O'Toole pleaded, scrambling to his feet. "If you'll just give me a moment to explain..."

Xander drew back and punched Warren in the face, sending him stumbling backward.

He fell into the waiting arms of Adam Genblade, either of his armpits wedged in the crooks of the killer's arms.

"Well well," Genblade chuckled, bringing the blade to Warren's throat. "Special Delivery from my good friend the Black Womb. And it's not even my birthday."

"Let him go." Xander ordered calmly, standing with his back arched. "He's mine."

"Didn't know you had a new boyfriend..." Genblade teased. When it got no response he continued unabated. "I'll tell you what. You wanted to go rescue the damsel? Fine. But only if you leave me here. I'm giving you and yours this one chance, Xander. You really should take it."

Xander clenched his teeth and balling his hands into fists.

"Do what you will," he said, then turned toward the doors.

"Ha!" Genblade yelled victoriously, then sliced through the tender flesh of Warren O'Toole's neck.

Blood squirting in all directions, lapping out onto the floor like red raspberry punch from the fountains that the school rented year after year for the prom. O'Toole did not speak or gasp or even barely move at all. His eyes were wide and white almost at once, and his cheeks were flushed. He did not reach for his throat or try to stop the flow the way people always did in the movies. Instead he stood there, propped by his killer's steady hand, and spewed thick blood the consistency of jelly out onto the last good shirt he would ever wear. His head toppled back and widened the slit, revealing the pink meat of his scrawny neck muscles as they wrapped around the barest hint of an adam's apple, clutching at it and making sick slurping noises as it sputtered and spat and spewed more blood out.

Genblade laughed hysterically, turned toward the three remaining Circe Operatives and Hale, and dropped the body to his feet in a bloody slump. "Kids these days, eh?"

Hale's eyes finally opened wide with fear as he watched Xander exit the room.

"Womb..." he said, softly at first, as the boy closed the doors behind him. "Womb! Don't do this, Womb!"

One of the Circe operatives stepped forward, holding his gun in both hands and intending to use it. Genblade had never had qualms about killing, especially not people in this line of work, but the full-body suits that they wore made it even easier. They all looked the same, their faces completely covered. It was like they weren't even real. This one was scrawnier than the rest. His muscles were toned, but there was no gristle on them. Genblade ventured that the man beneath the wetsuit was no more than twenty-five.

He stabbed the man in the chest, then swung him around on the tip of the blade and forced him to the floor, pinning him there.

There were screams, magnificent ones, as the man tried to move but couldn't.

Genblade kicked at the his head with his steel-toed boots, over and over again, his leg moving so fast that it was a blur. The screams had stopped, but the sounds that had replaced them were just as wretched. Each kick was accompanied by a wet crackling sound, like crushing a ripe bell pepper between your hands. Every so often there was a loud snap, but after a few kicks the sounds became slushier, like tossing a damp sponge into a dirty bucket.

The man's mask had filled up with blood. His eyes-pieces, like a diver's, were filled with the dark red liquid. It sloshed about them like water in a half-filled glass, and was the only outward indication from the neck up that there was even anything wrong with the man.

Genblade propped his foot against the man's shoulder for support, then pulled the blade from his chest with both hands the way Arthur had pulled Excalibur from the stone.

"Womb!" Hale called again, backing up one pace, then another. "For god's sakes, Womb! You can't leave us in here!"

Genblade grabbed another scuba-man and shoved his face into a wall. The impact sent blood spatter all the way up to the ceiling. He shoved the third and final man to the floor, now only interested in clearing the path between himself and Hale, stomping it methodically as Hale continued to back up.

"Womb!" Hale screamed, even as Genblade grabbed him, drew back the Spider-Sword, and aimed for the center of his torso.

BECOMING: CHAPTER NINETEEN

"Womb!" Hale shouted as Genblade drove the blade forward. It sliced clean through him, spewing blood out through the treads of the sword.

Genblade withdrew and let Hale fall to the ground, still alive. Blood was coming out of the gaping hole in the man's chest. It was so dark and bubbled out so furiously that it looked like oil escaping from a sprung vein, soaking through his clothes and into his skin. He was bleeding to death, and quickly.

"Isn't this interesting?" Genblade sneered, watching the life pump out of Hale's veins. He danced around Hale in a small circle, then leaned down to grin right in his face. "After all this time it's you that's going to fall, not me. Not like you always said. And I'm not even going to give you a decent death, you see that? You're going to die bleeding and mewing like a stuck cat and I'm going to watch. It's over now, do you get that? The Circe is done, do you hear me? Are we clear?"

"Crystal."

Genblade turned just in time to see Xander's claws coming toward his face.

They connected, all four of them ripping a different line through Genblade's skin, like tiny ditches dug for blood to flow through.

"Argh!" Genblade screamed, his head flying forward into his palm as his face burned. "Can't I ever be rid of you?"

The second Spider-Sword lay dormant in its holster against Genblade's back, the handle pointing toward Xander. He grabbed it and spun it around in his fingers as though it belonged there, the light gleaming off of it onto the walls.

"Apparently not," he returned, holding the blade at the ready. "No matter how much we both may want it."

He lashed out with the sword, bringing it down toward Genblade's downed head.

Genblade rose quickly, bringing his arm up and bending it until his blade ran parallel to it and blocked the path of the attack.

The blades met only briefly but made a spark so bright that it was like a camera flash had gone off between them.

Genblade spun on his heels and jabbed the blade out from his hip in a short, savage little thrust.

It had almost connected to Xander's hip when he brought his blade around and batted it away clumsily, then spun it back around to hold it with both hands. The momentum took Genblade's sword with it, sliding the blades together and making sparks fly as the blades locked into a stalemate and the both of them came nose to nose.

"How did this happen? How are you so deep into every part of my life?" Genblade spat, swiftly raising a knee and kicking Xander in the gut, forcing him back a pace. He slashed across Xander's face, causing the blackness to tendril off of the pink flesh underneath in long, swirling motions for a moment, revealing the bruised, scarred facial tissue beneath it.

"Just lucky I guess," he offered, his face slamming into lockers as he attempted to roll with the blow in the enclosed space. He felt a long, jagged tooth break off and travel down his throat, ripping everything it touched along the way.

"Shut up!" Genblade demanded, slashing forward with the blade again, ripping through Xander's chest. "Don't you get it? This is the day when you will finally fall!" He brought the blade up high, holding it with both hands, ready to slice Xander right down the middle.

Genblade brought the blade down, only to have the Womb catch it at the last possible second with his free hand. He gripped it tightly, drawing dark blood from a straight line across his fingertips.

"Maybe," he agreed, his voice gruff and painful to hear. "But that doesn't mean it'll be you!"

He pushed forward, forcing the sharp handle of the blade into Genblade's face.

"In case you haven't noticed, there are plenty of people around just waiting to do that!"

Genblade tumbled backward, growling deep within his throat. He raised his sword again and attacked blindly, full of rage. He slashed his sword again and again at the air, sometimes near Xander and sometimes not, raked grunts emerging from his throat with every push. He'd lost all the finesse he'd had a moment ago, and yet was still forcing Xander back. Glaring banefully, he locked eyes with Xander once more and drove his sword forward.

Xander dodged to the left to be free of it, springing up on his heels to get him further away.

In the distance, he heard sirens. An ambulance, and a police cruiser several blocks down.

"When I'm done with you, I'm going to find the Tees like you were talking about doing." Genblade hissed, holding his sword at the ready as he took step after step toward Xander.

Xander glanced over his shoulder with those deep, red eyes of his taking in everything, backing up again and trying to stay out of arm's reach.

Genblade slashed forward, taking a chunk out of Xander's leg.

"I'm going to kill them all and suck the marrow from their bones. Then if they haven't killed that little bitch you were talking about," he snarled, jumping forward a pace, connecting the blade with Xander's mid-section and narrowly missing his diaphragm. "I'll take those hollowed out bones and use them on her. She'll think those little two-pump chumps were nothing by the time I'm through with her. Oh, the blood'll taste so good..."

Xander sprung to its feet and lunged.

Genblade caught him by the throat and slammed him into the stone wall, driving his sword deep into his gut. The blade penetrated just above his naval. He was careful not to hit the Womb organ. He wanted this to last as long as possible.

"You won't touch her." Xander demanded, through pursed, dry lips.

Genblade chuckled. "That's the funny thing. I wouldn't have, if you'd only let me kill Hale in peace.. You see? You've doomed them all with your hero schick, get it?"

He twisted the blade, taking perverse pleasure in the moist, warm sound it made.

"I wonder if I can make Cathy make sounds like that, Xander?" he poised, smiling, watching Xander's eyes grow. "I never did thank her for that time she flirted with me in the visitors booth. I warned her what I was going to do. Bitches never learn, do they?"

He laughed, then got a thoughtful look on his face as he twisted the blade a full three-hundred and sixty degrees.

"Come to think of it, I learned that from another girl. Now who was that?" he asked. "Oh, yeah: Sara."

"Argh!" he yelled as both Xander and the Black Womb, forcing both his arms forward as he broke free of the sword's grip, ripping and rendering him own flesh to do so. Deep inside him, the Womb pumped ferocity through him, fueled by Genblade's words and the certainty that they were true. The organ stopped only for a moment, then began pumping to a different beat, quicker, readier.

All at once, Xander's eyes changed from red to aqua, a kind of blue-green shade that most people identified with the sea, but people who knew Xander Drew identified with merciless death, as his consciousness was forced away into a corner where it could not be heard, and only one thing ruled the Black Womb's body : itself.

All of its wounds healed over, all of its scars repaired themselves as the fight started over again for the creature, rejuvenating it as it looked upon its enemy with new eyes.

"BLACK WOMB LIVES!"

"That's more like it!" Genblade smiled, slashing his blade forward into the Womb's gut, spilling blackness everywhere.

The Womb barked, then slashed back. Its claws seemed longer now, and red blood dripped from their roots as they extended even further.

"That's it!" he shouted happily. "That's the man I've been waiting four months to see! Now show me the face you used when you killed my wife, you fucker!" he demanded, slicing long cuts into the Womb. He withdrew the blade, ready to stab it forward again, when the Womb caught it.

The creature held it for a long moment, squeezing with all its might.

"No..." it said, in Xander's voice. Suddenly, the creature's eyes turned red again.

"What..." Genblade gasped in disbelief.

The Womb broke the sword, shattering it into hundreds of tiny shards. They scattered to the floor like organ-pipes ripped from their moldings, each one making a loud clang as it hit the tile floor. Each sound was different from the last, echoing off the walls and becoming louder until a cacophony of cymbals assaulted Genblade's ears.

"I'm not going to give you the satisfaction."

"Argh!" Genblade yelled, leaping forward.

Xander swirled around the piece of sword that he still held in his hand, digging it deep into the side of Genblade's neck, then letting it go.

Genblade just stood there for a moment, blood oozing out of the open wound, his neck hanging half open, then he slumped to the floor just as Xander heard the paramedics pull into the driveway.

"There."

Inside Xander, a battle was still being fought as the True Womb tried to take over. "Ugh." he grunted, holding his gut.

"Hale..." he called, turning around. "Hale, help me."

When he looked, the man called Hale was nowhere in sight. There wasn't even any blood where he had been curled on the floor after Genblade had stabbed him in the chest.

Xander coughed up blood as the beast pounded through the doors, taking over again, turning his eyes a sickly green.

"BLACK WOMB LIVES!"

BECOMING: CHAPTER TWENTY

The front door to fifty-six Roberto Drive burst open, shattering the knob as Mike and Cathy stepped inside.

The house was dark despite the fact that all its lights were on, the beam from each fixture seeming to only make it a few feet. It was a long bungalow of the type that had gone out of style in the early eighties, with white vinyl siding that was burnt and charred on at one corner.

The inside seemed to be a trap for light. The carpet was the mixed fibre shade of a mongrel cat's fur or vomit after a day of eclectic tastes, with no discernible pattern or style. The result was uneven, but dominantly greenish-gray. It exuded shadows.

Walls that had started off eggshell had been stained a putrid yellow by nicotine.

The both of them stepped past the small inlet which was the porch (had to, in fact, so that they could both stand side by side) and into the hall. To one side of them was a quaint living room, and to the other was a mostly vacant dining room. Ahead was a small table with an old rotary phone on it, and beyond that was a hall that led into the bathroom. The furniture was passable in this light, but under brighter scrutiny Cathy thought that there would be chips and dings in them. They'd likely been purchased at the flea market that was held down by the Super Eight once a month.

She decided at once that this was a man's apartment. Everything was utilitarian. Nothing for comfort or to add warmth.

"Hello?" Cathy called out, cupping her hands over her mouth. "Is there anybody in here?"

"Cheap locks." Mike mumbled, closing the busted door frame.

"Hello?"

A fat head appeared from around the corner of the washroom, sticking out from the frame a little higher than they would have expected and looking like it was just floating there. It was completely hairless, even devoid of eyebrows. There were traces of white residue around his ears and a towel coloured the same wrapped tightly around the rolls of his neck. The flesh protruded around it above and below, as though it were trying to suck the towel in and swallow it.

There were boils behind the man's ears, but the head was otherwise smooth.

"Oh!" The man smiled an embarrassed little smile as we walked out to greet them. "I'm sorry, I didn't hear you come in. I was getting ready to take a shower."

"Okay." Mike said, raising an eyebrow. He looked at the man for a long moment, narrowing his eyes. He was shirtless with globs of condensation and sweat glistening underneath his nipples. There was a tuft of fuzz in the center of his chest that represented the only hair Mike could see, hovering between the two ends of the towel as though it were a part of it. And while his chest and arms jiggled with fat, his stomach was flat and toned as it went down into the denim of his jeans. He looked like he had been in shape, once, and was now slowly trying to be again. "We're looking for Randy, have you seen him?"

The man furrowed his brow, thinking.

"No... not for a few months." his expression changed then, from confused to concerned. "Why? Have you seen him? Is he okay? God, I haven't even heard from him since that day at school. I can't believe that that was my Randy..."

"You're his father?" Cathy asked, looking the man up and down.

Mike took a step to the left as Cathy's shoulder bumped into his in the narrow space. The light from the living room's bay window now played tricks with the water on the man's shoulder, making it glimmer. He didn't have any tan lines, Mike noted. The hairless look was not a new one for him. The man had almost the same pale fleshy tone to himself all over, actually. The only discoloured thing on his body was his ring finger, the flesh there much sallower than the rest in a smooth line.

"Yes." the man answered, offended by the question visibly.

"I'm sorry." Cathy replied honestly. "You just don't look old enough to have a fifteen year old son."

"I'm not." he sighed, chuckling a little. "My names Terrence. Terrence Owchar, by the way." His voice was deep and booming, but somehow very kind at the same time.

Mike took a slight step to the left again. Each time he did his perspective on the man changed slightly, showing a different part of him or the house around him. He could see the darkened oblongs of several doorways in the hall behind him now, where Terrence and Randy's bedrooms not doubt where. There was a table against the wall in between them that had a few crisp bills on it near the base of a picture frame that looked to be at least fifty years old. There was a vase next to it, glimmering blue with pascal flower print. At the end of the hall in the bathroom, he could see the mirror and the sink beneath it now. It was covered with steam, and he didn't know how he'd missed when they'd come in.

"So, you haven't seen Randy?" Cathy asked again, shaking her head and smiling.

Terrence shifted a little to the right. "No, of course not. Not since the police have been looking for him. I don't put up with those shannanighans in my house."

Mike shifted a little, tilting his head down. There was a shaving brush leaned against the faucet with bits of foam still stuck to its smooth brown bristles. Beside it was a small square made of black plastic, attached to a cover of clear plastic by a winch. It was open against the porcelain with a small wedge of sponge resting in it. The wedge was smeared and splotched with red and white.

"What did you say your names were?" Terrence asked.

"Oh!" Cathy smiled. "I'm Cathy Kennessy, and this is Mike Harris. We were... um, friends of Randy's before, you know..."

"I see." Terrance said, nodding. "You don't think he did it, do you?"

"I... can't say." Cathy said. "But if he did, I'm sure it's just because of the awful crowd he managed to get mixed up in."

"Yes..." Terrance nodded, shifting his obese body to the right again. "How do you suppose he got hooked up with those hooligans?"

"He's a legacy." Mike mumbled, turning from the bathroom and back to Terrance.

"Excuse me?"

"I always wondered what it stood for... never once occurred to me it was something so simple as the first letter of someone's name." Mike said, laughing humorlessly to himself.

"What are you talking about?"

Mike motioned toward the bathroom behind Terrence. "The makeup back there."

Terrence turned briefly to look where Mike was pointing, but didn't really have to. He knew exactly what the young man was talking about. When he turned back to them his eyes had shrunk into tiny black dots in the middle of his head. His brow was pushed forward like a caveman's, making a thick dark line across that shadows of his face, bisected by his thick Irish nose.

"You know now that I see it, I don't know how I didn't before --"

"I really think you'd better --"

"Roulette."

Terrence shot forward at Mike, crossing the distance between them in one great stride. He wrapped his plump fingers around the boy's neck and squeezed, forcing him against the wall that divided the living room from the hall.

Cathy screamed.

Mike reached up and tried to pull Terrence's fingers away. The flesh of his clubbed digits felt smooth and greasy, like plump Polish sausages. They were impossibly hard to get a grasp on, and Mike found his hands sliding fruitlessly around Terrence's bare arms rather than coming up with a good hold.

His face had turned pink immediately. Now it was a bright shade of red.

He made a sickly gasping sound as his mouth reached for air and found none, his windpipe held closed by Terrence's massive hands.

Cathy screamed again, louder than before.

Terrence's eyes were bulging now, his pupils so small and furious that they almost disappeared into the white marble of his sclera. His mouth had been contorted into a lemniscate that showed off all his teeth when he's started, but now was bent into a malicious smile. Spit frothed at the edges of his mouth and fell onto Mike's shirt as he shook the boy, pressing harder on his neck.

Mike kicked out, slamming twice into Terrence's stomach. It was like kicking concrete. A third kick connected with his groin. In registered a reaction, though not much of one.

Cathy screamed a third time.

"Jesus, what does it take for that bitch to shut up?" Terrence bellowed, turning to look over his shoulder.

Cathy smashed the blue vase into his face. The clay broke into hundreds of sharp little pieces that slashed at his cheeks as he fell over, slamming his head against the wall and releasing his grip on Mike. Ashes from inside the vase toppled down over him in weighty clumps, finding their way into his eyes and mouth. They stuck to his sweaty, moist skin even as the impact of his fall shook much of it off.

Mike looked at her as he gasped for air on his knees. "Thanks." he nodded, swallowing hard. It burned when he did.

"Not a problem." she frowned, dropping what remained of the urn to the floor. The ashes turned the multicoloured carpet a sickly but uniform gray.

From the floor, Terrence moaned. His hand was moving.

"What do we do about him?" Cathy asked, taking a step back.

Mike got to his feet, still caressing his neck with one hand. It still had the shape of Terrence's fat fingers pressed into them. He walked over to the puke green rotary phone that stood on the table and placed his hand on its receiver.

He stood like that for a moment without moving.

"What?" Cathy asked, taking another big step away from Terrence. "What is it?"

Mike did not respond. There was a drawer in the table that had been left ajar. Something twinkled in it now, the way the light had twinkled off the sweat on Terrence's shoulders a few minutes before.

Slowly, he took his hand off the receiver and picked up the shimmering object.

They were brass knuckles.

He turned a looked at Terrence's hand. The sallow flesh of the ring finger he'd seem before was still there, but now he saw what he'd missed the first time: all the fingers on that hand had sallow rings around them, forming a straight line across his knuckles.

"Are those?" Cathy asked, next to him now and glaring down at the brass in his hand.

"Yes." he replied, before she could even finish the question.

He finally picked up the telephone receiver, and handed it to Cathy.

With a vacant face and a throbbing neckline, he closed the distance between himself and Terrence again until he stood over the larger man. He slid the brass down over his fingers until it made a line roughly adjacent to where the line had been of Terrence's.

Cathy dialed the police, a number she knew by heart by now.

They would be a long time coming she knew, with everything that had happened at the school.

Mike drew his fist back as far as he could, then brought it down.

ʎʎʎ

Ian zipped up his fly, spitting down upon the beaten, bleeding body of Mandy Peterson.

"Everybody given her all they can?' Duncan asked, kicking her in the ribs as he spoke.

She didn't make a sound. She barely moved. Barely breathed. Her skull had been cracked open by one of them, matting her hair in blood. The vessels in her right eye had all popped, turning the white red and giving her a demonic appearance. Two of her teeth were missing, and another was chipped. Her face stung as fluids not her own seeped down it. Her nose had been broken, the roof of her jaw cracked.

They had sliced at her breasts with broken bottles and poured alcohol onto them, making them burn and ache. One of them had broken her legs while he had ridden her, and her left wrist was sprained. Blood and semen seeped slowly from her genitals as she stared wide-eyed into the darkness, her mind devoid of all thought, body broken and not her own anymore.

"Two's my limit." Randy admitted, sighing.

"Me too." Ian smiled, purposely stepping on her foot with all his weight as he stepped over her. He joined the others, then turned to watch her. "Should we let her heal up until we're ready to go, or -"

"Naw." Duncan snarled, taking out his gun. "She don't look half as pretty anymore. I think we're done with her, boys."

He pulled back the hammer on the gun, aiming it at her swollen, bruised face. "Bye bye. I'd love to say some kind, parting words, girl... but you weren't that good."

He paused.

"Come on, guys." he smirked, still looking down the barrel of the gun. "That was funny!"

He turned toward them, only to find that they were no longer paying any attention to him. They were facing the open doorway where the Black Womb stood, its eyes glowing blue-green against its silhouette, claws at the ready, hunched over and breathing so hard that it echoed off the unseen walls of the warehouse.

"Oh my god." Randy whispered, reaching to his pocket and getting out his taser. "Shoot it! Fast!"

Duncan turned his gun and opened fire on the Womb. The bullet hit its mark, sinking into its flesh where its human heart was. The creature did not flinch, did not move for a long moment, and even then, it only took a single step forward.

"Shit!" Ian cursed, fumbling about in the darkness for his gun. "Where the fuck did I fling it to? Stupid bitch made me friggin' forget, and now I..."

He looked up.

At first he saw nothing, only darkness. Then Duncan fired another shot, one that actually hit the darkness in front of him and made it bleed shadows. He tilted his head further up as the Womb knelt down until they were at eye-level. It hissed, long and snake-like, bending over quickly to bite Ian's throat with all eighty-four of its teeth and ripping it out, leaping onto him as he tried to scream but couldn't, its hind legs coming up and ripping at his chest with feet claws like a cat while its talons reached around to the rapist's back and ripped off two gigantic strips of flesh. The creature got up, covered in blood from the waist down, bent over and ate the two pieces of flesh in one bite.

Duncan fired again, this time hitting it between the eyes to no effect. The creature took a menacing step forward. Duncan fired again, hitting its mark in the central plexus. Nothing. It took another step forward, and Duncan pressed the trigger again.

-click-

Duncan looked down at his weapon with shock as the Womb slowly crouched down, then leaped forward with blinding speed and dug the talons of both its index fingers into Duncan's eye sockets. They ran down his face like tears made of jelly. He screamed so loud that his ears popped. So loud that he didn't even think the sound was coming from his own mouth, that it was someone else. It was only when a small trickle of his eye found its way into his own mouth that he came back to reality, though he wished he hadn't. The Womb drew back, then extended its arm right through Duncan's chest.

His heart fell to the ground on the other side of him, bouncing off the concrete from the propulsion of the blow.

The screaming stopped.

The Womb withdrew its arm from Duncan. It was coated from the shoulder down with dark redness.

The Womb turned, a wry smile on its face, searching out its next victim.

It snarled.

There, in the light of the doorway, Mandy Peterson lay in the arms of Randy Owchar. He had Ian's gun grasped in one hand, its barrel pointed against her chest. A taser shook in his other hand and he held it out toward the Womb, blue electricity coursing between its dual prongs and making the air smell like ozone. He held it out like a shield, as though he thought it would protect him.

"D-don't move!" he cautioned, stammering. "I mean it! I'll kill her!"

The Womb stood there, tilting its head to one side as Mandy watched it with sleepy but alert eyes, a smile somehow prying over her bludgeoned lips.

"You came..." she said weakly, blood coming out of her mouth.

"Yeah, well now I'll get to kill you both." Randy proclaimed proudly, gaining confidence with every word he convinced himself was true.

Slowly, the Black Womb crouched, tilting its head at Randy again.

"Bastard..." Randy whispered, tears flowing down his face. "This isn't the way it was supposed to go..."

"What?" the Womb said, its eyes melting from green to red. "You thought you were going to march into my school, kill people, kidnap and rape one of my friends, and then we were going to go outside and play jax?

"Grow up. Hand over the girl, before I get really mad again."

"No!" Randy yelled, putting first pressure on the trigger.

The Womb leaped, as fast as it could under Xander's control.

Randy fired.

BANG!

Mandy slumped to the floor, fresh blood soaking the wall.

"No!" Xander yelled in mid air, pummeling Randy and trying to wrestle the gun away. Randy brought the taser up fast and hit him in the right side. Electric fire spat out of it and shot through him.

The Womb sputtered, then died.

Even as the black liquid began to flow off of the naked Xander, he still tried to wrestle the gun away from the boy.

BANG!

BECOMING: CHAPTER TWENTY-ONE

Earlier that morning.

Mandy Peterson lay on the couch of Dr. Warren O'Toole, her hands folded in front of her, her eyes closed. She was asleep, or rather in a state of hypnosis, as the Counselor waved a golden pocket watch in front of her face.

"How do you feel, Mandy?" he asked her in a calm, steady voice, placing the watch on the table and picking up his pad and pencil.

"I'm a lot better today, actually." she smiled.

"Really, and why is that?"

"Last night I threw away all my old diaries and started a new one."

"Really? Why did you do that?"

"That was my old life. I didn't want to think about that anymore. I wanted to stop looking back and blaming myself and my mother and her boyfriends and my boyfriends... I just wanted to get on with my life, you know?"

Warren's lower lip quivered a moment, then he nodded, although she could not see him. He looked at her, at how beautiful she was, so sweet and innocent, healthily plump for a girl her age. The boys must love her.

"I do." he said finally, realizing that he hadn't verbally responded. "I do."

"I want to forget about them. I forgive them."

"You forgive them?" he said, dropping his pen.

"Yes, I do. I really do. That's why I had to throw away all the bad things I wrote about them all over the years. I want to start a new diary with good people in it. Like Xander, and they way he tries to make everybody okay, even when he's not. How he cares for me, though he doesn't have to. And Mike and Cathy, and how they love each other and how great that love is, even if they don't always see it. And Tommy... one of the only people to be so bad, and have something so bad happen to him... and then come out of it so good. So good.

"And Julie. I love her so much, I've never had a sister before.

"See? I want to write a new story, where nobody gets hurt and nobody cries. With people like my friends in it. And you, Dr. O'Toole."

Warren started to cry.

"I want to write something like that. I want that to be my life. And I can't wait to live it."

He wiped his tears long enough to say: "You can wake up now, Amanda."

Mandy awoke suddenly, her eyelids clicking softly as they snapped open. At first she wasn't quite sure where she was, looking up at an off-white stucco ceiling, her heart rate racing so much that she could hear it pounding in her ears.

"That was a good session." Warren said from where he sat perched on his chair across the room. He was still scribbling notes onto the sheet of paper attached to his clipboard, his hand going a mile a minute.

"It seems like I just laid down." she said groggily, sitting up and putting her hair back in a pony tail, pushing the hair away from her cute, plump face. Her sweater kept her warm on this chilly day, so big on her that it only stopped halfway between her hips and her knees. It made her look innocent and sweet, two words anyone that really knew her would probably not use to describe her.

"You always say that." he grinned, shoving his pocket watch into his breast pocket, his hand covered by a red and white handkerchief. "It's the truest sign of a good session."

"And you always say that." she pointed out, smiling at him just a little.

He smiled, but seemed distant. She wasn't sure, but she thought she caught the glimmer of tears in his eyes.

"So, when will you need to see me again?" she asked, stretching wide and then sighing happily.

"Hmm?" Warren hummed, lost in a stray thought. *"Oh, yes. I'm sorry... um, let's say next week sometime. Contact me on Friday and we'll see when's a good time for you, okay?"*

"Whatever." she chirped, then turned toward the door.

Warren watched her leave, then collapsed back into his chair, visibly exhausted.

"Oh, God..." he mumbled as reached behind his desk and pulled out a bottle of Jack Daniels and a short, wide glass. Throwing his clipboard into the nearest open cabinet, he poured himself a drink.

"Once more into the breach, my friends..." he murmured, downing the contents of the glass as fast as he could. *"We few... we happy few."*

BECOMING: CHAPTER TWENTY-TWO

Randy Owchar's hand slumped lifelessly to the floor, dropping the smoking gun as his last breath hissed from between his lips.

Xander, still dripping Womb-blood but not caring, rushed to Mandy's side. He propped her head up on his lap and he brushed the hair out of her broken face.

She tried to speak to him, but he shook his head.

"Shh..." he cautioned, hot tears streaming down his face as he held her close, her body... so cold. "Don't speak. It's gonna be okay. You're gonna be okay, I'm gonna get you help, love. Don't you -"

She raised a hand up to the side of his face and stroked it softly.

The last of the Womb's flesh dripped off of him.

"So," she whispered hoarsely. "You're the guy everybody's been talking about..."

Her hand fell from his face to the ground with an unceremonious thud, leaving only the blood that had been on her hand behind. Several long moments passed, as Xander listened to her heart slow... then finally come to a stop.

His lower lip quivered as he reached up and closed her eyes for her, those beautiful, sparkling eyes that now seemed so dull and faded. Tears pitted against her cheeks, but she made no move to wipe them off. Slowly, he wrapped his arms around her and began rocking back and forth, cradling Mandy as the tears rushed from his eyes and nose.

He wanted to sing to her, that Irish song Sara used to sing to him, but his throat was too raked with tears, ravaged in a way nothing had ever been.

So he stayed there, rocking her back and forth, sobbing and convulsing. When finally he got the strength to speak, he screamed:

"BLACK WOMB LIVES!"

BECOMING: CLOSING

Genblade lived.

Genblade and Roulette had lived, both of them in jail now.

Somehow he found that one of the harder points to get past. Of all the people that had died in such a short amount of time, a person like Adam Genblade had survived. His spinal column injured, unable to speak or breathe on his own, possibly forever... but alive.

"Ashes, to ashes..." said Reverend Gallagher, as Mandy's casket was lowered into the ground, a few flakes of snow falling from the sky. "And dust, to dust..."

Mandy had always loved the snow, or so Xander had recalled her once saying. Now, she would never get to see it again.

"Nobody's here..." Cathy mumbled, looking around at the surprisingly small crowd gathered.

"Julie's still in the hospital." Xander said coldly, not turning away from the coffin as it landed in its hole with a dull thud. "Tommy wanted to stay with her, since her whole family was going to be here. Mike doesn't go to funerals anymore."

Cathy nodded, remembering her lover's stance on the dead.

"She was special." he said, mostly to himself.

Tears started to stream down Cathy's face. "You did everything you could."

Xander thought back, thought of the choice he'd made to go back and fight Genblade instead of searching for Mandy, who was right where he thought she'd be.

"Sure I did." he responded, trying to hide the sarcasm in his voice.

Circe was nowhere in sight. Xander had checked everywhere for Hale, but there wasn't even a trace of his scent. It was like he had never been there.

School would start up again soon, and everything would get back to normal.

Without her.

Once again, they were forced to leave someone behind and to press forward. To commit to continuing to live, if only to honor the memories of those who could not make such commitments.

Once again, good people had died when the bad continued to live.

"It should have been me." Xander said finally, drawing Cathy's attention.

"What?"

"It should have been me. I should have been faster, smarter... or just plain ignored O'Toole. I made every wrong choice that day."

"Xander..." she sighed, crying, unable to think of a way to finish the sentence that would make him feel better.

"I have been asked by a shared friend of Mandy Peterson and I..." The Reverend continued, reaching down into his robe. "...to read to passage from the journal of Miss. Peterson."

Xander rose his head, eyes blank as he listened.

Gallagher opened the book, flipped a few pages ahead, then went back.

Tears started to flow down Xander's cheeks.

Though she wasn't quite sure why, when Cathy saw it, she cried.

Gallagher coughed.

"There is only one passage," he said, his lower lip shaking as he, too, started to cry. "It... It is dated the night before her death. It reads simply : 'I love my life. I can't wait to live it.'"

Cathy broke down crying, her tears washed away by the earth.

Gallagher stepped down, wiping his eyes in his sleeve as the rest of those gathered broke down as well.

Xander just stared down at the grave, as stone-faced as the headstone as his tears washed away his sins. He turned, looking up at Sara's grave on the hill, and listened.

"Hale said that I was becoming something." he said, to Sara as much as to Cathy, as he took her hand and lead her both away from the somber scene. "If that's true, then let it at least be something that I can stand to look at in the mirror."

ABOUT THE AUTHOR

Matthew LeDrew holds an Honours Degree in English from the Memorial University of Newfoundland with a minor in Anthropology, and studied Journalism at College of the North Atlantic in Stephenville, Newfoundland. He was honoured to be a jury member of both the 2018 NLBA awards and the 2020 Arts and Letters Awards.

He has written twenty-four novels for Engen Books: the ten book Coral Beach Casefiles series, *The Long Road, Cinders, Sinister Intent, Faith, Family Values, Fate's Shadow, First Aid, Jacobi Street, Touch Your Nose, Infinity, The Tourniquet Reprisal, Exodus of Angels, Garden of the Eighth Circle,* and *The Rats of Refraction* the latter five of which with his co-author and wife Ellen Curtis.

He lives in Chapel Arm, Newfoundland.